Andy Lake

Shades of Green

More about the book, the characters and additional features at

www.shades-of-green.info

More about the author at www.andylake.co.uk

Cover design by Steve Lown—www.stephenlown.co.uk

ISBN: 1-4818-0771-4
ISBN-13: 9781481807715

DEDICATION

This book is dedicated to

Helen Rose Lake

1924–2011

the greatest influence in my life

and a reader *par excellence*

PROLOGUE

At the end of a New Dawn

The convoy moved slowly through the newly-planted forests covering the hillsides. They could see the camp now, the wooden huts for all the world like lakeside holiday lodges. As the convoy descended the last hill and came round towards the entrance, the camp presented a different aspect. Barbed wire fencing surrounding the camp converged at a wooden gate, over which were the words: 'Entrance to a new world'.

The first wave of American and European troops had arrived several days before by helicopter. They had set up the first isolation units and treatment centre. Guards wearing decontamination suits waved the convoy to a halt, and immediately the new arrivals sprang into action to unload much needed medical supplies and body bags.

The liberating forces had found seven hundred bodies so far, here and at the satellite camp half a mile to the north. These had included the body of Terry Cairns, previously a member of the Green Earth government. The West Highland eco-camp in north-west Scotland would soon become the most notorious of the twenty-five camps around the country, in which some thirty thousand people perished. And these were only the first amongst the more than two hundred thousand victims in the country.

The final vehicle in the convoy pulled up. A young woman, dressed all in black, stepped out and surveyed the scene. She held a hand over her eyes to protect them from the sharp evening sunlight. Her investigation team began to unload their kit: computers, cameras, boxes and bags for confiscated documents and electronic hardware.

A senior officer recognised her and approached. 'Miss Kitson?' he enquired.

She nodded and took his outstretched hand. 'I'm Colonel Palmer, US Marines. I'm honoured to meet you—I just wish it could have been in different circumstances. I have a tent set up here for your team to work from. We can't tell if it's safe enough yet to work in all areas of the camp. But you'll be able to interview the survivors once you're suited up. I'm afraid though that two or three may not last out the day. ...'

Joanna Kitson took a deep breath, and replied, 'Well, we'd better get started as soon as we can. I want to get every last bit of evidence I can find...'

Despite her determination, her voice began to fill with emotion. Appointed by the new government as Special Investigator for the Commission of Inquiry, her motivation was not only professional, but also deeply personal. She intended to leave no stone unturned in her quest for evidence and justice—and in finding out exactly what had happened to members of her own family.

I
Four years earlier

It was, once again, an exceptionally hot summer. Europe was entering its fifth consecutive summer of heatwaves and drought. The spring had seen severe flooding in coastal areas of the UK, and the early summer brought 'tornadoes' to the midlands of England once again. Environmental anxiety was in the air, and in the absence of real news—as the editors saw it—the news media were competing to turn out the most startling environment-related stories.

The two men in the waiting area at BBC News found it refreshingly cool, an intermission between the summer heat outside and the intensity of the studio lights where the interview would take place.

An enthusiastic researcher in her late twenties bounced up.

'I'm Stella Walton—so pleased to meet you Mr Mason', she cooed, holding out her hand. 'You must be Dave Barrington—hi! I've read so many of your articles in the *Green Earth Review*. And that piece in *The Times* on Tuesday by Don Mason—you actually wrote most of that, am I right?'

She was right. Her degree in Medieval Literature at Oxford had made her an expert in textual and form criticism—she could isolate different styles and sources within any piece of work from way off.

'Very impressive,' smiled Don Mason. 'But I'm more impressed that you're a regular reader of the *Review*. Are you one of us?'

Stella warmly returned his friendly smile. 'A Green? Hmm. Probably no more than we all are these days—anyone who's working in our field has to be well versed in the latest environmental thinking. Don't you think?'

Mason nodded his assent, while Dave Barrington initiated conversation about one of the feature articles in the *Green Earth Review*, wanting to explore whether it would make a good programme or news feature. They walked down the corridor to the green room to prepare to be called to the studio.

Don Mason was the founder of the Green Earth Movement, a campaigning group promoting direct action to save the planet. The GEM focused on practical action rather than politics, and had been growing in influence over the years since it was founded. Don had sensed that people in the wider Green movement were disillusioned with the lack of success of the older Green party, and were ready for something new. And lately he had become something of a minor media star, the personable expert that the newspapers, radio and web channels turned to for a quick reaction to events.

'Now, superbeetles,' exclaimed Stella with a broad smile. 'Please take a seat and we'll go over the interview. Tell me about these bugs....'

That summer there were weird bugs and beetles everywhere. Some quite pretty, some exceedingly ugly, and some like the tabloid channels' Superbeetle were very large. And most of them were kind of tropical and exotic-looking. Dave Barrington knew they were mostly harmless, and none of them actually a brand new species. It was the media that had latched onto the idea of a new strain of pesticide-resistant 'superbeetle', and the confusion in people's minds with the hospital bacteria kind of 'superbug' had helped to create an atmosphere of public alarm.

Dave Barrington knew all this, but the story was a great hook on which to build greater Green awareness. And awareness of Don Mason and the GEM in particular. This was just the latest in the spate of summer stories about 'weird nature'. Eighteen foot sunflowers, ladybird swarms and tornado clusters had all been front page stories. Against the continuing flatness of the economy and a dearth of celebrity weddings, these made for good copy.

'Sure,' said Barrington. 'Did you get the images I mailed through?'

'Yes,' said Stella. 'Handsome devil, isn't he? What do they call him, a Rhodesian Ridgeback?'

Barrington smiled. 'That's a kind of dog—a very big dog. If we had beetles that size, I'd be on the next plane out the country! It goes by several names, one of which is a Sumatran Ridgeback—'

'And it's new?'

'New to Britain, for sure. It's been around for about seven or eight years that we know of, a kind of mutation of another tropical beetle. Why it's here, and why in such large numbers is the question to ask,' explained Barrington.

'It's a sign of our times,' said Mason. 'A sign of the impacts of global warming. That's what we'd like to focus on.'

Trevor MacLean, currently Science Correspondent at BBC News, walked up and introduced himself.

'We're just discussing the Sumatran Ridgeback here,' said Stella.

'Great', replied Trevor enthusiastically, shaking hands and swapping introductions with Mason and Barrington before putting forward his preferred editorial angle. 'You know what I'd like is a bit of colour in this story, some personal information about this thing. Something to make women gasp and children cry. I mean, do they suck the blood out of rats, or chew the nuts off squirrels or something gruesome like that? Do they bite the head off their mates when they get down to it? Do they get into fridges, eat raw meat and make terrible smells? Do they have oozing sores on their arses that we can do a close-up of? Brrr-r-r!'

He shivered theatrically as if a chill of horror was running through him, then leaned forward as if imparting a confidence. 'You know what I *really* want is some complaints if this airs before tea-time and young children are watching. I mean, they've lumbered me with being Science and Environment Correspondent for God's sake, which is scant reward for twenty years of cutting edge news reporting, in my view. But if I can get some complaints about this kind of item—my reputation will be redeemed.'

Mason watched this breathless performance with a quizzical smile on his face, while Barrington frowned.

'Well,' said Don, 'I think they are quite delicate eaters, in fact. And when they do "get down to it" I think it's generally best to look the other way. But they do look fearsome, don't they? I'm sure Dave's provided some close-up pictures which are ugly enough to scare the bejabers out of all viewers of a nervous disposition. Maybe we can have a close-up projected big and brutal behind us as we talk? After seeing that, you'll never need to be scared of a sci-fi alien again.'

Trevor MacLean looked closely at Don Mason. So this is the new rising star of the Green movement, he thought. Mason came across as a confident man in his late fifties, with greying hair that gave him a distinguished air. Trevor had heard Mason speak several times on radio, and seen some video on the Internet, and had been struck by his urbane charm and confident modesty. Not remotely convinced by the coherence of his ideas, nonetheless he admired his gift for promoting one or two simple ideas and making them seem irrefutable. Mason was a natural media performer, Trevor concluded—but was unsure how much he'd have to offer on the big stage.

'Stella!' exclaimed Trevor, suddenly overcome with a great idea triggered by the word 'alien'. 'Is there time to do a montage of one of these beetles clawing its way out of Sigourney Weaver? Do we need to get rights for using her? Or am I overdoing it here, chaps?'

'Maybe a little,' said Stella sourly.

Barrington tried to restore some order to the discussion. 'Actually we were just talking about putting the beetle in the context of climate change, as a sign of our times'.

'Oh God,' exclaimed Trevor, rolling his eyes up theatrically, 'Not global warming again. I hear the sound of a million kettles being filled, and another million people changing channels. Dull, dull, dull! Sorry, boys, climate change has been done to death–though "a sign of our times" isn't bad for a lukewarm soundbite, perhaps. We can build on that.'

'Well, Trevor,' said Mason. 'This is the BBC, isn't it? What about your duty to educate and inform? It may bore you and half the country, but the problem is no one's taking the issues seriously enough, despite all the signs of change around them. I'm sure we can make this entertaining enough, without forgetting the science.'

'Hmm. Appealing to my elitist tendencies is a good stroke to play, Donald. But for God's sake, if we must have global warming, make it *bite*. And I mean it's got to bite *now*, not some time in the future when we're all past caring.'

Mason looked at ease in the build-up to the interview. He looked up into the gallery, where he could just about see the director giving instructions to his team.

'Who's that?' Mason asked Stella Walton.

'That's Danny Malik. Do you know him?'

'No,' Mason said quickly. 'He looks very young. Is he in charge of this programme?'

'Kind of,' Stella replied carelessly.

Trevor MacLean hurried over to them, and began to brush some imaginary fluff from Mason's lapel. 'Now, Donald,' he began, 'we're going to take maybe fifteen minutes over this, but the viewers never see more than about thirty seconds of it at a time. So let's be clear and crisp so we don't have to cut you mid-sentence. We can put out bigger chunks online–so if you have any sentences longer than ten words, or words with more than two syllables, you can look for them later on the web channels. They're very good media for talking to your disciples and to foreigners, but if you've got something important to say on TV to all us dumbed-down common-or-garden Brits–make it simple and controversial, OK?'

Don nodded. He was becoming mildly irritated by MacLean's frivolous and somewhat patronising manner, but he knew the score. He looked at Dave Barrington, who was now scowling, and mouthed, 'Patience, patience!' Dave smiled. It was part of a mantra of Mason's that he urged on his followers. Patience and discipline.

They took their seats, and after some last minute changes to camera position, the interview began. MacLean had changed into a brighter colour jacket, and his manner changed to that of his front-of-camera persona—that of a somewhat eccentric seeker after truth, pitched somewhere between Dr Who and Hercule Poirot.

He began his introduction. 'Last year it was greenfly. In recent years we've had ladybird storms, locusts in Tunbridge Wells, giant sunflowers in Skegness. Now parts of the country are being overrun by king-sized beetles. Is nature getting weirder? Are these one-off freak events, or can we expect more of the same as the world heats up? We have with us environmental expert and leader of the Green Earth Movement—Don Mason.'

He turned to Mason. 'Don, you've been issuing warnings for some time now about the consequences for us all of our impact on the planet. Do you think the presence of these so-called superbeetles can be considered some kind of a man-made plague?'

'In a word, Trevor, yes,' Don replied. One of the ways that Don had endeared himself to the media was that he was always direct. He would always give a straight answer, unlike most politicians—even at the expense of accuracy.

'Of course,' he continued, 'no one has set out with the intention of deliberately introducing these kinds of bugs into an environment where they don't belong. All the same, it's the result of the careless way in which we live our lives, and the pressures we put on our planet.'

'What kind of pressures are you talking about, Don?'

'It's like this, Trevor. Nature always depends on striking some kind of balance. In the natural course of events, there is always change. We have warmer times, and cooler times. Different species flourish and become dominant for a while, and others fade away. But if nature is left to its own devices, generally a kind of balance is achieved.'

Trevor MacLean was nodding earnestly.

'But in the past hundred and fifty years—and especially the last fifty—the way we have altered the planet, and the way we consume resources has created a critical imbalance. Everything is out of kilter. These bugs and beetles we see—these summer plagues and infestations—all these are only the beginning. They are signs of the time—'

'Are these things actually dangerous, do you think, Don?' interrupted Trevor.

'Every imbalance is dangerous, Trevor. And I tell you, over the next five years, we're going to see a helluva lot more of these kind of critters, and some of them won't only be chewing the legs off greenfly.'

Dave Barrington cringed as he heard this. But MacLean liked it. He felt Mason was talking alarmist garbage, but garbage is good if it generates a response. Mason was consciously exaggerating for effect, to try to stimulate debate and reaction. Their aims coincided, one looking for political impact, the other for journalistic.

'What then should we do—reach for the DDT? That's a very potent bug-spray, by the way, for any viewers under fifty.'

'Heavens no!' laughed Mason. 'That's a great example of one of the ways in which we, in our arrogance, have caused almost irreparable damage to the planet. The main thing we need to do is *cut our consumption*. We are consuming resources at far too fast a rate. We need to reduce our "environmental footprint"—and do it fast. Shall I explain what we mean by that?'

'Isn't it a way of expressing graphically how much land on the planet each person requires to supply their needs?'

'That's right. And if everyone in the world were to consume resources at the same rate that we do in the West, we'd need at least four planets to supply all our needs. We're using up the earth, Trevor, and we've got to cut back. Human activity is putting too much of a strain on the natural functions of the Earth. The ability of the planet's ecosystems to sustain and support future generations just can't be taken for granted any more. It's not really about this beetle or that bug coming too far north for its holiday. It's about whether our children and their children will have enough food to eat. It's about how many of our native species of plants and animals will become extinct.'

'There are people, though,' said MacLean, 'who think a warmer Britain would be fine. I mean it would be no bad thing to have a climate like the South of France. Think of it, vineyards in Yorkshire. Kirkcaldy: the new St Tropez. That's not so bad!'

'It's not that simple. Climate change could mean the Gulf Stream will shift itself and Britain and Ireland may end up facing colder winters and more extreme weather.'

'Global warming will make us colder?' MacLean asked, feigning incredulity though he knew the arguments well.

'It could do—as our top meteorologists are warning us it might do. You know, part of the problem of talking about "global warming" is that it makes it seem like something the planet is doing to us—or at least a problem too big for us to deal with so we just have to find a way to live with it. If it's a global problem it's always someone else's responsibility. But I say to you, it *is* our responsibility, and we need to take urgent action. It's fine for politicians to talk the talk—but they never walk the walk. They run off to conferences, and talk about making international agreements to reduce pollution. But you know, every one of the government departments they run could cut their resource use by seventy or eighty per cent tomorrow, if they had the will. Every household could do the same. But they don't, and we don't.'

'So this freakish weather and the plagues of weird beasts—these are all our fault?' asked Trevor.

Mason gave half a smile. 'It is. Collectively, it is. But it's not a question of attributing fault, but of finding answers. It's a question of will, and a question of vision. We can see the problems, so why can't we do more than stumble towards half-hearted solutions? As a nation, as a world family of nations, we have no vision of the kind of world we want to live in in twenty years' time, or a hundred years' time. We need to have this as a basis for action, but are we anywhere near this?

'This is what our Green Earth Movement is about. Our vision is of a re-balanced and restored world, where mankind can live in much closer harmony with nature. And to do this we need to turn around from the path we are on. You know when I worked in the corporate world, people always said the key to growth is based on doing more with less. But I tell you, we need to turn right away from this path of endless growth. We need to re-learn how to do *less* with less! Can we have prosperity based on doing less, producing less, consuming less? I believe we can. Our vision is one of living in smaller, self-sustaining communities with production for our everyday needs centred around the home, and where our happiness is measured not in the quantity of our possessions but in the quality of our relationships—including our relationship with the rest of the natural world.'

'Including with these superbeetles?' asked Trevor, wide-eyed.

'Them and all their cousins too,' said Mason with a disarming smile.

'Your vision, though—is it achievable in the real world?'

'It has to be. The alternatives are too dreadful to consider. We have to change. You know, the time is getting short, and the day of reckoning will be coming unless we change our ways—and soon.'

••

'Did my take on global warming bite enough for you, Trevor?' asked Don after the interview.

'Well, I can't say I feel bitten, but I reckon I've had a determined gumming from a toothless old concept,' Trevor replied.

Don shrugged. He guessed that in five minutes this interviewer would have forgotten all about the topic and moved on to something else. That, though, was the name of the game. People like MacLean are hopelessly shallow, he thought, but they can be useful, and it's better to establish some kind of rapport with them.

Despite Trevor's withering remarks, Mason's 'day of reckoning' comment was played throughout the day on the news channels, and was picked up by the other news media with some relish, as a relief from stories about sunburn. They also picked up on his unscripted additions of colour. The 'chewing the legs off greenfly' quote, in particular.

Barrington, reluctantly amused, had complained on the way back. 'They don't chew the legs off anything—they eat crops, and that's the real worry. Talking like that can make us look ignorant, Don.'

'Lighten up, Dave,' Mason had said. 'Look ignorant to whom? The people who know what a Sumatran Hatchback eats will probably support us anyway. It's the other people we need to wake up to the issues. And if they do start to worry about big bugs biting their legs off, it's a first step to some kind of environmental awareness.'

'Look, Don, I'm making a big psychological concession by allowing all this doomsday talk about a pretty ordinary and harmless insect. Please give me some credit for my endlessly tolerant bullshit threshold.'

'OK. Point taken. But generally, how do you score the performance? How did you like the John the Baptist end-of-the-world stuff?'

'Pretty good. Amiable but challenging, just like we prepared. And the John the Baptist stuff? Well, you had me ready to repent, for one.'

These were jovial and almost carefree times for Mason and his party, the Green Earth Movement. Mason and his closest collaborators were rising media stars. And as a political alternative they were starting to be taken seriously, while having the freedom to be irresponsible that is enjoyed by opposition groups. But for Don Mason, behind the fun and the media performances lay a serious pursuit of influence and power.

2: The home front

Dave Barrington was thirty-seven by then, and working for the newly created Coastline Institute as Deputy Director—perhaps not the most obvious springboard for high political position and the 'state sponsored terrorism' of which he was later accused. But his career at this point is in some ways typical for members of the Green Earth Movement throughout the country at this time.

Dave Barrington and his wife Jessica Olsen struck their neighbours as a somewhat tight-knit couple—very pleasant but rather earnest, even a little intense at times. In looks they were quite dissimilar. Dave was slightly smaller than average, with dark hair cut somewhat severely around a fairly handsome face, with soulful brown eyes and an intense brow. Though he had a ready wit and was quick to make jokes and to laugh with others, it seemed he rarely broke into a full smile. Wry grins and muted chuckles were more his line.

By contrast Jessica was tall, Scandinavian in looks: strong boned but elegant, with long blond hair that she frequently tossed back as she readily broke into a glacier-melting smile or intense laughter. But this personal lightness was leavened by a certain severity of outlook, an intensity in all she did. This intensity was geared to maintaining a true green lifestyle.

The Barrington family—Dave, Jessica and the children Gaia and Adam, now aged eight and ten—enjoyed a completely free range and organic lifestyle. Home grown foods, locally sourced produce, home-produced energy from solar and wind sources, clothes repaired rather than new ones bought. They lived a kind of puritan green lifestyle. Practising what they preached, they spurned what they felt was the hypocrisy of armchair or academic greenism.

But it was not a life lacking in modern comforts or technology. Puritan, maybe, but not ascetic or excessively self-denying. Their home boasted a bewildering array of technologies, though every effort was made to reduce energy consumption and to use online activities to substitute for resource-intensive physical ones. Conferencing instead of travelling; downloading books and papers instead of buying books and magazines, and sharing their wisdom online were all highly valued as green activities in the Barrington household. And no equipment was ever left on 'stand-by'. The modesty of their lifestyle gave no hint of their ambitions to ensure that everyone should live in a similar way.

'How did it go?' asked Jessica as Dave Barrington returned home on the day of the interview. The dogs were still rushing enthusiastically round his legs, gradually returning to calm after the initial excitement of his homecoming. It was often like this—it could take quite some time to answer a simple question as animals and children demanded his attention. The children called questions to him and told him the latest happenings in their lives.

'Uncle Don's been on the news,' said Gaia, basking in the reflected glory of her father's connections.

'Talking about greenfly! And monsters!' added Adam, not looking up from his drawing at the kitchen table.

Jessica broke away from her cooking, shooing the dogs away to hug her husband at last. 'He was good—in his own Don-ish kind of way,' she said, smiling.

Jessica's affection for Don Mason was very strong, having worked closely with him for many years in the early days of the Movement. The intensity of family life had the strongest pull on her time now—and it was something she revelled in far more than she ever thought possible when she was younger.

For Dave, family life—and the 'Barrington Estate', as they jokingly called their two acres of land in Norfolk—formed a blessed refuge from the political labours and ideological struggles to which he had committed himself.

'I think it went well,' said Dave, finally answering his wife's question. 'You've had the advantage of seeing it on TV. What did they cut it to—about twenty seconds?'

Jessica nodded. 'And they showed more of the interviewer than Don.'

'Huh! Trevor MacLean—he's a bit of a berk, if you ask me. Thinks he's Oscar Wilde or something—always working hard to deliver the witty riposte. I think he's even more shallow in real life than he appears on TV. How's your day been?'

Before long Dave Barrington was outside, iced drink in his hand, preparing himself to do some work on the 'estate' for an hour or so while the children and animals played themselves into exhaustion.

It was 6.30, and still stiflingly hot, with barely a breeze to disturb the calm of the foliage on the trees and bushes. He looked around at the countryside that he loved, and that never failed to stir the romance in his soul. He loved the Norfolk countryside, always had. The gently rolling fields, narrow lanes, old farm buildings and quaint villages set against the ever-changing light of a big sky.

But already in June the land had that golden-brown parched appearance which in his youth you only saw in August, if at all. Norfolk now had the average temperatures that central France had had two decades before. And as he thought about this, all the determination of his political ambitions flooded back into his mind. Lost in thought, he did not notice Jessica come to his side.

She knew what he was thinking.

'We're edging closer. I feel it. People are more and more ready to listen,' she said, putting her arm round his waist.

'It's not enough, not yet. I think we're ready—more than ready, even. But we need that tipping point. Something to shake the country out of its complacency, and make them ready to turn to us.'

'It's coming. I'm sure of it,' said Jessica.

••

While Dave Barrington was preparing for the decisive action that would bring a new world into being, others were preparing for public life in more traditional ways, playing by the old rules.

Peter Kitson, a young Liberal Democrat politician, was also enjoying the summer. From a personal point of view things could not be better. A successful candidate in a by-election three years previously, the smallness of his party and his natural abilities combined to make for rapid promotion to the position of a 'shadow' spokesman. His brief was Environment and Climate Change, and he was pleased that issues in his domain were at the fore. He had also recently married, and his wife Heather was expecting their first child.

Life for Kitson was a breathless round of committees, debates, policy forums, working papers, electoral strategy planning, maternity classes, nursery decorating, dinner parties and relative-visiting. At the age of thirty-six, anything seemed possible.

Peter Kitson was an optimist. His optimistic and generous nature had been nurtured growing up in the midst of warm and close family relationships, a home where his precocious abilities and kind-heartedness were always encouraged and admired. But the death of his parents by the time he was eighteen brought responsibility early to his life. Now he felt he was in the process of recreating the warm family life that had been taken from him in his late teens.

Heather was talking in the kitchen with her sister-in-law Joanna. They had just come back in from the garden, where even at 10.30 on this Sunday morning it was already almost too hot to bear—or certainly too hot if you were six months pregnant.

Peter was in the conservatory with Evan Roberts and Sandy Honeyford. Evan was a fellow MP, and in charge of the party's electoral strategy. An election was due for the following year, and planning was in full swing. As a politician, Evan was everything that Peter was not. Glass half-empty to Peter's glass half-full. Cynical and suspicious, he had none of Peter's open-mindedness or willingness to think the best of others. His skills were in detailed planning, in identifying weaknesses in colleagues and opponents, in gaining tactical advantages and avoiding public relations disasters. He often made grudging asides about Peter's mercurial rise to prominence, and how he was an ingénue who needed more experience of life as ballast for his enthusiasm and idealism. 'Peter needs to get some mud spattered on those rose-tinted spectacles,' he had said to his colleagues more than once, emphasising the words with his distinctive Welsh lilt.

Sandy Honeyford was one of those bright young things who, fuelled by idealism and ambition, grace the corridors of all the political parties—working for almost nothing to support the political life of the party luminaries. She was earnestly making notes as the MPs spoke, pouring tea and punctuating her earnestness with flirtatious smiles that would have won the heart of any MP less engrossed with work and family than Peter Kitson.

Heather was staring into the conservatory in that special way that women reserve for other—especially young and attractive—women.

'Come on, Heather', said Joanna, gently pushing Heather's arm, 'You've nothing to worry about there. I've never seen Peter so happy as he is now'

'That's what worries me!' said Heather, turning back to her coffee.

'No—you can't think…! Heather, I really mean it. I have *never* seen Peter so happy as he has been over the past two years with you. I mean, I've seen him happy with his work and of course very, very pleased with himself. But I've never seen him so heart-and-soul to-the-bottom-of-his-boots *happy* as he is now. And I've known him a long time—all my life!'

Joanna was a thirty-two year-old lawyer with a passion for human rights work. Single, ambitious, and a tendency to be over-serious. Pretty, but not classically so, and very under-confident in dealing with relationships and men in general. She compensated for this by being very successful in her work as a human rights lawyer. To this she brought a lot of energy, commitment, insight and compassion, as well as her share of the inherited wealth that had seen her through the financially lean years after graduating from Cambridge.

'Hm, yes. I hope so,' said Heather, smiling. She knew it was true, but always liked to be provocative about the 'political groupies' as she put it, who buzzed around in the circles of power. And she also liked to exaggerate her husband's attractiveness to other women, when the truth was that he was, as a man, rather ordinary looking.

'Any interesting cases at the moment?' she asked her sister-in-law.

'That Mohammed Iqbal case is still taking up a lot of time,' Joanna replied.

'That's been going on for years, hasn't it?'

'Seven.'

'Seven! I can't believe it. Do you think he's a terrorist? Well, don't answer me—I mean, I know you're his lawyer and there's that confidential priesty confessional thing, isn't there...'

Mohammed Iqbal had been interned, and then released and put under house arrest, then put in prison again for over seven years now. Joanna was part of the team trying to secure his release, and she had pursued his case through the English courts, through to Europe and back as successive governments had kept shifting the goalposts and introducing new legislation to enable them to lock up or detain suspected dangers to the public.

'You know', said Joanna, 'I'm not sure the government thinks he is a terrorist any more. It's just they have so much invested in saying that he is that they can't back down. He's caught in this Kafkaesque situation where he still doesn't know the source of the information against him, or exactly what it is. He admits to having had sympathy with radical groups, but you know basically he's a bookworm—an academic who was studying the radicalisation of Middle-Eastern politics in the 1950s and 60s'.

'Oh,' said Heather, rapidly starting to lose interest, and still casting glances into the conservatory.

'But you know something else weird about this case—every now and then Mohammed just disappears—'

'Disappears?'

'Yes—it's been a feature since their last Criminal Justice Act which allows them to question terror suspects without access to their lawyers. By shifting the place where they are detained and the government body that locks them up, a new period of lawyer-free interrogation starts, and for about ten days or a fortnight I don't know where he is—his family don't know where he is and the Home Office goes all Guantanamo on us'.

'That's terrible. What do they do to him when he disappears?'

'It's kind of weird. It seems they do almost nothing, except wind him up a bit and cause his family a lot of anxiety. It's as if treating him and the others like him in this way is habit-forming. They can't charge him with anything, but they don't want to let him go either, so they just keep on doing whatever they can to hold on to him.'

'I guess that's the way things are these days, and we've all got used to it,' commented Heather absentmindedly. 'Have you seen how we've decorated the nursery—do come and have a look.'

'Sure. I want to see this—Peter's handiwork with a paintbrush. He was always so hopeless at art! But I thought you didn't want to prepare anything until the baby was born?'

'Yes, I felt like that—I didn't want to tempt fate if there was any risk of losing the baby...you know what I mean. But after getting to six months I feel much more confident. You know, I had such a bad feeling before, I was so sure my baby was in danger. I still touch wood all the time, but I'm sure now she'll be born safely.'

'She?? You know?'

'Maybe...don't tell anyone!'

They smiled at each other confidentially, and progressed upstairs to the newly painted nursery.

Downstairs Evan Roberts was talking political strategy on the basis of the party's latest opinion polling. 'We're getting some strong showing from the Greens this time. It could be seasonal, but the sampling and our focus groups indicate that they may make a strong showing in places where there are a lot of under-thirties: the university towns in particular. We used to do well in these places ten years ago or so—anti-fees and anti-war...' He paused while everyone winced at the recollection of their abandoned policy. 'But now the Greens seem a lot more organised and determined on the campuses.'

'How many can they win?' asked Sandy.

'Not so many. One or two maximum. But the main danger for us is that they suck away our vote in our target seats, letting in one of the other parties.'

'So we need to up the ante on our own green credentials,' offered Sandy.

Peter was looking thoughtful. 'Yes, up to a point. But we need to emphasise the realism of our policies—and the range of our policies too. The areas like health or policing where the Greens don't have any policies at all, or just have an incoherent pick-and-mix selection'.

He looked at Evan. 'But we've got more than one flavour of Greens to contend with. Some of their local campaigning doesn't seem to be up to much. Where do you think the threat is coming from?'

'Well, you're right, their performance is patchy as normal—perhaps even more so. But in the areas where they are better organised, I think they are *much* better organised than before. I think it's the areas where Don Mason and his crew have been taking a hand. Dave Barrington—he's a friend of yours, isn't he?'

'Well, not exactly a friend, but I quite like him. I've done stints with him on a couple of the "Sustainability Roundtables", and we've met up at several policy conferences. Heather knows his wife, too—they were at the same college, though a few years apart. She's an activist too—or was, I haven't heard much about her lately. You know Dave Barrington's quite pragmatic really—not like most of the others. He really knows his stuff, but he's also aware of the gaps in what we know. He doesn't bandwagon it like most of the rest of them do—I mean he doesn't just take the latest fashionable theory and say we all have to believe it. He seems kind of grounded in his approach, and he's willing to consider a variety of ways of achieving environmental goals.'

'Hold on here, Pete' said Evan, 'You're worrying me here. Have you gone over to the other side?'

Peter laughed. 'No, no, of course not. It just struck me that he's the kind of guy we could do business with if we had to. Maybe Mason's like that too.'

'Mason's a strange fish. At times it comes across like he's not too interested in getting elected; I can't feel the ambition there. But at the same time he seems to have the most disciplined following amongst the Greens. What's that all about?'

'I don't know. He's never said he wants to stand for election. His followers are part of the Green Earth Movement, and Dave Barrington says they are not a party as such. Maybe more a pressure group. A "movement" like they say. And they're not great fans of the mainstream Green party. Seems there's a bit of a battle on for the soul of Greenery.'

'Maybe he just wants to be a media pundit,' suggested Sandy. 'Power and publicity but no real responsibility for making decisions. Perhaps he just wants to stand on the side-lines and say "I told you so" whenever there's some bad news on the environment.'

'I don't think they're a threat,' pronounced Evan. 'Just a fact of life at the moment. And maybe they are helping to create a mood that can help us–help you, Peter–to get your eco messages across. Maybe you should even encourage your friend Barrington a little to get stories out that we can build on. Play the green card.'

As the others nodded their assent, Peter felt irritated. 'C'mon, guys. For me this isn't just about "playing the green card". This is really important, and to me it's central to what we're about.'

'Okay, Peter,' said Evan quickly, slapping Peter on the leg and giving a hearty laugh. 'We're all on the same page here. It's just if we can claw some more of the green votes our way, that's no bad thing, is it?'

3: Don's delusions

'For me, the prize isn't worth it, Ben.'

Don Mason was meeting with Ben Porter in the beer garden of a pub by the Thames. Porter was the leader of the largest mainstream Green party. He was in his mid-sixties, several years older than Don, and projected himself as the elder statesman in the Green movement. The two went back many years: colleagues, rivals and adversaries in the fragmented world of green politics and activism.

Ben sighed. They had had variants of the same conversation on numerous occasions over the past decade and a half, since Mason had gone out on his own to set up his Green Earth Movement.

'The thing is, Don, we need more boots on the ground for the election. It's only a year away,' said Porter. 'And your network of activists and sympathisers are just what we need. I really don't think we'll have another opportunity like this, not in my lifetime anyway, if we don't all come together to build on our local election successes and get more MPs into Parliament. Baxter's in the shit with the economy, Labour aren't getting anywhere, and the Liberals are just a waste of space. The country is really getting ready for something different. Anything different from the losers who've been running the country for the past ten years. We can win back Brighton and Norwich, and–'

He stopped when he saw how Mason was looking at him sceptically over the top of his glasses.

'Two or three MPs', said Mason. 'And at the local elections a handful of council seats. Maybe even taking control of one council. The usual protest vote at the European elections. You've been there before. And then it all slips back again. You had two MPs before, then lost them in the next election. All that effort. All that leafleting, canvassing, campaigning, fundraising. For what? Only to fail and dash the hopes of people who vote for you. And especially those who wear out their shoes on the campaign trail. It's just not worth it, Ben. If you play the game by the rules of the old Grey parties, they'll beat you hollow every time. We'll only win when we can change the game.'

Porter was torn between a having a full-on argument and the pressing need to make overtures to Mason and the GEM. He desperately wanted
their help. The problem was that Don Mason remained something of an enigma to him. He knew Mason was close to the more hard-line activist groups
within the Green movement. But all the same, he could not be considered
a 'fundamentalist' like them. On the contrary, to Ben he seemed to have
become someone on friendly terms with 'grey-green' sympathisers outside
of the Movement. But if he had become a 'gradualist', then it seemed he also
rejected the path of gradual change followed by mainstream Greens like Porter himself.

As editor of the *Green Earth Review* and author of several popular books,
it seemed that Don was now establishing himself as a respected figure capable
of making good connections with people of goodwill across the spectrum of
opinion. This was despite his pressing a 'deep green' agenda that would in
practice be far too radical for many of his wider circle of sympathisers. And
the truth was, despite Ben's largely recognised seniority in green circles, he
was starting to become a little jealous of Don Mason. Mason's success with the
media was giving him a more elevated platform than Porter had ever enjoyed.

And there was something else. Though Don's Green Earth Movement
didn't appear to do much in terms of political campaigning or recruiting,
it was clearly becoming a force to be reckoned with. Ben had no idea about
how big the GEM membership was, but its funds were growing and secure.
Enough anyway to maintain a robust infrastructure and to finance Mason and
his top level team in full-time positions, as well as a regional network and a
steady output of propaganda and 'think tank'-type research studies.

'OK,' said Porter. 'Maybe you prefer to sit on the side-lines while the
Greys hoover up all the power. But I've heard a bit about what you've been
saying to your GEM faithful. You know, about what needs to be going on before real change can happen. Like a continuing environmental crisis. Isn't that
building up right now? Like an enduring economic crisis that creates despair
and disillusionment with the old system. Haven't we had that for nearly ten
years now? Aren't we reaching the tipping point where we can break through?'

Mason smiled. 'Maybe we're getting close. But do you think there's a
chance of changing society by winning a few seats at elections? Even if you
won an election, do you think the old establishment would let you govern in a
way that made a difference? Not a hope in hell of that. It's going to take a much
sharper crisis than some hot summers and the economy flat-lining to give us
the chance to remake society.'

Porter laughed. 'Don, you're even more of a dreamer than I ever thought! You think winning a constituency or two is impractical, but you want to bring down the establishment and remodel society!'

Mason smiled. Ben Porter clearly hadn't got a clue about the strategy of the GEM and what its members did on a daily basis. 'I didn't say winning a seat or two is impractical. Just irrelevant. In the broader scheme of things.'

A familiar voice called out behind them: 'Hi boys!' It was Sarah Turner, one of the leadership team of the GEM. She was wearing combat trousers and what looked like a military vest, over which she wore a delicate floral-patterned top. Her sunglasses were pushed up on top of her head.

Both Mason and Porter greeted her warmly. 'What have you been doing today, Sarah? Tying yourself to a tree as usual?' asked Porter jovially.

Sarah Turner had come to prominence as a leading figure in the wood-land campaigns, and had helped score notable victories in seeing off developers. The recession was now helping keep pressure from developers at bay, and as an economist she had turned her energies towards policy and was the driving force in developing the GEM's economic ideas. Though, as Ben Porter had remarked to his party colleagues, little enough was known about those.

'What can I get you guys?' she asked.

But Don Mason was already on his feet and heading towards the bar. 'Cider? A pint?'

'Anything as long as it's really cold,' replied Sarah. She looked out at the Thames. 'That looks inviting. Fancy a dip, Ben?'

'I'm tempted,' smiled Porter. 'How's your day been? Don said you were doing something with students.'

'Yes, those that are still here during the summer. Getting some planning in place for next year.'

Porter looked interested. 'Planning? For next year's elections?'

Sarah smiled. 'We focus on practical things. Whole programme of practical activities for the year. People are tired of talking, you know. They want to do stuff to change the world.'

'You recruiting a lot of students?' asked Porter.

Sarah Turner smiled enigmatically. 'There's a lot of interest in our kind of approach.'

The truth was, though, that despite knowing Don Mason for many years Ben had little detailed insight into the GEM approach. His questions, and his expectations of how green politics should be played, seemed old-fashioned and out of touch to Sarah. Was it just because she was only a little more than half his age? That was not enough to explain it. It was a deep-rooted difference in mindset. Perhaps it came down to this, she thought. Ben had spent his life and career trying against the odds to raise public awareness of environmental issues. He seemed to have a touching faith in the democratic process as the way to make a difference. But Sarah was of a different generation. Awareness-raising wasn't the issue. Her generation had been bombarded with environmental messages since birth. The problem was, people were aware but they just didn't care. Or didn't care enough. So to expect them to turn up at the ballot box and vote against their narrow and selfish interests? It wasn't going to happen unless they got one mighty kick up the backside.

All the odds were stacked against being able to make a difference. And it wasn't just to do with elections. The way the British establishment worked—parliament, civil service, local government, law, police and media—all made for a system that stacked the odds against the kinds of changes that would be needed to save the planet. And Ben Porter, for all his good intentions, was in effect aligning the green movement with the processes of that same 'grey' establishment. On the other hand, the kind of direct action that she used to play a leading role in, that too had proved itself to be of limited value.

And it was precisely this kind of bind that Sarah had been wrestling with when Don Mason had first sounded her out about the Green Earth Movement. Mason's approach involved promoting environmental awareness through practical action rather than policy. But that was only one level at which it operated. The second level was to embed their members in parts of the establishment where they could rise in the ranks and be in a position to influence the powerful institutions of state. Some of these people, like Dave Barrington, also played a public and prominent role in the Movement. But there was also a third level of 'sleepers', a growing network of activists , or 'inactivists' as Mason like to call them, whose job was to move quietly into positions of responsibility and to be ready to be promoted into power when the time was ripe.

And it wasn't ripe yet. Don Mason had set out to his inner circle of followers the preconditions for a successful Green Revolution. In some ways, it was not so far from the circumstances that Ben Porter had been putting to Mason before Sarah arrived. A backdrop of deep disenchantment and economic gloom. An environmental crisis or two. But it needed more than this. There needed to be a sudden and unexpected shock. Something to unsettle the establishment, that knocked them out of balance, and that would enable a well-organised group like the GEM to take control. It needn't be directly to do with anything green—but if it was, so much the better. In the meantime, Don Mason had set out on a charm offensive with the media. Unlike Ben Porter, he recognised that British political life was evolving. More than ever, it was about personality rather than policy. In fact, being some kind of celebrity was a much more certain route to success than taking a traditional approach to climbing the political ladder.

If Ben actually knew the GEM strategy, thought Sarah, he would probably laugh out loud and condemn us as revolutionary dreamers. Who knows? Maybe he would be right, and change would indeed be a long time coming. Maybe we've calculated wrongly. But even so, at least the GEM had a solid strategy—not like the endless and futile tactical games of the mainstream Greens.

As Mason returned with Sarah's drink, he noticed with a smile that Porter was talking and Sarah clearly wasn't paying much attention. But Porter didn't seem to notice. Or if he did, perhaps he was so used to it that he didn't take offence.

'How's Lester?' asked Don, breaking into her reverie. Then to Ben, 'Sarah's latest.'

'It's over.'

'You sad about that?

'Nah. He was … tiresome!'

'In only three weeks? That's quick, even for you. How's Chuckles?' Then to Ben: 'Her house rabbit. Huge bastard. Very aggressive.'

Sarah smiled. 'He's my house companion. Lester hated him. Well, they hated each other. I thought he—Lester, that is—was going to ask to me to choose between them. So I got my decision in first.'

At thirty-five Sarah Turner had never been known to have a relationship for more than a few months. Her work was everything, and her passion for the planet drove her forward. She had been an inspirational activist with her apparently boundless energy, her insatiable appetite for learning and her ability to support and encourage new recruits in the never-ending round of campaigns. And it was Don Mason who had seen not only the value of her selfless work, but also her potential as a GEM leader. Someone who could draw together the various strands of Deep Green thinking and turn them into a coherent and radical economic programme.

Don Mason brought the conversation back to their reason for meeting. 'Ben wants us to work together for next year's elections. A kind of broad Green front.'

'Stuffing envelopes and posting leaflets?' said Sarah. 'Why would we do that?'

'There's a lot more to it than that!' laughed Porter, though he was starting to feel slightly nettled. 'We used to work together. And we're still all part of the one broader movement, aren't we? Pulling in the same direction. And you've clearly got people of huge ability, who would make great MPs. Yourselves. Dave Barrington. And Jessica—she'd make a fantastic candidate.'

'If she was interested!' interrupted Sarah. 'Which she is not. In the slightest, unless she's had a sudden change of heart about these things.'

'Times change, and we need the right people to step up to the mark,' persisted Ben.

'You've already got candidates in place everywhere,' said Mason. 'You think some of them would step aside for us? Or maybe you have a few vacancies in unwinnable places that no one else wants to touch!'

'These are details, Don,' said Porter. 'The first stage is to agree the principles, whether we want to cooperate or not. It's not like we're rivals or opponents, at least not in the ordinary sense. As far as I know, you've got no plans to get involved directly in the elections. But I imagine you'd prefer us to do well. How could it do any harm for the Greens to make progress, and set everyone thinking? We're an established party, we've got a well-thought out set of policies, and we're ready to go. But we lack some people-power on the ground. You have some of that. You seem to be reaching some of the key demographics, and winning them over. And you—both of you, and Dave—seem to be tapping in well to the media. And so … we need each other.'

Sarah Turner looked sceptical. 'But what if we don't agree with your policies? I think we're coming from a deeper shade of green, and your policies seem a little—pallid.'

Ben smiled and sighed. 'We have to operate in the world as it is. I doubt if our policies are so different from yours—but I'm not really sure what yours are, not in any detail. And we have the range of policies, not only environmental—the things that really concern most voters. I mean, what is the GEM policy for the health service, or law and order?'

'Why do we need policies for these?' asked Don.

'What?' Porter looked dumbfounded.

'This has been exactly the problem,' explained Mason. 'For years we've been swallowing whole the process of the Grey parties. Maybe there are no big problems with the health service, or with the police, except that they need to be run better. Political parties don't know how to run them. Nor do government bureaucrats. Our policy would be to leave the doctors and the police to run their own services. They would do hell of a lot better without all this meddling and constant restructuring. So why not? What we would do is make sure the environmental performance of these services is scrutinised and improved, vastly improved. That's what we should be about. Not pretending to be experts in areas where we clearly know very little.

'Now take your manifesto. There's a lot of good stuff in there, but it goes nowhere near tackling the fundamental problems we face. I know, I know, one step at a time, you'll say. But overall it's a mish-mash of ideas sucked in from other parties. Some socialistic, some libertarian, all of it well-scrubbed and politically correct. None of it really having any balls, I'm afraid to say. Even if we threw ourselves heart and soul into your campaign, we'd be nowhere near winning. And we wouldn't have done much to raise awareness of the real issues either.'

'That's harsh,' said Ben tetchily. 'OK. What are the real issues that you think we should be campaigning on?'

'That we're sleepwalking to disaster,' said Don. 'And your policies about so-called "green economic growth" are nonsense. We need a new approach to living that, in all probability, rules out economic growth for generations to come. We need to produce less and consume less. You know that. I've heard you speak about "prosperity without growth". But your party hasn't thought it through in any coherent way, has it?'

Ben Porter was now feeling exasperated. 'Don, do you understand what elections are about? You couldn't possibly sell negative economic growth to the electorate. We'd be murdered at the polls!'

'The way things are now, we'll be murdered anyway. The only way forward is to keep faithful to the true message. Like Churchill in the 1930s, being a lone voice against the dictators when everyone else was for appeasement. But when the time came, and he was proved to be right, he was the man for the hour. And when the crisis does come, Ben, you'll be knocking on our door to try and join us as the junior partner, not the other way round!'

Don Mason said this with an engaging smile that made it hard for Porter to know if he was being entirely serious. Did he really have such delusions of grandeur, or was it just banter to wind him up a bit?

'I see it like this, Ben,' continued Mason. 'We can't solve our problems with the same kind of thinking and the same kinds of actions that got us here in the first place. I know you agree with that. But let's take that idea to the next stage. Why do we accept the agenda set out for us by the same people, the same establishment, that has led us into this mess in the first place? I mean, the agenda of politics-as-usual, slotting into the structures that will ensure nothing *really* changes?'

Mason paused, then continued: 'You know in my dark distant past I used to work for an oil company?'

'Geologist, weren't you?' offered Porter.

Mason nodded. 'I was. I was one of the guys reading the landscapes, checking the data, finding the best sites for test drills—'

'He's amazing,' interrupted Sarah Turner. 'The way he can read a landscape. It's not just based on some scientific training and understanding land forms, he just has this connection with the Earth. He just *knows* stuff, somehow. It's in his DNA.'

'Some of my colleagues said I could sniff out the oil, like a water diviner can find water that's deep underground. It's not true, of course. But Sarah's right in a way. I did always feel a connection with the Earth. And I was working for a company, and with colleagues, who see the Earth as something completely separate from themselves. As an object on which to ply their trade, to ravage and plunder and strip her in one place, then move on to another place and do the same thing all over again. And I wasn't comfortable with that,' said Don.

'So you had some kind of Damascus moment, and joined up with us, the good guys,' said Ben approvingly. 'You did some good stuff back then, real environmental action sponsored by your company. Paid for by oil money. It was impressive.'

'It was window-dressing. But I want to get to my point. From there I was recruited by Nature and Habitat International, and then a couple of other jobs in the NGO world. All full of committed, caring and intelligent people. But you know what? I always knew it was not enough. Always on the back foot. Always trying to plug the gaps and make good the damage done by humanity's mainstream activities of self-indulgence and destruction. And you know the second thing I realised, and the one that really made me think hard about what I was doing? All these great organisations trying to change the game, in the end they are just playing the game. They become the reflection of the corporate world, only wearing woolly cardigans and always strapped for cash. You can't change the game when you've become the game, Ben. And that's what's wrong with the approach you're trying to sell me. Their game, their rules. They win. End of story.'

'You can't fool me, Don. I've known you too long,' said Porter. 'I know you want to be in that driving seat and making the big changes. You keep it close to your chest, but you've got your own game plan.'

'Sure, I'd like to be in the driving seat. Who knows, one day I'll make it there,' said Mason thoughtfully. 'Though maybe I'm too old, and it will have to be Sarah, or Malcolm, or Dave. Someone a decade or two younger. But my game plan is for a different game. And it's not going to happen until there's a massive change in consciousness, until we have tens of thousands of people who realise the danger we are in, and are willing to embrace the Truth. When we can mobilise tens of thousands on the streets, people who are ready for action—then we can change, really change the way things are done.'

Suddenly Sarah Turner's attention was diverted. She was looking over towards the entrance to the pub garden, and started to slide down in her chair.

'Uh-oh,' she said. 'I think this is someone I don't want to see. Too late. He's coming this way.'

'Another ex?'

Sarah shook her head. 'Police. Special Branch. Anti-terrorist unit.'

At this Ben Porter looked bewildered, and slightly alarmed. A tall man in his early fifties, wearing a beige jacket, approached the table where they were sitting. He seemed to be sweating profusely in the blistering heat.

'Ms Turner,' he said. 'Do you mind if I have a word with you?'

'Please, join us,' said Mason pulling a chair across from the next table. 'Can I get you a drink?'

'Not when I'm on duty, I'm afraid. Kind of you to offer, though.'

'May I introduce Detective George Cavanagh,' said Sarah. 'We're old … friends.'

'I'll get you a soft drink. Orange and lemonade or something, lots of ice. It's kind of my extended round,' persisted Mason.

'OK—thanks!' said Cavanagh.

Sarah Turner stood up to angle the parasol over the table so it shaded Cavanagh from the sun. 'You should take that off,' she said, touching the sleeve of his jacket. 'You don't need to be too formal with us. Oh, I should introduce you. This is Ben Porter, and that's Don Mason who has just gone off the bar. But you probably know that.'

Cavanagh and Porter shook hands.

'How did you know to find Sarah here?' asked Ben.

Sarah jumped in and answered for Cavanagh. 'Oh the usual. CCTV. Number-plate recognition. Tracking my mobile phone. Sometimes they just follow me. I am a woman with many shadows.'

Porter looked appalled.

'Don't worry about it, Ben. I'm used to it. I grew up in a peace camp, thanks to my implacable peacenik mum. So I've more or less been followed and harassed by the police since I was born. Just a fact of life.'

'A life in which you've never put a foot on the wrong side of the law,' added Cavanagh with mild sarcasm.

'I've always strived to live a good life, Officer,' said Sarah, with mock innocence and a wide smile.

Cavanagh laughed grudgingly. 'And always careful to side-step the issue. You see, Mr Porter, we know each other quite well. You don't mind if I ask Ms Turner some questions?'

'Fire away,' said Sarah.

'Were you anywhere near Cambridge on Sunday evening?'

'Cambridge? No. Why?'

'Where were you?'

'At home mostly. Near here, in Putney.'

'Any witnesses?'

'Sure. Not for all of the evening, but for some of it.'

'So you don't know anything about the destruction of two fields of genetically modified crops, and one very large greenhouse.'

'Nothing directly. Only what was on the news.'

'It was only in the local news. So you've been to Cambridgeshire since then?'

'Come on, George. Online news. I always watch out for the environmental news. *Guardian*, *Times*, *Independent*, BBC. And other specifically environmental interest channels. I read and watch a lot—it's my job.'

'Hm. You approve of this action?'

'Not especially. But I don't approve of what those biotech companies are doing either, or the people who fund the research.'

'We have some photos and video. Do you mind taking a look?'

Sarah Turner raised an eyebrow in response, which Cavanagh took for agreement. He pulled from his jacket pocket a small tablet computer and tapped the screen a few times, then turned it towards Sarah.

'Do you recognise these people?'

Sarah looked closely. 'You can't see their faces! They're all wearing some kind of protective suit.'

'Yes ... but the height, shape, stature; and the combination of people might give you a clue. Now here ... we have some CCTV from a bit of a distance ... you can see them moving. And one of them here lifts up his face mask—we think it's a him because of the size. Any clues?'

Sarah shook her head.

'No? This guy's really big. About six foot six tall. Size fourteen shoes. Built like a gorilla.'

She shook her head again.

'How about these ones. Please, just flick through.'

Sarah flicked slowly through the pictures. 'No sorry. Can't really make anyone out.'

'Hm. Look at this one. This person. About five foot four. Seems to be female. That isn't you?'

'No.'

'What's your shoe size?

'Five and a half.'

'She is wearing size six boots. Do you have any boots in a size six?'

'No!' Sarah laughed. 'Do you think these guys take their suits and boots home with them?'

'Do you know otherwise?'

'Listen, George—you know this isn't my style,' protested Sarah calmly.

'But it used to be?'

'Not really. Different kinds of direct action. I was up in the trees mostly, saving woodlands, not out in the fields. And I've been a model law-abiding urbanite for a few years now. Haven't I, Don?'

Don Mason had returned with a drink for the detective, and a new round for everyone else.

'Oh, thanks,' said Cavanagh, taking his drink and immediately drinking a good half of it. 'Oh, that's good! I wonder if you two recognise any of these?'

He handed the tablet to Mason, and both he and Porter both leaned in towards the screen, flicking through the pictures and video.

'No, sorry,' said Don, handing the tablet back. But Cavanagh had noted a flash of recognition when Porter had seen the first image of the larger man. He made a mental note to contact Porter later. And he was impressed with Mason's coolness. Mason was much more closely connected with the activists, so if Porter knew who it might be then Mason almost certainly would. But then again, the police were pretty sure already who it must be. The problem was getting a clear identification. And then finding him.

'So this is a fishing expedition, Detective?' asked Mason pleasantly. 'You have an idea who they are. You have no real reason to think Sarah was there. You just want to see if with a little prompting, something will turn up.'

'These are serious crimes, Mr Mason. Well-planned pre-meditated actions of substantial criminal damage. We're going to catch these people.'

'Maybe so,' answered Mason. 'But I think it's all a bit one-sided, don't you? All this chasing after people who damage property and commercial interests, but no one is chasing after the eco-criminals whose pursuit of profit is doing profound damage to the natural world. What do you say?'

'Well, that's your opinion,' said Cavanagh. 'But as I see it, my job is to enforce the law as it is, not how it might be or as you think it should be.'

'Fair enough,' said Mason. 'And if a future Green government passed laws to stop people being eco-criminals, you'd enforce them?'

'If it's all been through the system and passed into law, then I expect I would,' replied Cavanagh, who then finished his drink with a flourish. 'I should be going. Thanks again for the drink, and many thanks for your assistance, all of you.'

As he left Ben Porter leaned back in his seat and exhaled dramatically.

'That's absolutely outrageous,' he said. 'They follow you, accuse you, then ask you to turn informer. That's harassment! You should put in a complaint about him.'

'No point, Ben,' said Sarah calmly. 'This is what they do. It's a shot across the bows. It will all be authorised from the top. So you end up just wasting your breath.'

'And besides,' added Don, 'we need people like George when we get in. People who will enforce our laws without fear or favour. Our own Green Earth Javert. Don't you think so?'

Porter looked astonished, then said, 'Don, you're not just a dreamer: I think you're more deluded than I ever thought possible!'

'Then let's drink,' toasted Sarah, 'to Don's dreams and delusions!'

Hesitantly, then with a shake of his head and a sardonic smile, Ben Porter joined in the toast, little believing that there was any chance of Don's delusions becoming reality.

4: The shock that kick-started the revolution

Early August, and Peter and Heather Kitson were alone, enjoying the prospect of a peaceful and domestic weekend. Until the phone rang. It was Sandy. 'Switch on the news', she said. 'This is big.'

'What is it, darling?' asked Heather.

'Let's see', said Peter as he flicked onto a news channel. The news was from France—a growing crisis at a nuclear power station in the north of the country. Once the symbol of France's independence and modernity, these power stations were now over fifty years old and a powerful symbol of yesterday's tomorrows.

And now, it seemed, more than a symbol. A reactor in France appeared to be heading for a Chernobyl-type disaster. Troops had been called out to evacuate people from a hundred mile radius of the reactor on the Normandy coast. The circles showing the hundred mile radius on a map included a good chunk of the English Channel, taking in the Channel Islands and coming uncomfortably close to the Isle of Wight.

'Oh my God', whispered Heather.

Sandy was still online. 'Peter, I've got Evan and Howard online—can you connect to them?'

'Sure. Let me take it in the study where we can conference.'

'OK.'

Heather sat watching the TV, gently touching her stomach. Over the next half hour she would see a procession of experts talking about the French heatwave and the extra demand for power for air-conditioning, tales of rivers drying up and nuclear reactors unable to be cooled properly, repeated references to Chernobyl, Three-Mile Island, Tokaimura, Fukushima. She didn't understand a lot of the references, or the technicalities—but she got the message clear enough. Poor management of technology and poor stewardship of the environment was leading to a catastrophe—and one that threatened everyone in the West of Europe; not just herself and her husband, but her unborn child as well.

Peter sprinted to the study, flicking on the screens so he could have all three in view and the news showing too. The tight-lipped faces of Evan Roberts and the party leader, Howard Blackstone, came into view.

Howard spoke first. 'Peter, we need a fast response on this. I've had a call from the PM, and this is serious, really serious. There could be a lot of casualties in France, and possibly here too if the wind blows the radiation our way. He's preparing to declare a State of Emergency in all the southern and eastern counties of England. We're talking meltdown here, and it looks like we're in for a lot of fall-out making its way across the Channel. With the wind as it is, parts of Dorset, Hampshire, East Sussex and Kent are particularly in the firing line. They say London should be safe, but who knows if the wind changes? If the Met Office is right, then any fall-out will most likely blow north-east to Belgium, Holland and Denmark. Evan, can you fill Peter in on the discussions so far?'

Evan was champing at the bit to suggest how to approach this unexpected situation, as if he had been working all day on a new strategy. What could you read in his face? Peter, not usually the first to pick up on appearance, couldn't help noticing a kind of glow on Evan's face—a sheen of perspiration, perhaps. His eyes betrayed a mix of fear and elation. These were real events unfolding, and Evan felt somewhere near the centre of them. And he had a powerful urge to be closer still to the source of power.

'The PM wants the three main parties to agree an approach to this issue—to support the state of emergency, and help keep the lid on things, reassure people in the "cloud zone" and avoid making party capital out of this. And he's ordered an immediate review of safety and security at our own power stations—'

'That's just what I've been calling for this past year, and he's always refused', interrupted Peter.

'I knew you'd say that, Peter,' said Evan. 'Baxter knows you'd want to say that too, and he's specifically asked us not to make a point of it. They say it's not a response to your charges of complacency, but a prudent response to what's happening.

'And you accept that?'

Howard intervened. 'Peter, I think we'll look bad if we try to score "smug points" at a time like this. We all think we should be statesmanlike.'

Peter felt stung by the implied rebuke. 'So we leave the moral high ground to the Greens, do we?'

Evan responded. 'They can ride their moral high horse wherever they like, no one's going to take much notice. The point for us is to be seen to be on the practical and responsible side—we need to associate ourselves with doing things, not posturing.'

'How, exactly?'

'Tomorrow at 8 a.m. Howard, Baxter and Leadbetter will hold a joint press conference. All about solidarity and the national interest. Then you, and your Environment counterparts in the other two parties will hold a further press conference to deal with more detailed questions. How do you feel about that?'

Peter Kitson thought a moment. 'I've no problems with the approach. Now tell me what we know—how serious is the situation?'

Evan spoke again. 'Baxter's asked the head honcho from the Emergency Planning Unit to meet us online at ten past eight. He'll give the complete rundown on the situation. Peter—this is top level confidential. You should take this call completely on your own, no one else in the room, and maximum security—we have to get the story straight and do all we can to avoid panic.'

5: The Volunteers emerge

The traffic tailed back from the M25 around London, down every road to the south coast. It was not yet a panic, but few living in the so-called 'cloud zone' wished to remain behind and take the risk. Many Londoners too were arranging hasty weekends away up north, to be on the safe side.

The Barringtons were visiting Jessica's parents in the family home just outside Horsham. Sir James and Lady Frances Olsen, Jessica's parents, were anxious about the situation. But they were old school, not the kind of people to panic under any circumstances. They knew they had to leave the area, not only for safety reasons but because Sir James, as one of the country's top civil servants, would be urgently needed in London. As Permanent Secretary at the Treasury he knew that this kind of emergency would place heavy demands on public funds. The consequent reordering of budgets would be as much a political process as a financial one, and it would need a steady hand at the helm. Maybe for a day or two he could conduct business remotely and stay with the family—but in a day or two it might well become too dangerous to remain in the area. Mind you, Lady Frances had said, London might be no safer. So she had made judicious contact both with her relatives in Scotland and his relatives in Sweden. Possibly it would have been preferable to have some South American or Australian relatives at this time, to get as far away as possible. But she knew her husband would not like to be too far from the centre of activity, with his strong sense of public duty.

And there were Jessica and Dave and the children too. Visits had never been as frequent as both she and her husband would have liked. At first she had been inclined to blame Dave for this. But then again, she knew her daughter and her over-serious outlook on life. At one time she had hoped Jessica would meet a nice and 'normal' young man who would take the edge off her earnestness, and that she would mellow into a daughter who didn't want to take issue with the Olsen family's lifestyle and values. Instead she met Dave Barrington, and his over-seriousness reinforced Jessica's. They were well-matched, no doubt—but it was unfortunate for wider family relationships.

All the same, Jessica and the grandchildren all seemed happy and healthy; the Barrington Norfolk homestead, though a bit twee in her view, seemed a very pleasant and prosperous environment in which to bring up a family, and they had just had a very successful weekend together—one of the least tense she could remember.

There had inevitably been a few arguments. Well, she called them arguments. Jessica, Dave and Sir James referred to them as 'discussions'. But they did seem to get a trifle heated. And she could not bear Dave and Jessica's use of the word 'Grey', hurling it about as some kind of insult. As a trustee of a charity for the elderly and a dynamic proponent of 'active ageing', she resented the imagery—grey, old, out of touch, useless. In time they'd learn, she hoped.

Lady Frances was musing in this way, as she endeavoured to set up her irrigation system in the greenhouse—after all, it might be some time before they could return. Then she pulled herself up, thinking, 'My God! There could be a cloud of radiation coming across the water at any moment! And here I am thinking of all this trivial nonsense, just as if nothing unusual is happening.'

Lady Frances put down her gardening gloves and walked into the sitting room, where Jessica was trying to mobilise the children into packing all their toys and games into their travel bags.

'It's no use our just pottering around here, Jessie darling,' she said. 'We have to do something.'

Jessica was used to her mother's sudden bursts of enthusiasm, and it struck her as faintly amusing in these circumstances.

'Do something?' she smiled.

'And I don't just mean head for the hills,' her mother said. 'I mean, do something practical, right here, right now.'

'Like what, mother?

'Don't humour me, Jessie. You know better than that,' said Lady Frances with determination. 'Let's look at the situation. The roads are packed. There's around a quarter of a million people trying to get off the Isle of Wight, and all landing on the south coast to make their own way north. People are frightened out of their wits. It's August and it's unbearably hot inside, let alone stuck in a car somewhere.'

'Go on....'

'And there's not only the people on the roads. There'll be people who will refuse to leave. And there'll be others who would like to leave, but can't. And there'll be others who stick around because they want to rob the rest of us. So we need to do something.'

She said this with an air of finality, as Sir James and his son-in-law came into the room.

'Do what, dear?' asked Sir James.

'We can't just sit around here and wait for the roads to clear. Did you get out to have a look?'

'Yes,' reported Dave, 'but we couldn't get out past the end of the next village'.

'Exactly,' said Lady Frances. The others looked at each other quizzically.

'We have to mobilise for action. I know the PM has called out the troops and all the emergency services, before you say anything, James. But that's not the point. They'll take hours, maybe days to get here, and they're far too thin on the ground to cover everywhere. No, what we need is to mobilise concerned citizens.'

'But for what, darling?' asked Sir James.

'Honestly, James, how can you sit up there in Whitehall running everything when you don't know the first thing about anything practical?'

Sir James gave an affectionate 'Hrumph' and pretended to be affronted.

'What are we now, three hours into this crisis? Already there'll be families dehydrating on the A3 and the M23, and god knows where else. Now on TV they are talking about violent storms over the next couple of days, which could bring the radiation right down on our heads. So we need to take action. Action Number One: get some supplies to everyone stuck out on the roads. Tonight they'll need soup, and possibly blankets or a place to sleep. Church halls or anywhere. And if this goes on for a couple of days, what will happen to the food supply? Even now I'm sure there'll be nothing coming into anywhere south of London. Tesco and Sainsbury and all the rest will be completely out of stock—all this "just-in-time" nonsense. Hopeless in a crisis if you can't get the supplies in. So we need to plan a way to distribute all the food that can be sourced locally—that should suit your politics, Jessie!'

Jessica smiled, but Sir James was getting alarmed. He thought it time to intervene.

'Hold on a minute there, Fran,' he said. 'You're talking about emergency planning. What do you think the County Council is doing at the moment? They have all the responsibilities for disaster response, and they've done the planning. I'm sure they can achieve much more than we can. Let's not meddle.'

'Meddle?' retorted Lady Frances. 'They've faced nothing like this. And they don't have the resources to do what's necessary.'

'And we do?' asked her husband incredulously.

'Not only us, you chump,' she replied. 'We need to mobilise the voluntary networks—well as far as we can. A lot of folk will be on the road, or hiding under the sofa or who-knows-what by now. But we need a network of ordinary, local people who can support the authorities and carry out practical, low level action.'

'You call organising food distribution "low level action"?' asked Sir James.

'No, of course not. But this area is full of farmers and other people who grow or process food. There's even some fisherman still. Yes, it has to be coordinated. James can work out a system of vouchers to pay for everything that is pooled for the common good, and which can act as kind of government IOUs. You could get authority for that?'

Sir James looked flabbergasted. 'I could,' he mumbled, 'but I don't think it will come to that.'

'And I think it's very important that law and order and community spirit doesn't collapse, don't you?' she added, addressing all of them. 'We need to get those decontamination suits they keep talking about out to volunteers who are going to stay behind to maintain public order. You know the police and the troops will be far too thinly spread. And with those chumps of yours in Whitehall in control, they'll probably all be sent to the wrong places too. But if they can get the supplies in, our citizen volunteer force can do the rest!'

Dave Barrington thought it was a very good idea. He had already been in contact with Don Mason about 'doing something'. So far the GEM leadership had agreed it was a good opportunity to mobilise GEM activists, but the response so far was to try to organise a media campaign and mass rallies against nuclear power.

But Don Mason had felt this approach was too much like the old Green tactics, and was looking for a new approach which would put the GEM right at the centre of things. And when Dave called him back with Lady Frances' idea, he saw the possibilities at once.

'I think I can mobilise some additional labour,' Barrington said to his mother-in-law.

'Really?' she said, a little surprised. 'Oh, you mean your tree-climbers and tunnellers?'

Barrington smiled. 'Not only them. We've got more respectable people as well—ones who want to make less of a noise and more of a difference. But don't underestimate what the tree climbers can do. It's amazing what they conjure up at short notice.'

'Like producing chaos out of order?' muttered Sir James.

'Ignore that, David,' said Lady Frances. 'Now what can these people do?'

The truth was that the GEM activists and inactivists were taking flight or staying put in roughly the same proportions as any other group of people in the affected areas. And in the immediate area they had never been especially numerous. But for Mason and Barrington these villages in Hampshire would become an important pilot for social action. For Mason it dovetailed perfectly with plans to set up 'Earth Councils' across the country. It was imperative that these should not be purely political talking shops. They had to take the lead in practical action, and they had to help build the reputation and popularity of the GEM.

The work began. In the process Dave Barrington discovered just how resourceful his mother-in-law could be. She seemed to know not only the great and good of the county, but also anyone who could do anything. And she was very effective, even merciless in bullying people into voluntary action. Meanwhile Dave Barrington, a very organised and effective project manager, was soon coordinating the action. This was not without some difficulty, as all the communication networks were heavily overloaded. But by using volunteers with bicycles and motorbikes as 'runners' coordinated from the village hall and other selected hubs, and where possible the radio communications used by some farmers and taxi firms, relief was organised and a 'citizens' watch' set up in the nearby villages.

The next day the rains started to come: heavy 'monsoon' rains that within a further twenty-four hours led to flooding across large swathes of the south of England. The situation was now beyond crisis point, and the emergency services were stretched past breaking point. And with the rainfall, the danger of contamination from fall-out increased. The radioactive particles were coming down. Radiation-detecting equipment, medicines and protective suits began to arrive by helicopter and jeep.

Soon farm vehicles were making trips to and fro across the fields to the cars jammed on the trunk roads, with trailers carrying supplies of water, snacks and fruit to stranded refugees, and bringing away the sick and dehydrated for medical attention.

Just as Barrington was impressed with the abilities of his mother-in-law, so Lady Frances Olsen was amazed by the zeal, energy and organising genius of her son-in-law. He and Jessica worked effectively as a double-act, but there was no doubting where the direction was coming from. Sheltering under an umbrella in the driving rain, she and Jessica watched as Dave stood in a field with uniformed soldiers, directing the unloading of supplies and joining in quick decisions about the next priorities for actions. And they had a new house guest too, a GEM colleague of Dave the Olsens had never heard of before. A former captain in the army, his name was Malcolm Morton. Lady Frances thought it would have been impossible to have a more polite and correct guest in the house. And like her son-in-law he was both efficient and driven. He worked long, long hours, and was rarely in the house except to sleep.

The Olsen/Barrington formula for citizen action spread like a bush fire across the south, helped by the invisible hand of Don Mason as he called on the GEM membership to mobilise for action.

Soon a network of staging posts were in position, in part to encourage people off the roads for a time but mainly to create 'oases' where people could be refreshed, checked over and receive any help they needed. Mason told the GEM activists that they should clearly but modestly badge themselves as 'Green Earth Volunteers'. But on no account should they appear to be political. Many of them had until now been 'sleepers', and this was their first occasion to 'come out', as it were. And other environmentally conscious people asked for these badges too, so that they could identify with the good work being done. The field kitchens that were set up had a distinct green flavour to them, cooking predominantly free range and organic foods. But not exclusively so. Grocers and supermarkets were quick to donate tinned food, and tractors ferried the produce to the 'oases'.

In the south coast towns there were outbreaks of rioting and looting. Coordinated by Malcolm Morton, Green Earth Volunteers took up position to support the thin blue line of police, and coordinate a 'citizens' response' to law and order problems. As the contagion of fear spread to the South London suburbs, copycat looting met a similar Green Earth Volunteer response.

The army had been quick to mobilise—but not as quick as this. They were indeed thinly spread as Frances Olsen had anticipated. And army commanders, though at first a little nonplussed, welcomed the local initiatives as it helped them to focus their resources. And trusting in the safe hands of a forces veteran, Captain Malcolm Morton, there were many instances of effective cooperation, from rushing the sick to field hospitals to helping the army nip incipient looting in the bud.

Soon this activity caught the imagination of the news media. It is now a well-worn truism that in any crisis nothing will prevent the international news media from arriving en masse. There may be famine, floods or war, and food or medical aid may face insuperable obstacles—but nothing can stand in the way of a good story. 'Nothing is needed in a disaster area more than several tons of journalists,' Mason quipped. 'So make sure it's your story they're reporting.'

Trevor MacLean found himself amongst this shipment of journalists, and once again thrown into close quarters with Dave Barrington. He had brought with him a small film crew to catch the dramatic events as they unfolded. And he was very surprised at the Dave Barrington he found there.

The truth was that he had barely noticed Barrington the few times they had met before. He had seemed in one sense assured and professional, but had not seemed at all a strong personality. Quiet-spoken, he had always seemed to be playing second fiddle to Don Mason. A loyal sidekick, rather than someone with presence or sparkle. So he was somewhat amazed to find Dave Barrington as a commanding figure at the centre of events. Wherever Barrington went seemed to be the command centre for operations in the flooded 'cloud zone'—almost like a battlefield commander as people constantly sought him out in person, by phone and by field radio for decisions. And though it was disconcerting at first, it was also impressive how Barrington virtually ignored MacLean and his crew, so focused was he on the tasks at hand.

As the Olsen household seemed to be at the epicentre of much of the activity, Trevor MacLean negotiated to set up base there and permission to track Dave Barrington's activities for the next forty-eight hours. He would be delivering regular bulletins and hoped at the end to weave it all together into a news feature analysing the response on the ground to the crisis. Stella Walton had travelled with him and set to gathering background information on Dave and his family, and doing some further background research on the GEM and on the various local groups who were pulling together in the crisis.

MacLean was trying to grab some snippets of interview with Dave Barrington as they sped along country lanes in a LandRover driven by a Volunteer. But it was hard to get more than a sentence or two out of Barrington as he was constantly interrupted to take calls. The latest call seemed to be causing him particular concern.

'OK. OK. That's not far from here,' he said. Then to the driver, 'Take a left here.'

'I'm pretty sure it's impassable down there. The water's too high,' said the driver.

'Let's get as far as we can.' Then to MacLean, 'Seems there's a very sick child in the village down there. And there's not a doctor for miles that can get through. I want to take a look to see if we should call in an air ambulance.'

'Shouldn't we just call it anyway?' asked MacLean.

'The services are way overstretched right now,' said Barrington. 'They've said they want a doctor to confirm that it's a real emergency. I'm not a doctor, but I'll have to do. I've had first aid training, and I've had a fair bit of experience with my own children ...'

He trailed off into thought.

'OK. This is as far as we can go,' said the driver.

Trevor MacLean looked ahead, to where the road took a steep dip. The water looked as though it was more than five feet deep. Dave Barrington jumped out and surveyed the scene.

'It's only a few hundred yards, over there,' he called through the noise of the wind and the rain. 'If we can wade through this first bit, the land rises over to the right and we should be able to get through. Got your waterproofs on?'

Trevor and his cameraman grabbed some waterproof trousers and boots from the back of the vehicle, and hurried to the water's edge as Barrington took another call that was being relayed to his field telephone. Without another word he started off through the water. Trevor MacLean and his colleague looked at each other. The water did not seem to be fast moving, but there were no doubt many pages of company health and safety regulations advising against this kind of risk. The cameraman shrugged and set off into the water, with MacLean following gingerly.

Barrington had calculated right. After a few yards the water was up to his chest, but then he moved tentatively to his right, and the land did indeed begin to rise at the side of the submerged road. It was boggy, but he made his way forward, and before long the water was only waist height. As he approached the dry land beyond, he began to run toward a small group of houses that were just visible behind a line of trees.

As he approached the lane the houses were in, he could see water, slightly more than ankle deep, sweeping fast along the street. A man was waving frantically from an upstairs window. Barrington ran fast towards the house, and was bowled over by the force of the current. Holding onto a fence, he pulled himself up and made his way to the house.

'Watch the current! It's fierce!' he shouted back to MacLean and his colleague, who were just beginning to struggle out of the deep water.

'What did he say?' asked MacLean.

'No idea!' shouted his colleague, shaking his head.

Barrington was now in the house, and headed up the stairs, his boots squelching all the way. The high pitched cries led him to a room where a frantic mother was desperately trying to sooth her child, but with no success.

'Are you the doctor?' asked the mother anxiously.

'What's her name?' asked Barrington.

'Chloe,' answered the mother.

'How old?'

'Four,' said the mother, beginning to weep.

'Now Chloe, I just want to—she's not registering this, is she?' said Barrington

The child was very hot, and then he noticed some light spots on her arms.

'Can you get me a glass?' he said sharply, turning to the father. 'Empty.'

The father ran down the stairs, just as Trevor MacLean and his colleague came through the door. Ignoring them he ran through to the kitchen and in seconds was running back with a glass tumbler and bounded past them up the stairs.

'This way, I guess,' said MacLean. 'Keep the cameras rolling.'

By the time they came upstairs, Dave Barrington was already rolling the tumbler over the spots on the child's arm. Without a word he put in a call on his field radio for the air ambulance to come immediately. He was not happy with the response.

'An hour?! That's no good. OK. I understand. OK.'

Then without hesitation, he put in another call.

'The army are sending a helicopter. It should be here within ten minutes, but we need to get outside onto that dry ground over there,' he said.

'You said—meningitis!' exclaimed Chloe's mother.

'Suspected. I think it could be, and we can't take any chances,' said Barrington. 'I'm not a doctor—but I know enough to say this.'

The parents looked to be in shock.

'I'm sorry about these guys here. I'm coordinating some of the operations down here, and these guys are following me for a documentary. They're tracking us for a couple of days. Do you mind them being here?'

'Can we talk about that later?' asked the father. The implied 'let's see how things turn out' sent a chill through them.

Within ten minutes an army helicopter was overhead, looking for a spot to land. Barrington carried the child outside while the parents grabbed the things they would need to bring.

'Put the bloody camera down now and help me across the street will you,' he barked to MacLean and the cameraman. With MacLean holding tightly onto the fence, they formed a small human chain to help Barrington, the child and her parents cross the water that was racing down the lane. A few anxious minutes later the family were up and away on their way to hospital.

As the noise of the helicopter faded, Trevor MacLean let out a deep breath.

'I hope she's OK,' he said. 'How did you know that?'

'It's something I learned in training,' said Barrington. 'But what made it stick is that my nephew had it—it puts you on alert for your own kids.'

'I have kids,' said Trevor. 'And at the back of my mind, I know about the symptoms. But I'm not sure I'd have the presence of mind to do the right thing under stress. Or the confidence to make the call you just did. What if the symptoms had been more ambiguous?'

Barrington shrugged. 'Sometimes you have to just believe in yourself, believe that you are right. And act on it. Do you think we can get back to the LandRover?'

'I don't get why they were still here, why they hadn't left the area,' said the cameraman.

There were many instances during the crisis of people who stayed behind and ran into some kind of trouble. For people living in the area, there was an atmosphere of fear, edged with disbelief. People were calculating the risks differently. Most felt that probably they would be safe. But even if the percentages turned out to be small, the stakes were far too high for making the wrong choice.

So the wise choice was to leave the cloud zone. The bravery of the volunteers' decisions to stay was appreciated by all who took to the roads. Even so, most of the volunteers were developing a personal 'plan B' which would swing into action if things got worse.

It was the same for the Olsens. The reality of the situation hit Frances Olsen late on the third day, as radiation levels were reported to be rising in the coastal areas. She could make her choice, and Jessica could make hers—but what on earth were the children still doing here? With typical decisiveness she went to find her husband, who had been commandeered into loading flagons of bottled water onto a farm trailer.

'James, we've got to get Jessica and the children away from here. Get a helicopter! You're more use to the nation in London, and you can take them out with you. Pack them off to Norfolk quickly,' she instructed. 'I know Jessie will refuse point blank—but she'll have to agree. She can't risk the children's lives.'

'Get a helicopter', she had said. As if it were that easy. She always overestimated his influence. Yet once he thought about it, Sir James suspected he could get one sent, or hitch a ride in a military one, if he found out the right strings to pull. It was just that it these were not the kinds of strings he was used to pulling. It was typical of his wife to imagine that anything she thought of was achievable, not knowing the practical obstacles. His career to date had been very successful, but channelled along narrow paths. Now he accepted with reluctance that he would have to pull strings in different ways. And then, his son-in-law had proved he could commandeer helicopters—Sir James could not bear to think of himself doing any less.

Sir James wanted to bring Frances out too. But she refused point blank, until in the end they constructed their own 'Plan B' escape scenario for her and David should it become necessary. Simply enough, another helicopter would be on its way the moment there was further bad news from France or from the Met Office.

So it was that on the following day Jessica Barrington, her children and Sir James Olsen headed out to London, though not without a fight from Jessica. By this time people were on the move again, and being received by friends, relatives and hastily convened 'refugee centres' further north.

But Dave Barrington had a new project, about which Lady Frances was less enthusiastic—setting up what he called 'Earth Councils' to coordinate practical initiatives focusing on the environment. He had set up effective partnership working amongst the various Green groups and environmentalist sympathisers across the south of England. Now this had to be moved on to the next stage, building on the goodwill that the GEM had attracted in the early days of the crisis.

After a week of anxiety, the nuclear crisis seemed to be subsiding. The radiation leak was being contained inside the French nuclear plant, thanks to the collaboration of teams of experts from across the world. The power station would be unusable, and in Don Mason's words 'would remain a monument to human arrogance and folly until the end of time'.

But the chaos in the south of England was set to increase. As the flood water receded in the countryside, the water level rose inexorably in the rivers and canals—and most of these feed into the River Thames. The floods that now hit London were the worst since 1928 as the river burst its banks from Chertsey to Lambeth. Water flooded across Parliament Square, and lapped against the walls of Buckingham Palace. But it was south of the river that was worst affected, with tens of thousands of homes hit by water more than a metre high.

In their Battersea home, Peter and Heather Kitson had been busy moving their valuables to the upper floors of their Victorian home. Then Peter was out with his neighbours joining volunteer efforts to fill and distribute sandbags. It seemed nobody was doing their regular work, but lending a hand for the common cause. And Peter had quickly picked up on the news about setting up Earth Councils, and had become a leading figure in setting up the local one in Battersea.

It felt good to be working shoulder to shoulder with his constituents, and he felt the barriers dissolving between himself and those he represented in Parliament. He felt energised by the community effort, energised by the almost tangibly heightened awareness of environmental issues on all sides, and energised by the opportunities to make a difference personally.

Despite their efforts, catastrophe hit the parts of his constituency closest to the river, as the river level overtopped the defences. And as law and order began to break down and looting broke out, the Green Volunteers took on an additional role of supporting the police and patrolling neighbourhoods to help keep the peace. As the waters subsided, there was a massive clean-up operation to deal with. In London, as in the 'cloud zone', Green Volunteers were at the centre of everything that happened.

Three days later Prime Minister Patrick Baxter declared that the emergency was over. The main political parties congratulated themselves on making a common front in a time of extreme crisis, and for successfully managing an emergency.

But on the ground it did not seem like they had been managing anything. It seemed they were always several steps behind the actions of the Volunteers, and had no counter to the mounting criticism of Britain's own nuclear power programme and weak environmental protection. Nor did they have any answer to the collapse of confidence in the markets that was bringing on a renewed economic crisis.

The mood of the country was completely transformed. Just cross the Channel, dozens of people had died and a large area of Normandy made into an exclusion zone. Evacuations were taking place in France and Belgium. Parts of the south coast in England had been evacuated completely and placed under army control while radiation levels were monitored. News of the planned evacuation of London leaked out, and the names of the politicians who had led the way to safer ground. Though that evacuation hadn't been necessary, tens of thousands left anyway, just to be on the safe side, while hundreds of thousands were affected by the floods. The inadequacy of the planning became a stick to beat the government with. People knew that many things had to change, and the nation had to learn to live in a more sustainable way.

6: The truth is great

The two young women sat on the bench overlooking the Atlantic as the sun set on another hot summer's day.

'I've had confirmation from Titus. It's time,' said Juliet, her blonde hair blowing gently in the breeze.

Annie, her slightly-built, dark-haired companion nodded thoughtfully. 'It's not too soon?'

'It's the beginning. The preparation phase. We must be ready to do what we have to do. Are you ready?'

'I am well bedded in. No one else working there has my expertise in the required fields. When the moment arrives, I shall be more than ready. You and your friends will have to watch my back, to see that I am not reassigned.'

Me and my friends, thought Juliet. The conversation seemed almost unreal to her. She was only twenty-six, and Annie was maybe three or four years older. Yet here they were, preparing to change the world. It seemed impossible, but both fervently believed it could be done. It needed to be done, and they would play their part in seeing that it was done.

'The beginning has come a little sooner than we expected,' said Juliet. 'I am inside, but not so far advanced as I need to be. But there are others who will pull me up—on both fronts—if things go according to the script. By the next phase we shall be well in control.'

They spoke for around twenty minutes more, then stood up to leave.

'You are very brave,' said Juliet, putting her hand on the other woman's arm. 'You are at the centre of our hopes.'

'I am not brave,' said Annie, diffidently. 'But I hope I will be when I have to be.'

They watched for a few moments the waves crashing gently on the rocks and sand below.

'The truth is great,' said Juliet—a familiar quote, a comforting ritual.

Annie smiled and nodded. 'We cannot meet again until the time of fulfilment is close,' she said. 'We shall meet in the new dawn.'

The two embraced—stiffly at first, then with greater warmth as emotion flooded through them. Then they parted, and went their way to their separate hotels.

7: A single spark

It was as Don Mason had predicted. The event that set the Green Revolution in progress was unexpected—but after that the Revolution was proving unstoppable. *A forest fire can start with a single spark, but only if the forest is ready to burn.* One of his favourite aphorisms.

Fond of metaphors, he had previously given his followers constant warnings not to try to pick unripe fruit. Don't try to force the Revolution before the time is right. Now, though, the fruit was ripe, and ready for picking. The crisis had changed everything, and shocked the country into consciousness.

The nuclear disaster had helped create a climate of fear and anger against the government. Then the violent storms and flooding across the south of England. Set against the backdrop of nearly ten years of economic problems and austerity, this was the 'perfect storm' of opportunity.

'This is the Awakening,' Mason declared. As the focus of the Green Revolution promoted across the country by the Green Earth Councils, Don Mason was rarely out of the public eye.

Now he, Don Mason the 'media pundit', as they had liked to call him, was becoming more powerful by the day. The momentum was with him, as the media said.

And what momentum! he thought. Since the Awakening, the old order had either been swept away or reduced to irrelevance. The Green Volunteers marched daily in the streets throughout the country, demonstrating, educating. And at the same time, he ensured that they always carried out some purposeful actions to improve the environment. Practical action, not empty gestures. Deeds, not words. Mason insisted on this to distinguish his Green Earth Movement from the 'grey' politicians of the traditional parties on the one hand, and the divided and demoralised Green parties of old on the other.

'It seems God is on our side,' Malcolm Morton had said, referring to the 'monsoon' storms that hit England shortly after the disaster.

'Or the French, anyway,' Mason had responded, drily. 'Or maybe both. It's a powerful combination, anyway.'

'The years of folly and arrogance are catching up, for sure. And humanity is getting its just deserts,' said Morton.

It was the first face-to-face meeting of the leadership of the GEM since the Awakening.

'Steady on, Malcolm,' said Jessica Barrington. 'Remember who it was who almost got their "just deserts" then. We were down there visiting my folks, with our kids too, Don. It was pretty hairy at times, I can tell you.'

'From what I understand, Jessica, your parents played a big part in relief operations. Your father is a very formidable man,' said Mason graciously.

Jessica assented, somewhat grudgingly. Much of her life had been defined by opposition to her parents, wealthy and respectable pillars of the establishment. But she had to acknowledge they had pulled out all the stops in the crisis.

'Actually,' said David Barrington, 'Jessica's mother played a big part too. It seems she knows everyone, and mobilised the great and the good to do their part while we launched the Green Volunteers into action. It was a very British Revolution—spirit of the Blitz, Dunkirk and all that, everyone playing their part.'

'Except the people who should have been taking the lead,' laughed Morton.

That's how it had been. The weak leadership of the country had been found out in the crisis. And years of preparation for terrorist incidents proved to be ineffective as local emergency planners found themselves under-resourced and out of their depth. In the hottest summer on record, five million English people packed up their homes and tried to flee north as the invisible radiation cloud moved inexorably towards the south coast.

While the nation watched aghast and the authorities reacted slowly, Mason's Green Earth movement swung into action, with Dave Barrington at the epicentre of the activity. The Green Volunteers were born, and Malcolm Morton was now transforming them into a coordinated force across the country.

'This is the Awakening,' Mason had pronounced at every appearance on TV. 'This is our chance to get things right. We can't just respond to our current crisis, then sleep-walk back into the way things were before. We have to mobilise the tens of thousands of volunteers who have come onto the street to make a permanent difference.

'This is only the beginning of the beginning. We have to transform our way of life, transform the way we are governed, transform the way we do business, the ways we generate energy, the ways we work, shop, travel and have fun. We can still do all these things, but we have to do it in ways that have less impact on the planet. Don't you agree?'

It seemed almost everyone did agree. The GEM had been until now a small, well-disciplined group within the wider Green movement. The people joining the Volunteers were not GEM members, but ordinary public-spirited citizens responding to the crisis, to the GEM activities and the brand, and to Mason's values and charm.

New 'popular assemblies' were set up across the country to ensure the continuation of environmental action—the Green Earth Councils. Soon they were more influential than the local authorities and agencies they were set up to guide. And to coordinate them, a 'National Green Earth Convention' was to be set up, made up of representatives appointed by the Earth Councils—a 'third chamber of Parliament', according to some.

All the while, Mason was counselling his supporters not to be confrontational. *Not all fruit ripens at the same time.* Conciliation was the order of the day.

During the Awakening crisis, the Green Volunteers set the pace, but cooperated readily with the emergency services and the army, with voluntary agencies and with central government when these were ready to act. In doing this, they bypassed the official leadership of organisations, creating their own networks, making extensive use of the GEM 'sleepers' who were now roused into action and began to make their presence felt in their host organisations.

While Malcolm Morton coordinated the Green Earth Volunteers, a GEM 'sleeper' Douglas Cunningham, emerged as the leading figure in the Earth Councils. He had set up the first of the London Earth Councils for Camden and Islington, and it set the pace for exemplary environmental action in the capital.

Cunningham was a middle-ranking local authority manager with responsibility for environmental services, and taking the lead in setting up a new body with responsibilities for the environment seemed a natural thing to do. He swung into action to harness the voluntary energy unleashed by the Green Revolution. Soon programmes were created for waste reduction, reducing consumption, promoting local markets, forcing the public sector and encouraging local businesses to 'buy green', and holding all the public services accountable for their environmental performance. New funds were squeezed out of the local councils for local improvement programmes that were put forward and run by local volunteers.

Cunningham reported back to the GEM leadership about the progress in London. 'The energy is amazing. And it's coming from all sides. Only a fraction of the people involved are GEM at first–but they're signing up in droves!'

But Don Mason was concerned. Was it a problem of too much success too soon?

'This is all wonderful,' he said, 'but–we've got two potential problems here. One: this momentum will burn itself out after a few months. What we don't want is for them to become some new kind of institution or local bureaucracy, coming up with a whole bunch of tick-lists for environmental virtue. They have to remain the focus for strong, radical action. We have to keep the radicalism going.'

Everyone in the room was nodding in agreement.

'Two: I can see already there's a danger of the Earth Councils and Volunteers becoming all things to all people. As well as passionate citizens awaking from a long sleep, we're getting every kind of radical activist campaign in the mix. Anti-capitalist campaigners, Trotskyists, women's rights groups, Fair Trade campaigners, plus every kind of ambitious local politician jumping on board. This movement is not about socialism or attacking the 'fat cats'. It's not about equality. The rich are only in the line of fire if they are environmentally irresponsible, if they are eco-criminals. If they cooperate and open their businesses to be scrutinised and set onto a better path, so much the better. It's not about Fair Trade or any kind of international justice issue. It's not our business whether cash crops are grown ethically or not. The point is that they are shipped half way around the world to get here, and that's unacceptable. So: the Earth Councils must stand firm. The mission is to save the Planet, not to become a focus for each and every politically correct campaign. Those days are gone, and they can find their own way.'

'As I see it,' said Cunningham, 'our immediate challenge is to channel this massive energy and enthusiasm and at the same time bring it all together nationally, in a way that we can coordinate. Malcolm is building a central structure for the Volunteers, which is great. Now we need to do something similar with the Earth Councils. We've got calls from Earth Councils across the country to set up a national body to bring them all together. Malcolm and I have been working on a blueprint for this. It will be the spontaneous wish of the Earth Councils to meet in a National Assembly, and when it meets we will put forward proposals to turn it into a centre of power and action. We need to make this step at once, so it doesn't degenerate into some kind of useless talking shop.'

The GEM leaders talked through Cunningham's ideas and agreed the broad strategy.

'I want the Grey parties involved in this too,' said Mason, apparently thinking out loud. 'We have this revolutionary momentum behind us, but I don't want to leave any loose ends in terms of legitimacy. We're talking about having two delegates sent from every Earth Council in the country. Let's invite a couple of representatives from each of the parties as observers, and put them on the spot. Dave—you and Danny need to ensure the media coverage for this is spot on. The whole thing televised. Doug and Malcolm—you need to ensure absolute discipline amongst our people to see this goes the right way. The GEM may be in the minority in the room once all the delegates are selected, so we have to be firm and ensure this does not degenerate into anything chaotic.'

'At the moment the Earth Councils are run by groups of enthusiasts. People who feel they are all on the same wavelength,' said Malcolm Morton. 'Already many of them are discussing having elections so they become more representative. So Doug and I have drawn up a set of minimum standards for people standing for office. Some fundamental Earth principles they need to pledge to support. We can't have people standing for office who are against the whole thing—it wouldn't make any sense. Over time this will ensure that the National Federation, or Assembly, or whatever it will be called, doesn't become a focus for opposition groups to infiltrate and distort its purpose.'

'Agreed,' said Don.

He looked around the room at his team, enjoying the buzz and excitement of being at the centre of events. Sure, the feeling was similar to many previous gatherings where they had been in planning mode. But this was different. They were at the centre of the only events that mattered at the moment. And the decisions they took could be not only life-changing but history changing too. Earth-changing.

Sarah Turner burst into the room, late and breathless as usual, but with a smile and an energy that brought sunshine to any gathering. She threw herself down besides Jessica and was instantly involved in the planning, picking up the threads of the conversation without needing to be told. And opposite these two were the darker figures of Malcolm and Dave, both of similar build and now it seemed to Don almost like twins in their intensity. Dave had a more open and gregarious nature, though, while Malcolm had few close friends, and Don was one of the few people who knew him well. Both Malcolm and Dave had emerged from the crisis proving that they could scale up their organising abilities to the national stage. And Don could see their approach was rubbing off on Doug Cunningham who was now laying out his plans for the National Convention and the Earth Councils to operate as a more or less alternative state possessing the levers to 'get things done'.

Don felt there may be some moments in history when the right people come together. Had all his life been leading to this moment?

He felt his mood darken as the immense responsibility began to weigh on his shoulders. He recalled that many of the key moments in his adult life had been about walking away. Walking away from corporate life just at the moment when he should have been moving onwards and upwards into the most senior positions in the company. Walking away from his NGO job just at the time when he was receiving plaudits for the great work he was doing. Walking away from Ben Porter and the old Green Party, convinced that their time would never come. And shortly after that, walking away from the path of direct and guerrilla action in which he had dabbled and where he had met some of his key supporters. In the process, pursuing the development of his distinctive Green Earth path, he had also walked out on his marriage.

And now? Don could almost feel the future calling to him. He knew it would not be easy. But he would not walk away, and he knew that the people around him would travel with him, however difficult the road ahead.

8: The National Convention of Earth Councils

It had taken some time to get in. It was just a short step from Parliament to the conference halls in Victoria Street, but Parliament Square and all the roads joining it were thronging with people. A demonstration, a rally, a festival: it was all of them. Noisy, festive and assertive, with order being kept by Green Volunteers and a low-level police presence.

Peter Kitson was part of a delegation of eight members of Parliament—two from each of the major parties and two from the smaller parties—that had been invited as observers to the inaugural meeting of a 'National Federation' of Earth Councils. Delegates came from each of the local Earth Councils that had been set up across the UK.

As he made his way across, people alternatively shook Peter by the hand, harangued him, or pressed literature into his hand. He noticed that the MPs from the government party were getting a much harder time as they made their way across.

Once inside, Peter looked around the large meeting hall. There were more than eight hundred delegates from around the UK, all enthused and motivated to change the world—for the better as he saw it. He felt proud and privileged to be involved.

He and Terry Cairns, the deputy party leader, were the Liberal Democrat representatives at the meeting. Cairns was what the GEM side charitably called a 'grey-green'. That is, he had some eco-credentials, but these were dated and shallow in the GEM view, and always subordinate to other aspects of 'grey' thinking—traditional views about how to run a country.

Terry Cairns had been a strong influence on the young Peter Kitson as he entered politics, acting as mentor and guide. Tall and lean, a distinguished-looking figure, his dry wit and constant scepticism made him good company, but Peter felt that his scepticism often stood in the way of valuable initiatives. He always doubted other people's enthusiasms. He was fond of asking questions such as 'What makes you think this can work?' or 'Has this been costed?' or 'OK, you've given me the long words—now show me the numbers!'

Terry was, though, very sympathetic to the mood, as he saw it, of the present Green Revolution. Yet he remained sceptical about the practicalities. He listened patiently as a variety of young speakers urged the parliamentary representatives to endorse their proposals.

Douglas Cunningham was trying to manage the process as best he could, but managing Greens was always somewhat like herding cats. Yet despite the apparent drift towards chaos, there was a kind of discipline imposed by GEM representatives, who were building an argument and an approach between the digressions.

Terry, well experienced at sensing political machinations, pointed this out to his colleague.

'This is interesting, Peter,' he whispered. 'You know I recognise a fair number of these people. Been involved in one way or another with several of them over the years. They're all the ones not making a lot of sense. I can pretty much predict what any of them will say. Like Sean over there—he always talks about windmills sooner or later. And true to form he just did. Megan Jones there—she'll talk about fuel taxes in a moment. I'll put a fiver on it. Gabriella whatshername over there—she'll say something boneheaded about animal rights.'

He looked thoughtful for a moment.

'And?' said Peter, who was used to these pauses.

'And so—the predictable fruitcakes are being predictably at odds with reality. Nothing new there. But there's a core of other people here, most of whom I've never seen before. What they're saying isn't so memorable. But it is almost coherent. Like they've been prepared and coached.'

Peter shrugged. 'Is it important?'

'Important? I doubt it. It's pretty clear what they want. I'm just intrigued by an uncharacteristic discipline underlying the proceedings here. And it's these new faces that seem to be marching in step somehow.'

'You think it's sinister?'

'No! I don't think the Greens can be sinister, do you? Emotional, deranged, blinkered, obsessive—but not sinister. And usually not organised either.'

He spoke with a twinkle in his eye, not taking his own cynical commentary entirely seriously. He paused to reflect for a moment as one mini-speech ended and a young lady was invited by Cunningham to get up and address the meeting.

'My hunch is there's some kind of coup afoot in the Green movement. You know, like the far right, there's always some new splinter group trying to emerge and steal the clothes of the political leadership. But who's she?'

The young lady was now addressing the meeting in earnest tones.

'She's Jessica Olsen Barrington.'

'Cute. You know her?'

'Sure—you want me to introduce her to you?'

'Could do worse!'

'She's taken, I'm afraid. Wife of Dave Barrington.'

'Hmm. Lucky dog.'

'You recognise the "Olsen" part?'

'Olsen—you mean like our own Sir James from the Treasury?'

'His daughter. My wife was at college with her, you know.'

'You're better connected than I gave you credit for, young man. What's she saying?'

They listened—in fact the hall as a whole had quietened down.

'…So it's true we've come here as representatives of the local and regional Green Earth Councils, to open a dialogue with our elected colleagues at Westminster. It's right that we should do so. One speaker after another has put forward proposals for how a National "Federation" should be run. What its brief should be, how far its powers should run, whether it should control this or regulate that…. It is right we should talk with the MPs here. But we should not—I repeat, we should not—think of ourselves as in any way petitioners.

'We have not come here to have our legitimacy endorsed by representatives of the old grey order. Nor have we come here to become some useless advisory quango. We are appointed representatives of the Green Earth Councils across the nation, and have the authority of the people behind us. We come here to *ask* nothing, but to *assert* our legitimacy as a national representative body.'

While she spoke an appreciative buzz of approval had rippled through the audience. Now they broke into applause. Terry looked around. There were just eight parliamentary representatives amongst an audience of more than eight hundred.

'We welcome dialogue with Parliament. From now on, the House of Commons *must* consult us on all matters that come before it.'

Applause and cheers.

'We in turn assert the right to put before the Commons matters of national importance—and national urgency…'

Jessica now had to raise her voice as most of the audience were now on their feet, applauding continuously. '…And matters of extreme urgency that generation after generation of Grey politicians have neglected or sold out on! Our proposal is that from now on, this body shall sit in permanent session, as a National Convention of Earth Councils, to ensure that our voice is heard. We will ensure there is no sliding back!'

She sat down to tumultuous applause.

'Good god!' said Terry. 'I think she's trying to set up some kind of Green equivalent to take the place of the House of Lords!'

'It's about time someone replaced it with something,' smiled Peter.

Sian Novak, the Conservative Environment spokesman leaned over to them. 'We've been set up,' she whispered loudly. 'We're on a hiding to nothing if we reply to this.'

Jack Carsley, one of the Labour Party representatives, leaned in towards them too. 'I suggest we just let them let off steam. They can assert whatever they want—it has no validity unless we give it some. Stay calm.'

Terry responded quietly. 'First I suggest you both settle back in your seats. I don't want us to look like a cabal, not with the cameras watching us.'

Then Terry noticed Peter Kitson's expression. He was not part of this little exchange. Terry doubted if he had even heard it. He could see that Peter's mind was racing with new possibilities, and it seemed his heart belonged to this revolution.

'Stay cool, Peter,' said Terry, 'And don't say anything yet. Save any comments until we're outside of this cauldron, and can talk with a clear head. And check it out with Howard.'

But the pressure was not to be lifted yet.

The chairman of the meeting, Douglas Cunningham, eventually rose to call for calm and order.

'Ladies, gentlemen—it seems we have, uh, a very popular suggestion from our representative from North Norfolk.' A loud, almost deafening cheer and stamping of feet started up, and lasted for more than three minutes.

Holding his hands up for calm, Cunningham continued. 'We can see there is general acclamation for this—what can I call it? For this…'

'Demand from the people!' someone called from the audience.

'And the Planet!' shouted someone else, to great applause.

'Demand from the People and the Planet,' Cunningham repeated. 'Fine, that's good. General acclamation except, it would seem, from our rather silent Parliamentary colleagues here!'

The audience broke out into scornful laughter.

'But—I think we do need to fulfil the purpose of his meeting. We came here to draw up an agreement for constituting a National Federation of Earth Councils. But I think we have moved on from our original concept. We need to draw up a proposal, to be endorsed by ourselves, which constitutes this body as the National Convention of Earth Councils, to sit in permanent session and drive the Revolution forward at national level!'

More applause.

'So we'll vote on it—and then we get to work!'

More cheers, applause and stamping.

'I know that our representative from North Herefordshire had drafted an earlier more modest proposal. Malcolm? Yes—if Malcolm and Jessica could come forward—I suggest we take a ten minute break while we redraft this, then reconvene for the vote. Would any of our parliamentary colleagues care to cast their eye over this too? OK—back in ten.'

An explosion of chatter filled the hall. Groups formed themselves around the room, and a general surge towards the front took place, as delegates wanted to either join in the formulation or at least to witness it. They wanted to see, as they believed, history being made.

Each of the parliamentary delegations began talking amongst themselves.

'Jessica Olsen Barrington, what have you done?' Terry asked. 'This is quite a challenge to the status quo, wouldn't you say, Peter? Peter?'

Peter Kitson hadn't been listening. He was already making his way towards the throng surrounding Cunningham, Morton and Jessica Barrington.

'Peter!' Terry hissed, struggling to his feet.

'Don't worry!' Peter called back over his shoulder. 'I know what I'm doing. We won't have an opportunity like this again!'

Terry flopped back in his seat. He could see the Labour and Conservative coteries animatedly discussing—discussing what? How to extract maximum advantage from the situation, or how to minimise the fall-out for their party? And Peter was in his own way doing the same—trying to position his party well in the emerging events, and leave the others behind. But Terry could see he was also intoxicated by what was happening. What can be better than stealing a march on your opponents by doing something that coincides with your convictions?

Within just a few minutes Cunningham reconvened the meeting. A proposal was flashed up on the screen—a little wordy but it did the job. The 'National Convention of Earth Councils' was duly established and acclaimed. And Peter Kitson had positioned himself if not at the forefront, then close enough to be in touching distance.

Cunningham invited the parliamentary delegates to respond to the initiative on behalf of their parties. A theatrical gesture, as all but the two Liberals had already left.

'Where have they all gone?' asked Cunningham. 'Empty seats at the Revolution. Their absence speaks volumes!' The audience responded with jeers and whistles for the absent delegates.

'But we have of course two remaining—Terry Cairns and Peter Kitson. Gentleman—the floor is yours.' Cunningham gestured first to one, then to the other to take the stage.

Peter looked at Terry Cairns, who gestured to the younger man to continue what he had begun. As he looked around the room, he could see Peter receiving warm applause from most of the delegates. They seemed to appreciate Peter's supportive gesture and that he had thrown his lot in with them. Terry also noted an exchange of glances between Cunningham and Morton. It seemed that Morton was not entirely pleased with Kitson's interference. Cunningham returned Morton's frown with a shrug. Terry thought there may be method in Peter's madness after all. The GEM's little coup was, at least in part, being upstaged.

Peter spoke well—pressing the right green buttons to receive warm applause for the audience, and the occasional cheer. Then some heckling started.

Cunningham raised his hands for quiet, as Peter paused. Then he said: 'Mr Kitson—I'm sorry that you're being interrupted. But I think the gist of what they are saying is that they want you to endorse the legitimacy of this National Convention, and are asking if your party will support it? Do you support the status of this body as a legitimate national body, scrutinising parliamentary legislation and initiating new environmental laws?'

Peter looked confidently first at Cunningham, then at the audience. But he addressed his answer primarily to the cameras. 'As a long-standing campaigner for green initiatives, inside and outside of Parliament, and as a founder member of the Earth Council in my own constituency, I have no hesitation in endorsing the rights of this National Convention, and I look forward to its continuing role in our nation—'

'Are you speaking for your party, or for yourself?' called out an aggressive young man from near the front of the audience.

'Like yourselves, I'm a democrat. Today I speak for myself, but—' Here some members of the audience groaned theatrically. 'But tomorrow I will speak for my party. We have to agree this collectively, but from earlier discussions I am confident you will have our support.'

There was long applause for this statement. Kitson was being a little economical with the truth, and he could imagine the leader of his party, Howard Blackstone, cursing him when the news was broadcast. The Liberal Democrat leadership had indeed agreed to support the setting up of a National Federation of Earth Councils, but had not discussed at all how to respond to these far-fetched pretensions of being a legislative chamber of some kind.

Peter felt the Convention had little chance in practice of making any impact on the constitution. It would be up to Parliament to agree, and the other parties would stop it. Parliament, and the civil service, would never accept such an innovation. But he imagined it would become a highly visible and effective pressure group. To him this was no bad thing. As well as being the right thing to do, it was in his party's best interest to be on good terms with it and identify with the mood of the country.

Peter continued. 'We've a lot of work to do. We need to establish ways of working together between the government and this new representative body, and get everyone singing from the same hymn-sheet so we know who does what, when, and how. I can tell you there's some seriously dreary stuff we deal with in the Commons and in the committees. I can assure you that you don't want to get bogged down with all that—it will suck out the soul from this movement. In the meantime there are many urgent measures that this Convention can drive forward—'

Kitson was cut short by the entrance at the back of the hall of Don Mason. The applause began amongst those people that Terry Cairns had noticed as being more disciplined. Some of the other Green delegates looked a little bemused—after all, though Mason had publicly called for the setting up of this body, it seemed he had played no direct part in it. But he was the man of the moment in the national consciousness, and his presence here was not unwelcome.

The applause grew to a thundering crescendo, and Cunningham gestured for Mason to come to the front. He began his procession forward. Peter Kitson felt he had no choice but to give way and gesture to Mason that the floor was his. He resumed his seat next to Terry Cairns, who said nothing but raised an eyebrow, as if to say 'Do you think that was wise?'

Mason took the stage, standing where Peter had just stood. He motioned several times for the ovation to stop, and for delegates to sit down. It took more than five minutes for this to happen. Terry Cairns was almost the only person in the hall not standing—the others who remained seated were all prominent members of the traditional Green Party, clearly peeved at this upstart's current prominence. Up in the public gallery, Ben Porter looked down stony-faced.

Mason spoke. 'Comrades', he began, and again there was thunderous applause. 'Today the Environment has moved to the heart of national policy!'

Another ovation.

'Today you, democratically appointed representatives from every corner of the country, have changed this country forever!' More cheers and applause. 'The era of Grey politics is over. The Green Revolution is upon us!'

'And nature rejoices, I'm sure!' muttered Terry under his breath. Peter looked down at him, not quite hearing what he said, but sensing the tone. Thunderous applause and stamping followed for several minutes after Mason's proclamation.

Mason was continuing. 'Comrades! Have you felt it?' He was speaking more softly now, and a hush descended on the assembly.

'Can you feel it now? There is something happening here, on the streets, in our hearts, in our homes, throughout our green and beautiful land. And what we are feeling, I believe—I truly believe—is a new and profound connection to our Planet.'

Terry Cairns watched as almost everyone in the room sat wrapt, nodding their heads in silent agreement.

'For so long now we have been living our lives skimming over the surface of what we know is real. We have lived our lives in illusion, as if we are separate from the Earth, rather than part of Her—as if the Earth is simply raw material for us to fashion and shape and consume as we struggle and strive and fight for ... for what? A better life? There can be no better life if we live separated from who we are, from the Planet that nurtures us day to day. And which we repay by: destruction. And when we destroy the source of who we are, we destroy ourselves: bit by bit, little by little, every day. The pain of the Earth—is our pain.

'This is what we feel. This is what the tens of thousands of Volunteers on the streets are feeling. It is the connection with the source of our being, and with each other, and it is the guiding force of this rebellion against our old ways.

'But is it enough for us to be on the streets? Is it enough to be setting up our Earth Councils, to be sitting down together and planning a better future?'

Mason paused, and the delegates remained hushed, most of them sitting forward in their seats, waiting to hear his next words.

'Comrades, we are at a moment of crisis. A moment of decision. We are at a fork in the road. Down one road is the path of talking, and planning, and persuading, and, in the end, of compromising. And the other way? That is the road of transformation. It is the road where we tie our words, our ideas, our new connection and consciousness to practical action. We are not here to discuss the condition of the world, but to change it!'

As his voice rose, the delegates began to clap. Mason raised his voice further.

'The Revolution is here, but it is by no means complete. There is much hard work to do. So which is the path we will take comrades? Is it the path of talking and debating? Or the path of action?'

The hall erupted in noise as the delegates cried: 'Action! Action!'

'And where are the people to do it?'

The audience erupted with affirmations that they were the people to do it.

'Yes, I know that we are the people to do it! Together we can achieve everything that needs to be done. And I know there are some who will question our right to do what we will do. I say to them: "Don't stand in our way!"'

9: On the back foot

Peter Kitson was not wrong about his party leader being unhappy with his initiative. Howard Blackstone was furious. And it put Howard in a very difficult position as leader. It was an act of insubordination, as Evan Roberts kept reminding him. And it had come completely out of the blue, an uncharacteristically impulsive move by someone he trusted, and whom he had thought to be a safer pair of hands.

But the problem was, Howard felt, there was method in Peter Kitson's moment of madness. Though such a move should have been agreed with the party leadership, there was no doubt it had proved to be popular with the party as a whole, even if some of his fellow Liberal MPs were rattled and resentful. And more to the point, it was playing well in the country as a whole. The poll ratings the next morning showed a big boost for the Liberal Democrats, while the Conservative and Labour parties bore the full brunt of the 'Grey' label and were considered to be out of touch by most of the electorate.

And for forty-eight hours since the meeting, there had been three faces constantly on the news: Don Mason, Jessica Barrington, and Peter Kitson. He had successfully gate-crashed their party.

As he sat in his office in Portcullis House with Evan, there was a special focus on one of the 24-hour news channels on Peter Kitson, featuring interviews with his heavily pregnant wife and his crusading human rights lawyer sister.

'Was this scripted by his publicist or something?' sighed Evan sourly. 'We need to haul him in before this all goes to his head. I think we're getting a tail-wags-dog problem here, Howard.'

Howard didn't reply for a moment.

'You're not angry with him?' asked Evan, incredulously.

'You know I'm angry with him. Livid, in fact,' replied Howard in exasperation. 'We've worked so hard these past few years to rebuild the party, and this threatens to drive a wedge into it. But at the same time, we can't slap him down for taking what is turning out to be such a hugely popular initiative.'

'But it's reckless,' responded Evan. 'And sometimes the unpopular decision is the right decision. This all-encompassing enthusiasm for all things green is like a kind of hysteria. If we left it alone, it could be all but played out by Christmas. But if we all start paying court to the new gods of this so-called "Green Revolution", one of two things will happen. Either we'll give them a legitimacy they haven't earned and don't deserve. All over the country the Greens are our biggest rivals in key constituencies. What's the point of boosting the very people who are the biggest threat to us?'

'What's the second thing?'

'Well, the alternative as I see it is that we'll end up going down the plughole with them when the hysteria is over, and we return to a kind of shame-faced normality.'

Howard leaned back in his chair.

'In the meantime, we have to take a position,' he said. 'And we mustn't forget that we have long been arguing for tougher environmental policies—including scrapping nuclear power. A lot of our local councillors have endorsed the local Earth Councils in their area and helped to set them up. We're angry with Peter over procedure and discipline, more than the substance of what he has done, don't you think? I know you don't like him, but ...'

'Like him? I think under the wide-eyed naivety he's turning out to be a bit of a cunning bastard. Seems like he's decided to lead the party, wouldn't you say?' challenged Evan.

'Hmm. But I can't slap him down out of a wounded sense of vanity, can I? No, I think in some ways he's right. We do need to identify with the energy of this popular movement. I don't agree that it's just some kind of mass hysteria. It seems to be having some kind of transformative effect all around the country. And I think we can work with it. And we can benefit from it too, as long as we manage to maintain our separate identity. This is all very bad news for the Tories and Labour, don't you think? They are much more divided about this than we are, don't you think?'

Evan nodded. 'Yes, the formal position of each party is pretty much unchanged from before. Seem to think—like I do—what's required is to "keep calm and carry on". It will all blow over and then it will be politics as normal. But there are substantial numbers in each who want to accept this so-called National Convention and to snuggle up closer to Mason and all the rest of the Greens. Mason's unstoppable PR machine is already christening these people as "Grey-Greens" and denigrating their credentials. Calls them opportunists.'

'And we fall into that camp too?'

'Seems not. Not yet. Would it matter if we did?'

'On balance—yes! As a matter of principle, we are on the green side of the fence. Now, what time is it? I'm meeting Baxter over at Number 10 in twenty minutes. Do you want to walk with me over there?'

It took more than half an hour for Howard and Evan to take the short walk along Whitehall to Downing Street. The streets were thronged with demonstrators, Green Volunteers chanting slogans and handing out campaigning leaflets, with stalls selling all kinds of produce or giving it away to fellow demonstrators. Evan could see that Howard was enjoying his status amongst the campaigners as people grabbed him by the hand or tried to press him into taking Green Earth 'goody bags' containing campaigning materials, practical booklets and organic food samples.

'Are you feeling it Howard?' muttered Evan, scathingly paraphrasing Mason's well-publicised words. 'Can you feel your reconnection to Mother bloody Nature?'

Howard rolled his eyes at Evan's cynicism as they parted near the gates to Downing Street. 'Look around you, Evan. You can't ignore what is happening. Wake up and smell the coffee!'

Evans looked back towards the broken windows of Starbucks on the corner of Parliament Square, and the refreshment stalls set up for the demonstrators along Whitehall. 'All I can smell is camomile tea, Howard,' he called after him.

Howard was admitted to Number 10 and taken straight through to the Prime Minister's study. Dennis Leadbetter, the Labour leader and head of the main opposition party was there already. He was their third leader since the party had last lost power, and represented a return to the past. Having come up through the ranks of the trades unions, his main concerns were always jobs and employment rights. After ten years of recession and political failure, he wanted to get Labour back on the right track, looking out for the interests of the working man. All this 'environment business' puzzled him—where were the jobs in it, and what had it got to do with the price of fish? It had always seemed like a middle-class obsession to him. Yet now the streets were full of protestors and activists, far more than he'd ever seen turn out for a trade union rally. It didn't make a lot of sense.

Howard shook hands with him, and then with Patrick Baxter, the Conservative Prime Minister. As he looked into Baxter's face he was somewhat shocked. Suddenly it seemed that Baxter had aged. It was only a matter of weeks since the disaster that had kicked everything off, yet the stress was clearly getting to him. Baxter had never been the most popular of figures, but he had been respected and seen as a safe pair of hands, the right person to steer the nation through a prolonged period of economic adjustment. But it seemed that respect had evaporated overnight, and since the crisis he had been constantly pilloried in the press as incompetent and out of touch. For the Green Revolution, Baxter was the epitome of Grey.

Every day there were demonstrations calling for him to go. Parliament Square was still occupied, and every day Baxter had to run the gauntlet of chanting crowds as he moved between Parliament and Number 10 Downing Street.

'Are you OK, Patrick?' asked Howard. 'Bearing up? You're looking a little bit all in, if you don't mind me saying so.'

They were old adversaries, of a similar age and background. They had always been civil to each other, almost friendly perhaps.

'Yes, I'm fine, Howard,' said Baxter cordially. 'Just a bit harassed, and I've had a fearful cold I'm just shaking off. Time of year for it, I suppose. Please, take a seat.'

'Did you get here without having your ear bloody chewed off by the green brigades outside?' asked Dennis Leadbetter gruffly. 'All this was fine at first, but it's doing my head in now!'

'They have some points and they're trying to make us listen,' smiled Howard.

'And that's why I wanted us to get together,' said Baxter, becoming more animated. 'When the French nuclear crisis first broke, we came to an agreement. That we'd put aside party differences and stand shoulder to shoulder to do what was in the national interest. In my view, we need to do that again. The immediate crisis has passed—well, mostly passed—but I think we are still faced with a public order crisis. And with something new.

'All this talk of a "Green Revolution". For some people, no doubt, it's a bit of an excuse for a party. And the media love it. It's exciting. So many new stories and angles to report. And a good chance to beat us all with new sticks.'

'Yes, how are you taking to this "Grey" label?' asked Howard.

'I'd need more hair to qualify,' said Leadbetter, rubbing his hand over his smooth, bald head.

'Anyway,' continued Baxter, keen to keep the conversation on topic, 'things are moving on beyond some mild disorder. Demonstrations, rallies, even the occasional ugly confrontation—these are all part of the democratic process, the kind of things we can live with. Sometimes we need the people to give us a kick up the backside. But as I say, it's going beyond that. These Earth Councils, and now the so-called National Convention of Earth Councils. It may all fizzle and fade, but my gut feeling is that they are more durable than you might think. And they are a direct challenge to the constitution!'

'Isn't that a bit melodramatic?' asked Howard.

'Is it?' continued Baxter. 'Frankly I'm astonished at the speed with which they were set up, and the traction they've gained with the public. And not only the public. All across the country public officials are cooperating with them as if they had some official and legal status. And now they have these Scrutiny Commissions, poking their noses into how local public services are run. We've got local councillors and officers running backwards and forwards kow-towing to these new local emperors—and who are they? They are just a bunch of self-appointed activists, not even elected—'

'Not yet,' interrupted Howard. 'But they are planning to hold annual elections. They will become accountable.'

'Does that make it better or worse?' challenged Baxter. 'It seems like we're sleepwalking into letting a highly motivated group of extremists set up a kind of parallel state. Look at the pretensions now of this National Convention. You have these highly partisan local Earth Councils sending their representatives to London to set up a kind of quasi-government body—and they're demanding that the government and Parliament should be accountable to it.'

'Ignore the buggers. They'll go home in the end,' said Leadbetter. 'They'll run out of steam when they can't get their way. And when they get the bill for using that conference centre, they'll be out pretty bloody sharpish!'

'I wish it were so easy, Dennis,' continued Baxter. 'Already officials from government departments and agencies are starting to cooperate with them—enthusiastically, even. And last night I received a demand—a *demand*, would you believe—from the National Convention to cooperate in the setting up of some national Scrutiny Commissions. I've copied it for you. Look, there's a list of them. All ESCO-something. ESCO, for "Environmental Scrutiny Commission on" … ESCOHEALTH, to scrutinise the environmental performance of the health service, ESCOHED for higher education, ESCOTRANS, for Transport, ESCOLAW, ESCOMEDIA, ESCOMIL—for the military. It gets more and more worrying as you read it, doesn't it? All seems a bit Soviet too.'

'All seems a bit crap to me,' barked Leadbetter.

'But think about it,' said Howard thoughtfully. 'They've got a point. Our environmental performance in all these areas is pretty poor. I know we've got official standards and had odd bits of legislation, but really it's all been a bit bureaucratic, foot-dragging and, well, weedy, hasn't it?'

'You're missing the point, Howard,' said Baxter, a little exasperated. 'It isn't the rights and wrongs of the issue that's the problem. It's the setting up of these new bodies that want to make everyone accountable to them. Don't you see? And who are they accountable to?'

'Well, in the end, the people–if they have elections,' answered Howard.

'But that's our job!' said Baxter forcefully, lightly banging the table with his open palm.

'Well, I'm not as alarmed as you,' said Howard, though he was thinking that if Evan Roberts was there he might be agreeing with Baxter. 'And as for taking an active stance against them–I don't think that's really on, is it? I mean the public mood is ninety per cent in support of them, and in support of radical change. If we just stand up should-to-shoulder and say, "It's against procedure", or "It's not constitutional", we're just going to sound like we're idiots, and completely out of touch.'

'I half agree with that,' said Leadbetter. 'Like I say, better to just ignore the buggers. Sooner or later, we'll have to get back to the real issues: jobs and growth! All this environment business is icing on the cake. What good's the icing if you've no bloody cake?'

Baxter sighed.

'But I can see where this is going,' added Leadbetter. 'Howard's high-flying protégé Kitson the wonder kid is already cosying up to these new kids on the block. And you can see that Howard is already looking to go whichever way the wind is blowing–just like the bloody Liberals always do! Latest bandwagon–and they're on it!'

'That doesn't merit an answer, Dennis. You know we've always had much more thorough approach to the environment than either of the other major parties,' said Howard.

'Other major parties! I like it!' laughed Leadbetter. 'Your lot and the Greens fit well together, with your pretensions to grandeur. You know, even now people are talking about the "Kitson Greens". Are you one of them too, Howard? Ha-ha ha! So, Patrick, I think it's clear that Howard is going to go down the green populist path. But we're not. I know we've got our Labour Green fringe, but it's just the excitability of the moment, I'd say. So if you want to freeze out this National Convention and these Earth Councils, I'll not oppose you. But my advice is—and Howard has got a point here about the popular mood—play it calm and play for time.'

As he left the meeting, Howard Blackstone once again came face to face with the popular mood of Britain, and the party atmosphere in the streets. His mind was made up. That evening, in an online meeting of his parliamentary party, he recommended endorsing Peter Kitson's approach. It was time, he said, to play a leading role in this Green Revolution.

10: Reporting the Revolution

Stella Walton was exhausted. What she knew about green issues a month ago was practically zero. Now she was apparently a leading authority on them in the world's most prestigious media organisation. And as such, she was constantly in demand throughout the BBC and beyond. She had maintained throughout the crisis her contacts with Mason and his team, and developed new and useful contacts within the wider Green movement, and amongst the environmental cognoscenti. These included activists in other parties, and in no party at all: in academia, in government departments, in the literary world ('celebrity greens') and also the mavericks and sceptics that were needed for 'balance'. Or rather, for having a good argument.

Now she also had a small team of junior researchers working for her, constantly unearthing new angles and new information about every environmental topic under the sun, and bombarding her with emails and new websites to visit.

'God, there's such garbage out there,' she moaned to Trevor. He had developed the habit of dropping by her section at around six o'clock to review the day, confirm tomorrow's priorities and plan the next steps. 'I mean, who writes this stuff?'

'And who reads it?' Trevor replied, 'I mean, apart from you and your minions?'

Stella exhaled loudly, a sound halfway between a laugh and a sigh.

'We've got Peter Kitson coming in tomorrow.'

'Oh, you mean Mr Goody Dullsville. Please find some dirt on him, Stella. He's so insufferably nice and correct all the time. If you can tell me he makes coats out of puppies, or something, I'll double your salary!'

'I can tell you that if you like…'

'It has to be true, darling. We have standards, after all!'

Stella was sparked into a new train of thought. 'Actually, talking of puppy farming—what did you think of the idea from Juliet that I sent you a couple of days ago?'

Trevor looked puzzled. 'Who's Juliet?'

Stella gave him a look.

'Oh, one of your little girlies on Walton's Mountain?'

'Don't be so patronising, Trevor. You know who I mean and she's more than good at her job, which she does for bugger all money!'

'Very qualified for the job, I'm sure. Does she have a daddy in the corporate management suite too...?'

'Whatever. What did you think about her idea for a feature on the new wave Animal Rights movement?'

'As I recall, it seemed more like an idea for a mini-series.....'

'They do seem to be playing an increasingly important role in the Earth Councils—all kind of stuff is going on.'

'Oh, don't get me going on those dreadful Earth Councils—where I live you can't fart in the street without some unwashed person in a baggy T-shirt lecturing you about damaging the ozone layer!'

'Trevor, please....'

'So—you want an exposé of the "Animalistas—*Britain's new campaigners for inter-species equality*"?'

'Trevor, you're being facetious again—'

'No, no, no—I'd like to take the credit for making up that line, but actually I saw it on one of those baggy T-shirts. In Knightsbridge.'

'I'm not talking about an "exposé", as you put it,' said Stella. 'Just a good piece of balanced reportage.'

'"Balanced reportage",' Trevor mimicked, 'I'm all for that. But if you could throw in a talking donkey or something, I'd be most grateful. Just to spice it up a little'.

Stella looked at him wearily.

'The truth is, Stella,' said Trevor, 'We're being outflanked here. We're getting all the earnest political and ideological stuff to deal with, but the other teams are getting all the exciting cowboys-and-Indians stuff. Yesterday that skyscraper building site down the road was occupied by protesters. There've been—how many is it?—seventeen attacks on supermarket chains. All done by Green commando flash mobs. Police nowhere to be seen. But the media are there in force. I know we've got some of our boys and girls there, but where are *we*? Tucked up here in the office taking tea with bland political hopefuls and has-beens. I want to be out there, in the action! Don't you?'

The following day they were reviewing the plan for the interview. Despite Trevor's disparaging remarks about Peter Kitson, Stella had taken quite a liking to him. His unaffected 'goodyness' she found endearing, rather than boring or corny. He had a natural and warm smile, she felt. Most politicians learn to smile well, but Stella felt with Peter it was natural. And when they had met for the second time, she found he remembered many things she had said from their first meeting, not always a quality she had found in politicians. Usually they were there to be seen and to get their point across, fawning to the front-of-camera people while barely noticing the supporting team.

'You've got a crush on him!' Trevor had teased. True, she thought, Peter was not-bad-looking in a boy-next-door sort of way and had the aura of a rising star. And Stella was twenty-nine and single, well in need of a good stable man, as she said. In her own mind though, she said it was more a case of taking a shine to him than having a crush on him. She liked it that as he waited to go on air he took or made calls to his wife, and Stella could see that he was completely devoted to her. Oh well, she thought. The good ones are always taken—and good luck to him.

Trevor MacLean was not so sure about him. While Stella said Peter had a passion for the environment that was grounded in the social and economic realities of everyday life, Trevor scoffed and said that Kitson was a typical bloody Liberal, backing two horses at once. Was he for radical change, or for the old way of life? Fence sitters always eventually find their position painful and flip-floppers inevitably do themselves an injury, he would say.

A call came through that Peter Kitson had arrived at reception. Trevor MacLean gave a wry smile as Stella quickly said she would go and collect him herself, jumping in ahead of one of her team who was about to set off. As she went down to the main reception, she was thinking about why she found Kitson such an interesting man. She had been researching more about his background, and was surprised by what she found. Here was a man whose father had died while he was young, and then when he was eighteen his mother had also died suddenly, in a car crash. Peter had immediately postponed his gap year plans, and then put back going to university for a further two years to see his younger sister Joanna through her exam years. Now she understood more about the strong bond between them that had been reported. He had preserved the family home and tried to maintain a stable family life so that Joanna would have the best chance of discovering her own way forward in life. And it seems he had put his own ambitions on hold for this. Yet he never talked about it. Recent media profiles had talked of the tragedy of their parents' deaths and the big inheritance that had enabled them to pursue their chosen careers. But this personal insight into the man was missing. Though it would make a great new angle on Peter, she had not told Trevor. He would want to go large on it, and no doubt hope for some tears and camera close-ups too. But Stella preferred to respect his privacy.

All the same, she had found some interesting material about what Peter was doing between school and university. He had worked as an intern in an environmental charity, and been very active in the Liberal Democrat's environmental wing. So he had history in this field. And it was interesting how he had tried to assert his independence from the handful of uncles and aunts who wanted to manage both his life and financial investments from the inheritance. Peter had shown a stubborn and self-sufficient streak, determined to go his own way. And as a result he had mixed results in his investments, with a couple of disastrous ventures as part of his learning curve. Stella smiled as she thought that she'd happily trust him with her vote, but wasn't so sure if she'd trust him to manage her savings.

At reception, Stella found that Peter had arrived with Heather too. Heather was perched on the edge of a chair, and Peter gave gentle assistance as she rose from her chair. Peter greeted Stella warmly and introduced Heather to her.

'I hope you don't mind me coming, but I'm in danger of going stir crazy if I spend any more time at home. And Peter's out so much of the time now, it's nice just to get to spend some time with him and see all the interesting people he's meeting,' said Heather.

'Oh, it's lovely to meet you, and you're very welcome,' said Stella. 'We'll get you set up with a ringside seat and—maybe we could even grab a word with you, about the new world your baby will be born into and your hopes for the future? That sort of thing.'

'Oh no,' laughed Heather. 'I'm staying well out of it. And besides, I don't want to steal Peter's thunder!'

Peter chatted eagerly to Stella as they headed towards the studio about the maelstrom of events he found himself in.

'Are you happy being such a celebrity these days?' asked Stella with a smile.

'It's hard to think of myself like that,' he replied, returning her smile. 'But I have to say it is really energising being at the centre of everything.'

'Do you see yourself as a revolutionary then? A Green Revolutionary?'

'It's unreal to think of myself like that—'

'Not a cap that fits then?'

'No. It's just like, so many of the things I've wanted to happen and now—now there's a mood in the country, and the conditions are right to,

I don't know, *accelerate* everything. The barriers to change don't seem so high any more.'

'And you want the same things as Don Mason and Ben Porter?'

'Not the same. But enough of the same to make some progress, for sure. This is what Trevor's going to focus on in the interview, is it, the differences between our parties?'

As they arrived at the studio, Stella called over to one of her team, 'Juliet, can you help make Mrs Kitson feel at home?'

Juliet Coe rose from her desk, seemingly unwilling at first to relinquish the work she was involved in. She shook hands with Heather with half a smile, showing her to a sofa where they would shortly be meeting Trevor MacLean.

'Juliet's been invaluable to me these last weeks,' enthused Stella. 'She's got her finger on the pulse of the Green Revolution, so anything you want to know about it, just ask her! Unfortunately we're losing her at the end of the month. To a full-time post with the corporate Green Team. I'll miss her.'

Heather was intrigued by this quiet young woman who had no small talk, and who looked just a little out of place amongst all the other confident young things adorning the office. Then as Trevor Maclean came breezing in, causing ripples of laughter and bonhomie as he pirouetted his way through the office, Heather couldn't help notice the look of disdain that flashed across Juliet's face.

In the interview, Trevor challenged and teased about the Liberals leaping on the bandwagon of the Green Revolution. Peter was at pains to point out that his party had never sat on the fence when it came to the environment. They had always been much more progressive on this front than the other mainstream parties, he claimed, and their policies as a whole were much more coherent than any of the green parties and factions. In the current crisis, though, it was necessary to lay aside old differences and work with all people of good will to secure lasting change, for the benefit of future generations.

'And we all live happily ever after,' said Trevor, with a smile. Then, as an aside, 'I think I'm going to throw up!'

Kitson looked a little startled.

'Don't worry, Peter, we'll edit that out,' said Trevor. 'What did you just say? "Working with all people of good will to secure lasting change, for the benefit of future generations"—does that mean going into a coalition with Don Mason? The Green Earth Movement and anyone else following a Green agenda?'

Peter knew it was a long established tradition to duck this kind of question in the lead-up to elections. But times were different now. Riding high in the polls, there was a moment to be seized, but he still needed to be a little cautious, for the sake of his relationships with his party colleagues.

'We've long thought that we need a new kind of politics. People in public life need to work together, rather than create artificial differences. I think we and Don Mason's followers have a lot of things in common. Of course, we have to work on the basis of the people's verdict in next year's elections, and that's still some way off. A lot can happen in a few months. But if we can hammer out a common approach to practical action, and if the will of the people is that we should work together, then I can see no reason why we shouldn't work together in a common front.'

'So that's a "Yes", I take it?' asked Trevor.

'Let's just say that I want to work with these new realities, rather than against them,' said Peter firmly.

11: New realities

Peter Kitson was well pleased with the turn his life had taken over the past six weeks or so. Constantly in the limelight, treated with respect on all sides—or so it seemed—the birth of his first child coming closer and closer, and hopelessly in love with his wife, it seemed life could not be better.

Evan, the party's electoral strategist, was constantly stressing about the 'volatility' of the current situation. It was unstable. Hard to predict. And would probably turn out for the worse for his party.

But for Peter, the events unfolding seemed to bring new opportunities of developing a distinctive green and liberal way of life. He had always believed in a democratic and evolutionary approach to politics—bringing step-by-step change with people's active consent. And now that he saw people on the streets actively engaging in the issues of the day, he felt part of something large and dynamic. He was sure that it would change Britain in a lasting and positive way. And he was proud and excited to be part of what he felt were great events.

Heather was starting to miss him. Peter's days had stretched, his nights had shortened. For him this added to the intensity of the ride. For Heather, it meant breakfasts alone and evenings spent with her mother, or with Joanna, or sometimes a friend. And taking messages for him.

'I'm getting a bit bored!' she confided to Joanna. 'When he comes home, either he's too tired to do anything, or he's all pumped up and talking about this meeting and that meeting and the sea level rising and the species extinction and what Blackstone said and what Cunningham was saying and what a dozen other people I've never heard of were saying!'

But at the same time she felt a stab of pride whenever she saw him on TV or online, or heard people commending him, or even attacking him. She liked her man to be at the centre of things, and yet she felt a growing jealousy about this life of his that mostly existed without her.

Joanna, as always, tried to comfort her and allay her fears. 'I'm sure that this is only a temporary state of affairs. And maybe you're feeling a bit isolated because you've stopped work now. When the baby comes along there'll be a new intensity of family life. And that will put everything into perspective—for Peter I mean. He's sometimes a bit slow on the emotional uptake, but he'll always do the right thing by you in the end.'

Peter was working late again. But 'working late' in these heady days often meant sitting in pubs and restaurants with fellow MPs and co-workers, or networking with the ever-shifting alignments of factions in the other parties and in the newly-established National Convention.

As the leading standard-bearer of the 'green agenda' in his own party, in the changed political climate he was becoming more important than the more senior figures in his party. He was with one of them now, Terry Cairns. The wine was flowing after an energetic day in Westminster.

Terry was more than a decade older than Peter. People saw him as a sceptical intellectual, the kind of person to challenge and test policies and opinions. With a tendency to be sardonic, his natural appearance was to have a wry smile, a raised eyebrow, a sceptical twinkle in his eye. But he rarely put people down, and had a natural kindliness and openness that younger members of the party warmed to.

'I saw your interview with Trevor MacLean,' said Terry. 'You came across very well.'

'Thanks for the compliment. What do you think of MacLean? Bit of a strange fish–I'm never sure which way to take him,' said Peter.

'Oh, I think he's a grade A twerp, actually. But quite an effective one. I always thought his camp theatricality was affected, but they say he's just the same off camera.'

'Pretty much. In fact, I think he tones himself down a little when he's on air!'

'Really? But you know, he's quite effective as an interviewer. He never goes for the jugular. And by being wide-eyed and non-threatening he often gets people to open up and say more...perhaps say things they shouldn't have.'

'Uh-oh,' said Peter. 'And what did I say that I shouldn't have?'

'Well ... endorsing the "Revolution" is one thing, but Evan and Howard feel you're still aligning us too closely with these new kids on the block. Last night you more or less committed us to working in coalition with them if the time comes. They think you should hold fire on this. I don't agree, by the way. But it's what they're saying. Thought you should know.'

Howard Blackstone, the party leader, was someone Peter admired greatly and had always looked up to. But he was starting to feel that Howard was too 'old school', and maybe not up to handling the new dynamics of the Green Revolution. He knew all that Howard had achieved, weathering the storms of leading the third party in a two-party system. He had led a minor recovery after the bruising of being the junior partner in a previous coalition with the Conservatives. He had inched forward from one minor achievement to another, and in time built up a reputation for reliability and good judgement. But for Peter Howard looked old school, he dressed old school, he behaved old school. And there were things about this revolution that Howard would never truly understand.

Peter put down his glass and sighed heavily with exasperation.

'What else can we do?' said Peter. 'I mean, we're doing it already, right across the country. We *are* working together with them on the Earth Councils, in the Convention—we've made huge strides forward in our support by doing so. Look at our poll ratings!'

'And yours. Amongst all us "Grey" politicians, you have the highest "trust and integrity" ratings. And you've seen the articles tipping you to be our next party leader. Maybe even before the elections. Party leader by Christmas, say the bookies. It provokes some jealousy.'

'Are you saying Howard's upset about this?'

'No, on that score he seems strangely calm. Mysteriously calm, I'd say. Seems like he's weighing a lot of things up. But he did say to me you seem to be spending more time with the Barringtons and their ilk than you do with members of your own party.'

'Ouch. I hear Evan talking.'

'I said I'd have a word with you … and I am.'

'I accept your reproof. But—when we get together and I'm closeted with Howard and Evan, I feel like I'm wrapped in some musty cocoon, cut off from the real world somehow. They act like they are making big strides in the corridors of power, but these days they are just the corridors of inertia. We need to throw open the windows and doors! It's exciting out there! Unless we talk to these people, we're isolating ourselves from the changes that are going on. So much is happening, at every level. And we need to be part of it.'

'I know what you mean. Actually, there's far too much going on. It's impossible to keep up. Revolutions always throw up hundreds of new characters. But, Peter, most of them don't stay around for long. As the old guard fade away, everyone gets their fifteen minutes of fame. So it's easy to align yourself with the wrong people.'

'True.' Peter sighed and sat back in his seat, his brow furrowed in thought, as if weighing something up. 'But do you think the GEM are the wrong people?'

'No—they're more durable and disciplined than most of the Greens we've seen before,' said Terry. 'But we don't really know them. You know

Dave Barrington a bit—but we don't really know anything about who stands for what in their party, who really calls the tune and who wants to turn their party which way. So—caution isn't a bad idea.'

'But it's all change with the other parties too. Everyone expects their leaders to get the push, and there's a whole cast of wannabes lining up to take over in all the parties, tinting their policies with a bit of greenwash.'

'I was thinking,' mused Terry, looking around the bar and taking in the oak panelling and the ancient agricultural implements decorating the walls and the ledges, sensing their incongruity in a central London pub. 'It's like there's a Great Extinction going on with us older parties. Like old dinosaurs in their death-throes. Their heads can't control where their bodies are going any more. They flail around and bump into each other now and then, but mostly they lie on their backs roaring incoherently, with their tails thrashing about.'

'A very colourful image,' laughed Peter, 'And we're one of these old dinosaurs too?'

'Maybe—what's that?!' exclaimed Terry.

Outside the bar, there was a huge explosion of noise, and the sound of people running and shouting. They both got up to go to the door and look, as did most of the other customers.

In the streets was a throng of people, half of them wearing the uniforms of the Green Volunteers. Above their heads they were carrying two struggling individuals, both wearing suits. Both men had a plastic waste-paper bin taped to his head as a kind of hat, sporting the label: 'ECO-CRIMINAL'. A Volunteer was coordinating the action through a megaphone, and whipping up the crowd to shout, 'Make the polluters pay! Polluters will pay!'

Suddenly more Green Volunteers appeared in upper-floor windows either side of the street, brandishing ropes.

'Bloody hell, they're going to hang them!' exclaimed Terry. 'We've got to stop this!'

But he could not force his way through, or make his voice heard over the crowd.

'Eco-criminals!' chanted the crowd to the rhythm of a football chant.

'ECO-CRIMINALS!' CLAP-CLAP, CLAP-CLAP CLAP, rising to a crescendo.

'Where's the police?' cried Terry.

Peter looked around. He could see no sign of the police. It was a bizarre scene. As ropes were lowered to the crowd, Green Volunteers were waiting with their arms held high to catch the ropes, almost in competition with each other. And onlookers—passers-by, people from shops and bars, tourists—held up cameras and mobile phones to capture the scene. Many of the Volunteers themselves were taking pictures or filming the incident, smiling and laughing as they did so. In a few minutes the Internet would be full of film of the incident from every angle.

By now Terry was almost frantic, powerless in the face of a lynching. 'Let us through,' he shouted, Peter pushing with him to get to where the ropes were coming down.

They were too late. But as they got close, their fear subsided a little. They could see the Volunteers were making harnesses for their captives, not nooses. In a matter of seconds, the 'eco-criminals' were swinging upwards, bound across the chest and through their legs, then left to swing ridiculously halfway up the buildings, their suits pulled awkwardly around their hapless bodies, their faces contorted in fear, and the bins still taped to their heads.

The lynch-mob below began to laugh and jeer, before resuming their chanting and marching on to their next targets. As they left, a burly Volunteer pushed Terry forcefully in the chest, sending him reeling back.

'Useless wanker! You'll learn, you'll fucking learn!' he spat out as he stared menacingly at Terry.

Now the police arrived, with a small posse of concerned onlookers. Peter was already taking charge of efforts to rescue the two 'hanged' men, calling over the driver of an open-top tourist bus, which mounted the pavement under one of the victims. The passengers on the top deck supported the hanging victim on their shoulders while undoing his makeshift harness. Meanwhile some of the crowd of Green Volunteers ran back and hammered on the buses, resuming their chanting and jeering.

'We'll take over from here, sir,' said one the police officers to Peter and Terry.

'Good,' said Terry. 'Now how about stopping the bastards from doing it again?'

'Language, sir,' said the officer. 'I'd advise you to mind your language!'

Terry laughed. 'I don't think my language is the main problem here, do you, Officer? How come you're so thin on the ground when all this is going on?'

The policeman looked slightly abashed and tutted. 'They're just one step ahead of us all the time. And when we catch up with them, we're on orders not to go in hard and cause an incident—or at least escalate the incident.'

'But this is assault!' cried Terry. 'In broad daylight. Everyone saw who did it, but they're just going on their merry way to do it again to someone!'

'I'd advise you to calm down, sir,' said the policeman. 'Everything has been filmed. It's like the riots a few years back. There'll be detectives going through the footage, and we'll get who we need to get.'

Terry was looking round now, and finally caught site of Peter, who was being interviewed by a film crew. The sound of breaking glass and a huge cheer could be heard from further down the street.

'They might be one step ahead of the police,' said Terry, 'but they've got every media outlet hot on their heels. How does that happen?'

'They tell who they want to tell,' said the policeman. 'At the moment, they're in charge.'

'What kind of a bloody circus are we in?' asked Terry, as he made his way through the crowd of onlookers to find Peter.

••

It was headline news later in the evening. Now for the first time since the Awakening, Don Mason was put under pressure in the media.

He denounced the incident as being the work of fringe elements, and promised to use his best efforts to curb this kind of happening. But he was also able to make the point that though the GEM had a strong influence in the Volunteers, it did not actually control them. It was a pattern of owning and disowning that would be repeated over the next few days, as copycat violence against 'counter-revolutionaries' and 'eco-criminals' spread fast around the country.

So it was that the Green Volunteers acquired the nickname in the media of the 'Green Militia'. Malcolm Morton liked this, and reassured his colleagues that it was not something to worry about. 'It's like the Salvation Army—people know that. It suggests purpose, and structure and mission. "Volunteers" was OK at first, but it's too woolly in the long run. When people join up, we want them to know that they have a commitment and responsibility—it's not something they can turn up to or not as volunteers. And we need some discipline in there to control the mavericks, don't you think?'

'I recognised a few of them,' said Sarah Turner. 'Play it again.'

As they played the recording of the news story, Sarah identified some of the key ringleaders.

'That's "Fast Eddie" there,' she said, pointing to a face of a volunteer holding ropes at a window. Remember him? We called him that because no one could climb a tree as fast as him back in the woodland protest days. And that's Carl Fullerton, next to the woman with the megaphone. He seems to be orchestrating things.'

'He's always rejected our way as being too tame, hasn't he?' asked Jessica Barrington. 'What's he doing in the Volunteers? We need to root out his kind. He's a complete nutter!'

'Jessica's right,' pronounced Mason. 'We do need to get a grip on the Volunteers. That's down to you, Malcolm. And Doug, you need to rein in the Earth Councils a bit if you can. There's a fair bit of negative reporting about some of the more extreme ideas coming out of them. While these incidents help to keep the momentum up, we have to be sure that nothing backfires. If one of those guys being strung up had fallen and cracked his head open, this would be a different story altogether for us. We have to stay in control. Forceful, fun, and educational. No serious violence. No injuries.'

Everyone nodded their assent.

'And we need to ramp up our efforts on media management,' Mason continued. 'Find out what those eco-criminals were up to, and shift the focus to *their* irresponsible behaviour and its damaging impacts.

'We've had an easy ride so far, but the truth is it won't stay that way for long. Our activists need to get into position as fast as possible. This government may not last until the elections next year, and we need the media completely onside if we're to take over.'

12: The Green King

When the King of England, Henry IX, met Prime Minister Patrick Baxter a few weeks later for one of their weekly meetings, it could have meant something or nothing. The King had long had a strong interest in the environment. And not only a theoretical interest, as he had initiated many environmental reforms on the royal estates and was a strong advocate of organic farming. His interest in the current turn of events was entirely natural.

Privately he was very enthusiastic about the Green Revolution. Baxter, in the tradition of Prime Ministers before him, had regular audiences with the King, and returned again and again to warning about the dangers posed by the Green Earth Councils at local and national level. This bored the King enormously. He was knowledgeable about constitutional affairs, but as someone used to exercising authority, albeit with a limited remit, he couldn't see the problem.

'Frankly, Baxter, I can't see why you get so hot under the collar about this. Whatever power they claim, the point is this: if you like what they suggest, do it. If you don't like it, don't do it. It's as simple as that. They can huff and puff all they want, but they can only get their way if you let them.'

Baxter looked exasperated. Events were taking their toll on him. The country hadn't been irradiated, though men in radiation suits were still collecting soil samples all across the southern counties and several of the coastal towns remained unoccupied. After the initial confusion he had successfully organised, as he saw it, the evacuation from the South of England of all who wanted to go. There had been no serious unrest or looting in the area. He had set up a Royal Commission to investigate alternative sources of energy and how to speed up bringing them on stream. And new flood defences for London were being commissioned already. Yet he was under daily attack from all quarters, and lambasted in the media as a witless and incompetent buffoon.

He had also tried to stand firm against the Green Earth Councils. But standing firm was not as easy as His Majesty would have one believe. Events had acquired a momentum of their own and everything was slipping out of the Prime Minister's control. The support of the other two parties at the moment of crisis had proved valueless. He was under daily attack from within his own party for ignoring warning voices while making common cause with the opposition parties.

What he wanted to do was issue an Order-in-Council that no government official at any level should deal with these wretched Earth Councils. But when he had suggested it to his own inner circle, they had rejected it as being an impractical course of action. And maybe they were right. It would provoke a crisis in the party by cementing his unpopularity. And possibly it was unenforceable.

'If I can speak frankly, Sir,' he said, 'We have a problem with the Earth Councils. You've told me you think that on balance they are a good thing—a "positive force" I think you said.'

The King nodded. They were walking in the gardens at the palace, the King walking with his hands clasped behind his back, slightly stooped and creasing his face as he set his mind to considering the issues. Baxter was talking and occasionally mopping his brow—the sun seemed unbearably hot on this late September afternoon.

Baxter continued. 'Initially the Earth Councils set themselves up—appointed themselves really. Then they went through a kind of election process, though not the same across the country. Then they co-opted representatives from the local authorities, the hospital trusts, the emergency services, the chambers of commerce and God knows who else. So they have a kind of democratic legitimacy—in the eyes of many people, at least. But they are … irregular'

'Please explain to me what you mean by—"irregular",' the King asked.

'They have no status within the system of government. And yet they are affecting it profoundly. These Scrutiny Committees they are setting up are interfering more and more in the process of government. They are persuading public bodies across the country to adopt regulations, change procurement policies, alter planning policies and do all kind of things that are really beyond their powers, or in the case of some of the procurement policies break European law. And we've got local government officers running around like ninnies seeking approval from these meddlers when they should be looking to their local elected councillors.'

'And to you—central government, I mean,' added the King, with a wry smile. 'You mean they're encouraging local government to defy the dictates of central government.'

'Well, Sir, I wouldn't have put it quite like that. But now we're starting to have the same problem in central government with that wretched National Convention. Suddenly all the Whitehall Mandarins are outdoing each other trying to paint themselves green and cooperate the most with this upstart Convention.'

'I can see you're not too well enamoured of these new bodies, Baxter.'

'With respect, Sir, my feelings are not really the point. The point is that the elected government—your government—is losing the ability to govern.'

The King thought for a moment. Then he asked simply: 'So what are you going to do about it, Prime Minister?'

'You know what I want to do, Sir.'

'I do, my "spies" have told me.' The King was fond of referring to his political staff and informal contacts as his 'spies'. 'You want to use all the means at your disposal to order all public servants to stop cooperating with these new bodies. Some things you can do yourself, so long as Parliament supports you. For others you would like my consent.'

Baxter nodded. 'Yes indeed. To regulate the Civil Service. And the army, of course. You're the commander-in chief.'

'I'm afraid I don't share your view. I have these powers on paper, but to exercise them would be tantamount to a royal coup! We don't do things like that, and I'm surprised you suggest it. You say the constitution is under attack. Certainly there's a little, shall we say, ferment. But is it entirely bad if the establishment learns to take on a greener hue?

'To take the steps you want would be unnecessarily divisive at this time, and provoke a major confrontation. Take my advice. This National Convention may be a bit of an upstart, but it is not the Petrograd Soviet. Mason isn't Lenin and neither Barrington nor Kitson make a plausible Trotsky, wouldn't you agree? These are middle-class intellectuals, who wouldn't know how to run a whelk stall. Ride the storm, and stand firm on individual issues, not as a matter of pride or principle. The British establishment has a way of absorbing and regularising the irregular. Today's innovation is tomorrow's tradition. It'll be business as usual—only a bit greener—in two or three months, you'll see.'

Baxter sighed. 'I have always kept you informed, Sir, about every aspect of our government. Your position as sovereign is, amongst other roles, to be the guardian of the constitution. I am telling you today that the constitution is being subverted and altered without the clear mandate of Parliament, King or the will of the people expressed through an election. Your government is being put in the position where it cannot govern. My view is that the ship of state is being buffeted from all sides, and unless we take firm action...'

'...we'll be all at sea?' suggested the King with a wry smile. 'No, Baxter. I'm surprised at you. It seems like you're being uncharacteristically melodramatic. If these new environmental bodies become permanent features, as you intimate, then possibly we can look back and say that the Constitution is evolving, as it has always done. I see no evidence of its being "subverted". Surely everything that's being done has been done in the open, and I have to say seems to be wildly popular. And they seem to be doing some bloody good work too.'

The King then began enthusiastically to describe initiatives promoted by the Earth Council in Windsor, and with which the Crown Estates were happily cooperating.

Baxter looked down to the ground, only half listening. He knew what he had to do.

Prevented by his party and by his monarch from taking the strong action that he firmly believed was necessary, Baxter resigned.

13: Forcing the pace of change

The collapse of the government took the country by surprise. Patrick Baxter believed that the situation could only get worse over the next six months. So he reasoned it might be possible to limit the damage by calling an early election, while the opposition was unprepared.

'I can't believe it!' said Sarah Turner. 'It's suicidal. There's no way they can win!'

The GEM leadership was indeed caught off guard, and Malcolm Morton was not at all pleased. 'Maybe we can't, either. We really needed another six months to prepare, to get the right people and the organisation in place. Now we've got six weeks!'

'Maybe Baxter is more shrewd than we think,' offered Don Mason. 'I mean, he believes that the country is sliding into chaos, and he is unable to stop that slide. He probably believes, the way things are going, that he will have no more chance in six months than he does now. And he also believes that the green movement overall is a bit of a rabble. Until now he has been the focus of opposition. We all unite to hammer away at him. Now he's thrown the ball in our court. So we have to sit down with the other groups across the green movement and sort ourselves out so we can win. This will bring all the petty jealousies and rivalries to the fore, as well as the ideological differences. And he must believe that we'll end up tearing lumps out of each other, and that our inexperience will show. We can't let that happen.'

'And he'll also get a fairer crack of the whip in the news, as the media fairness rules come into force for the election period,' added Dave Barrington.

'I would think Ben Porter is rejoicing now,' said Sarah Turner. 'After all, it's his Greens who have the infrastructure to fight elections. And like Malcolm says, we've never fought a proper election before—we need more time to organise. But we don't have it.'

'And that could be a big problem,' said Morton. 'The risk is that Ben Porter's Greens and the Kitson Greens make all the running.'

'Our strength is in the Earth Councils and the Volunteers,' said Mason. 'We need an initiative from them to put us back in the driving seat. But I think we need to be realistic. We've enjoyed a following wind for a couple of months, but not enough to put us into power on our own.'

'A coalition?' asked Douglas Cunningham, with obvious distaste.

'But one we set the terms for,' said Mason. 'Anyone who wants to run with the Green Revolution needs our support. So we can set the terms for that.'

'A charter. An Earth Charter,' offered Sarah Turner.

'And we should press all the parties and all the candidates to sign it,' said Don, nodding appreciatively at Sarah's idea. 'The Grey parties won't allow their candidates to sign that. So however much they green up their image, their true colours will show through. But more importantly, we can use it to set up a process that puts the Earth Councils in charge of who the candidates should be in a unified front. As the voices of the wider green movement, the Earth Councils should choose who the candidates are on our side. So Porter will end up in conflict with the Earth Councils and the National Convention if he insists on having all his candidates in place.'

'Agreed? We need to move fast on this,' said Morton, already on his feet and with his phone in his hand.

'And–direct action,' continued Mason. 'No let-up in the direct action. We have to distinguish ourselves as doers, not talkers'

••

There had never been an election campaign like it, or at least not since the 19th century. The country seemed to be on the verge of exuberant chaos. Everywhere Green Earth activists and their supporters were taking direct action to curb anti-environmental behaviour. The Green Revolution had a momentum on the ground that was even more dynamic and dramatic than the high theatre of national politics. Everywhere activists were seeking to force the pace of change, and few people sought to oppose them.

Direct action was the order of the day. Campaigns sprung up all across the country, emboldened or empowered by the Earth Councils and Scrutiny Commissions. It was no longer enough for businesses to have an environmental policy document. Green Volunteers or other local pressure groups came in to the buildings to check environmental performance, forcing companies and public bodies to limit waste and modify production methods. In some supermarkets, Green Volunteers stood by the shelves and advised people about the food they should buy, like how to recognise and avoid products that had been transported long distances when more local products were available, and how to avoid battery-farmed foods.

Elsewhere they courted the countryside vote by forcibly re-opening post offices, bringing the old postmasters or postmistresses out of retirement and supporting them with help from the Militia. Don Mason promised them that this would be properly funded when the GEM came to power.

Some of the most headline-grabbing action was taking place in Coventry. A blockade was set up there that was to last for several months, but it was the early days that were the most spectacular. The blockade was coordinated by a coalition of pressure groups calling themselves Coventry EcoFront, and was supported by the local Earth Council. One of the world's largest makers of off-road and popular utility vehicles had for a couple of decades been enjoying large sales of its 'City Cruiser' SUV range—large, gas-guzzling four-by-fours seen as ideal by city dwellers for carrying children, pets and the family shopping. For almost two generations of greens, these vehicles had come to epitomise everything that was wrong with 'consumptionist' values, even though the manufacturers argued that the cars' environmental performance had improved markedly in recent years.

The blockade of the car plant was not the first—there had indeed been several over the previous ten years. But they had always been short, and as time wore on, the media became less interested. This time, with the mood of the country as it was, the blockade was headline news again. On the first day several thousand activists turned up to form a human chain around the plant, so preventing the morning shift from getting to work. The management, under pressure from the police, advised the workers to go home so as to prevent a confrontation.

But the blockade, instead of fading away, became a focal point for national activity. For the next two weeks the numbers who came there increased, becoming almost a point of pilgrimage for the environmentally concerned from around the country.

Trevor MacLean called in some favours and was sent to report, taking with him Juliet Coe, one of Stella Walton's young researchers. Juliet, as a committed GEM activist, was rising fast and enjoying a great deal of influence by her active role supporting the BBC 'Green Team', the body entrusted by ESCOMEDIA with improving the BBC's environmental performance. They were using a local film crew who had been covering the blockade for the local news.

Britain had been enjoying and enduring an epically sweltering Indian Summer, but continuous rain formed the backdrop to the day's filming in the Midlands, and they were all taking shelter in a somewhat stuffy BBC van.

'Grim here, isn't it? You know, I'd rather people stopped talking to me than actually being sent to bloody Coventry,' Trevor whispered loudly to Juliet.

Trevor had made it his task for the day to make Juliet laugh, or at least smile. This almost worked. Juliet nodded towards the local film crew in the back, to remind Trevor that the crew were local and might be offended by his banter. There were a few moments of silence as they watched the rain bucketing down.

'Which side are you on, then, Jules?' asked Trevor.

'Can't you guess?' Juliet replied. 'And please Trevor, don't call me "Jules". I'm Juliet.'

She looked away as she said this, being slightly embarrassed to be rebuking the larger-than-life Trevor MacLean.

'OK…'

Trevor sighed, and leaned around to talk to the crew.

'Is the weather always so good here?' he asked, by way of making conversation.

The cameraman nodded.

'Global warming hasn't reached the West Midlands yet?'

'Nothing comes to Coventry unless there's no alternative,' muttered the cameraman gloomily in his heavy West Midlands accent.

'I almost didn't get here, you know,' said the soundman, in equally gloomy tones.

'Why's that?'

'I was stuck on the M42.'

'Seems like most of the country's been stuck on some motorway or other for most of the last few weeks,' commented Trevor. 'Nothing nuclear, I hope,' he added drily.

'No—just the bloody anti-roads brigade. Some sort of protest. They were blockading both carriageways. It was getting a bit feisty with some of the truck drivers. You know what I did?'

Trevor and Juliet shook their heads.

'I just walked up to them, through the traffic, flashed my BBC pass at them, and told them I was coming here to do a report with Trevor MacLean. And you know what they did?'

Trevor and Juliet shook their heads again.

'They came back with me to my car, wearing those luminous green and yellow safety jackets they wear now, and ushered me through onto the hard shoulder and let me through. I had the motorway all to myself after that. It was really cool!'

'You see, Juliet,' said Trevor, 'my name opens doors. You should try it sometimes.'

Juliet rolled her eyes and looked out the window again.

'I think it's starting to clear again now,' she said.

'Time for some more vox pop, then!' said Trevor, trying to sound jolly. Then winking at the film crew he added, 'But Jules, could you get me a few less plebs to interview this time? The editors will want some people who can actually be understood in the rest of the country. Things being as they are, we can't afford subtitles.'

Winding up Juliet was a mildly entertaining sport for Trevor, a way to pass time on a wet day. She was so humourless and politically correct, in Trevor's view. The only problem was that she didn't respond. It would be fun to get a bit of banter going with her, or even with the crew. As they got out of the van, he whispered to Juliet, 'I think those lot in there are the gloomiest people I've met this year. And I've met all the Green leadership too!'

'You're not going to bait me, Trevor,' said Juliet. 'And I think you should go easy with the "let's insult the locals" routine—just because you're from London doesn't mean everyone else is a yokel, you know.'

'Point taken, miss,' said Trevor in mock dejection, holding out his hand for her to slap.

Juliet ignored him, and went off to set up some interviews, both with the activists blockading the camp and with the car workers and their families.

Trevor's first interview was with a very damp activist, a young woman in her early twenties, or so it seemed to Trevor. Juliet had established that her name was Karen.

'Where have you come from today, Karen?' Trevor asked.

'From Solihull.'

'You enjoying the weather here in Coventry?'

'It's much the same in Solihull, you know,' she replied, beaming up at him through her long bedraggled hair.

'So, Karen, what made you decide to join the blockade here today?'

'I just wanted to add my voice to the protest, you know, to draw the world's attention to the damage these kinds of cars do to the environment. It can't go on, you know!'

'Do you think this blockade will make a difference? I mean you may close down production for a few days, but can it make a difference in the long term?'

Karen became animated. 'Yes, I think it can, you know! We're not going to go away until somebody does something—the car industry, the government, both of them, all of them!'

A small crowd around her began to cheer as she became more emphatic.

'But what exactly can they do?' Trevor asked.

'First they can ban making all these gas-guzzlers,' Karen replied, to more cheers. 'Then the government can set up new tough standards to control pollution from cars. And they should invest more in cars that run on alternative fuels.'

'What do you feel about the car workers here—if your blockade carries on, and if you succeed in your aims, they could all be out of jobs. Do you care about them and their families?'

'Of course I care,' she quickly responded. 'I don't want anyone to be out of work! But we have to do something about the way the motor industry destroys the world we live in. No one needs to be out of work, you know—if they switch over to making more environment-friendly cars they could become world leaders.'

'You think people would buy electric cars now—they haven't done so in great numbers so far, have they?'

'The mood's changed now, you know,' she replied exuberantly. 'People are ready for change! Look at the numbers here now. I was never into this kind of stuff before—I didn't even think about it. I want to do my bit to help, like all the others here. I'm sure if eco-cars were available, we'd buy them!'

'That's brilliant, Karen,' said Trevor, ending the short interview. 'Watch the news bulletins after two o'clock: I'm sure you'll be in there.'

Trevor then interviewed a succession of demonstrators, but became increasingly bored. He was sure he couldn't improve on Karen's short interview. And besides, he thought, she was very cute and would look best on screen.

'Juliet—where's the other side?' Trevor called to his colleague. 'Where are my workers' families? Where's the Coventry Cratchitt family? There must be a Tiny Tim here somewhere about to fade away if his Dad can't earn a crust!'

'I've got someone just about to step up,' replied Juliet. 'I asked him to fetch his wife and kids, so they'll all be here in a moment. But Trevor, it's actually a problem finding the other side here. It's like twenty-to-one in favour of the blockade.'

'But we need to have some balance, Juliet.'

'I'm giving you balance,' Juliet insisted. 'Representative balance. True balance!'

Phil Carpenter and his family were able to provide the balance Trevor MacLean was looking for. He had worked for around ten years in the factory, and had met his wife Linda there. Now they were both somewhat sheepishly in the full glare of national TV with their two young children. Trevor did his best to set them at their ease with some inane banter before the interview began, but they still felt more than a little nervous.

Trevor began. 'I'm joined here outside the factory gates by Phil and Linda Carpenter. The factory is central to their lives. Phil has worked there all his working life, and even found true romance on the production line, marrying one of his former co-workers, Linda. They live just over there, in the shadow of the factory. Let's start with you, Phil. What does the closure of the plant mean for you?

'Well, er, at the moment it's not too bad. I know I've not worked for two weeks, like, but we're still getting paid, at least for now.'

'And if it goes on?'

'The blockade, you mean? Oh, right. That could be bad news. They can't pay us forever to do nothing. In the end they might have to lay us off. And it's not only the workers in the plant. There's hundreds of other companies in the area, large and small, who'd be in trouble if it was closed a long time.'

Trevor then turned to Linda.

'Linda—I think you now work for one of these smaller firms that Phil mentioned? Is the blockade starting to have any effect on you or your company?'

'Well, like Phil says, it's early days yet,' replied Linda. 'But it's starting to be worrying. So far we've mainly had to hold off delivering parts, but you know the protesters are also stopping the office staff coming in to the factory. And this means they haven't paid us on a couple of contracts. We're only a small business, so unless something's done soon, things could get a bit sticky!'

Trevor sensed a chance to generate a little passion, and decided to probe a bit further.

'"Unless something's done…" What do you mean by that, Linda? What can be done, and who should do it?'

'Well,' she said, 'first of all this lot should clear off home. They've made their point, and now they should take it up with the government and the bosses, and leave us to get on and earn our living.'

As she said this, some of the protesters listening began to jeer, and calling out 'We're not going!' and 'No chance! We're here for the long haul!'

Now Phil took exception to his wife being jeered at and sprang to her defence.

'Go on, piss off the lot of you! Go back to college, or London or wherever you bloody come from.' Then turning to Trevor and the camera he added: 'None of this lot are local, you know—never seen any of 'em before!'

Some of the protesters began to react angrily and were shouting back at him. 'This is great!' thought Trevor, and then he whispered to the crew, 'Are you getting all this?' They nodded or held up a thumb in acknowledgement.

Then Trevor noticed a small ruckus developing around Juliet and three policemen. It seemed they were holding back some angry men who wanted to get through to the cameras, or the protesters, or both. Trevor gestured to the crew to turn and film the incident, and apologising to his interviewees he began to march quickly towards the scene, all the time providing an excited commentary.

'As you can see, a disturbance seems to be developing over to my left… I can't quite see what is happening, but it seems tempers are rising. Some people are trying to get through….are they car workers? They seem to be shouting at the protesters … Did somebody just throw something? I think it was just a plastic bottle….'

He could hear people on both sides shouting and swearing at each other. There was a small group of about twenty car workers, who were shaking their fists and remonstrating with the protesters, and it seemed, with Juliet.

Trevor arrived at the scene. Switching off his microphone, he asked Juliet what was happening.

'These guys wanted to come and join in the interview, 'she explained.

'Is that all?'

'I was holding them back, or trying to. I think we already have enough from their side, and they seemed a little aggressive!'

Trevor noticed she looked both determined and a little afraid.

'Good girl!' he said. 'Nothing I like better than a good fight—though I'm sure that's not what you intended!'

'Of course not!' she exclaimed angrily.

'Ah! Here's a lesson my dear: never deny yourself credit for something that turns out well. Come on—let's sort this out!'

Trevor moved round a policeman, muttering 'Excuse me officer', and placed himself in front of the largest car worker, a very tall man with close cropped hair and tattooed arms. He grabbed the man by his hand and introduced himself.

'Excuse me, sir—I'm Trevor MacLean from the BBC... I can see you have some forceful views you'd like to express. How would you like to express them on air?'

The man looked both surprised and a little disarmed for a moment, then his anger rose again.

'Of course I bloody would, you pillock! That's what I was telling your little girlie there, but she wouldn't let us through. Then this lot started. Right bloody shower they are!' he said, gesturing to the protesters, who immediately began jeering and cat-calling again.

'Apologies, apologies,' Trevor replied, 'my fault entirely. I'd said we'd done enough for the day, and I was going to get on to editing the report for the next bulletin, et cetera et cetera, but that was before you and your friends arrived, and it seems like you've livened things up a bit. So I really want to hear what you have to say!'

Juliet had coloured up, and stood angrily to one side.

'Now,' said Trevor, 'I know exactly what I'd like to do, if you agree. There's a lot of people out there who don't really know what this is all about. So I'd like to set up a small debate here—a couple of you and a couple of them, each to put their point of view. What do you think?'

The big car worker turned to his mates. 'Sounds good to me,' said one.

'OK,' said the big guy, rubbing his hands together. 'Let's get this party started!'

'Right,' said Trevor. 'You guys decide who'll be on your side, and my researcher, Juliet, can find a couple of protesters to put their point of view, and we'll start in about five minutes, over there by the gates, if that's OK. Just one thing: don't hit anyone, however much you're tempted. Especially me!'

They all laughed.

'Just watch your step, son, and you'll be alright!' joked the car worker.

'That's very reassuring! Oh, and one more thing,' added Trevor in a confidential tone. 'Be nice to Juliet. She's a sweetie, really. Just a bit inexperienced. I don't think she's ever met a real worker before!'

'Well, tell her I'd be very happy for her to make a closer inspection of one!' joked one of the workers.

'Better not be you,' added another. 'Frighten her off for life.'

Juliet was burning inside as she went to find some of the leaders of the blockade. She couldn't hear all they were saying, but she recognised the ribald tone of the laughter, and felt humiliated. 'Just focus on the task,' she told herself.

The representatives of the protesters were soon found—a young man called Tim and a more mature woman called Delphine, a veteran of *Reclaim the Streets* campaigns. It was agreed they could put their case first, and the car workers Colin and Steve would respond.

Trevor introduced the two sides and put his first question to the protesters. 'The blockade of the plant has been going on for quite some time now. Don't you think that's long enough to have made your point? Isn't it time to start thinking about the livelihood of the workers and their families?'

Delphine responded on behalf of the protesters. 'Well Trevor, we're making our point for sure, but I don't think we've made it completely yet. I mean, what will happen if we just pack up and go home now? Within a day everything will be back to normal, and they'll be trying to push out as many of these gas-guzzlers as possible to make up for lost time.'

'And what's wrong with that? It's a bloody car factory. It's what we do!' interrupted Colin.

'What's wrong with that?!' asked Tim in disbelief, as if the wrongness of it were self-evident. 'It seems our message hasn't been getting home to some people—'

'And the message is?' asked Trevor.

'The message is that these cars, these little trucks dressed up as cars, epitomise all that's wrong with the way we live. About eighty per cent of them are being sold to people who live in towns, and they just have no place in towns. They're built to drive over rough land and do a tough job of work. But they're being marketed and sold as status symbols, when they are of no practical use in towns. And all this at a time when more responsible manufacturers are developing much more fuel efficient cars and cars that run on alternative fuels.'

'And we're also trying to get a message to government,' added Delphine. 'They are not doing half enough to promote cars powered by alternative fuels. They're too timid, and far too close to the roads lobby. They need to promote what we call "new generation mobility" with more incentives and investment and more penalties against gas-guzzlers.'

Colin was champing at the bit to respond, and Trevor invited him to do so.

'So you're trying to put us out of work to make a political point, are you? You should be making your human chain around bloody Downing Street, not us. But the police would never let you near there—so you picked on a soft target to get yourselves in the news. And the police do nothing. Look at them! Just let you intimidate decent law-abiding people like us!'

'Are you intimidating them?' Trevor asked the protesters.

'Of course not!' replied Tim. 'It's a peaceful demonstration!'

'Peaceful my arse!' exclaimed Steve. 'You mean you'd let us just walk in there if we want to start working, and do nothing about it?'

There was no reply at first.

'There, you see!' shouted Colin, taking their silence as evidence that that the protesters would get rough if anyone tried it.

'It's your own bosses who have locked the gates,' said Tim weakly.

Trevor turned to the car workers. 'Don't the protesters have a point though? We're especially conscious at this time of the damage we're doing to the planet, and using these cars in urban areas just can't be justified can it? Tell me what's the point of having them in towns?'

Colin and Steve looked at each other to see who would reply, and Steve gave Colin the go-ahead. 'What do you mean "what's the point?" Why do you need to have a point? It's a free country, after all!'

Steve interrupted. 'Speed humps!' he said pointedly. 'And pot-holes. These days it's worse driving on the bloody roads than driving off-road! And if you've got kids and dogs and the family shopping, why not have something like this? Their beautifully made, very safe, very robust, bags of carrying space….'

Now his co-workers around him were all cheering. 'Tell 'em Steve!' 'He's better than any bloody advert!'

And the protesters began shouting back. Trevor held up both his hands to call for calm, but this was exactly the kind of heated debate he was looking for. He turned to the protesters and asked: 'OK. OK. Steve and Colin say they do have practical value, and in a free country people should be able to choose the car they want.' The car workers cheered. 'How do you answer that?'

Delphine looked a little rattled, but tried to appear calm. 'Sure you can carry children and shopping. But you can do that in any vehicle—why produce such environmentally-unfriendly vehicles to do it in? As for your other point, it's all very well to say it's a free country and we have choice, but people should not be allowed to choose to do things that harm the world. All the laws we have are to stop us doing harmful things, and so restrict our choice. We need to understand more about the harm we do to the planet, and to future generations. Then I think we'd accept these restrictions without question.'

'What about our jobs?' someone called out from the crowd.

'Yes, Tim, what about their jobs?' asked Trevor.

'We don't want to put anyone out of a job,' Tim replied. 'All car manufacturers need to shift their production to more sustainable forms of mobility....'

Some of the car workers began to mimic his middle class southern accent, repeating in exaggeratedly effeminate high-pitched voices 'Ooh, more sustainable forms of mobility!' Tim looked embarrassed, but soldiered on.

'Why not? There can be as many jobs producing eco cars, and we can become a world-leader in this field!'

'What about this, lads—couldn't you make cars that run on electricity, or hydrogen, or sugar or cow shit, or whatever?' asked Trevor.

'I'm sure we could,' replied Colin. 'We could make anything. We could stick Timmy here in the tank and maybe they'd run on bullshit! But I don't think this young man has any idea of the time and investment needed to work up new models...'

'You've had years to do it!' a protester called from the crowd.

'All that's fine,' added Steve. 'But your average punter isn't going to want to go to work in a bloody milk float, are they!'

And so the argument went to and fro, now generally good natured though with a good deal of cat-calling. Then Trevor had an idea.

He turned to the protesters' representatives and put a question to them.

'Delphine, Tim—at the start of this interview you insisted that this was always a peaceful protest. But you didn't commit yourself when Steve here asked whether you'd stand aside and let them go back to work. I'm asking you now for a direct yes or no answer. If they wanted to go back to work, would you use physical force to stop them?'

Again they hesitated, and it seemed to Trevor as if Tim in particular was looking into the crowd for some kind of prompt or signal before answering. Again Delphine volunteered a response.

'We're committed to non-violence, and would use all non-violent means possible to prevent the factory starting up again.'

'What do you mean by that?' asked Trevor.

'Just what I say. But we've always been successful in the past by not giving away our tactics, so I'm not going to tell you now!'

Trevor decided to push the point. 'But say, for the sake of argument, that the big Boss arrived with his key and opened the gate to let his employees in. Would you physically stop them?'

Again hesitation.

'I expect so,' said Delphine. 'But we'd use physical *presence*, rather than physical *force*. We'd put ourselves in a position where violence would need to be used *against us* if they want to get in and reactivate the factory.'

As she spoke, twenty or so large men from amongst the protesters began to move into what seemed to be prearranged positions in front of the gates.

Before Trevor could ask another question a policeman tugged at his arm and asked for a private word. Trevor signalled to keep the cameras on.

'Sorry sir,' said the officer, 'but I suggest you move on from this line of questioning. It could lead to a confrontation, and as you can see we don't have enough officers here to keep the lid on things if it gets ugly'.

'Sure, sure,' said Trevor. 'But I've seen, and reported on, many occasions when the police have held back protestors and pickets to let workers get in to do their jobs. What's different this time?'

'Oh, I'm not really the right person to ask about that, sir. But I think it's the national mood at the moment, don't you? The manufacturers don't want any more bad publicity than they already have, is my guess.'

'And maybe your bosses don't want to be seen supporting gas-guzzling car producers when the police force is having its own environmental performance taken apart by the Scrutiny Commission, what do you think?'

'As I say, sir, I'm not the right person to ask about these things. By the way—I think you did a good job of work in calming this lot down before—shame to let that go to waste by winding them up again, I'd say. So I strongly advise you to wrap things up here now, before tempers get frayed again.'

By nature a stirrer rather than a fighter, Trevor graciously accepted this advice, and went to thank all his interviewees and to record his closing words.

As he did so he noticed Juliet and the police officer talking earnestly to each other and shaking hands. It seemed like they had known each other for longer than just today.

The journey back to London with Juliet was rather frosty. His attempts to goad her mildly were met with silence, and he could see he had upset her, but he was not entirely sure how. Still, professionally it had been an excellent day. In the café at the train station they had seen on the News Channel that their item featured in the headlines, with footage of both angry confrontations and extracts from his impromptu debate.

For Juliet it was a good day's work too. She couldn't bear Trevor's imperious and patronising manner. She felt that as a journalist he had no values, and was motivated only by the vanity of seeing his work ahead of everyone else's. But she had to hand it to him. He had brought the blockade back to the forefront of attention, and however inadvertently helped to raise awareness of the issues. And though he had risked pushing things too far, his report helped to give the impression that the Green activists were completely committed to non-violent methods.

Still unsure of what exactly he had done to offend Juliet, Trevor thought maybe he ought to make it up to her somehow. She had proved herself to be quite an effective assistant, if a touch biased towards the 'green bandwagon', as he saw it. But then, half the country was in the same space emotionally at the moment. He decided on a peace offering.

'You know Stella told me you had an idea for a feature on the rise and rise of the animal rights folk,' he said. 'How about sending me what you have and we'll have a planning session in the morning?'

Juliet looked at him. 'Thanks. I'm sure we can do something very interesting!'

And she smiled.

'I've been trying all day to make her smile,' thought Trevor. 'It seems nothing works. Except giving her what she wants.'

When he looked back at her, she was already asleep, with her head against the window of the train.

14: Animal behaviour

There was indeed a great deal of activity on the 'Animalist' front. The Green Revolution had brought animal rights activists centre stage. The heightened guerrilla activity of the animalist 'balaclava brigades', often working with other fringe elements in the wider environmental movement, was only part of the story. The majority of activity was above board and law-abiding, coordinated through the Earth Councils. It both tapped into and generated local enthusiasm for adapting the way we live to be in closer harmony with the natural world. Local energy across the country was being thrown into nature conservancy and habitat restoration or creation projects, as well as programmes to support food production without cruelty.

All this activity—and indeed popularity for the cause—was new to Titus Whitaker. As Professor of Moral Philosophy at the University of Wessex, he had established a modest academic reputation in the field, noted for his controversial take on environmental issues and animal rights.

Now the Green Revolution had flung the doors of his ivory tower wide open, and so far he was enjoying the ride. Having played a leading part in setting up Earth Councils in Wiltshire and Somerset, he had enhanced his standing amongst environmental activists and had attained the status of a regional celebrity. After that he had been delegated to represent the area on the National Convention of Earth Councils, and he was beginning to enter the national consciousness too. This was both enjoyable and, he felt, a touch unsettling.

But Titus Whitaker's was already a well-known and celebrated name amongst the host of activists on the far fringes of the deep green and animal rights movements. His books and pamphlets were read hungrily by the proponents of radical change and of direct action, though he had rarely taken any part in direct action himself. His words and ideas were often on the lips of those who took part in actions such as destroying fields of genetically engineered crops, or liberating animals from laboratories and research centres.

Now he was sitting alongside one of the leading 'Animalist' guerrillas and member of the National Convention, Gabriella Pearson, as they held court in a seminar room at the University. Around twenty activists were gathered around, lapping up his every word. But they were far from a passive group. All had been involved in various kinds of direct action, and were keen to press the case for particular kinds of direct action and guerrilla activity.

As Whitaker looked around, he was aware that by some distance he was the oldest person there. Gabriella Pearson and a couple of others maybe were into their early forties, and they were the older ones amongst the rest. He himself was in his early sixties. And the youth and energy of the movement gave him hope. Not that he would in any way belittle the efforts of the other old stagers who had kept to the faith throughout the years, but this new wave of younger activists was a joy to behold.

'We are approaching a new dawn,' he said. His voice was deep and soft-spoken, but seemed to echo out somehow from the back of his skull, carrying a kind of gravitas as if coming from a deep source of erudition. 'The ferment of this Green Revolution gives us a chance, as never before, to carry forward our ideas. But we can't do this alone. No, there are just not enough of us yet. I know some of you are concerned about collaborating with the mainstream Greens, or becoming too close to the GEM who seem to have stolen a march on us all. But if on fifty or sixty or even seventy per cent of the issues we are on the same side, then let's work with anyone of good will who will take forward those elements of our programme.

'At the moment, I'd say that most of the country is with us to some extent, and we must capitalise on this moment. As a result of the Awakening, the Great British public is in its salad days of true Earth awareness, and everyone is wearing at least a little greenery! This moment, I believe, can last of its own accord for a year or eighteen months: we need to make that enthusiasm last for two to three years to bring our best efforts to fruition. So we need in every area to implement our most engaging and attractive projects, while we embed ourselves in the ranks and leadership of the Green Volunteers. We need to make this movement our movement. And I'm sure we can win new friends from amongst people of good heart, people who already have or who will grow to have true Planet-awareness.

'Up until now we've pursued our aims with purity and pugnacious idealism. Now, without abandoning our ideals, it's time also to win friends and influence people. Now I believe our comrade Juliet has some ideas here.'

With the aplomb and charm of an old-school English gentleman, Whitaker bowed to Juliet Coe and gestured to her to take the floor. She stood up with a somewhat diffident and unassuming manner, but spoke determinedly and without hesitation. Having been embedded as a GEM sleeper in the BBC, speaking openly here felt to her like coming out of the shadows.

'What Titus says is true. And I'm an example of someone who has spanned the apparent gap between our movement and the Green Earth Movement. The GEM has the right approach, and the discipline to make our dream of a Planet-loving government a reality. I believe with my whole being in this vision, just as you do. But if there have to be compromises on the road to taking control, we have to ensure that within that process there are people like ourselves who will stay true to the true path. And if we can convert others on the way, so much the better.

'But we have some problems of a negative public perception to overcome. And I'm delighted to be able to tell you that I've secured agreement for a short series of programmes about our quest for true equality between the species that share our Planet with us. And what I'd like from all of you is examples of the best and most light-green-friendly work you've been doing in your localities so that I can weave them into the programming.'

People jumped in with many suggestions about activities in their localities that would fit the bill, and Juliet diligently noted them down and good contacts to get in touch with.

Juliet also set out one of her main challenges. She had to collaborate on the programme with Trevor MacLean. His name brought a round of knowing laughter. 'He'll probably want to have some kind of phoney angle, like: "Animalists—Saints or Subversives?" But I'm getting plans in place to neutralise his influence.'

Just one of the assembled group sat back, arms folded across her chest and an irritated frown growing all the time. She exchanged a sardonic look with Gabriella Pearson, who now raised her voice to attract everyone's attention.

'Hold on a minute, everyone. I think Tara is not entirely happy with what's going on here. Come on Tara. Don't hold back. You're among the best of friends. Tell us what's on your mind!'

Tara Collingworth took a gulp of her drink and, without changing position, waited for everyone to turn to her. Tara was herself becoming well-known in Animalist circles for her writings as well as for her activism. As a Christian Environmentalist she held strongly to the view that the role of humankind was to act as stewards to Creation, a role we have abandoned in pursuit of selfish 'species self-interest'. Her most read pamphlet was called *The Noah Principle*, exploring the story of Noah and his Ark as a parable of the role that a virtuous humankind should play in protecting and saving the diversity of species in the world. Her writing was infused with the fire of the Old Testament and the call to action of Liberation Theology and Christian Marxism.

When she was sure she had their attention, she spoke. 'Well ... I don't want to be the wet blanket at the party here. And I'm sure Juliet is doing great. But I'm not so sure about this approach of trying to win the hearts and minds of everyone across the spectrum from Ben Porter to Mr and Mrs Oxfordshire who want to look at a nice country view out their window. We have to keep our eyes on the prize and not get distracted by petty bourgeois greenery. All these minor achievements have no value in the long run.'

'Tactics, Tara. Tactics,' interrupted Gabriella Pearson. 'You can have no doubt that our eyes are set firmly on the prize. But we have to get there step by step.'

'Yes, well, so you say,' answered Tara. 'But tactics have a way of becoming the strategy if we start focusing on how other people think about us. Compromise becomes a way of life then an end in itself when you want to be onside with the media. Just look at what the Grey parties have done over the years. All image, no substance.

'I mean, do we need to be acceptable to these people, to the general public? You know we don't want them or need them in the long run. If we tie ourselves to them, they'll drag us back from our true aims. They are many, and we are few. And that's the way it has to be. It's only by being few, and by being dedicated to the true rebalancing we aim for, that we can keep our radicalism and save the Earth. Am I right or am I wrong?'

'Of course you are right,' exclaimed Gabriella Pearson. 'And you know I've never been one to compromise. And I never will be one to compromise. But Titus and Juliet are right too. We have a unique window of opportunity, and we must use it. There's a favourable climate of opinion right now—but it won't last forever! So we have to do everything we can to extend the moment for as long as possible, as long as we need to. You know we all—everyone in this room—is signed up to the principles you and I believe in. It will just take some time, and if we can hold our nerve we can use the power of this wider movement, we can use the energy of the Green Volunteers, to take a huge leap forward.'

'Patience and discipline, as Don Mason is always telling us in the GEM,' interjected Juliet Coe. 'Until the time is right.'

'And the time is almost right,' added Titus. 'We have to trust each other on this. You know in our movement we've had to keep a cellular structure and work on our more far-reaching operations on a "need to know" basis. Well, can you trust me on this? There are other wheels turning, and we just need a little time for all to be in place.'

He looked at the faces around the room, and could see that the trust was there. Finally he fixed his gaze on Tara Collingworth. She smiled graciously, and nodded her assent.

'And Tara, we can't always draw too hard a line between "us" and "them",' added Whitaker. 'We are few, as you say. It's our strength, but our problem too. We need to draw towards ourselves people with the right skills and attributes if we are to succeed long term. After all, in the new balanced communities we aim to set up we will need butchers, bakers and candlestick-makers. A community made up of provincial professors like me or political activists like Gabriella might struggle to survive the first winter!'

'Not so sure about the butchers!' laughed Pearson, like most of the activists a life-long vegetarian. 'But we get your drift. The new communities must be diverse, energetic and capable.'

Whitaker smiled, as he recognised the phrase. 'Well, I'm glad someone's been reading my books,' he joked. 'We have to listen to Tara, and keep our eyes on the prize. And what is the prize? It's to restore the balance of the Earth. And now is the time to start to lay the foundations for the new world. The new mood in the Revolution will give us the opportunity to build our new communities and to begin the important works of renewing nature. Reforestation. Rewilding. Reintroducing indigenous species that mankind has wiped out, not only in special areas but throughout the country. Completely transform food production. It's what we are called to do. We cannot sit on the sidelines, but have to engage at every level to make this happen. We are the vanguard of the New Dawn, and we have to lead the way there.'

15: A common front

Sandy Honeyford let herself into the Kitson's house, though she suspected that maybe Heather was none too pleased when she did this. But Peter had said not to stand on ceremony, to treat it as her own home now that they were working together so much.

And this time she carried a very large and beautiful bunch of flowers, as it was the first time she would see Heather since the baby—Andrea—had been born. Sandy had already congratulated Peter, smoking cigars with him and drinking beer the night after the birth. This, she suspected, was something else that might rankle with Heather. Still, Heather would have to accept this—she and Peter were close colleagues working all hours in exceptional circumstances. And above all it was—at least on Peter's part—innocent. Tired but happy and relieved to be home, Heather was willing to be gracious as Sandy asked after her health and cooed over little Andrea.

Heather had already noticed the difference in the questions that women asked. Mothers ask the kind of questions that women without children cannot. And they ask them in a way that speaks of their own experience. In fact, more often than not their questions were simply a disingenuous cue to talk at length about their own experience. But women's conversations, she had noticed, were often like this. I say something about my experience, you pick up a trigger word and talk about your experience, and so on and so on, until in the end you build up some kind of imagined empathy. Women who haven't had children can't play the part, even if they ask the right questions, ones they have heard being asked by others. It would become more like a man's conversation—questions followed by answers, or something equally unsophisticated.

Heather came to with a start, realising that Sandy was asking her something, while she had been off in some meditative dream-world musing about the way people communicate. She was aware that Sandy was floundering, like a fish out of water in this new-born domesticity. Suddenly Heather felt more compassionate towards her, and a need to be gracious, even though deep down Sandy's presence grated on her.

'Sorry, Sandy,' said Heather, pushing her hair back away from her face. Sandy noticed that it had been cut to shoulder-length. Is this a necessary ritual for becoming a mum—to cut one's hair and prepare to look more motherly?

Heather continued, in a gently flustered kind of way. 'You know I've been like this since Andrea was born. Kind of inattentive and dreamy. Maybe I'm still on cloud nine—a kind of sore-down-below cloud nine! Or it could be I'm still floating with all that pethidine. '

Sandy felt the friendly tone of what Heather said, but the words were alien and a little bit discomforting. And she wasn't sure what pethidine is. She guessed some kind of drug used in childbirth, or was it perhaps some kind of hormone? Best just to laugh and say how marvellously Heather is coping.

'Listen, Sandy' said Heather, 'I know this is short notice, and it's also really stupid to be doing this so soon, but we're having some people to dinner on Friday week—and I wonder if you'd like to join us?'

'Oh, thanks, Heather, I'd love to. But are you sure, it is so soon, and you can't want too many people—'

'No, really, Sandy. I wouldn't ask if I didn't mean it.'

Sandy was sure that was true. And she was genuinely pleased that Heather was being friendly to her.

'OK. But on one condition. I know nothing about babies, so in that way I feel totally inadequate as a woman. But I do have credibility in the kitchen. So as long as I can help out with the cooking and everything, I'll be there.'

Heather looked at her for a few moments. 'OK! It's a deal.'

••

When Sandy came through to Peter's home office—a rather large home office crammed with technology and ceiling-to-floor shelves of books—he was talking with both Terry Cairns and Howard Blackstone on screen.

A mutual trust and friendship between Peter and Howard had been re-placed by a tense and uneasy relationship. Howard was still inwardly smarting at Peter's unilateral initiatives in manoeuvring the party into a kind of coali-tion with the Greens. They'd had another blazing row, though now the dust had settled they found they were still able to work together. In truth, Howard felt he might have been inclined to do something similar. But it had needed discussion and consideration by the party as a whole. Peter had just announced that he accepted the 'Earth Charter' when journalists questioned him directly. Evan Roberts was still livid, and refused to deal with Peter unless absolutely necessary. Peter felt this was to a large extent sour grapes. His strategy was sound, and Evan should in principle love it. But Evan was the party strategist, and his opposition was of the 'not invented here' variety. In short, Peter felt Evan was sulking.

Terry Cairns acted as the peacemaker and bridge-builder. He felt a responsibility as Peter was a kind of protégé of his. And he also felt a little taken by surprise by Peter's increasing impulsiveness—not something that he had previously noticed as a character trait in this otherwise careful and correct man.

Now they were talking about the 'rubber stamp', as the Earth Charter had come to be called. Howard was voicing his reservations about it.

'It's a matter of principle, really. If we sign up, we're accepting that an outside body has the right to approve our candidates—I feel it's a slippery slope.'

Peter protested. 'But we've done it before. We signed up to a Charter for Disability last time around, a Charter to end World Poverty, a Common Statement against Age Discrimination—and several more before my time as well, I believe.'

'But Peter,' Howard said, 'it's just not the same. Those were statements by charities on single issues, which coincided with our own views and we were happy to endorse. This is altogether different. It's like being asked to sign up to someone else's manifesto, and giving another party the right to approve or disapprove of the candidates our local parties select.'

Terry was more pragmatic. 'But what's the fallout if we don't sign up? We set ourselves on collision course with a popular movement we have so far endorsed. Ah, Peter. I see you've got Sandy there now too—Hi Sandy!'

Sandy leaned over Peter towards the screen, putting one hand on his shoulder, and said 'Hi!' She felt good being in the company of some of the most important people in the country, even if two of them were only there on screen.

'What do you think, Sandy?' asked Howard.

Sandy responded without hesitation as she sat down beside Peter. 'Sign. It's the only option. And I think we have to sign up without delay. If we grumble and debate, or try to negotiate, we put ourselves hopelessly in the middle. It would be as well in that case to throw our lot in with the others, and take a combined stand against it. But I think if we resist, we risk throwing away everything we've won back over the past three years.'

'That's a bit dramatic, isn't it?' suggested Howard.

'Hmm—I don't think it is,' said Sandy. 'Environmental policies have been one of our unique selling points over this time. Our core supporters expect it. Whatever words we could use to try to explain our opposing the Charter, the green parties will play it like we were insincere all the time. They'll be able to portray themselves as the only true believers.'

'But how much would that matter?' asked Howard.

'It only matters,' said Terry, 'if they have any chance of doing well.'

'And we all think they do have a very good chance of doing well,' added Howard, and they all agreed.

'If we don't sign up to it,' said Terry, 'We're on the defensive from day one, with something to justify all the time. I suggest we sign up then shut up about the principle of it—I mean sideline it as an issue, and just focus on the positive. Let the other two "Grey" parties slug it out about whether its right to sign up to this kind of thing.'

This now became the agreed approach of the Liberal Democrats. The party leadership would sign up to it on behalf of the party as a whole. Then they would allow individual candidates to make their own final decision about whether to sign or not, in the confident expectation that everyone would follow suit.

After the video conference, Sandy spoke candidly with Peter. 'I'm sure this is the right thing to do, Peter. Howard's not so sure. It seems he's losing his way. He used to be so decisive, and now he's hesitant. The game has moved onto to a new playing field, and he's not sure of the rules any more. It's down to you to take the lead, Peter. Effectively, you have been the leader for the past few weeks.'

'Not everybody likes that, I know,' said Peter. He knew that Sandy kept her ear close to the ground, and he was inviting her to tell him if she had heard anything. She had.

'That's true. Evan is still really mad at you. He thinks you're dividing the party. But he's also behind Howard agreeing with you over the Charter tonight.'

Peter looked puzzled. Sandy continued.

'The way Evan sees it, you've boxed us into a corner over relationships with the Greens. But he is sure it will all blow over in a few months, and it will be politics as normal. What he wants is to hang you out there to dry. Everything that goes wrong can be laid at your door. You've hijacked the party, and sent us down a risky path. He expects you to pay the price for taking the risks.'

'I see,' said Peter. 'Not much I can do about that, is there?'

'Only stand firm. And watch your back!'

16: The last moments of freedom

What fills the days of an emerging leader during a revolution? Everything except rest, according to Don Mason. Even moments of relaxation were spent high on the excitement of events—planning, discussing, firing off advice to people who rush in with messages, arranging meetings, putting people off—there seemed to be no end to the activity.

Mason was having a late supper with other leading figures in the GEM—Dave Barrington, Douglas Cunningham, Sarah Turner and Malcolm Morton. When these five got together, it always seemed like old times: a strong sense of shared experience and comradeship. But there was a difference now. In earlier times they had bonded through a feeling of campaigning in adversity, always with the odds stacked against them. Now they had the growing feeling of being on the brink of something—something great and wonderful, that would bring them to the fulfilment of their dreams.

They sat together having a working supper—a selection of takeaway food from the nearest restaurants that weren't fast food chains. Sarah Turner noted the change as she chomped into her vegetable kebab.

'I love this kebab. Mmm! But are we all selling out or something? This is our thirty-second consecutive meal of convenience foods. Not like the old days!'

Sarah had been a phenomenal activist. An economist by training, she was an apostle of 'sustainable consumption' and had a fervent commitment to protecting the natural world from human excess. Graduating through anti-roadbuilding protests, she could climb a tall tree in seconds and chain herself to almost any branch. With her lean but muscular build and her long brown hair tied back in a loose ponytail, she had become an almost familiar figure to the nation for a few years as she swayed in the branches, unfurling banners or haranguing construction workers through a loudhailer.

Many were the times when she also swung down from the branches and with seemingly limitless energy and good cheer would unfold her home-made barbecue, throw together some rissoles and cook a meal for her fellow activists. While others in the protest camp fell to sleep, Sarah could always be seen reading text books or scribbling in notebooks by lamplight.

Douglas Cunningham had never been a tree climber—far too big a man to haul his large frame up trees. But he was a self-taught ecologist with a gift for organising people in swift-moving events. He could mobilise a swarm of activists on his cell phone and constantly took his opponents by surprise, whether developers in their hard hats or the police. Now munching his fish and chips, he often felt nostalgia for the old days. He could almost smell the leaves and the rissoles when Sarah spoke of 'the old days'.

'Do you remember that day in Yorkshire,' he asked, 'when Don said "I think it's time to come down from the trees?"'

They all laughed gently, between mouthfuls of food.

'What was that ridiculous extended metaphor you used, Don?' asked Dave Barrington.

Malcolm Morton chipped in, trying to imitate Don's voice, which had a trace of a Scottish accent. 'It's time to come down from the trees, my friends. We need to surge across the plains, gathering strength and numbers, and hide in the long grass until the time comes to ...'

'*Pounce!*' they chorused, then broke into laughter.

Don wasn't sure whether he had actually said this at the time. But over the past few days he had indeed said many times that it could be time to pounce on an unsuspecting enemy. He never minded being teased by his close comrades. Some, like Morton, he had known for more than twenty years, and their relationships were firmly rooted.

'I'm more than ever sure of it,' he said. 'There won't be another opportunity like this, not in our lifetimes. Everything is falling into place. And you know what? Something I hadn't expected. The world is coming to *us*—it's beating a path to our door! We've started something rolling, and we're in danger of being run over by it unless we keep a tight grip. I had no idea we could possibly be so busy, and spend so much time reacting to other people.'

Almost on cue, the door opened and Jacqui, Mason's PA, came in waving a post-it. 'I've got Ben Porter on the line. Says it's urgent. But if you want to call him back I have his mobile number.'

Mason opened his arms wide as if to say, 'What did I just say?'

'Can you tell him I'm in a meeting and I'll call him back?'

Jacqui nodded and left. She was enjoying this new turn of events. All this busy-ness meant that she now supervised a small team of staff, instead of doing everything for Mason at all hours without help.

'Porter. More than ever, he wants to be friendly with us now,' said Mason.

Ben Porter as the long-suffering leader of the older, more established Green Party, had led his party to a brief resurgence ten years previously, but had been condemned to see his dreams fade and die. That surge of greenism had not been his hoped-for 'tipping point', but a short-lived protest against the ruling party of the time.

'I hear Ben's pissed off with our dominant role in the Earth Councils,' said Barrington.

Doug Cunningham guffawed, then wiped his mouth with the back of his hand. 'So he should be!' After all the years of foot-slogging, posting leaflets through every door, lost deposits....'

'I'll drink to that—Ben Porter's lost deposits!' toasted Dave, raising a tea-cup.

'And here we come along just when everything should be swinging towards them, and we steal their thunder. He must think we're a right bunch of upstarts. And you, Don—the media have been ripping him to pieces for twenty years, and then make you their sweetheart. Why should he be happy?'

'Why not?' said Don. 'Aren't we all basically on the same side? We're just that bit more well-organised, that's all. And much more dynamic. Without our Earth Councils, what would Ben and his followers be doing now? Posting leaflets somewhere, I suppose. Getting excited about winning a council seat in Oxford or Brighton, perhaps. They'd squander the moment, again. But we shouldn't feel any enmity towards them. We've worked side by side with so many of them in the past. We may be a faction in the wider green movement, as he says, but we can't afford to have a factional spirit. If we sometimes treat the Old Greens with contempt, let it be an affectionate contempt!'

The others were nodding and smiling. The mood changed, as it always did when Mason was dispensing his wisdom.

'We don't have enough people to run the Earth Councils—and if we ran them alone they would not be so effective. Remember what we agreed. We have to be inclusive—but also indispensable. We want people of all parties and none to be enthused with new initiatives to change the way we live. But we must set up and run the means to deliver everything. Even if there are mavericks and lunatics, we should let them have their head for the moment. They can always be reined in later. Doug—what's the picture like overall? I mean, in terms of running the programmes of the Earth Councils?'

'Pretty good, I'd say, Don,' replied Cunningham. We've got Earth Councils up and running in about 85% of the country. Most of them are our initiatives, but there's about a dozen districts where we're thin on the ground, and others have taken the lead. But they're following our model in pretty much every case.'

'Where's the 15% of the country with no Earth Councils yet?' asked Don.

'Mostly in Scotland and Northern Ireland. The wilder areas,' Doug replied.

'Sounds like we need a Plan B for the remote areas, Doug.'

'It may not be too much of a problem, Don' said Malcolm. 'These are mostly areas we've targeted for major initiatives when we get in—reforestation, habitat re-creation, natural education camps, new model communities and so on. We'll be pulling plenty of people and resources in then.'

Everyone nodded sagely. *When we get in*, Morton had said. And he said it with confidence.

Morton and Cunningham had also noted their leader's suggesting the need for a 'Plan B'. This was the way GEM decisions were often made. A suggestion from Don Mason would be taken up by his colleagues, who would bring back a more detailed proposal for consideration. Mason liked to encourage initiative, and then authorise the action. He believed it brought the best out of people.

All the same, it seemed he had an almost photographic memory. Sometimes colleagues felt he wasn't paying much attention, only to find later he could recall almost every aspect of a discussion and every detail of a policy paper. Often his suggestions were about areas where he thought too much was being left to chance. He disliked giving direct commands, but was successful as a leader because people respected his views and wanted to please him.

••

A week later Don Mason was relaxing at home for maybe the first time in two months. The kind of countrywide tour politicians take in election time was inescapable, even for a man who liked to do things differently. It was a time to pause and reflect on how things were going.

They were going well. Remarkably well, he reflected as he walked through his empty apartment. At meeting after meeting he had been greeted as he had been at the inaugural meeting of the National Convention. Wild applause, stamping, cheering, ovation after ovation, and people hanging on his every word. His team decided the tour should be turned into a celebratory procession. Bands, some famous, some local, provided warm-up support and post-rally partying, attracting crowds of thousands wherever he went. Impromptu stages and large screens were set up to ensure he could be seen and heard by as many people as possible.

He had been assigned a police guard. As a public figure he was as much a target as other celebrities and politicians. 'Any nutter might have a pop at you', his police escort was wont to say. And in addition, Malcolm Morton had assigned a small team of Green Militia to guard and assist him round the clock.

But Don had tired of this constant company. He wanted to be alone, and to achieve this had rented the empty apartment opposite for his bodyguards to set up in rather than have them in his home. Their door was constantly open, so they could watch the corridor. But behind his own door, alone, he felt more secure, more able to relax.

All the same, he felt a slight emptiness, a small pang of loneliness. He had bought this London apartment after the break-up of his marriage several years earlier. For him, it was partly a necessity—he needed somewhere to live. It was also a statement of intent. Here, without all the distractions of family life, he could focus on his writing and campaigning and organising the Green Earth Movement. And it had worked well enough. Even before his more recent celebrity he had produced a steady stream of books that sold moderately well, and articles for which he could command a reasonable fee. And he had a small income from the GEM as its leader.

As he wandered idly from living room to kitchen, to study and back to living room, he hankered for the home he had left behind. His ex-wife still lived in their family home in a prosperous commuter-belt village in Surrey. His grown-up children, recently out of university, still maintained a base there, and called it 'home'. He talked to them often, and they were proud of their father's new status. But they seemed to meet less and less often. It was Mason, after all, who had left home first. He remembered all the work that he had put into that home: his garden; the children growing up there...so many things. It had also been the epicentre for the embryonic GEM. All his close colleagues had warm memories of the atmosphere there. Don had fond memories of his wife, too. And he recognised them for what they were—memories.

Valued, but there was nothing to be rekindled with Stephanie on that front. And there was no one else.

••

Sunday morning. Don Mason awoke with a start. He had slept on the sofa all night, falling asleep watching *Match of the Day*. Sunlight was forcing its way through the curtains, and someone was clattering about in the hall, and then in the kitchen.

It was Sarah Turner. She burst into the living room. 'Don?' she called, then recoiled a little.

'Jesus, the air's ripe in here! Did you sleep here all night?'

Mason grunted.

'In your clothes?'

'You want me to sleep naked?'

'Never mind!' she said as she propelled herself through the living room, threw open the curtains and opened the windows. It was Don's turn to recoil as the sunlight hit him full on, and the sounds of London traffic entered the room.

Sarah picked up the take-away trays and the empty bottle of wine. She examined the bottle.

'Have company last night?' she asked with a wink.

'Chance would be a fine thing,' Mason replied in a gravelly voice.

'I thought your doctor told you to keep off the sauce?'

'He was talking about beer and whisky.'

Sarah looked dubious. She knew about Don's nagging stomach complaint, one which he did not tend to complain about. But sometimes his close friends noticed him wincing, especially after over-eating or drinking too much.

'It's in the Bible, Sarah. "Do not drink water only, but take a little wine for the sake of your stomach". St Paul said it. You should know that.'

'I'm Jewish, Don. What would I know about St Paul? And anyway, I think the operative word there is "little". He says "Take a little wine", not "Knock back the whole bottle with a lamb pasanda".'

She looked solicitously at Mason. 'Is everything all right, Don?'

'I'm fine, I'm fine,' he replied, rubbing the side of his head through tousled hair. 'After all this frenetic activity, I just needed to zonk out. You wouldn't believe the crap I watched on TV. It seems nothing has changed on Saturday night TV in fifty years!'

'I wouldn't know about that, Don—I'm far too young!'

'When we get in, I'll change all this. We'll put on some worthwhile programmes—some animal documentaries, and maybe a tree-hugging sitcom! To remind you of your activist roots. What do you think?'

Sarah gave him a wry smile.

'One essential thing, though,' he added. 'I'll command *Match of the Day* to be put on earlier in the evening. No one over fifty can keep awake! You endure an evening of dross, and then when the programme you really want to watch comes on, bang, that's it! You wake up frozen on the couch at three in the morning!'

'Or nine in the morning! But don't blame your age, Don. There are other factors at work here, I think!' She held the empty bottle up in front of him. 'Now I'm going to cook you breakfast. You've had twenty-four hours of mental collapse—today the show must go on!'

A few minutes later, as Mason prepared to go into the shower, he could hear chopping and frying in the kitchen. When he came out of the shower, he could smell bacon, and could hear several voices. A working breakfast. The campaign continues. And he felt ready for the challenge.

In the kitchen it wasn't quite the usual line-up. Malcolm Morton was there, but no Dave Barrington. He'd flown home to his nest for the weekend, to recharge his batteries. Doug Cunningham was there, and also the impressive young Danny Malik. Danny jumped up to greet him. After some general pleasantries, Cunningham pressed forward to the point of the meeting. A new media strategy for the remainder of the election campaign.

'I thought we were doing quite well,' Mason commented. 'But you know me, always open to new angles.'

'Well, Don,' said Doug, 'Danny has come up with a new approach which we think could boost our polling'

'Go on.'

'It's like this,' said Malik. 'The problem we have is that we're pushing out too much paper—and paper only has a limited reach. And the media limits us by its rules of balance. Everything we get on TV has to be balanced by input from the other parties. The main news channels take these rules online too. So we need to move outside of these constraints. Let's start from basics: a picture is worth a thousand words, as they say. And a movie is worth several thousand pictures. We need to put our movies in front of the whole nation, for as much time as possible.'

Mason looked around the room, not appearing to be very impressed. So far it seemed like the enthusiasm of the inexperienced. Danny Malik, it seemed, was passionately stating the obvious.

'Now what I'm proposing,' he continued, 'is getting out movies to every household on memory cards. I know this kind of thing has been done before, but this is different. These cards will contain a number of short movies, targeted at different issues, and with links to more online resources that people can follow.'

Mason still looked unexcited. 'Mmm, this bacon is wonderful, Sarah! Good of you to cook it for me!'

Danny looked slightly disconcerted, but carried on. 'That's just part one of a three-pronged attack. The second thing is billboards. The other parties are still working with paper. We need short message-movies on billboards—like some of those new adverts you see on the sides of buildings. Your face needs to be everywhere, Don, laughing and smiling—and looking firm or serious according to the message.

'And the third thing: all this touring the country is just too knackering. And inefficient. Now you've physically visited every region of the country, so no area will feel left out. But how many people have you met? Maybe point zero-zero-zero-one of the electorate. We can do better than that! We can use new technologies to get you in front of so many more people—the whole nation! What we are proposing is simultaneous rallies across the country. Well, we can take a few areas at a time, and in every town and city—even some villages—set up a screen, and you can have a public meeting even when you're not there! And they must be interactive. We can coordinate questions from several places, so each rally has an impressive geographical reach. As well as the local experience, we can broadcast them online from our own web channel—there's nothing to restrict that.'

'And the great thing about it,' added Cunningham enthusiastically, 'is that we can conduct a campaign that chimes with our policies. I mean, you don't travel, people attending the rally don't have to travel far, and we use our local resources as far as possible. We have several donors around the country who can come up with the kit we need.'

Don was nodding now. He was interested. 'Can we afford this? And can we stay within the election expenses limits?'

'Sarah's got that covered,' said Danny.

Sarah held up crossed fingers, and made a mock-nervous smile.

'I like it so far,' said Mason. 'I like the media approach—well done, Danny. And I also really like the idea of running a campaign that illustrates our principles. Can we take this further?'

He looked around at them. No one was entirely following his drift, as they were all focusing on media issues.

'I mean, for example: we are trying to get a message across about buying locally—localising production and consumption. At some of the rallies, could we organise local produce markets? Could we set one of the rallies at an Earth Council tree-planting scheme, and get participants doing a little digging?'

And so the ideas came tumbling forward, until Mason asked: 'Have we got time to do all this?'

Then the brainstorming turned to a meticulously detailed action plan, in the true Mason-Morton style. The addition of Danny Malik to the team had added a new dimension. And it also signalled the beginning of the end for Dave Barrington as the GEM's Director of Communications. There were some worries about Barrington not being a party to this change of direction, especially as his project management abilities would be crucial to the success of the campaign. But for this he was happy to pass on the baton to Danny Malik, and throw himself into the kind of detailed planning and organisation that he relished.

17: Hanging in the balance

All elections throw up some surprises. This one threw up more than most. Each of the traditional parties was divided into those who went with the Charter, and those who didn't. The two larger parties were the most split, with only minority factions identifying themselves as 'Green Labour' and 'Environmental Conservatives'. The Liberals endorsed the Charter, though some candidates rejected it on an individual basis. They did well–their upward path continued from the previous election.

But the main 'Grey' parties–Conservative and Labour–were devastated. Clearly out of step with the popular mood, their representation was more than halved. The majority of those who remained were 'Grey-Green' candidates who had accepted the Charter.

The biggest surprise of all though was the strong showing of the 'Animalists'–animal rights candidates. Where had they sprung from, and why so successful?

The local Earth Councils had given them a platform, and the opportunity to take part in some practical politics. Their leaders, the somewhat eccentric Gabriella Pearson and Titus Whitaker, were now household names thanks to their role in the National Convention. With their gospel of compassionate farming and proposals to ban animal experimentation and all forms of hunting, they were in tune with the new mood of middle England. Overall they achieved 10% of the vote, and in a couple of places they gained over 30%, coming in second. Under the British system, there are no prizes for second place, so they had no MPs. But their influence was enhanced in the local Earth Councils and in the National Convention. Their numbers would grow in these bodies in the annual elections.

The dominant party was Mason's Green Earth Movement. Effectively mobilised and organised for the election, they had coordinated with the other Green groups so as not to tread on each other's toes. To come from nowhere to over two hundred MPs was a tremendous feat. With the support of the other Green parties they would come close to having a majority. So the Parliament was 'hung'. They needed support from at least one other group. In Mason's calculations, it had to be the Liberals.

There was a lot of debate in the Green parties about what to do. Ben Porter, leader of the old Green Party, was very active in trying to knit together a majority. He met with Mason and Morton on a daily basis, as they strove to agree a common programme and alliances. One thing Porter did not want, however, was any deals with the Liberals. There had been too many past conflicts at every level of electoral contest–city, county, European, regional and national. Wherever the Liberals were successful, the Greens always moved in behind them. They felt they could appeal to the same kind of people. Battles between the two had grown at times very bitter, as the Greens frequently stood between the Liberals and success, just drawing enough votes away from the Liberals for one of the other larger parties to win.

Mason and his followers, however, felt there was no alternative to a coalition with the Liberals. Porter urged a deal involving Animalists from the Convention and 'Green Labour'. The Convention could then be used to initiate legislation that the hung Parliament would be challenged to accept.

Mason was direct. 'Ben, it's not practical. Gabriella is too much of a fundamentalist. And they will demand so much that our programme will be compromised–severely compromised, I think. And the more they want, the less we'll be able to keep Green Labour with us. And you'll have to rein in some of your Green fundamentalists too. We need to be able to demonstrate stability and fitness to govern before we can pursue our more radical aims.'

Ben protested. 'We've come too far to throw it all away in some kind of dreadful fudge. If you depend on Kitson–or especially Blackstone–that's what you'll get. Some wishy-washy insipid apology for green policy.'

Malcolm Morton was nettled. 'You struggled for years and achieved nothing. In just a few weeks, look what we've achieved! You've seen us in the Earth Councils and the National Convention. Does that look wishy-washy to you? And don't forget other combinations are possible–we could drop your Green Party from our coat-tails and work with both the Liberals and Green Labour–'

He cut himself short. This was possibly going too far. They still needed to keep some unity amongst the Green movement as a whole. But Porter saw the truth in the threat. And he had seen Mason's party in action in the Earth Councils, and was beginning to understand their ruthless discipline. When they wanted to do something, they did it with clinical efficiency. So far he had been on the same side as them–he did not relish the thought of being on the other side.

He looked darkly at Morton.

Mason intervened. 'Ben, I can assure you that any long term arrangements with the Liberals are the last thing on our mind. This is only the beginning. If we do well, we won't need them for long. But I am a believer in practical politics. We can't afford the indulgence of being utopian. The Liberals are here. They've got ninety-two MPs. And they could throw in their lot with the "Grey Remnant". We can't allow that to happen.'

Indeed a Green government was not the only possible outcome, in principle. The Liberals could throw in their lot with the remaining Conservatives and Labour groups to make a majority. It was an option, but one which no one was in a hurry to propose. An exhausted Patrick Baxter and Howard Blackstone met privately. 'Give Mason a chance to fail' was the Conservative's preferred strategy, and Howard Blackstone saw some merit in this. If necessary, it would be better to be rescuing the situation with the Conservatives, rather than trying to take an initiative with them in the face of determined opposition and the current public mood.

This was high-risk for Howard, as in that case the Liberals would have to change ships in mid-stream—but he was sure it could be justified in the circumstances of the Greens messing up. And he was inclined to think that might indeed happen. In the meantime, there was the real prospect of having Liberals back in government again, which he felt could only be good for the nation. And if they could make the coalition work—so much the better.

Despite Baxter's private view, the Conservatives were reluctant to hand over power to a GEM-led coalition without exploring all the options. The nature of the 'hung' parliament meant that there were many permutations possible.

18: A common language

Heather Kitson found there was something disturbingly traditional about this evening. She, Sandy Honeyford and Jessica Barrington were beavering away in the kitchen, while in another room three men were drinking beer and talking politics. Dave Barrington and Peter Kitson were joined by Martin Lang, one of Joanna Kitson's colleagues and an emerging figure in the Scrutiny Commission for the Legal Profession—ESCOLAW.

They were talking shop, of course. There was serious business to be done in terms of Green/Liberal liaison. But after a day devoted to making progress in this, the evening was intended to be more relaxed, especially as there were to be other guests for dinner. As well as Martin, Heather's close friend Rachel Dean and her husband were expected, and Joanna too if she could be back from Edinburgh in time. Rachel was lecturer in History at a London University college, and Heather had invited her to witness close up, as she put it, 'history in the making'.

Martin felt a little awed sitting talking to two potential members of the next Cabinet—but he tried not to betray this. He was pleased to be asked about his work and that of ESCOLAW. 'You know the legal profession works in very traditional ways, and is good at resisting change. Despite all the electronic systems we all have these days, it's a profession devoted to churning out paper, and duplicating work at every possible step. The Scrutiny Commission is having a hard time auditing environmental practices—but I think we're making some progress at last! You know, every bad practice has a reason. Not necessarily a good reason, but a reason all the same, and there are people who will defend it to the death as being a non-negotiable bastion of freedom or accountability, it seems.'

'I did Jury service a few years back,' said Dave Barrington. 'It was a real eye-opener.'

'In what way?'

'The sheer inefficiency—it was astounding. From the dodderiness of the geriatric judge, who fell asleep at least twice during evidence, to the ineptitude of the prosecuting counsel who drew up the charges wrongly, right down to the stupidity of the police who had failed to record statements from witnesses whose evidence was vital to the defence. It was a shambles from start to finish. A case that should never have come to court, or taken half a day at most, took eleven days to complete. That's not only the legal fees to pay, but twelve jurors plus reserves not working and losing money.'

Martin felt a little uncomfortable with this diatribe, but did not feel an inclination to defend his profession. Dave continued.

'What I couldn't believe, Martin, was how low-tech the whole performance was! Each team came in with armfuls of paper files, and didn't seem to know what was where. And although there was a recorder typing up the transcript into a computer, the judge insisted on hand-writing his own notes. He even stopped the witnesses to ask them to repeat what they said so he could note it!'

They all laughed. Martin said, 'I think I know the judge you are talking about. Actually, we've had one plan after another since, oh, the 1990s to make the whole thing seamless and computerised. But it's one helluva job connecting up the criminal justice system. So many agencies, involved, and archaic systems and data protection issues, and all the rest. I'll give you an example. A teenager is arrested for trying to steal a car. How many agencies have a finger in the pie? At first you think it's the police and the courts. But then you find there are social workers, youth offending teams (or whatever they're called now) educational welfare officers, the probation service, legal aid, CPS, solicitors, barristers, and Uncle Tom Cobbleigh and all. You know it would be cheaper to give him the bloody car and be done with it!

'So when it comes to carrying out a "sustainability audit"—where do we begin? None of these agencies share information effectively, they all have massive paper archives, their own palaces of bureaucracy—which are mostly a long way from environmental high performance—and no one has the authority to bang all their heads together! So when you guys get in—how about sorting out this lot?'

'We'll do it,' said Dave with a smile, 'And maybe we can call on you to give us a hand with it!'

A casual comment, but one that pleased Martin to hear. His ambition was well-known—and it was not only to be a successful lawyer. Politics attracted him, yet his opinions were far from fixed. With embarrassment he remembered a conversation he had with his tutor at college, when he said he was interested in going into politics. When his tutor asked straight away, 'Which party?' he found he didn't know. It was not something to which he had given a lot of thought. He just like the idea of legislating for the nation, and one day standing up in Parliament to speak, and earning the respect of his colleagues for his insight. Which party? Now there was a question!

His background would incline him to be a Conservative. But he had reforming ambitions, a liking of innovation and improvement, so this inclined him to the 'New Labour' that had emerged back in the 1990s. These were the only serious parties of power at that time. It seemed weird that twenty years later he was dining with people poised to enter government—and that they were Liberal Democrats and Greens. Greens! Who would ever have thought it? But his reformist instincts had attracted him to the Earth Scrutiny Commission for his profession. Other instincts attracted him to Joanna Kitson, but sadly for him nothing had developed in that direction, except professional respect and a kind of 'missionary friendship' as they endeavoured to reform the unreformable.

Supper was served. Rachel and Mark, her husband, had arrived. Rachel was thrilled at sharing a meal with leading personalities from the news. Her husband, a businessman in the IT field, was making a show of not being especially impressed. He had a low opinion of politicians as a breed. All he could foresee from a Green/Liberal government would be more regulations to comply with, and no doubt a whole new range of taxes. But Rachel had instructed him to be on his best behaviour.

And he was. He was being pleasant and friendly, but it seemed to Heather he was a little too quiet. So she tried to involve him in the conversation. 'Mark, have you been involved in any of the new initiatives—an Earth Council, or professional scrutiny commission?'

'No, I haven't,' he replied. 'Though regrettably they've been involved with me!'

Rachel looked daggers at him, but the others smiled or laughed, including the Barringtons.

'Are you a polluter, and are they making you pay?' asked Jessica, with an openness that surprised him.

'Not a polluter—though I guess the things we buy and install were made by some pretty dirty processes. But not in England! No, the problem is we have a business to run, and clients to deal with—but these new bodies meddle with everything. It's costing us a *lot* of money, without any apparent gain for the environment.'

'How's that?' asked Dave Barrington.

'Some of our biggest clients are public sector: local councils, central government departments, parts of the health service. We've got about half a dozen cases of contracts being held up, or being renegotiated, or being asked to re-tender. Why? Because these Earth Councils or whatever are spending all their time writing new policies that all contractors have to comply with—even on existing contracts. It costs them nothing to write this nonsense, apart from time in meetings yapping and drinking herbal bloody tea. But it's cost us about half a million pounds already, and they've only been going a few weeks.'

'How?' asked Peter, looking baffled. It was not a possibility he had thought of, and he assumed Mark must be exaggerating.

'It's a council contract, and their local green gurus—'

'Mark!' hissed Rachel, disapprovingly

'- they've come up with the notion that one particular provider of components has a poor record on environmental things, I don't know what or why but I guess they think the manufacturing processes they use or their suppliers use is especially noxious. Or something. And the upshot is that I've got to use different components. But I'm already locked into contracts with my supplier. In the end, the cost to the council will increase—but I've also got to take a hit on that as I need to stay in the frame for new contracts.'

'And it sounds like you'll have to implement new environmental policies for yourself—cast a more watchful eye over the environmental impact of what you do,' said Dave Barrington, still friendly but a little challenging.

'Of course, and we're doing it. And that has a cost too. But what I ask myself is, what do these Earth Councils actually know about technology, industrial production and about business? Sweet F.A., I'd guess. I've asked for the evidence on which they base their view about our supplier. That seemed to throw them into a spin for a bit. Then someone sent me this piss-poor article in *New Earth Times* or something—a piece of flabby journalism based on a few bits of crap on the Internet.'

He paused for breath, and brief reflection on his tone of language in this company, then continued: 'I'm actually quite happy to beef up our environmental practices—we've always had an ethical strand to our business—supporting technology for charities and all kinds of thing. But I've also got a business to run. We've got a few hundred business clients, and we employ four hundred and fifty people directly, plus about another hundred or so who are dependent on our work in some way—smaller businesses or freelancers we subcontract or that our clients use to manage what we install. So whoever conjures up new policies and sets new hoops to jump through needs to know something about what they're doing, and base their new policies on real evidence!'

The others looked to Dave Barrington or Peter Kitson to answer.

'I'm with you about the evidence—it has to be scientific or we lose credibility, and maybe cause a lot of problems as you say. So you think we ought to rein in the Earth Councils?' said Barrington.

'Maybe—one way or another they need to be accountable. I mean, here they are holding everyone else to account, but what if they are up the pole on something? Who challenges them? Or they could be given clear guidelines about what they should do.'

'I think there's another problem here too,' said Peter. 'Mark has never liked government. Full stop. Whatever any government does is bound to impede the smooth workings of capitalism, and cost him money. If he was in charge, we'd still have small boys cleaning our chimneys...'

'Yeah, yeah!' Mark cut in with a wry smile. He and Peter were used to this kind of sparring. 'You've got to have regulation to protect the innocent and all that—but it's got to be soundly based.'

'And you think the evidence to support strong measures to protect the environment isn't there?'

'I didn't say that—but honestly I don't know. What I've seen seems, well, arbitrary. Just based on the whims of politicians and activists—and none of them understand business.'

'So we need more business people on the Earth Councils,' said Peter.

'But who has time, Peter, when you're running a business?' asked Heather, her own experience being on the business side of the equation.

'It's a question of priorities, I guess,' offered Sandy.

'Not only priorities,' Mark replied sharply. 'It's easy for bureaucrats and politicians to spend time in meetings. They are paid to do it. It sounds trite to say it, but time *is* money. For you guys in the public sector, money is a free resource—you can just tax people! But we have to earn it.'

'You want the Earth Councils to pay you to be involved?' asked Jessica.

'Why not? A little consultancy wouldn't do any harm. All the bureaucrats are being paid for turning up!'

'You're missing the point, Mark,' said Martin. 'All these initiatives depend heavily on voluntary effort—Joanna and I aren't paid for being on a Scrutiny Commission. The movement wouldn't have this dynamism if people were only in it for the money!'

Dave Barrington thought it was time to end this stream of discussion. He had learned something, but he felt it was becoming a bit heated, and further discussion would not be illuminating right now. 'Mark, why don't you come and see me next week sometime? I'm interested in what you say. It sounds like a dimension is missing from the way the Earth Councils are operating. I'll see if I can get Doug Cunningham in on it—he's much more directly involved with the Earth Councils than I am. And maybe you can bring along a couple of other business people, from different sectors maybe, and we can identify where the fault lines are and how to get round them.'

Everyone was impressed with this suggestion, not least Mark Dean.

Conversation now ranged over the whole range of topics and issues that come up at such London dinner parties—food, music, families, second homes in France and Italy, mutual friends, things that drive people mad, holidays to exotic places, fine wines and languages.

With so many ambitious people around the table on the brink of national eminence, it was only natural that there should have been a certain amount of name-dropping too. Their conversation produced a remarkable who's who of London society—not only the politicians but also millionaire entrepreneurs, senior civil servants, the directors of art galleries, football club owners, members of the aristocracy, professors, theatre producers and playwrights—a long list it would have been if they were all noted while the diners chattered.

But the mention of one eminent connection brought an uncharacteristic silence—Jessica's father. Jessica had always wanted to make it clear that she owed nothing to her father—they were two different people. Heather instantly detected Jessica's sensitivity on this, and tried to widen the discussion. 'With your family name, Olsen—does that mean you have a Scandinavian background?'

'My grandparents were Swedish, and I've got a lot of cousins who live in Sweden.'

'She speaks fluent Swedish, you know,' said Dave Barrington. 'French too'.

'I'm no way fluent in either!' protested Jessica. 'I would guess that just about everyone round this table speaks at least one other language.'

It was almost true. Britain had certainly become more international in recent years, and despite the dominance of English as the world's common language, aspiring people such as these prided themselves on knowing a language or two. All were also well-travelled, and the Kitsons, Deans and Martin Lang also owned property overseas.

The real linguists though were Sandy and Martin, having studied Modern Languages at university. Both could speak fluent Spanish, and they rattled off a jokey conversation with each other that no one else could understand, though everyone laughed at the theatrical gestures that accompanied the dialogue. Sandy also spoke some French and German, while Martin had set himself the challenge of learning some Arabic and Chinese. They were, he said, with English and Spanish the two most important world languages at the moment. He had studied them part-time, as a kind of useful hobby, while progressing on to his legal studies and then practice as a lawyer.

Heather could see an interesting friendship develop between these two—and she would be glad if her dinner party were to be the genesis of a new romance. She had long thought that the one thing Martin lacked in his life was a good woman. She wasn't yet sure if Sandy was a good woman—but she could see enough to think they could be a good match.

Joanna Kitson finally arrived, having completed her mission to 'green' the lawyers of Scotland. 'Bloody hard going up there,' she said. 'You're going to have your work cut out to make serious headway amongst our friends north of the border....' These remarks she directed to her brother and Dave Barrington.

A throwaway comment, but it was something that was a source of concern to the GEM leadership—for it was true that the enthusiasm for the Green Revolution was much more marked in England and Wales than it was in Scotland or Northern Ireland. The conversation quickly took a more positive turn, however, as they looked forward to the big rally and demonstration which would take place the following afternoon.

Joanna looked across the table at Martin Lang with an amused expression. His broad face was flushed with wine, and was he actually flirting with Sandy Honeyford? Martin had become a close friend, and Joanna knew well that he had wanted to be more than that. For her, the feeling was never mutual, but she liked his intelligence and quick wit. He was always good company. And seeing him with Sandy, she felt a mixture of amusement and anticipation, tinged with just a hint of friendly jealousy. They seemed well suited, and would make a handsome couple if things were to take a romantic turn.

She turned to Jessica Barrington, who was sitting next to her. 'Your guys have done well, haven't they? But you didn't want to stand as a candidate?'

'Not all,' confessed Jessica. 'I'm on the local earth Council, and that's enough for me. I've become too much of a home lover these days.'

'But I've seen your face everywhere in the news. I have to say, you're just as beautiful in real life,' said Joanna graciously.

Jessica smiled sheepishly. 'I've been an activist most of my life, and I know how to rally the troops. But they keep pressing me, in the nicest way, to do "one last thing" and then wheel me out as a kind of Green Earth cheerleader. I'll do the rally tomorrow, and that's it. You don't have to play the same role for your whole life, do you? Or you shouldn't do, anyway. And in a strange way I'm finding it a bit demeaning, being the poster-girl for the Green

Revolution. We need to be a bit deeper than that, I think. Anyway, I'm happy enough doing my bit locally and lending Dave to the Revolution on the big stage. And what about you? Are you going to go into politics like Peter?'

'I'm not really attracted to it,' said Joanna. 'I follow politics, maybe I'm even a bit of an anorak about it. But I'm passionate about my work, the human rights stuff. So maybe I'm political with a small "p". And the work I'm doing with ESCOLAW is fascinating too. I'm getting a lot of insights onto how everything works. So, it's human rights and the environment from here on in. The two things I'll never make any money out of!'

'So you're a campaigner, like me,' said Jessica. 'For myself, I'm not sure if I've got the talent or temperament to be in the driving seat.'

'Well, I guess we'll soon see if Dave and Peter have, won't we?' said Joanna.

19: The March on London

Eight days after the election, it was still not clear who would form a government. But the GEM were mobilised for action, and were preparing a large rally in Trafalgar Square. Thousands of activists were ready to march into central London to demand a Green Earth government, with parallel rallies in all the major cities.

It was a sunny but chilly November afternoon and already Trafalgar Square was packed. Jessica Barrington and Sarah Turner were providing warm-up speeches, keeping the crowd enthused. But between every speech there were cries of 'Mason! Mason!' Then several celebrities were wheeled out to endorse the idea of an Earth Charter government. A couple of ageing rock stars followed. Then Ben Porter came on stage to huge cheers, probably addressing the biggest gathering of his life. He spoke eloquently about the 'thirty year struggle', careful to stress his own role at the forefront of it. Then Peter Kitson came forward, urging the principle of a 'Charter government' and meaningful change, challenging Baxter and the other parties to get out of the way if they can't form a majority government.

The police and Volunteers were now having to prevent any more people entering the square. The side streets were full to bursting with people, and for the sake of safety they were being channelled off towards Hyde Park and Green Park, where Danny Malik had ensured large screens had been set up. All across central London the cry went up, 'Mason! Mason!', with a spontaneous call and response developing between the different open areas. The screens now showed other rallies around the country in Bristol, Cardiff, Birmingham, Manchester, Glasgow, Edinburgh and many more as they took up the cry. There were literally millions on the streets demanding a government led by Don Mason and the GEM.

As Mason prepared to go on stage on cue at three o'clock, Malik caught his arm to hold him back. 'Let it build it up some more. Go up to the stage through the crowd, and let as many people as possible shake your hand on the way. OK?'

Mason nodded and began to make his way through the crowd. The cameras caught it all—his being hugged, embraced, grabbed all the way to the stage. Green Volunteers had to move in to rescue him to get him through the final few yards to the stage. As he went up the few steps to the stage the noise became deafening. For a full ten minutes Mason was unable to speak as he soaked up the acclaim of the crowd, a big smile on his face but at the same time appearing modest and overwhelmed, humbled by the adulation and support. The atmosphere was completely electric.

At last the roar subsided enough for him to address the crowd, and the millions watching throughout the country. Throughout his speech he was interrupted by cheers and applause, and he had to stop frequently to let the ovations subside. He was perspiring gently, and this lent his features a fervent glow. There was a slightly tremulous edge to his voice as he spoke.

'Comrades!' he began, 'Ladies and gentlemen! Citizens of the United Kingdom!'

It seemed whatever he said would receive deafening cheers that day.

'What's happened to global warming today?' he asked humorously.

The crowd responded with laughter and cheers.

'Comrades, you will be pleased to know I won't keep you standing still for long. Of course you're welcome to stay and party through the night—there's plenty of music lined up all over town, and if we get the result we're all looking for, there'll be dancing until dawn!

'But what is the result we are looking for? In a word, it is "Change"! Isn't it about time?'

There was a roar of people shouting 'Yes' and then 'Change! Change! Change!' rising to a deafening crescendo until Don held up his hands to still the storm.

Eventually he continued. 'How long have our leaders been turning a blind eye to the crisis facing our planet? For hundreds of years we have ravaged and plundered the Earth, in the remorseless pursuit of power and profit. Most of this time, for sure, people acted in ignorance. All the same, our prosperity, our way of life, is based on this destruction of the Earth.

'But for the past thirty or forty years, our leaders have *known* that this environmental destruction was unsustainable. They knew before the rest of us the growing impact of global warming. And they did nothing! They knew about the degradation of the ozone layer, and the melting of the ice-caps, and they did nothing. They knew about the destruction of the rainforests, and the extinction of one species after another—and still they did nothing!

'And they hid from us the impact this will have on our way of life. They know that if we carry on at this rate, we will face environmental and economic crises of unimagined proportions. Already we see and feel the impacts.

Each summer is hotter than the last. Which may be good for our sun tans, or for ice-cream sales! But what about this?'

Here the giant screens came back to life, with images of the dried river-beds and reservoirs of the last few years.

'And this?' Now there were images of late summer floods that had caused so much death and damage over the past decade.

'And this?' Now footage of the sea reclaiming hefty chunks of the east of England, with rocks and cliffs and several houses crumbling into the waves. A family weeping by the remains of their house, half disappeared into the North Sea.

'And these?' Now footage, including handsome close-ups, of the various plagues of strange insects seen over the past few years, a sequence culminating in the most recent, the so called 'superbeetle'—with thousands of them devouring a field of crops in Lincolnshire. Danny Malik had done a fine job in coordinating the visuals for the demonstration, and these sequences dovetailed effortlessly with Mason's speech. More images like these now formed the backdrop to the continuing speech.

'The Grey parties always said: "These are global problems! They must be tackled at International level!" They took pride in swanning off to one worthless jamboree after another—achieving what? Achieving nothing!

'Of course in one sense they are right—international action is needed. But at the same time they have misled us into believing it is someone else's problem, or that signing some pointless Protocol will lead to a better world. It will not!

'So what is it we offer instead? *Leadership* and *action*!'

Massive cheers erupted, in particular from the green-jacketed volunteers. Mason waited for the cheering to subside. 'But there's a serious question. How do you know we can deliver? I'll tell you how. You've seen the achievements of the Earth Councils in your area. Waste has been cut. Resources are being recycled at an unprecedented scale. Harmful development has been stopped through tougher planning action. New homes are being built to genuine eco-standards—all the pretence is being washed away!

'All this has been done, and we're not in government yet! Think what could be achieved if there was a genuine Green government, supported by the Earth Councils, and working hand-in-hand with *you*, citizens of Britain, mobilised for action!!'

Again there were deafening cheers. The crowd looked almost ecstatic, euphoric with expectation.

'This, my friends, is a Green Revolution!' More thunderous applause and ecstatic cheers. 'And you are the vanguard of the most peaceful, most effective and most promising revolution the world has seen. The way the country works has been changing before our eyes. Has one person been hurt or injured? Has there been one confrontation with the police or authorities? Not one!

'Today there are millions of citizens on the streets. The immense power of the people is being unleashed! But we must use it wisely and responsibly. This is a critical moment. Your demand is for a government based on the principles of the Earth Charter. We will not rest until we have this demand met!'

Don waited for the cheers to die down, and then paused a little more, and his tone became more sober. 'But I tell you, this is not something to be seized by force or intimidation. Together we will apply pressure—but we will do this the right way, so that no one can doubt our legal right to form a government!

'And I don't presume to say that the Green Earth Movement, though it is the largest of the parties now, will lead the new government. We will cooperate fully in any government that adopts the principles of the Earth Charter!'

And so his speech continued for a few more minutes. He briefly went through the Green Earth programme—renewable energy, sustainable consumption, local markets, utility reform, higher eco-standards for housing and transport, taxation based on the 'polluter pays' principle, and all the rest. How much people understood about what these would mean in practice was open to question, but they cheered every item.

When the speech ended, the music began—the GEM wanted to create a carnival atmosphere. On the big screens there were scenes of celebration from all over the country and around the city, inter-cut with scenes of Don Mason meeting and greeting people backstage.

But the drama was only just beginning. Two policemen arrived to see Dave Barrington, accompanied by a man in a suit who looked very serious, a little out of place amongst all the euphoria. It soon became clear it was a drama of quite a different nature unfolding. The man was an official from the Palace. As yet, the King had never met Don Mason, and was anxious to do so at Don's earliest convenience.

Dave led the palace official to the front to meet Mason, who was busy receiving plaudits from the crowd, and told Danny Malik to make sure this was all picked up by the cameras and projected onto the screens.

The message was given. Don accepted the invitation, but spent another few minutes greeting his supporters before edging away to catch up with the messenger and his escort. If he were to meet the King, why not now, in the full glare of publicity?

Despite the crowds, the messenger had arrived in a royal limousine, authorised to use the narrow routes the police had kept clear for emergency vehicles. Mason refused a lift, judging that a potential Green Earth Prime Minister should not arrive at the palace in a car. He chose to walk.

The police estimated there were some two million people on the streets, and Don's walk down the Mall to the palace became like a coronation procession, filmed all the way by Danny Malik's team. The crowds already there on the route cheered him as he went through, and many climbed over the barriers to fall in behind him. Mounted police moved in ahead and behind him to bring some semblance of order.

He was let through the gates of Buckingham Palace accompanied by another roar of applause.

During the course of the rally, the Conservatives had finally given up any hope of forming a coalition government. The King was anxious to meet Mason, and judge for himself whether he was a worthy person to hold office. He told Mason of his feelings of frustration at being a spectator over the past week. Normally the incumbent government would keep him appraised of events and what the options were. Civil servants and Palace officials did pass on the news, but he felt they were trying to keep him at a distance from events. After seeing today's demonstrations, he wanted to hear at first-hand about the 'Green Revolution'. As the sovereign, he said, he had a right to know what was going on.

Don remained in the Palace for more than an hour. On his leaving, the crowd around the Palace greeted him as if he was already the new national leader. Officially he was not, but everyone assumed it was so, that he had the approval of the monarch and that the rest would be a formality. In public life, appearances are often more important than the realities that lie beneath and after this everything else fell into place.

With this development, the Conservatives finally gave up any hope of forming a coalition government. The agreement between the GEM and the Liberals was concluded later that evening. There was partying through the night. Bars stayed open all night, people danced in Trafalgar Square until dawn.

In the morning, Don Mason was invited back to the Palace. Despite never having set foot in the House of Commons, he was invited to be Prime Minister. He duly accepted.

II

20: The First Cabinet

The new Minister for Production and Energy, Peter Kitson, looked around the cabinet office at his new colleagues. It was hard to believe that he was in here, sitting at the famous boat-shaped table as a member of His Majesty's Government. Sunlight streamed into the corner of the room, fine particles of dust rising and wafting as the other new members of the government took their seats and arranged their screens and papers.

There was an awkward moment as finally Donald Mason entered the room, flanked by Douglas Cunningham and Malcolm Morton. Should they all stand, as per custom? Terry Cairns led the way amongst those who stood up, while Sarah Turner giggled awkwardly, then looked around at everyone with quick movements of her head, a beaming smile spreading infectiously across her face. Mason motioned his colleagues to sit down, and indicated that this deference would not be expected in future.

'Bloody hell, we're here!' he exclaimed, and with these words he opened the first Cabinet session of the most radical government in Britain since the days of Oliver Cromwell.

Mason's exclamation helped to put his Cabinet a little more at ease. Terry Cairns noted that Donald Mason played continuously with his pen, flipping it round between his fingers. He had not seen him ever show any signs of nerves before. Malcolm Morton, by contrast, was ice cool. Morton was now the Home Secretary—one of the top four positions in government and which amongst other duties put him in charge of national security.

People had been talking about it, but it was only as Terry looked at the faces around the room that it really struck home just how inexperienced this government was. Possibly the most inexperienced in British history. Only one person had spent a significant amount of time in government, Lord Ashley Felton. Felton had been a minor star in the New Labour days, but when put out to grass in the House of Lords had drifted over to the Green Party. Now he had an honorific post and was included in the government to make use of his experience. Howard Blackstone and Terry Cairns had been junior ministers the last time there was a coalition, so were considered by comparison 'elder statesmen', having long experience of the workings of government and all the parliamentary procedures.

'This could be an interesting ride,' Terry thought to himself.

Looking around the table again, he found it hard to suppress a smile at seeing Ben Porter as Deputy Prime Minister. And he had arrived wearing a suit—maybe the first time anyone could recall seeing him in a suit in Westminster. But the badly knotted tie was working its way loose already, as he unbuttoned the top button of his shirt.

Terry and Peter Kitson had been joking about Ben's elevation to high office before the meeting.

'How long do you think Ben and Mason will be able to stomach each other?' Peter had asked.

'Hmm, yes,' Terry replied. 'It's not exactly a marriage made in heaven, is it? How long do you think before Ben realises he hasn't got a real job, and flounces out?'

'Oh, I'll give it six months. The trappings of power may seduce him for that long.'

It was true that while Porter had negotiated high office for himself, Mason had not left him any real work to do. At one time the Deputy Prime Minister ruled over a sprawling collection of departments, with no real coherence, bound together only by the Deputy PM's personal foibles. At another time, the Deputy office was connected with constitutional and government reform. But there was no way the GEM would let Porter near any of that.

Douglas Cunningham had the powerful role of Minister for Local Government and Communities. Coupled with his dominant position in the Earth Councils, he would certainly be a major force.

'How's your friend Barrington going to save the environment then?' Terry had asked Peter. Barrington was now Minister for Environment, which in principle gave him a very wide brief.

'He's got a special brief to work on a range of large-scale projects to green the nation,' Peter explained, although he was still in the dark as to what this meant in practice. 'I'm not sure how it cuts across my role at Production and Energy. Like with the transition to renewable power. Who's going to run that process, Dave or me?'

'Maybe you'll have to work together. You keep telling me he's OK. Are you looking forward to being Minister for Windmills?'

Peter had smiled patiently at Terry. 'You know, if you take the piss out of the best endeavours of our earnest colleagues all the time, you're not going to last too long!'

'Maybe none of us will, Peter. I mean look at us. What do we actually know about doing anything? Maybe Howard's right, and this won't last more than six months. But by then we'll have enough experience to head a new line-up. Remember what he said?'

'Yes—how many times did he say it? "Do the right thing, do it well, but watch out for the grass stains if you snuggle too close to the Greens." '

'He has a way with words, Howard.'

'Yes, if he had a little more political dynamism, or the charisma of Mason, then maybe we'd be in the driving seat, don't you think?'

'Maybe. I wouldn't want to be too hard on my old friend and colleague. He's Foreign Secretary, you know.—the highest office we've held in nearly a century. Actually, it puzzles me, Peter. Why do you think Mason gave away such a high post so cheaply?'

'Because he wants us on board,' said Peter. 'Otherwise who does he have? From his point of view we're the least bad option. Or it could just be inexperience?'

'Or maybe,' Terry pondered, 'maybe he's just not interested in foreign affairs, and wants to keep Howard occupied with affairs outside of the country. Same for me—as Minister for Europe I'll be tangled up in all kinds of diplomatic nonsense, getting nowhere fast. And you're in a well-contained position with both Turner and Barrington to keep a close eye on you. '

'God, you're such a cynic, Terry.'

'Maybe I've been in the game too long!'

'Well, it's a new game now. Maybe the old rules don't apply. Maybe Mason genuinely wants to get the best out of all of us. Let's face it, without us he can do nothing, right?'

So it was that the Liberals had gone into their first Cabinet intrigued by what it might hold, but also feeling secure in their position and their options should things not go well.

The meeting was duly called to order. After some friendly and team-building words, Don Mason launched into the main business of the day—the new government's programme to be announced in the King's speech the next month at the opening of Parliament. Everyone around the Cabinet table had a screen in front of him. Cunningham made the presentation. The non-GEM

Cabinet members had not been advised of any of the programme beforehand, though they could guess at the content from the election campaign. But they had not expected such an extensive programme as this.

It was all there. New taxes to tackle pollution, and that would hit motorists particularly hard. Major projects, to be run by Dave Barrington, on reforestation and sea defences. New legislation to curb carbon emissions, with a monitoring unit to collect much more data and provide evidence for enforcement. A commission to come up with comprehensive plans for carbon rationing. A programme to switch the country over to renewable energy—Peter looked pleased when Cunningham said that Kitson's department would have additional resources to develop the programme and drive it through. This was an extensive programme already, and then Cunningham announced some new bombshells.

'On local and regional policy', he announced, 'we're cancelling investment in the Growth Areas, and rescinding their designations as areas for substantial housing and job growth. Now I know some of you cynics thought we were just playing for votes in rural areas when we first put this forward. But catering to this kind of unsustainable development is not the right way to go. Employment needs to be spread across the country. There's no reason why, with the technologies we have now, everyone should be charging towards one end of the country in order to work. The last few governments have peddled the myth of building "sustainable communities"–but pouring concrete over several million hectares of green fields in the south of England is anything but sustainable!

'We will announce measures to stimulate home based enterprise, including home-based and localised food production.'

Terry raised an eyebrow.

'In terms of food and agriculture policy,' Cunningham continued, 'we will be focusing government support and subsidies on small producers and in particular on organic producers. There will be substantial subsidies to switch production to organic.'

Terry and Howard Blackstone looked at each other in alarm.

'Wait, wait, wait a minute,' interrupted Terry. 'Hasn't anyone advised you that you can't do that?'

Mason intervened. 'Yes they have, Terry. But we don't agree,' he said in an assured and friendly voice.

'I think it's advice worth considering, Don,' Terry responded. 'This cuts across European agreements. We can't just go off and do our own thing when we've bound ourselves by treaty to do something collectively with our European partners. Don't you know we're in the middle of negotiating the removal of most subsidies, a very ticklish issue for the French and also for world trade policy? And, if you don't mind me saying, Don: you've appointed me Minister for Europe, but neither you nor Doug or anyone has consulted me about this.'

'A couple of points, Terry,' said Don. 'First—we're in the middle of nothing. We are a new government, and we won't be bound by what any previous government was doing. Secondly, about taking the advice of our legal advisers. One of my axioms is that in any legal contest, 50% of the lawyers must be wrong! So, Terry, we listen to their advice, but that's all it is: advice! We act on it, or not. And once we pay them to support a different view—our view—they will argue our point in any court of law!'

'Good God!' Howard muttered, but most people around the table were laughing.

'Seriously, Terry,' Mason continued, 'this meeting is exploratory. This is what we want to do, and we want your input. We didn't want to announce any of this before, and you are bound by Cabinet rules not to leak any of it. Once we've formulated the right policies, we'll announce them in the proper way. With all the detail. But I know you've been very critical of the way the European Union works. I wanted you to be Minister for Europe so that you can help us push matters like this through. Europe can be a force for good, but it shouldn't set up inflexible systems that stop all innovation—it has to allow member states to innovate and bring forward better ways of doing things to share at the common European table. Actually, those aren't my own words. Do you know who said that?'

'I did,' Terry had to admit, with a wry smile and a shrug. A ripple of laughter went round the table.

It was a long programme, and a long meeting ensued. Each policy proposal generated a great deal of debate, and sometimes some heated arguments. Much of the friction was caused by Ben Porter's abrasive attitude. Porter was very devoted to certain ideological views and would always challenge approaches that didn't meet his exact prescription. He and Barrington clashed often. Terry noted that Barrington was by temperament a patient man, but he had no tolerance for people who, in his view, got their facts wrong. Terry could see where some of the fault lines were emerging in this motley Cabinet crew already.

Thursday morning stretched into Thursday afternoon, with plenty of mineral water and sandwiches. Howard Blackstone was thirsting for a beer, and by 2 p.m. an unforgiving headache was setting in. He'd been having headaches like this quite frequently in recent months, and they made him tired and irritable. He looked more and more pale, and by 4 p.m. had not ventured a comment for nearly three hours, even though he thought he might be failing in his duties as party leader in keeping so quiet. Most of the debate, he felt, was pointless. What was needed was just a little interaction, after which it should be up to the responsible ministers to draw up the detailed policy and circulate for review and feedback. But he wasn't too unhappy. All this confirmed his views of the probable ineptitude of the GEM leadership. But as the meeting drew to a close, he felt there was a need to say something.

'Well, if there's nothing else for today...' Mason was saying.

'There is actually,' interjected Blackstone. 'All this domestic stuff is, of course...interesting. But I'm Foreign Secretary, and there were a number of items we discussed in negotiating this coalition that I'd like to see included in the Speech. Most importantly, the foreign aid measures we proposed and the goal of eliminating poverty. How does all this fit in? And why is there nothing in your draft programme about it?'

'Well, Howard,' replied Mason. 'You are the Foreign Secretary. You propose something, and we'll all discuss it. I know the poverty issue is close to your heart. But I'd also like you to think about the environmental implications of economic growth throughout the world, and how we can export the Green Revolution.'

The meeting broke up shortly afterwards. 'Christ, I'm dying for a pint!' Howard exclaimed. 'Are you two coming?'

Terry agreed.

'I'll catch you up,' Peter said, 'I've got a lot to discuss with Dave and Sarah.'

'Oh, Dave and Sarah is it?' harrumphed Howard when Kitson was out of earshot. 'Have we lost him, Terry? Has you protégé gone over to the dark side?'

'Dark Green side, maybe,' Terry replied with a laugh.

A rather distressed-looking Lord Felton had walked up to them. 'Dark Green? I think they call themselves Deep Green. But I like Dark! And—do you mind if I join you for a drink? You know, they rope me in to give them advice, then they don't listen to a word I say!'

'Probably too busy talking to listen,' suggested Terry.

'There's some of that!' laughed Felton. 'But you know it's as if all these GEM people have got everything worked out in advance—I don't think anything we say or do will make a jot of difference.'

'They'll learn,' said Howard. 'When nothing works, they'll learn!'

21: A Few Degrees Either Way

Trevor MacLean flopped back on the sofa he had brought in specially to the production office—his 'creativity couch' he called it. Today he felt exasperated, after another run-in with the Directorate Green Team. His inner demon urging him to political incorrectness was more than straining at the leash. It was finding its way into his programme making. First he produced a sceptical documentary on methods for estimating global warming. Then he had produced a programme focusing on the follies and frivolities (as he called them) of several Green Earth Councils.

Now the Directorate Green Team was taking him to task. Not only were his programmes irresponsible and badly researched, they alleged, but his programme-making techniques were shoddy and wasteful.

After this roasting, he felt he certainly deserved a lie-down. And to be creative—that is, creatively plot his revenge. Stella Walton saw him as the Green Team left, and could tell from Trevor's body language that all had not gone well. Stella went to the door of the office—in part to offer tea and sympathy, and in part to be entertained. There was nothing like a Trevor bitching session for serious amusement, so long as one wasn't the object of his wrath.

'Don't ask, don't ask!' he exclaimed, theatrically putting his hand to his forehead as Stella came into the room.

'I was only going to ask,' Stella responded with mock-nervousness 'if you would like some tea.'

'Oh—you can ask that. Ask. Ask. The answer's "You're a life-saver, darling—I'll be your slave forever!"'

Stella already had the drink prepared outside, and brought it in. 'Your favourite anti-depressant. Industrial strength BBC tea.'

'Oh, you're a 21st century Florence Nightingale. An angel of mercy in my hour of need.'

He took a big gulp and lapsed into silence.

Stella stood in the doorway. She waited patiently for him to offer up some information.

'This room is incredibly hot. You could do with a fan in here.'

'You can stand in the doorway and cheer, if you like!' Trevor joked gloomily.

'Well?!' Stella asked pointedly, raising her eyebrows. 'Aren't you going to tell me what happened?'

'Is that why you've stayed late, to have a good laugh at my expense?'

'I always work late, Trevor. Haven't you noticed? But a good laugh at the end of a hectic day is good therapy!'

'OK. They didn't like *"A Few Degrees Either Way"*. One of my finest and most objective documentaries, I'd say. What did you think?'

'What do I think? I did the research, what do you expect me to think?'

'I know, I know. Wonderful it was too! But just look at the trouble you've got me into!!'

'Just tell me what they said, Trevor!'

'Well, item 1: *Our programme lacked integrity and impartiality.* I–I mean "we", because I want to share the blame with you—we gave far too much time to an "unrepresentative maverick viewpoint challenging methods of modelling historic climate conditions".

'Item 2: *The programme violates recently agreed editorial policy.* Recently agreed by whom? Not me, for sure. What happened to editorial independence, I ask?

'Item 3: They say I *should have consulted with higher authority* before it was aired. But "higher authority" commissioned me to do the programme in the first place!

'Item 4: They say I *employ careless and environmentally unsound production techniques* ....'

'Well, that last one is true, Trevor,' said Stella.

'I'm shocked you can say that! What do you mean?'

'Come on Trevor—we've worked together for a while now. I know how you pack programme budgets to give you some leeway. Then you can overspend on locations, you have crews and casts worthy of costume drama rather than news and documentaries—and how much equipment have you bought that you only use once?'

'Some of it I've never used at all!'

'Exactly—don't boast about it!'

'But why is it any of their business? The end result is fine by everyone else. We've been through four Heads of News and Docs since I've been here. Have any of them ever complained about my work? Then these cretins come along with their E-for-environment-Vision. E-Vision, by god. When I first came here E was for Efficiency—do you remember that?'

'I don't think I was born then, Trevor.'

'Yes, those heady days of the 1990s: the Efficiency Vision, or How to Print Money for Consultants. They had us all jumping through hoops. You know, you've never seen this place so full of people. Instead of going out and making programmes, everyone was dribbling manically in the corridors, waiting for the next reorganisation.

'But what pisses me off the most, Stella, is that just like then there's a bunch of salami slappers who've never made a programme in their lives passing judgment on what we do! They have their policy checklist: tick 'em all and bugger the production quality—it either fits with their list-ticking or no! Have I bored you with this before, sweetie?'

'Yes—but never with such passion! But you can't say that about Craig—he's won awards for his work.'

'Awards? One award, you mean. I see he's treated you to his "I'm really a programme-maker but they don't take me seriously" soliloquy? He won an award fifteen years ago for one schools programme he made—I think we only made two new ones that year. Since then he's spent all his time hobnobbing with the Suits in a ceaseless quest for promotion. If we stuck a camera on his tongue we'd get some wonderful insights into the large intestine of the Director-General, don't you think?'

Stella snorted with laughter—a bad move she thought, as it only encouraged him.

'Actually, I think this could be a whole new sub-genre of Reality TV—the "fly up the arse" documentary. What do you think?'

Stella waved at him with the back of her hand, a gesture for him to stop with his nonsense. He continued for a while: 'You know I've made up news, I've plagiarised facts, I've libelled God knows how many people, insulted the entire management hierarchy—and I've never come under fire like this. In fact they've always defended me if I got into hot water—defended my journalistic freedom or some such nonsense. What the hell's going on, Stella?'

••

What was going on? Craig Delaney was the senior representative from the BBC who sat on the Environmental Scrutiny Commission for the Media—ESCOMEDIA for short. Long involved with policy initiatives in the corporation, it was his fortune to be leading an environmental policy audit at the time the Green Revolution gained momentum. Genuinely enthused by this turn of events, he had thrown himself into the task of setting up a Green Team for each directorate in this sprawling organisation, and coordinating with ESCOMEDIA when it was set up.

To his continuing annoyance, despite support from the hierarchy the Green Teams faced the same problem as all managerial initiatives at the BBC. The programme-makers took not a blind bit of notice, or at best sought to find a way round this unwanted interference. The atmosphere of these cat-and-mouse games was always coloured by the contempt that the 'Creatives' (the programme-makers) and the 'Talent' (those in front of camera) held for the 'Suits'. These were the seemingly endless supply of managers and accountants whose mission appeared to be to frustrate the will of Creative and Talented people.

Craig had tried to put himself in the position of someone who could bridge the divide–a Creative who could also manage and make policy. But he found his career had faltered, and he was the butt of endless contemptuous comment from his former colleagues. Despite his basically friendly nature, he was a man with several chips on his shoulder, as are many talented people in all fields of life who find they have not risen to the level that their abilities merit. And in particular, he had a downer on Trevor MacLean, a man who had snipped and sniped at him and mocked his initiatives for nearly a decade now. So he was more than a little pleased when Trevor, with typical arrogance (as he saw it), kept sticking his head above the parapet. It was time to shoot him down.

Craig had also acquired, in a way he did not quite understand, a side-kick called Juliet Coe. She had kind of 'appeared' on his team, and her presence was endorsed by ESCOMEDIA, possibly even paid for by them–she no longer appeared to be working as a junior researcher in News. Serious and hardworking, she also had a direct line of communication to Danny Malik, whose meteoric rise to sit at the right hand of Donald Mason was one of the wonders of the media world. Juliet's connections were useful–but also a little unnerving for Craig.

Craig and Juliet were now meeting with the Director-General, Miles Campbell and the Head of News, Michaela Cavaliero. The two senior managers were uneasy about having this meeting at all, and became more uneasy as the discussion progressed.

After some small talk about the weather and the progress of various corporate green initiatives, Miles Campbell addressed himself to the agenda that had been sent through by Juliet.

'I recognise that we have an agreement with ESCOMEDIA to respond to reports and suggestions brought to us by their representatives—but I can't say I'm sure that a meeting like this is an appropriate way to deal with the issues you're bringing before me. Getting right down to the nitty gritty, there are two issues of substance for this meeting: your suggestions for a "protocol for accuracy in environmental reporting", and "issues and actions stemming from the journalism of Trevor MacLean"—by which I think you really mean the disciplining of Trevor MacLean and Stella Walton.'

Craig Delaney looked slightly uncomfortable—he was not used to having face-to-face meetings with the Director-General. Juliet was taking notes, and met the eyes of the D-G with a steady gaze.

Campbell continued. 'Let's deal with the first of these issues. What you are asking for could be seen as an attack on free speech and on the independence of the BBC. All our reporting has to meet some standard prescribed by … by who exactly? By you? By ESCOMEDIA, that is, by a government quango? It seems to me you're effectively asking for a veto on what we can report.' He had thrown down a challenge, and waited for the response.

Craig cleared his throat and steeled himself to reply. 'With respect, it's taking things too far to call it a "veto". What our report suggests is that we need a clearer approach to editorial policy. The issues at question are not simply a matter of opinion, where two sides of a debate want to make themselves heard. These are issues where it is important that people have the facts, and where misrepresentation of the facts can be very damaging. In *A Few Degrees Either Way*, well-established facts about climate change were portrayed as simply a matter of opinion, and maverick views shared by almost no one in the scientific world were given equal prominence—'

'So people are not entitled to hold wrong opinions?' cut in Michaela Cavaliero, whose dislike for Craig Delaney was almost palpable.

'They're entitled to hold any opinion they want, of course. But we don't have to report it.'

'You are making it sound like we are trying to break new ground in compromising editorial independence,' added the soft-spoken Juliet Coe. 'But look at it like this. If we had produced a programme giving equal weight to the views of racists and non-racists, we would be in trouble. Or if we focused on the views of people who said that women were inferior to men, and that all evidence to the contrary was politically correct falsehood, we'd have had the Equality and Diversity Unit down on our heads like a ton of bricks. Those two mavericks on Trevor's documentary were saying exactly that—that global warming is no more than politically correct falsehood. They don't just have a bad attitude, or wrong opinions: they are wrong *in fact*. What this—'

'Whoa, whoa! Hold on a minute!' interrupted Michaela. 'You're saying you want to censor everyone who says something factually incorrect in a news strand? I can't believe we're even talking about this! We'd never be able to interview a politician, or a social campaigner, for fear they've got their facts wrong!'

She slumped back into her chair to emphasise her amazement, and feeling that her point was proved.

'I think, with respect,' said Craig, 'that's taking things to extremes. In the case under question, it's not a question of someone just getting their facts wrong in an interview. It's about a journalist and programme-maker, and his research team for that matter, deliberately setting out to make a programme that distorts the facts, using extreme selectivity to highlight one incorrect and unrepresentative viewpoint. We need to protect ourselves against this kind of sloppy journalism.'

'Why? Because we've offended the government? We've been through these sort of issues before, and I'm satisfied that we have good policies and protocols already for working them through. We will from time to time offend governments—it's the nature of journalism, and also a sign of our independence. It will be a sad day when we always do what the government wants!' argued Michaela.

'Agreed, agreed,' said Craig. 'But there are times when as a public body with a mission to educate and inform we throw our weight behind socially responsible campaigns—like for AIDS awareness, combating racism, child abuse, etc etc. Educating and informing the public about the destruction of our planet falls into this kind of category. We should avoid making cheap controversialist programmes just for the sake of the ratings.'

'I don't think we have a problem in informing people about environmental issues. We have a track record going well back before the current situation. I daresay Don Mason and half his supporters gleaned a lot of their environmental knowledge from the BBC as they grew up,' said Campbell.

'May I ask one thing about current editorial procedures?' asked Juliet.

'Go ahead.' said Michaela.

'Did Trevor MacLean's programme proposal or his script come across your desk for approval—and did you approve it?'

Michaela pursed her lips thoughtfully. There was no point in denying it, though she felt unsure of the consequences. But she hadn't got to where she was now by being timid.

'Yes. And yes. Yes to both questions'.

'I see,' said Juliet. 'So essentially you're in this meeting now both to protect Trevor MacLean and to protect yourself.'

'If you mean, "Do I stand by my decision?" the answer is, again, "yes"! But I have to ask *you* something. Who are you? I mean I know your name, but who are you? Why are you here? On whose authority are you grilling the Head of News and the Director-General?'

Juliet blinked a couple of times, as if stunned by the attack on her credentials.

'I simply represent the scrutiny function of ESCOMEDIA, and assist Craig with coordinating our Green Teams. My report represents the considered view of ESCOMEDIA, and my job today is to discuss it with you, and to report back on your response. Simple as that.'

She determinedly held Michaela's gaze.

Miles Campbell broke in. 'Well, this is my response. You can note this down. We are taking your report under advisement, and will consider the issues it raises. Now onto the other matter: Your report recommends disciplinary action and "re-education" for two of our staff, Trevor MacLean and Stella Walton.'

'Yes,' said Craig. 'In a nutshell, Trevor for all his merits is a loose cannon, a disruptive element. I know he's been a very successful—and a very recognisable—figure for a few months now. But officially he's still a science news correspondent, and it must be time to get the musical chairs going: and he needs to be put somewhere where he can learn to be a responsible journalist again.'

'Demotion,' said Michaela emphatically.

'Reassignment. Somewhere where he can't do so much damage to the BBC and its reputation,' Juliet corrected, inclining her head to one side and raising her eyebrows, as if looking for agreement.

'I note your recommendation,' said Miles with a sigh. 'And what's your recommendation for Stella Walton?'

'She's basically a first-class researcher. We think if she is away from MacLean's influence she can still be an asset to the organisation. But someone senior needs to keep a close eye on her work for a while.'

Michaela exploded now. 'Miles, I don't know about you, but I can't take much more of this! If these members of our staff have done something wrong, there's a disciplinary procedure to go through. They need to defend themselves, and they're entitled to representation from the union and advice from HR. Yet here we are, two senior managers and two...two...random ... somebodies sitting in judgment on them and being asked to make a key decision about their careers.'

Miles was nodding thoughtfully as she said this, while Juliet and Craig both looked down. When Michaela finished speaking, Juliet looked up and spoke with determination.

'You could take disciplinary action. Or they can always invoke the grievance procedures if they feel they are being badly treated. Punishment and doing nothing are two ends of a spectrum of options. In view of your sensitivities about editorial policy, I'm proposing a middle path. Every day decisions are taken about who works with whom, and who is assigned where. You can make such decisions about Stella and Trevor. Then it's up to people to interpret your actions as they will. But I should let you know, ESCOMEDIA is determined that some action will be taken in respect of these two journalists, and that measures must be put in place to monitor the quality of output with greater vigilance. Maybe more professional management is necessary.'

Juliet turned and looked steadily at Michaela as she said this.

Before Michaela could respond, Miles gestured to her and declared the meeting at an end. 'We will let you know our decision,' he said frostily.

'Thank you for your time,' Juliet replied, and left. Craig nodded at both of the senior managers, and let out a kind of muted grunt as a way of bidding farewell.

When they had gone, Michaela threw her head forward, then back, running her hands through her hair.

'What the hell was that, Miles?!' she asked. 'At the end there—was she threatening me? Miles—are you listening to me?'

Miles Campbell wasn't listening. He was deep in thought.

'Oh Miles,' said Michaela, 'you're not thinking of giving them what they want, are you?'

'Michaela, this isn't the only issue we have with our new green government at the moment. They're planning to shake up the Board of Trustees, to get some reliable people on board.'

'Some of their cronies, you mean...'

'And not only that. I've got the first report from the ESCOMEDIA into our overall environmental performance–the corporation's performance, that is. It's very detailed, and quite damning in places. And much of the blame is laid on poor management. That's me. That's us, the corporate management team.

He paused.

'What are you saying, Miles?' Michaela asked gently.

'I feel I'm being caught with a pincer movement, Michaela,' Miles said, opening his drinks cabinet. 'Want one?'

'Make it a double, please!'

Miles poured two large Scotches, but his pensive mood continued.

'Let's leave aside our anger about this meeting and its irregular nature for a moment, and look at the situation in its wider context. If we end up in a conflict with the government in the current mood of the nation–I don't think we'll come off too well. Juliet Coe was maybe proposing a solution we can live with. No, hold on Michaela, hear me out. We can talk to Trevor. I think he'll be theatrically miffed, but he'll understand. Let's send him out of the firing line for, say, three months. There's actually some useful work I could get him to do in Edinburgh where we're reorganising regional news-gathering–and isn't his family from around there?

'About two hundred miles north of there, but it's the general direction, I'm sure...'

'And Stella. Assign her team to Miranda Lebowsky–she's a safe pair of hands. But I want you to bring Stella to see me. I have a special, highly confidential research operation for her in her spare moments. I want to know everything about this Juliet Coe. I want to know where she's coming from, why she's so influential, who she talks to, who she's shagging, what she has for breakfast, everything!'

Michaela was composing herself now. She raised her glass, and they gave each other a world-weary look as they said 'Cheers'.

22: The Green Mandarin

'Be honest—you never thought we'd do it, did you, Dad? In power, still here after six months and still popular. Maybe even more popular than last November!'

Jessica Olsen Barrington was strolling along the riverside walk through the village with her father, Sir James Olsen. They had just enjoyed a pleasant evening at the Olsen's Hampshire home, a family meal where old hatchets had been, if not buried, at least politely kept out of sight. Everyone at the table knew that there were many things to be said, both about the past and about the new events that had made Sir James' son-in-law a cabinet minister. This was a role that would make their paths cross often and could create many delicate situations for both of them in their personal and professional lives.

It was early spring: the daffodils were out and the blossom was out early on many of the trees and bushes after another short and mild winter. Jessica remembered how when she was young, she would love to walk in the countryside with her father—a somewhat remote, mysterious and all-wise figure in her life. It was a time when she could have him completely to herself, and escape from the frenetic and smothering devotion of her domineering mother.

That changed. As she grew into her teens and developed her own rebellious take on her mother's charitable conscience, Jessica felt increasingly frustrated by the calm assurance of her father's views. While they walked in the countryside he would talk to her in, as he felt, an adult way about the issues of the day, imparting his wisdom in response to her precocious questioning. He didn't understand her growing antipathy to her upbringing, the smugness of their privileged way of life. Jessica could not understand why, as a man of principle, he could change his views to please whichever government was elected. She didn't accept his ideas about 'that's how democracy works' and 'you have to take the longer view' and 'the need for stability and a professional civil service'. She had accused him of having a 'flexible morality' and putting his personal ambition before doing what is right.

At the time these arguments stung him. They also pleased him, at first, as he saw his little girl's growing intellectual maturity. He accepted the rough edges, and expected them to rub off in time. Jessica felt this in him, and reacted fiercely against what she felt was his patronising attitude. In his own calm way, she felt, he was just as domineering as her mother.

By the time she was sixteen she had abandoned these country walks with her father. At times, she would barely speak to him. Instead, she would saddle up a horse and ride on her own to a solitary spot, where she would sit, read and reflect. Her thoughts became passionately occupied by the growing threats to the environment from the way we live, and the ways in which governments and businesses always took the wrong decisions. It was time for a change, and Jessica wanted to be in the forefront of this. It had guided all her choices since then, and without ever breaking completely with her parents, led to conflict and mutual disappointment—not least over her marriage to 'that romantic and impoverished dreamer' David Barrington. The arrival of grandchildren softened the impasse, but Jessica felt that the weight of parental disappointment always remained.

Now things had changed. The views Jessica had championed were now in the ascendant, and the establishment was having to adapt.

'These are indeed interesting times,' Sir James replied.

Jessica smiled. 'Is that the best you can do?'

Her father gave a short, self-deprecating laugh. 'OK. It has taken me by surprise. And congratulations. Your team has played its hand well.'

'I'm glad you approve! And how does it feel to be working up a Green Earth/Liberal economic programme?'

They walked amiably on without speaking for a few minutes, soaking up the sights, sounds and smells of the warm evening. This was almost like old times. Jessica had never expected her father to hurry his replies, and as a young girl had liked his thoughtfulness—until the times arrived when she had been impatient for an argument. Now part of the reason behind his pause for thought was a sincere wish to avoid such an argument.

After a while he spoke, at first hesitantly. 'I'm not sure how much we should talk about this, Jessie. Where the boundaries are. Whether we should be setting up some Chinese walls in the family. But I'll say this. It's probably the most radical programme I've seen from an incoming government, and very challenging for us in the civil service.'

'Challenging in what way? You think it's not workable?'

'I'm trying to approach the workability of it with an open mind. There are aspects of the programme that takes us into very new, untested areas. We have all kinds of economic and financial models into which we feed any proposals for change. But our models are based around traditional assumptions around growth, how markets work, around how labour markets work, around the impacts of taxes and benefits and so on, so on. Now the government and its advisors are pulling these models to bits, or challenging the assumptions they are built on. And of course, it's always a good thing to challenge and test the assumptions involved. But they are replacing the old assumptions and certainties, however misguided from their point of view, with a whole new smorgasbord of untested hypotheses and assumptions—'

'So you don't buy it?' interrupted Jessica.

'It's not that. It's intellectually challenging. Even exciting in its own way. But Sarah Turner went so far as to tell me I had to "rip up the rule book". She and her team run up and down their narrow channels of ideological certainty, but where are the tools to do the job? What if the real world of a nation of 65 million people and what they do every day doesn't fit into their mould? What if there are too many variables they haven't thought of?

'Our job is making the mechanisms of government work. And everything I've looked at so far says that government income can only reduce year on year, even if we only do half the things they are considering.'

'Prosperity without growth. You think it's not doable?'

'We don't know how to do it yet. I can see the "without growth" bit well enough. But the "prosperity" bit? I can't see where that's coming from. And whatever the current enthusiasm, I can't see people being very happy with this in a year or two.'

They were arriving back at the house now.

'I know you, Dad. This is what makes you happy,' said Jessica, gesturing with her arms to the countryside all around. 'And us—I hope. It isn't money that makes people happy. Getting more and more things isn't what makes us happy. Prosperity is more than this.'

Sir James stopped by one of his cars in the drive. 'Get in,' he invited, holding open the passenger door for his daughter.

'What are you doing?' aske Jessica, quizzically.

'Go on. Trust me. I want to show you something.'

'O...K...?' said Jessica with mock distrustfulness.

Sir James drove out of the village, then pulled out on the dual carriageway towards Eastleigh. After ten minutes, he turned off, saying, 'Here we are. This is it!'

'The superstore?' exclaimed Jessica.

'Indeed,' said Sir James as he carefully parked the car as close to the store entrance as he could find a parking space. 'Let's just sit here a while and watch.'

His daughter was completely bemused. It was a 24 hour store, still busy at well after nine in the evening.

'What do you think of this place? Most of the locals protested before it was built. Ugly. A blot on the landscape. A monstrosity of monopoly capitalism, said some. I don't especially like it, myself. What do you think of it?'

'You know what I think of it!' laughed Jessica.

'Do you remember your Grandpa?' asked Sir James, apparently going off at a complete tangent.

'Are you losing your mind, Dad? Or having a stroke or something? Of course I remember him!'

'He was a young Oxford don, not long been in England, actually, when the war broke out. He volunteered but was deemed not fit for military service. But he volunteered for the charity relief efforts from Oxford to relieve the famine in Greece.'

'I know the story.'

'But it's not just a story, Jess. For me, it's within a generation that there were people starving in Europe. When I was born we still had rationing. And think about it, as change swept across Eastern Europe in the 1990s, when you were a child, millions came close to it again. So what you see here is a kind of historical miracle—'

'I can't believe you're waxing lyrical about Tesco!'

'No, Jess. Every day now I have to hear the new team of politicians decrying the evils of the ways we produce, transport and sell food and groceries. We can all do some blue skies thinking about how it can all be done differently, sure. But this is *real*. Think of all the hundreds of thousands of choices and transactions that focus on this point, this very place where we are now. On the one hand all the networks of producers, wholesalers, distributors, logistics providers and so on, and then on the other hand all the individual decisions and movements that enable us to feed tens of thousands of people in such an orderly way, so that none of us is short of food. And from this we provide thousands of jobs, skim off a predictable amount of tax to build the infrastructure and provide the services people want ... And the thing is—it's actually all so precarious. So many variables and dependencies. We've seen how easy it is for it to be disrupted, whether it's a petrol strike, or fear of a radiation cloud, floods, or whatever.

'What I'm saying is, it may not be the best of all possible ways to organise how we do things, but it works. And across the world it works on a scale never seen before. Never before in human history have so many people been free from hunger, with a roof over their head and with prospects in life. So if we want to rip up the rule book, if we want to scrap all this in favour of local markets and home-grown food and things we haven't really known how to do for forty years or more, we'd better be sure—absolutely sure—that we know what we're doing. I fear we may be throwing out something we know works in favour of a roll of the dice. It's a huge gamble!'

Jessica was taken aback by her father's passion about this. For the first time in her life, she could feel real anxiety on his part about his work.

'So you really don't think it can work? I'm sure it can. You talk about Grandpa. I remember trotting behind him in his vegetable garden when I was only four or five years old, with him teaching me all the names of the plants and patiently tolerating my efforts at helping. Maybe he has a lot to answer for about the way I am! But we can do things differently. Most people in the world don't shop at any kind of superstore. We *can* recreate the networks of producers, and consumers and all the links in-between without the sky falling in. And it will be a better world for it. I know if we're all giving each other our home-produced goods and bartering services with each other, you'll have fewer things to tax and in some respects government won't know what to do with itself. But this isn't going to happen overnight. It will be step by step—and you'll be there to make sure we don't run away with ourselves, won't you?'

'Hmm,' said Sir James, doubtfully. 'While we're here—didn't your mother say we needed some more sherry?'

'Yes. And bananas. And some juice for the kids.'

They got out the car and went into the superstore, continuing to debate the chances for success of the new programme.

23: Re-education

'I'm not paying it! That's all there is to it!'

Sam Sharma slammed down his tea cup on the breakfast table.

'I told you. You and your big mouth! Would it have done any harm just to do what they want, just for once?' Kelly, Sam's wife, spoke calmly but firmly as she mopped up the tea spilt on the table. She sat down and topped up his cup.

'Here, drink some more before you burst a blood vessel!'

Sam looked at her and gave half a smile.

'Kelly, it's two hundred pound! Two hundred bloody pound. I can't pay it!'

'We'll have to, love,' she said, putting her hand on his and giving a little squeeze. 'And we can get the kids to sort the trash out from now on. They need to take some responsibility. And it's not like we can't afford the fine.'

'It's not the money—it's the principle of the thing. They can separate whatever they like from their bins, but I'm buggered if I'm gonna sort it myself. What do I pay the Council Tax for? We pay through the nose, then have to be the bloody bin man an' all. I'm not paying it!'

As a market trader, Sam Sharma was one of the first people to fall foul of the Camden & Islington Pollution Tribunal. These were local courts set up by Earth Councils, and sanctioned by one of Don Mason's first Acts of Parliament. Now, after six months of the Revolution, these Tribunals met on a weekly basis throughout the country to deal with offenders who persistently flouted environmental regulations.

All the local market traders had been annoyed by the attentions of the 'bin police' as they called them. New regulations from the Earth Council put obligations on all homes and businesses to carry out more recycling, and new services had been introduced to make this more extensive. But it was a duty of the individual to separate all their waste into the various bins provided. Sam had always done this to some extent. Cardboard here, everything else there. Now it had become much more complex.

Sam, an anti-authoritarian by nature, had refused to take the new requirements seriously, and had felt that his offences were too trivial to be noticed. But he had reckoned without the tenacity of the local Green Volunteers and the Waste Control Officers—or WaCOs, as people liked to call them.

Initially it had been a game of cat and mouse. The waste from his market stall—mainly various forms of packaging—were put into a row of communal bins. So if he could sneak it in, no one could pin it on him that he was the one putting the wrong kind of waste into the bin. So after his first couple of warnings he took to trying to ensure he only disposed of it when the WaCOs weren't around. His fellow traders were amused at his antics, and he played to the crowd as he carried out his furtive trips to the bins.

But eventually he was caught. Green Volunteers had been deployed to keep an eye on him, and they had extensive photographic and video evidence of him flouting the regulations. And so he had been hauled before the Pollution Tribunal.

Even then he hadn't taken it seriously, smirking at the po-faced citizens on the bench. Until they made their decision. A £200 fine and compulsory attendance on an Environmental Awareness Course which was being run for offenders at the local college. And the President of the Tribunal solemnly warned him of serious consequences if he failed to comply with the penalty. He was given forty-eight hours to pay.

For possibly the first time in his life, Sam was dumbstruck. That evening he joked with his friends and family, that he would never have got into college if he hadn't been a bin criminal. But overnight his amazement at the verdict turned into a righteous fury. With every fibre of his being he wanted to turn the tables on those 'jumped-up idiots' on the Tribunal. And he had a plan about how to do it. Make fun of them.

••

Don Mason was calm, but Malcolm Morton and Danny Malik were seething with anger. This was their first experience of having the media turn on them since they had become the government. Malik felt a personal sense of failure. It was his role to infuse the media with the spirit of the Green Revolution, and also to present the GEM in the best light.

It had started with the London *Evening News*, and had spread from there to the national tabloids. The *Evening News* had a long tradition of tweaking the tail of London local councils, even when it broadly agreed with what they were doing. And Sam Sharma had passed on the 'Evidence for the Prosecution of Mr S Sharma' to them. Only he'd given it a different spin. He calculated the person hours of all the people who had been involved in tracking him and videoing him. And he totted up the hours of the officials involved in preparing and presenting the case, and of the Tribunal panel. His prosecution had involved more than a thousand hours of activity. Half of that was time by paid officials, and the rest was volunteer time. But using the local government formula for costing volunteer time, the media came up with a figure of £44,000 to prosecute him.

'They could have employed two bin men to sort everything for that', Sam had commented. 'And times that by the number of cases they deal with. They're wasting money prosecuting innocent citizens, when they could be getting people into work to do the job properly! Maybe they should put those wallies on the Tribunal to work sorting the bins—at least they'd be doing something useful!'

Mason read this, and chuckled. 'Danny—this kind of mockery may be new to you. But for us old timers, it's familiar ground. For decades, we were the butt of everyone's jokes.'

Morton protested. 'It's different now, Don. We're the government, and we can't be made to look foolish. We need to take a firm stand on this. First we had the BBC backsliding with all that nonsense from that prancing pansy MacLean—now this. We need to stop the rot.'

Don looked at Danny, and raised his eyebrows, inviting his opinion.

'I agree with Malcolm. Image has been crucial in our success so far. I know we expected something like this. The media won't voluntarily be on our side forever. But we need to do something about the Sharma case.'

'What's your plan?'

'Well ………'

'Come on, Danny. You know how I work. I want people to come to me with solutions, rather than problems. Or at least a range of options…'

'OK,' Malik replied. 'The first part is easy, and is in place already. We respond with positive stories: the successes in improving recycling all over the country. Without these tough measures, this wouldn't have been possible. And we can highlight the more substantial cases, where businesses have been hauled over the coals and forced to change dangerously polluting activities.'

'Good,' said Mason. 'Now what about the hard part?'

'We have to bring the press into line. You know generally I think they're on our side. But they can't resist a good story. And knocking us is always the easiest option. So we have to rule that out.'

'How?'

Danny Malik looked at Morton, who took over the proposition. 'Go for the journalists. And the editors. I've had some Volunteers watching Philips at the *Evening News*, and Stitchwell at the *Record*. We can bring Philips before a Tribunal. They've done hardly anything to green their business. And Stitchwell. Danny knows him. By nature, he's a coward. He's happy to drag people who can't defend themselves through the mud. But he's easily intimidated by rich people who threaten legal action. We should meet with him. And talk about Tribunal proceedings. And about his womanising. And about his drink-driving offences. And about the need for a strong front in promoting the Green Revolution. And you know, what he really likes to do is hang around important people. I think we can turn him into your number one boot-licker!'

Don chuckled, but continued to look serious. He thought for a moment.

'OK. But let's be subtle about it. We don't want people to think we go about threatening people when we don't like what they write. You know, I think Sam Sharma is doing us a favour.'

Malcolm and Danny looked surprised.

'OK, so he makes our local people look a bit ridiculous. We suffer by association. But highlighting his punishment gives everyone a message: they know we're serious! I think we'll see an increased level of compliance after this. Most people don't want to risk a fine. A few high impact cases of "exemplary justice" are just what we need. Malcolm, I take it he didn't pay up in forty-eight hours? Then the Tribunal needs to be on him like a ton of bricks—and the whole country needs to know about it! Is he going to his awareness classes?'

Malcolm nodded. 'He seems to like them!'

'I think his fine needs to be increased, and he should get community service—on a green project. One of the eco-colleges, don't you think?' said Mason.

'I'll pass that message down to the local Earth Council,' said Morton, 'but of course the Tribunal will make its own decision.'

'Of course,' Mason agreed. 'But—and this is one for you, Danny—we can't afford to have a reactive policy towards the media. We need a clear plan to harmonise the media with the principles of the Green Revolution. Nothing too overt—we can't tell them what to say, or we'll forever be enemies of the freedom of the press! But we need a clear programme of how to draw them closer and how to deal with anyone who wants to move into an oppositional position. Can you do that?'

'Sure,' said Danny. 'Juliet's got ESCOMEDIA working along those lines already—we just need to draw it all together.'

As the meeting ended, Danny Malik pulled Morton to one side.

'Would you like some insight into MacLean, Malcolm?' he asked. 'You called him a prancing pansy. Actually, he's straight. Married to his childhood sweetheart, and has a couple of kids. All that camp theatricality—it's mostly an act. He told me once that the way to get on in the media is to be larger than life, wave your arms around a lot and be unthreateningly eccentric. Back in the early 1990s when he started it, he said, being a straight white male made it hard to get on in TV. He couldn't change the "white" and the "male", but he said the "straight" was up for negotiation!'

Malcolm gave half a smile. 'Is he a problem for us?'

'Probably not,' said Malik. 'I've always had a soft spot for him, but Juliet is still very suspicious. She forced Miles Campbell to sideline him in the frozen north, where it seems he's behaving himself. She wanted more of an example to be made of him.'

'What do you make of him, Danny?' asked Morton.

'I've always thought he's a great communicator, a great interviewer in particular. By playing to the gallery and being a bit off-the-wall, he could always put someone at their ease and egg them on to say more than they really want to. I always liked him, to tell the truth, quite fun to be with. He's quite a snob about art and music and literature and all that: a touch elitist. But he's shallow—a bit of a hollow man. No deep convictions, for us or against us. He wanted to ride the green bandwagon, but only until the next bandwagon came along. He's a shit-stirrer, and that's what made him a problem. But so as long as he's not in a position to stir the shit there's nothing to worry about.'

'I just thought he was a pillock,' said Morton. 'Someone needs to keep an eye on his work, make sure he toes the line, OK? We don't want his kind coming out of the woodwork to fan the flames of dissent. This is a critical time, and how we manage the media is crucial to the success of the Revolution.'

●●

Sam Sharma's second visit to the Pollution Tribunal was not so comfortable. He went into it, he believed, with the weight of public opinion behind him. Messages of support had come from all over the country. But as the proceedings unfolded, he felt the ground shifting beneath his feet.

The Tribunal Panel was clearly very angry. The President of the Panel asked him what new evidence he had to offer to justify his non-compliance with the previous order. He had none, but started to justify himself on general principles. The President interrupted him, and challenged him to explain why he refused to pay the fine.

'The £200 fine, sir, is completely out of order. I'm an honest man, and I pay my taxes. To my mind, I'm being fined because the local council is failin' to provide a proper service. They've got a duty to clear the rubbish. And that's that. There's no way they should be sneakin' around spyin' on honest citizens to force 'em to put their rubbish out this way rather'n that way. It's an infringement of my rights. I'll take this all the way if need be, all the way to the European Court of Human Rights. And I hope you guys are prepared for the costs they're gonna award against you!'

His family and friends in the public gallery had been cheering him throughout his short speech. Now they stood and applauded. The President of the Tribunal looked over his reading glasses at the public gallery, then at Sam. Then he conferred with his colleagues for a few moments while calm was restored.

He coughed twice, then pronounced the Panel's verdict. 'Mr Sharma. It seems that you have learned nothing from your Awareness classes, and are determined to persist in your obstinate defiance of the local recycling regulations. You make it sound like these are some illegal imposition on you and your fellow citizens. They are not. The regulations are properly constituted, and have the full force of the law behind them. They are sanctioned by the democratically elected local council, and the democratically elected Parliament of this nation. You seem to see yourself as above the law, and the views and opinions of the majority of your fellow citizens as being of no account. And Mr Sharma, I must say I can't understand your resistance to something so simple as separating your waste into different containers for recycling. I do it. My wife does it. My grandchildren do it. Yet you seem to think it beneath you to do this?

'By the powers vested in this Tribunal by the Camden & Islington Earth Council, we hereby impose an additional penalty of £5000, to be paid to this court within seven days. We also feel you to be in need of further development of your environmental—and social—awareness. After completion of your short course at the local college, you will report to the newly established West Highland Eco-College when it opens at the beginning of next month. There you will carry out community service for six weeks on appropriate environmental projects to be determined by the college's management. If you complete this programme successfully, and this Tribunal receives a good report of your progress, the fine will be commuted to £2,500, with the balance of £2,500 returned to you. Next case!'

For maybe only the second time in his life, Sam Sharma was dumb-struck. A Tribunal official and a police officer came to lead him away. As it sunk in, he turned and shouted at the Panel, 'You can't do this! You can't do this! You'll regret this! I've got a business to run! I'll bloody 'ave you, I will!'

His wife and sons rushed forward to comfort and calm him, and the next minute he was enveloped in a tangle of journalists and photographers who wanted to catch the drama of his reaction to the verdicts.

For the Tribunals, this was only the beginning. Across the country business owners, bus companies, lorry drivers, council leaders and warring neighbours found themselves brought before the Tribunals, and many were sentenced to fines or community service in the eco-colleges. So when Sam, after rejecting the option of fleeing the country, reported for transportation to the eco-college, he was not alone. Along with him were representatives of all trades and classes, including the editor of the *Evening News*. Then Sam realised he may have got off lightly. Philips had been given eight months at the eco-college, and his newspaper fined half a million pounds.

'So you didn't sort your rubbish into different sections either, then?' Sam asked him.

'I leave that to the sub-editors,' Philips replied drily.

24: A future with teeth

'Well, it seems your green future has teeth,' said Heather Kitson, as she put down her newspaper on top of the others that her husband had been trawling through over breakfast.

'It would seem so,' Peter mumbled, still absorbed in the edition he was scanning.

'A touch illiberal, hauling all these people off to work camps in the Highlands and Islands, and the wilds of Wales, don't you think?' Heather asked.

'The Tribunals mean business. But you know, some people volunteer for that kind of work.'

'Are you volunteering, honey?'

'Not at the moment. Got a country to run!'

'What does Joanna think of this? Has she launched a crusade to rescue Sam Sharma?'

'Oh, please spare me Joanna's crusades!' said Peter, looking up at last. 'She hasn't said anything about the Sharma case, but she's on at me every day about Mohammed Iqbal. Seems to think I can do something.'

'But you have the ear of important people... you are important people!' Heather offered.

'I guess so. I have mentioned it to Morton. More than once. He says he's looking into it. Do you know, I think he doesn't actually know where Iqbal is. It seems to worry him a bit—I think he wants to get the security forces under firmer control.'

'Maybe that's not such a bad idea. It seems they've become a bit of a law unto themselves. I agree with Joanna—they need reining in. Do you think your friend Morton is up to it?'

Peter thought for a moment. 'Having seen him at close quarters, I'd say he's a formidable party manager. Now he and Doug Cunningham seem to be imposing some discipline on the maverick fringe too. But I'm not sure if he's up to controlling the professionals who've been giving politicians the run-around for years—the civil service, I mean! But it's our own fault.'

'Our fault?'

'Politicians, I mean. We've given the security services more and more power, and then get alarmed when they go and use it.'

'And what can you do about it?'

'Me?' asked Peter, as if the idea surprised him. 'At the moment we Liberals can only investigate and lobby. But once we get stronger, we can get more influence in this area. I mean, we've gained a lot of influence in some areas, but the GEM seems to want to dominate home affairs.'

'You mean, they want to run the country...' Heather smiled.

'It would be a surprise if they didn't. But I'm not sure they can do it. And when they start to struggle, we need to be in a position to assume control.'

'You sound like Howard, or Evan,' said Heather.

'There's a difference, though,' said Peter. 'Howard expects them to fail on all fronts. I want them to make real progress, working with us, on the environmental front. That's why I can put up with the Tribunals and the Scrutiny Commissions. They do some odd things sometimes, and can be a bit harsh—but it's clear people are changing their ways faster because of them.'

Heather looked long and hard at her husband. High office was changing him. She knew that in opposition he would have condemned any 'illiberal' measures out of hand. Yet now he talked glibly about 'the irresponsibility of opposition'. In government, he said, there is a duty to get things done. In opposition you can always find fault: it's so much easier to be destructive than constructive.

And he was so absorbed in his work. Now he spent more time with his officials and with Dave Barrington than with his own family, Heather had complained. It seemed to her that Peter felt he had the hand of history upon him, and that he was determined to produce lasting achievements. Well, so politicians should. But it seemed he was getting too carried away, that's all.

Still, he was proving to be an excellent father. Despite his longer working days, he couldn't wait to get home to see Andrea, and liked to bath her, feed her and play with her before bedtime. And sometimes it seemed, he just wanted to hold her for the sheer pleasure of holding his child in his arms. And when she saw this, all Heather wanted to do was to pack their bags and move away to somewhere where they could live a happy family life, away from all the politics, away from all this intensity and ambition.

But she knew it couldn't be so—at least not yet. She had supported Peter every inch of the way in fulfilling his ambitions, and she knew he could never be happy, never completely be himself outside the world of politics.

Heather loved Peter for his honesty and, as she saw it, his simplicity. She had had a couple of relationships with more worldly and sophisticated men before she met Peter. They had been much more adept than Peter at weighing up other people's motivations, game plans and weaknesses. They could outmanoeuvre and manipulate people in ways that would never occur to her husband. She felt there was a shallowness in their approach to life, a lack of steady commitment to anything except their own interests, and that undermined their close relationships.

Peter, on the other hand, tended to believe in the basic goodness of people. Sure, he knew there were rogues and egomaniacs out there—especially in the political world—but it was always his first instinct to take people at face value and believe in their good will until proved to the contrary. Some politicians always feel their opponents must be bad people. Peter would just think they were to some degree mistaken.

And he never seemed to see through people whose opinions matched with his own; never suspected they might have other agendas. Like Sandy Honeyford, for instance. Peter projected his own innocence onto other people, that was his failing. Like many failings, it was a good trait carried to extreme.

'Peter,' said Heather, 'I think you should listen to Joanna more. She should be your conscience, your little Jiminy Cricket sitting on your shoulder reminding you of your real self in the face of all this temptation...'

'What, now I've become a "real boy"?' laughed Peter.

'I'm trying to be helpful, honey,' protested Heather, smiling.

'I know, but I'm surprised. I thought Joanna bores you when she witters on endlessly about her cases and civil liberties and all that?'

'Yes—well it's true, but isn't that my failing not hers? She's not wrong, is she? She's your sister, and I'm really close to her too. Well maybe that's beside the point, but we always agreed with her before, and I'd hate to see you two sliding into different camps. See if you can help her out, yes? Don't just accept what your new GEM colleagues tell you they are doing without checking it out. And—just don't forget who you are!'

Peter looked across at Heather affectionately. They used to talk together for hours, putting the world to rights, but lately it had been different. No less affectionate, but their lives had been devolving into separate worlds.

'I don't think I need Joanna whispering in my ear, when I've got you,' said Peter, smiling.

The phone rang. It was Sandy. It seemed a crisis was brewing up in Parliament, and Peter ought to be there. He drank his tea quickly, kissed Heather and Andrea each on the forehead, and left.

25: Ins and outs

Peter Kitson conferenced with Sandy, Howard, Terry and Evan Roberts as the taxi took him to Westminster. He knew the background to the issue. The Scrutiny Commission for Parliament, ESCOPARL, wanted to include the running and working practices of the political parties within its field of scrutiny. Baxter's Conservatives and Leadbetter's Labour Party were trenchantly against this. They were calling it 'an attack on democracy' for a government agency to interfere in the running of opposition parties. Now they were threatening to walk out of Parliament if ESCOPARL persisted.

Evan, as the Liberal Democrat's Chief Whip, had taken soundings from his own MPs about what to do in the current crisis. A comfortable majority felt it was right to support the government line, but that left a significant minority wanting to work with the old 'grey' parties and make a stand against external interference in party matters. Evan was one of these. He put his viewpoint across forcefully.

'Guys, I think we're sleepwalking to disaster if we simply back Mason and his crew on this. Firstly, I think it's the thin end of the wedge. OK, it doesn't look so terrible in itself, but once we accept this principle that the Scrutiny Commissions, Earth Councils or whoever can meddle in our affairs, what next? Believe me, once Morton has his knife into you, he'll start twisting. And secondly, think of the numbers! If Baxter and Leadbetter keep their people out like they say they will, our position is much weaker. Mason will in effect have an absolute majority. And if he wants to keep up the image of a broad coalition, he could do a deal with one of the smaller groups–so-called Green Labour, or a combination of nationalist groups. Don't you see?'

'So what are you saying,' asked Peter impatiently, 'that we leave the government, and boycott Parliament? On this feeble issue?' Peter suspected that Evan's agenda was as much personal as political.

'Not necessarily. If Mason knows we could side with the opposition, they'll moderate their proposal. That could keep the other parties in Parliament, and maintain unity in our party.'

'Or not,' interrupted Sandy. 'The other parties want to bring this government down. If they can't make a crisis out of this issue, it will be another.

We are part of the government now, and we've got to act like it. We can't always be seeking our moment to bring them down. Or maybe that's what you want, Evan?'

'You know my view, Sandy,' Evan replied. 'You know what I've always said, "Don't get into bed with the enemy". It's as true now as it's ever been.'

Now Terry added his views. 'The problem is, Evan, that we've never at any time argued against this work by the Scrutiny Commission. I think ES-COPARL—and I hate these stupid names, by the way—has actually been doing quite a good and responsible job. It's got everyone thinking about how they do their work, and it's really helping the modernising of government. And about time too! We can't just leap around from issue to issue seeking tactical advantage. I have my reservations about some of the things Mason and his lot come up with. But I think we can support the best and moderate the worst—'

'Not if we don't have any leverage, we can't,' countered Evan. 'Howard?'

'Well,' said Howard slowly, once again appearing more indecisive than he normally was, 'I tend to agree that this is the wrong issue for a fight. And besides—we've only been part of the government for sixth months. We've hardly started to do anything, as yet. I think, Evan, you should work on bringing that ten per cent of dissidents in the party round to our view. Peter, what do you think, or need I ask? Peter?'

Peter Kitson was still on the other side of the river near Vauxhall. His taxi had become stuck in traffic and a sea of people. 'Can you hold on a minute? I'm just getting out of the taxi...' he said. 'We can keep the conference going as I walk...'

'He's getting out of the taxi..?' asked Sandy, puzzled.

'He probably thinks he can walk across the bloody water,' muttered Evan, loudly enough for the others to hear. Howard let out a muffled laugh.

On the way in to the centre of London, Peter had been noticing a visible difference in his surroundings. After the mild but wet winter, it was now a baking hot day in late spring. He had always loved London, and took pleasure in seeing all the different sides of it. Now he realised how things had been changing over the past ten months or so since the first Earth Councils had been set up. People were taking possession of the places they lived in, and had been transforming them. They were cleaner and brighter; there was new planting everywhere; many more 'home zones' had been created where pedestrians had priority over cars; everywhere there were people working with the Green Volunteers to 'make a difference'. Everywhere people were on bicycles, and a using a range of other bicycle-based contraptions: tandems, tricycles, cycle rickshaws, bikes pulling buggies, bikes pulling carts with shopping in—the London streets were starting to look more than a little Dutch.

As Peter got out of the car to investigate the cause of the hold up, he activated the camera in his phone and invited his conferencing colleagues to see what he saw. His journey to Parliament had become bogged down in a kind of street party. An area of long derelict land, one that Peter had often passed on his way into Westminster, had been 'reclaimed' by the community. A band was playing, and some people were swaying to the music as they drank wine from biodegradable cups. Others were taking turns at digging over the land, while others were consulting plans about the landscaping and planting.

'What are you planting here?' Peter asked a bystander.

'Oh, it's going to be a mix—we've got a fair bit of land here. Some is going to be landscaped as a toddlers' play area, then there's bit for some flowers—but also a place for a local co-op to grow some fruit and veg. And a communal herb garden, for…hey, aren't you…aren't you…'

He hesitated as he recognised Peter. 'Hey everyone, we've got a government Minister come to visit us!'

People rapidly turned to see Peter, and recognised him at once from the TV. People came rushing towards him, and some broke into applause, thanking him for coming to see what they were doing. Peter motioned to his police bodyguard that this was fine. Someone pressed a cup of home-brewed beer into his hand. As people pressed closer to talk to him, he held up his phone and said:

'I've got a few other people on the line here, and I was just showing them what you're doing here. When I say a few other people, I mean a couple of other members of the government, MPs, people like that…'

The people crowding around him laughed.

'In fact we were just talking about some of the great things that are going on at the moment, and I think what you're doing here is bloody amazing, actually. People are just getting up, getting out, working together and transforming the country. It's great! Here's to your success and a fruitful year ahead!'

He raised his cup of beer to toast them. The crowd followed suit and then everyone clapped and cheered. Though they pressed him to stay, he said he had to go.

'I'm afraid I've got to help sort out some crisis in the House. Apparently there's a bunch of politicians making asses of themselves over there while you folk here are doing all the donkey work!'

He looked around and saw that the taxi was still stuck in the melee.

'Can someone lend me a bike?' he asked.

While he was talking to the crowds, his colleagues saw a shaky video stream of the digging party. Sandy rammed home the point for him.

'There's still a lot of momentum in the Green Revolution, Evan. It would be suicide to turn against it now. You said it would be over within three months or so. Well, it isn't. If we jump ship now and snuggle up to Baxter, we'll be defining ourselves as forever "Grey". We can't do that. We don't want to do that. And we'll be betraying a lot of people if we do.'

The decision was taken to keep supporting the government. All Evan could bring himself to say was, 'Well, I hope Golden Boy remembers to pay the taxi driver. The last thing we want is bad press about being cavalier towards the working classes!'

••

The vote was taken, and the government won it easily. Baxter and Leadbetter led most of their MPs out of the House of Commons, moving into offices on the other side of the river. The 'South Bank Secession' had begun, with the parties there proclaiming themselves to be the protectors of the true traditions of Parliament.

Meanwhile MPs met in groups all across the House to discuss the significance of the events that had just taken place. Gabriella Pearson had collared Terry Cairns and Peter Kitson in the Terrace Bar, clearly excited by the drama that had unfolded. Gabriella, as the Animalist leader in the National Convention, was a regular guest in Parliament.

'They're such a shower, that lot! What have they got to be afraid of?'

'Nothing much, I would think, apart from GEM sympathisers poking around amongst their list of shady donors, perhaps! Or else it's a matter of democratic principle,' Terry replied.

'Pfaaw!' Gabriella exclaimed. Terry discretely wiped Gabriella's spittle from his chin, and checked to see if there were any ripples in his beer glass.

'They just don't get it, do they?' she continued loudly. 'Politics has changed forever. The fact is we have some new fundamental principles incorporated in the constitution. Protecting the environment is non-negotiable. If you don't like it, tough.'

'I think they've twigged politics has changed,' said Terry. 'We seem to be living in an age of multiple parliaments—you've got your one in the Convention up the road, so why can't they have one of their own over the river?'

Gabriella guffawed, and was about to respond when Malcolm Morton came into the Commons bar, evidently looking for someone. Catching sight of Peter, he nodded and came over to him.

'Hi Peter. Gabriella, Terry. Do you mind if I borrow Peter for a moment?'

Peter got up and walked with Malcolm a few steps away.

'Everything OK?' asked Peter.

'Yes, fine,' Morton replied. 'I've got some news for your sister about the Iqbal case, actually.'

'Good news?'

'Well, yes it is. Could you ask her to come across and meet with us, as soon as she can?'

Peter called Joanna straight away, and within half an hour Joanna, Mrs Iqbal and Peter were in Morton's secretary's office. Then they were called in.

As they went through the inner door, they could see there were two other people in there with Morton. One was Don Mason. The other was Mohammed Iqbal.

'My God!' exclaimed Joanna Kitson softly, as soon as she saw her client—a client she had only ever met once before despite fighting his case for seven years.

Mrs Iqbal was also praising God, and tears cascaded down her face as she saw her husband and then clung to him as if she would never let him go. Soon tears were streaming down Mohammed's face too. Between soft words of comfort and endearment to his wife he looked back and forth between Mason, Morton and the two Kitsons. Joanna, too, was wiping tears from her eyes. This had been the last thing she expected when she received Peter's call.

Eventually an emotional calm was restored, and the five of them took their seats. Morton sat behind his desk in the oak-panelled office, while the Iqbals and the Kitsons sat on the two sofas in the room. Don Mason pulled a chair over towards the sofas and sat there with them.

After a lot of smiling and polite words, Mason began to speak more formally.

'Mr Iqbal, Mrs Iqbal, I can only apologise to you for the suffering and anguish you have been through. It must have been a complete nightmare for you. I can't really begin to comprehend what you must have been through during these past seven years. I know we have been in government for some eight months now, and if we have seemed slow to act, then I am sorry for that too—'

'Please, please,' interrupted Mrs Iqbal. 'You have done something. You have ended this. That is the main thing!'

'And we have learned a lot from this,' Don continued. 'It took some prodding by your representative and her brother to get things moving. And quite frankly, I don't think we fully appreciated how these things worked until Malcolm really got his teeth into it. Even then, it was quite a process to track down where you were, and to get through the legal and security machinery to ensure your release. But I think we now have our finger on the pulse of all this—which will be good for future occasions, I'm sure.'

Having recovered her equilibrium, Joanna Kitson began to move back into professional mode, as the representative of Mohammed Iqbal.

'If I can get this straight, please, Mr Mason—'

'Please, feel free to call me 'Don'—'

'Don—can we assume now that all charges, all accusations against Mr Iqbal have now been dropped?'

'Completely,' said Don. 'One hundred per cent.'

'Actually,' Morton intervened, 'It seems there were never any substantive charges, or any substantive evidence, against Mr Iqbal.'

'Then why did they take him?' asked Mrs Iqbal, incredulously.

'Well, it seems to have been largely circumstantial evidence. A question of connections and associations,' explained Malcolm. 'Mr Iqbal seems to have had some connections with people being monitored for suspected terrorist activity. Most of it is very indirect. He communicated with people who communicated with people who were close to some people suspected of inciting terror. It is actually very thin, but I suppose if you're an intelligence officer you can convince yourself that putting together a lot of thin evidence makes thicker evidence, when actually it's forcing a case out of things that don't fit together at all.'

'What are you saying there, Malcolm?' asked Peter Kitson.

'Well, maybe I've said too much, but—in confidence—I think we've got a lot of work to do sorting out investigative techniques and priorities in the security services. But as you can see, we've made a start with your release, Mr Iqbal.'

Iqbal nodded thoughtfully, then broke into a beaming smile again as he looked at his wife and considered his freedom.

'So—you're admitting the government is at fault here? You're admitting liability?' asked Joanna.

Now Don Mason intervened. 'Well, Joanna, I think it's inevitable we will do. But we haven't entirely thought that through, as yet. And I'm sure you can understand that in this case "we" is not a straightforward concept. "We", that is the government that includes Malcolm, me and your brother, had nothing to do with arresting your client and moving him all around the country, and so forth. But then "we" as the head of the system have to bear some responsibility. I can tell you a couple of heads are already rolling for this. People who have repeatedly obstructed and frustrated Malcolm's investigation. Others may follow. And we're happy to compensate Mr Iqbal appropriately. I don't think we have a leg to stand on in regard to this case, so we'd rather not go the expense of any kind of legal case. I've asked the Attorney General to work this through with you and your client, if you're agreeable to this approach.'

Joanna looked stunned. It was as if everything she had been fighting for was coming to her in one fell swoop. Recovering her composure, she said:

'It sounds like I have something worthwhile to discuss with my client! There are though, a number of others…..'

Mason and Morton looked at each other. 'We know,' said Malcolm, 'and we're actively looking at them. I think Mr Iqbal—'

'Please, call me Mohammed!' urged Iqbal. 'I have had no friend to call me by my name for many years, you see!'

Malcolm smiled. 'Mohammed is the first of quite a few. There are some things to clear up, and actually there are a few people, it seems, who do have a case to answer. But we need to regularise their situation, don't you think? What I would like to do, though, is come up with an agreed approach about how we handle this. I think we can establish a lot of goodwill here, and it's best if neither side makes public statements that the other side might find hard to live with, or might jeopardise the process of releasing other detainees. What do you think?'

It was agreed. Clearly there would have to be media briefings, and the release of Mohammed Iqbal would be big news. Mason made it clear he did not want to try to claim credit for doing something that was long overdue: the government would issue a short statement and leave the limelight to the Iqbal family and their lawyer.

There were handshakes and warm words all round as everyone left Morton's office. Outside Joanna gave her brother a big hug.

'You know, I had almost stopped believing in you,' she said. 'And then, you come up trumps, as always. You've always looked out for me, haven't you?'

'And I always will,' he said, planting a brotherly kiss on her forehead.

••

When Peter caught up with Terry, he was back with Howard, Sandy and Evan at their favourite Westminster bar. Howard was on to his fifth pint, and the others were polishing off their second bottle of wine. Their police escorts sat at a neighbouring table, looking wryly on and enjoying a relaxing time, apart from the professional necessity of having to drink only coke and orange juice.

After being greeted somewhat rowdily, Peter told them about the release of Mohammed Iqbal. They were astounded and delighted, although the news put Evan into a pensive and political mood.

'What are they up to?' he asked softly, as if talking to himself. 'What are the bastards up to?'

'Oh, come on, Evan!' the others chorused.

'No, think about it,' he urged. His voice sounded conspiratorial. 'This is Malcolm Morton, who has proved himself to be the best political fixer since...since ... since I don't know who! There has to be a reason.'

'Yes, there is a reason,' said Peter. 'The guy's innocent. He shouldn't have been in prison. So Morton released him. End of story!'

'No, no, no, no, no. There's more to it than that. I'll bet they've done a poll, and have found their environmental policies are playing badly with the Asian communities. Well, we've found something like that too. We all know Asians are more concerned about the economy, about the business climate— and that's playing bad right now. I'll warrant this is a move to try and engage Asians more with the Green Revolution.'

'Evan! Stop stereotyping!' exclaimed Sandy.

'OK, OK, I'll prove my point. Hey Golden Boy!' he said, addressing Peter. 'How many Asians were there at your street party today? Not many, I bet!'

'Well, I didn't count...But the band was Asian. Kind of jazz with Middle-Eastern and Asian flavours. And the women organising the home produce co-op there are Asian.'

'Organic business, eh? So...inconclusive on theory number one,' said Evan, still in pensive mode.

'You know, I'm not too worried about his motives. Their policies are motivating people to do great things in their communities, and their latest policy it seems is to release innocent people from prison. These used to be our policies too, Evan, so let's be happy about it!' said Peter, slightly exasperated.

'Oh, they *are* suckering you, aren't they?' said Evan, raising his eyebrows. 'I can guarantee you would care about the motive if my theory number two is correct. OK, here it is. Theory number two: He wants to keep us sweet. Or more particularly, he wants to keep Peter sweet. Now why?'

'You tell us, Sherlock,' said Howard.

'I'm sure he will,' added Terry.

'This must be it!' Evan suddenly exclaimed, with a wild and mischievous look in his eye. 'You know, Morton's unmarried. Your sister's single...'

'Oh no!' everyone groaned.

'That's it, Peter! Malcolm Morton's got the hots for your sister!!'

He said this very loudly, causing many people in the bar to look round. Peter put a friendly hand on his shoulder, and urged him to calm down. Then Evan continued in a quieter conspiratorial voice:

'The question is, how can we use this?'

'I'm out of here!' laughed Peter, and left.

26: Keep it local, keep it healthy, keep it simple

It was a warm July afternoon. Rachel Dean's south London suburban garden was looking a picture. The delicate pink clematis that climbed up the bower over the patio was in full bloom, casting floral shadows on the white cotton baby clothes of Andrea Kitson, who rested snugly in Rachel's arms.

'Maybe we should go … ' suggested Heather. 'I don't think Mark—'

'No, no—he'd feel embarrassed later if he thinks he drove you away. Just leave him to it.'

Mark Dean had arrived home early from work, threw off his suit jacket and tie, poured a ferocious Scotch, drank it, poured another then headed upstairs with hardly a word to his wife or her guest. He emerged a few minutes later in shorts and T-shirt, and headed for the garage. Hauling out the motor mower, he began to mow the extensive lawn with a fierce determination. Heather had seen him fly off the handle before, but never look as black as this.

Rachel began to explain.

'Mark's really upset. He had to lay off some staff today. Fifteen of them. It's not something he's had to do since the very early days, when he started his first company. He's angry and wracked with guilt. When he went into work this morning, he was still trying to think of ways to avoid it. Obviously he couldn't find a way.'

'Shouldn't I just go, and you can talk to him and comfort him?'

'It's not his way. Me, I want to cry on someone's shoulder, or just hide in a darkened room. But Mark's not like that. If he gets angry or upset, he has to do something. Some mindless activity, he says, to get him quickly to the other side of the adrenalin curve. It's just his way. Then he'll talk about it. But he never wants comforting if he's feeling guilty about it. Just says he has to face up to what he's responsible for. And he thinks he's responsible for the livelihood of everyone he employs. Mind you, he's never been shy of sacking someone who isn't up to the job. But he recruited these people specially to expand the company. They all left good jobs to come and work for him. And now....'

'Is the company in trouble?'

'Yes. A bit, anyway. Mark says there's a new recession and it's beginning to bite. There's nothing coming from the private sector. No business confidence at all. Most of their remaining contracts are public sector—hospitals, government agencies, local government. But some of that is looking dodgy too. And they're such bad payers! Very bad news for the cash flow. It takes months to get any money out of them. Anyway, anyway... I love this sunhat Andrea's wearing! It's so sweet on her!'

Heather smiled. She never tired of hearing compliments about her baby. *She is my life and soul*, she thought, as one of her dreamy moments washed across her. Then she snapped to and thought about Mark and his problems. She watched him for a moment as he mowed the lawn.

'He does that very methodically, doesn't he?'

'Yes,' Rachel smiled. 'He always tries to make what he calls "Wembley stripes". You know most men fantasise about playing for England at Wembley, or scoring the winning goal in the Cup Final. Mark fantasises about being the groundsman!'

'Aren't you a stone's throw from Wimbledon here? Maybe he could help them out there!'

'No. Tennis courts are too small. In his dreams he needs something the size of a football pitch to express himself! What does Peter think about it—I mean the economy and all that?'

'We haven't talked much about it. He seems to think that the new environmental industries will more than make up for any problems, and will generate new opportunities. He's pretty upbeat about business confidence returning. But never mind these men. What do you think? You're a historian, what can we learn by experience?'

'Oh, ask me anything about the past, but don't ask me about the future! Like they say on your pension plan, "past performance is no guide to future performance"! But if you press me, I'd say that as long as we don't try to do too much too fast, it will be alright. No Great Leaps Forward—unless we all want to starve!'

'Yes, just tiny steps for mankind,' chipped in Mark, confusing his historical references as he poured himself some lemonade from the large jug on the wrought iron patio tables. 'And tiny steps for her too, eh? Or is it too soon? When do they start walking?'

'Mark! You ought to remember. How many children have we had?'

'Oh, God knows! Where are they, by the way?'

'At the Junior Volunteers, darling. Saving the planet.'

'I'm glad they're doing something useful. Not like you girls. Just sitting here chewing the fat.'

'Actually, Mark, we were talking about history, politics and economics. Not bad for two dippy mothers on a hot afternoon.'

'I heard, I heard,' said Mark, and a gloomy shadow seemed to return to his brow. 'The prospect really depresses me—the next few months, or years. I can't see the light at the end of the tunnel. Especially after my meetings with Dave Barrington and his strategists a few months back. If ideas were money, the country would be rich! But I can't see how their ideas will do anything but shrink the economy. I know what Peter talks about. But there's no way these new industries can create enough real value to keep the economy healthy. And it will take years before the investment in Dave Barrington's big projects will trickle through to benefit smaller suppliers. And reducing consumption? People are buying less all across Europe and America, and this is hitting every economy. Especially the Chinese economy. If that starts to stall again now, we're all in deep shit. Everything is interconnected these days. It's like that butterfly flapping its wings in our garden and causing a typhoon somewhere in the Pacific. Still, what can we do but ride it out?'

••

Economics was on the mind of Terry Cairns as well. He sat on the government's Economic Strategy Committee, along with amongst others Donald Mason, Sarah Turner, Ben Porter and Howard Blackstone. And this was what Mason called a 'milestone meeting'. A small team of civil servants, headed by Sir James Olsen, were in attendance. It was time to prepare to launch the new economic strategy in earnest. And Terry hadn't liked what he'd seen so far.

Don Mason was presenting the plans himself. Terry's face grew darker and darker as he heard Mason outline the GEM's proposals for 're-naturing' farming, creating quality products for a more discerning market. In a post-industrial age, Mason explained, the industrial approach to farming was no longer relevant.

'We subsidise large agricultural corporations to over-produce and to keep prices artificially low, while small farmers go to the wall. And in the name of "sustainability" we subsidise farmers to keep fields out of production. Every year we negotiate with producers and argue furiously with our European partners, all in an effort to tinker on the margins of an economically senseless system. And public money, our money channelled through Europe, supports intensive farming methods that wipe out wildlife and pollute the environment.

'The present system has emerged not from market forces, but in a market distorted by the monopoly power of the big supermarkets and by government policy and subsidies. So I have no qualms about trying to reshape the market, and returning power to smaller producers and to consumers. The key to our new proposals are: keep it local, keep it healthy, keep it simple.'

Sarah Turner went on to explain how the government would support the setting up of regional markets to help small producers to supply the supermarkets, and incentives and targets for the large retailers to supply from local sources. There would be incentives for organic farmers, and incentives and targets for retailers to switch to organic foods.

Sarah's face glowed as she outlined this programme. Finally she briefly discussed how this was only the beginning. Similar policies would be brought forward for non-food production.

All the while Mason and Turner talked, Terry Cairns was flicking backwards and forwards through the presentation slides and the pages of the supporting documents. Looking alternately at the screen through his reading glasses and then over the top of them at Mason and Turner, he became more and more uncomfortable with the generality of it all. The principles behind the policies he found enticing, but the more he listened, the more he became convinced they were not well thought out, and would probably be unworkable.

As Sarah Turner finished, Ben Porter leapt in with comments praising the initiative, saying how it had been a key plank of Green policy for many years, and how delighted he was to be part of a government bringing in these initiatives.

Terry felt otherwise.

'An ambitious and innovative programme, for sure,' he said. 'But to me, what I've just heard sounds more like a brochure than a plan of action. I mean, where are the numbers?'

Mason and Blackstone gave wry smiles, and Sarah Turner looked a little piqued.

'What I mean is: we are talking about subsidies, incentives, targets. How much? How and when will they be put in place? Basically, what I've just heard is high on politics, but low on economics. Someone needs to do a lot more work on this. And I think one of the key questions is, can the methods of production and distribution you're proposing compete on price? One thing the supermarkets do is squeeze the cost to the consumer right down. I mean, we have local shops and markets in most towns, but they can't compete on price for the most part. And they certainly can't deal with the volume that the big four supermarket chains do. So what are the projections about price increases?'

Sarah Turner looked very exasperated by the time he finished his questions.

'You know, Terry, you're so annoying! Sometimes I wonder why you're even in this government. You think we're not aware of the difficulties? And do you think the officials at the Treasury and at Food & Agriculture haven't been saying much the same thing? We're talking strategy here, but as always you're impatient for the details. We're working on that. And you can help too, by working on it. We've got some serious work to do on realigning the subsidies, and if you're onside you can be a great help with that. What do you say?'

Terry stroked his chin and pursed his lips thoughtfully, before continuing.

'Sure, I'm broadly onside with what you're aiming to achieve.'

'Terry, you keep on saying "you" and "what *you're* trying to achieve", and so on. Don't you think it ought to be "we"?' asked Don.

'OK, point taken,' said Terry. 'What I'm trying to say, is that it makes a difference whether what you—we—propose is workable or not. For that you need to know a fair amount of detail. It's quite possible to do some economic modelling, and create various scenarios that will give us an idea of the impact of different approaches. Do we have those?'

Mason and Turner now looked at each other. After a moment, Mason nodded.

'OK,' said Sarah. 'The economists have been doing some work…. But frankly we don't think what they're saying is entirely right. Their projections are too pessimistic.'

'Pessimistic?' asked Howard Blackstone, raising his eyebrows.

'Yes—in the sense that they haven't factored in all the range of new measures we are proposing. We don't have a level playing field at the moment, and they seem to assume that nothing substantial will change. On that basis, it will be very hard to make an impact.'

Ben Porter was very agitated. 'Why weren't we given all this information in advance? It would have been far more helpful! As it is, we are kind of discussing all this in the dark! Can we see the papers?'

Mason and Turner looked at each other again, and then Mason nodded to Sir James Olsen. One of his underlings then started working energetically on his touchscreen, and duly sent the relevant documents round to each of the participants in the meeting.

As the documents were being distributed, Sir James said, 'As you see, there's rather a lot of it. Some of it you have had before. But not all the modelling work or the treasury's evaluation of the impacts.'

Howard Blackstone sighed heavily. But it was Ben Porter who spoke.

'I think we need a break to consider all this, don't you? Not necessarily to read in depth, but to get the flavour of it.' They agreed to break for an hour.

'Before we break,' Mason said, 'I'd like you to think about something. We are a radical government, committed to innovation. This isn't only a matter of economics, it's a matter of will. The popular mood is with us. If ever there was a time to drive through changes in patterns of production and consumption, it's now. Sure, there are some challenges, big challenges. But if we let everything we try to do become bogged down by the conservatism of the economists and bureaucrats, we'll never get anywhere! We have to be bold—otherwise we might as well just pack our bags and go home. If you see obstacles, don't just tell me there are obstacles. Tell me the how to get over them!'

And throwing a sharp look at Terry Cairns, he got up and left the room.

27: Boscy's

'We need to talk,' said Don Mason to Terry Cairns the next day. 'How about lunch?'

'Fine,' said Terry.

'12.30 at Boscy's?' Boscy's was Don Mason's favourite restaurant, just off the Strand, serving high quality organic and vegetarian food.

'I'll be there.'

'Why don't you bring Sandy–I'll have Louise Adams come along. In case you need some numbers. There may be some actions we want to document from the meeting, so as well to keep our advisors in the loop.'

Terry liked Boscy's too. It had a very tasteful, relaxing atmosphere. As its name implied, there was plenty of greenery, and this was used to provide a degree of privacy for each group of diners. Through the middle ran a small stream, gently babbling over several sets of rocks and boulders, and down each side were a series of connected water features. Well-chilled jazz, provided either by musicians in the restaurant or through the sound system, reinforced the mellow atmosphere. Don's choice of venue for discussions with Terry indicated that that he wasn't looking for conflict. And the food there was something special. Perhaps Mason was trying to make a point about what his policies were designed to achieve. The food was also pretty expensive, even by London standards.

Terry was talking about his 'baptism' into organic meat. 'I can remember to this day my first taste of organic bacon. I was at a music festival, maybe thirty years ago. And there was a stall selling organic bacon sandwiches. And when I bit into it, it was like a moment of revelation. The taste took me right back to my childhood, when meat was meat and tasted like meat, and not like a factory product. I was hooked, and have been hooked ever since!'

Mason nodded and smiled.

'I had a similar experience. I think we're about the same age, and come from similar backgrounds. But what I'm not sure about is how much we share the same outlook, the same aspirations. That's why I wanted to talk to you, informally. So we can get to know each other a bit better, and understand where we're going. Sometimes when we're in Cabinet, or committee, I find you a little bit puzzling–what I'm saying is that I just want us to see eye to eye.'

'Sure, I think it's a good idea,' said Terry.

'Maybe you can start off by telling me a bit more about yourself—what brought you into politics, and what impelled you towards the greener wing of your party.'

And so Terry gave a potted version of his life history. How he'd worked for one of the top five consultancies, and then become a senior finance officer in a blue chip company. At this stage, he said, he only 'dabbled' in politics, but was involved with the local Friends of the Earth and got involved in campaigning to save ancient woodlands from development.

'I liked that practical side of things. And I met some really good people, who influenced me strongly. But on some of the big picture issues, I thought they were too ready to let their hearts rule their heads. It's right to have ideals. But we have to remember that ideals are aspirational. We can aspire to them, but may have to realise that they may be unattainable, or at least unattainable in the short term. There are some things we may be able to achieve at a personal level, but in terms of public policy they may be unachievable, or only partly achievable.'

Mason was nodding, and seemed genuinely interested.

'You're a pragmatist, and I understand that. I respect that. You want to achieve the achievable, and not be seduced by dreams. But you know, "what's achievable" is a matter of judgement, not a matter of fact. Louise here has been with us for a few years now. When I met her, and I said we could form a government in the near future, I think she thought I was mad. She was just too polite to say so.'

Louise Adams nodded and gave a beaming smile. She was a political assistant to Sarah Turner, but had a wider role advising the GEM group on business issues and the economy. With a degree in business and economics from Harvard, not to mention a very bright and sunny personality, she had had a mercurial rise in the ranks of the Green Earth Movement. She fixed her gaze on Terry as Don spoke, her smile subsiding into a kind of sultry pout as she rested her chin on her hand, with the rippling LED lighting shimmering on the waves of her long blonde hair.

'But now we are in government,' Mason continued. 'And Louise has helped achieve that, giving great support to Sarah in particular. The "unachievable" is often achievable, with hard work, discipline, and a strong focus. And you, Terry. You joined the smallest of the major parties, but presumably you always had a belief that the party could achieve something, and would edge forward to greater things. But most importantly, you believed that your outlook and ideology would benefit the country.'

There was nothing Terry could argue with here, and he was warming towards Don Mason a little more.

'It's all about where you set the bar. How high are your aspirations? You can set the bar low, and easily jump over it. Setting it higher will pose some challenges. And you'll have to take some risks.'

Terry noticed how Sandy was reacting to Don's little speech. She was nodding enthusiastically, and her eyes seemed to be glowing. Maybe the wine, he thought.

'I want your genuine opinion, Terry. Do you think we are setting the bar too high? Are we setting ourselves up for a fall with our localist policies and by pushing for much more self-sufficiency?'

'Well,' said Terry, 'at the risk of sounding like I'm trying to do the high jump with lead boots on, my concerns are rooted in some pretty basic economic principles. This is superb wine, isn't it? Well, it's a top-notch organic Australian wine. And we love it. And in principle, it could be possible to produce wines of this quality in the UK, under glass, using artificial sunlight and all that. But we don't. And we shouldn't. It would be local, for sure. But the cost would be too great. The energy and resource cost would be too great. And the cost to consumers would be too great. If locally produced things are the only choice, and they're more expensive than things transported from afar, then that has a wider impact on the economy. People don't have so much money to spend on other items.

'Now wine is an extreme example. But it applies to almost everything else. Tomatoes, wheat, beef, butter, nails, ladders, fridges, cars, software—you name it. The market will largely determine where it is most cost effective to produce it. If you say everything has to be produced locally, then you guarantee that many things are going to be produced inefficiently, using resources inefficiently, and costing much more—because they are being produced in the wrong place!

'When Sarah told me one time about how terrible it is that green beans are produced in Kenya and transported thousands of miles to us, she was talking like it's self-evidently wrong. But is it? African countries have been pressing us for years to make it easier to export to us. The fact is that they can produce them more efficiently, and we can only produce them more expensively. Let's follow through the process of how we actually make local production work. This is the challenge. First, we have to get people to buy the more expensive local beans. We can either persuade them, or we have to deny them access to the cheaper beans. And in our proposals, I don't see how we're going to do this. In fact, I can't see how it can be done—at least not in the short term. What's the answer?'

Mason was nodding thoughtfully. But it was Louise Adams who ventured a reply.

'I think you're right up to a point. But only if you're operating in a free market. And we're not really operating in one now. The choices presented through the supermarkets are very distorted ones, disadvantaging the organic producers. And the cost of transporting goods internationally is distorted by the lack of duty on aviation fuel. A key plank of what we want is for producers and distributors to pay the full environmental costs of what they do. Once we have these measures in place, it will mean a more level playing field.'

'So, what you're saying is, prices up across the board. Starting with food. Are we prepared for this?' asked Terry.

'Prepared—in what way?' asked Sandy.

'I mean, are we prepared for the economic impact of having everyone's monthly grocery bill increasing? And increasing by how much? Ten per cent, fifty per cent? It's not just the supermarkets that would take a hit, as people have to trim their total monthly spending on other items. That reduces the prospects of economic growth, and it means people out of work. Increased travel costs means a hit for the travel industry... Can you see why I keep asking for the numbers? An awful lot depends on the detail.'

Mason shrugged. 'I know you think we're all economically ignorant. But I'd say your liberal-economic approach is ecologically unrealistic. Wasn't it Einstein who said, "We can't solve our problems with the same thinking we used when we created them"? You seem to assume that more and more growth is the framework we have to operate in. But we're engaged in saving the planet, not helping people fill their lives with useless possessions—'

'But this is the crux,' interrupted Terry. 'People want to be prosperous. They want more. And they don't want the things they need and value to become more expensive. How can we keep people onside and at the same time reduce their standard of living?'

'It is the crux, isn't it, Terry? Your answer seems to be that it can't be done. But if you believe that, why are you sitting at the Cabinet table with us? You seem to want me to come up with the answers, and don't want to try to find them yourself. I can tell that your heart is with us, but your head won't let you believe. Why? Because you've absorbed too many traditional "grey" assumptions about how the world works—as if it can only work in these ways.'

'I don't know how we do it, Don,' said Sandy, intervening to prevent Terry making a possibly antagonistic response. 'What is your answer?'

'My answer? My answer is that it will indeed be difficult. But I am sure the way things are is not the way things have to be. I firmly, unshakeably believe that we have to reduce consumption. So what Terry says about a lack of economic growth doesn't worry me too much. But—and it's a big "but"—people will only be happy with this if what they have in the way of reduced consumption is of much higher quality. Like your first organic bacon sandwich, Terry! So part of our focus must be on improving quality. You know in Germany they have higher engineering standards than here? Most people think there are the same standards all over Europe. But in Germany for many goods, they have their own higher standards, above the European standards. People are prepared to pay more. And they expect to have engineered items that will last a lifetime. Here we are prepared to buy imported, cheap rubbish and hope it will last a year or two. Aldous Huxley said in the post-war years that the "Western economy is built on the twin pillars of built-in obsolescence and armaments". He was right. The role of armaments has reduced, but we've ever more addicted to waste!

'What we're talking about is achieving a whole culture change. Yes, fewer things will be consumed. Yes, they may cost a bit more. Or they may cost less, as we aim to incentivise people to grow their own food and make more of their own things. But either way there will be a new emphasis on quality, and satisfaction, and on valuing what you *have* rather than always wanting the next new thing, however worthless. We're talking about a transitional process. And it's much more complex than your traditional outlook can deal with. Let's take your beans. I'll bet ten pounds that your parents and grandparents did what my parents and grandparents did—they grew their own vegetables. They didn't go into Sainsbury and pay £2 for imported vegetables all wrapped up in plastic—they grew their own. At practically zero cost. So when we talk about increased prices, this can be balanced by reducing other costs.'

'I've been working on projections that factor in various levels of home production, as well as the cost impact of localised production,' said Louise.

'I'd like to look at what you've got,' said Terry. Sandy raised an eyebrow at Terry.

'You know, Terry,' said Mason, 'I'd really like you onside in this process. I know you have your doubts. Here's the rub: I don't think a "light green" version will work. All that will happen is that localised and organic production will become a niche for the wealthy. Like Boscy's. We've all got immense respect for your knowledge and abilities. And Sarah needs help in dealing with the conservatism and obstruction of the civil servants. Can you help us? I think it would be such a shame if you put yourself on the side-lines trying to pick holes in what we do.'

Terry leaned back in his seat, and looked up to the ceiling before replying. He noticed that the ceiling was a screen of the sky, complete with slowly moving clouds and birds flying overhead. And he felt that the wine was beginning to get to him. He looked across at Mason, then at Louise and Sandy. He noticed that they were two very attractive women.

'I'm part of your government, Don,' he said at last. 'Point me in the right direction, and I'll see what I can do to find a way through.'

••

What had happened? Terry was struggling to remember. His head hurt. A very liquid lunch at which he'd agreed to help Mason somehow. He remembered how the lunch had continued very convivially, chatting away to Mason, then Louise, and finding lots of interests in common with her. And Sandy and Mason hitting it off well too. Then in the afternoon sitting through a meeting on something-or-other, probably with a glazed expression on his face. And then? Had he really asked a woman more than twenty years younger than him out to a club? And had they really ended up back at his place?

Now she was gone, but she had left behind a pot of coffee and a very sweet note beside it. He looked at it and smiled. He thought, with a pang of guilt, about his intermittent partner back home in his constituency. A kind of on-off relationship-of-convenience in which he had found some comfort since his wife passed away some ten years before.

'Talk about sleeping with the enemy,' he thought. 'This really complicates things.' But then he smiled as he thought about Louise. For the first time in about ten years, he felt a spark of happiness within himself, even if he felt deep inside that such happiness could not last for long.

28: Old and new loyalties

By the end of the year Sandy Honeyford and Martin Lang were quite definitely an item, though possibly not quite a couple. The problem was they were just both so busy. Martin was now the leading figure and driving force in ESCOLAW. What had begun as environmental audits had now transformed into a full-scale attempt to drag the judiciary and legal professions kicking and screaming into the twenty-first century.

He was meeting some determined opposition. Outright in-your-face opposition is relatively easy to deal with. But the British establishment, Martin found, does not work like that—or only does when it comes in for the kill. Mostly it works by stubborn inertia, and by skilfully manoeuvring to undermine one's position. He could feel the knives in his back, as well as the ground shifting under his feet. But at the same time, he had the ear of the government, and had been given a position where he could exert great pressure on senior figures, including the ailing Lord Chancellor. Lord Denby was a politically neutral figure, brought in by the previous government and diplomatically left in place by the Mason government until one of their own people could be installed. Martin Lang cherished hopes that he could be Denby's successor.

Sandy too was exceedingly busy. And tonight she had some special news she wanted to discuss with Martin. Don Mason had offered her a special political role coordinating strategy preparation between the parties in the coalition government.

'Well, Martin, what shall I do? It's a fascinating offer!' said Sandy, as she leaned into him on the sofa in his apartment, sipping her white wine.

Martin nodded thoughtfully. 'Fascinating indeed. Are you going to take it?'

She looked up into his face, and smiled. 'I was asking for your advice. I'm not sure.'

'What is there to be not sure about?'

Now Sandy sat up straighter, and leaned a little way from him, looking him in the eye. 'Are you serious?' she asked.

'Go on.'

'It's about Peter, and Howard and Terry—and everybody else, of course! How can I betray them?'

'Is it betrayal?'

208

'Of course it is! Or kind of. I know I'll still be working with them. It's just that I won't exclusively have their interests at heart. And damn it, I'm a Liberal, and always have been. And a green-tinged Liberal at that! How can I abandon my convictions and work for the enemy!'

'Are they the enemy, then?'

'Well, they're our partners at the moment. But they weren't. And in the future they might not be again. Where would that put me?'

'Maybe the question is, where do you want to put yourself?' suggested Martin.

'For Christ's sake, Martin,' snapped Sandy, 'stop giving me the Socrates treatment and just tell me what you think!'

'OK, OK,' said Martin. 'You haven't told me much about the job, but what I think, off the top of my head, is this. Yes, it's a good opportunity. But— if I can ask another question—what's in it for Mason, apart from having a very talented and beautiful advisor by his side?'

'Very smooth, I'm sure,' said Sandy, smiling. 'What Don says he wants is for the coalition to work more seamlessly. It seems to him that every time they bring forward something new, it causes a fight in the Cabinet. Usually it's Terry or Ben Porter who reacts badly. They feel like they're always being caught on the hop, and have to make decisions without enough information and without enough time to think about it. What? Why are you looking at me like that? OK, what do you think his motives are?'

'Actually,' said Martin looking a little puzzled, 'I can't quite work it out. It seems a little naïve on the face of it. I mean, to ask a political advisor from another party to take on this role. One would expect such a person always to be running back to their old friends with state secrets...'

'Unless he trusts me?'

'Or thinks he's turned your head enough to become his faithful new disciple. Has he?'

'No more than you, I wouldn't think!'

'You think he's turned my head?'

'Isn't he your new guru?' asked Sandy teasingly.

Martin shook his head with a grin, and reached for the wine. 'You know what I say, honey. I'm in their world, but not of their world. It's the only way of keeping focus, and keeping your head from being turned.'

'And what are you focusing on, Martin?'

'Achievement. And the high position that comes with it.'

'I don't believe you're so cynical. You believe in what you're doing.'

'Hm, maybe. But I keep my eyes open. It's their game at the moment, but in the course of a lifetime it won't be the only game. The same applies to you and your Liberal friends. They're not the only show in town, even if they are the ones you've been most comfortable with up till now.'

'It's not just a question of comfort,' Sandy protested. 'It's friendship, shared ideas, shared history. Damn it, I was virtually born a Liberal, what with my mother taking me everywhere on her campaigning. It was natural I fell into this role. And it feels like home!'

'But ambitious girls like you don't get where they are by staying at home. We're both ambitious—that's why we're good together. I think you're more idealistic than me. You know, the higher you rise, the more chance you'll have to put your ideals into practice.'

'I get the feeling from the tone in your voice that there's another "but" coming.'

'Well, I'm still trying to understand Mason's motivation. One thing I've learned this past year is not to underestimate them. Your friends Howard and Evan have. They thought it would all be over by Christmas last year, and everything would be back to normal. But these Green Earth guys are shrewd operators, and in their own inexperienced way, they're quite cunning.'

'You think so?'

'If you accept the post, what has he done? He's successfully detached you from Peter Kitson's group. From what you've told me, you've played quite a key role in keeping them all together.'

'You flatter me.'

'And also, you know where they're coming from. Whether you mean to or not, you're bound to provide insights into their way of thinking, their strategies and so on.'

'Sure. That's why I'm worried about betrayal.'

'But maybe it works the other way. By getting closer to you, maybe you can be an avenue for him to influence them more.'

'Naturally. You know there's all this "greening" of everything going on—well, of course you do, you're doing it to all those stuffy lawyers. I think it's not just a question of getting the parties in the cabinet working together. I think the GEM want to suck them in ever closer. You know, the word they use a lot these days is "harmonise". Everything and everyone is going to be "harmonised" with the Green Earth principles. It seems like Don may want to integrate those he sees as genuine green-thinkers, and divide them more from the grey-thinkers. You know, Don's been making great efforts with Terry Cairns, to clear up misunderstandings and draw him closer ...'

Sandy trailed off, as a new train of thought developed. A mischievous gleam lit up in her eyes. 'You'll never guess the rumours flying around about Terry?'

'Terry?'

'Yes, it seems Terry's been casting off his grumpy old mentor image and is having a fling with Louise Adams—one of Sarah Turner's advisers!'

Martin looked impressed. 'Wow, she's kind of hot, isn't she?'

Sandy whacked him with a cushion. 'Hot? What do you mean hot? When have you seen her?'

'Well, she's nowhere near as hot as you, of course! I've seen her on TV. And she was at a reception, once, at the US embassy. A Supreme Court judge was there, you know, Lewis, and he wanted to meet some of us English legal eagles and chat about how we're modernising the legal system here.'

'Lewis—that old reactionary? You were hobnobbing with him?'

'Actually, he's quite a moderniser, even though his views are a touch... traditional.'

'Downright illiberal.'

'American. They're not the same as us. Anyway, tell me more about Terry and his cute girlfriend.'

'Nothing more to tell, really. Except I was there with him when they hit it off. At Boscy's. Terry and Louise, and me and Don...'

'Terry and Louise, you and Don—this does get interesting. Did the Prime Minister hit on you?'

'Of course not. But the next best thing—he obviously took to me, because he offered me this job.'

'Hm. What was Terry's chat-up line: did he ask her to show him her numbers?'

'Yep, kind of!' laughed Sandy.

The doorbell rang. Sandy's face fell, and she flopped back into the sofa. It would be Joanna Kitson. Martin had said she would be calling round: some ESCOLAW business. And she had some other things on her mind too that she wanted to share with Martin.

Sandy had known Joanna for many years now, and had always been quite friendly, though never the best of friends. It was devotion to Peter that had been the bond. But such bonds can also breed a certain unstated rivalry. Now perhaps that rivalry was shifting its centre to Martin.

Sandy knew that Martin had previously been close to Joanna, infatuated even. Or more. Now he seemed very happy with his relationship with Sandy. Yet Sandy always felt unsettled when Joanna joined them. Something changed in Martin, almost imperceptibly, but there all the same. His expressions were different. His touch was lighter, and his affection seemed a little restrained. Maybe he still had strong feelings for Joanna. And Sandy had always felt Joanna was somehow a bit more classy than her, with her Oxbridge background, natural good looks and easy professionalism.

She heard Martin and Joanna kissing in the hall as she entered, then Joanna came through and embraced Sandy in the same breathless, affectionate way. They chatted and gossiped, and when the shop-talk about ESCOLAW became too impenetrable, Sandy went through to the kitchen to throw together the light meal they would share.

'God, I wish I could do this, Sandy,' said Joanna between hungry mouthfuls of lasagne. 'All I seem to eat these days are shop-bought sandwiches and instant noodles. This is so delicious! By the way, have you heard from Peter?'

Sandy nodded. 'Yes, we had a conference with him today. He seems to love Reykjavik. All that green energy production. I think it was turning him green with envy, actually!'

Peter Kitson was on a tour that would take in Iceland, then the Scandinavian countries, before meeting with European Energy Ministers in Luxembourg. They chatted easily about his tour, about the foibles of some of the European politicians he would meet, then about Heather and Andrea. Martin noticed how everyone always spoke about Peter with a kind of protective affection. He wondered about how a man could become so likeable. As he listened to Sandy, he understood more the challenge of split loyalties posed by the job offer from Mason.

Finally as they finished their tiramisu and moved onto coffee, Martin asked Joanna about the problems she wanted to talk about.

'Oh, I decided maybe I shouldn't bore you with them,' she said.

That's never stopped you before, Sandy thought to herself.

Before long, though, Joanna was talking about her new difficult civil rights cases. Kelly Sharma and several other people had come to her on the back of the reputation she had gained from the Mohammed Iqbal case. And they wanted help with their 'disappeared' relatives—all of whom had been arrested or detained since the new government came to power.

'I thought Sam Sharma was out and about again,' said Martin.

'He was,' said Joanna. 'And now he's back in. We think he's in one of the new eco-camps, you know the eco-colleges as was, only with some tough love. But it still seems a little chaotic. No one knows exactly where. Unless, of course, like Mohammed he's being passed from pillar to post amongst the security services ... '

'Do you think Malcolm can help out this time?' Sandy asked.

Joanna noted Sandy's referring to Morton in this familiar way. Peter's colleagues had always tended to speak of the GEM leadership by their full names or surnames only. It seemed a new closeness might be developing between the leading figures in the two parties—or perhaps Sandy might be name-dropping.

'I have asked him,' Joanna replied. 'Well, I've tried to contact him and left several messages.'

'Last time he came up trumps, didn't he, even though it seemed Peter was getting nowhere with him?' suggested Sandy encouragingly.

'That's true,' said Joanna, 'but isn't this a little different? I mean, this time it's Malcolm's own people who are responsible, or so it seems.'

Sandy looked nettled, but it was Martin who answered her. 'We don't know that, Jo, do we? Or even if it is his people who are responsible, you know how these things work. Often the people at the top aren't really in control. They spend all their time reacting to situations created by their underlings.'

Joanna looked thoughtful, and troubled. 'I hope you're right—both of you. But the rate of new detentions is worrying me, whoever is ultimately responsible. It's impossible to get the full picture yet, but it seems the Tribunals are sending off more and more people each week for re-education at the camps.'

'What kind of numbers are we talking about?' asked Martin

'Well, some Tribunals are much more active than others. I've got my researchers working on trying to build up a full picture. But in the past three months, it seems they've each been sending off an average of about five a week. Multiply that across the country, and you'll get an idea of the scale. Around five hundred active Tribunals, each having sent off about sixty people in the past three months—that's thirty thousand people. Can you believe that?'

'Whoa,' said Sandy, 'hold on a minute. Most of these people have come back too! What's the average penalty? Three or four weeks? You're making it sound like we've got a massive network of gulags sucking in more and more people. But they let them out as well. And then they make fun of or slag off the system when they come out! It doesn't seem much different from the system we had before for dealing with persistent social nuisances!'

'Sure, until recently most of them seem to be turned out quite quickly. Lately though, things seem to have tightened up a bit. They're trying to make the camps a more serious proposition. People coming out are saying the work is tougher, and the discipline is much tougher. There's a special brigade of guards or something that's been formed to enforce the camp regime. It's no picnic for sure! And say only one per cent of people fall into the "missing" category. That's about three hundred people. And I've got forty-three on my books. Other relatives must be going through other channels to track down their lost relatives. We're taking on some extra staff to help do the tracking down.'

'I'm sure it will be something to do with the newness of the system,' suggested Martin. 'The eco-camps or eco-colleges or whatever, they're a new phenomenon. And there's bound to be teething troubles. And the Tribunals, they're new too. From what you say it's clear they don't have their reporting systems completely worked out. Probably no one's coordinating their decisions—so they may sentence someone and send them to a camp, but maybe that camp can't deal with it at the time so they get sent to somewhere else….'

'So they end up in a kind of judicial limbo? Could be. But it's a strange process, don't you think? This new legal body created out of nowhere, staffed by some species of instant magistrate, and able to pull people out of their regular life and send them god-knows-where….how did all this happen?'

'What are you saying, Joanna?' asked Sandy. 'That the Tribunals are somehow shadowy and spiriting people away? How did it happen? Ask Peter! He's part of the government, and both Martin and I are working for this government too—so are you as a member of ESCOLAW! None of this has been done in some dark corner: everything's right out there in the open. We're all part of this Revolution—and maybe some things aren't going as smoothly as they should. You still think in "them and us" terms, as if it's still the old government in there. Maybe you're naturally oppositional, but I think if you try to work with the system rather than suspecting everyone of malicious intentions you'd get somewhere faster!'

Joanna felt a bit stung by Sandy's words, and by the tone of voice too. Martin sat quietly, not knowing what to say.

'Thanks for the advice, Sandy,' Joanna said at last, somewhat icily. 'You might be right—maybe I'm too quick off the mark with my suspicions. But our clients are worried sick. Put yourself in their position, if someone you loved was in trouble with the authorities, is sent away for three or four weeks, and you are unable to make contact with them in all that time. Then when they should come back, there's no sign of them. Actually, there's something more positive you can do than just think about it. From what you say, you're pretty close to the leadership now—if I supply you with a list can you see if you can come up with more than Peter can?'

Now Sandy looked a bit taken aback. This was an area she did not want to become involved in. All the same, she said: 'Sure. I'll see what I can do!'

'Thanks,' said Joanna. 'Is that the time? I really think I should be going. Although...'

Joanna hesitated, then decided to do her thinking aloud.

'At the risk of sounding paranoid—has anyone else noticed something strange? Sam Sharma was always in the media, criticising the government and the Green Revolution. Now he's gone. And his wasn't the only protesting voice. But where have they all gone? When was the last time you read or saw something in the media that's critical of the Revolution and its foibles? You may find some mockery and cynicism from the overseas media, but our media has become entirely tame. Which is why I ... Never mind—that's enough of my paranoia! I'll go now and leave you in peace!'

29: Sister acts

Reykjavik had been exciting, stimulating, motivating. A country powered almost entirely on renewable energy. The journey through the Nordic countries in fact had provided plenty of food for thought for Peter Kitson. Stockholm in particular had provided many useful contacts as well as examples of innovative approaches to energy production and conservation.

While in Stockholm he also had what seemed a chance meeting with Sir James Olsen, at the time on holiday meeting members of his Swedish family— or so he told Peter. He invited him to a reception he was going to for mainly British and Swedish business leaders, funded by an organisation to promote Anglo-Swedish industrial cooperation. Peter, at his assistant Haliburton's urging, agreed he could spare an hour for the sake of goodwill. But once there he found that the reception was not all it seemed, as most of the people he met were in opposition to the Mason government. Sir James also introduced him to 'an American friend' who probed him gently about the inner dynamics of the coalition, and the Liberals' position on this or that policy. Still, Sir James was extremely well connected with high ranking Swedish and EU officials, and brought him a number of useful introductions. Then it was on to Brussels to meet with his counterparts from the EU nations.

This tour had, amongst other things, given Peter the chance to see how the Green Revolution was progressing across Europe. And the truth that he learned was that the picture across Europe was very uneven. He had seen in Iceland and Scandinavia many interesting and innovative initiatives—but all of them generated in a 'politics as usual' situation. Always one step ahead on the environmental front, no one in these countries seemed to see the need for the kind of far-reaching changes being introduced by the Mason government. In general, though, his interest was received cordially, and the dignitaries he met were keen to hear more about the UK's plans.

In Brussels, however, Peter felt like an outsider trying to come in from the cold. The general consensus was that the UK was becoming once again a disruptive force in the European Union. This was something he had half-expected, though the frostiness of the reception from some of the officials and ministers still took him aback.

The fall-out from the nuclear melt-down had not produced a continental consensus in favour of radical change. The initial surge of green fervour that had swept the west European countries had subsided. In France new fault lines had developed in political life, overlapping with the more traditional ones. A typically Gallic stand-off along more or less geographical lines had evolved after protests had turned to blockades and then violence. One French government fell, but was replaced by another composed of largely the same personnel, only now more than ever determined to resist radicalism from the periphery.

The governments of the east and south European countries were far from impressed with the UK's new ideas. What they saw more than anything was one of the richer countries reneging on its commitments in agricultural and trade policies, and withholding payments. And to add insult to injury, a delegation of members of the European Parliament came unexpectedly to Brussels to corner Peter about suspected human rights abuses and violations of freedom of the press taking place in Britain. As a life-long Liberal, he felt a special humiliation in being put on the back foot about such issues.

Peter, however, was still convinced of the rightness of the programme of the Green Earth coalition government in Britain. Never one to back down from political debate, he vigorously made the case for the changes his government was making, which he insisted were an example to the whole of Europe.

It was while he was in Brussels that he got a call from Sandy Honeyford. He poured out his woes to her, and lamented the image of the Green Earth government that was becoming pervasive in Europe. Sandy had always given her colleagues sound advice about strategy and tactics, and usually she provided encouragement too in difficult situations.

'I'd say just focus on two things. One, remember why you are there—to develop new directions in energy policy. This is a time for Europe to back up its fine words about renewable energy with some serious investment. Not in more R&D, but in real, commercially viable projects. I'm sure you can get support for that. Two, accentuate the positive. Get yourself some air time, and make the case for what we're doing, what we've achieved already. See if you can set up a debate with one or two of your critics. You can politely show that they've done fuck all for the environment. Challenge them about what they are going to do. You succeeded here by setting the agenda—do the same for the garlic munchers and the sausage eaters! And everything else, about human rights etc etc—just tell the truth! That is, there's been a certain amount of chaos and maybe some over-enthusiasm at local level, and if they hit you with specifics, just say you'll look into it. By the way, Joanna was laying it on us the other night, with her list of fifty missing people...do you know about this?'

'Yes,' Peter replied, 'and I passed it on to Morton a few weeks ago. He said he'd set his people onto it. But I hadn't really thought about it since. But thanks for the advice. You're right, of course. I could have done with you here to pep me up, instead of this deadweight Haliburton from the Ministry they've landed me with. He's all statistics and completely dismal company. I think it's his first time over here, and he's memorised all the guide books. Can tell you everything you never needed to know about the royal palaces and museums. He's so useless in meetings when I'm under attack, I've encouraged him to go off and do as much sight-seeing as he wants.'

'Peter, there's something I've got to tell you...' Sandy said anxiously.

So Peter Kitson came to know about the defection, or half-defection as she put it, of one of his closest and most trusted advisors. In a magnanimous way, though, he could see that this was possibly a good move for Sandy, giving her a position pivotal to the government as a whole, rather than just to one party. As he congratulated her, he nonetheless felt a hollowness behind his words. In his fair-mindedness, he didn't recognise that Sandy hoped, even expected him to try and persuade her to stick with him, and that she felt a little hurt that he didn't make any attempt to talk her out of it. She told him that Howard Blackstone had been furious, and called her a traitor amongst other insults, saying he couldn't possibly work with her again. But she expected him to calm down, and Mason had advised her that if Howard wanted to remain in the government, he would have to get over it and work with her.

Sandy's news came as a shock, but not as great a shock as the one he received the following morning at breakfast in the hotel. When Haliburton came to join him at breakfast, he passed over to Peter a copy of *The World This Week*, the top American current affairs magazine. On the cover was a picture of Joanna, and the headline: *Sister Acts: Making a stand against the green fascists.*

As he read the article, with its peculiarly American slant, Peter's jaw visibly dropped several times, or so Haliburton told his colleagues later. The article, based on an interview with Joanna, told of her campaigns to free people who had disappeared 'into a kind of Guantanamo limbo', and her fears about the over-exuberant and unaccountable activities of the local Tribunals. A handful of case histories were inserted about people who had fallen foul of the Tribunals for seemingly innocuous activities, or activities that in most other countries would clearly just be a matter of preference. And Joanna's fears about attacks on the freedom of the media were accompanied with stories from other sources of direct and indirect pressure exerted by government and the Earth Councils. A number of journalists had left the country, including the former BBC News chief Michaela Cavaliero, who had jumped at the chance of a senior post with an American news network in Europe. In a boxed insert Michaela pulled no punches about the political interference of ESCOMEDIA in her work and their compromising of editorial independence.

The article infuriated him. To him it seemed a typical piece of sloppy journalism. There was no hard evidence behind any of the accusations, only a lot of 'he said, she said'. Joanna had infuriated him, although he took a certain amount of brotherly pride in how glamorous and poised she looked in the photos. He couldn't stop asking himself, 'Why has she done this?' Maybe the tone of the article was not at all what she intended. But she was no fool. She had talked to a prestigious overseas publication in the full knowledge that the results would put pressure on the government.

Most of all, though, what irked him was the reference to 'green fascists', and the implication that Peter himself was one of them. The phrase in the headline seemed to come from Joanna. But in the article it was not her who came up with it: it was part of a quote from an unnamed 'White House spokesman'. That was worrying too. If that was the view of the right-wing President, Johnson Wilding, then Anglo-US relations might be taking a bit of a nose-dive too.

'Green fascists! Unbelievable!' he muttered.

Jasper Haliburton was about to take a mouthful of bacon, but paused holding his fork in mid-air.

'Hm, yes,' he said. 'Not a nice brush to be tarred with. Somehow I don't think your sister will be serving on ESCOLAW for much longer. Unless maybe the powers-that-be want to make a point that they're not fascists!'

He raised an eyebrow, then tucked into his bacon.

Before he could respond, Peter's phone rang. It was Danny Malik, the Minister for Culture and Media. He didn't sound pleased.

'Peter, I guess you've seen *The World This Week* magazine?' he said.

'Sadly, yes,' said Peter. 'Just now.'

'We all assume you knew nothing of this in advance?'

'Nothing at all, I'm afraid.'

'This puts us, and you in particular, in a difficult situation, don't you think?' asked Malik.

The icy coldness of his tone irritated Peter. Who did this young upstart think he was? But Peter was a bit at a loss to think how to respond. Joanna had put him in a tight spot, perhaps, but she had a right to her views.

'It's bad PR, for sure,' said Peter.

'And we need to counter it as soon as possible. Can you help us here?' said Danny sharply.

'Well, I'm bound to be asked a few questions about it today. The family angle will, I'm sure, make it hot news for a day or two. But my advice is not to over-react. Most stories come and go in a day. Putting up vigorous denials or smokescreens only encourages them!'

'I'm glad you take it so lightly,' said Malik. 'The rest of us don't take so kindly to be branded as fascists, even if it is by the celebrity lawyer sister of a government minister.'

There was silence for a few moments, as Peter bit back the words he wanted to say. It seemed Malik was almost trying to provoke him. Then another voice came in on the line.

'Hi Peter. This is Malcolm here. Danny's really fizzing over this one. I'm sorry he didn't give me the chance to greet you at the start. But of course I'm quite concerned as well, as it's me who's being misrepresented to a large extent in the article. Joanna doesn't seem to remember how I helped her before. And now she's turning this "List of Fifty" that you gave me into some kind of sound-bite accusation. It's very damaging you know. To all of us.'

'I know,' said Peter, softly. He was feeling quite torn. His inclination was to disassociate himself completely from her comments. They had nothing to do with him, and he felt she was way out of order in this article. But on the other hand, he was her brother, and their relationship had always been very close. He felt a revulsion against taking any position that he felt was disloyal to her.

'Have you been able to talk to her?' asked Danny.

'I've only just read the article. What about you guys? Have you tried to contact her?'

'Perhaps that's something you should do,' suggested Malcolm.

'Maybe,' said Peter. 'But if you called her, you could make your feelings known—though she must be aware that you won't be best pleased. And you could give her an update on the progress in tracking down her clients. Maybe that's all it needs to take the sting out of this, a bit of transparency.'

Peter was regaining his political equilibrium, and was fighting his—and Joanna's—corner. 'No harm in putting these arrogant bastards on the back foot a little,' he thought.

'I'll think about it,' said Malcolm curtly.

Danny took up the initiative in the discussion.

'OK, Peter. What we need to do is agree a strategy of response. Whatever else you try to talk about out there, however much you want to set the agenda, the hacks are going to chase you about this. They're going to ask you about Joanna, about whether you agree with her views, whether we're all a bunch of green fascists. So we need to make sure we're singing from the same hymn sheet, don't you think? You need to be ready to counter to all the accusations in the article -'

'Wait, wait, wait,' interrupted Peter. 'There's no advantage in being defensive. I think the best thing is to be dismissive of it in a friendly and jocular kind of way. I can handle the family side of things. Joanna's clearly been quoted out of context, and the article is mostly baloney. This won't run. Americans can't take a sustained interest in any news that isn't about food or guns or baseball, and *The World This Week* has a limited circulation in Britain— so the damage here will be limited.'

'Yes,' said Danny, 'the damage here will be limited. But no thanks to you or your sister. We've impounded this week's edition. Almost no one will see the article first-hand unless they go hunting for it online. It's more an issue for you as you're out there now, and for our image abroad. We've done our bit limiting the damage. Now you can do yours.'

The call ended abruptly.

'I take it they're not happy?' said Haliburton.

'No, Jasper, they're not,' sighed Peter. 'I think they're over-reacting. I mean, today's news sensation is tomorrow's chip wrapping.'

'As a matter of interest, I read that the Belgians claim to have invented chips. I always thought they were British' said Haliburton, wiping his mouth with a serviette. 'More to the point, I've heard that today the National Convention is going to propose making 'defaming the Revolution' a punishable offence. I think your sister may need to mind her Ps and Qs a little more if that gets through.'

30: Securing the Revolution

Malcolm Morton looked round the room, at the various members of the Joint Intelligence Committee and their advisors. He was conscious of his own inexperience set against the many years' experience of the heads of the intelligence service—MI5, MI6, GCHQ, plus key section heads from the Ministry of Defence. And he was sure they were also conscious of this imbalance. He felt that they both patronised him and withheld important information from the government.

Here, in an oak-panelled meeting room in Chequers, the country residence of British Prime Ministers, the elite of the intelligence community clearly felt very much at home. Morton, however, had a surprise in store for them that would shake their complacency to the core.

Sir Max Fernley, Director-General of MI5, was presenting an assessment of revised security priorities following a falling away of terrorist threats from Islamic extremists.

'There are rumours,' he said, looking over the top of his glasses in an apparent aside, 'that there have been secret negotiations between members of the government and representatives of terror groups.'

'Who has been saying that?' asked Morton.

'Well, we are the ears of the nation,' said Fernley.

'And what's the deal supposed to be?' asked Don Mason.

'We withdraw our troops from their bases in all Islamic countries within two years, and they leave us alone. And we release Islamist detainees. That's about the sum of it,' said Fernley.

'It could have advantages,' said Mason.

'Though not for our alliances,' said Fernley.

'So this intelligence is from the Americans?' asked Morton. 'We know how reliable their intelligence services can be!'

'Anyway,' said Fernley, happy to air the topic and then let it lie, 'the point is that we are able now to devote more resources to tracking and infiltrating some of the more extreme and disruptive elements at work in these volatile times. Direct action can be contagious, and we're finding some unlikely groups combining. It's not news that there is an American-style Christian Right activist movement kicking off here, attacking doctors and clinics that provide abortions. But now we find some of them working in tandem with extreme animal rights groups—not their natural bedfellows, one would think. But what's bringing them together is opposition to genetic engineering and cloning technologies. The dangers of "playing God", and all that. We think jointly they have been behind several arson attacks on laboratories and companies involved in the field.

'But we have some sensitive issues here. In the current, er, ferment, there are many cross-currents and connections. And some of these connections stretch to people in the National Convention and the Green Militia. By the way, I do wish we could revert from Green Militia back to Green Volunteers. It's the sort of terminology that makes us in the defence and intelligence communities a little edgy.'

There was a small ripple of laughter around the table. But Malcolm Morton was a little stung.

'We can deal with the sensitivities around infiltrating these extremist groups by reporting directly to me. But I gather the term "Militia" isn't the only thing making the intelligence and defence communities a little edgy?'

There was silence around the table.

'I mean collaboration with ESCOMIL. It seems the military and the intelligence services are not keen to have their environmental performance scrutinised.'

'Well, to be frank, we find ESCOMIL to be somewhat over-eager and intrusive, straying well beyond their brief,' said Lieutenant-General Sir Roger Terrington, the Chief of Defence Intelligence. 'You yourself used to be in military intelligence, Minister—the matters we deal with are extremely confidential, and we can't have all kinds of people from outside trampling all over the place.'

'Yes, these scrutineers seem to be becoming a kind of permanent presence, a bit like political commissars to keep us on the right track,' added Fernley.

'Perhaps that's necessary,' said Morton. He waited a moment for the significance of what he was saying to sink in, before continuing. 'It seems to us that there are people in the intelligence services who are not being quite straight with us. Who are continuing to monitor the Green Earth Movement as if we were a subversive group, rather than the government of this country.'

Several people round the table tried to object and interrupt, but Morton raised his hand.

'You will let me speak,' he continued. 'I asked you all a month ago for all the files relating to monitoring of the GEM and members of this government. And you all sent me various bits of information. But not the truth. In fact, I already had full access to all the monitoring that took place—and which continues to take place. What do you think you are doing, spying on Cabinet Ministers and their advisers?'

'Home Secretary, this is normal procedure,' protested Fernley. 'It's not spying. We have to keep a friendly eye on what Ministers are doing, the contacts they make—it's to keep them secure more than anything else.'

Morton sighed. 'Fernley—I've read the files. I've seen the videos. I've listened to the people who have been listening in on us. This goes way beyond our security. We are going to get to the bottom of this unauthorised and treasonable activity. Your services will be cleaned up root and branch, starting today.'

There was silence around the table, and members of the Joint Intelligence Committee looked towards Don Mason for support. He smiled grimly, and nodded.

'All of you are suspended from your posts with immediate effect,' said Mason calmly.

'You will not return to your offices. The phones and computers you left with security at the door will not be returned to you,' continued Morton.

'This is outrageous!' blustered Terrington.

'Not as outrageous as spying on your own government!' said Morton sharply. He waved his arm towards a group of plain-clothes policemen who had entered the room. 'From here you will go with these gentlemen to Scotland Yard, where the investigations into your own conduct in these affairs will be, shall we say, "scrutinised". As we speak, our own people are moving into your offices and making arrangements for running the services until the situation is resolved. And no need to worry about "outsiders", as you put it. We shall be promoting from within.'

There was a stunned silence.

'I'm disappointed in you, Morton. I thought you were one of us,' said Terrington at last.

'I don't think that's the issue,' said Morton calmly. 'The question is whether *you* are one of *us*. And the answer so far is not looking good.'

'The meeting is over, gentlemen,' said Mason, standing up to leave the room.

As the heads of the intelligence services grappled to take in what had happened, they were unaware that in a coordinated move, senior members of the military were being arrested across the country. They were taken to separate police stations, with the officers involved unaware that they were part of a coordinated national operation. The 'harmonising' of the military and intelligence services with the aims of the Green Revolution had taken a big step forward.

Within the civil service, rumours of this putsch were rife. Sir James Olsen, who always kept his ear close to the ground, could now see a pattern across the various sectors of government. When a few weeks later he needed to attend a family funeral in Sweden, he and Lady Frances packed their bags and set off for Stockholm. From there, citing ill-health, he submitted his resignation. He had no plans to return until the Mason government was over.

31: Howard's end

Howard Blackstone sat back in his chair and let out a deep sigh. He had a deep affection for this room, where he had always found a refuge from the world. The walls were lined with books: novels, political books, biographies, travel memoirs, art books, scientific works and many, many reports of all kinds. Howard had been in political life for over thirty years, and had accumulated a monstrous amount of both paper and electronic documentation.

Now he looked around at it all, and wondered if the effort had all been worth it. He was widely respected. People said he was a decent man; a thoughtful, cultured and honest man. And successful: the most successful leader of his party for nearly ninety years.

He looked out through the French doors which led from his study into the garden, his other favourite abode. He had created this garden from the wasteland left by the builders who had restored and extended his Victorian cottage in the Hertfordshire countryside some twenty-five years ago when he and Margaret had first settled there. Now the walls were covered in climbing clematis and wisteria, and the fruit trees he had cultivated produced a bumper harvest every year. Well before the likes of Mason and Porter came on the scene, he and Margaret had developed their own organic kitchen garden and 'orchard'. Self-consciously he had imitated Gladstone who used to start the day with forestry work followed by some reading or academic work: so Howard would rise early to tend his small estate before retreating to his study to read through his latest acquisitions, or pen an article.

But what did it all count for now, he wondered? How would people judge his legacy to the country, and to the nation? The most successful party leader since Lloyd George? Or the man who led his party up a blind alley, as Evan Roberts believed, and the man who presided over its dissolution?

As he continued his nostalgic and gloomy meditation, Margaret put her face round the door. It was a picture of affection and concern.

'They're all here now, darling,' she said softly.

Howard had summoned the leading figures of his party, both elected members and senior party officials, to his home on this sunny February morning for a working breakfast. Such breakfasts had been common during campaigns, but were otherwise rare. Everyone knew it had to be something important. Picking up a glass of orange juice on the way through the kitchen, he joined his colleagues on the patio where they sat at the wrought iron tables, helping themselves to croissants and coffee. It was unlike Howard to be aloof like this, not greeting people as they arrived. But he had wanted to avoid responding on a one-to-one basis to a very simple question: 'How are you?'

Evan Roberts, Peter Kitson and Terry Cairns were amongst the ten leading figures gathered there. Howard greeted them all warmly, and thanked them for abandoning their family life on the day of rest, assuring them that there was an important reason for doing so.

'Some of you may have felt that I've been a little quiet of late. And I feel myself that I haven't perhaps been providing the kind of leadership I should have been over the past year or so. I apologise for that.'

He paused, as if summoning up the effort to say what was on his mind. Some of his colleagues looked puzzled, others anxious or alarmed.

'I don't know how to say this—I guess the only way is just to come out with it. Two weeks ago I suffered a seizure. Here in the garden. I was halfway up a ladder at the time, over there in my little orchard. Luckily I was not hurt too badly, no broken bones. Afterwards I felt fine—but Margaret was so alarmed she more or less dragged me to the doctor. And he arranged for tests….and on Friday he called me with the results. I have a brain tumour. And judging from the size of it, it's probably been there for some time. I'm not done for yet, but it's not straightforward.'

At this point, Gill McDonald, the party President, couldn't suppress a gasp, and felt the tears welling in her eyes. Margaret Blackstone, who had remained standing, moved behind her and put a comforting hand on her shoulder, squeezing it gently.

'Howard, I…' began Terry Cairns, one of Howard's oldest colleagues, as well as deputy leader of the party.

'It's OK,' interrupted Howard, holding up a hand to halt any comments. 'I know you all want to say something, offer me kind words and express your concern. And at the same time it's so hard to say the right thing, not to say something insensitive: something conveying either too much hope or too much fear. I'll give you a few moments to let this sink in, and then I'll tell you all the doctor has told me. Then I'll tell you what I intend to do.

'But first, I want to say this. Every one of you here is someone I have worked with for many years, and for whom I have the greatest respect and affection. Over the years we have worked fantastically well as a team, and achieved great success—and I want that to continue through the difficult times ahead.'

His mouth felt dry, and he took a long sip of juice.

'OK—now about me. The doctor has told me the tumour is operable. And there are chances of a successful outcome. They'll operate next week. After that, assuming I'm still here….there'll be months of chemotherapy and maybe radiotherapy. It will be rough, I'm sure. But I can't imagine not pulling through. That may just be vanity, or denial, or something, I don't know.

'In these circumstances, though, I have to consider my priorities. I've devoted my life to politics. To changing the world! But now I have to take my eyes off the horizon, and focus in on my family, on my home. I told my children yesterday—they're all on their way here now. I want to spend time with them, and with my grandchildren. I'm sure I'll see you all, and often, during my treatment and convalescence. But it will be as friends, not as colleagues at work. Today I'm resigning as your party leader, and tomorrow I'll meet with Mason and resign my post in government. Please don't try to persuade me out of this. For me there's no other way. If these are my last days, I don't want to spend them reading committee papers and sparring with Whitehall bureaucrats!'

There was a moment of stunned silence. Gill McDonald came across and hugged Howard, trying not to cry. Terry Cairns felt profoundly moved, feeling for one of his oldest friends as he confronted his mortality. One by one the colleagues expressed their sympathy and concern, wishing him well and offering to help in any way. Then Howard addressed them all again:

'Now, to business. Let's have another round of coffee. Have some more pastries. Life goes on. Or is that the wrong phrase? The show must go on, maybe that's what I meant! Now I've always felt that I'm a realist, or maybe that's just wishful thinking, eh, Evan?'

Evan smiled sheepishly.

'So we have to work through the implications. We've never faced the situation of electing a new leader while we're actually in government. Makes a difference, doesn't it? I'm not sure what the rules say. But in the interim, Terry as Deputy Leader needs to step into my role. I'm sure between you, you can handle this side of things brilliantly. More tricky is the coalition issue. We had to negotiate ourselves into the positions we have, and we can't assume when I step down as Foreign Secretary we can just pop someone else in my place. Over the next hour or so, you need to come up with a renegotiation strategy. Something I can make the first move on when I meet Mason tomorrow.'

He looked at them all intently, then continued.

'I have some words of caution though. I look back on my year in office as Foreign Minister and I think I've achieved–bugger all! Well, pretty much bugger all. We've been spared a major international crisis that might have forced us to react quickly or invade somewhere, thanks be, but I haven't been able to do any of the positive things I was hoping to do. None of the initiatives on world poverty, for example, or disarmament. Our GEM colleagues just refuse to make these a priority. They have their own agenda, and just seem to want me to be a kind of international spin doctor for the Green Revolution. So it would be better to have a less prestigious post with more internal clout, perhaps.

'Though even then I think they may still try to pull the strings. You know, I think we–and that includes me, maybe especially me–we've consistently underestimated the GEM since they surfaced. We thought we'd have the upper hand as we have the experience. But they've changed the rules. Our wisdom applies to a world of government that no longer really exists.

'I've had this emphasised to me while I was in America last week. I had a long session with the President and Secretary of State. They seem to be remarkably well informed about what's going on here. And they seem to have some inside knowledge of what goes on within Mason's magic circle. Wilding is very troubled by what he believes they are planning, which he thinks will lead to economic disaster: that is, very drastic reductions in production to bring about negative economic growth. He also warned me that the GEM are prepared to withdraw from the European Union and from NATO too, if they think isolation is the only way to pursue their plans.'

Peter exchanged glances with some of the others. 'With respect, Howard–he would say that, wouldn't he? We know his outlook,' said Peter, 'and we know how their intelligence likes to exaggerate to please the views of the White House.'

'Granted,' said Howard. 'I'm only telling you what he said. And there's more. Morton's got them worried. Especially with these camps. Maybe they're extra sensitive after the long inquests into Guantanamo. Wilding claims that Morton's preparing the machinery to turn the country into a one-party state. And he had a message for you, Peter: "Listen to your little sister!" Far-fetched? I can't take this on. But if any of it is true, it's really up to all of you to do something about it. There–I'm failing to exercise leadership again!'

With a grim smile he ended his address, on a note of humility and self-mockery. As the discussion ensued, Howard could see that his hope for party unity after his stepping down was but a remote possibility. Evan argued more strongly than ever that it was time to end the coalition, to try to leave with hands relatively clean. Peter and Terry argued the opposite view, that there were important achievements to build on, and that the GEM would be more manageable if they remained close to them. Howard could see that both Peter, and more recently Terry, had been seduced. He—Howard—had been seduced by the prospects of bringing the party into power. Peter had been seduced by his idealistic vision of the party leading the way in environmental achievements. And Terry had been seduced in more ways than one.

That was it, that was the end, as far as he was concerned, Howard thought as he heard a car pull into the drive. Time to put family before the party, and before saving the planet. Time to put his own humanity before humanity in general.

A large white Mercedes crunched its way into view up the gravel driveway. Howard's daughter and her husband hurriedly got out, followed by their three children. Megan Blackstone hugged her father long and hard as he arrived to greet them. His grandchildren hugged his legs, then ran noisily and playfully to greet their grandmother.

As Megan released her grip on her father a little, she glanced with an instinctively jealous hostility at the interlopers on the patio. Howard quickly sensed her feelings, and whispered softly to her. 'I invited them, Megan. Please, be friendly, they'll soon be going. Help me now—I need to do this. I need the transition to go smoothly. Will you help?'

Megan nodded, wiped a tear, and went over with her father to greet his old friends and colleagues, thanking them warmly for their support at this time. She would remember this occasion, the last time she saw them all together.

32: Going inside

The seascape was changing off the Welsh coast. Heather Kitson could see from the cliff top the towers rising dramatically out of the mist over the Irish Sea. The sea spray in the wind was cold on her face, and the wind blew back her shoulder-length hair.

It was an impressive achievement. Vast ranks of wind turbines, most as yet incomplete, like columns of headless soldiers, about a mile off the coast. And she was married to a man who could share in the credit for transforming the country's energy supply.

Holding back her hair against the wind, she looked down the coast where she could see the construction site that had become home to the workers assembling the parts and transporting them out to sea. More platforms were being assembled at the port, waiting to move into position and erect more turbines. This was a government that was going to deliver what it promised, she thought. It would be a far greener Britain that Andrea would grow up in.

As she looked further inland, into the National Park, she could just make out another camp, the Snowdonia Eco-camp. Here there were also lines of huts, as at the coastal construction site. But here there were also watch towers, and in their travels in the area they could not fail to notice the signs designating certain areas off-limits, and the patrols of the Green Militias in their characteristic green and yellow high-visibility jackets.

The Kitsons were staying at Terry Cairns' country cottage not far from Machynlleth, a beautiful remote retreat he had just bought for himself. Now that he was party leader Terry felt a stronger urge than ever to get away from the pressures of London from time to time. And with his new relationship with Louise Adams, he also felt a strong urge to have a romantic hideaway. Now he was also pleased to be able to pay back some of the hospitality the Kitsons had lavished on him over the previous few years.

Heather had left the others in the cottage and driven to the coast to get the sea air. She was thinking about her new family life, how she felt totally immersed and warm. Yet with this security she enjoyed all the more her rare moments away from everyone, giving her time to reflect. Just five years ago she had had her life and career mapped out before her, as a public relations executive. Now that all seemed so far away. There was nothing to stop her returning to work, but it was the last thing on her mind. Terry and Louise had been having a discussion about 'how do you measure happiness?' But she couldn't help feeling that happiness is something to be enjoyed, not measured. At least enjoyed while you have it.

As she returned to her car, wet and windswept, she reflected also on the transformation of Terry Cairns. Some of his hard-edged cynicism had evaporated. Whether it was the warmth of Louise or the charisma of Don Mason, she didn't know. But he seemed to have a renewed appetite for life and for activity. All the same, his enthusiasm for the Green Revolution sat a little uncomfortably with his sceptical nature—and that made his relationship with Louise something of an enigma.

She got into her car and headed back to the cottage. The rain began to lash down fiercely. Driving down a particularly windy country lane, she had to brake suddenly as she came across a minibus parked in the road. A couple of Green Militia officers turned suddenly as her car braked. Heather could see two militia officers by the minibus consulting a map, and several others heading into an adjacent field. One of them came over to Heather's car, and she lowered the driver's window to talk to him.

'Excuse me, miss,' she said. 'You wouldn't happen to have seen anyone wandering around these roads, wearing an Eco-Camp uniform, would you?'

'Sorry, I haven't seen anyone,' said Heather, above the noise of the wind and the rain.

'We're a bit worried,' said the officer unconvincingly. 'A bloke has wandered off from the camp, and it's not at all a good idea to be out on these hills in this weather.'

'Doesn't bear thinking about, does it?' said Heather.

Another militia officer came over, a tall man joining his slightly built female colleague. Heather noticed he seemed to take a good look into the car, as if suspecting something.

'Where are you heading for, madam?' he asked in a friendly tone, still checking out the car.

'Oh, not far—just by Machynlleth,' said Heather.

'Wait a minute...' said the female officer. 'Do I recognise you? I'm sure I do!'

Within a few moments she had correctly identified Heather, and she beckoned over to her nearby colleagues to share the news of her discovery. Soon there was a group of five or six of the militia crowded round her car and asking questions. Heather refused the offer of some tea from a flask in the bus.

She knew Joanna would be arriving soon to join Terry's house party, and she ought to be getting back. And she had an instinctive wariness about getting into a bus with a bunch of strangers, however friendly they appeared.

But the thought of Joanna reminded her of her sister-in-law's view of the camps. On an impulse she started asking them about what projects they were working on in the camp, and then made an unexpected request: 'Would it be possible to have a look round the camp, and see what you get the inmates doing there?'

The militia officers looked at each other briefly. It was the tall man who answered. 'We don't get many sightseers coming round...I'll have to check. Do you have a pen and some paper? OK, if you ring this number in the morning and ask for Kate Selsnick, we'll see if we can arrange a tour. Would it be just you, or your husband too?'

'Maybe—and maybe more, I'm not sure,' Heather replied. 'There's five of us—eleven if you count all the security that goes round with us now. But we wouldn't all descend on you, don't worry!'

••

It was late afternoon, and already dark when Heather returned to the cottage. As she pulled up she could see her friends and family through the windows, as they chatted and laughed in front of the open fire. She could see Joanna, standing behind the sofa, holding Andrea, stroking her still wispy hair, and rocking gently from side to side. For sure, Joanna would make a good mother one day, she thought. Louise Adams was nestling gently against Terry, and he looked as content as she'd ever seen him. Louise reminded her of Sandy—one of the girls who was one of the boys, never more at home than amongst all the political strategising and manoeuvring. As always, though, Heather quickly shook herself away from any intruding negative thoughts. Louise had been pretty much the perfect hostess these past couple of days, warm and welcoming and inclusive.

Joanna was first to notice her sister-in-law's arrival in the driveway, and rushed to unlatch the door, keeping up a running commentary to the sleepy Andrea all the time. Andrea perked up a little, holding out her arms at once for her mother. Joanna hugged Heather, and soon everyone was chatting and asking Heather where she had gone for her walk.

Soon Heather told them about how she had invited herself into an eco-camp. Terry and Peter looked impressed with her initiative. Joanna looked delighted while Louise looked grave and thoughtful.

'This is just the kind of chance I've been looking for, to get behind the shroud of mystery that surrounds these places,' said Joanna softly.

'Phew,' said Terry, 'this is some news! But if anyone would be *persona non grata* in an eco-camp, it's you, Joanna!'

'Do you think they won't let me in?' she asked anxiously.

'I wouldn't bank on it,' said Peter.

'What about you, honey?' Terry asked Louise. 'The situation must be a little more delicate for you, given who your employers are.'

There was a pause.

'Do you want to check it out first with Sarah, or Don or Malcolm?' asked Terry.

'No,' said Louise, regaining her composure and smiling. 'It'll be the weirdest way I've ever spent a holiday, but what the hell! OK, we'll see what they say in the morning.'

Towards the end of the evening, Louise suddenly turned to Joanna, and asked:

'It's probably bad taste to raise this, but in your profile in *The World This Week* you seemed to be saying we're drifting towards a dictatorship. Do you really think that?'

Joanna was surprised at the directness of the question. She didn't know Louise well, and in seeing her with Terry she had almost forgotten that Louise was actually a high-flying GEM economic strategist.

After a few moments pause for thought, Joanna replied: 'I don't exactly believe that, but I fear it. It seems many of the things we all protested about under previous regimes have intensified. Tribunals, Green Militias—we've come to accept them as a normal part of life. Now we have these EBOs—Environmental Behaviour Orders—which a Tribunal can slap on someone. They provide a catch-all provision so if someone is accused of anything—just accused, not convicted—they can be shipped off to an eco-camp. Most of the people coming out of the camps have an EBO slapped on them as a matter of course now, and in the blink of an eye they're back inside as a repeat offender.'

'Sounds like you do think it's getting tyrannical,' Louise replied.

'But what I don't get, really,' added Joanna, 'is the lack of consistency. People get shipped off for doing not very much, and other people are released. Newspapers, journals and websites are closed down for criticising the Green Revolution, but the leaders of the Grey parties are still at large, saying whatever they want. And what about me? I'm sure they think I'm a real thorn in their side—'

'Or pain in the neck…' suggested Peter.

'Oh, brotherly love for all to see!' retorted Joanna. 'But anyway, why don't they re-educate me?'

'Is that what you want?' asked Heather, a little alarmed.

'Maybe it's because your green credentials are quite good,' suggested Louise. 'You clearly haven't opposed the essence of the Green Revolution, and you're even helping it with ESCOLAW—greening the greyest institutions and professions in the country!'

'But other people with big mouths have run into trouble. Why am I protected? Is it because I know you guys?'

'Maybe it's about the power to influence other people. If they're denied access to the media, all the grey leaders can do is talk to each other—they become the most ineffectual of chattering classes. And the same goes for you. That's why your article upset Malik and Morton so much, because it was intended for a mass audience,' said Peter, with an accusing look at his sister.

'So you're implying that we have become a kind of dictatorship?' Louise asked Peter.

'I don't feel that,' Peter replied. 'I think there are things we need to get to the bottom of. But to me the idea of "dictatorship" implies something systematic, and crushing your opponents ruthlessly. I don't see that happening. Of course I don't agree with all the GEM's ideas. But to me it seems that people like Don don't claim to have all the answers, and we can work with them as partners. Stubborn on some things, open to suggestions on others. Just like you expect a coalition to be.'

Now Terry offered his own insights into the nature of dictatorships. 'Well, dictatorships can be more or less efficient. Most people imagine they are more efficient than they are. Mostly, though, they're *arbitrary*. When people try to change too much too quickly, you always get a fair amount of chaos on the ground. You get competing interests and jurisdictions—little empires being built. And there's a lot of ambition and enthusiasm from the volunteers on the front line. People picking up where the politically correct brigade left off, only actually *doing* stuff instead of just moaning about what other people do. It's they who are denouncing people to the Tribunals and seeking EBOs. And then there are people with scores to settle just denouncing each other for the hell of it.

'It's the burgeoning security apparatus that's worrying me, frankly. I'm sure Malcolm wants it to be even-handed, if a touch scary. But in practice it's bound to be arbitrary. Because at the end of the day it's a system run by ordinary people. For most of them a pay packet is more important than the ideology. Maybe not in the beginning, but as it gets routinised it ends up that way. Unimaginative people do humdrum jobs, but with more power and authority at their disposal than is good for them. In the end, people are branded as enemies or friends without good reason. It just happens.'

'What are we, then?' asked Heather. 'Friends or enemies?'

'I think they see us as moderately useful fellow travellers, and they'll ditch us as soon as they feel safe enough.'

'That's a bit gloomy, isn't it?' said Louise.

'I think it's got the potential to get like that, but we're not at that stage,' said Terry. 'The Green Revolution has a democratic deficit, and we have to prevent it getting out of hand. It's true there's still a strong groundswell of support for the Revolution. And the lack of criticism in the media seems to be as much self-censorship and political correctness as fear of being brought up in front of a Tribunal. All the same, too many unaccountable things are happening, and it's down to us to get things back on track, don't you think?'

Louise looked troubled. 'In the GEM we've always accepted that we'd have to implement some unpopular measures. You can't rely on democracy as we know it to deliver all that's necessary. As a species, humans are selfish. Like any species, I guess. But we have the knowledge and ability to do better for the planet. We're in a transitional phase where we have to run ahead of public opinion. But the GEM doesn't have a gospel of permanent revolution, and things will settle down.'

'And is the momentum for revolution exhausted?' asked Joanna. 'There's plenty still to do according to the GEM programme, and I hear many people in the party and the militias want to go even further.'

'Sure, there's more to accomplish...' said Louise noncommittally.

'I can't imagine these measures will be any more popular with some people,' continued Joanna, 'so how will dissenters be dealt with? More eco-camps? More purges of the professions?'

'Steady on,' said Terry. 'Aren't you a member of ESCOLAW, carrying out your own purge?'

'That's a problem,' admitted Joanna. 'When we began ESCOLAW, it wasn't meant to be carrying out any kind of purge. We were looking at the way the whole *system* performed, to make it greener. To be fair to Martin, he's always stuck to the line that it's systems, not people, that we must focus on. But things are changing. At first it was only people from the legal profession on the Commission. That's changed. Now about a quarter of the Commission are "experts" invited in and government representatives. Most of them are GEM, and they carry a lot of weight. They always say you can't change the systems without changing the people. Some people have resigned from ES-COLAW because of what they see as political interference. It's only because of Martin that I'm still on it–he persuaded me not to resign. He's trying to maintain some balancing act, between his principles and his ambition, maybe.'

'You really wanted to resign?' asked Peter.

'I had the letter written,' said Joanna. 'I've got a couple of cases going to the House of Lords against the government, and then maybe onto the European Court. So how can I be both working for the government and hauling it through the courts at the same time? But I think the courts are the only ways at the moment of maintaining that accountability we've been talking about. The only trouble is the government just ignores most of the judgements, or passes a new law to neutralise the judgment.'

'These are complex times we live in,' said Terry.

'Well, it's fine to criticise,' said Louise, 'but what would you do if you were suddenly put in power at this point? How would you be able to maintain the achievements of the Revolution–or would you wind it all back to politics as it used to be?'

'That's a good question. The short answer is that we'd be doing much the same, only without the authoritarian streak,' said Terry. 'And we'd be treating the economic crisis with a little more urgency. I think the big projects are all going to run into a fair bit of trouble soon unless we can boost the economy, or get some outside investment into them. But the business climate is not right for that at the moment.'

'You're part of the government though. You have to take the blame for anything that goes wrong–or quit the coalition. What would it take for you to do that–I mean to quit?' asked Louise.

'Good question,' laughed Terry, aware of Peter's concerns about discussing party matters in front of Louise. 'Maybe we need to go into private session to come up with an answer to that!'

Despite his renewed commitment to the programme, Terry felt in one part of his head that they should have left the government already. But they were enjoying the ride, and despite their concerns, it seemed too early to get off. All the same, in the light of Joanna's probing questions, he felt it was time to prepare an exit strategy in case they were unable to reverse the drift. Later that evening, he spoke to Peter privately about this, and called Evan to arrange a meeting of the party luminaries. Even though there was no decision to leave the government, Evan was delighted to hear the news.

••

In the morning all the adults of the house party piled into Peter's people carrier and headed for the eco-camp, escorted by most of their security detail in two other cars. Detective Sergeant Julia Masters, part of the Kitsons' security team, had volunteered to look after the baby so that both the Kitsons could go.

Halfway there they were met at an improvised checkpoint by a detachment of Green Militia. The visitors were invited to transfer to a bus, and left their car by the side of a field. The bus wound up and down several hills, then suddenly as they turned a corner they could see the entrance to the camp through rows of newly planted trees. They could see two watch towers at the corners of the camp, complete with search lights. Other lights were strung over the top of a barbed wire fence. In the centre of the fence was a tall archway, with its two big gates wide open. A checkpoint and a barrier stood a little way in front of the gate. A detachment of workers in orange overalls were digging in trenches either side of the road, which had narrowed the approach to the camp to a single lane. Several stood up and stared at the bus as it approached. A couple waved, intrigued at seeing visitors not in uniforms.

Joanna felt a chill on seeing this—but also a thrill of excitement at seeing one of these mysterious places at last. There could be people inside that she was looking for. Heather too felt a distinct chill of fear, she wasn't sure exactly why. Probably prisons do this to most people. But she noticed Peter and Terry were fascinated, discussing the layout of the camp and the reforestation around it in animated tones. Louise looked pensive, and remained very quiet.

After passing through the checkpoint, the bus proceeded through the gates. Everywhere there seemed to be an air of purposeful activity, although what the inmates and Militia were actually doing was hard to gauge. Beyond about fifty metres of open space was a small village of barracks and huts. From one of the buildings stepped a tall and imposing man, putting on a Militia jacket over his smart-but-casual clothes, dark grey corduroy trousers and open-neck shirt under a Norwegian-style woollen sweater.

He strode purposefully towards the bus, flanked by two members of the militia. As he came up to the group, the visitors noticed that he was much taller than average, about six foot five, broad-shouldered and very athletic. A man in his late thirties, both Heather and Louise later commented on how handsome and imposing he looked, with his slightly long blonde hair and fading sun tan. In conversation his piercing blue eyes held people's gaze a little longer than most felt comfortable with.

'Welcome, welcome to our humble village!' he said enthusiastically as he reached the visiting party. 'I'm Carl Fullerton, Overseer of the Eco-Camps, and this is Kate Selsnick, Camp Warden, and her Deputy Keith O'Connell. We're delighted to welcome members of the Cabinet and their guests to an Eco-Camp. Apart from Malcolm Morton, you're the first ever to visit. I hope you find what you see here interesting and inspiring!'

With that he greeted each of the visitors in turn, before explaining that Kate Selsnick would take the lead in showing them around the camp. He would meet them later for lunch and answer any questions they might have.

Terry, as the senior member of the group, took the initiative in speaking on behalf of the group. He assured Fullerton that their visit was impromptu and informal, and thanked him for the opportunity to get some insights into what the camps did and how they work. Fullerton's attitude was intriguing to Joanna. Her view of the eco-camps was that they were a somewhat illegitimate offshoot of the legal system, but Fullerton's view was that they were an under-valued innovation. Rather than being sheepish and defensive, as she had anticipated, he was bullish and assertive about their purpose and achievements.

Louise's impression was different. Unlike her fellow visitors, she had met Fullerton once before, although he seemed not to remember it. Within activist circles, his exploits were legendary, involving protests and guerrilla actions, often involving confrontation or violence. In fact the previous time when she had met him, she recalled, he had hauled a construction worker out of a bulldozer, jumped in himself and then rammed the bulldozer into several other construction vehicles before it stalled. He leapt out and easily outdistanced several chasing policemen into the woods, before circling around and rejoining his fellow demonstrators.

As she recalled, he had been no great fan of either Don Mason or Malcolm Morton. Yet here he was in a key position happily flaunting his badge of authority. She was puzzled. Given his extreme and subversive views, what could have brought him round to supporting the GEM? Maturity and mellowing, perhaps? From his manner, she doubted if there had been much mellowing in the intervening years. She would try to catch a private word with him later, she decided.

Terry was grateful to Heather Kitson for her impulsive initiative in setting up this visit. He realised he had not given any real thought to the extent of the eco-camp operation. His first thought was, 'How much does this all cost?' And how had this slipped under the radar of all the Cabinet meetings and briefings? Definitely something to bring up with his Cabinet colleagues.

First stop was the refectory, a log cabin kitted out with long wooden tables. A kitchen worker wearing the green overalls of the inmates, was laying out tea, coffee and home-baked biscuits on one of the tables. Kate Selsnick started to explain about the operation of the refectory.

'The refectory operates on a cooperative basis. All the meals are prepared by the campers. Most of the food is grown on site. Everything we do is based on the principle of minimum waste. We're always conscious that although the campers are not here of their own choice, they are not prisoners. The aim is always to educate, so people learn by sharing new experiences, probably the kind of experiences they would always reject in their previous life outside. The work is quite hard. But these refectory workers will leave here with an understanding of what organic food production and healthy food preparation involves. And many are fitter and healthier than before. We've actually had people write to us afterwards saying how a spell here helped them to lose weight, as well as find a new purpose in life! Hard work, healthy eating and lots of fresh air, that's the secret! Later on, I'll show you where and how we grow our food. But for now, please get yourselves a hot drink to warm yourselves up before we go out into the cold.'

Keith O'Connell talked them through how the camp had developed over the past year. Everything they could see had been built by the campers. Joanna winced every time she heard the word 'campers', not knowing whether to snigger or be outraged at this incongruously twee description of the inmates. A village of tents had gradually transformed itself into this small settlement of log cabins. They had built their own solar, wind and even hydro-electric electricity generators, which now supplied almost all their own needs.

As they moved around the camp, they found it was huge. They saw inside the barracks where the inmates slept in bunks, much as in the army. The conditions were Spartan, but warm, clean and dry. They saw the lecture theatre, dug into the hillside as a kind of cave. Many of the other buildings were half underground. Kate Selsnick and Keith O'Connell explained the design principles, ventilation and heat retention qualities with a vast amount of technical detail that passed right over the heads of the visitors.

The 'kitchen gardens' were huge, with many campers working on them. Terry noted it was unpromising soil to grow food in. Much of the production was under glass, with soil and organic fertiliser shipped in from outside. There was also a bakery, with the inmates producing their own bread and pastry for cakes and pies, which were also sold outside the camp.

There was also a compound of laboratories being built, for developing new low-energy production techniques and horticultural innovations, O'Connell explained. The inmates seemed to be involved in various kinds of chemical, engineering and botanical wizardry. It was all very impressive to the visitors. And everywhere there was new planting and landscaping—herb gardens, flower gardens and reforestation around the buildings.

There were also animals—sheep, a small dairy herd, goats, pigs and chickens, as well as horses and ponies, not to mention the dogs used to guard the perimeter.

The visitors managed to exchange a few words with some of the 'campers' on their tour. Mostly they were in there for small-scale environmental offences, and all seemed at least to some extent appreciative of their experiences there.

Peter seemed moderately impressed, but Joanna instinctively felt there was something phoney about the tour, reminiscent of the tours of Cuban collective farms that were a highlight for tourists in the Castro era. She longed for a chance to talk to some of the inmates without the attention of any of the Green Militia. But she couldn't see how this could be done, and feared embarrassing her brother again by doing something untoward. She was also desperate to find out if any of her list of 'disappeared' were at the camp, or had been there.

They were led back to the refectory for lunch. The food smelt delicious. The head cook seemed eager to discourse at length on the wholesomeness of the menu. Joanna now had a chance to quiz her and some of the other people serving about why they were there, what the conditions were like—and also if they had seen any of her missing clients in the camp. They clearly did not want to talk about this.

'Look sweetie,' the head cook eventually said, 'have a little more sensitivity for our position here. We just don't talk about other people's affairs here. A lot of people come and go. Only a few of us have been here for more than two months. Now please, take your food and move along. I've got work to do!'

Joanna did not wish to leave the camp empty handed. When Carl Fullerton marched up to join them, she wasted no time in asking whether he could answer some questions about people who had been through the camps.

'You can ask,' he replied with a smile, 'but I can't guarantee I can provide the answers.' It was very hard to tell if his smile was forced or genuine, Joanna felt. He confirmed that Sam Sharma had been an early inmate at this camp, but he wasn't sure where he was now.

'Miss Kitson, you must understand something about your client, Mr Sharma. He is a continuously disruptive element. It's just in his personality to be difficult, I think. We have to maintain some kind of order in these camps. And he just breaks one rule after another. So one sentence follows after another, and that's the way it is. We move him about because he is such a bad influence. I'm sorry, but it's in his own hands.'

'Wait a minute,' said Joanna. 'You said "one sentence follows another": who sentences him to what? As far as I know, he's twice been sentenced by Tribunals, but for limited terms. There's no record of any further sentences.'

'Come on, now, Miss Kitson. You must know how it works. He has to complete his re-education before he can be released. His behaviour shows that he hasn't changed, and so he needs to start over.'

'So someone can stay inside indefinitely?' asked Joanna, in disbelief.

'I shouldn't think it will come to that,' Fullerton replied with a casual laugh. 'But let's see what we can do for you. I've heard you have a list of people you want to track. Let me have it. I can't keep a list in my head of who's where, but I may be able to help. I'll get back to you.'

Straight away Joanna got out her phone to make a call to her office.

'There's no signal here,' said Fullerton. 'But go to the office, and call from there: they can email the list right to us here.'

'OK, I'll do it now,' said Joanna, and got up to head for the office. Fullerton nodded to a Militia officer, who opened the door for her and escorted her to the office.

Terry now took the opportunity to quiz Carl Fullerton, asking probing questions with gentle humour: 'Carl, all the development that's been happening here: as far as I can remember, this kind of thing just isn't allowed in National Parks! How on earth did anyone get planning permission for it?'

'Well, we're the government now, and everything from the old grey world is up for rethinking. I mean, Terry, just think about the concept of "National Parks". Special areas safeguarded from development, preserved in aspic, while at the same time trying to be a focus for tourism. So National Parks, Green Belts, Sites of Special Scientific Interest, Areas of Outstanding Natural Beauty…just think about the hypocrisy of it! Why give these areas the kinds of special protection we fail to give all the rest of the country? It's like going to church on Sunday, then back to the brothels and casinos on Monday!

'We need to be more consistent and more rigorous about the way we protect the environment *everywhere*. And what we are doing here has national, even global significance! In two ways. First, we aren't trying to "freeze" an era of landscape history for the area, as the National Parks have traditionally done. We're actually trying to recreate and restore its ancient, pre-human flora and fauna, as a prelude to allowing it to continue its natural course of evolution after an intermission of several thousand years.

'Like Jurassic park?' offered Terry mischievously.

Fullerton threw his head back and laughed. Heather noted how when Fullerton did anything, he did it with an engaging, even exhausting, boyish energy and enthusiasm. And he was very attractive when he laughed like this. Fullerton's laughter subsided into a warm smile, then he carried on.

'The second thing is, we're trying to develop a new style of human settlement and society, much more deeply integrated into the natural world. Sure, it's experimental, and we'll get things wrong. And sure, we can't go into Manchester and Birmingham tomorrow and apply the same principles and techniques. But we can learn many lessons, and apply them to new development while stage-by-stage "greening" existing settlements.'

'By "integrating people more deeply into the natural world", what exactly do you mean?' asked Heather. 'We've seen people living more or less in caves here, as well as log cabins: is this your model for the future?'

Carl smiled, and fixed his piercing blue eyes on her, as if trying to speak to her soul.

'It's one good model for eco-homes, building underground or partly underground. Less wasteful of materials, and with the right engineering the thermal qualities can make for vast energy savings. You can run a home on far less energy. It's not hard to generate enough of your own energy to meet domestic needs. And you can grow your own food on the roof. We're not the first to try this, but maybe the first to attempt to on such a scale—here and at the other camps.

'And we want to do more than that. The re-education here is for real. It's not just a question of slapping the wrists of recycling renegades like your Mr Sharma. We believe that if we can show the most recalcitrant members of society how to live a green and sustainable life, they can go from here and spread the message. Joanna seems to think we make people disappear. On the contrary, we want people to reappear in their communities, but carrying something with them from their experiences in the camps that will transform our towns and cities, restoring a truly workable balance between humanity and the rest of the natural world.'

As he spoke, Fullerton became very animated, making sudden movements with his arms and jerking his powerful body in one direction and another to fully face towards each of his visitors. His passion and conviction were overwhelming. It seemed almost necessary to agree with him, or risk an excessively passionate confrontation.

All the same, Terry continued his questioning, though from a slightly different angle.

'If you don't mind me asking, Carl, who funds all this? I mean the initiatives here seem to cut across several departments. Apart from yourself, who's running the show? I'm only a senior government Minister and our party's spokesman on finance, so I guess there's a good reason why nothing about this has ever crossed my desk?'

If Fullerton was a little surprised that a senior member of the government was ignorant of how the camps fitted into the government's budget, he didn't show it.

'You're right about it cutting across departmental boundaries. Of course the Treasury allocates most of the funding through the Climate Change Projects programme. But the leadership and funding for the Green Militia here comes through the Home Office—it's a security thing, of course.'

'So the camps are part of Dave Barrington's jurisdiction as well as Malcolm Morton's?' asked Peter, a little surprised by this connection. Barrington had never discussed any of this with him.

'Not really. It's complicated,' said Fullerton. 'Dave Barrington's programme supports much of the work we do here, and we ask for funding from him for particular projects. But in a day to day practical sense we're part of Malcolm Morton's world. Dave tends to deal directly with him, rather than with me. You know Malcolm has taken a whole new approach to how the Home Office works. His secretariat has its fingers in most pies—mainly because it relates to the priorities of the Green Volunteers—or Green Militia as I should say. But of course you know that.'

He fixed Terry Cairns with an unfathomable stare.

'Broadly, I know that,' admitted Terry. 'But actually I've had few direct dealings with the Home Office recently. Maybe you can tell me if Malcolm has a department dealing with foreign affairs as well!'

Fullerton smiled a cryptic smile. 'He probably has. Visas, immigration and all that. Homeland security. That's where his department interfaces with foreign affairs.'

••

'I don't exactly get it' said Terry suddenly on their way back to the cottage. 'What don't you get?' asked Louise.

'What we've just seen. And Carl Fullerton in particular. He's so excited and animated—about what? Everything we saw was so damned ordinary. There's all this investment in nothing that's remotely new. The half underground eco-homes, the self-sufficiency—we've all seen it done much better elsewhere, ten or even twenty years ago. So what's the point? Carl was acting like it's some great new experiment in human living!'

'Surely the point,' said Peter, 'is what he said about persuading the unpersuadable to become apostles of green living.'

'It seemed more than that,' said Heather. 'He was talking about "a new style of human settlement and society, much more deeply integrated into the natural world", wasn't he? And "learning the lessons from it to apply all over the country." ' She humorously imitated his deep voice as she quoted him.

'The whole thing struck me as phoney,' said Joanna. 'Well, not completely phoney, but today we only saw the top layer of whatever's going on. And I found some stuff out.'

'What kind of stuff?' asked Heather.

'People stuff. I called Martin from their office. He's got a copy of my lists, and I asked him to buzz it over to me. Well, to their office, in fact. There was quite a helpful girl in the office who opened it up for me, and I got her to scan through the list, and asked her if she knew any of the names, if they were there or if they'd been there. And about fifteen of them had passed through at some time or another. She was very candid. I guess she assumed we were entitled to know all this, being dignitaries or something… Anyway, it took me some way forward. Until the militia guy who escorted me there got edgy and said she should get clearance from Kate whatsername or Carl before cross-checking any more of the list.'

'Who did you find?' asked Peter.

'Several of the missing journalists on my list have been there. Miles Campbell, DG of the BBC, is there now, working on building a new satellite camp.'

'What?!' they exclaimed in unison.

'I didn't know he was missing—you've never mentioned him before,' said Peter.

'Celia Hill, his partner, came to me the day before yesterday. Said he'd been taken for questioning on Boxing Day, and hadn't returned. He'd been in trouble with ESCOMEDIA in the middle of the year, then put before a Tribunal like so many others. He had an eight week spell somewhere, was released, and now it seems he's back inside. Celia thinks it's because he had some long calls with Michaela Cavaliero and some other overseas dissidents. She's sure now that her phone has been tapped.'

'Wow!' exclaimed Heather.

'There's more. Sam Sharma has had several spells there. The girl in the office seemed to think he was some kind of lovable rogue—kept them all entertained, but was always in trouble. Just before the militia guy stopped her, she went into her system to find where he is. Last week he was sent to off to help construct somewhere called North Camp, at the West Highland Eco-Camp. Anyone heard of that? I haven't.'

Terry noticed that Louise seemed to tense when she heard this. As the day had progressed, Terry had in fact become more and more annoyed at Louise. The things Carl Fullerton and his officials had said to them must have been known to Louise already, he felt. They had maintained 'Chinese walls' between their domestic life and their separate work lives, as far as was romantically possible. But all the same it grated with him if she had been concealing any extensive and expensive programme from him. Her bosses shouldn't have been doing it, and she shouldn't have been complicit in it.

Terry decided to see if he could flush her out a bit.

'Lou, honey, do you know anything about this North Camp?'

Louise looked sharply at him. She felt it was unfair to put her on the spot about her work in front of the Kitsons. It broke the rules of their relationship.

'Not a lot. Actually, I didn't think it was active yet. It's a planned offshoot of the West Highland camp. They are building satellite camps at all the eco-camps, for special projects. But don't ask me what it does—I just assumed it would just be doing the same as the others, only in a different area. In the north, like it says on the label!'

'Do you think it's for especially stubborn offenders, like Sam?' asked Joanna—more thinking aloud than asking anyone in particular. But Louise felt she was being quizzed, and snapped in reply:

'Look, I've said all I know, OK?'

There was an icy silence, in which the Kitsons exchanged glances while Terry looked steadfastly out of the window at the countryside, becoming absorbed in its melancholy beauty in the rain.

Heather broke the silence. 'I'm not sure if I'm ready for a trip to North Camp yet. All this fresh air has given me an appetite. Soup and baked potatoes when we get back—I'm volunteering Peter to make it! I'll supervise, of course, to make sure he doesn't poison us all! How does that sound?'

••

Louise and Terry readied themselves for bed in an atmosphere even colder than the weather outside. Finally, Terry brought himself to apologise for putting Louise on the spot like that. She thawed more quickly than he expected, hugging him and giving him a quick kiss on the chin, before pressing her head to his chest.

After a few minutes just holding each other, Louise eventually said:

'I shouldn't have been so prickly. It's awkward, isn't it? Two people in a relationship will usually share everything, or at least try to. But there are some things we can't discuss. You don't know the difficult situation I'm in, being pulled in several directions all the time. More than you could guess. I'm saying too much even hinting at this. This is a Revolution, and the Movement is a ferment of ideas. In my position, I have to keep abreast of all that's going on. But of course, whenever people tell me something, they want me to be on their side. There's a thousand new ideas being worked up, most of which will never get close to being realised. That's the way it is.'

'Sure, honey, I—'

'I can tell you this: it wouldn't be good for you to know some of the things that I do. But I do need to know something, to help me get things right.'

'Go on.'

'In the last few months you've moved a bit closer to the GEM, working closer with us. I'm asking you, just between ourselves—I promise, this is only between ourselves—how comfortable are you now being part of the government? Have you become less of a sceptic, like Don wants?'

Terry sighed, and looked thoughtful.

'Tell me honestly, please,' asked Louise encouragingly, and snuggled closer to him.

'OK, it's like this,' Terry answered. 'I can't help being sceptical. And the problem with the times we live in is that it's not possible to be an environmentalist *and* be sceptical at the same time. You have to be a believer. You're either in the faith, or you're an infidel. A Green or a Grey. That's it.'

'You mean, even after Don's pep talk, you're still don't believe?'

'I've tried. I'm trying. How does the prayer go? "*I believe—help thou my unbelief!*"' Terry exclaimed.

'Whoa, hold on a minute,' said Louise. 'Are you saying you're a member of this government and you don't believe in what we're doing?'

'You won't shop me, will you?' joked Terry. At least, he hoped he was joking. 'Of course I'm committed to a Green course of action. Of course, of course. But I can't swallow everything hook line and sinker, just because I need to *belong*. We have to doubt and to challenge what we're told, and most of all what we plan to do. Most of the boneheads in the Green Militia would believe the moon is made of organic cheese if they read it in the *Green Earth Review*.'

Louise's jaw dropped in a shocked smile as he said this.

At last she said, 'So tell me what you don't believe. Global warming, perhaps?'

'Should global warming be something you "believe" in?' asked Terry. 'That's just the problem—it's become an article of faith, rather than an object of free and rational enquiry. Sure, I think it's overwhelmingly *probable* that human activities are contributing to a greenhouse effect. But I reserve the right to doubt the evidence, most of which is computer simulations built upon other computer simulations, all based on very thin historic data until after the 1960s.'

'Am I hearing this?' gasped Louise.

'OK. Try this. The next time you're in a meeting and someone witters on about "average temperatures" rising, ask them what exactly an "average temperature" is. They won't know. And ask them how long temperatures have been accurately and systematically recorded across the world. They won't know that either! The British Empire did its stuff collecting some data, I'm sure, but for any credible record it's all since the 1960s. Before that it's a case of filling in the gaps with assumptions and computer simulation. Anything before the 1880s is more gaps than record. And sea temperatures? We've got bugger all of a historical record there. So if anyone tells you they know what the Earth's average temperature was in 10,000,001 BC, you can be sure they're talking out their arse!'

'How can you say that, Terry! I've read the reports–'

'And all their speculative deduction from other indicators like tree rings in North America, and -'

'And the geological record–'

'Geological record? You know, now we talk about change year by year, or decade by decade. But with the geological record we're talking about is "give-or-take-a-hundred-thousand-years!" And then we fill in the hundred-thousand-year gaps with computer simulation, then draw fancy graphs showing changes of fractions of degrees. We talk about one or two degree rises in average temperature–but the margins of error in the calculations are up to five degrees either way!'

'Terry–what *are* you doing in this government?!' exclaimed Louise.

'Well sometimes, I ask myself too. I don't want to give a political speech, but to me it's quite clear we need to tackle how we use the world's resources, and to limit the damage we are doing to the planet. The destruction of the natural environment and species extinction, to me, are bigger and more tangible issues than global warming. About these, I know we can make a difference. But when it comes to restricting liberties and shackling the economy, we need to be clear that the evidence stands up to scrutiny.

'What the believers do is start with a big theory, and then squeeze all the evidence to fit it. It's like you have five pieces from a ten-thousand piece jigsaw, and you want to connect those five together because it's all you have. Or it's like the constellations in the stars.'

Terry pointed out the bedroom window, guiding Louise's gaze towards the clear night sky. 'We can just about make out Orion or the Great Bear because we've been told we should–actually you could draw any kind of bloody shape you like up there by joining the dots! It's the same with the shards of historic evidence we have! OK, don't look at me like that, I know I'm going over the top! Of course the evidence *points to* the reality of global warming! But is it really some kind of moral perversion to question this or that piece of evidence?'

'OK, Mr Smart-ass: you've apparently got all the answers. Don't interrupt! What would your lot *actually do* if power fell into your hands tomorrow?'

'Well, first of all, my sweet Believer, I've never said I've got all the answers. What I'm saying is we don't know all the answers, and it's dangerous to act like we do–'

'So, you're a typical bloody Liberal: you can criticise everything, but have no clear ideas about what to do!'

'Oh, so harsh, honey! No, I can tell you what we would do. Number one, continue with the switch to renewable energy—it's been Peter driving this anyway!'

Louise gave a theatrically sceptical look.

'But here's the clear difference between your lot and us: we'd go for sustainable growth. That's "sustainable" in the green sense, and "growth" in the old-fashioned economically sensible sense. You and Don say it can't be done. We say it can be done. What I mean is, we know how to do economic growth. The point is to "green" it. Everything else is a leap in the dark. An act of faith.

'Don and Malcolm and Sarah can't know what the outcome of their ideas will be. They can *believe* what they want. But all the wishful thinking in the world won't guarantee success. We're just guinea pigs in some grand political eco-experiment. All their plans will disrupt the economic foundations of our society: we'll run out of money to pay for schools and hospitals, and we'll have millions unemployed. That's the reality.'

'You mean, that's *your* belief,' said Louise quietly. 'So what are you going to do? Quit or stage a coup?'

Terry laughed at the thought of him staging a coup. 'Please, give me some credit for trying—trying to swallow my common sense and work with the Believers. What I'm saying is I can't be a blind follower of anybody. I can follow, and I can be loyal, but always with my eyes open.'

'Hmm, what an interesting self-assessment for a man: "I'm a good follower"! Can you lead, Terry?'

'You know in some things I'm happy to take the lead!' Terry replied, putting his arms around her and pulling her back on to the bed.

33: Local business

Over the next few months Terry Cairns threw himself into trying to make sense of the localism programme, and seeing that it was put into practice. He was put in charge of a new 'Department of Market Transformation' which not only provided incentives and made regulations, but also had a brief to stimulate voluntary activity.

Local energy and enthusiasm were the keys to making things happen, and Terry would find himself one day in charged meetings with supermarket executives, and the next on a regional tour endorsing and supporting local initiatives. This work often brought him into close contact with the Green Militia. In most areas, Green Militia personnel still carried forward much of the volunteer spirit of the early days, energising and supporting local people to produce and consume goods and services locally.

The summer of the second year of the Green Earth government was a good time to test the success of the new approach. By this time 'citizen planting' was yielding results as the programme was now benefitting from a full year's preparation and the local trading mechanisms which were now in place. Good weather had helped deliver success in producing a healthy amount of domestic and community crops. And where this was taking off, local people seemed more than happy to use the local markets. There was a momentum of goodwill behind them.

New regulations and the 'food mile taxes' introduced in Sarah Turner's budget incentivised supermarkets to buy locally too. This, though, was creating pressure on supplies in some places.

Not only food, but local production of clothes and other textiles, and all kinds of crafts came under Terry's department. And working with Peter Kitson, they developed an approach to domestic and community energy production to complement the large-scale energy programme of Peter's ministry.

Terry also spent hours with Danny Malik, as the new approach had to be sold to the nation, with its achievements promoted on TV and the Internet. Terry's department provided a regular diet of 'achievement stories' for the various channels, and Danny Malik had a team working day and night with social media to promote the best ideas and help people share problems and solutions about being 'domestic producers'.

This was a great time for Terry and Louise, who often worked together and sometimes toured together. During this time they met the King and other members of the royal family, who made a point of getting out and about to show top level support for these kinds of initiative.

But in truth, Terry was finding there were two sides to the local voluntary effort. The good side was where the systems of incentives he introduced were used wisely, in his view, by the local Earth Councils to seed-fund and support local projects. The downside was the tendency of the Green Militia in many areas to take direct action against people they thought were not complying, and against existing companies they felt were undermining the new approach. Their direct action could include blockading retail parks, or haranguing and threatening their customers. Groups of Militia surrounded people and asked them questions like 'Why are you buying a rug here? Why are you buying clothes here? You can buy them from the local Earth Market, and support local production'. They found that filming people in these situations quickly got people to leave the store, for fear of being brought before a Tribunal.

Similarly, people who made no effort to install their own renewable energy system or take part in a community energy system could be put under continuous pressure. In this way the Green Militia provided a different kind of incentive to complement the positive incentives that Terry Cairns was promoting.

Through this work Terry worked tirelessly to overcome his 'unbelief'. But the concerns he had were not only about the tendency of the Militia towards coercive tactics. Despite the apparent success of the local markets programme, he remained pessimistic about the economy as a whole.

He expressed his fears to Don Mason as their 'Local Markets Magic Bus' took them back to London from a rally in the West Country. Mason was delighted with the markets he saw and with the still rapturous reception he received at the rally.

'So have we made a Believer of you now, Terry?' he asked. 'What you achieved is little short of miraculous!' Then he leaned over and added in a whisper, 'Have you seen Ben Porter at the back of the bus, grinding his teeth? He's green with envy, about not being involved in this, and about the rising of your star! He's feeling a touch left out.'

'If he's left out, Don, isn't it because you wanted him to be left out?' answered Terry.

'You could say that,' replied Mason. 'I know you were puzzled by why I was anxious to involve you closer in our work. But what we've seen today is the answer. I much prefer to work with a sceptic like you who can do things, than a dreamer whose ideas are closer to my own, but doesn't have the ability to deliver anything. Your role has put a few noses out of joint. But nothing has upset people quite like harnessing Sandy's energies to the cause. She is like you. She can deliver. And her ability to work across boundaries–the different parties and with the departments and agencies of government, make her worth her weight in gold, don't you think?'

Terry nodded thoughtfully. 'And so you work with people outside of our coalition too–like Carl Fullerton?'

Now Mason nodded. 'I always admired his energy. It just needed better channelling, and perhaps he needed a little more maturity. Like all of us, he's a little older and wiser now. And he always bridged the divide on the activist side between our various shades of Green and the Animalist tendency. He has a certain charisma, too, that can keep people motivated when otherwise they would be flagging. You don't approve of him?'

'I barely know him,' said Terry. 'But I've seen what the Green Militia do under his leadership, and I think they often cross the line. And you know, I've never been comfortable with this "Militia" idea.'

Don Mason looked squarely at Terry. 'Hm, yes. Volunteers, Militia … to me it's all of a muchness really. It's about the people being on the march. And it still is, you know. You've seen yourself how people on the ground are over-fulfilling our targets and expectations. It's by no means all the Militia as such. Often as not it's local initiative, and the leadership only hears about it after the event. Carl, and Doug, and Malcolm–all those most involved in interacting with the grassroots–encourage this kind of bottom-up initiative. We don't have all the answers! And we ourselves learn from what's happening out there. We get to see what works, what doesn't, and where there are gaps and where more should be done. Our role is to do as you've done: put in place the supportive structures and incentives to enable the transformation to be done by the people themselves.'

'What about when those actions go too far?' asked Terry.

'Like what kind of thing?'

'Like when people who are slow to change have "eco-criminal" painted in big letters on their homes, or cars, or have their offices ransacked? Or these attacks on chains of furniture stores, the "grey monopolists" as they are being called. I saw where half a retail park had been burnt to the ground last week. Six large stores, burnt to the ground. This has got to stop.'

'Yes, yes,' agreed Mason. 'Malcolm and Carl are trying to get a handle on this kind of thing. But it's not the official Militia doing this. Hmm. Did I just say "Official Militia"? I'm not really sure if even I could put my finger on what that really is. It's all still quite fluid. And there are people out there who will never willingly submit to any kind of control. We can but try. All the same, no one's been hurt, and in the long term, these kinds of out-of-town retail centres don't have a future. Maybe you and Louise can start to think about how they can be phased out, how we can bring our city centres back to life, building on your local markets. And what we should do with these out-of-town centres; with the land, I mean, when they cease to be viable.'

That, for Terry, touched on the big issue. While the local markets were proving to be successful and popular so far, the same could not be said for the rest of the economy.

'This is where we are having a problem, Don,' said Terry. 'The viability of the rest of the economy. The economy's been sluggish for nearly ten years now. And parts of it seem to be heading into free-fall. I'm really concerned about this, even more than about some maverick wildness on the fringes. This is really affecting ordinary people in their daily lives. The success of our local markets and the boost to home-based businesses falls a long way short of making up for the decline in output across the board.'

'It's still the issue for you, isn't it, Terry?' chimed in Sarah Turner, who was sitting in the seat opposite, apparently engrossed in calculations on her tablet. 'Whether people can have enough, and be happy, without a return to growth, without increased consumption. You doubted our localism approach. But it works. Patience, patience, and you'll see the rest. It's a market adjustment, but not the kind you're used to from the old economics.'

'If this carries on, it will be an adjustment for sure. The question is, how painful should it be?'

Sarah put down her tablet in exasperation, but Don Mason looked attentive.

'People are losing their jobs, but they still have mortgages and rents to pay,' explained Terry. 'They have local taxes, and utility bills, and so on and so on. Now perhaps they can take the edge off this a bit if they can grow their own food, or generate their own power, or trade through a local exchange system. But in the end, they still need money. They can only get that through paid work, or benefits. Unemployment is rising as the economy shrinks. And our benefits bill is something we've got to get a grip on too. Our expenditure is rising, even as our government income is plummeting. We can't fill the gap by borrowing indefinitely–soon no one will want to lend to us anyway. You know, Sarah–you've got the figures there.'

'Well–for some it may be a hard landing,' said Sarah. 'But we have to help people to take responsibility for their own lives. At the risk of sounding like an old Tory, this may just be the jolt people need. You know, for too long most of us have been sucking at the endless teat of somebody-else-providing. Give me a job. Give me training. Give me benefits. Feed me. Clothe me. Bring all this stuff to me from somewhere else, I don't know how to go there and get it myself! It's all crap, you know! Capitalist, communist, one way or another they've infantilised us all, dragooning us into one collectivist system or another–'

'I think it's called Society, Sarah,' said Terry.

Sarah gave half a laugh and continued. 'No, you don't get it. It's not about that, it's about dependency. Dependency on big, wasteful systems that make idiots of us, that make us like helpless infants. And here's the thing: these big wasteful systems, whether corporate or government-owned, do immense damage to the planet we live on, and they're taking us to the brink. So we've got to help people break free, and make their own way in life. But in a new framework that supports self-sufficiency and self-reliance. You know that only fifteen per cent of the workforce are self-employed? It's been more or less the same for over thirty years, despite all the talk. We need to push that up to fifty per cent. Yes, *fifty* per cent. And support community enterprises to provide local services. We need to revolutionise expectations so that we all become producers, so that most of what we consume we have produced ourselves. I can see that sceptical look of yours, Terry. So what's your solution?'

'I'm not sure I have one off the shelf. But my advice would be: go slower. You want to create this new economy, but a) people aren't ready for it yet and b) we need to head off the kind of recession that will stop our new approach in its tracks. Can the change not be managed over a longer timescale, with the two systems existing side-by-side in the interim? You're not going to push up your self-employment and self-sufficiency rates to the level you want overnight. And in the meantime we'd have big questions to address, like: how can you run a modern health service against the backdrop of a grow-your-own and barter economy?'

'A snail's pace revolution?'

'Maybe walking-pace, rather than full-tilt, is how I'd put it. At a speed most people can cope with.'

'That's your problem!' exclaimed Sarah. 'Always concerned about people. "People, people, people". I never hear "Planet, Planet, Planet" from you, Terry. These people—*we* people—have ravaged the planet. The Earth has had to absorb so many shocks from human behaviour. But any adjustment the other way, and it's "Oh, let's take it slowly, so as not to upset anyone!" The fact is that we are going to have to have a few jolts—otherwise we'll never change. But adaptable is what we are. And we can, we will, adapt to a way of life more integrated with the needs of the planet.'

'I agree. Totally,' said Mason. 'But—Terry is right I think about managing the transformation of the old economy better, rather than just letting it disappear down the plughole through sheer negligence. Let's get to work on this, shall we?'

34: Conspicuous Consumption

A small convoy of four-wheel drive vehicles raced past Mason's 'Magic Bus' in the opposite direction, honking their horns. Engrossed in their conversation, Mason, Cairns and Turner barely noticed them. Ben Porter, dozing in the back of the bus, sleepily turned his head to look at them speed past. Inside were young people, shouting and gesticulating at the hydrogen-powered bus. Clearly off somewhere to party, thought Porter, who resumed his dozing, unconcerned.

A short way beyond, the cars turned off into a country lane. A few miles further along, similar expensive gas-guzzling vehicles and a mix of older, beaten-up or customised cars joined in from other lanes, music blaring from most of them. Inside, people were already dancing in their seats, drinking and whooping. There was now a small traffic jam as the cars slowed to file one by one through a wooden gate onto a field. Some sped fast, others bumped slowly down an incline towards a small wood.

Just beyond the wood, and out of sight of the country road, a party was already in full swing. Sound systems had been unloaded and music was pounding. New arrivals unloaded drink, food, drugs and anything else needed to make the party into an instant festival. As it said on the banner now being unfurled, a *'Festival of Conspicuous Consumption'*. This was a deliberate parody of the 'sustainable consumption' mantra of the Green Earth government. The idea had started as a student prank, and then was taken up with gusto by several groups of well-to-do young people. Extreme self-indulgence was the order of the day.

One of the ring-leaders, Justin Talbot-Smith, fell out of the back of a Range Rover, laughing all the way. He was the grandson of Lord Talbot Smith, one of the leading landowners in the region, and son of a leading Tory MP who was an implacable opponent of the new regime. But whereas his father and grandfather fulminated on the politics, Justin preferred simply to party. And to poke fun. A party-loving young man of twenty-two, he was by nature addicted to fun and reckless behaviour, like many young people born into money. And he was quick to identify the soft underbelly of the Green regime: its earnestness. The new overwhelming 'political correctness', the new institutions, the local markets and all their worthiness, the taxes on 'unethical' consumption, the endless stream of propaganda and 'green achievement' stories: these were all ripe for mockery. For being subverted by humour.

Justin was hauled from the floor by a small bevvy of bejewelled beauties in designer clothes, already clearly intoxicated. One of them fell sprawling to the ground herself as she tried to help him up, laughing all the time. Hugs and greetings done, they pulled Justin over to the drinks table where his close friends embraced him or clapped him on the back.

'Bloody brilliant, guys!' exclaimed Justin as a large glass of unnameable punch was poured from a jug, summer fruits and ice tumbling in with the alcohol. And it was indeed impressive. One of the best they had organised. Tables were laid out and overflowing with food. And not just any food. Young people who as students might have made do with anything instant, or for special events gone to expensive restaurants or used professional caterers, had now in this time of growing shortages developed a talent for sourcing fine foods and laying on amazing spreads of gourmet fare.

'You must try the truffles!' exclaimed Lisa, Justin's girlfriend, dragging him over to the next table. 'Oh my god! Natasha, where did you get that handbag?!'

Natasha, whose mouth was too full of venison sausage hot-dog to reply, pointed to a small truck parked on the other side of the encampment. Here was an alternative type of instant market, and it was doing great business. All the best brands of clothes and accessories were displayed on portable racks and fold-away tables. People were trying on clothes in front of full-length mirrors, and getting the advice of friends on how they looked and the best accessories to go with their selections. Wads of cash were exchanging hands, and the people selling were taking orders when stocks ran out or a different size was needed.

Away from the top-end items, Lisa was looking over the fastest selling items at the party: T-shirts in various designs and colours emblazoned with slogans such as 'Glad to be Grey!', 'I consume, therefore I am', 'Who cares about the future? Live for today!' and 'On Earth to make an impression'.

Nearby a group of boys were looking at a computer screen. One of them was editing scenes of their last instant festival being broken up by Green Militia. As always, the Conspicuous Consumptionists had had their escape plans in place, and were able to evade the small numbers of Militia trying to get hold of them. Now the boys were laughing, as they edited scenes of the Militia giving chase. They were making it look like a Keystone Cops sequence: speeding up the film, cutting in scripted scenes they had filmed later of Consumptionists dodging behind trees and popping up behind people dressed as Militia, then adding in music so it presented like an old and jerky silent film. Their previous efforts were already going viral on the Internet.

Back up the hill, the 'chase and exit' team was already laying out some hay bales and traffic cones to mark out a path down to the party. Except the route they were marking out now would lead the Militia if they arrived into boggy ground where their vehicles would get stuck. If this chase panned out as they planned, it would be hilarious. At the same time, their own exit routes had been planned across neighbouring fields. It was all fun, a big game. It was reckless, exhilarating, and they did not expect the consequences to be too serious if they were actually caught.

'Is Hunter coming?' asked Lisa.

'He should be, but you can never tell,' replied Justin with a smile.

'Will he have the horse?'

'He might do—but it could be too far from home unless he can borrow one.'

Hunter was the so-called 'Hunter Hoy', a new Internet sensation for this age group. He appeared at most of the Conspicuous Consumptionists' events in a hunting jacket and carrying a bugle, sometimes on a horse. Heavily disguised, he wore mutton-chop sideburns and a twirly moustache. 'Hunter Hoy' masks were already on sale, and 'Hunt Ahoy' had become a catchphrase in the movement, especially in confrontations and chases with the Militia. It seemed that protest against green government was becoming conflated with other, more traditional forms of conservatism.

Suddenly they heard the sound of a bugle, and people started to look around, gesturing to the people with the music systems to lower the noise.

'Over there!' cried Lisa in delight.

In the twilight they could make out some figures racing across a nearby field. There was Hunter Hoy, in his riding pink, alternately blowing his bugle and waving madly. And alongside him was a quad bike, with someone clinging perilously on the back, filming Hunter charging along. Several figures were running along behind, occasionally taking a tumble, then quickly getting up and running again.

'What on earth are they?' someone asked.

'Some kind of fancy dress, I think,' said someone else.

Then, as they all got closer, they could see. There were several people dressed as hunting dogs, one dressed as a fox, and two others each wearing half of a pantomime horse costume. Now everyone was laughing uproariously, as the new arrivals lined up for a procession over the last couple of hundred yards to the party. The film that would be made of tonight's chase would be special. Now all it needed was for the Militia to arrive.

An hour later, word came in from the outlying sentries that the Militia and police were on their way. And many more of them than on any previous occasion.

••

Don Mason couldn't help smiling when he saw the video. He was meeting with his 'kitchen cabinet' at the request of Danny Malik. Danny had half a smile too, but he took it seriously. It was his responsibility after all to ensure that the media were onside.

'I think it's one of the funniest things I've seen for quite a while,' said Mason. 'Just a shame that it's us having our tails tweaked.' He chuckled again.

Juliet Coe was furious. 'This is doing us a lot of harm. We are being made to look ridiculous!'

'Or rather–the Green Militia look ridiculous,' corrected Sarah Turner. 'We'll only look ridiculous if we come down too hard on it. We should leave this kind of thing to the police. Just treat it as an illegal rave, pick up the drugs offences, and so on.'

From her frown, it was clear Juliet Coe did not agree. 'The problem is, Sarah, that this kind of thing undermines all the hard work we are doing in news management. This has to be stopped before it sets the tone of how people think of us. Especially the upcoming generation.'

Juliet Coe had indeed been working hard. Having purged the BBC and promoted GEM sleepers and others she considered reliable into top management, she had been elevated to deputy head of ESCOMEDIA, and been tireless in 'harmonising' the other mainstream media outlets with the GEM approach. This was no small task. There were more than two thousand broadcast and media channels to deal with. Foreign media remained a problem. And the host of social media sites where people could freely express themselves and upload content–like the Conspicuous Consumptionist videos.

Juliet now had a growing reputation for her dogged determination and attention to detail. There were stories of her sitting in on script-writing sessions for soap operas, to ensure that environmental issues were brought to the fore. 'Why not?' she reasoned. 'They always prided themselves on dealing with the issues of the day, such as teenage pregnancies, AIDS, drug addiction, gay marriage and the like. So why not the future of the planet?' And when some script-writers and actors had overstepped the mark in revenge by portraying Green Militia leaders as pushy prigs, she had had them arrested and sent for re-education. It was important to her to set clear examples.

'Sarah, doesn't something in the video remind you of your early days,' asked Mason, seemingly going off at a tangent. 'Look at the spread they've put on, out in the middle of nowhere. And how quickly they set it up and cleared it all away–though that could be the editing, I guess.'

Sarah Turner smiled. 'I can't remember anything I did involving pate de foie gras, pheasant or champagne, Don. But I take the point. The subversive power of their organisation, and their ability to improvise are–impressive.'

'The difference is,' said Mason, 'the form is there but not the substance. I can't see any *real* subversion going on here. Nothing with the sense of purpose that we had. These are kids, clearly stoned out of their heads, having fun by thumbing their noses at authority. And showing a good deal of enterprise in the process. We're seen as the establishment now, so we must expect to be the focus of anti-establishment reflexes.'

'That's very liberal of you, Don,' said Malcolm Morton. 'Are you sure you're not spending too much time with Terry Cairns?'

Mason grunted and gave a slight smile in acknowledgement. 'Maybe so. All the same, I'm not convinced we need to go all Tiananmen and clamp down too hard. Getting all serious and over-reacting to humour only makes us look humourless and pompous. I'm with Sarah on this.'

The resulting batch of videos from the event had indeed proved extremely popular on the Internet, and had spread fast around the world. The Green Militia had indeed turned up in force. And as the Consumptionists had intended, the Militia had driven their vehicles into the boggy ground and got stuck. When the Militia and police then got out of their cars and vans, many had then sunk knee deep into the bog, and were forced to help each other squelch slowly to drier land. And as they did this, Hunter Hoy arrived on his horse, and after a few initial blasts on the bugle, he swapped it for a megaphone. As the people dressed as dogs, fox and horse performed a surreal dance, he bellowed at the Militia through the megaphone, 'In the name of all normal people on the planet, you are all under arrest! For offences against partying and against everything in life that is fun! I order to you to report to the nearest circus in the morning for re-education. Hunt ahoy!!' All the partygoers laughed and clapped, then began to run as the first of the Militia got through the mud and the last vehicles to arrive found their way around the bog. Then the chase ensued. This footage, though, was heavily edited to include people dressed as dogs comedy-wrestling with 'militiamen', and Hunter Hoy riding past to slap militiamen and police around the head with what appeared to be a large salmon.

'You do realise,' said Morton, addressing everyone, 'that this was in fact one of our more successful raids. We managed to block off one of their exit routes, and in all we caught around thirty Consumptionists out of the two hundred or so there. None of them seem to be the ringleaders, though. But we have a better idea who they are now.

'As for the general issue, Don and Sarah are perhaps right up to a point. We have until now not taken it too seriously. But it hasn't gone away. Instead they have become emboldened. There are copycat flash-events elsewhere. And as Juliet says, it is undermining, and I think corrosive. We could perhaps tolerate these things carrying on out in the countryside. Treat them as illegal raves, emphasise the drug arrests and criminal damage. If we didn't send in the Militia, we might avoid some of the more damaging video in these ridiculous chases. What worries me more is what they are starting to do in cities now. These kind of flash-mob demonstrations. It makes it all much more like a political protest movement—just at the point where we have been successful in neutralising most of the rest of the opposition by one means or another.'

'So what are you saying, Malcolm?' asked Danny Malik.

'For the moment, anyway, we need to avoid further confrontations where they can turn the tables on us. But we have some good leads. We can step up the surveillance, and we're preparing some people to infiltrate them. And we need to find if they have any connections with more serious opposition—which I think they have. While we try to avoid embarrassment, we need to see who else is attracted to them, and when the time comes we can scoop them all up at once.'

'Meanwhile, Juliet and I can see that the other side of the story gets out,' suggested Malik. 'In the end they left quite a lot of stuff behind. There must be stories about their branded goods being made by children in Vietnam or something, as well as anything plain illegal. We could explore their values, contrasted with the ethos of the local markets. Dumb, spoilt, rich kids flaunting their wealth compared to down-to-earth, honest, hard-working people making their own way and saving the planet. That kind of thing.'

'Sounds like a plan,' said Mason.

35: Under pressure

Joanna Kitson left the High Court in a state of barely suppressed fury. For months she had been applying all the levers available through the justice system to secure the release of several eco-camp detainees, including Sam Sharma and Miles Campbell. And four weeks ago she had succeeded with an injunction to secure their release. Then nothing happened.

She had spoken with judges privately to no avail, and now she had returned to court to try to force the issue, only to find that this time the court would do nothing. Clearly some pressure had been applied, and Joanna was at a loss how to go forward. She had been left with the small group of relatives, feeling humiliated and impotent, and conscious of having let them all down.

Now on her way back to her office, she considered her options, and dismissed them all one by one as futile. Her pondering came to an abrupt halt as she turned into the side street where her office was based. Lined along each side was an imposing line of Green Militia, who went completely silent as she entered the street.

Shocked and immediately fearing for her safety, Joanna looked over her shoulder. Any thoughts of retreat were cut off by a group of another half dozen Militia who sauntered menacingly into the road, closing off the way out.

Holding her nerve and trying to preserve her dignity, Joanna walked slowly forward towards her office. 'They're just trying to intimidate me,' she said to herself. 'And they're succeeding!'

One of the Militia muttered 'She's here' into his headset. Joanna now noticed how they all had identical headsets worn over one ear, one of the latest and most sophisticated models. And their uniforms seemed different. Much smarter than the days of the Green Volunteers, or even than the Militia a few months ago. One of them threw the dregs of his drink at her as she approached the building. She could feel it sliding down her cheek, but for the moment chose to ignore it, for fear of encouraging the others. It smelt like a strawberry smoothie. 'Could be worse!' she thought.

She swiped her card and opened the door of her building. Several Militia pushed through the door with her. As she went into the lift to go up to her office two Militia men joined her, saying nothing but just watching her constantly. They followed her into her office. As she went inside she found her assistant, Monica, almost in a state of panic, which intensified as she saw several of the Militia following Joanna through the door.

'There's some of them in your office...' said Monica weakly, her voice almost failing her.

Joanna nodded, fearing her voice would fail her too. She went inside. There were four Militia officers in her office. One, a man, sat at her desk, while another, a woman stood looking out of the window, keeping her back to Joanna for the moment. The other two were going through her shelves and cabinets, and seemed already to be downloading information from her computer to a nearby tablet.

Joanna tried to appear nonchalant, taking some tissues from the box on her desk to dab at the drink that was soaking into her suit. 'You could always have made an appointment,' she said. 'There's absolutely no need to force your way in.'

The man sitting at her desk raised one eyebrow and sniggered.

'Any luck at the High Court?' asked the woman by the window, without turning round.

'I would think you know by now,' replied Joanna.

'Did you expect your sabotage to succeed?'

'I would have expected the law to do its job.'

'But the law is not what it was.'

'Evidently. Perhaps you'd like to tell me why you are here, or is it only to gloat?'

Now the woman turned to face her. She was a young woman, less than thirty years old, her brown hair tied back loosely. Her face, which might otherwise have seemed quite attractive, was contorted in anger. 'This is your last warning. Why are you doing this? Why do you keep on trying to sabotage the re-education of eco-criminals, Ms Kitson? Why?'

Joanna said nothing, just looked her straight in the eye.

'This can only end badly for you. You know that.'

'Have you got what you came for?' asked Joanna icily.

'Mostly.' The Militia woman came closer, and stood face to face with Joanna.

'You think you're so clever, little Miss High-and-Mighty, with your Cambridge degrees and your inherited wealth and your friends in high places. But you are nothing. Nobody. Your old-world fantasies count for nothing now.'

'Then—why are you so afraid of me?' asked Joanna quietly, trying to hide the fact that she was trembling almost uncontrollably.

'Pah!' exclaimed the woman, and just for emphasis spat directly in Joanna's face. Joanna flinched. 'You are the most pathetic, deluded, bitch.' Her anger seemed to well up further inside her, then she continued her tirade against Joanna.

'Afraid of you? We can end this any time. Any time. I came here to give you a friendly warning, that's all. What will you do now? Call the law? We are the law! Or go and cry on your big brother's shoulder? What can he do, when he's one of us? You are beneath contempt.'

She signalled to the others and they slowly left the room. As he left, the man who had been sitting at her desk knocked her screen with his elbow, sending it shattering to the floor. He nodded with a sardonic smile as he went by.

As they left Monica broke into a flood of hysterical tears. Joanna put her arms around her and hugged her close, comforting her and in the process calming herself. After a minute or so, Joanna said, 'Let's go and get a coffee. Or something stronger. I just need to go to the washroom to wash my face.'

In the washroom Joanna took some deep breaths to calm herself further, than leaned over to wash the remaining saliva from her face. She dabbed her face with a paper towel, and was preparing to retouch her makeup when she heard the toilet flush in the stall behind her. In the mirror she saw the Militia woman who had confronted her emerge from the stall.

Joanna couldn't help smiling at the bathos of the situation. 'Please, don't mind me. Go ahead and wash your hands!'

The woman nodded curtly, and started to wash her hands at the other sink. 'Kind of bizarre this, isn't it?' said Joanna. 'Comic, even.'

The other woman looked sideways at her.

'I mean,' said Joanna, 'All that drama and aggression in there. Now we two in here, on our own, all normal, woman to woman, even sharing a mirror. You're not so big and, what's the word, authoritative, or pushy, when it's just you and me in here. Little you, and me a good three inches taller, and with my kickboxing belts and everything. Do you want to try something now maybe? Whatever I did, it would be self-defence ….'

The militia woman opened her mouth as if to speak, then said nothing and shot out the door.

Joanna smiled. It was a small and cheap victory, but it did something to restore the day.

••

Despite this minor victory, Joanna was still trembling when she reached her brother's house. It was Andrea's second birthday, and they were hosting what was turning out to be a somewhat chaotic party for toddlers, their parents and a range of friends and colleagues.

'What on earth has happened?' cried Heather when she saw her sister-in-law. 'You're as white as a sheet. And is that blood on your jacket?!'

'Oh, it's nothing. Just an upset at work. Let's not talk about me. How's the birthday girl? I've got something for her right here...'

The two-year-old Andrea was running towards her aunt with faltering steps, arms stretched out.

'Ah, you want to give your Aunt a big hug!' said Joanna.

As Joanna scooped her up, instead of throwing her arms round Joanna's neck as usual, Andrea struggled and kept her arms open. Joanna looked a bit puzzled.

'Uh-oh,' said Peter, 'She doesn't want you any more, Jo—she wants a present. She's learnt something new today!'

They all laughed and made a big fuss as Joanna squatted down and retrieved a wrapped present from her bag. Andrea was coaxed into a cute 'Thank you' that had all the parents cooing and laughing. Peter went to get Joanna a drink while Heather introduced her to the various other parents there. This was a whole new world that Heather was now part of, and Joanna could see some of the charms. A world away from the hassles and frustrations of her own life. After a chaotic game of 'pass the parcel' involving several toddler wrangles and some tears, the cake was brought out, everyone sang 'Happy Birthday' and the party descended into a free-for-all.

Now Peter and Heather and Rachel Dean pressed Joanna to know what the trouble was, and Joanna gave them the outline of what happened.

'You said you had kickboxing belts?' asked Peter, incredulous.

'A small fib, I have to admit,' said Joanna. 'I did have a couple of lessons at college, though I mainly learned how to do press-ups and how to fall over!'

'Why did you give up? It could have come in handy some day—like today!' asked Rachel.

'Oh, I don't know. Somehow it all seemed a bit too, er, physical for me! Enough about me now. I hear you've been under a bit of pressure at college, Rachel.'

'Oh, please. Let's not talk about that,' replied Rachel. 'There's some fanatics on campus trying to "Green" everything we teach. They're scoring my history classes low for environmental awareness. I'd like you to come in one day to kick-box the butts of some of these ignorant little shits. But I have to bite my tongue. Especially with things as they are at home.'

Joanna didn't actually know how things were at home for Rachel. But she had noticed Mark Dean, her husband, slumped quietly in a corner and clearly drinking far too much. Mark at a kiddie's party in the afternoon didn't quite add up. There had to be problems at work. And there were, as Rachel explained quietly. He'd had to close down his business, laying off all the staff, and the business had substantial debts that he wanted to honour, but had no idea how.

'The bottle offers some relief, but no answers,' said Rachel sadly. 'I don't think we can take much more. I'm trying to get a post in America—I've got my feelers out. I can't see any prospects here for us.'

'Wow, that would be a wrench for us,' said Heather, glancing across at Peter. Peter nodded emphatically.

'Come with us!' said Rachel. 'At least till things settle down here. Although...I suppose you're kind of central to getting it settled down, Peter.'

'I expect I am,' said Peter thoughtfully. The truth was, he was having a lot of doubts about his role in these times, made worse by what he had heard from Joanna and Rachel.

The problem was, he felt two very strong reasons for staying involved in the government. The first was, he genuinely felt the renewable energy and eco-business projects he was involved in were valuable for the nation. He enjoyed the work. The second was that if he and Terry and their junior colleagues left the coalition, what would come next? He could see things that were not right, but what could he do from the side-lines? No, tomorrow he would go to have strong words with Don Mason and Malcolm Morton about the need to get a grip of the radical elements that were out of control at grass-roots level. And he and Terry needed to get to work on pushing measures to stimulate business, before more businesses went the way of Mark's.

It was certain he would need to have some in-depth one-to-ones with Don Mason about the fault-lines and excesses in the Green Revolution. After two years, it was surely time for things to settle down and be regularised.

36: Annie Lee's journey north

The phone rang. Even before she picked it up, Annie knew who it would be.

'Hello, Ma.'

She knew the first questions her mother would ask: What are you doing? Are you busy? Have you eaten? Maybe only the answer to the last one was of any actual interest to her mother.

Annie's parents had come to Britain before she was born, from mainland China via Hong Kong. Selfless hard work was a trait she had inherited from them. They had worked day and night to build a living, and to save money so their children could succeed. A dutiful daughter, Annie nonetheless knew she was a disappointment to them when, in spite of her grades, she chose not to go to medical school, choosing biotechnology instead. Initially, it was awareness of her father's increasingly incapacitating kidney disease that led her in the direction of wanting to do pioneering research. Naturally academic and idealistic, as a bright fourteen year old she had dreamed of finding new cures for all kinds of chronic diseases. While her friends at school read teen magazines and talked endlessly about boys and fashion, Annie read books about biotechnology and genetic research.

Gradually her friends drifted away, and she spent most of her time on her own or in the company of adults. Her science teacher persuaded the senior librarian in the university library to allow her to study there. Charmed by her precocious earnestness, he provided her with a password to read all the electronic journals. Many were the times her parents found her glued to her computer when they returned from work at two in the morning—not chatting, not gaming, but reading papers in medicine and biology.

Gradually her horizons widened, and she became more and more interested in applying biological science to solving environmental problems. This was her route into green activism, and how she fell under the spell of Don Mason and Sarah Turner. It was Sarah Turner who had first taken her under her wing. This pretty and petite Chinese girl had at first looked so out of place at the rallies and protests. One day Sarah had found her shivering behind a tent, reading an academic text on new techniques in organoponics.

'Can you cook?' Sarah asked.

That she could certainly do, having almost grown up in restaurants. It was second nature. For two years she was a fixture at protests all around the country and had bonded with a new group of friends. Then, it seemed, she disappeared from all activist activities, devoting herself first to her studies and then to her work.

The activist phase was a mystery to her parents, and a source of great worry to her father in particular. Having escaped China at the tail end of the Cultural Revolution after much suffering in his family, he distrusted all kinds of politics, and especially any that involved extremes of enthusiasm and devotion to an ideology. She would sit quietly through his tirades against the follies of that era and, as he saw it, the idiocies of his countrymen.

Despite their disappointment at her not going into medicine, though, she gradually won her parents' approval for her choice as she rose in her career. That she worked for the British government seemed a good sign for them. It seemed unfortunate to them that she would never be as rich as a doctor, but if she had security and status that would be good too.

'This place you go to,' said Annie's mother, 'Will there be many doctors there?'

Annie smiled. 'If I can't be one, you want me to marry one?'

'You're not getting younger, child. You're very pretty, but at your age you can't expect to get any prettier. For me it was downhill all the way after I was thirty. Good thing I met your father before that, or you wouldn't be here with us now!'

Annie knew what would be coming next. She could almost mouth the words as her mother said them.

'I'm sixty now, and I would like to see my grandchildren before it's too late.'

In fact, Annie's mother was only in her early fifties, but it had been an idiosyncrasy for as long as Annie could remember that her mother would round up her age to the next multiple of ten.

'You must have a lot of money saved up now, Annie. Living on your own in that tiny room. And up there in Scotland you'll be living rent free? You should really put down the deposit on a small place near home, some place you can come back to. And it would be an investment you can cash in when you get married. So many couples are struggling now, but you would be in a much better situation. And of course we could add to that—maybe you could buy something outright, and have no debt.'

Annie saw out the rest of the conversation, giving away as little as possible about where she would be staying and the miniscule salary attached. When she was younger, she had tried to enthuse her parents about the eco-projects she became involved in, but her involvement just left them baffled and bemused. All the same, she never wanted to argue with them. Her respect for them was boundless, and her love for them immense, inexpressible. That made her choices all the more difficult. For now her heart and her head were turned to larger issues, and the completion of a mission that had started some eight years ago, when she had first become a 'sleeper' for the GEM. It was at that time too that she had first met Titus Whitaker, and his philosophy had, for her, joined up all the dots. In her mind, there was no contradiction between the ideas of Don Mason and those of Titus Whitaker—only a reinforced necessity for action.

She packed the last of her sparse belongings in her luggage, and looked one last time around her neat and modern studio apartment. She had two cases. One for books, the other for clothes and bits and pieces of technology. More than half of her clothes she had taken to the charity shop, and even some of her treasured books.

Two framed photographs remained. One of her with her parents when she was about nine years old. And one of her younger brother, now training in London to be: a doctor. Annie went to the door, leaving the photos behind on the small desk. Then at the last minute, she walked quickly back, snatched them up and put them into the top of one of the cases.

Outside, a taxi was waiting to take her to the train station in Salisbury. From there she would travel north to Glasgow, and from there by bus with the Green Militia to the new research facility at North Camp, a satellite of the West Highland Eco-Camp.

'Don't look back,' she told herself. 'The rest of my life, my new life, begins here. I will never be the same again, and the world will never be the same again.'

37: There is no big picture …

Don Mason wanted to export the Green Revolution. And he wanted to neutralise the hostility he felt building up in the US administration of President Johnson Wilding. So he arranged an official visit, accompanied by Peter Kitson. He felt that Kitson would be an asset to him, as a coalition partner representing one of the older and more respectable parties, and Kitson's role was to forge links with government bodies and private companies engaged in sustainable energy initiatives. He would be a very acceptable face for the Green Revolution.

Peter had had sharp words with Don and with Malcolm Morton after Joanna's experience with the Militia. It was a new experience for Don and Malcolm: they could not recall ever having seen Peter angry before. And it worked. They promised him that nothing would ever happen again. And for good measure, several people on Joanna's list were released as part of a highly publicised programme of selective releases of detainees at Christmas. The former detainees were interviewed on TV and spoke in glowing terms about the new practical skills they had learned and their awakened understanding of the need to live in harmony with the Earth.

Mason anticipated that the reception in America from President Wilding would be correct but frosty. But it did not worry him unduly. His aim was to capitalise on Wilding's low poll ratings and present an alternative to him to the American people and their media. For Mason, the chat show appearances were more important than the sessions with Wilding, and the meetings with Mayors and Governors more important still.

The fact was that the USA was having its own kind of half-hearted Green Revolution. Certainly the President opposed it. But many mayors of large cities and some state governors had been elected with environmentalism at least as part of their ticket, and many were pushing though ambitious green initiatives. Leaving Peter Kitson for talks with officials in Washington, Mason went on a five day national tour, in which he was greeted either as a hero or at least as an 'A List' celebrity.

Huge crowds turned out in the streets to see him, even though in February the weather in many places was far from welcoming. He spoke about the historic connection between Americans and the natural environment, quoted Thoreau, Emerson and various Founding Fathers, appealing both to liberals and the more romantic strain of conservatism. As in the early days of the Green Revolution in the UK, Mason made a show of his openness and directness. Politicians, journalists, and members of the public asked him tough questions, and he was happy to reply, never ducking the issue though often challenging the assumptions behind the question.

'What about hunting?' asked an angry caller on a phone-in. 'Isn't it your people who banned hunting in England?'

'No, it wasn't, though some of our people campaigned against it. That was more than fifteen years ago, now. And that was hunting for sport, not food. I actually think there's something more honest about confronting your food before you eat it, rather than buying factory-farmed cuts of meat from a shop. Don't you?'

On another show the host tried to cajole Mason into condemning the President's record on the environment. Diplomatically, Mason refused to do this.

'You know President Wilding stands in the Bush tradition, and that is an outlook that is often condemned by environmentalists around the world. But I have to say, I think there are many things that the President is getting right. Number one: not signing any pointless agreements about pollution reduction targets or emission quotas. In my view these have missed the point entirely. Number two: American government investment in new greener technologies has been second to none, and is very extensive under President Wilding. Now I'm very happy about that. I think there's much more to be gained by countries pushing ahead with their own ways of dealing with the environmental crises we are facing. We need to support and encourage each other, and learn from each other—not sit a bunch of bureaucrats and politicians in a five star hotel somewhere to cobble together some useless compromise that everyone then ignores.

'So I welcome his initiatives, and I welcome the many initiatives I've been seeing as I journey around the states. What is needed now in this country, I think, is a larger measure of involvement from everyday people in transforming their own local environments. We've found that it's not all about big expensive projects. The root of the Green Revolution in Britain is the care and concern of ordinary people in improving their local environments. That all adds up to helping the Planet.'

'Seems he wants to set up a branch of the Green Volunteers here,' President Wilding growled to one of his aides when he saw this interview.

Mason's toughest grilling came in an in-depth news interview with Ted Waterstone on one of the national news channels. Ted focused in on the Mason government's growing reputation for illiberal measures.

'Now tell me about these re-education camps, Mr Mason. This doesn't sound like a British way of doing things—it sounds more like Pol Pot's Cambodia than the England of tea and cricket that we all know and love, don't you think?', said Ted challengingly.

'Whoa, that's a far-fetched comparison. You can't compare planting trees in Scotland or building wind turbines in Wales with wiping out the entire middle class in Cambodia!' Mason replied.

'OK, but isn't there a lot of concern about people who just disappear into these camps and are never seen again?' asked the interviewer, leaning forward meaningfully.

Mason looked thoughtful and concerned as the camera zoomed in slowly for a close-up.

'Don't you think it's a bit early, Ted, to be talking about never being seen again? I mean, these environmental work camps have only been around in their current form for around nine or ten months. Ninety per cent of people who've been in one are out and about now. It seems there have been some intermittent problems in communication and tracking people down sometimes—it's a new venture. You know, Ted, half the people mentioned by Joanna Kitson in that article you talked about are out right now walking the streets of London, or Liverpool or wherever they come from.'

'But those figures you quote, Don, don't they include the early stages of the so-called "eco-colleges" as well? If we leave those people out of the equation and concentrate on the last six months, there's a lot of people who've gone in and not come out. What's the population of the camps, Don?'

'The latest figures I have, from about two weeks ago, are eight thousand people in the camps, and their average length of stay is eight weeks. We're talking about work experience here, and giving people the opportunity to learn and change their outlook on life. You know, our way of life is so urbanised, so detached from the natural world, that it's very hard for people to change unless they get the opportunity to live close to it.'

'You make it sound like fun, Don, like some kind of team-building course. But this is not something people choose to do—people are forced into it and treated like criminals aren't they?' interrupted Ted.

'Well, the team-building analogy is not a bad one. And if you work for a company, going on the teambuilding course is usually not optional! You have to go if you want to keep your job, don't you? And what's the aim of running a course like that? To help people become responsible members of the team. We're doing much the same, to help people become more responsible members of society and take a more responsible and knowledgeable attitude to the world we have to share together.'

'That's fine—but treating people like criminals, Don?'

'Criminals? We think that people who have been sent to the camps have shown themselves to be criminally irresponsible towards the world we live in. They are usually people who have done something seriously wayward—like dumping toxic waste in rivers—or else they're persistent low-level offenders. And we're trying an experiment where some of these are everyday criminals in the last part of a prison sentence, and we're preparing them for active and responsible citizenship. It's true we've got a bit tougher in the camps. But I think most Americans can identify with that. It's no good pussy-footing around. All the same, the way people are treated in Greener Britain is not as tough as how a common-or-garden criminal is treated here. I mean, here in America *suspects*—people not even convicted—are shipped around in chains. There's nothing like that with our camps. People are given a time to turn up for a bus! And the camps are nothing like your prisons. No gun-toting guards, no drugs, no gangs, no rapes: I'd bet most of your prison population would rush to sign up to serve out their sentence in one of our eco-camps!

'You know the way I like to think of it is this. Until now we basically had two kinds of law that affected most people: criminal law and civil law. If you are sued in a civil court, that doesn't make you a criminal. Now we have a third kind of law: "Earth Law", we like to call it. It comes back to our respect for what I call "mute interests". Democracies are great at defending and promoting the interests of the people who live in them. But who speaks up for the mute interests? There are two kinds of these: the interests of the natural environment, and the interests of future generations. They have no voice, but their interests have to be enshrined in law, to prevent the present generation from wrecking the planet.

'It's like you have your constitution. You set out the basic sacred principles, and all governments should abide by them. I reckon if the Founding Fathers had seen how future generations would plunder and ravage the beautiful country they revered, they'd have added in a few Green clauses to protect her, don't you think? That's what we're doing—setting the British Constitution on a new footing. It's a transitional phase, and some people don't want to co-operate. So we're dealing with that. Some people don't like it, and some don't want to cooperate. But the mood of the country has been to *do* something—they don't want a whole lot more posturing and talking. So we're exercising leadership, and I think that's what people want.'

Mason's tough but thoughtful attitude played well with the American public and media. But it cut little ice with the Administration. At the end of his tour Mason returned to Washington for further meetings with the President. Reluctantly Mason agreed to a round of golf. The President liked to play golf on every possible occasion, and being a fine player he especially liked to play when entertaining foreign dignitaries and political opponents. A chance to get an upper hand from the start.

'Have you played much golf, Don?' asked the President.

'Only the odd game here and there,' Don replied. 'I'd have liked to play more.'

'Here's your chance,' said the President as they arrived at the first tee. 'Don't you think it's just beautiful here?'

Mason looked around, taking in everything. It was indeed a beautiful, managed—even manicured—landscape.

'Just glorious,' said Don.

'But maybe not natural enough for you?'

'I was wondering how many thousands of gallons of weedkiller, insecticide and fertiliser per year it takes to achieve this....'

'I'll ask the greenkeeper,' said Wilding with a wry smile.

Mason smiled too.

'Maybe you'd prefer it if we covered the greens in horseshit?' suggested Wilding.

'It might make things more even for me,' Mason replied, then took his first shot. It didn't rise very high but travelled quite a distance nonetheless.

'Not bad, not bad!' said Wilding. 'Straight as a die—you really have played this before!'

'Just beginner's luck,' Mason replied modestly. 'You know, you could have more natural golf courses. It might inject more character into all the different courses....'

'Like crazy golf?' suggested Wilding. And he took his shot. It soared into the sky, pretty much straight down the fairway, landing a good distance beyond Mason's. 'Do you want to walk or take the buggy?'

'Let's walk,' said Mason, 'It's a nice day for a stroll and a quiet chat.'

Later President Wilding would recall his surprise at Mason's character. He had expected from the reports he received some wild-eyed ideologue who would lecture him on the sins of America and the righteousness of being Green. Instead he found a quick-witted affable man with a ready smile, firm handshake, and it seemed a willingness to listen to others. But behind the amiability he sensed a determination which at this stage seemed to manifest itself in a genial stubbornness. In the face of growing international pressure, it seemed Mason wanted to win some time for his programme to make more progress.

At the ninth green, Mason attempted a fifteen foot putt, which he hit a little too hard: it swung off the lip of the hole and rolled a couple of feet to the right, almost stopping before the slope took it down, gently accelerating to the edge of a bunker.

'Very nearly one Tiger in his heyday would have been proud of!' said Wilding.

'As my father always used to say, "A miss is as good as a mile",' said Mason with mock gloominess.

'Really? Your father said that? So did mine. Endlessly!' said Wilding, preparing to putt. '"No prizes for coming second". He said that too. Endlessly. Until I believed it.'

He confidently sunk his ball from around ten feet.

'Tell me,' said Mason suddenly, 'what do you want?'

Wilding looked a little puzzled. 'What do you mean, exactly? I want re-election, like all good Presidents—but I don't think you're asking that.'

Mason looked thoughtful for a moment, and swept his greying hairs back over his temples.

'It's partly a personal question, partly a Big Issues question,' explained Mason. 'I know why I'm doing what I'm doing. I'm trying to change things, and I have in front of me some big Goals, capital "G" Goals! I'm wondering what *you* want to achieve, what America wants to achieve. You have all this power, and your country still has this huge global domination, but what do want to do with it?'

Wilding blew out his cheeks a little, then pursed his lips. 'That's quite a big question for the ninth hole. My answer might be different at the nineteenth, after a few beers. Come on Don, you read the papers, you must know what I want!'

'I know what's in your programme, but that's not what I mean,' Don replied. 'I'm asking you about what it is ultimately you hope to achieve, how people will remember you in the future.'

'I know what you mean, Don, I'm just stalling for time a little to get my head round the answer,' said the President, smiling. 'The thing to remember is, Don, that we're different. You're a radical, I'm a conservative. You want endless amounts of change, but I like where we are and I want to draw out the best of what we have now.

'You know, Don, there are different trajectories of achievement, all in motion at the same time. As a conservative I don't have one big all-embracing goal. For the leader of a great and powerful nation, just holding it all together is an immense achievement. To give people the security and the opportunity to enjoy life, liberty and the pursuit of happiness. And to enable people to create wealth, stimulate enterprise, and motivate people to realise their dreams. There doesn't have to be a big picture. The big picture is all the little pictures put together, that's all. I'd be proud to have carved on my gravestone, "Here lies President Johnson Wilding. He kept things ticking over, and we were all happy"!'

Wilding had stopped as he spoke, and with the sun streaming down on them between the trees, they stood talking half-way to the tenth hole. Mason was smiling and nodding at his answer, as it grew more impassioned.

'But if I was a dreamer, Don, this is what I'd add. I'm no isolationist. I see America's role in the world, now that we have this immense power and responsibility, as being to spread liberty and prosperity. I want to give the chance for all peoples all across the world to enjoy what we enjoy. And if in every nation we are all busy raising our families, building our homes, making money and trading with each other, I believe there'll be less space for conflict. It's when people are forced to put ideologies ahead of their own and their families' well-being that we get violence, disorder, terrorism and war. I won't go on. You get the picture, I'm sure!'

They walked on for a few moments in silence, then Don spoke:

'It's a vision I'd believe in but for one thing. There's a great cost attached to it. Prosperity and self-advancement come at a huge cost to the world we live in, as we suck more out of the planet to put into our own lives. Within two generations we'll come up against the limits to growth, and where then? Maybe we just leave it all to our kids to sort out, telling them it's a price they must pay for having higher levels of income.'

'I don't share your pessimism about the future,' Wilding replied. 'Greater prosperity can give us the means to deal with our problems. Stagnation or poverty would mean we tackle the world's problems with our hands tied behind our backs. Do you think when people have less they'll adopt higher principles? No, Don. If we stop becoming richer, people will soon revert to barbarism, superstition and incessant conflict.

'You know we have our own environmental programmes. And we can do more than anyone else because we're richer than anyone else. I heard you even said some kind words about our programmes the other day. Thanks—and did you mean it?' he chuckled.

'Of course, of course—I'm always sincere in my praise!' laughed Mason. The tone was light, but both knew they were getting closer to the real issue. Now Wilding spelt it out.

'You know what worries us about you, Don, is not any of your up-front environmental initiatives. It's the mindset that there's something wrong with economic growth. We've heard your folks are seriously talking about "negative economic growth". Do they really know what they're talking about, and what its impact will be? Your country still has the sixth largest economy in the world. The impact will be global—and maybe you want it to be: hit us all with a renewed recession. And the word is you're thinking of taking Britain out of a whole range of international agreements, ploughing your own isolated furrow. But you ought to know, there's a whole lot of people who don't want this to happen. Including most of your fellow countrymen, I would think. Even people who swallow the rhetoric now, when they begin to experience hardship will think again. And, Don, if what people are telling me is true, I'd like you to think again too. A green and prosperous future is a fine goal, and one we can all share, though we might take different paths to reach it. But reducing prosperity to achieve your goals—the outcome doesn't bear thinking about.'

Mason was a little taken aback by the President's passion and eloquence. When he'd asked the question, he had anticipated the President not being able to come up with much of a vision. Wilding's views did not strike Mason as ecologically realistic, but his little speech changed Mason's view of the President. He had imagined him as a mediocre political operator, in the pocket of big business. Instead he found a very confident and successful man, with a strong belief in what he was doing.

'A green and prosperous future,' Mason repeated pensively. 'It would be fine—so long as we could agree what "green" and "prosperous" actually mean. Endlessly acquiring useless possessions which will be redundant in a few months is a poor kind of prosperity. And asking multinationals to plant a tree here and there after whole ecosystems have been ravaged is not exactly green. We've got a long way to go before we talk the same language.'

'Fine,' said the President. 'Let's start the conversation. But we can only have a successful dialogue if it's built on trust. And that means we have to trust that your government isn't about to do anything … precipitous.'

'Sure,' said Mason, 'and we have to be sure the dialogue isn't just a way to prevent us doing anything, while you protect the status quo. We have to talk about real things that we can do together. Things that will happen within our own lifetimes!'

'Understood. We've been boiling some things up, and Zara Alderney, I believe, should be sharing them with your Peter Kitson right now. You know, I like that young man! Kitson's sharp, Don, got his feet on the ground, and his ideas rooted in reality as we know it … '

'Can't be one of ours then!' said Mason, raising an eyebrow.

Wilding hesitated a second or two. 'That's British humour, isn't it, Don?' he said, and after a moment of reflection laughed out loud. 'Come on, let's play!'

'Play on indeed,' said Mason.

III

38: Stella's files

Stella Walton was alarmed at what she had found. The question was, what to do with it? She had seventy-two hours to do something. ESCOMEDIA had ordered her to appear before a Tribunal as a result of general dissatisfaction about her work at the BBC, and the upshot was that on Saturday morning she had to report at 8 a.m. at Manchester Central coach station, to be transported to a re-education camp. But it seemed that whatever her alleged offences, the authorities didn't yet know what she had found from her research into Juliet Coe. At least, research that had started by investigating Juliet Coe, as Miles Campbell had requested nearly two years before, but which had since moved into new territory.

'Call Trevor,' was her first thought. She had hesitated. Finally she concluded that for all his much vaunted cowardice, he was someone she knew she could trust.

Trevor MacLean had been migrating northwards as his previously spectacular career went into reverse. The former Director-General, Miles Campbell, had assigned him to a special advisory role in Edinburgh. Then the heat was turned up by the Scottish Media Scrutiny Commission, and his boss there had protected him by reassigning him to local radio in the Highlands. He bought a small cottage in a village a few miles south of Inverness, close to his wife's family. Caroline, Trevor's wife, had never entirely taken to life down south, so a return north of the border was not in the least unwelcome to her. She realised though the setback it meant to Trevor's career. Despite Trevor's theatrical grumbling, they settled down quickly to life in the wilds. Their two daughters rapidly settled into life at a local private school. The MacLeans could foresee some financially stretched times ahead, but agreed there could be no better place to weather the tornado that had hit the media world.

Stella Walton's call brought the old world rushing back in.

'Stella, how wonderful to hear from you!' he cried when he heard her voice for the first time in more than six months. 'Which gulag are you calling from? Do you want me to send food parcels, or some blankets?'

'Trevor...'

Stella's tone of voice let him know that within just a few seconds he had, as always, opened his big mouth too wide.

'Oh, God!' said Trevor. 'I've put my foot in it again. Something's happened, hasn't it?'

Stella was trying her best not to feel too anxious and upset. 'I'm sorry—I wasn't going to hit you with the bad news straight away. Still, it's not that bad. You were joking, but you were right. I'm being packed off to an eco-camp somewhere. Twelve weeks, they gave me, but from what I hear, the sentences can be a bit flexible either way. Hopefully I'll get some time off for good behaviour!'

'Oh, Stella, I'm so sorry. But I'm sure you'll be alright. Here's some serious advice. If you're being sent anywhere in these parts, take plenty of woollies, and thermal underwear too. Anyone who works outdoors up here has a good supply. I can send you some, if you don't object to me buying your underwear, darling! Where are they sending you? I do hope it is up here, then I can come and visit. Be like old times!'

'Well, one thing I've found out is that these days they never tell you: you only find out when you arrive. But I'll let you know if I can. And—don't worry about sending anything: I go on Saturday. But I'll take your advice and go shopping for my thermals tomorrow! Anyway, how are you? How's the family?'

'Oh, I'm fine, we're all fine! You know, I did a piece today about an apparent epidemic of sheep-shaving. Young wastrels shaving graffiti into the wool on live animals, would you believe! It's a serious problem in these parts, these days. Not quite the same as interviewing Prime Ministers, is it? At least we can say we rode the tiger for a few months. Shame it turned around and bit us, isn't it? But you know, life up here is good. I'm even growing vegetables ... '

'I can't believe you're growing your own food, now!' laughed Stella.

'Well, potentially. I must be doing something wrong. Everything I plant grows perfectly formed, but absolutely miniscule! The neighbours keep asking after my "bonsai vegetables"! The kids love it up here though. Carrie too. The scenery is just amazing, and the air is as clean as you could imagine. And so much less stress in my life. I'm genuinely happy here! But how are you, I mean apart from the sword of Damocles having fallen?'

'I've been fine, Trevor, just fine. Life has been hectic, and kind of precarious too, as you can guess. In some ways, when the Tribunal came down on me, it was sort of a relief—bringing a resolution to months of maybes.'

'And how's your love life—as eventful as ever?'

'I wish! Still no Mr Right. But maybe that makes my situation more bearable. I've only got Me to worry about. Having my career trashed doesn't affect anyone else.'

They talked some more, exchanging news about family and mutual friends and colleagues. Finally Stella got to the purpose of her call. 'Trevor, there's one thing. I want to ask you a favour.'

'Sure,' said Trevor. 'Anything. Except—oh my God—you don't want me to take in that cat of yours, do you?'

'No,' laughed Stella. 'I've found a good home for the mog. What makes you think she'd like to stay with you, anyway? She knows what you're like! Seriously, though, it's about some research I've been doing. It needs a safe place to be—or even for someone to carry on the investigation for a while. What do you think?'

Trevor felt alarm bells ringing. 'I'm listening, but I'm promising nothing, yet.'

'That's fine,' said Stella, unconsciously lowering her voice to a more confidential tone. 'You must feel free to say no. This could be quite hot—maybe even too hot to handle.'

'I'm getting worried now, Stella!'

'I have to confess that I did some digging into Juliet Coe's background…'

'Stella! What are you doing?!' hissed Trevor, also lowering his tone. 'Is this why they're sending you to Siberia?'

'Funnily enough, I don't think it is. I got no hint they knew I was up to anything like that. I've been very discreet.'

'And what about now—is this what you call discreet, talking to me on the phone?'

'Maybe you didn't notice, but this is a secure call I'm making.'

'Nothing is that secure!'

'Do you think either of us is important enough for our calls to be monitored? I can't imagine we've gone that far yet. Well, briefly: in my covert diggings I found a whole lot of leads that set me to thinking there are wheels within wheels in the Green Earth Movement. Not everything is as it seems, and not everyone is who they seem to be. There's a darker green agenda bubbling underneath. I'm not one hundred per cent sure yet who are the main people driving this. Or whether this is the "real" GEM under the surface, or whether there's some level of infiltration by other groups.'

'OK, OK, Stella,' interrupted Trevor. 'I don't think I want to know any more about this. I'm really, really sorry! The last thing I want to do is let you down. Maybe you have something, maybe you don't. But the fates have conspired to mark this file "None Of My Business". You know what a born-again coward I am! A card-carrying chicken-worshipping coward. And I have a good life here. I don't want to jeopardise it, or do anything against the interests of my family. God, I feel a heel! But do you understand? I can't touch it!'

'Sure, I understand,' said Stella, trying not to sound too crestfallen. 'I just wanted to make sure…OK, never mind. What do you suggest I do with my work so far, just bin it?'

'Stella, if the powers-that-be, ESCOMEDIA or whoever, think that you are trying to subvert the Green Revolution, you could be in re-education for life. My strong advice is, however much it disappoints you, take it no further! Maybe another day things will be different.'

Reluctantly, Stella agreed. She knew she was taking a risk by contacting him, but security on Internet calls could be pretty sophisticated these days with the right software. Maybe, though, she hadn't appreciated enough the danger she might put him in. Still, she had achieved one thing. In the event that something might happen to her, someone knew she was on to something big.

And Trevor wouldn't be the only person she would let know. Next on her list was Peter Kitson. He, after all, might be the main loser from the 'wheels within wheels' she felt she had discovered. Stella had met him three or four times in the election campaign and just after: she felt, like most others who met him, that he was a decent and trustworthy man. She just needed some time to work out how best to contact him, given the security that now surrounded him as a government minister.

Stella thought back to the unexpected commission from the then Director General, Miles Campbell, that had put her first onto this train of research. She had begun it with enthusiasm, only for Miles to pull her off the work a few days later. A few weeks later he was dismissed. He must have known it was coming, she thought, and wanted to protect me.

Since Michaela Cavaliero had left the BBC and fled overseas for a lucrative post with CNN, Stella had found herself pushed more and more out into the cold, with little useful work to do. She knew that she had fallen foul of the increasingly powerful Green Team at the BBC. Then one day about six months back she had chanced to be leaving Media City at the same time that Juliet Coe was coming in for an ESCOMEDIA meeting. How times had changed. Juliet was now surrounded by a small troupe of flunkies, each eager to gain her attention and carry her bags.

On impulse Stella caught Juliet by the arm, and beamed a friendly smile. Stella had given Juliet her first job, and they had worked together for more than a year. Juliet's reaction was frosty, and she seemed affronted by the physical contact.

'Hi, Juliet!' Stella had said. 'How are you?'

Juliet's reply was hostile in the extreme. She berated Stella for the harm she had done to the Green Revolution, and warned her that she no longer enjoyed the protection of powerful friends, so she should watch her step. Stella had little choice but to endure this tirade. Embarrassed, humiliated and fuming with resentment, she marched out of the building. On the way home she resolved to get even with the little upstart. She resolved to do an even more thorough investigation of her background and career, going beyond anything Miles Campbell might have sanctioned. Using some illicit software she'd acquired some years before from a tabloid journalist she had been seeing, she began to monitor Juliet's communications and contacts. As her dossier on Juliet began to build up, Stella realised that she would have to search wider to put Juliet's dramatic rise in context. And the picture that emerged was far more than Stella had suspected. For some six months, Stella used her spare time to build up her dossier on Juliet Coe and her fellow travellers. And now she urgently needed to share it with somebody.

••

Juliet Coe's schedule became more pressing by the day. It was quite rare for her to set foot in the BBC these days, though the grand old institution was still officially her employer. She had become the dominant figure in ESCOMEDIA, due to the fact that she had the ear of Danny Malik and Don Mason.

Juliet knew the issue she had brought before ESCOMEDIA had ruffled some feathers, and alarmed a few of the less radical members. It was important work, and it had to be done. And the issue was close to her heart—the question of 'accurate and balanced reporting'.

The GEM leadership, despite their increased control of the press, were concerned about the nature of much of the reporting in the media. Criticisms from the 'alternative parliament' on the South Bank were still occasionally reported, though not with much prominence. In the place of real news, there was often scurrilous speculation about the private lives of members of the government and of the National Convention.

The tabloids, as ever, liked to pick up on the apparent absurdities of the revolutionary institutions, at all levels. And now some of the more heavyweight papers were probing into some of the 'disappearances' in the prelude to legal action brought by Joanna Kitson's clients.

'We have to get some perspective on this,' Mason had told Danny Malik and Juliet Coe. The *Code on Accurate and Balanced Reporting* was their response.

Word of the Code had got out to media owners and editors shortly before the meeting that Danny Malik had called, and they responded with a mixture of alarm and rage. But they had been sufficiently intimidated by the detention and 're-education' of hundreds of journalists, and were rather muted in their response. Danny and Juliet were talking on the way to the meeting.

'We're OK,' said Juliet. 'Pendlebury at *The Guardian* is upset—but he does support the Revolution. We can bring him round. Jackson at the *Mail* has resigned, thank God. Her likely successor is one of ours. The main problem, frankly, is the Horton media empire. They have a couple of the biggest circulation dailies, plus all their satellite channels and online channels. But most of all, they're largely based outside our reach. All the same, the Code will apply to their operations in this country.'

'They'll have to accept that,' said Malik firmly. 'And I don't think they're the force they were, now that the old man has gone. They seem to be a bit rudderless.'

Juliet nodded. 'And they want to be friends with the government. We have leverage.'

They arrived at the meeting and were warmly greeted by Craig Delaney. To his great surprise, Craig had found himself as Acting President of ESCOMEDIA after the unexpected resignation and disappearance of the previous incumbent. Craig had told his wife 'I feel uncomfortable with this big suit on', but he hid his discomfort well as he carried out his duties diligently and wallowed in his new found high status.

Of course he still had his 'sidekick', Juliet Coe, who was always one step ahead of him. If not pulling all the strings, she was at least the direct line to the people who were. He often pondered his game plan. To serve with credit, and establish himself as an enduring figure of respect in the broadcasting world. This was the kind of phrase that came into his mind in his more reflective moments, as he brushed his teeth or took a shower. He would look into the mirror after he shaved, angle his head to one side and say to himself 'This guy's OK. He's made it!' Then he would smile or chuckle, feeling that his tongue was firmly in his cheek and that he had everything in perspective.

Craig now had the status he had always felt he deserved. Over breakfast he could pick up *The Times* and see his face. Or turn to the media supplements and read the report of an in-depth interview he had given. He could tolerate the spin that journalists felt obliged to throw into such articles as if to prove their superiority over their subject matter: in the end he was the person people were talking about, not the hack who wrote it. He could also laugh out loud at the gossip in the tabloids, however scurrilous or off-beam.

At a time when many people were feeling the pinch, Craig's income had rocketed. Not that being President of a Scrutiny Commission was rewarded with a vast salary. But it was more than respectable, nearly double that of his former role once all the allowances were counted in. On top of that was the freelance work, writing several opinion pieces a week for domestic and foreign press, plus appearance fees for TV and conferences. He knew he wasn't the most dynamic or charismatic of men. But people seemed to like him. He felt he was, in another of his own phrases, a personable apostle for the Green Revolution.

He was a great believer in the value of public service media. He often started his musing with the words: 'I'm a great believer in ...' The fact of his belief in this or that carried great weight for himself. In his elevated position, what he believed not only should be listened to, it was listened to. And acted upon. He felt the reforms he had helped introduce to the BBC had helped to put it back on the right track, with a renewed emphasis on serving the public interest. Now he could take this further.

He was especially proud of having helped to oust such shallow and ratings-driven people as Trevor MacLean and Michaela Cavaliero. News and documentaries had now moved away from sensationalist and shallow infotainment and were once again serious and issues-driven, in his view, with detailed analysis that didn't revolve around personalities and opinion polls.

And he was proud of the introduction of what he called 'achievement news'. He agreed with Don Mason that too much of news reporting focused on the negative. Under the old regime a news story on wind farms would have focused on local self-interested protests against them. Now the focus would be on the fact that renewable energy was contributing nearly thirty per cent of the nation's needs. Which was the more important fact to report? The big picture had always been obscured by dogged pursuit of sensational or controversial trivia. But no more.

Not only the government's achievements were highlighted, of course. Personal and corporate achievements could make the news headlines too. This was not to everyone's taste. From the safety of her new home in Italy, Michaela Cavaliero had commented that following his guidelines the BBC news would be pitched somewhere between China Daily and the Cleethorpes Clarion.

Through ESCOMEDIA, Craig had helped to take these reforms beyond his former employer, and helped bring the other media channels into a more responsible position. Jonathan Austin, Chief Executive of Channel 17, was a contemporary of Craig and an old adversary, barely less insufferable than Trevor MacLean in his withering disregard for Craig. Austin had soared past him in his mercurial rise a decade ago, yet now he was coming to Craig as a supplicant. It felt good.

Now Craig found himself greeting two people who used to be junior to him but who were now calling the shots in the media world. One of them, Danny Malik, was now a government minister. The other, Juliet Coe, was inexplicably powerful and seemed to be able to pull all kinds of levers. Craig himself was seen as the third figure in this triumvirate, and that was good enough.

The new *Code on Accurate and Balanced Reporting* was accepted without a fight. Meetings between ESCOMEDIA and media organisations that had formerly been quite lively with debate were now dominated by sullen faces, sycophants and empty chairs. The empty chairs mostly belonged to representatives from the Horton media empire.

'They can run, but they can't hide,' said Juliet icily.

'Craig, we think it's time to use the emergency powers vested in ESCOMEDIA to take over and administer the renegade media outlets,' said Malik. 'Don't worry about the overseas divisions—we'll have to find another way to deal with them. The technology is almost in place to block access to foreign counter-revolutionary influences. Just get the home team on message and we'll all be very pleased.'

39: An unexpected gift

Peter Kitson had arrived home from Washington with a curious mix of feelings. Exhaustion, elation, a sense of achievement and an undercurrent of uncertainty all competed for dominance. Most immediately, however, he felt intense comfort and relief being at home with Heather and Andrea.

There was a lot of catching up to do, on both the domestic and the work fronts. Heather was excited to hear about Peter's meetings with the President, bombarding Peter with questions about what he was really like. And she was itching to hear the inside story about Zara Alderney, the glamorous celebrity-turned-politician who as US Secretary of State had spent a fair amount of time entertaining Peter and Don Mason. Given her reputation, the questions Heather really wanted to ask were 'Did she come on to you?' and 'Did you flirt with her?' The second question was, however, ironic–from long experience she felt her husband was incapable of flirting.

The early evening was dominated by Andrea, delightfully so for Peter. He had brought back armfuls of presents for her, and for Heather. In fact though he didn't know it, it was the enthusiasm of his shopping that more than anything had endeared him to Zara Alderney. She had asked him in the middle of one exhausting session with White House officials, 'Do you really want to be doing this? Wouldn't you rather be back home playing with your little one?' Peter had smiled a rueful smile, and thought that he would. 'This business, like show business, has a huge cost for family life. I've been through several families. Take it from me, I'm an expert!' she added.

As Peter and Heather snuggled together on the couch, Peter told her all about this. Heather wanted to know the details of the rooms, the décor, the furnishings–all the things he tended not to notice.

'And what was she wearing?'

'Who?'

'Who?' echoed Heather. 'Now that's always the first answer of a guilty man! Secretary of State Alderney, of course.'

'I don't know,' said Peter, 'Something white I think one day, and on another day maybe it was something...'

'Black?' smiled Heather

'Possibly,' Peter confirmed. 'Don't you want to hear what we talked about, or maybe I should analyse Zara Alderney's make-up for you? Or the President's?'

'Peter, don't patronise me like I'm some celebrity fixated moron! Remember I was in PR. Being shallow is being professional, for me!' said Heather, pretending to be affronted. Then she added with mock seriousness, 'Tell me darling, how were the high level diplomatic discussions? Fruitful, I trust?'

Peter outlined the range of issues they discussed, and how he had come to admire but also be exasperated by the stance the Americans took across the board. 'They have this self-assurance that comes from being confident in their power. On every issue they drew a line in the sand, so a whole lot of things appear non-negotiable. Then they set an agenda of things they want you to do or not to do. At times it felt like being in school, with the teachers telling you the rules and what's expected of you!'

'And what do they want?' asked Heather.

'They were very interested in our national projects, especially the energy ones. They want American companies to have the option to carry out the construction and engineering projects. Zara kept calling Dave Barrington's approach "socialistic". They don't like all this state control. That's something we may be able to do a deal on. And they were worried about a whole load of world trade issues, and what the British self-sufficiency drive means for American exports. They seemed to know an awful lot about the GEM's future plans—much more than I do, if they're right! And they wanted more assurances over our defence policy—that we'll continue to support everything they do. Zara seemed to have a whole file on me—my past political views going right back to student days when I helped to organise demonstrations against the Iraq war. They'd done their homework.'

'What did you ask from them?'

'Well, Mason's approach for this trip was all about reassurance. And to promote the Green Revolution in America, without directly confronting the President. He spent a lot of time on TV. And a fair amount of time seeing Green activists there. They're a bizarre and disparate bunch, on the whole. Many different factions of them, coming from all sorts of directions that seem like another planet. Mason thinks America needs a GEM—a green movement with teeth and self-discipline to pull everything together. But America's a different sort of country. I don't think that model could work there.'

'No one thought it could work here either,' observed Heather. 'You must have spent a lot of time at close quarters with Mason—even more than normal, I mean. What do you think of him?'

'We talked a lot, especially when we were travelling,' said Peter. 'Most of the time it was practical things—how to handle particular issues, and not only to do with America. And we talked about our personal lives, a bit. It was funny though. My personal life was all present tense, but his was nearly all past tense. It seems like he's really put his personal life completely on hold. And you know, he can drink for England! My God, he can put it away! Wilding trounced him at golf, but Mason could out-beer him any day, with capacity to spare!'

'What's the President like with a sore head?'

'He seemed to have some added respect for Mason. It's a macho thing, I guess.'

'You didn't try to keep pace with them?'

'No way! I'm not a man's man. Just a woman's man, maybe!'

'Did Zara think so?'

'Please, honey! Don't forget she's more than twenty years older than me!'

'She was twenty years older than some of her husbands, too. Still used 'em up and threw away the husks, by all accounts!'

'I love it when you're jealous!' said Peter. 'By the way, Don Mason said to send his best wishes to you and Andrea. He said he'd heard a fair bit about you from the Barringtons, and all of it complimentary. And he was falling over himself with apologies for how Joanna was treated. You know, there's something about him that's a bit hard to fathom. He should be under a lot of stress, with the economy on the slide and his popularity waning. Even though we don't see much in the news, the GEM relentlessly commission polls about the government's performance, and it's all downhill at the moment. It's almost like he expected this, and is waiting for something. But enough of all this. Tell me more about what's been happening here.'

So Heather poured out the news from England. Joanna's coming and goings and her campaigns, and her emerging credit as a 'good aunt'. A call from 'that treacherous bitch Sandy', as Heather and Joanna now invariably called her, who wanted still to be pally. News from Margaret Blackstone: Howard was doing moderately well, recovering from surgery in Germany but still not out of the woods. Terry's cross-party activities with 'Luscious Louise' had hit the online scandal sheets. Jessica Barrington had become the poster girl for a programme called 'Our Nation's Food': a kind of organic 'Dig for Victory' campaign. The royal family were hardly ever out of the papers, always launching or endorsing some new environmental initiative. Mark Dean was languishing in the depths of depression, and was looking very stressed all the time that he was not completely drunk.

'And something really weird happened this morning, when I was taking Andrea to nursery,' said Heather.

'What kind of weird?'

'Well, I don't know what to make of it. But I've saved it to last so it didn't get in the way of all our other catching up. I'd taken Andrea in, and this woman I vaguely recognised came up and greeted me a little theatrically as if I was a long lost friend. It was Stella Walton. Do you remember her? Tall, dark, early thirties maybe, fringe—only this time her hair was blonde, not black. From the BBC.'

'Yes, I remember her. She worked with Trevor MacLean, I think.'

'That's her. It was strange. After greeting me, she said, "Please act normally, like we're old friends. I want to get a message to your husband, but I don't want anyone to know. It's really important. The day after tomorrow they're sending me away for re-education. I don't know where. I have some really important information, and Peter really needs to know about this. I don't want to leave anything with you, for your protection. But I want the briefest of meetings, that's all!" It was so strange, so cloak-and-dagger. And do you know what she asked me to do? She wants you and me to go shopping tomorrow lunchtime. Somehow she knows your schedule for tomorrow, and that we'd have time to meet at one-thirty. If you want to do this, we're to go to Next on Oxford Street, the kids' clothes section, and just look at a few items. She'll make contact there. If we don't want to do it, we just don't turn up and she says she'll understand. This creeps me out, you know!'

'Wow!' said Peter. 'That is weird. What do you think she wants? I do remember her, and MacLean singing her praises. She seemed a genuine kind of person. Warm and likeable. But if she's off for re-education, I guess she's in some trouble with her work. Do you think it's some kind of grievance?'

'Peter, you know how many crank letters we get. It could be someone trying to set you up. Even assassinate you! I don't think we should go. Maybe we should tell your bodyguards. But I wanted to discuss it with you first.'

'Why both of us? If she wanted to meet me, it would be quite easy to arrange.'

'She seemed frightened, genuinely frightened. But for all we know, her fear could be some paranoid delusion. She said if we were together your bodyguard would give us more space, and almost certainly wouldn't go all the way with you into the kids clothing section.'

'That's probably true. How important can it be?'

'She said it would give you a very significant insight into the GEM and their plans. And it's in the national interest for you to know…'

'Well, if it's in the national interest! I don't know. Let's sleep on this and decide tomorrow, OK?'

••

The following day Peter and Heather met for an early lunch at the National Gallery, having cancelled his last meeting of the morning. He'd had a busy morning of briefing sessions, and now was looking distinctly jaded and jet-lagged.

'Let's not do this,' Heather advised.

'I want to know what this is about,' Peter replied. 'My curiosity has overcome my natural caution. I tell you what. We can just go casually to the entrance of the kids section and look in. If Stella is on her own, and doesn't look completely crazed, we go in and see what she has to say. If it looks like she's with someone, or anything else is odd, we turn back and we can just look at some clothes for us. OK?'

'OK,' said Heather, sounding uncertain. She was a little fearful, but the adrenalin was also running. This sort of thing didn't happen to her every day. 'Shall we walk or take a cab? I think I'd prefer to walk.'

'Walk?' exclaimed Peter. 'It's about minus ten out there!'

'Yes—exhilarating isn't it?' said Heather excitedly. 'A real winter. We haven't had one of these for how many years?'

Their bodyguard, two special branch officers, had other ideas, and hailed them an electric taxi. At Next, one of the bodyguards stayed outside, while the other one accompanied them inside. As Heather began to look through some racks of women's clothes, the bodyguard let them wander further from him. Peter glanced into the children's section. As far as he could see, there was no sign of Stella.

Suddenly Heather recognised Stella, still blonde but this time wearing glasses, and bundled up in a warm brown winter coat with a high faux-fur collar. She walked through the shop making straight for the children's section. The Kitsons could hear her asking the sales assistant a question, something about a warm coat for her seven-year-old niece.

After a minute or two in the women's clothes section, Peter said:

'I thought we were coming in here for Andrea, not you!'

'OK, OK!' Heather laughed. Then to the bodyguard she added, 'Are you like this when you go shopping with your wife?'

'I never do,' he replied solemnly. 'That way our marriage will last. Are you going into the kids section, then? OK, I'll just lurk out here. Shout if you need any fashion advice, won't you!'

The bodyguard had already checked out that area of the shop to his satisfaction, and had observed a new and unthreatening customer come in. The Kitsons went through, and started looking at the range of outfits for two-year-olds, rapidly becoming engrossed in the task despite the covert nature of their mission.

Stella Walton brushed past once as she sought out coats for her niece. Eventually, after shaking off the over-helpful sales assistant, she came opposite the Kitsons and spoke softly to them as she looked through the rack, pulling out occasional items.

'I can't thank you enough for coming. What I have is potentially so hot, I couldn't entrust it to any third party. Peter—I've just dropped a memory stick in your pocket—don't look for it now. Everything's on there. You need a key to access it. It's in today's personal ads in the *Evening News*. Look for the "woman seeking man", third one down: "Attractive graduate nurse, 40, seeks new man to set her pulse racing". The last word and the box number provide the key—you'll see how it works easily enough. Don't write it down anywhere, just in case. Oh, isn't this coat just wonderful?'

Peter looked up and met her gaze. 'Yes it's lovely, but a bit big for our little one!' he said. Then lowering his voice, he added, 'Why me, Stella? Why like this, so cloak-and-dagger?'

'You'll see when you open the files. And don't open it on any computer that's connected online—you're probably being monitored all the time. Don't share it with anyone until you're totally sure you can trust them. Definitely no one from the government or security services. You'll see what I mean. I have to go. God bless you for coming!'

Stella turned quickly and walked up with the coat to the sales assistant. 'I think this one's perfect. I'll take it. But can we bring it back if it doesn't fit?' Then she went off to pay for it, while Heather and Peter chose a couple of items for Andrea.

Outside, their bodyguards hailed another taxi. As the taxi was pulling away, they saw Stella surrounded by some police and other officials. One of the bodyguards noticed this too. 'She's the woman from the shop, isn't she? Seems to be in some trouble now.'

'She didn't seem like a shoplifter,' said Heather.

'They never do,' said the bodyguard.

••

Peter decided not to look at Stella's gift to him in his Westminster office. After all, it might not be secure to do so, assuming she was correct in her fears. And if her intent was malicious, it might contain a virus or similar to be unleashed on the central government networks. He and Heather opened it together at home, after Andrea was in bed. He plugged the memory stick into an old laptop not connected to his home network. He took her advice about this, but nonetheless remained suspicious of her motives.

As Stella had said, the memory stick contained an encrypted directory. Heather had already opened the *Evening News* to the personal ads, and they had had some fun reading some of them out over supper. They could see that the key required fourteen digits to be entered, and duly put in the letters and numbers from the message. A video message from Stella Walton started up. Her hair was its normal colour, so clearly this was something she had put together at least a few days before.

'Hi, and thanks for taking the trouble to look at this. I hope it doesn't mean trouble for you—it probably means trouble for me if anyone finds this. There are about three thousand documents here, which are the fruits of my research into the inner workings of the Green Earth Movement and background on several of their key personnel. Unfortunately, I don't have time to complete my work, as I'm being shipped off for "re-education" soon. My research into what happens in re-education shows that I may not be back in action for some time, certainly longer than the sentence I've been given. Maybe knowing what I know I should just run away. But I want to see for myself what happens there, how this Green Revolution is playing out on the ground. Journalistic instinct, I suppose. Or just recklessly nosey!

'When I come out, I hope to continue this research. And maybe you can help. The people I'll be sending this file to can all in their own way, with their own contacts and specialisms, add to the knowledge. I'm afraid some of my findings are only partial, and many of the connections are only circumstantial. But I *know* there is a big story here, and one that people need to know.

'I also know what some people may say if my partial findings become public. They'll say I'm motivated by a personal vendetta against Juliet Coe. I helped get Juliet her first post at the BBC, and later she pushed me and many of my closest colleagues out of work. She repaid kindnesses with treachery thanks to her blinkered ideology. So maybe there is some revenge motive that helped me begin my research. That's not the whole story, though.

'What I have found, I believe, is a sinister strand within the GEM and Animalist movements, dedicated not only to reducing production and consumption, but also to strictly controlling the human population, in the interests of "ecological balance". If this is their aim, it's something that's being kept very much under wraps. We need to ask, why? And if it's part of their future plans, in a democracy it needs to be brought out into the open for an honest debate, don't you think?

'And that brings me to another strand of my research. In the GEM there is a determinedly anti-democratic strain. We've seen anti-democratic tendencies building over several decades, in every party that gets into power. But at least some of the GEM leadership are preparing to make a step-change in the nature of government control over our lives.

'Take a close look at the documents I've prepared and see for yourself. I have brought this to you because it's no use going to the British media. So the media overseas and people in privileged positions at home are our only hope. We need to get the truth out into the open, and confront it. I look forward to your support. Thank you.'

As the message ended, a menu of other enclosed documents popped up.

'Wow!' exclaimed Heather.

'Wow indeed!' echoed Peter. 'A touch dramatic, even melodramatic, don't you think, honey?'

'I don't know, but she gets "A star" for presentation! Look at this list of documents, all neatly linked together—documents, charts, databases, presentations, and I can see several more videos in here too,' said Heather. 'But I guess this could be awkward for you. If she's right, you and Terry and your supporters are right in there up to your necks with these sinister forces.'

'Um, yes,' murmured Peter uncomfortably. 'Do I look like the sinister type, honey? Let's have a look at some more.'

They combed through the files, and realised that it was going to take more than one sitting to digest it. Heather was particularly struck by one file. It was like a rock band 'family tree', tracing the histories of individuals and the groups they belonged to, showing the cross-currents and influences, complete with photos and some embedded movies showing some of the key protagonists in action. The chart could also be rotated in three dimensions, showing a matrix of key themes in the speeches or writings of the people being researched.

'My God,' said Heather. 'Whether it's accurate or not, this is a work of art!'

At the level of themes, the chart showed a bright constellation of connections to the themes of 'reducing consumption'. Then there were smaller stars with lines radiating to fewer individuals, labelled by themes such as 'population restraint', 'rights of species', 'active populations rebalancing', and 'need for coercive measures'. Right at the extreme edge were some fringe ideas with a few connecting strands such as 'the Voluntary Holocaust', 'the Malthus Trigger' and such like. Clicking on these labels brought up a summary of the key ideas and further quotations from leading advocates of that viewpoint.

A further button labelled 'Caveat' provided a candid assessment of the value of the research from Stella. It warned that guilt by association was a dangerous path to go down. Nonetheless, an accumulation of associations indicated something definitely worth investigating further. It also noted that in many of the documents she had found, the ideas were posed as debates and questions rather than definitive statements of intent. So population control was most frequently put forward as an idea to be discussed as the logical extension of other policies. She had found few clear statements that this was the right thing to do, let alone the advocacy of any specific measures to do it.

One thing caught Peter's eye in particular. 'Look at this, honey,' he said. 'Look at the "career path" chart, how often people move in the last couple of years from fringe groups to the centre. Especially recently: look at the numbers of apparent mavericks who are now in the Green Militias. Wow! I recognise one or two of these names–they're people quite high up now on Morton's staff. I need to check out the ideas they're credited with...'

'And look at this, honey,' said Heather. 'There's quite a lot of interconnection between Greens and Animalists...though when you think about it I guess they would have many issues in common.'

'But Mason is often very scathing about them—especially about Gabriella Pearson and Titus Whitaker.'

There were also databases of people who had been taken into re-education camps. Apparently Stella was trying to find if there was any pattern in who had been transported to them. It seemed she was trying to prove that the government was targeting certain type of enemies. But she had to admit the evidence was too patchy and diverse to have firm conclusions. It did seem though that a relatively large number were from the media. This information could be drawn from public sources made available by the Tribunals. But there was also information about where people had been sent.

'This information isn't freely available. Stella must have hacked into it somehow, or she's got contacts in the system. Joanna would give her eye teeth for this information,' said Peter.

'You must give it to her!' said Heather quickly. 'Oh, let's check for someone she's looking for. I'm trying to think of those names she keeps mentioning...'

'Sally Meredith, that outspoken science teacher who told her students not to believe everything they heard or read about climate change,' suggested Peter.

Heather leaned across him and ordered the database records alphabetically, and clicked through until she found the name Meredith. There were three of them, and one was indeed Sally Meredith, a science teacher from Lincolnshire. Her penalty was twelve weeks re-education, and she had been sent to the West Highland eco-camp. There was a recommendation that she 'might require more intensive and longer re-education, due to the stubbornness of her greyist views and hostility to ecological reality'. Her record also included a note of subsequent transfers to other camps, and a note of some hospital treatment. Peter felt a chill as he read this.

Peter made copies of Stella's files—one for Joanna, one for Terry Cairns, and one for back-up. He now began to realise that it was time to prepare to separate the Liberals from the GEM. Zara Alderney had dropped heavy hints to him in America that the time would come. He had felt then these were clumsy attempts to undermine the coalition. Now it seemed there was enough in Stella's research to pose serious questions about the direction the government was going. He'd talk to Terry in the morning. But how was he going to broach the subject with Mason, without revealing the sources of his information?

40: Betrayal

Peter Kitson never met Terry Cairns to give him Stella's files.

At breakfast time the next day the phone rang. Heather answered, then handed it over to Peter. 'It's Sandy,' she said with a withering look.

Sandy sounded upset and excited at the same time. Something dramatic had happened overnight. 'Oh, thank God you're there, Peter. Something unbelievable has happened. And Terry's in trouble because of it. It's Louise Adams. She's a spy or something! It looks like Terry's going down with her!'

'Hold on, hold on!' Peter interjected. 'Tell me slowly, from the beginning—what's happened?'

Sandy didn't know exactly. She had come into work early to prepare for the morning's meetings, to find the GEM leadership all there with Ben Porter. She told Peter she felt a distinct chill in Morton's look as she came in, and everyone went quiet. Mason was looking pale, a little shocked. He had invited her to take a seat, and told her the outline of what had happened. This she now passed on to Peter.

'It seems impossible, but Louise has been working for the Americans—no one knows for how long. Morton's people were monitoring the activities of American agents working out of the U.S. embassy, and found Louise was in almost daily communication with one of them before Don's trip to America.'

'But why—why would she do that?'

'That's what they were all wondering. They all worked with her for several years even before they came to power, and of course she's been helping to guide their current policy. It doesn't really make sense. Though she did go to university in America. It seems too far-fetched to think she might have been recruited there and then assigned to track such a fringe party as the GEM was at the time! But maybe she met someone back then who entered the intelligence world and followed her up—oh, I don't know. Everyone's speculating!'

'Where is she now? And what's happening to Terry?' asked Peter.

'Well, Louise is under arrest, under lock and key somewhere. As for Terry—Malcolm wouldn't say except he said Terry's not under arrest. But naturally he's under suspicion and he's being questioned somewhere.'

'The idea of Terry being an American spy, or in cahoots with one—it's ridiculous!' exclaimed Peter.

'It is, I know,' agreed Sandy. 'But look at it from the angle of the security services. He was, shall we say, romantically involved with her. And because of her trusted role in our government he may have let her in on all kinds of things—and not only about the government and the GEM. The Americans were probably interested where the Liberals stand on a range of issues and how robust the coalition is. She could spy on both sides. Or as Sarah said, "She was screwing him for information while he was screwing her for fun". I guess she could have put it more delicately.'

Peter paused for a few moments, as all kinds of thoughts and possibilities rushed through his mind. 'Let's think about this coolly for a moment. Louise was a key adviser to this government, and she already knew most of what there was to know about both us and the GEM. She can't have got any great advantage through getting so close to Terry. And as for passing secrets to the Americans. They're our allies, for God's sake! We've always given them bucket loads of information, and carte blanche to operate here. Apart from disliking the general principle of the thing, I can't see there can have been much damage done. Unless there's something the GEM aren't telling the rest of us…'

And as he spoke Peter began to think of the files from Stella, and of his own thoughts after the visit to the eco-camp. This could all tie up. Or maybe Stella's paranoia might be starting to affect his view of the GEM. But he couldn't tell Sandy about Stella's files. At one time he might have confided in her, sought her advice, but now it seemed her loyalties were more diverse.

'Sandy—is there something the GEM aren't telling us?' asked Peter.

'Oh, Peter! Don't put me in a difficult position. I have to work with three parties: the GEM, the old Greens and you. There's lot of things I find out—and there's my whole history with the Liberals. I know all kinds of things about you guys, personally and politically, which I don't spill to the others. There are lots of things the GEM aren't telling you—or me for that matter. There's private meetings I'm not invited to. I get hints of stuff going on. But if you're asking me is there anything earth-shatteringly important that you don't know about, my answer is a definite "No". Not as far as I know. You've got to believe me!'

Peter was still thinking. Sandy was always unable to bear gaps in conversations, and so continued: 'Listen, Peter. I first met Terry when I was two months old. Can you believe that? My parents knew him well. I campaigned for him when I was sixteen, and worked in his constituency office. I love the guy. I'll do anything to help if I can. But we have to face it, he's in a difficult situation. It's like Profumo—only sleeping with a different enemy...'

'Enemy?' exclaimed Peter. 'I know it's not great to spy on your allies, it's true, but since when have the Americans been our enemies?'

'Oh, maybe I phrased that badly,' said Sandy. 'But I think it's all to do with the America trip last month. Don and everybody were very negative about Wilding and his people before. Then they go there, and seem to be kicking off a new more cordial relationship. Then it seems the Yanks have been playing false, and have got a mole right into the heart of the Green coalition. It seems like they're trying to play us. As you can imagine, the transatlantic lines have been buzzing a little!'

'Sandy—can you find out where Terry is? I want to speak to him. And maybe get him a good lawyer.'

'Sure. I'll get right on it. A word of advice though: don't let your kid sister near him. She's tolerated because of you, but as far as some of the GEM are concerned, she's pretty much Public Enemy Number One. Associating with her wouldn't help his cause! Sorry to be so frank!'

'So guilt by association is order of the day, now, is it?' said Peter with some bitterness.

'Don't go there, Peter. Stay focused and practical, and I'll help you all I can!'

The call ended. When Peter mentioned guilt by association, he wasn't only thinking about the conversation with Sandy. He was also thinking about Stella Walton's family tree of extremists. He had feared that too might be a house of cards built on networks of knowing the wrong people.

Despite his misgivings about Stella's findings, he knew what he had to do now. With Terry being indisposed, and Howard too ill to be called back into play, he was the senior figure, and had to take the lead. It was time to call Evan, and prepare to leave the government without delay. There were just too many things he was now uncomfortable about, and he feared what he would find if he scratched the surface a bit more.

As Heather looked at Peter waiting for an explanation of the call that she had half overheard, the phone rang in Peter's office.

'Peter? Zara Alderney. We need to talk.'

They talked for a good twenty minutes. At first Peter was quite brusque. 'Zara, this Louise Adams affair—why the hell are you spying on us?' he almost shouted.

Zara tried to calm him down before getting to the point. Yes, they were sincere in wanting to develop better relations with the Mason government. And the President had taken a definite liking to Peter, and wanted to work closely with him. But their intelligence services were flagging warnings about certain elements in the GEM and in particular the Green Militia. As Zara spoke, there was a distinct echo of Stella's findings. A cloud of depression began to settle over Peter. Everything he had worked for and hoped for seemed to be stuttering to an end, in a haze of suspicion and uncertainty.

Suddenly the screen flashed that another call was coming in. It was Don Mason.

'I think I'd better take this—can I get back to you? It's Don Mason, and we may need to follow up after I've talked to him. I'm planning to take us out of the coalition,' said Peter.

But he didn't get the chance to resign. Mason made it clear at once that the Green-Liberal coalition was over. Peter, and Terry, all the Liberal Democrat junior ministers were dismissed from their posts. Mason would announce new arrangements over the next few days. He spoke firmly, but added his regrets that it had come to this, and his appreciation for all that Peter had done in his time as a Minister.

After the call, Peter picked up his conversation with Zara. 'They got in first—but in the end it adds up to the same, I suppose.'

'I'm sorry, Peter. In my view, though, it's for the best not to be associated too closely with them. I have some advice for you now. Don't get involved in open opposition. Take your lovely wife and daughter and leave the country, as soon as possible. Our intel says things could get nastier, as I think you already suspect. You and your family can come here. Spend Easter in Washington! I'll personally show you and Heather all around our beautiful capital. My door is always open for you.'

41: New partners for the Planet

The GEM leadership was shaken to the core by the unmasking of Louise Adams as an American spy. It was clear the long honeymoon was over, and people at home and abroad were falling out of love with the Green Earth regime. Don Mason felt himself to be on shaky ground, and all their achievements under threat. This was the crisis point that he knew would come sooner or later, and it felt very uncomfortable.

Sarah Turner was mortally embarrassed that someone so close to her should turn out to be a traitor. Malcolm Morton too was embarrassed—he thought he had things more under control than they turned out to be. But every problem is also an opportunity, and he was swift to act.

First act was to set up a new squad to monitor and purge the GEM itself, the Militia, the Earth Councils and any fellow travellers with dubious track record or connections. This came to be known as Morton's 'Jack Russell Squad', trained to go and sniff out any other rats. All the cabinet agreed to have their phones tapped, so that any contacts they had could be efficiently monitored. Their advisers and civil servants would be monitored too, but without their knowledge.

Apart from the security question, there was a political difficulty to deal with. Without the Liberals, technically the GEM government did not have a majority. Did it matter? After two and half years, the structure and habits of government had changed. Parliament had changed, and the main opposition parties had put themselves into splendid isolation on the South Bank, or left the country altogether.

With Parliament more or less reduced to rubber-stamping and ceremonial functions, the centre of activity was now the National Convention. Its members elected by the Earth Councils, the Convention did not run along traditional party lines. The GEM were dominant there, and there were various 'Green Labour', 'Green Liberal' and independent members. But since the elections to the Earth Councils the previous May, the most active group after the GEM were Gabriella Pearson's Animal Rights Party—the 'Animalists'.

Though some of the GEM leaders were sometimes scathing about the Animalists, there was a certain logic to working with them, at various level in the Green Earth Movement. And especially the Militia, where many members were champing at the bit for more radical action. At local level, GEM and Animalists frequently cooperated on projects to change the face of Britain. And at grassroots, GEM activists viewed the coalition with the Liberals as a brake on the Second Revolution. There was much internal debate about what this should be and how far it should go. But whatever it involved, it would be a rejection of any 'snail's pace' change as advocated before by Terry Cairns and Peter Kitson. It was time to embrace the concept of a future without growth, absorb the shocks and learn to live in a new harmony with the environment.

Dave Barrington was aghast at the prospect of bringing the Animalists on board. He saw them as a potentially unstable and disruptive element, while his approach was always about clear planning and good order. But Don Mason reminded him of the maxim to keep your friends close and your enemies closer. If the Animalists were not on board, in the new circumstances they could be extremely disruptive if they took on the role of being the Opposition.

'You should get to know them better,' Mason advised Barrington.

Dave Barrington felt that he knew Gabriella Pearson and some of her followers well enough. And Titus Whitaker's guru-like status was inexplicable to someone like Barrington who prided himself on his scientific credentials. He remembered that in her earlier days as a front-line activist, Jessica had crossed paths and crossed swords with Gabriella Pearson on several occasions. They had taken an instant dislike to each other. Jessica's dislike of 'Gabriella and her kind' had influenced her husband, and he felt her dislike quite understandable. But he had had very little to do with Gabriella since she had been a raw and hyperactive youth, until an unexpected meeting just a few months previously.

Malcolm Morton had invited Dave over to his house in rural Herefordshire. He had bought himself a fairly isolated farm house in Herefordshire. He said he needed seclusion, peace and quiet as an antidote to London life, and to unscramble his thoughts. With his personal bodyguard, which grew over the years in office, he also felt more secure there. Unwelcome visitors could be spotted a long way off.

When Dave arrived there, his first surprise was that Morton had a secret passion. On arrival, Barrington was escorted up the long drive, and taken past the imposing front door of his residence to a group of partially restored outbuildings. Morton was there in the courtyard in shorts and T-shirt, smudged all over with grease, working on the engine of a classic car. He greeted Barrington with a wide smile, and seeing his surprise, he opened his arms wide and said, 'Welcome to Malcolm's Motors! Would you buy a used car from this man?' He gestured to the other outbuildings, in which Barrington could see a fair number of other classic or vintage cars.

'Bloody hell!' Dave said. 'Morton the mechanic, who would have thought it? Malcolm, I may be wrong, but don't these cars run on petrol? In fact one hell of a lot of petrol? It looks like you're on a one-man mission to warm the climate!'

After that, Morton introduced Barrington to all his cars. Most of them were in beautiful condition, thanks to the tender loving care he lavished upon them. Two or three were in the process of being restored, and in one large barn there were a couple of cars being cannibalised for parts, plus many spares neatly stacked and labelled on shelves running the length of the barn. As a hobby, it was a very large and expensive one.

Over a beer on the veranda of his house, overlooking the Herefordshire countryside on a blissfully warm early September afternoon, Malcolm explained his unexpected passion. 'To me these cars are beautiful. Exquisite pieces of engineering. Innovative. Imaginative. And relics of a bygone age. Soon the era of the internal combustion engine will be over. And rightly so. But it's still possible to appreciate the achievements of a heroic age.'

It was a sentiment Barrington could understand.

'I love getting my hands dirty! I love the sheer physical pleasure of handling the engine parts, or polishing the bodywork,' Malcolm continued. 'Even repairing the upholstery. It's all very tactile. Actually, more than tactile. It involves all the senses. The smell of the metal, and the oil and the grease, or feasting my eyes on the coachwork, or listening to hear how the engine is running!'

He seemed to go into a reverie and looked into the distance. Still unable to take him entirely seriously, Barrington said: 'You missed out one of the senses—taste. Do you lick them as well?'

Just then Barrington heard a noise from Morton's office, which was next to the veranda. Then he had his second surprise of the day. Morton then told him that he had another visitor with him, and he called through the open window for her to come out and join them. To Dave's complete astonishment, it was Gabriella Pearson. She looked very much at home, tall and leggy in her shorts and loose shirt tied in a knot above her waist.

Dave was indeed astonished, as he knew how disparaging Don Mason had often been about Gabriella and her team. On later reflection he appreciated that some cooperation was natural—even though at that stage it seemed un-thinkable that Mason would bring them into the government. However, gov-ernment has always in part worked through committees that involve all the parties. And the National Convention did likewise. At grassroots level, Ani-malists and Greens had often worked together, and even more so after the Revolution. Moreover 'Animalists' was a very broad term encompassing many shades of animal rights campaigners, from the stereotypical sweet but eccen-tric old ladies who took in stray cats through to the balaclava guerrillas who planted bombs or burned down research labs.

Gabriella's Animal Rights Party was formed from activists who tended towards the extreme end of the spectrum, but not exclusively so. Many ani-mal rights campaigners who supported her party had also joined the Green Volunteers, and were subsequently absorbed into the Green Militias. Many of the hottest activists who emerged as Militia leaders had earned their spurs as animal rights liberationists. People like Carl Fullerton had always straddled the boundary.

Malcolm soon explained the reason for inviting Gabriella to his home at the same time. She had some particular ideas for eco-projects that she felt would be suitable for inclusion in the eco-camp programmes that were on the agenda that weekend. At this time, the work camp programmes were still in the process of being reformed. Morton reminded his colleague that they had included in their election manifesto references to the restoration of ecosystems and extensive habitat creation. Some of Pearson's people had strong ideas backed by a good deal of knowledge and experience. So Morton felt it was quite reasonable at least to sound her out on these. And he said her ideas could be valuable. Dave Barrington was in charge of the Climate Change Projects, and the integration of these with eco-camp activity was the reason he was there that weekend.

This was the first time that Dave had more than a fleeting discussion with Gabriella Pearson. She was a very different person, he found, in these relaxed circumstances where she evidently felt quite at home. Not at all the wild-eyed witch that the tabloids—and possibly Jessica—had portrayed her in the pre-Revolution era. In the Convention she always seemed a woman with a mission, intent on winning an argument. In private, she was far less preachy. Her voice was just as loud, which made conversation a little uncomfortable, but she was willing to be interrupted and also displayed a confident and some-times self-mocking sense of humour. Dave wondered whether there was some romantic connection between her and Malcolm now. As he observed them, he felt there probably was not, though there was clearly some kind of chemistry there. Possibly an initially professional relationship had gained a degree of friendship and even affection.

In some ways they were similar people. Both strong-minded and determined, both very ideologically committed. Neither had a partner or children, and this maybe enabled them to have a more single-minded focus on their political life. They had no family life to put their other concerns into perspective, as Barrington had. It was quite a contrast to his own life, he felt, where he was always conscious of a desire to strike a balance between home and work.

Gabriella joined them on the veranda, putting her feet up on the edge of the table and tipping her chair back as she swigged her beer straight from the bottle. She swept back her long red hair and shook her head a couple of times, as if clearing it before speaking. Dave was expecting her to say something aggressive or sententious, but all she did was smile widely at him, comment on the wonderful weather and the great view, and say how pleased she was to have a chance to sit down with him to 'chew the cud'. The one sour note was when she asked, 'How's Golden Girl?' which was the way she always referred to Jessica Barrington.

The discussions that followed were good natured and practical. Gabriella Pearson expressed admiration for Dave Barrington's scientific approach to environmental issues, and for his logistical and organisational abilities, qualities which she said she lacked. This was said modestly, but it was also true. She saw herself as a 'big picture' person, and feared she might not have the abilities to get things done. Barrington was flattered. But warning bells also rang. There was just a hint that she saw herself as a general, while casting others in the role of functionaries carrying out her will.

During the conversation, Pearson gave some insight into the Animalists, often through casual remarks she made. She clearly liked and respected Whitaker, whom she regarded as the party's great thinker and philosopher. Barrington had always regarded him as a windbag, and his philosophy as incoherent and often incomprehensible. But now he learned how he was a man with an international reputation in the Animalist movement, based in part on his writings in philosophy and later his pioneering work in animal behaviour studies. He had also long been an advocate of direct action, and had become a guru to the animalist guerrillas. Morton had once shown the GEM leadership intelligence papers from MI5 that identified Whitaker as the inspiration for numerous acts of sabotage. He had always been willing to justify direct action, though Morton had doubted his ability to direct particular acts of violence. Gabriella Pearson, on the other hand, everyone had always felt was capable of terrorist activity.

The thing that struck Barrington most about her during this meeting with Morton was her complete identification of animal rights with the GEM's environmental concerns.

'Every square millimetre of our environment is a habitat for a myriad of life-forms,' she enthused. 'You, David, have devoted years of your professional life to studying the coastline and improving sea defences. How many times have you stopped to think of what the sea actually is, and what the coast consists of? Each wave that hits the shore carries millions of organisms, and each piece of the shore that is struck by a wave is the home or hunting ground of billions of others.'

Indeed Dave hadn't quite thought of coastline ecosystems in that way. But once she had said this, he still hadn't been quite sure what to do with the concept in any practical sense. For Gabriella, though, this was only one step in an argument that ended in the notion of the equality of all species, including humankind. Humans had unbalanced the whole of nature, both by overpopulation and by our ability to control, exploit and distort the natural environment. Now it was our duty to rebalance nature, using our abilities and technologies to try to 're-attune' things to the way they should be. And she criticised both the old Greens and the GEM for being too focused on human interests in devising remedies for the damage we ourselves have done.

All this came by way of preamble to the purpose of the meeting. They moved on to more practical matters, and in particular her ideas for habitat recreation and promoting biodiversity across the country. By the end of the day, they had agreed on a programme that included both eco-camp activities and Barrington's other Climate Change Projects. Collectively they would transform the landscape, and the balance of flora and fauna of the United Kingdom. All the same, though that meeting had modified Barrington's picture of Gabriella Pearson, he still felt her a very unlikely and potentially unreliable partner for a coalition in government.

In the end, though, the GEM cabinet members all agreed on the new approach: coalition with the Animalists. The brakes were off, and it was full steam ahead for the Second Revolution.

42: The Trimmer

'Mason's just being realistic,' said Martin Lang, momentarily breaking off from brushing his teeth. 'I know you grew up with them, but you have to admit it was a marriage of convenience. It couldn't last, could it? I mean, going just over two years with them is not a bad innings.'

Sandy was sitting on the bed, looking sad and pensive. She said nothing. Martin was talking objectively, and maybe he was right. But Sandy's connection with Terry and Howard and the Kitsons wasn't just professional, it was personal. Martin did not have strong emotional connections with any of the people involved, only pleasure at being close to the centre of intrigue. He didn't understand how this development tore at her loyalties. Maybe that was something Martin could never understand, and she felt resentful towards him for that. Fleetingly, she thought that their relationship could never work.

Now he was by her side, holding her hand and stroking her hair. 'Sandy, I know you feel bad. But it's the way things go. Both sides were trying to use each other. And the stronger side wins—that's the way it is. We're not made to be party people. We should ride the currents to go where we want to go. Don't you think so?'

Sandy didn't answer, but just fell back on the bed and said, 'Oh, God!'

While Sandy was feeling anxious and not a little devastated, Martin was still riding high on his personal success now that he had been elevated to being the President of ESCOLAW, the Scrutiny Commission for the legal profession and judiciary. Men and women he used to revere now came to him as petitioners. The rumours were stronger than ever that he would be Lord Chancellor on the retirement of Lord Denby, the present holder of the post.

Martin enjoyed his connection with the Mason regime, but he felt no loyalty to it. To him the regime was there—it was a fact. Personally, he felt sufficiently strongly about environmental issues to believe in what he was doing, and not feel himself to be a hypocrite. All the same, his enduring respect and admiration for Joanna Kitson made him susceptible to arguments about abuses of human rights, and he felt uncomfortable about being associated with this. But he was not so uncomfortable as to sever his connections with the government that was, allegedly, responsible for these abuses.

Now Martin reflected on his connections with the people that Malcolm Morton had begun to refer to as 'the Kitson Circle'. He and Sandy were, of course, part of that, though he had never perhaps been an inner member of that group. Now that Peter Kitson had been cast out into the wilderness, he wondered what this would mean for him. He would need to distance himself from them. But he did not want to distance himself from either Sandy or Joanna. 'This could be difficult,' he thought to himself.

Sandy did not want to discuss the day's distressing events. Eventually she asked Martin, 'You've gone quiet. What are you thinking about?'

'I was thinking about a sixteenth century statesman, Sir William Petre. He served under four successive Tudor kings and queens—not easy when everyone was getting their head lopped off for backing the wrong horse. Someone asked him how he managed it. He said it was because he was more like a willow than an oak: he could bend with the wind. That's how we should be. We can work with the Kitsons and Cairnses of this world, we can work with the Masons and Mortons, and we can work with whoever comes next. Don't you think so?'

'I wish it could be so easy,' Sandy replied, both unconvinced and a little annoyed by Martin's little historical lecture. Clever, perhaps, but just not connected at any emotional level to how she felt.

'You have to move on,' urged Martin.

'But I feel I'm betraying my family if I do that!'

'You mean, you want to make some grand gesture and resign? Where's the value in that?'

Sandy sunk back again. She could see little value in it either.

'Why wreck your career for a bunch of naïve has-beens?' Martin asked rhetorically. 'Come on, Sandy. We both know you're ambitious. So am I. Ambition is a good thing. From positions of power you can do things—really achieve something! And from a position of power you can do more to protect your friends too. This is not a time for quixotic gestures, like those lemons on the South Bank!'

A little stung, Sandy protested she was not about to commit career suicide. 'I know what I'm going to do, but that doesn't mean I'm going to feel good about it. Maybe you could feel a little more sensitive to what I'm going through. And maybe a bit more compassionate towards Terry and Peter and Joanna and everyone too!'

Even as Sandy talked, Martin realised he might have to bite the bullet, and have nothing further to do with Joanna. He knew that her days being tolerated by the regime were coming to an end. And Sandy? There was a question. If she became tarred with the same brush as the Kitsons, would he stand by her? It was a question he wanted to put to the back of his mind. The regime would not last forever, and it might be better to keep up good relations as far as possible with its opponents too,

Now Martin reflected some more on events in the legal world during the last few weeks. Having discovered the whereabouts of several of her missing clients, Joanna Kitson had served a further injunction on the government, demanding their release. The courts supported her petition. But the government refused to release them, and warned the judges of serious consequences if the matter was taken any further. It was at this point that Martin had found the judges were not made of heroic stuff any more than the journalists and editors who had been intimidated before. Though her case was won, Joanna was unable to obtain the release of the detainees. The courts proved to be unwilling to take forward any enforcement measures.

As Joanna saw it, she faced a series of procedural delays. She was not aware of the intense personal and professional pressure that was brought to bear on judges and senior officials. This pressure wasn't only about Joanna's cases. ESCOLAW investigators conducted a series of inquiries that probed every aspect of judges' conduct, and the Green Militias leaned heavily on people they considered unsympathetic to the Green Revolution.

Though Martin was now the President of ESCOLAW, he was not fully aware of the extent of its operations either. These were largely orchestrated by Malcolm Morton through the permanent officers that had been taken on—all of them former GEM 'sleepers'. Martin was being played, and did not realise it. For Morton and Mason, it was valuable to have an apparently neutral and energetic figure such as Martin on board. It was also convenient, in an ironic sort of way, to have Joanna Kitson on board though she rarely attended meetings now. It showed to the outside world that the Green Earth Government was willing to have its critics participating in the Scrutiny Commissions.

All the same, by this time the government's patience with Joanna was almost at an end. The one saving grace was that the strict control of the press meant that her initiatives had little impact inside the UK. Like the political parties that had walked out to set up a protest parliament on the South Bank, the government could afford to let her do whatever she wanted, as long as the public was generally unaware of her activities. But the Louise Adams affair seemed likely to change this toleration, or so Martin judged.

'Martin, don't you think this has all gone too far?' asked Sandy, interrupting her partner's train of thought.

'Too far…?' Martin asked, not sure what Sandy was referring to.

'It doesn't matter,' Sandy sighed. 'Just hug me.'

43: Declaration on The Rights of Species

Gabriella Pearson was more than pleased with the recent turn of events. She felt the strength of her position, which she contrasted with that of the Liberals before. As coalition partners, the Liberals seemed to have jumped into bed with the GEM without achieving any substantial concessions. There had been no distinct item from their election programme that they had been able to put into practice, only elements that coincided in a pallid way with Green Earth priorities. All they had got from the coalition was a few cabinet posts, and in the end these proved to be of almost no value. She guessed that from a Liberal perspective their coalition had been largely tactical. They had not expected the Green Earth regime to last.

Her approach was different. There would be a price for Animalist support of the GEM government. And now the price—or at least the first instalment—was about to be paid, as the National Convention prepared to debate a *'Declaration on The Rights of Species'*.

This move had divided the GEM's inner circle. Mason and Morton said that it was a pragmatic concession, that in reality would mean very little. Sarah Turner and Douglas Cunningham felt it was a sign of unnecessary weakness, while Dave Barrington disliked such a 'metaphysical' approach to important issues.

Barrington was at home when he received the news from Mason that this debate was to take place. He barely skimmed the documentation—making grand statements about animal rights seemed to him an unwise course, but as he told Jessica, it was not something to be unduly concerned about.

Jessica had thrown herself into the 'Nation's Food' campaign that had run alongside Terry Cairns' local markets programme, but as the peak of that passed, she had become increasingly withdrawn into family life, professing almost no interest in the political world that had once drawn them together. It seemed she had not heard Dave's brief and dismissive comment at first. After several minutes preoccupied with re-potting some seedlings, a frown grew over her face. Eventually, she put down her little tools and said:

'Dave—don't have anything to do with this. If Whitaker and Pearson are involved, don't have anything to do with it!'

Dave thought for a while.

'Any particular reason?' he said at last.

'It's hard to put my finger on. It's just… a gut feeling, if you like. Bad ideas, and bad people circle around them. I think…I think things are slipping away from us. And if we tie ourselves to these people, things will just slip right out of control.'

Dave could feel his wife's great anxiety. And he was aware that lately a kind of numbing distance had been growing between them. He was relieved by this conversation, a chance to get things out into the open. All the same, he was disconcerted by the nature of her concerns.

'Who in particular, are the bad people, do you think?' he asked, his tone gentle.

'You know … we all knew them. Or knew they were there, even if we didn't know exactly who. The people in balaclavas. The Big Yogis of this world.' She attempted a half-hearted smile.

'Big Yogi' was a semi-mythical character in the early days of environmental and animal rights extremism. Wherever there was confrontation to be had with the police, or animal testing centre to be vandalised or burned down, Big Yogi would turn up—a big bearded bear of a man who always claimed to be 'smarter than the average bear'. No one knew his real name. There had been many guesses as to his identity, including that he was really more than one person—a kind of Ned Ludd for the early 21st century. Such mythical characters romp through history, accruing legendary feats of heroism and bravado. They act as recruiting sergeants for whichever movement they are associated with.

'Or if you want real people—there's Carl Fullerton. You remember him in the early days? An Animalist guerrilla, always hovering close to Titus Whitaker. Now he's reinvented himself as a Green Militia leader, and he's becoming ever closer to Malcolm. Or Tara Collingworth, and her "Noah Principle"…'

Dave guffawed, and regretted it at once. He was contemptuous of people like Collingworth, but was worried it might seem he was contemptuous of Jessica's line of thought. 'She's a complete crank, a maverick. No one takes her seriously,' said Barrington, trying to be reassuring.

'No one outside his charmed circles took Titus seriously either a year ago. I'm worried about the drift. That maybe even Malcolm doesn't know the dangerous waters he's getting himself into.'

Dave looked sceptical.

'And I'm worried about you. About you being in the firing line.'

'Thanks for worrying about me, Jess. But I know what I'm doing. I'm not exactly happy about this new tactic. But I think that's all it is, tactical. Temporary. I didn't like the marriage of convenience with the Liberals, but it was by no means as bad as some of us feared.'

'We have to work with the lie of the land as it is: when we own it, we can change it,' said Jessica, quoting one of Mason's aphorisms.

Dave nodded, and smiled.

'Owning the land is fine. It's joint ownership with Titus and Big Yogi that worries me,' Jessica added, picking up her tools and carrying on with her planting.

••

The inner circle of the GEM met in Mason's office at Number Ten to work out their approach to the *Declaration of the Rights of Species*. Doug Cunningham, as President of the National Convention, was chairing this session.

'We have before us, colleagues, a proposal to make a *Declaration on the Rights of Species*. And not for the first time. As you know, this is the fourth time our Animalist friends have brought one forward. And on each of the previous occasions, we have kicked them into touch.'

'As we should do again,' Sarah Turner cut in.

'Well, Sarah, we'll come to discuss the issue in a moment. But we're all aware of the different circumstances we find ourselves in this time around, so I think we have more at stake, as we need to keep our friends happy.'

'Gabriella Pearson, man's best friend,' said Sarah in a stage whisper.

'You all have the full text—and the supporting documentation from our policy unit,' continued Cunningham.

'And I trust you've all read it,' interjected Mason, looking around the room at everyone pointedly. Dave Barrington nodded, but avoided Mason's gaze, as he had barely looked at the documents.

Cunningham continued. 'I know it will be difficult to avoid, but I don't think today we should be discussing the philosophical merits of the Declaration. Nor Whitaker's convoluted—even impenetrable—prose style in the preamble. We should focus on the political and the pragmatic. The view of the leadership is that this time we should allow them to have their way. Don will explain the merits of this approach. In his view, that is...'

'And not yours, Doug?' said Mason with a wry smile.

'I reserve judgement, Don,' said Cunningham, and settled back into his chair, exhaling loudly.

Doug Cunningham had developed a fairly jaundiced view of the Animalists from his time as President of the Convention. They irritated him to distraction at times, but he found that in committee they were often more amenable. He felt they could be managed without making significant concessions to them.

'You all know my opinion on this by now,' said Don, 'and that it's entirely pragmatic. For the time being, we need the Animalists with us in the Convention. They want something from us, as the price for their support. And I believe this Declaration is the least concession we can allow them.

'In fact, in our own programme we have already enacted many of their aspirations. We are enforcing natural farming. We have prohibited live animal exports. Dave is taking us way ahead on habitat restoration, through the CC projects. The point is, we're doing those aspects of their programme that are good environmental practice. What they want next from their programme is much more hard-edged—do-able things that are unacceptable to huge swathes of the public, plus the complete head-banging stuff. The campaigns they've been working up lately focus on banning leather, and ultimately the use of any animal skin for clothing—say goodbye to your sheepskin coat, Sarah! And banning all animal testing, even for medical research.'

'Well, actually I kind of agree on that one,' admitted Sarah.

'These are complex issues, for sure,' continued Mason. 'They are quite a volatile lot, and you can't be sure what idea they will focus on next. Internally, they're in a big ruckus about banning fishing. I'm told a recent meeting came to blows about this.'

'Yes, they have a strong lobby to end what they call "fish torture" ', added Morton. 'Another pressure group is working on Whitaker to make it a commitment to provide vegetarian-only meals in schools. Another lobby is working on making it illegal to "own" any animal.'

'Even pets?' asked Barrington.

'Tut, tut, Dave,' said Morton. 'You should know better. The word "pet" is patronising and robs an animal of its dignity. We must refer to them as "companion animals". And, yes, Whitaker seems persuaded that no one can "own" an animal. He is however happy to entertain the notion of "designated animal carer" as a substitute concept.'

'Ye gods!' exclaimed Cunningham.

'Anyway,' said Mason. 'I know we're all more pragmatic, and not so dewy-eyed about animals. But we do have a vision about animal rights, in the context of a balanced environment.'

Everyone in the room nodded their assent.

'We can live with this Declaration. In one sense, it's just words, and can't harm us. The spirit of the Declaration is even broadly in line with our views on animal issues: and we've negotiated out some tricky lines about animal freedom and freedom from ownership. I think this is the way to keep them onside. And I have to say this. We may take the piss out of them at every opportunity. But we also know that amongst the activists are some of the best-hearted people you can find, motivated by high ideals, compassion and concern for the planet. Ever since the GEM began, we've worked with many of them individually on one issue after another. Keeping them close to us, we can accentuate their positive aspects and rein in their follies. OK—over to you guys. Sarah: I think you don't agree with this approach?'

'Well, I don't, Don,' said Sarah emphatically. 'And that's the first time I've heard you get dewy-eyed about the Animalists!'

Everyone laughed, including Mason who threw his head back in laughter, then angled his head, nodding, as if to say, 'Point taken'.

'Two reasons I don't agree with Don's view,' continued Sarah. 'One. We assent to this Declaration and we tar ourselves with the same brush as the Animalists. True, they're getting more and more activists in at the Earth Council elections—but they're *not* getting any more popular! It's because people aren't voting in Earth Council elections like they did at first. The Councils seem too extreme, and the Animalists are the epitome of the extremes people don't like. We mustn't lose the distinction between us and them.

'Two. The Declaration itself is not harmless! Why do you think they are so keen for it? Not because of the fine words, as Don says, but because it's the basis for further action. It legitimises the rest of their programme. And it constrains what we can do—Dave was telling me just the other day about an "eco-fort" Animalists have set up at an estuary where new sea defences are being built. They think the rights of a mollusc—not even a rare one—should take precedence over a vital climate change project. If we support this Declaration, they can stop all our projects in their tracks by dragging us into court on the grounds of violating animal rights!'

'I broadly agree with Sarah,' said Cunningham. 'And also, I don't think it's necessary. We can call their bluff on this. After all, we had the Liberals on board with us for the best part of two years, and we gave them bugger all. Just

had them working their tender little arses off on our projects. The Animalists are different—not as domesticated as the Liberals—but I think they can be
house-trained! We've been edging that way in the Convention. And at the end
of the day, they want to sit in that Cabinet every bit as much as Blackstone and
Kitson did. You don't need to give them anything—vanity and ambition will
suck them in, just like the Grey-Greens before them!'

The *Declaration of the Rights of Species* was a remarkable document,
unique in modern political history. It didn't only call for better treatment of
animals, but stated the basis for their better treatment—their inalienable rights
as co-inhabitants of the planet. Dave Barrington glanced again at the Preamble
to the document.

> *While the amelioration of human suffering and inequality are laudable aspira-
> tions, the pursuit of justice and equality has remained blind to the sufferings of
> our fellow Earth Co-Inhabitants—both flora and fauna—and hence our rapid
> progress as a species has been made at the expense of all other species, their
> ecosystems and the resources of the planet.*

> *'It is time to recognise and act on the hitherto unacknowledged principle of the*
> ***inalienable rights of all species on this planet to their existence and
> to freedom from the harm caused by the activities of the human
> species.*** *We recognise that this harm is caused by predatory activity, reckless-
> ness and neglect, arising from an inequitable single-minded focus on individual,
> national and species-specific self-interest.*

> *'There have been historic struggles against discrimination in all its forms: on the
> basis of colour, ethnicity, religion, gender, sexuality, age and disability. Specie-
> sism, whether wilful, unconscious or institutional, is the last remaining form of
> discrimination.*

> *'Therefore, the freely elected, democratically constituted and nationally repre-
> sentative National Convention of Earth Councils of the United Kingdom takes it
> upon itself to declare on behalf of all living entities on the planet a Declaration
> on the Rights of Species.'*

Barrington now skimmed through the following pages of the Preamble, taking in the key paragraphs of the Declaration:

> *'All living entities come into their existence free and equal and with
> equal rights to continue their existence as Co-Inhabitants of this Planet*

· *The right to a continued existence pertains at both the collective and individual levels*

· *The Government of the Human Species of the United Kingdom, on behalf of the Human Species as a whole, freely assents to maintain and preserve the rights of all species to a continued existence*

· *All species have a right to be maintained and preserved in their indigenous habitats, with access to the necessary resources within their ecosystems.*

· *The Government of the Human Species will take all necessary steps to restrain harmful human activities which damage the interests and impinge on the Rights of non-human species.*

· *All species have an inalienable Right to be free from externally-induced genetic modifications. Arguments from human welfare are not sufficient to overcome this Right. The Government of the Human Species rejects categorically all measures for genetic modification of animals, plants and microscopic life forms.'*

And so the Declaration of Rights continued, becoming more specific and in turn outlawing the mutilation of animals (such as de-horning, de-beaking and the docking of tails), the use of animals for entertainment and all forms of hunting for sport.

Dave had not been listening to the discussion taking place around him, until he suddenly became aware of eyes turning towards him. It seemed that Mason was volunteering him to be spokesman for the Government in the debate on the Declaration.

'Well?' asked Mason.

'Did I hear you right, Don? You're asking me to manage this garbage through the Convention?' asked Dave, incredulously.

'Yes—and why not?' asked Mason. 'You're one of only two of us Ministers who also sits in the Convention. Doug chairs it, so who else? It seems quite natural to me.'

Barrington protested some more. 'We've got plenty of other good people in the Convention, even if they're not in the Cabinet. And I know nothing about Animal Rights. Absolutely zilch.'

'Ideal,' said Mason. 'I doubt if anyone could do it better. You've been with us from the beginning, and before assuming your current technocratic mantle, you were our number one communicator. The debate requires an entirely pragmatic response. We need to sense the mood and direction of the majority on the Convention, and put the government's weight behind it. If we can water it down, so much the better. If they push for more, we need some fine judgement about what we can allow. You'll have to think on your feet, and you won't be swayed by any emotional arguments.'

'So, my ad-libbing will determine government policy? And the wording of the Declaration?' protested Dave.

'In a sense, yes,' said Don. 'But in other ways not. We'll supply you with ample signals during the course of the debate. But I can tell you, our direction is already determined. We want to ensure the outcome helps us move onto the next stage. If we get it right, this can be of use to us as a springboard for speeding up the pace of reform.'

'The Second Revolution?' asked Sarah.

'If you like!' smiled Mason.

44: Between a rock and a hard place

His head hurt and his mouth was dry. The handcuffs that held his hands behind the chair had now worn red grooves into his wrists, and he felt disoriented from lack of sleep. The interrogator had not said anything for maybe twenty minutes, and just sat on the edge of the desk, watching. Occasionally he studied his tablet, as if acknowledging some incoming new information. Eventually he spoke, clearly and slowly.

'So it comes down to this, Terry. It can only be one of two things. Either you were in this together—but you deny this. Or, she was playing you—and you don't want to believe this. So, what we want to know is what you passed—together—to the Americans, or what you passed on to her and then she passed to the Americans. Your only way out of here is to tell the truth.'

The questioning had gone round in circles for days, weeks. Terry Cairns was sure they knew all there was to know. What more did they want?

For Terry the distress of his interrogation was just a fraction of his torment. He had not been beaten—just low level bullying, really. He was a big man, and could easily cope with this kind of harassment, or so he felt. And despite his tiredness, he felt he could cope with the psychological techniques that were being used to soften him up for questioning.

But what was eating at him was Louise. He felt bewildered, betrayed and at the same time out of his mind with anxiety for her. To him she was small, fragile and vulnerable, and he was more in love with her than he could ever have imagined. Despite her apparent duplicity. They had shown him the facts—it was pretty incontrovertible. But it made no sense.

He tried to remember every conversation—though he would tell his interrogators almost nothing. Some things she said—perhaps she had been sounding him out on whether he could lead an alternative green government, one the Americans could live with. But what was the plan? There seemed to have been no realistic way to oust the GEM, with their control of the state apparatus and the backing of the Green Militia.

More importantly, what were her feelings? What were her real feelings for him? Or was it all lies? Depression washed over him.

'Tell me about Stella Walton,' the interrogator said suddenly. This was a new angle.

Terry looked puzzled, and shook his head. He could remember no one of this name.

'When was the last time you spoke to Peter Kitson?'

Behind the glass, Carl Fullerton and Malcolm Morton were watching the interrogation.

'I've seen enough,' said Morton. 'He's a fool. But he knows too much.'

An hour later Morton was reporting back to an anxious Don Mason. 'Cairns is a broken and lovesick old fool. He's passed nothing to the Americans, and knows nothing about security leaks. But he did initiate all those enquiries about North Camp after his weekend in Wales, and it's possible he found out some things that Louise Adams didn't already know. He may have told her. And even if it was nothing new, then it may have provided confirmation for her. He's a stooge, probably an unwitting one, but we can't let him go. We're sending him off indefinitely to the Snowdonia Eco-camp. This is his chance to contribute something practical at last to the Green Revolution.'

'I regret this,' sighed Mason. 'Sarah's really shaken up by it too. It seems anything of significance that Louise passed on she gleaned from Sarah and her advisers. It's a mess.'

'I've got one of my people in Sarah's team now, replacing Louise. There will be no further embarrassments,' said Morton with determination.

••

Hooded, handcuffed and blindfolded, Terry Cairns was shipped out that evening to the Snowdonia eco-camp. It was a long and uncomfortable journey. Two Green Militiamen pulled him roughly from the back of the van, and frog-marched him to the cell where he would spend the next two weeks in solitary confinement. Occasionally he was hauled from the cell and questioned. But by comparison to when he was first arrested, the questioning seemed half-hearted. Then he was given a note book and instructed to write his 'testimony'—everything he had done since entering government, his true feelings about the Green Revolution, and where he thought he had gone wrong. In particular, he had to include the actions, conversations and ideas of people he had associated with—particularly his Liberal colleagues and Louise Adams.

At first Terry refused until he had some information about Louise Adams, and until he could speak to a lawyer. This prompted an angry response from the Militia officers in charge of him, and he was dragged back to his cell and thrown into a corner. The notebook and pen were thrown in after him. In the end, he decided to comply. Writing would break up the extreme boredom of being there. But he was determined not to write anything that might implicate anyone in something that could land them in a similar situation.

He found himself unable to sleep. Every muscle in his body hurt, from the rough handling and the manacling of his arms and legs, and the hardness of the bed in his cell. But what hurt most was not knowing about Louise, and not understanding her motivations. Conflicting thoughts replayed themselves again and again in his agitated mind. And it also hurt that when he was taken for the first time from his cell for questioning, he realised where he was. Barely ten miles away from the camp was his own cottage near Machynlleth, which for a time had been his perfect retreat with Louise. Now all that happiness had evaporated, and he could see no way ever to restore it.

Eventually he was moved out of his solitary cell and into a shared barracks. The others in the barracks were an eclectic mix of professions: several workers from an intensive turkey farm, a doctor, a lorry driver, a teacher and two young Conspicuous Consumptionists who looked like they'd been having quite a rough time. They formed a motley and unlikely crew as they worked twelve-hour days together on building and planting projects.

Over the next couple of weeks Terry got to hear their stories. The turkey farm workers had worked at a factory farm in Norfolk which had been taken over by the local Earth Council, and its workers sent to an eco-camp in the area. That was back in the days when it was still described as an 'eco-college'. The aim was to re-educate them in organic and free range farming practices. There was a logic to this. As people used to handling livestock, they could be retrained to work in more ethical ways with the birds and pick up new work locally once the system of farming had been changed. But they had failed to take the process seriously, one of them absconded twice, and they were sent back for a second time. This was just at the time when the National Convention decided to remodel the eco-colleges on a more punitive basis as work camps. A new specially trained corps of Green Militia was brought in to run the eco-camp more rigorously. 'Reformation through work' was the new mantra—and the work had to be all absorbing. Time not spent on work or preparing meals had to be devoted to self-criticism and study of Green Earth principles. For these young men, the work was bearable but the study elements were not. 'If I could study, I'd never 'ave been working in a bloody turkey factory, would I?' said one of them. These signs of bad attitude had led to a longer sentence, and they were transported to the Snowdonia eco-camp. Terry felt that maybe their ability to work hard for long hours might also have been a reason for sending them to this place.

The lorry driver's case was straightforward. Karol had taken part in a fuel protest, where several hundred truck drivers had in a time-honoured tradition protested against high fuel duties by running a 'rolling blockade' of slow moving lorries along a motorway. Three days afterwards he was in front of a Tribunal and sentenced to eighteen months at a camp. These types of longer sentences were now becoming routine. What concerned the driver most was what his family would do for money while he was gone, and he had no way of knowing.

None of the inmates were particularly welcoming to Terry when he arrived in the barracks, but Karol was particularly hostile. 'You helped them. Without you, none of this can happen!' he said sharply, and spat on the ground by Terry's feet. And Terry had no real answer to this.

The doctor was in the camp because his department had failed to change their suppliers of clinical goods, despite warnings from ESCOHEALTH. The teacher said he was there because he had been denounced by someone, falsely accused of mocking the Green Revolution. This was a growing problem for anyone involved with students, it seemed. And the two Conspicuous Consumptionists had been rounded up at one of their flash-festivals of consumption. They had suffered at the hands of the local Militia before being sent on to the eco-camp. One of them had been to an elite boarding school, and adjusted quite well to the constant low-level taunting and bullying he received from the camp Militia. The other, though, seemed completely lost, thrown into an environment where he had no control and where his formerly carefree attitude to life won him only punishment and humiliation. This one, Marco, was also desperate about his girlfriend, Natasha. She had been caught at the same time and had experienced similar rough treatment. She had a congenital heart condition that needed constant medication, and the last he had heard she was running short of her tablets and being forced to work long hours at one of the new satellite camps being built nearby. These young people had each received three year sentences.

After a month in the camp, Terry was becoming used to the routine. Physically, it was survivable, he felt. What was harder to take was the overwhelming feelings of despair and regret that overtook him. When his young wife had died many years back, he had fallen into a severe depression. He often thought of her now. He remembered how inwardly, and sometimes to his circle of friends, he had raged against fate. And it was fate. She became ill, and there was nothing that could be done. But now, this situation he was in—there were so many things he could have done differently. He felt responsible, responsible for the sufferings of those around him as well as his own. But it seemed beyond his power to do anything to put it right.

In his feelings of depression and powerlessness, he accepted without comment the daily humiliations from the guards. On a daily basis, the worst people to deal with were the 'Stage Two' trustees: people with time left to serve but who had progressed through the rankings into a position where they could oversee other prisoners. Terry and most of those in his barracks were 'Stage Zero'. Karol and one of the turkey farmers had progressed to 'Stage One'.

Terry soon learned what these gradings meant. A camp committee met regularly to decide if anyone's work and improvement in attitude and thinking merited progress to a higher level. Stage One brought small privileges to make life more comfortable. Stage Two raised the possibility of being a team leader or overseer. Stage Three could mean either early release, or being assigned to one of the 'new model communities' that were being built around the country. In the minds of the camp leadership, this seemed to be the ideal outcome, to be selected to play a part in the new world they were building.

Terry was pretty sure though that he would not make it past Stage Zero. As in most prisons, there is appearance and reality. The reality was that one's progress could be set back at any time by the arbitrary power of the guards and the Stage Two overseers. And they clearly didn't like him.

After another month everyone in the barracks was sent to work for three weeks at one of the satellite camps. This raised Marco's spirits as he hoped to be able to see his girlfriend Natasha once more, or at least find out something about her by coming into closer contact with female prisoners. They boarded the bus and drove further in to the hills, away from the coast. Terry knew this area well.

It was a warm, bright but windy day as they left the bus and looked around at the building site. It was a hive of industry, with orange-suited inmates carrying timber, pushing barrows and pulling carts, climbing wooden scaffolding and hacking at rocks with pick-axes. Men and women worked side-by-side on these labour-intensive tasks.

'Christ!' exclaimed Terry. 'They're building their new world by hand!'

'Our bloody hands,' said Karol softly.

'No machinery at all!' observed the doctor.

'Probably can't afford the bloody petrol,' said Karol as a guard came over, barking at them to get in line.

Terry and Marco were having similar thoughts. Seeing the women working here, maybe there was a new chance to find out something about their girlfriends. The difference was that Marco didn't hesitate. He ran straight over to a group of women prisoners who were pulling a cart of broken rocks away from a cave being sculpted in the mountainside.

'Oi! Where are you going! Come back here!' shouted a guard.

Terry could see Marco talking rapidly with the women, before he was pulled away by several Militia guards. One of the women was mouthing 'Sorry' to him. Marco was dragged back into line beside Terry, being lectured all the way by the guards about his behaviour and what was expected of him. As they let go of him, Marco began to crumple to the ground. Terry and Karol quickly grabbed him to support him.

'What's up, man?' hissed Karol.

'She's gone. She was here, but she's gone,' Marco said almost inaudibly.

'Where to?' asked Karol.

Marco didn't answer, just looked blankly ahead, with tears trailing down his cheeks.

'Oh, Jesus!' muttered Terry.

It was in this satellite camp that Terry discovered what hard manual labour feels like. The daily routine was exhausting. And for minor misdemeanours there were punishments like having to work through the fifteen minute rest break or receiving reduced food rations. Unofficially, there were physical beatings and humiliations. Sometimes a day's hard labour could be followed by being hauled off for questioning about what he had written in his self-criticism. The experience was gruelling, but Terry was surviving.

Marco, however, was not. He seemed to disappear off into another world at times. An overseer or guard would then whack him with his baton on his legs or back to get him moving again. At meal times he would sometimes sit and not eat. Terry did his best to protect him and encourage him to snap out of it, at least to do enough to avoid being punished. The guards, it seemed, were well versed in what each inmate's 'eco-crime' had been, and their treatment of prisoners reflected that. Marco was targeted not just for his vulnerability, but because as a Conspicuous Consumptionist he had openly set himself against the values of the Green Revolution and intentionally committed one eco-crime after another. Now they would make him pay. Often they taunted him about the fate of his girlfriend. 'How's your Gucci girl?' they would call out. 'Do you want to join her out the back?' 'We'll dig up her body if you'd like a last poke!'

Finally Marco snapped. He and Terry were sawing planks of wood, but Marco was going slow. An overseer stood next to him watching, but Marco did not pick up the pace, as most prisoners would do. Eventually the overseer prodded Marco on his cheek with his baton, then hooked it under Marco's chin. Terry couldn't hear what the overseer was saying, but it seemed to galvanise Marco into activity. Suddenly he grabbed the baton from the overseer, who stood there for a moment, dumbfounded. Before he could put his whistle to his lips to call for help, Marco smashed the baton into the overseer's head. Then he began to run, heading across the building site towards the trees. Someone blew a whistle to sound the alert.

'Ah, we've got a runner!' said a nearby Militia guard with evident enjoyment, as Karol rushed forward to tend to the injured overseer.

Everyone had stopped working to watch. Terry moved forward as far as he dared, to see Marco running down the hillside towards the trees. Militia started to converge on him, and soon he was penned in. He flailed around them with the baton. Eventually a senior Militia guard pulled out a taser from his belt and fired it at Marco, who collapsed to the ground, jerking uncontrollably. There was a gale of laughter from the Militia guards as the one firing the taser said, 'Consume that, shithead!'

Terry stood watching this, his head in a spin. This was the most full-on violence he had seen, but it was the threat that had been lying there in wait every day. And he found it impossible to square what was happening on the ground here with what he had been doing every day in the Coalition government. It was hard even to reconcile this with what he had seen before when he had visited the camp with Louise and the Kitson family. He knew he must get out of here, but at the same time knew it was impossible.

Terry felt a hand on his shoulder. 'Don't think about it,' said a voice he half recognised. 'Better get back to work.' The person he now turned to face was very thin, almost emaciated. 'You don't recognise me?'

'Miles Campbell?'

'The same. I was bussed in from another satellite camp this morning. This is how it is now, and I can't see any signs of it getting any better.'

45: Crises of leadership

It was time to leave. Of that there could be no doubt. Patrick Baxter, the former Prime Minister, reviewed his options, and decided there was only one.

After the election that brought Don Mason into power, Baxter had been persuaded to continue the leadership of his party in opposition. But he found opposition to be futile. He'd been Leader of the Opposition for a brief time before he became Prime Minister. But this was nothing like it. The opposition now was completely neutered. There was absolutely no way to call the government to account. The setting up of an alternative 'parliament' on the South Bank had been intended to provide a focal point for rallying the opposition. But it had been a meaningless talking shop. His old adversary Howard Blackstone had warned him of this at the time. But Howard's Liberal Greens had achieved no more by hanging onto the coat tails of the GEM.

Now he realised that exercising leadership involves looking hard into the mirror and acknowledging where you have been a failure. And then to make the appropriate choices. He was well aware of the tightening security grip of Malcolm Morton at the Home Office. Foreign travel was now being closely controlled. He knew of several people within his party and senior civil servants who had been prevented from travelling. Ironically, these travel controls were part of an effective package of measures that had reduced immigration to practically zero—a policy aim long advocated by strong voices in his own Conservative party.

Baxter had tried to keep in close touch with the growing opposition centred in Stockholm around Sir James Olsen. But the almost total control the government exercised over the communications networks and the Internet was now making this impossible. There was no alternative: it was indeed time to leave.

What spurred him to continue in opposition until now was, despite his failures, a conviction that he had been right all along. The Green institutions had created a new system of government without the checks and balances of the old British Constitution, which he still believed in strongly. Now, though, it was time to seek help from wherever it could be found to help put Britain back on the right track. Calling in a few favours, he flew out the country in the private jet of a wealthy supporter. His cover story was that he was flying up to Scotland to play golf, as he had done many times before. As they flew close to the east coast, the plane turned and headed out over the North Sea towards Scandinavia. As he looked down at the coast below, he wondered how soon he would be back, and what kind of circumstances would bring him back.

In Stockholm, he was made welcome by Sir James and Lady Frances Olsen. It felt like the old British establishment was re-establishing itself in exile, as a succession of visitors came and went: high ranking soldiers and former soldiers, former civil servants, business people and people from the worlds of art and culture.

Several foreign diplomats came to make contact and see what they could find out about Britain under the GEM. Because the truth was, Britain was becoming more and more cut off from the outside world. To Baxter this isolation became extremely apparent as he looked at his home country from the outside. The question was, what was to be done?

Baxter was briefing Sir James Olsen and some of his colleagues about the situation back in the UK, as he saw it. 'When the coalition with the Liberals ended, and Mason got into bed with Gabriella Pearson, so to speak, I knew there would be absolutely no prospect of politics as normal. At least until they were ejected from power. And I was picking up signals that they were planning to postpone the next elections. Even if they didn't, the way Morton and Malik were controlling the media I was sure there could be no chance of having free and fair elections. It seems so odd to be saying such a thing about our country. Sounds almost Third World. But that's the way it is now.'

Sir James was nodding thoughtfully. 'We've been picking up similar noise from our contacts in the service. In fact, it's getting ever harder for them to keep in contact with us. In the wake of the Terry Cairns affair there was a round-up of suspected moles from several departments, including a few who had been keeping us informed. Did you hear about this?'

'Only echoes and rumours. That was the trouble with our alternative parliament on the South Bank. We were out of touch with everything, several steps removed from the action. And I know the GEM were laughing at us.

'Terrible about Cairns, though. I know Peter Kitson's been pulling out all the stops trying to find out what's happened to him. But, in all honesty, what can he do? These disappearances are commonplace now. There's an atmosphere of fear developing. Mason always protests that parts of the Green Militia are out of control. But it suits him to say that, while at the same time the fear they create lets him tighten his grip on power. He's a very dangerous man.

'How he manipulated Terry Cairns into taking a leading role in his local markets agenda, I'll never know. I thought the fellow had more sense. And this business with Louise Adams—completely unfathomable. She seemed to be sucking him further into the Green Earth agenda, and then suddenly she's unmasked as an American infiltrator. Or so I hear on the grapevine. Or did she just upset the leadership somehow, and they've used her as the excuse for a major purge?'

Sir James knew from his American contacts that she was indeed passing information to them. 'From what I hear, Adams was recruited after she graduated from Harvard. They asked her to get involved with some fringe environmentalist groups that they felt posed a threat on both sides of the Atlantic. Then it seems she went native, as they say, under the influence of Sarah Turner. But something happened last year, we don't know what. And out of the blue she got back in touch with her handlers and was passing them—I don't know what exactly. But it's got Wilding and Alderney very worried. They are convinced there are wheels within wheels in the Green Earth Movement. And this current cosiness with the Animalists. Alderney thinks Mason was blowing smoke in everyone's eyes when he appeared to be hostile to them before. She feels there is some inner circle that binds together key people in the two movements. Are you aware of anything like that?'

'Not at all,' said Baxter. 'I just saw it as another piece of opportunism by Mason. His GEM seem far more disciplined than the Animalists, who still seem a chaotic bunch despite their elevation into government. That doesn't mean I think they can't do anything effective. I think these two organisations together can cause a lot of mischief, each egging the other on to more radical and extreme measures.'

One of Sir James' junior colleagues now looked up from his screen and nodded to him.

'Ah,' said Sir James. 'It seems Secretary Alderney can join us now.'

They all looked towards the big screen at the end of the room, where Zara Alderney's face now came into view.

'Gentlemen, good to see you and thanks for inviting me,' she said. 'Patrick—a while since I've had the pleasure of your company. I'm so glad you've taken the step you have. You were no good to anyone hiding away on the South Bank, if you don't mind me saying so.'

Patrick Baxter in fact did mind her saying so, but nodded graciously all the same. 'Indeed, Zara. I felt it was time to get out into the wider world and see what I can do from over here.'

'That's great,' enthused the Secretary of State. 'The President thought it would be good idea if I make our position plain. We're gravely concerned about the state of our closest ally right now. Let's make no bones about it. The government over in the UK is extreme, anti-democratic and as we can see hell-bent on radical measures that will do great damage to your economy and to the international community too. And we don't think for one minute we can stand by and do nothing while your people suffer.

'I know you want to change this government. So do we. And you can count on us to support you in any way possible to make this happen. If it's about funding an election campaign, we can fund it. If it's about other measures, let's talk about how to do that. Hopefully it won't come to that and the regime will collapse under the weight of its own contradictions. But from what I've heard, they won't let go of power easily. So what we need to do is to create a joint strategy about how to achieve what we want. Anything you need—just let me know.'

And so in the course of a three hour meeting, they explored the options. Mason's continued popularity with a substantial and energetic minority of people was a key problem, as Baxter pointed out. Morton's thorough purges of the old establishment and tight grip on the security system was another. And despite occasional protests, the people of Britain were proving themselves to be quite adept at adapting to the new circumstances. There was no large groundswell of opposition or resistance. Perhaps the majority were just waiting stoically for it all to be over. But what if it wouldn't be over? In the end they decided that what they needed to do was to build up networks of resistance. They had to find the people in the government, in the military and in the intelligence services who were prepared to work against the Mason regime. And they desperately needed more information about what was going on in the eco-camps, and what new radical plans were brewing at the highest levels in the government.

●●

Back in the UK, Don Mason was winding up a meeting with Dave Barrington and Sandy Honeyford. She hadn't often been included in these meetings between Barrington and Mason. But when she did she was amazed at the galvanising effect they had on the Prime Minister. These days he was looking increasingly care-worn. But there was something about the meetings with Dave Barrington that brought Don to life. Barrington more or less set the agenda, and would arrive with plans and visuals for new and ambitious projects. These ranged across plans for new small-scale eco-communities, closely integrated into nature; plans for converting specific towns and cities to zero carbon living; huge new renewable energy schemes; nationwide plans for more effective and environment-friendly water and waste management; plans for huge sea defences against rising sea levels, and alternative plans to adapt to rising sea levels and integrate human living into the new environments that would result. Barrington's energy seemed inexhaustible and his attention to detail remarkable. Whether they were workable or not, Sandy didn't know. But Don Mason relished these sessions, critiquing the plans, making suggestions, challenging assumptions and always encouraging Dave Barrington to keep up the good work. The future it seemed was more interesting than the present.

As the meeting ended and Sandy and Barrington left, Malcolm Morton and Gabriella Pearson entered the room. As she passed by Gabriella said, 'Hi, Sandy–little Miss Useful!' and gave her what Sandy considered to be a strange and enigmatic smile. It was a big smile, and not unfriendly. But kind of weird all the same. Coupled with the words of greeting, Sandy felt patronised. And Gabriella always did it.

'Ignore her,' advised Dave Barrington, noticing Sandy staring quizzically after Gabriella as she shut the door. 'She's an acquired taste. If you don't like her, that's OK. Lots of other people don't either! Jessica can't stand her either. A long story.'

'Oh, it's not that I don't like her,' protested Sandy. 'She's made it quite easy for me to work with her team. But why does she always look at me like that?'

'Like what?'

'Like I'm some vaguely amusing pet or something?'

'It's just her. I think she likes to mess with your head at first, until she gets to know you. And then get you looking for crumbs of approval. She likes to set the emotional agenda, the dominance agenda, before she gets down to dealing with people. That's what Jessica says, anyway.'

'Interesting approach. I'll remember that for future use!'

Dave smiled and left for his next meeting. As Sandy returned to her office she was burning with curiosity. There were an increasing number of meetings between Don Mason and Malcolm Morton that she was excluded from, and it rankled a bit. Not that she wanted to attend every meeting. There were far too many meetings as it was. But what was so special about these ones? Was it at Morton's request that she was excluded? Was it because he did not trust her personally, or was it that there were top secret matters of national security?

The additional personnel who sometimes attended these exclusive meetings were also intriguing to Sandy. Pearson. Fullerton. Occasionally some other people that Morton brought along, sometimes in military uniform or Militia uniform. Very occasionally Titus Whitaker or Danny Malik. And the meetings were never minuted. Not officially, anyway. But the same was true of his meetings with Dave Barrington. Sandy was sworn not to divulge what went on in the meetings with Barrington, which to her was a little puzzling. Though they might be controversial at several levels, there did not seem to be anything requiring top level secrecy. Maybe it was all a sign of the creeping paranoia she had observed amongst the leadership since the Louise Adams affair. Or just habits from years of subversive activities.

Inside the meeting, Gabriella Pearson was giving Don Mason something of a hard time. 'It's really reaching crisis point now, Don. Time for decisions. We've got to decide now whether it's tick along gently without causing too many waves, or go for a Dave Barrington big tech "bright green" agenda, or go full out for the kind of Restoration we all think is needed in the end.'

Mason was looking thoughtful. 'It's not only about the final destination, Gabriella. It's about the pace of the journey.'

'Well, I'm not for hanging about. We know we can't bring everyone on board. So every day we delay is a chance for us to lose our grip, and for the Greys to get bolder and bring us down, one way or another.'

'But if we move too fast, too soon, we also risk falling short and the whole project will come to an end. We could set back the cause by decades, by generations even,' said Mason.

'But time is a luxury that we don't have,' urged Gabriella. 'The Planet doesn't have the time! Every day hundreds of species die out, every day another—'

'OK, I don't need a lecture,' interrupted Mason sharply. 'We're barely ready yet for the Second Revolution, let alone a Third Revolution and the kind of restoration and rebalancing that will bring. In your dreams all things are possible, but this is the real world we are dealing with now. And we have imperfect control of one small corner of that real world. We haven't got here by underestimating the nature of power or the strength of the people who would oppose us. It's about—'

'I know, "patience and discipline",' interrupted Gabriella. 'But you can be too patient. Like what's with all this farting around with the likes of Terry Cairns and Little Miss busy beaver Sandy Honeyford? What a waste of time and effort! Look how Cairns let you down. It was inevitable, wasn't it Malcolm?' She looked to Morton for confirmation. 'Honeyford will do the same. I can't see why you insist on playing these games.'

'I make no apologies,' replied Mason. 'Terry Cairns was sharp. He wasn't one of us, but I liked him. And unlike most of our people, he understood how the system works. For the time being, we still need to be able to work in and then alongside the old economy. He was making that happen. And there is still work to be done there because, let me spell it out, we are not ready to move faster yet. You know, running all these projects and supporting the Volunteers and all our national and local initiatives costs a shitload of money. We don't have that money. Running the everyday services people expect costs money. Like schools, hospitals, transport. We still have huge debt repayments. In the long run, we can change this. But for now we have to keep all this going—ticking over as you say. So we need the support of as many people as possible who know what they're doing, while we need to harmonise and contain those elements that we cannot win to our side. Your way is to unleash chaos and hope that something good shakes out at the end. It won't do.'

'But Don, we need a clear strategy,' protested Pearson. 'We're developing two or more different strands simultaneously, and we need to know in the end whether it's going to be one or the other, or both for a limited time, or what. Are we looking at one year, two years, ten years, a generation? There are very practical reasons for needing to know this. We have detailed plans to put in place, and people to motivate to do what is necessary. '

'OK. Point taken. I note your impatience and—'

'It's not just my impatience!' Gabriella shouted. 'We have people champing at the bit to do what we need to do. Good people! And we have projects half developed—really challenging projects—that need the go-ahead. Or not. This waiting is causing us a lot of stress and headaches. And soul-searching too. We *cannot* afford to lose momentum. But maybe you've lost

your momentum, and are enjoying the good life in Downing Street, hobnobbing with Kings, generals, ambassadors and captains of industry. Have you
gone native, Don?!'

Don Mason gave a short laugh, and then sighed deeply. 'Let's get all the
options on the table next week, and we'll plan from there. Now Malcolm, I
need you to bring me up to speed with the state of the opposition following
Baxter's scampering off to Sweden. Does it mean anything?'

While Gabriella threw herself back into her chair and exhaled loudly,
Malcolm Morton calmly went through the latest security assessments. 'Baxter has clearly decided to build up resistance to us from outside. At some
point he's decided to abandon any hopes of fighting and winning an election
here—not that we'd necessarily have given him the chance. It's gone down
very badly in his party: some Conservatives sticking it out here feel very betrayed. In Stockholm he hooked up straight away with James Olsen, and had
a three hour conference with Zara Alderney. Now he's doing the rounds with
officials from various other countries. I doubt he's saying how great the Green
Revolution is. We must regard him with the utmost suspicion. Both he and
Olsen still have good links with many in government circles here, so we need
to redouble efforts to monitor people at this end who might be in contact with
him.'

'But no sign of any plan to undermine or topple us?' asked Mason.

'Not yet...'

'But it's exactly why we have to get a bloody move on!' interposed
Gabriella.

Morton continued. 'There are also some developments around the
Kitson Circle.'

'Oh?'

'There was something we missed. Back in March we uncovered a journalist who was intercepting Juliet Coe's communications, using some old hack
techniques. Not very sophisticated. She was already on our lists as under suspicion, and was due to go off to an eco-camp for re-education. All this flared
up just as she was about to leave and we raided her flat in Manchester. And
we found she'd been doing a lot more than tracking Juliet. She was building
up some kind of dossier about all of us, and delving into areas that are strictly
off limits. She had thousands of documents, which our people are still going
through.'

'Is she working for an external party? Baxter, or the Americans?' asked Mason.

'That we don't know yet. Cairns and Adams seem genuinely not to know about it, though some of our interrogators feel they are holding back on something. But there are a couple of interesting leads. Shortly before she left she contacted that buffoon Trevor MacLean. Remember him? She tried to run security around the call, but we can get through that. The thing is that MacLean completely refused to listen to her after she said she'd been investigating Juliet Coe. He told her to drop it. I can play you the tape if you want.'

'He offered to buy her some thermal underwear,' laughed Gabriella Pearson. 'For her time in the eco-camp.'

'We've monitored MacLean for three months now, and he's as clean as a whistle. But the other interesting thing is that after that she shot down to London. We lost her for a short while, but then picked her up on CCTV in Oxford Street. She was going to see her sister and was going to buy a present for her niece. So she said. And we missed something at first. We were getting nowhere in finding out who she was sharing information with. So we reviewed all the CCTV tapes from the time she was arrested and guess what? Going into the same shop just before her and coming out just after was none other than Peter Kitson. And his wife.'

Mason opened his eyes wide. 'Coincidence?'

'Maybe. The pictures in the shop are grainy, but we checked with their security and the records show they were there for sure. One of the pictures seems to show a short exchange of words between Peter Kitson and this journalist, Walton. We know they knew each other, so in fairness it could be a brief exchange of words on a chance meeting. But to me, it smells bad.'

'So what are we doing?'

'So far we can't find any evidence that Kitson has done anything with the data. If he has it. No evidence of transferring it, or following anything up online. But my instincts tell me something is up. We're introducing some more intrusive surveillance. There was some data about eco-criminals in the camps. If he has it, he may have given it to his sister. That could be his angle. If he's up to something, we'll find it.'

Mason thought for a while as the information sunk in. 'How potentially damaging are the files that Kitson has?'

'Walton did a lot of digging, but it's more a fishing expedition than a completed project. I think she was side-tracked by a vendetta against Juliet, looking for things like personal scandal or fiddling expenses. And of course there's no whiff of scandal around Juliet. Then she started to follow up lots of associations between Juliet and key people in the underground. A little while longer, she might have dredged up something potentially very dangerous to our cause. She was starting to investigate Operation Cyrus.'

'And if it were published now, what would the impact be?'

'Everything is deniable. But it would be embarrassing and set us on the back foot. Worse though, it would set a lot of hares running. If our opponents were to get hold of it, and match it up with their own sources, get professional intelligence agents working on it—we could be in big trouble.'

'So we need to contain it.'

'Absolutely.'

'Which brings us back to your Sandy Honeyford. A pivotal member of the Kitson Circle,' said Gabriella.

'Previously, but not now. I understand there's a rift there. The Circle, such as it was, has been broken. And Sandy is useful,' replied Mason.

'And pleasant company, for sure,' mocked Gabriella.

Mason looked irritated for a moment. 'If it wasn't her, I'd need someone like her. There is a job to do to bridge the gap between us and the old establishment, the grey way of doing things. She is part of that bridge. Without her, every day would be struggle from beginning to end. You don't know how wearing that is. No. We need to keep this show on the road, for the time being at least.'

'Sooner or later, Don, we either have to give up or go for broke. Either we choose the time of that, or our enemies will force our hand and choose it for us. I say the sooner we are ready, the better. We can talk all we like about Second or Third Revolutions. At the moment we haven't even got half a revolution—it's time to get our act together.'

46: The blow that lit up reality

Peter Kitson's life had collapsed in on itself. He felt isolated from all the things he had been trying to achieve. Now he no longer met his team of civil service advisers each day, or his Cabinet colleagues and their advisers. He had lost his ministerial pay and allowances, and had to lay off some of his support staff and advisors. Along with his fear and suspicions about the new direction of the Green Earth government he had a feeling akin to grief. And he felt embarrassed, even humiliated, about his demise.

Old colleagues such as Evan, who had never agreed with the 'Kitson Green' approach spoke to him in a friendly way, but their sympathy was unwelcome to him. They felt they had been right all along. And though his pride stood in the way, he was beginning to believe it himself.

Then there were half-hearted overtures from the South Bank Secession, and the self-styled government-in-exile: Patrick Baxter and his almost forgotten Grey-and-proud-of-it rag-tag coalition. How often had Kitson been contemptuous or withering in his comments about this motley reactionary crew? Now they held out the hand of friendship to him. But it was not as if he was powerful political figure that they longed to entice over onto their side. With Terry Cairns and Howard Blackstone out of the picture, Peter Kitson cut a sorry figure. In theory he was at the helm of a significant parliamentary party. But in practice, this group was now rudderless and divided, with Evan trying to pull them in a new oppositional direction. In his depressed state of mind, Peter could not throw himself into this new political world of opposition.

Life became more depressing when he attended events such as the official opening of Don Mason's first 'Truly Sustainable Community'—the first of the eco-settlements that had replaced the old hypocritical 'concrete over the countryside' sustainable communities. As a leading Member of Parliament Peter was invited to attend. But he had to endure not only the Green Earth dignitaries heaping praises on themselves, but also the new Green Energy Minister Rhoda Sackville taking the plaudits for initiatives he had overseen throughout the whole development phase.

The eco-settlement was entirely energy-self-sufficient, and radically low in energy consumption. The need for car use had been entirely designed out in the village: every service was accessible by walking or cycling. A community of self-sufficient eco-enthusiasts with a balanced range of skills had already moved in, most of them working in craft workshops, studios or surgeries embedded in their earth-covered homes. A local market had been established based on trading skills and services, rather than money. A special fair was held on the day of the launch, bringing people from all over the country to sell and promote their eco-products and expertise. Danny Malik was there in person to mastermind the media coverage of the event. Peter saw one after another Doug Cunningham, Rhoda Sackville, Gabriella Pearson and eventually Don Mason interviewed. Finally, as a magnanimous gesture, Malik guided a local TV crew over to have a word with Peter—this was after all, an initiative with cross-party support.

After this, Peter could bear no more. He could see real value and achievement in this new community, but he felt empty and worthless inside. He longed to be centre stage. But he also knew this longing was itself shallow and worthless, and he felt revulsion towards himself and his ambitions.

He could write his memoirs. That was always a possibility. He had no stomach for working with Baxter in die-hard opposition, or for the machinations of Evan in trying to form a new Parliamentary front against Green Earth extremism.

What was left to him now?

Family life. The enchantments of family life—and having the time to enjoy it—rescued him from retreating into himself. Heather seemed to understand him completely—possibly he never appreciated her, or loved her, more than at this time. And Andrea was growing up fast. Every day brought a new discovery, new delights. Each day he could sink into blissful family exhaustion after Andrea was finally asleep. Toys and all the baby paraphernalia could be cleared, meals a deux prepared. Finally, he and Heather could sink back in close embrace on the sofa and watch a film, or just chat about everything and nothing. Normal life had resumed, and it was more than good.

And if his political life was over? Then maybe, so be it. The value, Peter felt, was in real achievement, not in the posturing or the glory. In future he would always try to add real value, and use the experience he had gained to the best effect, regardless of party politics.

This was not to say that his interest in political life came to an end. Often he and Heather would talk over current events, commenting on and criticising government initiatives, or sometimes praising them. He found visits from Joanna became more enjoyable again, now that he was not in a position to press her cases at the highest level. Joanna was doing her best to advise her brother on tracking down Terry Cairns and Louise Adams: they, like many others, had disappeared without trace. Eventually, after two months, there was an unexpected call from Terry. He was being allowed one call, and clearly wasn't being allowed to say very much. He assured them that he was alright—but was desperate for some knowledge of what had happened to Louise. On mentioning her name, the call was abruptly ended.

During his time in government, Peter had enjoyed working with Dave Barrington. They used to play squash two or three times per month. This sporting camaraderie had also evaporated, but not before one last game a couple of months after the end of the coalition.

It was a day or two before the debate on the Declaration of the Rights of Species that they played their last game. Barrington noticed how much Peter Kitson had changed since being bounced out of office. Their friendship had naturally become a little strained, a little artificial now that they were not Cabinet colleagues working together. He also seemed a worried man—and this seemed to give an edge to his play: more aggressive but also more wayward than usual.

Between games, in hushed tones, Peter Kitson confided his fears to his former colleague, but they struck Barrington as bordering on paranoia. 'Mason is a cunning bastard,' he said, 'though whether it is him or Morton, I don't know.'

A little taken aback, Dave asked him to explain what he meant.

'Listen, my phones are all bugged,' he whispered.

'Why?' Dave asked, apparently surprised—although with his own phones being bugged after the Louise Adams affair, he couldn't help feeling that this was now par for the course.

'Why? It's your lot! Terry's disappeared God-knows-where, and they want to get me too, I guess.'

'And yet you trust me?' Dave joked. 'I'm one of them, don't you think?'

Peter did not respond, but just sipped his drink nervously.

'I can't believe anyone is trying to set you up for anything. But the security services might be interested, as you spent a fair amount of time with Cairns and Adams. It's kind of natural,' said Dave. 'Surely if anyone is really out to get you, it would have happened by now. Don't you think?'

'It's coming,' Peter said, standing up and retrieving his racquet. 'It's only a matter of time. I feel I'm under constant surveillance. And so I'm like walking on eggshells—watching what I say, who I meet…'

Dave shrugged, feeling there was nothing he could say. If it was true, it was beyond his control. Peter continued expressing his fears. 'I have no power or influence now. It makes no sense to keep a watch on me like this. I hear what you say about Louise—but she wasn't in our party, she was in yours, wasn't she? But it seems she was using Terry to brief her paymasters about us too!'

Barrington became a little annoyed by this protestation of innocence. 'Half your supporters have at least one foot in the Dark Grey camp. If not her, then someone else could have betrayed us.'

Peter seemed shocked by this. 'Perhaps I shouldn't trust you, then, if you can say things like that. But I've said so much now.'

There was a long pause, then he continued. 'Listen. There's been a major, major erosion of civil liberties over the past 18 months or so.'

Dave rolled his eyes upwards and got up to resume play. He felt a lecture coming on, and wasn't in the mood for it. Peter got up and followed him on court, talking all the time.

'There has, Dave—but maybe you think it's acceptable. All the same, you must have your suspicions about Morton's secretariat, his control of the police and his Jack Russell Squad! I think most members of the Cabinet, the Convention, and Parliament, are being spied on.

'But that's not the point, or not the whole point. It's my firm belief that Mason and Morton are preparing a major package of "deep green" measures that will entail a lot of compulsion and coercion. Which means a drastic curtailing of traditional liberties. These measures—and those of your Animalist colleagues—won't be popular. And where consensus fails, coercion is the only alternative. You like to think you are all pragmatists. And as you believe much more in environmentalism than civil liberties, compulsion is the pragmatic thing to do, unless you are prepared to look defeat in the face. Come on—let's play a last game.'

They played a last game, which Peter won in very aggressive fashion. At the end of the game, he took one last parting shot. 'What about you, Dave? I hear that you drew the short straw, to be the Chief Hypocrite in the Rights of Species debate. Take my advice: watch yourself. It could be a set-up. No doubt Mason sweetened the pill with some flattery. But ask yourself: why you? I'll tell you why. Mason isn't sure whether this new tack with the Animalists will work. If it all falls flat on its face, you'll be the guy who stuck his head above the parapet.'

'Quite a conspiracy theory!' Barrington laughed.

'I can smell a rat here. Your problem is you've been living wild with them for so long that you just can't smell it!'

That hadn't occurred to Barrington, and he was irritated by the suggestion. He felt that relationships at the top of the GEM had always been marked by high degrees of trust, and this seemed a crude way of trying to set them against each other.

'This kind of sour grapes isn't like you, Peter,' he said. 'OK, you're out of power now. But there's still a lot you could contribute if you remain constructive and focused.'

'I wish it could be so, but I reckon I'm done for politically. As for you, Dave—I don't know. I'm confused by your attitude. Either you know what the game plan is, and you've been playing some kind of cat-and-mouse game with me over the past months. Or you're being kept in the dark by your colleagues as much as I was. Who's really calling the shots, Dave? Is it Mason? Morton? Pearson?!'

'You accuse us of a fiendish plot,' Barrington replied quite sternly. 'But if I didn't know you better, I'd suspect you of attempting to put a wedge between my colleagues and me, and draw me towards you and the other the other Grey-Greens. Well, let me remind you: I'm no moderate. I'm a radical and proud of it. For me, politics has always been a means to an end. I believe in our mission: to end the destruction of our planet. We have become friends, and have worked well together. But equally I will work with anyone who will work towards the same goals as me.'

It was the last time they met.

Disillusioned with politics at the top level, Peter threw himself into his constituency work. Through this he began to understand the real day-to-day problems that people were facing. The lack of work and money. Failure to pay benefits. Food shortages. And almost every day he heard complaints about the GEM government, the overbearing activities of the Militia. The cost of gas and electricity in what was turning into the coldest year for a decade. But he focused his activity on case-work: trying to help people solve their individual problems at a practical level by liaising with the appropriate authorities. This struck him as a more rewarding approach than trying to tackle things through political opposition, which held few prospects of success at the current time.

And then, there was the information from Stella Walton. After ignoring it for several months, he finally went back to it. He began to spend more and more time going through it, mulling it over, discussing parts of it with

Heather. The more he dug into it, the more awfully fascinating—and alarming— it became.

And the more he looked into it, the more he admired Stella too. She was clearly a very resourceful person. And a risk-taker. She had intercepted phone conversations and messaging between leading figures in the GEM and the Animalist movement, in particular conversations involving Juliet Coe. It seemed Stella felt Juliet Coe was pivotal to the more radical directions of the new coalition—and there was something personal in there too.

In the early autumn, Peter received an unexpected email. It said simply: 'Still chewing it over? OPEN YOUR EYES. You could be our only hope. READ THE NOAH FOLDER. S.'

The sender address was clearly fake—but he had no doubt it was from Stella, wherever she was. If she was still in re-education, he had again to admire her resourcefulness.

Peter called Heather over, and together they found their way to the folder marked 'Noah Project'. In Stella's system of linkages, he had seen several references to documents in this folder, but so far had not explored it. There were over two hundred documents in the folder, and they split the task between them. As they read through, they became more and more appalled by what they read.

The files in the Noah Project folder explored a variety of approaches to human population 'stabilisation', 'rebalancing' and 'reduction'. Some explored more regular political channels—incentive-based one-child or even no-child policies, completely free contraception, financial rewards for early sterilisation, voluntary childlessness campaigns and the like.

More chilling were documents from supporters of concepts like the 'Voluntary Holocaust': voluntary population reduction. Euthanasia techniques were popularised, with a green angle added. One campaign was called 'Renew the Earth through Suicide', and provided a network for people to form suicide pacts.

'Aren't these just the usual Internet freaks and loonies?' asked Heather. But then they looked at the linkages that Stella had provided. Some of the identifications were through association of the authors. Where the documents were anonymous, she had subjected them to a textual analysis that linked them to identified authors. If her identifications were correct, most of the documents could be tied directly or indirectly to influential people in the Animalists, GEM or Green Militia.

Titus Whitaker was frequently quoted—often critically for being too tentative in his approach to population rebalancing. Gabriella Pearson was referred to many times in the documents. Although the authorship of none of the documents could be directly linked to her, several could be linked to people identified as her close Animalist collaborators. Peter was shocked to see Rhoda Sackville identified as an advocate of the Voluntary Holocaust. It seemed quite out of character with the mild-mannered and unassuming person he had handed over to. Louise Adams also came up as a name associated with this view. How was this possible? Was she acting as an 'agent provocateur' to flush out extremists and pass information on to her American paymasters?

Then there were advocates of more extreme and coercive views. The metaphor of Noah's Ark was frequently used, to signify a rebalancing and cleansing process. And the religious tone didn't end there—the writings were infused with a moralistic tone, and references to sin and redemption. 'Creation' was referred to reverentially. Then in the next breath, various measures of population reduction—human population reduction—were considered coldly and pragmatically. Exporting of weapons of mass destruction to unstable countries. Unleashing plagues in more populous areas of the globe. Contaminating water supplies to induce infertility. Using terror to reduce undesirable population elements.

Voices arguing for such measures were countered by others concerned about the knock-on effects on the natural world as a whole. Others still said not only the human population had to be rebalanced. Other species had declined unnaturally due to human predations, while others like rats had expanded unnaturally. At times the arguments became abstruse, debating what constituted 'natural' and 'unnatural' rates of increase and decrease.

Linked to these more extreme views several names came up repeatedly. Most frequent among these was Tara Collingworth, author of a pamphlet called 'The Noah Principle', which was cited everywhere, though not always approvingly. And there were frequent references to two people identified only by their code names, 'Samson' and 'Cyrus'. And the public figure most to these linked in Stella's constellation of extremism was none other than her bête noire Juliet Coe.

Heather and Peter now had to decide what to do.

'Pass it on to Zara Alderney,' advised Heather. 'Make this information available outside the country. The media is too controlled here now, don't you think?'

'If Louise was mixing with these people, maybe there's nothing here Zara doesn't know already,' Peter replied. The thought that Zara knew all this, and Stella too, made him feel foolish. He'd been acting as if he was in control of events, while all around him were all kinds of currents of activity, wheels within wheels of machinations.

He began to feel that Mason was a master politician, who had played him and his colleagues very skilfully. He had played Peter himself, bringing him on board and in effect splitting the party. He had seduced Terry, not once but twice, sucking Terry further in when all his sceptical instincts had been telling him the Green Earth solution was unworkable. And he had seduced Sandy, taking away one of the party's key organisers.

But what was Mason's role in the more extreme tendencies before them? Mason was often quoted or criticised, but none of Stella's identifications pointed to him as sharing in these extreme views. Unless he was 'Samson' or 'Cyrus'.

'You sent copies to Terry and Joanna, didn't you, honey?' asked Heather.

Peter looked slightly pained. 'Terry was arrested before I could give it to him. And Jo—I only gave her the camp databases.'

Heather looked puzzled.

'It's what would help her most,' Peter continued, 'and I didn't want to compromise her further by having information from illegal phone taps and all that kind of thing...'

'You must get it to her, and to Zara,' Heather insisted. 'If we're the only ones with it, the data is very vulnerable. Do you think you can send it out securely?'

'In theory, yes,' said Peter. 'But I'm sure I'm being watched. The state security apparatus—they can intercept just about anything. I don't think we can risk sending anything online.'

'What then?'

'Let's make some copies now, and take one to the American Embassy tomorrow. I'll find a pretext for going there. And then I'll go on to meet Joanna. And there's also a journalist from a German news agency I think I can trust. Stella said she was sending it to other people. Journalists I'd guess. But we've never seen anything come of it. So how solid do you think all this stuff is? After all, there are cranks in all parties.'

'There are cranks, and there are cranks, honey! These cranks are something else, with friends in high places too. We *must* get this information out into the open.'

Resolved on this course of action, they made the copies and went to bed. Peter had in the meantime formulated another possible course of action. He was hesitant about broaching it with Heather–he was well aware what her response was likely to be. Finally he felt he had to share his idea. 'I know you're not going to like this. But one other possibility is to share this with Sandy and Martin.'

Immediately he saw the change in his wife's expression. Her face, which was naturally predisposed to smiling and laughter, took on a pinched and tense aspect. Though he should have known better, Peter continued with his train of thought. 'We don't know how much Mason and the other top dogs know about this. Maybe one way of dealing with it is getting her to ferret around a bit. Or she may be able to get the GEM people to do their own dirty work, and weed out the nutters. And Martin's in a powerful position now–he could set up his own independent investigation, maybe'.

Heather exploded in exasperation at this proposal. 'How can you still trust that woman after all she's done? And Martin, he's no better. I remember Sandy told you to watch your back, then she's the one putting the knife into it! She's betrayed you all, and now she sits at table with the people who've destroyed the party she grew up in. Sandy and Martin, they're both trimmers: they'll just sail with the prevailing wind. They've got no principles! None at all. All that spurs them on is their vaulting ambition. What do you think they'd do with this? They'd probably pass it on to Morton then his boys would be round and we'd all be sent off for re-education. And what would happen to Stella if Morton's people got hold of this? I can't believe you're seriously thinking of this!'

Peter didn't share his wife's violent dislike of Sandy. As always, he liked to see the situation from all sides. But he agreed that it was perhaps best not to risk the contact with Sandy.

At four in the morning, they woke suddenly to the sound of violent banging on the door and the baby crying. Peter leapt out of bed and rushed to the stairs, Heather rushing to the baby's room. Despite her alarm, Heather hissed to him, 'Hide the memory sticks!' It had been playing on her mind all night.

But it was too late for him to do this. As Peter reached the bottom of the stairs, armed police broke down the front door, flanked by officials of the Green Militia. A warrant was briefly flashed in his face, and two police officers roughly manhandled him to the side of the room. In all it seemed upwards of twenty people surged into the house, all of them apparently with a clear mission. Trolleys and packing cases were brought in to gather his computers and files. Police technicians began disconnecting the computers and packing them into the boxes. Others began searching his office. The whole operation seemed to be conducted with determination and a barely suppressed violence, as books and files tumbled off shelves and household items were trodden underfoot.

From the top of the stairs where Heather stood trembling with Andrea in her arms, she saw Peter begin to resist the militiamen who were forcing him to the wall. She could hear Peter protesting and saying something about his 'rights'. And she let out a scream when she saw the blow that fractured his cheekbone and knocked him to the floor. As she started down the stairs a woman police officer sprinted up to restrain her. Heather was yelling—she didn't know what.

Peter was silent, and dazed. The blow had opened up to him a whole new reality. 'So this is what it boils down to,' he thought. He wanted to fight back, and then it dawned on him. He had never hit anyone since he was a young child. He didn't know how to hit anyone. And up until now he had considered that a virtue.

IV

47: Bugger the mice ...

Trevor MacLean hadn't had a full night's sleep since Stella Walton had contacted him. His anger towards her had mounted over the following three or four months, until he was almost spitting blood. Though he said nothing, his wife and kids had noted his increasingly sour moods, and found it safest to keep out of his way when he started 'growling', as they put it.

Why had Stella tried to involve him? He had often taken risks in his journalistic work. But these had been *career* risks, not *life-and-limb* risks. That was quite a different proposition. And he had been happy laughingly to describe himself as a 'born again coward'. That too meant little—until he was brought up face-to-face with a colleague's own courage. Now his own vaunted cowardice bit deep into his conscience. Yet he had responsibilities to his family, and to his own well-being. Stella's actions, he came to feel, were a kind of moral blackmail, impelling him to action. He cursed her often in his mind, in between feeling anguish for her situation. Why had she done this to him?

And she had not only asked him for help, she had dropped into his hands the means of helping, whether he wanted to do so or not. In their phone conversation some months before, she had asked in a nonchalant way if he thought she should just 'bin' the work she had done so far. To Stella and Trevor, this carried a double meaning which would be unknown to anyone monitoring their conversation. In their old days of investigative journalism, they often left information for each other in places they called 'bins', sometimes a real place, other times an online location. Trevor was certain that Stella would want to keep her information available, and had deposited it in one of their 'bins'. And this tortured him all the more as it created the real prospect that he could do something to follow up her work, and not just feel sorry for her predicament.

Eventually he began to crack. And it made him even more livid to think that she had probably anticipated this! Visiting or accessing any of these bins, of course, carried risks. Maybe he was being watched. Maybe the authorities already knew where her bins were, and were waiting to see who else knew about them. Only a bad conscience made him constantly revisit the issue: he knew the wisest course of action was just to forget about it all. But he couldn't.

Finally he confided in his wife. He hadn't wanted to involve her, but felt her consent was now necessary if he were to take any further steps. He chose his moment to speak to her, when they were walking home from the village shop one afternoon, and he could be sure of not being overheard. It saddened him to think that already it was common practice for people to think like this—a mild paranoia about saying the wrong thing at the wrong time had become normality.

To his surprise, Trevor found that Carrie agreed readily to his taking the next step—so long as he did it discreetly. He should at least find out what it was that Stella had unearthed, and then he could decide for himself whether there was anything worth pursuing.

'Worth pursuing?' Trevor had mused aloud. 'Worth pursuing where? Even if I find out the most incriminating, most sensational evidence of evil afoot—what do I do with it? With the press controls, I can't publish, I can only be damned. And I'm not some kind of William Wallace figure who can rally the clans to drive out the wicked English...'

'He lost, anyway,' added Carrie, with a wry smile. 'Best try another role model!'

'So if I find out some more, I'm no better off. Where does it take us?'

'To the next step. And then you make another decision.'

'One step at a time,' said Trevor thoughtfully. 'With no clear destination and no road map. By the way, aren't you impressed that I've avoided being headstrong and impulsive? Completely out of character!'

'Very impressed, of course,' smiled Carrie. 'And you can use your new-found skills in self-effacement and avoiding publicity to take the next steps. Quietly, like a mouse. Not like the bear with a sore head who's been blundering around the house for the last few weeks!'

'*Wee, sleekit, cow'rin, tim'rous beastie / O, what a panic's in thy breastie!*' quoted Trevor. 'Aye, that's me, a'richt. Panicked up tae mah eyeballs an' beyond!'

Carrie smiled. They walked on in silence for a while, then Trevor recited some more of the Burns poem: 'How does it go? *'I'm truly sorry man's dominion / Has broken nature's social union...'*'

'Hmm. Very apt, for these times. Makes you think, doesn't it?' observed Carrie.

'Yes, it makes you think,' agreed Trevor. 'But not for long, unless you've got a screw loose! Bugger the mice! Let's get on with being human! Do you

357

think we'll be able to get any petrol this week? My arms are going to fall off if I have to carry any more shopping up this hill...'

••

A family trip to Edinburgh was the cover for Trevor visiting an old friend and collaborator, Donny Patterson.

Edinburgh had changed. At first rather sluggish in its response to the Green Revolution, the Scottish capital was now the epicentre of Don Mason's mission to 'convert' the country. Green zealots from across the whole nation converged in Edinburgh to support the initially beleaguered Earth Council. The City Council had now been purged of its trenchant Grey elements, as had the Scottish Parliament and the Scottish Executive. A Scottish National Convention had been set up on the same lines as the one in London. Squads of the Green Militia roamed the street, enforcing the new green regulations on businesses and citizens alike. Along Princes Street and the Royal Mile various campaigning groups held continuous rallies and handed out leaflets.

Animalist campaigners were strongly in evidence. A group of vegetarians were claiming that now more than 50% of the country had given up eating meat.

'Bloody hell, I could eat a steak!' whispered Trevor to his family.

'Dad!' hissed his children.

'Look at their T-shirts,' Trevor whispered. The T-shirts featured cute pictures of animals' faces, and written in bold letters: 'If it has a face, I don't eat it!'

'Why do they never say, 'If it has an arse, I don't eat it'? It would be just as true, though the pictures might be less appealing ... '

'Dad!' the children hissed again, urging him to silence.

The streets of the capital were bustling with people. The shops were less busy, though, and most had fewer goods to sell. Several shops had their windows smashed, mostly for failing to sell local and organic goods, or using excessive packaging. Words like 'Grey Profiteer' or 'Counter-revolutionary scum' were spray-painted across the walls.

Though not outlawed, meat had become hard to buy through the regular outlets. Many supermarket meat shelves were bare, and most butchers in the capital had been put out of business apart from a few organic ones that provided financial contributions to the militias or green campaigns. Meanwhile, a black market had sprung up in 'forbidden fruits', as the non-organic produce—mostly meat—was now being called. It seemed there were problems in exporting the Revolution from the capital to the rural areas, and there were new channels for the unreconstructed supply to meet the unreconstructed demand. All this Trevor and Carrie found out as they met old friends in Edinburgh. These were indeed interesting times to live in.

The following day, Trevor met with Donny Patterson. In the past, Trevor had often used the technical wizardry of Donny both for putting programmes together and for carrying out investigations. Donny always boasted that no door could remain closed to him online.

Donny also boasted that whatever he did, he could cover his tracks. No one had so far traced his illicit activities. Now he agreed to help Trevor get Stella's material out of any online hiding places without being tracked—if indeed she had stored the material electronically. Despite his professional boasting, Donny always put his achievements into perspective. 'It's not like I'm robbing banks or hacking into the Pentagon—just doing a bit of harmless digging,' he would say. But Trevor was aware that Donny knew his way around most government systems and the channels of political parties and campaigners. And what motivated Donny was not money but the challenge, plus an old-fashioned beard-and-sandals idea of freedom. He believed that all governments are up to no good most of the time, and felt he was doing mankind a service by exposing their machinations.

After two days and nights of exhausting work, Trevor and Donny had not only verified most of Stella's sleuthing, but substantially built on it too. They could now identify 'Samson', but 'Cyrus' remained elusive. Donny was gripped by the challenge, and promised to keep working on it.

'Samson' they identified as none other than Carl Fullerton. And he was an advocate of the more extreme coercive measures for population reduction. As a public figure, he was not well known. So the second stage was to find out if he had any real influence—and they found that he did. He had been elevated to the position of coordinator of the eco-camp re-education programme. And his name cropped up as an increasingly close confidant of Malcolm Morton.

'It seems these guys are moving their way close to the centre,' said Donny.

For Trevor, this wasn't enough. Wild talk and positions of influence were still only circumstantial. What was needed was evidence of people actually doing something to put these ideas into action.

Donny worked his way through secure systems by having multiple personalities. Where he had previously infiltrated a system, finding the information he needed was child's play. The skill lay in being untraceable, so that no one could establish where his fictitious identities were operating from. Getting into new areas was more challenging. And this was just what Trevor was now asking him to do.

Carl Fullerton, they found, had established a new elite unit within the Green Militia, which was based at a newly built eco-camp called New Dawn. Of the people they could identify so far, only Fullerton and Malcolm Morton had access to the network dealing with New Dawn activities. No one identifiable from the security services had access to it. Donny was unable to find a way into this network, so until he could do this they gathered what information they could from other sources.

There were Cabinet briefing papers relating to New Dawn: financial details, plans for building, estimates of labour demand, and a reference to its being a 'new model camp for taking forward re-education projects'. Nothing particularly incriminating here. Only the centrality of Carl Fullerton to the project, and the extreme secrecy surrounding it, made New Dawn a cause for special concern. And what of Morton's role in this? Was he a part of whatever was going on, or was his security apparatus being infiltrated by radical extremists?

'What do you think is going on there?' asked Donny, not for the first time that day.

Trevor thought for a while, going over in his mind all the snippets they had found. 'Let's put all the pieces together: they call the camp "New Dawn". They speak of it officially as a "new model camp". Fullerton's really into it. And it's so top secret maybe only one or two of the Cabinet really knows what's going on—but maybe not even they really know. And Fullerton, as "Samson", has written a whole bundle of stuff in recent years about population rebalancing, and "HPR"—human population reduction. Maybe they are doing some social experiments up there, like creating environments where humans live much closer to nature—like cave men or something...'

'Have you read some of this stuff from Titus Whitaker about "*The Unbalancing of the Human Race*"? Quite chilling survival-of-the-fittest stuff,' said Donny.

'Go on,' said Trevor.

'He says humanity started to get out of kilter with the natural world because we learned to overcome genetic weaknesses, through social interaction. Our civilisation developed from that.'

'Nothing new in that idea.'

'It's where he takes the idea, though. Natural man would be fitter, and stronger, and more athletic: swift as an arrow and hard as iron, he says. But also more stupid, if I can paraphrase a bit. We wouldn't have needed to develop complex social systems, technologies etc. We'd be truer to our animal nature. And our ability to reorganise the natural world would not have developed. He gives an example: simple visual defects like being short-sighted or longsighted. In the wild, people with poor sight would tend to die early and be less able to reproduce. But by protecting people with dodgy eyesight, we aided higher population growth, albeit of weaker humans. He sees this as a bad thing, given the long-term results. Too many of us, too addicted to restructuring the world for our own benefit and creating the conditions for weaker specimens to survive.'

'So, it seems we didn't so much come down from the trees, but fell out of them as we got old and kept missing the branches!' joked Trevor.

'Maybe they're putting the camp inmates back up the trees, as a way to get back to our true nature. They're certainly planting a helluva lot of trees. And reintroducing bears and wolves and who knows what else,' said Donny, skimming through some project finance documents.

'No woolly mammoths or sabre-tooth tigers yet?' asked Trevor.

Donny grunted and swivelled back to face his screens. Then he swung back.

'You know, there's a lot of lab work going on there. It's not all log cabins and camp fires, you know.'

'I hope you weren't taking me seriously—you don't think they're reconstructing prehistoric animals in the labs, do you? That's just nuts!' chuckled Trevor.

'Well, some of these guys are nuts. But I doubt if they're that far gone. Though reconstructing predators to keep human numbers down might be within their frame of reference, who knows?'

'Well, there's no idea so stupid you can't find a hundred followers, I reckon. In the Internet age, maybe that should be a thousand followers,' said Trevor.

'True enough. But let's look at the lab work. In all the camps there are research facilities. I can track all the specs and procurement. The camp reports from all round the country refer to all kinds of biotech stuff—organic biotech, I guess. But the spending on research at New Dawn is off the scale—far more than all the others put together. And they've been bussing in hundreds of inmates who were previously building satellite camps at the other eco-camps round the country,' said Donny, flicking his way through several documents on his screens.

Trevor sat up sharply. 'What are they doing there?' he asked.

Donny sighed and angled his head on one side. 'I can't say yet. Nothing spells it out directly. But I can tell you what kind of kit they've been shipping in, where it comes from, who they're working with, and... oh my God!'

'What?' asked Trevor impatiently. It seemed the colour had drained completely from Donny's face.

'I've come across these project names, these coded references before...'

'For Christ's sake, what, Donny?'

'I was doing some digging for a peace organisation on WMDs a while back, and I came across the same kinds of patterns. It all points to Porton Down.'

'Porton Down?' asked Trevor, puzzled. Then the penny began to drop. But it still didn't completely make sense. From day one the Green Earth government had vowed to get rid of all of Britain's weapons of mass destruction. The media regularly reported progress in working towards this. Now it appeared that a top secret government project was setting up a new facility in the far north of Scotland closely linked with Britain's research centre into chemical and biological weapons at Porton Down in Wiltshire.

'This is big, man!' said Donny softly. 'I've got goose bumps on my goose bumps!'

Trevor nodded. 'I'm shitting myself here. God, I wish I'd never touched this. Why did you do this to me, Stella?!' he cried, looking theatrically up to the ceiling.

Then he added, with determination: 'This isn't enough. We need to have more pieces of the jigsaw. We need to know who else is inside this project, find out where they've been and what they're doing. And we need to find exactly who and what has been coming out of Porton Down.'

'It could all be innocent, you know,' suggested Donny. 'I mean, if they are genuinely closing down a major research facility like Porton Down, maybe they're just recycling some of the bits and pieces—you know, tables, chairs, workbenches, kettles, filing cabinets....'

'That would be nice. Unlikely, but nice!'

The digging continued.

48: The interrogation

The interrogator looked with contempt at Peter Kitson's crumpled figure slumped in the corner of the room. Peter hadn't eaten for two days, and had been given very little to drink. The left side of his face was swollen and heavily discoloured with bruising from the blow he'd received at his arrest. Leaning over Peter's dishevelled form, the interrogator gave a short snort of laughter, then turned to the desk. He kicked round the chair on one side of the desk.

'Sit, and join me at the table, Mr Kitson,' he said in mocking tones.

Peter thought about ignoring him. He sensed a slight nervousness in the man's contemptuous tones. Here, he thought, is someone not used to being in authority. He decided to leave his response long enough for the man to become anxious about the next step. Then slowly he got up, and walked painfully to the table. The interrogator gestured to sit. Peter smiled weakly, and took his place opposite, and leaned back. His ribs hurt. Movement was painful.

'Thank you. Very gracious of you,' said Peter, half-attempting a smile.

Peter had thought deeply about the time he had spent since his arrest. At first he had been too shocked to know how to react. Everything was too confusing, too irrational to cope with, and the pain from his initial beating was too searing.

Two months had passed, and he had time to get back some of his equilibrium. Now he was determined that whatever happened, he would not allow his accusers to have things their own way. In his mind he had worked through strategies to try to turn the tables on them a little, even though he risked further beatings.

A few hours earlier he had frustrated one interrogator enough that he had stalked out and sent in a couple of Militia men to soften him up. After which they had flung him like a rag doll into the corner of the room. Now someone new had come in, possibly someone more senior. But he did not seem to have the grit of some of his earlier tormentors. It was time to test him.

The interrogator feigned boredom, and leaned back in his chair. 'You think you are being clever, Kitson. But you don't seem to realise the seriousness of the situation you're in.'

Peter didn't answer, but just fixed the interrogator with a prolonged stare.

'You think?' he said at last.

'You must understand,' said the interrogator, 'that your interview with me represents your last chance to tell us what we need to know...in a cooperative manner. After this...I cannot be responsible for what will happen. Think about it.'

Peter shrugged. 'Tell us what we need to know. Or maybe you mean "Tell us what we want to hear".'

Now the interrogator shrugged. 'They are the same. We want to hear what we want to know. There's no point in playing games with me. Let me remind you, you could be facing charges of treason.'

Again Peter paused, and looked long and hard at the man on the other side of the table. He was a red-haired man, young but already balding. He was shorter than Peter, and slightly built. Peter tried to imagine a background and career path that had led him to be in his position, several ranks up in the opaque hierarchy of the Green Militia. A local activist, probably. A campaigner, thrust into a position of forcing rather than persuading people to act as the Militia wanted. Maybe, like Italian Fascist squadristi, or Mao's Red Guards, or Stalin's party apparatchiks, he had jostled his way amongst people who find themselves in the position of having to outdo each other to prove their enthusiasm. And this guy had made it up the ladder into a position of some authority. But, Peter wondered, what was he made of?

'I can make things easy for you,' said Peter.

'Go on,' said the interrogator.

'I want three things. Then I'll cooperate fully. You'll look good. And I'll feel better.'

'Go on, I'm listening.'

'First—tell me who you are. I want to know who I'm talking to. A small thing, but it makes a difference.'

'And the second?'

'I want something decent to eat and drink, then I want to be able to clean up. Feel like myself again.'

The interrogator angled his head to one side, as if considering this.

'Third—after we've talked, and I've made my statement in full, I must be released into the custody of the regular police.'

Peter noticed the interrogator look both to the guards in the cell, and then to the CCTV camera in the corner of the room. So someone higher up was watching this.

'Perhaps you need to consult someone with more clout than you? It's OK, I can wait,' added Peter.

The interrogator hesitated.

'Just think of it this way,' Peter continued, in a whisper. 'My fate is sealed, one way or another, by forces neither of us control. You can take home to your family the consolation that you, in a small way, acted properly when everyone around you was violating every tenet of justice and human decency.'

'Huh!' said the interrogator dismissively. 'You're in no position to lecture me or make demands, my friend!'

Peter leaned back. The interrogator was taking in some instructions on his headset.

'I'm not making demands, just stating facts. If this, then that. If not, then it's a different story. Let's start. Introduce yourself, just like real policemen do in an interview. It's not hard, just say.'

The interrogator smiled. 'My name's Perry Jones. Principal Investigator with ESCOSAFE–the Scrutiny Commission for the Security Services. But you must know what ESCOSAFE is. We now have a special service that carries out its own investigations, supplementing MI5, MI6 and all the rest.'

'So you're the Green 007?'

'If you like.'

'Except maybe you don't get out so much.'

'You treat your situation too lightly, given the stakes.'

'As I said, I'm sure whatever I do makes no difference to the final outcome. So no point in being more miserable than necessary, don't you think?'

The door opened, and two burly Green Militia men came in.

'More beatings?' asked Peter, raising an eyebrow, pretending not to feel the fear rising up again in his body.

'What can you think of me?' asked Jones. 'These gentlemen are here to escort you to wash before dinner.'

An hour later, fed and refreshed but still in pain, Peter Kitson was questioned again by Jones. 'You were found with classified information in your computer. We'd like you to confirm the source of this material.'

'You know this already.'

'We know. But your confirmation is important.'

'Have you seen all the material?'

'Of course.'

'Then that's more than I did. The source identifies itself. She even videos herself in the introduction. And as far as I know, you have her in custody.'

'Then you confirm the source of the material as Stella Walton?'

'You know as much as I do.'

'You confirm you did not receive this material from a third party?'

'There is no wider conspiracy, if that's what you're getting at.'

'How long had you been in communication with Stella Walton?'

'I've said all this before. I barely knew her. But like a lot of people, she knew me, and got in touch.'

'Kitson, you must understand. This is one of the key questions: why you? She must have had reasons for seeing you, amongst all people.'

'You know, I've been wondering that too. And why I went to meet her.'

'And maybe why you didn't go straight to the authorities with it?'

'Tell me something, Principal Investigator Perry Jones: how much of what was on that memory stick is true?'

Jones thought for a moment, then said: 'It was a mixture of classified information and malicious gossip, as far as I could see.'

Peter smiled. 'They haven't let you see it, have they?' He watched as Jones' face coloured slightly. 'Would you like me to tell you what was in it?'

'Let me show you this,' said Jones quickly. He swung the screen on the table towards Peter. A video began playing. It was the grainy footage of Peter and Heather's meeting with Stella in the clothes shop. Their voices could not be heard, but the meeting was clear.

'Furtive. Secretive. You knew what you were doing was criminal. We can plainly see your wife was involved. Now we need to know who else was involved in your circle. Your sister—we can take her complicity for granted. Now there are several others we want you tell us about. Terry Cairns. Louise Adams. Zara Alderney. And we know about your meeting in Stockholm with Sir James Olsen. And who are the intermediaries you use to communicate with Alderney and Olsen?'

'I've been shown a lot of videos these past few days. I've had private conversations replayed to me. You guys have been monitoring everything. Doesn't it strike you that if there are gaps in your conspiracy theory, it's because there's actually nothing to fill them? The evidence you have is evidence of no conspiracy!'

'You're playing games again, Kitson. We know that Walton couldn't have produced all this on her own. It's clear she had help. And it's clear she gathered information that was of direct relevance to your sister's cases. Why did she go looking for that?'

Peter was silent. Questions that brought in Heather and Joanna always made him very wary. He needed to divert the conversation from them. But he felt uneasy saying anything that would implicate Stella Walton further as a sole 'culprit' in all this. He needed to divert the interrogation.

'How well do you know Juliet Coe?' asked Peter.

Jones looked nonplussed. 'She's far too eminent for me to know her,' he said self-effacingly.

Peter then went on to quiz his interrogator about the Voluntary Holocaust, the Noah Principle and Population Rebalancing, all things that he had read about in Stella's files. It was clear that Jones was not one of the inner circle in this regard.

'Well, Mr Principal Investigator. It seems you have something worthwhile to investigate now. Get Stella Walton's files. Follow up what she says. Focus on Juliet Coe. Find out who "Samson" and "Cyrus" are. I'd guess they're people you know.'

'Enough!' shouted Jones angrily. 'You've said you would cooperate, but you're just wasting time.'

'I said I'd tell you everything,' Peter said firmly. 'That includes both what you want to know, and what you don't want to know. If your job title means anything, you should follow up the leads I'm giving you. I'm telling you, get those files and read them!'

Peter noticed his interrogator glancing nervously at the camera. Then one of the militia guards came over, and grabbed Peter by the hair, forcing his head back over the back of the chair. The pain in his ribs made it hard to breathe, and one side of his face felt like it was on fire. Not for the first time, Peter felt a sensation of panic.

Jones leaned over the desk towards him. 'Now, Kitson, it's time for you to tell us what you know. Let's start with your sister, the lovely Joanna. What classified information did you give her, and what more were you planning to give her?'

Peter tensed at the mention of Joanna. He was well aware of her vulnerability in the present situation. It was something of a mystery to him why she had been allowed to remain at large for so long. And Heather, too, had been compromised by her knowledge of Stella's information and joining in that cloak-and-dagger meeting.

He remembered clearly their conversation with their bodyguards when they saw Stella Walton being arrested. In all probability, they had not been intended to witness that. But he guessed that whichever agency had been watching for Stella had probably been watching them too. And listening. From the interrogations he had experienced, Peter knew that the authorities had been listening in on many conversations he had thought to be private.

'I think you know this,' said Peter at last. 'My home was bugged, for sure. You'll know that I gave Joanna information that was relevant to her cases. The databases of who was at which camp. She used it to get further court orders for the release of her clients.'

'So you admit to possessing and passing on official secrets?'

'Secrets! On what basis do you call this information secret? It's information that was being illegally withheld from members of the legal profession, and from members of the government—such as me! And it was being withheld in defiance of several court orders to release it.'

'You expect this hair-splitting to impress me? The fact is this information was stolen, and you passed it on to a third party or parties. Who else did you give it to?'

'I was planning to pass it on—all of it—to Terry Cairns. But he was arrested and hasn't been seen since. Except by you, maybe? Do you know where he is?'

Jones looked at the militiaman, who hit Peter heavily on the side of his neck, making him gasp for breath.

'And did you plan to give it to Louise Adams?'

'No, of course not. She was one of yours—at least as far as I knew!'

'But it's strange, don't you think, that she is the lover of your best friend and you have private conversations with her paymaster, Zara Alderney?'

So his phone had been tapped, for sure. Now for Peter some pieces had begun to come together, and he could see the reasoning in his accusers' paranoia. The unmasking of Louise Adams, Stella Walton's investigations, her passing the files on to Peter, and his contact with Zara Alderney were all being woven into a paranoid conspiracy.

And no doubt the Americans must know something of the wheels within wheels of the GEM and their fellow travellers—he remembered Zara's warning to him: '*take your lovely wife and daughter and leave the country, as soon as possible*'. And he had been too blithely self-confident, too full of himself, too complacent to take note of it.

He sighed as he realised the nebulous substance behind their conspiracy theory—a theory in which his actions and friendships were pivotal. Peter rested his forehead on one hand, his elbow on the table.

Jones leaned forward and hissed at him, 'Who else, Kitson?'

••

Malcolm Morton sighed as he finished reviewing the video of the interrogation. Jones and Carl Fullerton were with him.

Morton had hoped the interrogation process would get more out of Kitson. The lack of substantial results was depressing, as far as exposing the full extent of the suspected 'Kitson Circle' was concerned. And Morton was also personally repelled by seeing the fruits of violence on the damaged body of Peter Kitson. Despite his active service background and his readiness to be ruthless, he had not like being faced with brutality—unlike Carl Fullerton, for whom theory and practice were one. Fullerton seemed to relish doing the dirty work, as if it proved his commitment to the cause.

That was why Morton employed people like Fullerton, and why Fullerton had risen to the top. He was the right kind of person to take the Revolution to its proper conclusion, where others might be too fainthearted.

'Kitson disgusts me,' Morton said at last. 'Here's a man who has everything going for him. Very intelligent, capable, hard-working, and aware of the crisis facing our planet. But at the same time he's a complete idiot! He blindly refuses to follow through where his understanding of the crisis should lead him. And he blunders along, always thinking he is in control, making one mistake after another when it comes to the power game! Even now, he miscalculates all the time. When he falls from power, he thinks he can succeed as a subversive! First he goes to Dave Barrington and tries to play him against the rest of us. Dave doesn't bite, of course, and sends him away with a flea in his ear. Then he tries to sow seeds of doubt in your mind, Jones—but of course you don't bite either. So amateurish, so naïve.'

Jones didn't know what to say, or if it was his place to say anything. He looked from one to the other, and awaited a cue to do or say something.

'What next for him?' asked Fullerton. 'We can turn up the physical pressure, or play with his head a little...'

Morton thought a little before answering. 'One thing I will grant the fool, though, is he's resilient—much more than I would have expected. And I think he wants to keep the pressure on himself, to keep it off others. People he is close to. You notice how every time he's asked about his wife or sister he changes the subject? It's time to bring in wife and kiddie, to exert a little leverage.' He nodded to Jones, who stood up and went in to the next room to take the appropriate action.

Fullerton raised an eyebrow. 'Not his little sister? He's protecting her, too.'

'No,' replied Morton. 'I want her out there in the field a little longer, a beacon to all the bugs that come out at night. There's time yet, and she serves as an outlet for all those constitutionalist dreamers who stake their hopes on words, courtroom drama and pieces of paper. Her time will come.'

Jones returned and hovered until he got Morton's attention. 'It seems Heather Kitson is not at home. She's driving up into East Anglia at the moment. Took the toddler as well. She didn't mention to anyone where she was going, or we'd have picked it up.'

'What's out there? Who does she know in those parts?' asked Fullerton.

'Well, according to the monitoring team, the only time she's been out that way in recent times is to visit the Barringtons.'

'Really?' asked Fullerton. He looked surprised, but also amused. 'You think...?'

'Of course not!' said Morton dismissively. 'Dave and Jessica are straight down the line. Dave's fed back a lot of intelligence about Kitson and his colleagues. And Jessica is mortally embarrassed by her family connections.'

'But Kitson did meet old Sir James when he was in Stockholm...'

Morton shrugged. 'Nothing to do with Jessica, I'm sure. No, Heather's desperate. She's going to see if Jessica can help get Peter out of his situation. Let them meet, and find out what she's after, or if she lets anything slip. And don't let her go anywhere else. Pick them up on the way back, when she's tired and disillusioned. Get a couple of women officers onto it too. Don't lean on them too heavily yet. It's Peter Kitson we want to sweat over this.'

Once Jones had left the room, Morton and Fullerton looked at each other.

'Do you think he's a safe pair of hands?' asked Fullerton.

'He doesn't impress me, so far,' Morton replied. 'I know he's climbed swiftly up the ranks, says and does the right things—but he seems a little wet behind the ears. Kitson didn't tell him as much as I expected.'

'What should we do with him?'

'After he's arranged for Heather Kitson to be pulled in, have him transferred to New Dawn. See how he copes with the hard stuff, and we'll make a decision from there.'

Fullerton nodded slowly. 'He comes across a bit lightweight. But I think he has the necessary steel within. And a desperate need to be approved of and to belong. My bet is he'll do the business for us.'

49: Jessica's help

Heather knew she was being followed, but it didn't worry her. How did Peter refer to it? 'Having the benefit of a stealth escort', or something like that.

She pulled suddenly into a petrol station, and watched the vehicle tailing her go past. There were far fewer cars on the roads these days. She retained Peter's permit as an 'essential user' to buy petrol, and no doubt the people following her also had one. She filled up the car, then took Andrea out of the car seat and went inside to pay. A second car pulled up, and she could see the occupants craning their necks to see where she was.

It's only a matter of time, she thought. They're stepping up the surveillance. Maybe by visiting them the Barringtons too would be compromised, but she felt little compassion for them, if that turned out to be the case. Back in the car, she reversed and stopped parallel to the car that had been following her. She looked straight at the people inside and nodded to them before setting off again. A brief smile gave way to a look of steely determination.

After another hour's driving, Heather arrived at the Barringtons' house deep in the Norfolk countryside. Security officers briefly detained her before waving her through into the driveway of the house. Heather had expected to have to argue her way in—remarkably easy so far. As she drove up the drive, she remembered how idyllic the house had looked last time she was here, with its tree-lined track leading up to the old wisteria-covered farmhouse, English cottage flowers then high in front of the windows. Foxgloves, lupins, hollyhocks, cornflowers—and a bed of lavender casting its strong summer scent over arrivals at the doorstep. Now in this bitter December, the aspect was much bleaker.

Hearing the tyres crunch on the gravel, Jessica came to see who had arrived. She was hoping it would be Dave. These days they seemed to spend more and more time apart.

At first a little nonplussed, Jessica soon turned on a smile and welcomed Heather and Andrea in. She quickly guessed Heather's reason for coming. She knew that sooner or later she would have to disappoint her. There was little she could do. She felt all her influence in the Movement was gone, and so devoted herself to her family and to cultivating her garden.

For half an hour they avoided the inevitable subject, filling the time with cooing over Andrea and talking about their families and mutual acquaintances.

A welcome pretence of normality. Andrea was getting restless, and Jessica used this as a pretext for suggesting a walk outside.

'Wrap up warm,' Jessica advised, 'the wind has a wicked bite in it'.

The wind was indeed very sharp now, a north-east wind bringing in heavy grey clouds that looked as if they were full of snow.

'A white Christmas, maybe' suggested Heather, smiling as she looked at the clouds.

'They say it could be the coldest winter for thirty years,' said Jessica.

They walked far into the Barrington's extensive gardens, through well-ordered beds of vegetables and into the developing orchard, the trees now bare of fruit.

'Was it a good harvest this year?' asked Heather.

Jessica was looking at three year old Andrea, tottering hurriedly around the trees, with the Barrington's two dogs frolicking good-naturedly beside her.

'I know what you want to ask, Heather,' said Jessica, without looking at her. 'And I have to be honest with you—I'm not sure what I can do.'

Heather responded with a crestfallen, softly spoken 'Oh!'

'I don't have much influence these days.'

'Even with Dave?'

Jessica smiled. 'I have plenty of influence with Dave, but not in the political field. And Dave has little do with security affairs. He's so wrapped up in his projects. He wants to leave some lasting achievements behind before—'

She stopped suddenly.

'Before what?' asked Heather, puzzled.

'Before....before we're thrown out of office in the elections. I shouldn't say it, but it's only a matter of time. Next year, or the following one at the latest. We don't say it, but it's no secret. They're all worried shitless, and don't know how to turn it around. There isn't much vocal opposition, but there's a dead weight of sullen hatred in the country about what we're doing.'

Heather was astonished at what Jessica was saying.

'I feel it wherever I go. The euphoria has long gone. I feel people staring coldly at me. You know I used to resent the security around me. Now I find myself looking around to make sure it's there. And this coalition with the Animalists. For me it's the last straw. I know some of these people from old. I could never work with them. And I found, I don't have a taste for high politics. Maybe my mother was right—I'm only fit for kicking against authority!'

'Could you kick against authority now?' pleaded Heather. 'And at least help me find out what's happened to Peter. If you or Dave could take an interest, maybe he could be released. Whatever he's accused of, I'm sure Peter would want to stick around and clear his name—he's not the type to run away.'

'Of course I'll try, Heather,' said Jessica, putting her hand on Heather's arm. 'But you have to know, I'm kind of tainted these days. My father. It's not reported, but he's done a runner. He shuttles between Sweden and America, trying to rally as many people as he can against Don's government.'

Heather noted the way she said '*Don's government*'. She said his name with affection, but she no longer spoke of '*our government*' as she used to.

Jessica continued. 'I'm under constant surveillance. Malcolm was good enough, in his own warped way, to tell us about it. He said they want to monitor all contact between us and my family. I'm probably being paranoid, but that's the reason I brought us out into the orchard. I don't think they can hear what we're talking about down here, even with their James Bond listening kit—not in this wind, for sure.'

'Anything you can tell me, Jessica, any hint about what's happening... I've got no idea what's happening, and every other avenue, even Joanne with all her contacts, draws a blank. Where is he? What's he actually accused of? What are they planning to do with him?' Heather threw her arms out in a despairing gesture.

'Let me tell you what I know,' said Jessica. 'You've got to understand that what's happening to you is part of a bigger picture. I mentioned my father. He's actively conspiring against the government—he and Patrick Baxter.'

'Since when is it a crime to oppose a government in this country?' exclaimed Heather.

'Usually, it's not. But Daddy's doing more than organising an opposition, or so they think. It seems he's maintained a network of contacts in the machinery of government, and could be plotting a coup with foreign enemies—or so they say.'

'It's unbelievable!' gasped Heather. 'Is it true? You seem so calm about it!'

'My father's a resourceful man, and the way he left the country was—not straightforward. Kind of suspicious. I knew he wasn't fond of the government, but I always thought he'd see it through... They tell us he's developed close contacts with American agents. Probably he always had close contacts. But then came the Adams and Cairns affair. That shocked us. You can imagine. And it's unfortunate for me that my father is seen as being in cahoots with

Wilding and Alderney. Then Peter comes along. He meets with Daddy in Stockholm. And he's reputed to be quite thick with Zara Alderney. And of course intimate with Adams and Terry Cairns.'

Heather knew there was no substance to any of this, but was beginning to understand how it might look from the other side. And what a serious situation Peter could be in.

Jessica continued. 'I don't know what triggered his arrest—you probably know more than me. Frankly, I was surprised. I gather Malcolm was fond of referring to my father and your Peter and Joanna as "beacons". Lights that will attract all kinds of bugs out of the darkness towards them. So he was leaving them alone. You know in GEM circles they speak about "The Kitson Circle"— a whole range of people associated with Peter and Joanna. Then there's the "South Bank Circle"—people who had gravitated to Baxter and those poor saps with their "alternative government". Do you think they ever wonder why they're left alone? But left alone they are, while they serve a purpose. So something must have changed about Peter's position—have you any idea what? Was he planning something?'

Heather knew the answer, but did not think it was one she could share with Jessica. It must be to do with Stella Walton. If Peter was a 'beacon', Stella had been attracted to his light. But what she had given to him must have had extra significance, something that triggered Peter's arrest. But then again, why had they not arrested Heather as well? Unless they didn't know she had seen almost as much of Stella's data as Peter had. Heather considered what she should say. Jessica was talking some more, but Heather lost track of it as she pondered what to say.

'Peter came into possession of some disturbing information,' Heather said at last.

Jessica raised an eyebrow.

'I won't say how—the background is kind of strange anyway—but it related to secret agendas within the GEM and Animalist parties.'

'Go on—let's see if you surprise me. Sounds like something cooked up by our old Grey enemies.'

'I don't know about that. In a sense, I hope it is. Do you know anything about the Voluntary Holocaust movement, and Population Rebalancing? Or the Noah Project?'

'Oh, that stuff!' Jessica laughed.

'You know about it?'

'Sure, I've read some of that—all hogwash and senseless ranting, for sure. There's been a handful of freaks around for as long as I can remember writing this kind of stuff. Fantasy. You can't believe that Dave or Don, or Malcolm or Sarah are into this kind of stuff? No way!'

'No, nothing indicated they are involved. But are you so sure about your Animalist friends? It seems Titus Whitaker is well into it, and some of your people like Juliet Coe are closely connected with these "freaks" as you put it.'

'I think it's pinch-of-salt time, Heather. If Peter received information like this before his arrest, I can only think it's a coincidence,' said Jessica reassuringly. 'Unless someone has been leaking secret information about government ministers, and it's an official secrets investigation. You may have to face the possibility as well, Heather, that Peter had other irons in the fire that he didn't want you to know about. Something more directly oppositional.'

Jessica could tell by Heather's reaction that the information was not from a source inside government. And she could also see that Heather knew more than she was prepared to say.

'What kind of country are we living in, Jessica? Since when do people get arrested for opposing the government?'

Jessica shrugged, and turned away to look at Andrea and the dogs playing happily. She held out her hands. Snow was beginning to fall.

'Is this really what you expected?' continued Heather. 'The camps, the muzzled media, the silenced opposition, arrests, disappearances, militia squads harassing people in their daily lives, food and fuel shortages, the climate of fear...is this what you and Dave and Don always planned and wanted?'

Jessica looked down to the ground for a few moments. Snowflakes settled on her hair. Then she looked up and firmly met Heather's gaze with a look of both candour and regret.

'In the old days we talked often about how tough it would be, of how determined we needed to be to change the way people live in this country. And we said that we couldn't pull our punches. Revolutions are usually messy affairs. But somehow I always thought we would still be fighting the old enemies. Big business, developers, the roads lobby: all our old demons! And I thought apart from that it would be like it was at first—like you and me, Dave and Peter, talking, debating, working things through. People of goodwill working together with a common purpose. This hard phase is too hard for me, for sure.

'I'll do what I can to help, Heather. I doubt I can influence what happens, but I'll try my best to find out something about Peter's...situation.' Jessica only just managed to stop herself saying 'Peter's fate'.

Heather stayed for a while longer, but refused an invitation to stay over as the snow increased in intensity. She joked that if the weather became too scary she'd stop the car and get a lift with the jackasses following her.

She didn't need to stop her followers and ask them for a lift. Five miles down the road, a police car pulled her over, and two other unmarked cars pulled up, one ready equipped with a child seat. Heather was ushered into the car, and told her she was being taken in for questioning.

'She's sold me out,' Heather thought with bitterness and despair.

50: A solution for humanity

Morton was calm.

Gabriella Pearson and Carl Fullerton were screaming at each other across the table, while Titus Whitaker and Tara Collingworth looked on nervously, occasionally trying to intervene to restore rational debate. But what could be rational in a discussion like this?

Three other people looked on. One, Russell Pointon, was designated as 'Procurement Officer' in this highly secretive context. Another was Annie Lee. The third was Juliet Coe.

The key question for this meeting, on the shores of Loch Lomond, was not if, but when and how. And from Morton's point of view, the debate had become side-tracked on the rather bizarre ethical issues of the 'species rights' of viruses and bacteria.

In the opinion of Morton, Fullerton and Lee, the most efficient method was to release a genetically modified strain of the plague. One that would target humans more effectively than previous strains, yet ensure that it would remain harmless to non-human species. Pearson argued with typical vigour against this view. Humans should not take this godlike approach. They—the GEM—should not have taken it upon themselves to experiment on a species at the same time as signing a *Declaration on the Rights of Species*. Their recklessness could create new imbalances in the natural world. And in any case, bubonic and pneumonic plague in their natural form were sufficiently deadly to reduce the human population. What was needed were mechanisms to ensure it was spread sufficiently.

Titus Whitaker felt extremely uncomfortable. This was the moment his entire career had been leading him too, and where all his philosophical writings had led him. Yet he now felt extremely uncomfortable about the outcome, whichever way the argument turned out. It is one thing to map out and work through improbable scenarios: it is quite another to be caught up in the middle of executing one of them.

While he felt quite comfortable advocating the rebalancing of the natural world, he felt distinctly uneasy about plotting the deaths of millions—eventually billions—of people. And here he was, sitting opposite the people with the power and the will to carry out his dream. Suddenly he felt light-headed, and in need of a stiff drink.

'I–I think we should break at this point for refreshments, don't you think?' he interjected.

Morton nodded, and Fullerton sank back into his chair, a broad smile breaking across his handsome face.

'Let's find a way through this,' said Morton. 'We're all on the same side, aren't we? And we all know what we have to do.'

Pearson glared at him. She'd had the argument with him before, and knew his pragmatic view. She bit her lip. He looked at her with a twinkle in his eye. He had prodded her before about her always needing the last word. And she knew he expected her to try to get the last word on this occasion too. In the end she could not resist.

'Fuck you!' she exclaimed, and stalked out the room.

Managing Gabriella Pearson was an art he had developed over the previous few months. With his calm authority he had succeeded in a way that Whitaker could never have done. And clearly there was a special chemistry between Pearson and Morton. Despite their greatly differing temperaments—he ice-cold and calculating and she heated, volatile and impulsive—they recognised in each other a single-minded determination that they both respected. Morton knew he would carry the day: he just needed her storm to blow itself out.

All the practicalities were in favour of the genetically modified strain. Annie Lee and Carl Fullerton had presented the evidence, gathered through experiments at New Dawn re-education camp. The modified organism multiplied quicker. It was immensely more contagious, and would spread quicker, but posed no new danger to animals. It also killed quicker.

Vaccines and antidotes were not hard to prepare, so the spread of the plague had to catch the world by surprise. Other variant strains were also being prepared for second, third and fourth waves. Though again vaccines would not be hard to create, the surprise of new resistant strains would keep health authorities and foreign governments on the hop, giving the disease time to spread. Their researchers had undertaken sophisticated social-geographic modelling to project the likely movement of vectors of the disease and its consequent dispersal. They had no doubt that this was the optimal approach.

And timing was vital. The disease needed to be released in the UK and be sent out through passengers infected at airports almost simultaneously, to prevent other countries isolating Britain. It needed to be planned with military precision, and unparalleled secrecy. What they were planning would change the entire course of human history and the natural world.

The technical team had calculated that they were about four months away from being able to deliver sufficient quantities to meet the objectives. Experts had been co-opted in from universities and biotech companies. Security was vital during this stage until everything was ready.

Annie Lee had assured Morton that Porton Down was secure. Previous governments had been in the habit of sharing secrets with the Americans. But the ostensible closing down of the biological research programme had been used as a cover for getting rid of people close to the Americans or other allies. Malcolm was sure that Annie was completely reliable. She was a long-standing member of the GEM and had been subject to rigorous surveillance. She had contributed greatly to the rebalancing programme, sacrificing any hope of family life, career or personal academic glory to the higher aim of transforming the world.

Though born in Britain, Annie Lee was proud of being Chinese. And within Morton and Pearson's agenda, she had a personal mission. To reduce the population of her parent's motherland to manageable proportions, and so save it from the results of two great follies—Mao's population drive and the current regime's madcap industrialisation policies. In her view, the combination of overpopulation and breakneck industrialisation was destroying the environment of her country and causing irreparable damage to the planet. It could not be allowed to carry on. Of all the populations of the world that needed to be 'rebalanced', the Chinese had to be top of the list. She would see that the plague was successfully exported to the Far East, and then to the population south of the Himalayas. Morton approved of and supported her plans.

Titus Whitaker was on the veranda, scribbling energetically in one of his ever-present notebooks. He looked up from his writings, out towards the loch. Juliet Coe and Annie Lee were talking by the water's edge, and trying to skim stones. They were not very good at it—but better than he had ever been himself. He had always lacked that necessary physicality, that in-touch at-home-ness with the world of objects that came so easily to so many other people. So many people who would now die, while he lived on—for a while, at least, until all was accomplished.

As he watched, Gabriella Pearson strode up to the other two women, talking and laughing loudly. She took the stone that Juliet was holding in her hand. Then she tossed it aside, picking up instead a smoother, flatter stone. She hurled the new stone with a very masculine action and follow-through, shaking her clenched fist in triumph as the stone bounced once, twice, in the end twelve times across the surface of the water. At last the stone kicked up for a final hollow-sounding but satisfying 'plop' into the deep water twenty meters from the shore.

••

'Will it work?' asked Tara Collingworth as the meeting reconvened.

'Annie?' said Morton, inviting Annie Lee to explain the mechanics of the process. Keeping the discussion on a practical and scientific basis would help to calm the emotions.

Annie Lee spoke quietly but clearly. 'We have developed seven strains of the bacterium. Four of them have been modified to make them fast acting. Three of them are slower acting, to give the hosts a greater chance of travelling–ideal for use at airports and international railway stations. Three are forms of bubonic plague that can be injected. Once inside the host they will spread not only to the lymph nodes but also through the bloodstream and to the lungs, so the host is more or less guaranteed to become a transmitter of pneumonic plague. The remainder are forms of pneumonic plague to be spread through aerosol distribution–through ventilation systems and then from person to person.'

'Why seven strains?' asked Tara.

'Yersinia pestis–plague–is curable if caught early enough,' said Annie in the same matter-of-fact tone. 'And we need it to be curable. We need to be able to control it. Each one has been modified in a slightly different way to give it a degree of resistance to different antibiotics. This is to keep the enemy off balance, keep them guessing. Standard treatments won't work, but it won't take long to find a treatment for the strain that is least resistant. But then they will find it doesn't always work. All this is designed to give the plague the greatest chance of spreading as far as possible. And we also needed to be able to develop vaccines to ensure those we need to survive do survive. This is truly a scientific breakthrough–this has never been done before! We also have stocks of fake vaccines to release to the health authorities. The first bottles in every batch will be a genuine vaccine, but the rest will be contaminated with versions of bubonic plague. When used, these will create a further wave of infection and contagion.'

'Vaccines,' said Pearson emphatically. 'Is it true we're all going to be immunised against the disease?'

'It's not true,' said Fullerton. 'But it's a choice we'll have.'

'How can that be justified?' she interrupted fiercely.

'The show must go on. Rebalancing the population is only part of our programme. We have to create the model society for a rebalanced world. It's too important to leave to chance.'

Titus Whitaker shifted uncomfortably in his seat. 'Don't you think there's something a trifle unethical about this? We could even be accused of hypocrisy.'

'I've been accused of all sorts of things,' Morton retorted. 'It makes no difference what people think, as long as the right things are done.'

Tara Collingworth now intervened. 'Is it true we're building up stocks of vaccine for the Green Militias?'

Morton shrugged. 'As I said, we need to manage the progress of the Revolution. Things could get out of hand in a national health crisis. We can't risk a breakdown of public order.'

'And think about who the Green Militia are! We will build the basis of a new society–balanced and cleansed and in harmony with nature!' enthused Fullerton.

'A new heaven and a new earth!' muttered Whitaker, without enthusiasm.

Fullerton looked surprised. 'What's the matter, Titus? Isn't it all there in your books, about the rebalanced society?'

And it was. Whitaker thought of the things he had written. Of small, self-supporting communities, living on land where sprawling suburbs had once stood. Of a non-materialistic way of life, based on shared ownership, shared responsibilities and a common purpose towards stewardship of the natural world. Of voluntary clans where four couples out of every five denied themselves the right to have children, and the chosen ones raised children on behalf of, and with the help of, the community as a whole.

But when he looked at Fullerton, and when he thought of the Green Militia, he could not see these people as truly representing a better way of life in the future. The communities he envisaged were purposeful, idealistic and innocent. Morton's people seemed too driven, too hard-edged and within their movement lay a dangerous self-righteousness and egoism.

'Oh, don't worry about me,' Titus replied, as he emerged from his musings. 'I worry though about the bandwagon tendency in the Militias, don't you? I mean, already there are signs that people have joined up with the Militias as a meal ticket, or gravy train … whatever, whatever. It brings privileges, and is essential on the CV if you want to get on in public life. And it can give status to some weak-minded people who like to throw their weight about. Don't you think?'

He stopped short of mentioning the beatings and exemplary punishments reportedly being carried out by Militia squads across the country.

Fullerton was nettled, but he knew there was some truth in what Whitaker said. 'We're on top of this kind of problem. It's all the more reason for maintaining an effective and committed leadership throughout … all this. We can purify the party and the squads in the process—but we can't do that if we're all dying like flies.'

Tara objected. 'It won't be five minutes before people know that the Militias have been immunised—and they'll all be flocking to join. Or attacking them in the streets.'

'We can manage that,' said Morton authoritatively. 'We know the first plague outbreaks will be in the camps. Most of the Militia in the next four months will have a spell in the camps on programme work or training weeks. They'll be inoculated then. As far as they know it'll be against a new strain of flu. Now, I want us to go over the issues in a more orderly manner. We have a timetable, and it's vital that our people are ready to do their part, on a need-to-know basis.'

The atmosphere in the room changed, to one of quiet and intense concentration. Morton mapped out the key events of the next four months, and the tasks that were expected and who would do them.

Stocks of the modified bacteria were being developed as they spoke, and would be distributed through the camp network, under the strictest secrecy. There would be a number of ways to distribute the agent. On Earth Day, 22nd April, a wide-ranging amnesty would be declared and thousands of inmates from the camps would be released and allowed to travel home. Without their knowledge, they would all be infected.

The timing was crucial. The holiday period during Earth Week, which had replaced Easter as the main Spring holiday, would mean that millions of people would be on the move, allowing the disease to spread far and wide. It would also mean that medical services would be scaled down during the break, and people would wait longer than usual to seek treatment. The most virulent strain of the modified disease needed just three hours to incubate, and after a further three hours was almost untreatable.

Juliet Coe's influence in the media would be crucial, first for building up the amnesty and then later suppressing, or at least delaying, news about the spread of the plague and the scale of casualties. At this meeting Juliet said little, content that she was at the epicentre of the true revolution. This deep green planning could not come into the open. It was not a time for egoism. Quite the reverse: it was the time for the extinction of ego, as mankind was subsumed back into a proper position in the natural order.

The second wave of distribution would be through the public transport system, Morton explained. This would happen in part from people travelling, but would also be assisted by targeted infusion of ventilation systems—primarily shopping malls, the underground railway stations and airports. The restrictions on air travel would also be lifted a week or so before with a fanfare of public-spirited generosity, encouraging tourists to visit again and allowing the disease to leave the country. High-yield aerosol delivery mechanisms had now been tested and perfected at the camps. Further field trials would refine the techniques.

Over the several waves of diffusion, if all went to plan, the country's population could be reduced to around 30 million—halving the population.

'What's your ultimate target population?' asked Whitaker.

'Our target is your target,' said Morton, fixing him with a faint smile. 'Around the population of Tudor England, didn't you say? Four or five million. We start with a fifty per cent reduction. Then a further wave after six weeks to halve the population again. Economic collapse and other measures should lead to further reductions over the next generation. This first wave will put us on track.

'We don't have such a direct influence over the rest of the world. But we reckon that a week after Earth Day around seventy per cent of Europe's population and a quarter of America's will have been in contact with the disease. Remember, we're aiming to cut out the danger to other animals. That's why it's so vital to be pragmatic and use the modified strain: it's far more virulent and much more contagious on a person-to-person basis, and less contagious to other mammals. We have special teams who will go to China, India, Pakistan, Japan and America to get things moving. Further waves with new strains will follow.

'As I've said to the Militia elite trusted with this mission, it will be an unwritten chapter in human history. But one of the most important in the history of our planet. And you, here around this table, are the ones who hold the future in your hands.'

51: A leader's responsibilities

Don Mason had been drinking heavily again. It was not the first time Sandy Honeyford had seen him like this. Sarah Turner had been covering for him, and asked Sandy to put it about that he was suffering from a stomach complaint. After a late start to the day, he had seemed to Sandy to be uncharacteristically morose and uncommunicative. Now, by 11 o'clock he was perking up a little, and could at least make some kind of conversation. But he looked terrible. Sandy understood why Sarah had wanted to keep him away from meeting people.

These are one-offs, Sarah had explained. Meeting the obvious question, *Is he an alcoholic?*

But Don Mason wasn't an alcoholic. He could go long spells without drinking any alcohol at all. Or he could enjoy a glass or two of wine, or a pint of beer, then stop. At this stage of his life, or career, Mason had discovered a need at times to go over the top in his drinking. And he always did so on his own. Sarah was worried—these episodes were definitely becoming more frequent. Yet always he recovered, and his capabilities did not seem to be diminished when he got back on his feet.

Sandy felt less comfortable in her coordinating role now that her former colleagues were no longer part of the government. She had offered to resign. Mason persuaded her to stay on. The fact that she was neither GEM, Old Green or Animalist made her more like a civil service advisor, he said—her apparent neutrality would be useful in managing a volatile coalition. And Don had flattered her about her insights into both policy and political relationships. He said he had come increasingly to depend on her. In truth she had not needed this flattery. She was still sufficiently seduced by being close to the centre of power that her offer to resign was not entirely sincere.

And the nature of the government's table talk had begun to infiltrate her thinking. The almost siege mentality. The tough talking 'Second Revolution' language. She knew things were being kept from her, and that people like Morton, Pearson and Cunningham didn't trust her. As personalities, she liked Whitaker and Ben Porter. They were always civil and gentlemanly, both of them very cerebral but with a dry, intellectual sense of humour. Sarah

Turner and Dave Barrington were the most open and friendly with her. Despite her past associations, it seemed that through working closely with her a professional respect had developed, and it was mutual.

And what of her relationship with Mason? It seemed he had seen something in her, and had taken on the task of moulding her into—into what? He let her into many confidences, and liked to bounce ideas off her. He had never tried to use her to get intelligence about her former colleagues, although she knew that they had come under suspicion. And though she had spent her whole career until recently working with the Liberals, that all now seemed a long time ago. It frightened her a little to think how quickly she had accepted the new way of doing things, and had adjusted to the general feelings expressed around her about the complicity of Terry Cairns and Peter Kitson in disloyal actions. Following Martin's advice, she had not made it her business to intervene or to find out what was happening to them.

Mason was freshening himself up in his bathroom. Sarah was now working with Sandy to prepare for the business of the day—both Chancellor's and Prime Minister's business. Mason had reverted to operating mostly away from 10 Downing Street, saying he felt insecure there. *The ghosts of another establishment were too strong there*, as he put it.

In all this, Don Mason seemed to be separating himself from direct contact with the machinery of government. He had evolved the role of Prime Minister into being a motivating force rather than having a hands-on, directing approach. Sandy's role had evolved too. As Mason avoided much of the routine business of government, senior civil service officials sought her out as 'someone we can deal with'. She had never felt more important or powerful.

Underneath this, however, Sandy still had feelings of unease. Perhaps, she felt, this communicated itself from the top, from Don Mason himself. She recalled the conversation with some of his colleagues the previous evening, when Mason was just beginning to get into his cups, in which he expressed some rare self-doubt, or so it seemed.

'You know,' he had said, 'sometimes I think the responsibility is too great for me. I often think I'd rather be an adviser, or philosopher, someone who just writes their ideas on paper. I have to write on human skin, which is ticklish to a different degree, as someone once said!'

It was Sandy who had picked up the historical allusion. 'I remember Howard quoting that, Don. Catherine the Great, isn't it? Well the thing is, that was her reason for never carrying out most of the ideas that her philosopher friends were suggesting. So maybe that's the way to get off the hook. She just did the usual things that Tsars do—build palaces, fight wars, have lovers. Carry on as normal!'

Mason chuckled. 'Two out of three of those sound interesting! But unfortunately I don't have that luxury.'

Those who were there took this as Mason showing his commitment to the Second Revolution, and the conversation had turned to the need to speed up the pace of reform. It seemed, though, that all this was taking its toll on Mason.

••

The Cabinet meeting broke for lunch. Sandy Honeyford was waiting outside to see if there were any actions pending. As usual the meeting of some twenty-four people broke up into smaller groups to talk about issues from the meeting, upcoming proposals or other business. Dave Barrington and Malcolm Morton were talking quietly together. Sandy Honeyford, though engaged in one conversation, as always was picking up 'noise' from many others. And she could hear the word 'Kitson' coming repeatedly from the Barrington/Morton conversation. Sandy broke away from her conversation to move closer.

As Barrington was leaving, Sandy caught up with him. 'Hey, Dave! You OK? Did I just hear you saying something about Peter Kitson?'

Barrington looked a little angry and flustered. It seemed, despite the polite tone of the conversation, that he and Morton had exchanged some heated words.

'Of course, he's an old friend of yours. Why are you asking me this?'

'I haven't heard anything about him. Natural curiosity from an old friend. I want to know if he's OK.'

They continued walking out into the street towards Whitehall.

'Actually, that's what I was trying to find out.'

'Really?'

'Uh-huh. Heather and the baby came to see Jessica yesterday—seems like they've not heard anything about him either. Heather's desperate, by the sound of it. She persuaded Jessica to get me to see if I can find out anything.'

'Did you?'

Barrington looked at her sternly. Sandy realised she might be overstepping some of the boundaries she had established. After a short pause Barrington answered.

'Not about Peter. Malcolm told me that Heather was picked up by the Militia on the way home. That's why you may be seeing smoke coming out of my ears. I'd like to think someone can visit my wife without being taken in for questioning on the way home! I made the point, maybe too forcefully.'

'Andrea was taken in too?'

'I guess so.'

'It doesn't make any sense!'

But even as she said it Sandy could see a range of possibilities. Perhaps it was to do with something Heather had done. But unlikely. It was probably something to do with Peter, or even Joanna. Or possibly it was something to do with the Barringtons. They would want to know what Jessica and Heather had talked about—no wonder Dave was uncomfortable.

'Why is Peter being held in custody for so long?' asked Sandy.

'As far as I know, he's not being very co-operative about his dealings with subversive groups…'

'Peter—subversive!' exclaimed Sandy. 'Someone must be joking.'

'I can't really talk to you about this, Sandy. But—I think Heather and the baby are being brought in to exert some leverage over him.'

'What?' cried Sandy. 'How can—that's not possible. We don't do that kind of thing—'

But Sandy could tell from the look Dave gave her, that these days the authorities did do that kind of thing. Exactly what kind of thing wasn't clear. Maybe they just wanted to frighten Peter, maybe more. Sandy's chest began to feel tight, and she felt a pain in the pit of her stomach. Her face went white, and she stopped walking, pulling at Barrington's arm.

'Where are they?' she asked.

'I don't know exactly. Somewhere in town. One of the usual places, I guess.'

52: Sandy's turn

Sandy took her leave of Dave Barrington, saying she had shopping to do. Thoughts crowded into her head—all the thoughts she had held at bay until this moment. All the reports about disappearances, about thuggery, about the role of Morton's security services. Like many others, she had willingly allowed herself to be taken in by the occasional releases of prisoners and had been persuaded that the need to take exemplary action for environmental crime was a short-term measure.

But what was she to do? Let matters run their course, perhaps, and trust that British good sense would result in their release. Go to Don? Mason would talk to Morton, and that would just show her up as being unreliable, and too attached to her Liberal roots. She needed to find out more—and the best place to start would be with Joanna Kitson. Calling her would be difficult—her calls would certainly be monitored. She had to see her personally. She needed to think fast—this would not be easy.

Sandy took one of the new electric cabs, stopping at a café round the corner from Joanna Kitson's office. As she travelled the short distance in the cab, Sandy noticed the strong contrast between people's appearances in London. Many people looked as smart as ever. But there was a marked increase in the number of people looking shabby and down-at-heel. The recession was biting as sharply as the weather. There were more beggars than ever sitting by the doors of shops and offices.

As she got out of the cab, a young man shivering on the pavement in a sleeping bag held up a biodegradable cup, rattling the small change inside.

'How would you like to earn £20?' Sandy asked.

The young man almost sprang to his feet. 'I wouldn't have thought someone as cute as you would need to pay for it, darling!' he said.

Sandy was repelled both by the suggestion and the aroma that wafted from his body and sleeping bag. But she could see he was sharp enough for the job she had in mind. And being one of society's victims, she imagined he would be welcome in Joanna's bleeding-heart office. Ignoring the disapproving glances of the serving staff, Sandy took the down-at-heel young man inside the café with her.

'Are you clear what to do?' she asked as she handed him a mug of tea to take with him.

'Yeah, yeah' he replied.

But Sandy repeated it all the same. 'Go into number 16, the glass door, straight up the stairs to the first floor. Ask for—?'

'Joanna Kitson.'

'And?'

'Bring her here to you.'

'And if she's not there?'

'Find out where she is, how long she'll be there, and come back to tell you.'

'Exactly. And tell no one. But if you talk to her, stress that it's extremely urgent, and it's about Heather. OK?'

'Sure. But you know—this sounds dodgy. Or dangerous.'

'£50. Twenty now, and thirty on your return. OK?'

The young man smiled, and went.

Sandy sat nervously for ten minutes, fifteen, twenty, nursing her mocha. Then she noticed a slim, attractive figure in the doorway, bundled up in thick coat, hat and scarf. Joanna looked at Sandy with unveiled hostility, then walked briskly towards her.

The down-at-heel young man loomed behind her. Sandy gave him the £30, and with a wink he went outside to resume his begging position.

'Sandy,' said Joanna icily. Sandy knew better than to hold out her hand, or to hug her as would have been natural in the old days.

'Joanna, I'm so glad you came.'

'Interesting approach. If you wanted to see me, all you had to do was send some of your Militia friends, and I don't think I could have refused.'

'Jo, I know you've no reason to like me or trust me. But this is serious, and we don't have much time. Heather's been arrested.'

Joanna looked shocked. She clearly didn't know about this yet.

'When?'

'Last night. It seems she went to see Jessica Barrington to try to find out something about Peter, and was picked up on the way back.'

'The bitch!' exclaimed Joanna. 'And they used to be good friends, I thought.'

'She might have set her up, but I don't think it's like that. I only know about this because I heard Dave Barrington ask Malcolm Morton about Peter, just like Heather wanted. And it was Dave who told me that Heather had been pulled in. It seemed like he was fuming about it, as if he thinks Morton's people are trying to get something on Jessica.'

'Their paranoia runs deep, it seems,' said Joanna. Then her face clouded over. 'Look, Sandy, I can't take this in. I have a hundred questions to ask you, but frankly my skin is crawling just to sit here with you. When I think how you and Martin have compromised yourselves throwing in your lot with these people—'

'Didn't Peter and Terry do the same?' asked Sandy sharply.

'Point taken—but after what happened to them, and what's happening all around us in this "Second Revolution", how could you be so wilfully blind? You know, a part of me thinks you're setting me up now.'

These words were very bitter to Sandy. 'Do you know the risk I'm taking coming to see you here?' she whispered. 'Never mind. There's no time for this. I'm going to do all I can to get Peter, Heather and Andrea out of wherever they are—'

'Andrea?' Joanna gasped.

'Yes, Andrea—as far as I know they're keeping her with Heather, somewhere in town. I think they want to use them as some kind of leverage to make Peter co-operate, at least that's what Dave Barrington thinks.'

'Oh my God! They'd do that?'

'I doubt if they'd harm them in any way, but who knows what Peter would believe? Maybe just the thought of them being sent to a camp might persuade Peter to do whatever they want, who knows?'

'Wait a minute—you think Peter is in London, and they've brought Heather here? I thought he must be in a camp somewhere, being "re-educated".'

'Joanna, I'm completely out of my depth here. I know nothing about the police and camp system, or the Militia if they're involved. But you do. Where do they usually keep people for interrogation before sending them to camps? I want to narrow down the options and make discreet enquiries.'

'There's several places. Sometimes at MI5, or at Scotland Yard, or one of the more central police stations. Oh, and lately they've been using Green Volunteer House in Smith Square, you know the Militia Headquarters. I can do some checking too.'

'If you can do it without anyone knowing you're involved, OK. I'm sure you're next, Jo, I just feel it. They don't say nice things about you. Has it ever puzzled you why you remain free? Perhaps it's because of your international status as a fighter for civil rights. But they also say it's because Morton wants you at large, for the time being. And there's Carl Fullerton who's itching to have you brought to book.'

'Do you think I haven't thought of that? I know they must have reasons for leaving me alone, so they can bug my office, tap my phone and open my mail. I've developed habits of extreme caution. Though I know it's only a matter of time before they come for me, too. Every morning I expect the knock on the door, or a bunch of Morton's cronies to burst into the office and clap me in irons!'

'If they're watching you so closely, maybe they can see us now. That's my goose cooked! Don't worry, I'll handle that. I need you to do something. Can you go to Peter's house, collect all their passports, and get ready to leave the country? I know you've got your work and all, but … Get ready to go now. I'm going to do what I can to get the family out, and when I contact you again, be ready to move instantly. Pack an overnight bag, and put in some nappies and baby food too!'

Joanna put her head to one side and looked hard at Sandy.

'Why are you doing this, Sandy?'

'Just say it's for old time's sake. And to make up for my negligence. Now tell me where you'll be over the next twenty-four hours. I'll get a message to you somehow—maybe even use Dogbreath with the aromatic sleeping bag again!'

Joanna told her simply where she would be: office until eight, then over to Peter's house as Sandy asked, then home, then in the office again at seven in the morning, in court at two. This could all be a set-up, she thought, but there was no point in hiding her whereabouts from Sandy when she knew she was being watched twenty-four hours a day in any case. With half a smile, Joanna stood up, then reached over and squeezed Sandy's hand. Then she left, still not knowing whether Sandy could be trusted.

Sandy finished the last dregs of her coffee, and set off into the cold. As she left she crouched down to have a quiet word with the man she had uncharitably christened as 'Dogbreath', speaking to him for two or three minutes. Then pulling her lapels up close to her chin and her scarf over her mouth, she hurried off into the icy wind.

53: Eyes into the soul

It was a good half hour walk back to her office in Whitehall, but Sandy walked all the same rather than take a cab. Though it was freezing, she needed to get some fresh air into her lungs, into her brain—to think clearly about what to do.

She was now determined to rescue Heather and Andrea, Peter if possible too. But it was preposterous—how could she 'rescue' anyone? She was just not cut out for this kind of work. In fact, everything seemed preposterous. That she had an office in Whitehall. That she visited 10 Downing Street and the Prime Minister's personal residence on an almost daily basis. That she was working for a Green, not a Liberal party. That she was probably going to marry the man who would soon be Lord Chancellor. And that she was about to risk everything she had achieved and stood to gain. For what? She asked the question of herself, but knew the answer with a deep certainty. For friendship, loyalty, and self-respect. And for love.

She had two courses of action in mind—both of which ran the risk of losing everything. She could approach Don Mason, and negotiate a way to let Heather and Andrea go. The risks were less to her, though her loyalty would be put under scrutiny at the very least. But even if successful, there would probably be little benefit to Peter and Joanna. Or she could try something unofficial, using her position somehow to spirit them away, and out of the country.

Sandy stopped suddenly in her tracks. It was beginning to snow, and she just stood there rooted to the spot. Passers-by eyed her warily.

There was Martin to consider! She had spent the past how many hours thinking only about the Kitsons, and what she would do for them. She had thought of Martin only in passing, as almost a remote factor to be considered in her crisis. He was now the most important factor in her life, and it would be impossible to act alone, leaving him to pick up the pieces. But if she consulted him, she was sure he would want to play it safe. He would have no reason to risk all for the sake of the Kitsons, she thought, especially as his relationship with Joanna was now so frosty.

By the time she reached her office, she knew what she would do. She would start with Mason. They had plenty of business to discuss, but Mason guessed that there was something else on Sandy's mind.

'Don, do you trust me?' asked Sandy.

Mason appeared surprised. The question of trust had never been raised between them. 'Of course I do, Sandy. You've proved yourself in so many ways. But there must be a big reason for your asking that.'

'You know all my background, and maybe you suspect I have divided loyalties.'

'Not at all,' said Don reassuringly.

Sandy frowned anxiously at him. 'But I do, Don, I can't help it.'

Don raised his eyebrows in surprise at this confession, then smiled again in an interested but reassuring way.

'I offered to resign when my old friends went their separate way from you–but you pressed me to stay on. Now I find I'm torn. Not by politics, no, not at all. But by old friendships and loyalties. I know Peter Kitson has been held for questioning. Deep inside me, I can't believe he's done anything wrong–but I can understand why he might come under suspicion.'

Mason was pouring a drink, and raised a glass to offer Sandy some wine. She gestured with her hand to say no.

'I understand Peter being questioned, the way things are. But I've heard that Heather, and their baby, have been brought in too. I know Heather. Actually, we've never entirely hit it off. But I know she can't be involved in anything underhand, I mean, it's Heather! You've met her. She's almost apolitical. Her idea of doing something wrong is to eat white bread instead of brown! Her horizons don't extend beyond the kitchen and the nursery! What's going on with her being arrested?'

'Arrested?' exclaimed Mason.

'You didn't know?'

'Who told you this?'

'It doesn't really matter–but I think it was a reliable source–someone with no reason to make this up.'

'OK.'

There was a pause, and Mason seemed very thoughtful.

'I want to ask you, Don,' said Sandy nervously, 'to tell whoever has authorised this to let her go. A police station, or holding cell, or wherever, is no place for a mother and young child.'

'Sandy—have you ever heard of someone called Stella Walton?' asked Don.

'Sure, she used to be at the BBC, but she's been off the radar for a while. How does she tie in to this?'

'I'm not sure I know exactly. It's her connection with Kitson that is the reason for his detention. And I think his wife's as well…'

'I don't understand…'

'Nor do I, really, but Stella Walton had been under surveillance for some time. She was suspected of peddling in government secrets. Acting as some kind of investigative journalist or something, then using what she found to pass on, or sell, to opposition groups. Making a living by embarrassing the government. That may not be a capital crime, of course. But it brought her into regular contact with all kinds of criminals and subversives. And Peter Kitson, for some reason. And Heather too.'

'Heather? I can't believe it!'

'Sure. At first the security services focused all the attention on Peter Kitson. No one thought Heather could be involved in any way. We know she had a covert meeting with Walton—but at first we put her being there down to chance, that Peter was using her for cover. I've seen the surveillance—it was all very cloak and dagger. Innocent people don't behave like that!'

'But how can we know that Stella wasn't leading them on somehow?'

'That could be right. We're sure she approached them. Maybe something tickled their curiosity. But after their computers were impounded, we found that both of them had been working on files containing government secrets—information they had no right to.'

'Oh.'

'Oh, indeed. And not only that, we know that Peter passed on some of the information to other people. His sister for one. And, we believe, the Americans.'

This was hard to take in. Not just the accusations, but the fact that Mason so readily involved himself in the security issues.

'Would I be able to see them? Maybe I could get to the bottom of what this is all about,' suggested Sandy.

Don looked surprised. He knew that there had been a distinct cooling between Sandy and the Kitsons.

'Maybe,' said Mason at last. 'But I'm the wrong person to ask. Carl Fullerton has oversight of the investigation. Go through him.'

'A word from you would clear my way—you know what these security types can be like. I can't imagine Carl listening willingly to a suggestion from me.'

'I'll think about it—I'll see what Malcolm has to say, too.'

Sandy nodded. This was progress, of sorts.

As she was leaving the room, Mason called to her:

'Sandy—be careful about this. I know you and the Kitsons go back a long way, but it may not be too wise to identify yourself too closely with their Circle.'

••

At home Martin offered the same advice. He was at a complete loss as to why she would stick her neck out. She risked losing everything she'd gained. The Revolution, he said, had rough edges, for sure. But it would just be a question of time before everything was regularised. It would take people like Sandy and himself to ensure stability and order. As for the Kitsons, he admitted that Peter was in a jam, but largely of his own making. And he was sure no harm would come to Heather and Andrea.

He could sense that she didn't accept his view. He made her a promise: 'I'll do whatever I can to see that no harm comes to them.'

Sandy looked at him thoughtfully.

'Tell me Martin—about ESCOLAW. It has a mission to examine all aspects of the legal system and prisons. Does it investigate the actions of the camp system? And the activities of the Green militia?'

Martin hesitated, then shook his head.

'Who keeps a check on them?'

'Well, we have discussed this. But the majority view in ESCOLAW was that the camps and the militia are revolutionary bodies, with the same aims as ESCOLAW. Their environmental credentials are beyond reproach. What ESCOLAW does is to scrutinise the environmental performance of the penal and legal systems. We're not there to investigate everything they do.'

Sandy now knew that Martin would be unable to help her. She was touched by his concern for her. She could feel the warmth of his instinct to protect her. But she was also saddened by his lack of concern for others, for people he used to call his friends and were now in trouble. She knew what she had to do.

The next day Sandy set off to work with her heart thumping. She had faced many challenges before, but never had she felt as if her career were irreversibly in the balance, and that she even risked her freedom if things didn't go right. Martin's words, 'Is it worth sticking your neck out?' rang in her ears. She didn't really know the answer to that. All the same, she felt she couldn't sit by and do nothing. She had an overwhelming feeling that Peter and Heather were going to be harmed, and she couldn't shake off a feeling of responsibility for them.

At work, she found that Carl Fullerton had responded to her message, and wanted to see her to discuss her request. Sandy had met him several times before. His intimidating charisma both attracted and repelled her at the same time. She was prepared for this, for the way he would lean forward and fix her with his piercing stare. His lips would curl into a gentle smile, but his eyes seemed always to be trying to find a way to get through to your soul. Either your eyes would betray you, or you would fall under his spell—neither seemed an attractive prospect to Sandy. She would need all her resolve to find her way through.

'You want us to let you interview Peter and Heather Kitson, I hear,' said Carl with the benign smile of a tiger.

'Yes,' said Sandy, steeling herself not to avoid eye contact, but not wanting to say any more until she had an idea of his opinion.

His smile seemed to become more amused, even playful, as he said: 'So you think you can get something from them?'

'Something...it depends what you are looking for.'

'The truth.'

'Truth should be easy,' Sandy responded. 'But I have to say, if you're looking for evidence of complicity in something—something to do with Louise Adams, then I think you'll be disappointed. Look, this is the way I see it. You know I've known Peter for years. And I can't believe he'd deliberately do anything harmful to this country, or to the Green Revolution. So I'm not impartial. He'll trust me, and if you watch how we talk, you'll know what he is saying is true. He's not a schemer—he's always been a touch naïve. Enthusiastic, capable, but in the political world a bit naïve. That's why he always needed people like me and Evan Roberts to organise him.'

'You're telling me, you're on his side. You'll believe anything he tells you.'

'Possibly so. But your people don't have to. They can observe everything we talk about, and draw their own conclusions'.

'It seems to me, Ms Honeyford, that you're being a little naïve too. You think this is all to do with Louise Adams and Terry Cairns? Let me tell you, it's not. I wish it was so simple. It would make my life much easier, and Peter Kitson's too.'

Fullerton leaned forward and spoke confidentially to her, telling her the outline of what they knew—the secret meeting with Stella Walton, his apparent closeness to Zara Alderney, whom they felt was responsible for Louise Adams' infiltration of the government, and his passing on of top secret information to Joanna Kitson, and suspected others. What they wanted to know was who else he had passed on the information to, and what exactly had he learned from the stolen files. With this, Fullerton agreed she could go to see Peter Kitson. They would secretly record the whole interview, and afterwards she must cooperate with the interrogators.

Sandy readily agreed. 'I need to see Heather and Andrea as well. The first thing Peter will ask me is if they are alright. I haven't seen them for a while, and I've only heard worrying news. We've known each other so long, I'm sure he could tell if I'm lying or flannelling. And if he's reassured, maybe he'll open up a bit more.'

Fullerton looked at her steadily, and she returned his gaze.

'OK,' he said crisply. 'I'll prepare a note of authorisation for the investigating officer. You can go this afternoon, at two o'clock. Ms Honeyford, this is a big responsibility. I know you have divided loyalties. Actually, I admire that—your loyalty to old friends. Loyalty is a quality greatly to be admired, and something I demand absolutely in the Green Militia. Please don't be offended if I ask you to remember also your loyalty to the Green Earth government. They have treated you well, given you a great opportunity to help achieve unprecedented and historic achievements. Please don't do anything that makes us think you've compromised that loyalty. Don Mason speaks highly of you. Don't let him down, will you?'

'Carl, I want you to understand me. It's obvious I'm torn apart by this situation. Don has inspired me like no other man before. But you know it was Peter who was the first person to fire me with enthusiasm for green issues. He was always so passionate and articulate. Something's happened, and I want to understand it. And I want the situation to be…resolved.'

'I'm sure it will be,' said Fullerton.

'One thing,' said Sandy. 'What information can be so secret it has to be hidden from me, and would be so upsetting to the Americans if they got to know of it?'

'What can I say? If it's something you don't know, then I guess you're not meant to know it. Your clearance status is something you can discuss with Don, perhaps.'

'You've seen it?' asked Sandy.

'I can't go into detail. But you know, I'm sure, that all kinds of policy options are being worked up right now. Some very far-reaching measures are being discussed, modelled and costed. And probably most of them will never see the light of day. But our enemies can always make capital out of half-formed ideas, and disrupt our programme. Now, Peter Kitson seems to have bought into some far-fetched conspiracy theory, and seemed intent on spreading it around. It could potentially be very damaging for us and the real work we are doing.'

Elections, Sandy thought. It seems the GEM are thinking hard about a second term already, and want to keep a lid on anything that might be damaging.

As Sandy was leaving, she turned back and asked Fullerton: 'Oh, one more thing. Peter's likely to ask for any news on Terry Cairns—is there any?'

Fullerton's faced changed rapidly, becoming very solemn.

'Cairns is dead. Died a few weeks ago—a heart attack. It's not widely known, and maybe it won't help Kitson to know. I leave that to you.'

Sandy felt the room tilt, and her knees began to give way. She leaned in the doorway to support herself. The colour drained from her face.

Pulling herself rapidly together, she asked after Louise Adams. Is she OK—and does she know about Terry?

Fullerton's gaze became colder as he offered Sandy a warning. 'Take my advice, Sandy. Don't show too much concern for enemies of the Revolution. It can only reflect badly on you.'

After Sandy left, Fullerton called Malcolm Morton, who was expecting his call.

'So, it's all set,' said Morton. 'It will be a true test of her colours. We've given her enough rope—I have no doubt she'll hang herself.'

'The PM seems quite protective of her,' ventured Fullerton. 'Maybe he won't be happy if she does show her true colours.'

'Don't worry about Don, Carl. He knows what he's doing.'

Back in her office, Sandy's shock at the news about Terry Cairns gave way to a renewed and determined focus on the task. She sat in silence for an hour or more, refusing all calls, and running through her options about how to deal with the afternoon ahead. Then she left to perform a few errands, before making her way to Green Volunteer House.

54: In the lion's den

Green Volunteer House in Smith Square was an imposing eighteenth century building that had served many purposes in its long history. Family home, commercial offices, union headquarters, political party offices. A wealthy benefactor of the GEM had bought the lease, and now it served as the nerve centre of the Green Militia.

In the early days of the Revolution, it had been a hive of chaotic energy, almost a centre of pilgrimage as enthusiastic and ambitious Volunteers descended on it from all around the country. Many came with ideas for policies and projects, and found at Green Volunteer House opportunities to get the ear of people who had the ear of the great gods of the Revolution, or people who were on their way up. They could bump into Members of the Convention, MPs, gurus, advisers, officials and, of course, like-minded individuals who would welcome and reinforce their commitment to the cause.

People compared those carefree and optimistic times to the 'Summer of Love' in the 1960s. Anything and everything seemed achievable. The approachability of the leadership then was in sharp contrast to how it was three years later. In the early days, it was possible to turn up and find oneself in an informal meeting with Don Mason himself. Word would spread and soon thousands would flock to the Square to hear his words of wisdom and encouragement. Mason still came to meet the Militia. They received him rapturously, but the occasions were now much more guarded and stage-managed.

Sandy approached the building with a degree of trepidation, but also excitement. She had not had occasion to come to the building often—maybe no more than half a dozen times, even though it was no more than a stone's throw from Parliament. She had noticed, though, that people below the top level of the GEM and the Militia treated her with great respect, as if she were a senior member of their own party. She assumed that her close connection with Don Mason was the reason. In fact, their reasons for it went further than this. It was widely assumed that Sandy Honeyford must have been a GEM activist all along, and had been assigned as a 'sleeper' to work within the Liberals. Her word carried even more weight than she realised amongst Green activists.

On her arrival she was greeted respectfully, even warmly, at reception. A high ranking Militia officer, Laura Colson, waved her through the security gate and shook her by the hand. Sandy noted that security was actually quite light, and she guessed at Militia HQ they had no particular reason to feel insecure. So the levels of security at entry were much like any other government building. And there was a lot of coming and going: a very busy building, it seemed. People entering and leaving, many but not all in uniform, were usually acknowledged with a friendly smile. It seemed more of a community than a paramilitary base.

As they went through, Laura Colson briefly explained what they expected her to do. First she should see Heather Kitson, and see if the 'good cop' approach could elicit more information from her about Stella Walton and the information she supplied. Sandy should also try to get some insight into who had been in contact with Peter, and who had been supplied with classified information by either of them. She should also try to find out in as much detail as possible, what Heather had discussed with Jessica Barrington. After that Sandy would be taken deeper into the building to do likewise with Peter Kitson.

Sandy asked Laura Colson if there were any notes of interviews so far that she could look at. Without hesitation Colson asked a colleague to prepare copies of some notes. A few minutes later, Sandy was handed a slim tablet containing the interview files.

'What happens at the end of my interviews with them?' asked Sandy. 'I mean, will there be a debriefing session with you or someone else?'

'Yes, you'll meet with me—I'm not sure about anyone else. The Senior Investigator, Perry Jones, has been called away to Scotland, though we may be able to conference with him.'

'And what about Heather Kitson? She's not actually been arrested, has she? So assuming we find nothing untoward, you'll be letting her go?'

'Oh, I'm really not sure about that,' said Colson. Sandy nodded, not wishing to press that matter any further at this stage.

'What's happening to Peter Kitson?'

'Well, he's another matter. We're expecting him to face charges—the only issue is at what level they pitch the charges.'

'So, has he got a lawyer?'

'Not yet—you'll be meeting him on his own. Lawyers come later in this kind of case.'

Sandy felt a sense of outrage at the complacent way Colson said this, as if denying people their right to representation was a common occurrence, and a matter of no great concern. But she knew she could not betray any such a feeling. She skimmed through the files she had been given—far too much to take in at this point.

A Militia official came to the door.

'OK, we're ready for you to meet Mrs Kitson now,' said Colson.

••

Heather Kitson was sitting alone in an interview room close by. She had been told she had a special visitor, and was nonplussed to see Sandy Honeyford come into the room. She had never particularly liked Sandy, though at times she had tried hard to. She had resented the fact that Sandy wanted to be more than professionally close to Peter—the friend and confidant role was more than Heather was happy to allow. And lately she had resented the way Sandy had changed ships seemingly without a care. The betrayal seemed complete when she stayed with Mason after her previous party fell from grace.

And yet, when Sandy walked in the door, hope came in with her. Here was a friendly face—or one that could be friendly. Here was also a high-ranking person who might help to make sense of everything that was going on.

'Sandy!' exclaimed Heather.

'Heather…how are you?' asked Sandy. She had been allowed to come in alone, but in the full knowledge that everything they said and did was being watched through CCTV and recorded. She saw that Heather looked tired and strained.

'How am I? At my wits' end, Sandy!' Heather replied. 'Do you have any news of Peter?'

'Not yet. But I'll be seeing him later. Where's Andrea? I thought she was here with you.'

'She's in the building, hopefully being looked after. Actually, there's quite a nice girl they have here who's been taking care of her when I've been interviewed, or interrogated, or whatever's going on. She came in today with armfuls of toys and treats to help keep her occupied. God, it's so strange. They're such a mix here. Some people seem so sweet, while others seem to want to rip you apart! What about you, Sandy? Are you going to be sweet to me or rip me up into tiny pieces?'

Sandy smiled at what she hoped was a joke. 'I came as soon as I heard what was happening. You must believe that I'm here because I want to help both you and Peter. I've got authority from the highest level to come and talk to you, and to try and resolve this situation.'

'You mean from Mason?'

Sandy nodded. 'Yes. Don Mason is anxious for everything to be resolved as soon as possible.'

She said this partly for Heather, but mostly for the benefit of the Militia investigators whom she knew would be watching.

'You should know that our meeting is part of the investigation. Everything we say will be recorded, and may be used in evidence—'

'Evidence in what?' Heather interrupted sharply.

'Well, evidence that might be used in any legal case that might come out of all this. Wait, please, let me finish. I told Don quite plainly, and anyone else I've talked to, that I don't think Peter is guilty of anything. I'm sure of that. But it seems that circumstances surrounding him—and you—can be interpreted otherwise. I really want to help. And the only way to do this is to get everything absolutely out into the open, tell them everything they need to know.'

'Sandy, I've been over everything a hundred times. They keep asking me about Stella Walton and those damned conspiracy theory files she sent, and which ones I looked at, and what did Peter do with them, and how many times he spoke to Zara Alderney, and what was his relationship with Louise Adams. His relationship, mind you! I thought that was Terry's relationship!'

Sandy winced as she mentioned Terry's name.

'What is it with all these women, Sandy? Louise, Zara, Stella—all with their own agendas and we get dropped in the middle of it! Tell me what you know about Peter, you must know something!'

Sandy looked hard at her, opening her eyes a little wider, willing Heather to trust her and not make things difficult. With her eyes she motioned to the CCTV cameras, then continued.

'Heather, let's go over everything that happened, if only for my sake, OK? '

So Heather told her everything that had happened, from the moment Stella Walton first contacted her, and how they'd taken things forward more out of curiosity than anything else. And when they looked through the files, they thought they were a work of art, very professionally presented. But a lot of it seemed to be adding two and two together and making five, or eleven, or seventeen! She had read several of the files, to help Peter get through them. Peter, she said, had put them aside for several months. Then he got another message from Stella somehow, urging him to look at particular files. But as far as she knew, Peter didn't pass anything on to anyone, apart from information about who was in the eco-camps to his sister. But he made some copies for back-up, which he always did as he never trusted computers to be reliable. As for Zara Alderney, she had apparently been quite charming in Washington. And she had called him once. It seemed she was anxious to separate him from the GEM—something he had refused to do.

Heather spoke convincingly, though she was a little economical with the truth. Unlike Peter, she didn't hesitate to say things that might drop Stella Walton further into trouble. As far as she was concerned, Stella was the root of all their troubles, whether she intended to be or not. The most important thing was to be able to get Peter out of trouble.

'Tell me about your trip to see Jessica Barrington,' Sandy asked.

'Not a lot to tell, really,' said Heather. 'Except that it's probably the reason why I'm here—stepped out of line somehow. I went to ask if she or her husband could find out something—anything—about what's happened to Peter. I've been frantic with worry, can you imagine? Joanne with all her contacts couldn't find out anything. I just thought the Barringtons might be able to help, that's all. And then she calls someone to get me arrested.'

'Actually, Heather, I don't think she did. She asked Dave and he did actually make some enquiries, I believe. I interrupted him while he was talking to Malcolm Morton about it—that's how I've ended up here with you now.'

'Oh, maybe I misjudged her...'

'What did you talk about?'

'Oh, at first nothing much really ... kind of pretending like nothing had changed since we used to meet regularly, when Peter and Dave were working together. It felt very false. Then we went outside into her garden because Andrea was restless. Jessica really lives the life, you know, the green life. I asked her if she could find anything out about Peter, but she wasn't very encouraging. And I asked her about the, you know, general drift of the government...I probably shouldn't say too much to you, really...'

'Please go on, it's important.'

'Well, I mean the drift into harsh government—how did she feel about it. But she wasn't very forthcoming. She's hard to make out. On the one hand, she's the most political woman I've ever met—except for you, maybe! On the other hand, it seems she likes to withdraw from time to time, to retreat into the safe world of her family and her garden. And I think this business with her father has cast a shadow over her—she's embarrassed by it.'

'Did you discuss the files from Stella with her?'

'Yes, well, I asked her about them. I mentioned some names, some of the theories in there.'

'How did she react?'

'She laughed out loud—a really genuine laugh. She described them as crackpots or something, said they'd been knocking around for years and nobody took them seriously. It shook me, actually.'

'Why's that?'

'It was like a moment of clarity. I'm sure after speaking to her that Stella Walton's investigation is a house of cards. She's a journalist, not a real researcher. So superficial. But as a result, we're up to our necks in this Kafkaesque situation. The only thing I couldn't understand is why this over-reaction if they're just a bunch of crackpot theories. Jessica hinted that they're worried about being slandered: Stella's theories could be quite damaging if they got out into the open, particularly with elections coming up. It shows how far they've lost their way, if elections are all they're worried about! But I tell you this, Sandy. If your friends would just let us out, I'd take a solemn oath, I'd swear on the bones of my mother or the life of my child, that I'd never breath a word about these ideas, nor would Peter. We'd happily retreat to the countryside like Jessica, and lead a humble and virtuous life! No more politics! Ever!'

They talked for almost an hour, then Sandy decided it was time to move on. She went to the door, and asked the Militia guard to have Andrea brought up to the interview room to be with Heather until she returned. Then she spoke to Heather.

'I'd like you to wait here until I return. I'm not sure how long I'll be. I'll be seeing Peter. Anything you want me to pass on?'

Heather became very animated. 'Is he really here in this building? Please, if you can, persuade them to let me see him. He's really here?'

'Possibly. Or it maybe it will be a videoconference, I'm not sure yet.'

'When you see him, tell him that we're fine, we're both fine. And Sandy, tell him how much I love him, we both do, and how much we both miss him! I love him so much, you can't know how much. Nothing is worth this, nothing, to be separate like this...Promise me you'll tell him!'

'I promise I will,' said Sandy warmly. 'I wish I could promise more, that you'll soon be back together. I wish I could ... '

Then Sandy left, fearing her tears would betray her. 'Tell him how much we both love him,' she thought. 'Sure!' she said under her breath as she was led down the corridor into the interior of the building.

Laura Colson escorted Sandy along a series of corridors, through two steel gates that had to be unlocked for them, until they reached a central stairwell where they began to descend to the basement level. The atmosphere here was very different to the relaxed atmosphere at the front of the building. The militia guards wore different uniforms, more like soldiers. Sandy noticed there was no natural light, the corridors were lit by naked light bulbs. She noted the coiled and ugly design of the energy-saving bulbs. It was like a prison. She was surprised that, apart from the light-bulbs, a green prison was no different from any other, apparently. Colson didn't call it a prison, though, preferring to call it a 'holding area'.

They went through another gate, then finally through a steel door. Sandy was handed over to a grim-faced guard, who silently led her past a short row of cells. The air smelled bad. She could hear someone shouting, and someone else sobbing. By this stage she was feeling very frightened.

At the last cell in the row, the Militia guard said, 'He's in here.'

Slowly and deliberately he unlocked the outer steel door, then the gate behind it.

'I'll leave the outer gate open, and I'll be sitting just here. Call me when you're finished, or if he gives you any kind of trouble. They say he's a violent one, so watch your step!'

Sandy was left to step inside on her own, with the guard watching warily from behind. The crumpled shape of Peter Kitson lay on a low bed.

'Peter?' she called softly.

With difficulty Peter Kitson jolted himself up onto one elbow.

'Peter?'

'Sandy? Christ, is that really you?' he rasped. His voice was very dry, and broke as he spoke.

'Yes, Peter, it's me,' Sandy said softly.

Now Peter pulled himself fully upright. Sandy saw at once that he had lost a lot of weight. The she saw the discolouring all down one side of his face, and let out a little gasp. Peter smiled grimly.

'I guess I'm not a pretty sight, eh?' he croaked.

'Oh, Peter,' she said, moving towards him. Then she checked herself, remembering why she was there, and that every move she made would be watched.

Peter smiled again, and said: 'Sandy, I'm so glad you're here. You can't know how good it is to see a friendly face.'

He paused and his face clouded over. 'You can't imagine what it's like to be anxious every time you hear a key turn in the door, always to be expecting

408

the worst! But, as they say, "what doesn't kill you makes you stronger"! This won't go on for ever, and I know there's a life beyond this misery.'

He paused again. Sandy was too shocked as yet to say anything.

'Have you seen Heather? How is she?'

Sandy nodded. 'She's fine. Andrea's fine, too. I saw them earlier today. She told me to tell you how much they both love you, how much they miss you.'

Peter bowed his head, overcome with relief and emotion.

'Heather hasn't been arrested?'

'No. She's been questioned, but not arrested. She's fine.' Strictly speaking, this wasn't a lie. 'She went to see Jessica Barrington, to see if she could help her find out some news about you. Things kind of filtered through to me, and here I am now. But the deal is, I have to ask you some questions.'

'They told me she'd been arrested, that they were holding her. Are they just playing with my head?'

'They've spoken to her more than once, for sure. Peter, how did you both get involved in this?'

Peter raised his head, and looked hard into her eyes. For the first time, he questioned in his mind whose side she was on. He sighed. 'Do you think they'll let me see them? Heather and Andrea, that is...No, wait, wait, wait. I think they should keep away. I don't want them to see me like this, they'd be so scared and upset. Maybe once they've decided I don't know anything else, if they don't let me go...maybe then.'

He looked down again. Peter seemed confused, befuddled. She'd never seen him like this, never seen him vulnerable. It was painful to see him like this.

'What happened to your face?'

'Apparently it happened while I was resisting arrest. Can you imagine me resisting arrest? They just hit me. And since I've been inside, they've carried on hitting me. Almost every day. I think some of my ribs are broken.'

Sandy winced. 'Have you had any medical attention?'

'Some. Basically to see if I'm fit enough to take some more beatings.'

Sandy was shaking her head. 'I can't believe this...'

'What, this is England, and we don't do things like this?'

'I did think that.'

'Me too, actually,' sighed Peter. 'Joanna was the only one who understood. Why could she see it, and none of the rest of us did?'

Peter instantly regretted mentioning her name. It kindled in Sandy a new respect for Joanna, and she remembered with regret her annoyance when

Joanna had gone on interminably to Martin about her cases. *So this is what it is all about*, she thought.

'I'm sorry, Peter,' she said, 'I have to ask you some questions. I really want to clear this up. And if we can get everything out into the open, maybe we can get you released. Or if you're really going to be charged with something, perhaps you can be out on bail. That way, at least you'd be with your family and out of...all this.'

'Sandy, I'm sure you're going to ask me about Zara Alderney. Do you know what she said to me? She said something like "Take your lovely family and get out of there. Come here and I'll personally show you all the sites." And I keep asking myself, what did she know? She plainly knew something that I didn't. Or maybe not. Maybe she was just trying to split the coalition. I don't know. They keep asking and asking me what information I gave her. They listened in to our conversation. Why can't they see that she knew much more, much sooner, than I ever did. She had her own sources.'

'Louise Adams.'

'Sure. But America is the richest, most powerful nation on earth. They spy on everyone and everything. Louise Adams wasn't their only source, for sure. Why would they need me? I was contacted out of the blue, and I have to admit, I was curious. I don't know what my real motives were for meeting Stella Walton. But after Terry was arrested and I was dropped from government, I was suspicious and dug into them a bit more.'

'How well did you know Stella?'

'Not well at all. I only knew her because she used to arrange interviews and briefings for TV. All I knew was that she was intelligent and personable. Confident and pushy too, like most of these media types. I guess I felt that she wasn't a fool, or an idiot, or timewaster—she might have had something interesting. You know, they keep talking about classified material, that I stole classified material. All the time they say this. Nothing appeared to be like that. Most of it seemed to have been gleaned from public sources, or maybe she hacked into some private forums on the Internet. But not government stuff, for sure. Only the stuff I gave to Joanna about eco-camp inmates might have come from government sources. At least as far as I could see. There were thousands of files, and I never got through them all.'

'I haven't seen any of this, Peter. What was it all about?'

'If you really don't know, Sandy, I'm not going to tell you. It's obviously got me into a tight spot. You're safer not knowing. But I'll tell you this. If any of it is true, Britain isn't going to be a pleasant place to be in the months and years ahead. Do you know what I'm talking about?'

It was plain to Peter that Sandy had no idea.

'It's not the kind of place I'd like to see my child grow up in, even if she had the chance to. I want you to think about that, and remember that. Will you remember what I said?'

Sandy now felt very confused. She was used to Peter being clear-headed and incisive. Now he seemed to be confused and was speaking obliquely.

'Sure, I'll remember.'

'You know, it's so ironic. They accuse me all the time of being in collusion with Zara Alderney. And I didn't even listen to her! My God, if only I'd listened to her. Don't you think I should have listened to her? Two mistakes. Two mistakes. I didn't listen to her. And then I met Stella Walton. I should have ignored her. Or maybe not, what do you think? Ignorance is bliss. It would have been bliss, unless…but now I know, at least there's a chance. A chance for some of us, at least, don't you think, Sandy? It's not too late, is it?'

Peter was now perspiring heavily, sweat dripping from his forehead. The guard had risen to his feet, and hovered in the doorway. Sandy looked round at him.

'I think he's severely distressed. I've never seen him like this before. He needs help.'

'Yes, I think it's best if you go now. I'll get some help in here.'

'Do you have a doctor in the building?' asked Sandy sharply.

'Not a doctor, but we have a First Aid team—'

'Not good enough,' barked Sandy, as fear for Peter rose within her. 'Where's the nearest hospital? Get Laura Colson down here NOW!'

Sandy was surprised at the effect of her words. Guards leapt into action and were running around doing everything she asked. When Laura Colson and one of the guards protested that they needed to consult with their superiors Sandy snapped: 'Your chain of command only goes to the top of the Militia. I am here with Don Mason's full authority. Cross me if you wish, but be prepared for the consequences.'

At the same time, Sandy was thinking all the time about the consequences for herself of what she was doing. She was sure it wouldn't be good. When she thought of Peter Kitson's injuries, she knew she was risking the same for herself. All the same, she revelled in the exercise of direct authority, even while she felt her knees trembling.

An ambulance arrived in minutes. Paramedics rushed in, and were ushered into the depths of the building. Heather Kitson rushed to the door of the interview room in time to see paramedics and panicking Militia officials running past. She feared the worst. The guard by her door asked her to stay inside and keep calm. A second, third and fourth ambulance arrived.

Downstairs Sandy had ordered all the cells to be opened and the inmates examined for injuries and psychological stress. More doctors arrived. Militia guards and officials milled around, some confused, some angry, and some just curious. For several of them, it was their first time to see into the secure area.

Peter Kitson was helped onto an ambulance trolley. He struggled and began to panic as he was strapped in. Sandy leaned forward and whispered something in his ear. Instantly he relaxed. Laura Colson looked on curiously.

'I just told him his wife and child are upstairs. They will go with him to the hospital.'

'I–' Colson began to protest, but then thought better of it. Seeing the pitiful condition of two or three of the inmates, she felt that Sandy was right. But she also knew heads would roll. Probably hers would be first.

A small procession of trolleys was manhandled up the narrow stairs, and a couple of walking wounded followed. Howls of anguish followed from the four or five detainees who had been declared medically fit and were left behind, cries that would haunt Sandy in the days ahead, often waking her at night.

As they approached the front of the building, Heather Kitson rushed out of the interview room, recognising the bruised face of her husband on the trolley. She hugged him and kissed him as she ran alongside, passing Andrea to Sandy to carry. Sandy hugged Andrea close to her saying softly: 'Shhh, shhh, it's alright. Mummy and Daddy are fine. See?' And thinking over and over, 'This is what it's all about. My God, my God, this is what it's all about!'

Outside the patients were being loaded into ambulances when Carl Fullerton arrived. He had been called several times by anxious Militia guards, caught between their old instructions and Sandy Honeyford's pulling rank on them.

'Sandy, it seems you've caused quite a stir. What have you been doing?' he asked with a grim smile.

Sandy walked boldly up to him, her five-foot-five-inches body dwarfed by his huge frame. She poked him sharply in the chest as she spoke to him. 'Carl. You've got some explaining to do.'

He looked taken aback, but his lips maintained their tiger's smile.

'This is not how we do things,' she said slowly and emphatically, poking his chest with each word.

'Well, well, Sandy,' he said. 'Since when have you taken over running security?'

'Huh! These people are on their way to hospital. I'm going with them. If they need security, it will have to be from the police. We'll talk about this later, but I can assure you Don is not going to be happy.'

Fullerton threw his head back in laughter.

'You're damn right there, Sandy! But let me tell you something. I could have them taken back downstairs just by clicking my fingers, and you'd be down there with them. I'll allow you your moment of triumph. It means nothing.'

Then he nodded his head curtly to Heather Kitson, turned and walked away. Putting his arm round Laura Colson's shoulder, he walked with her into the building, leaning over and talking animatedly to her all the way.

••

At the hospital, Sandy continued to keep herself busy. A contingent of Green Militia had followed the ambulances, but Sandy had called ahead to the Metropolitan Police and several officers were there waiting for them. She asked them to see that on no account would the patients be moved without contacting her. In the meantime, she wanted the officers to take statements from the patients about how they had received their injuries.

A message came through to her phone. It was from Don Mason. He wanted to see her at six o'clock that evening in his office at Number 10.

She couldn't decide what to do yet. Sandy was aware that she had created chaos and exploited that to exercise her authority. But she was sure the normal structures would soon be reasserting themselves. Carl Fullerton and Malcolm Morton would now no doubt have spoken and given their version of events to Mason. She could be in very big trouble. She could try to fight her corner, or she could run—as yet she wasn't sure.

Peter Kitson was hauled off for a series of tests, always accompanied by Heather. A doctor told her that he had a broken jaw, which hadn't set properly and seemed to have become infected, and a broken eye socket. He also had two broken ribs and two broken fingers. They also thought that he had suffered kidney damage, and were waiting for test results. He was also extremely distressed. In part it was because of the trauma he had been through.

His main cause of anxiety now was the safety of Heather and Andrea. He told them repeatedly to leave the country—he would join them later when he was fit to move. He said the same over and over to Sandy, to urge them to leave the country.

Sandy agreed. And she had already made arrangements for this. The hard part now was to persuade Heather to do so. Heather was adamant that she would never leave him. Eventually, as Peter was sedated, he began to calm down. He spoke slowly and rationally, saying how he could never rest if he thought they were in danger, and might be used to get at him. Heather argued that they could all leave together, after he had recovered from the operations he needed to set the broken bones in his face.

In the end, with huge misgivings, Heather agreed. Then she leaned forward and whispered in his ear. Peter instantly propped himself up and hugged her close to him, evidently overcome with emotion. Nurses came to calm him, asking Heather gently to move away. But Peter did not seem distressed. Through the tears he was smiling wildly.

Heather came across the ward to talk to Sandy again. 'OK,' she said, wiping away tears, and smiling. 'I've agreed to go. Will they allow that? I'm meant to be being held for questioning, or I was.'

'I think you're floating between jurisdictions at the moment. You have to seize the moment, and go now.'

A police officer and a Militia guard were talking at the entrance to the hospital ward. Sandy spoke quietly to Heather, but within earshot of the Militia man.

'It's all arranged. You fly to Holland at eight o'clock tonight from City Airport. The tickets have been bought. Someone will be waiting for you with your passports.'

'Sandy! I can't believe you. You're amazing—we owe you so much.'

'Stop now, please!' said Sandy. 'I've always thought of you as family—what else could I do?'

Heather embraced her, and started to move back to Peter's bed as the nurse pulled back the curtains again. Then she returned to Sandy.

'There's one other thing...' she said hesitantly. 'I would never usually tell someone this early, because anything can happen, you know...'

Sandy raised an eyebrow and looked at her expectantly. Heather continued.

'I've just told Peter. I'm expecting another child.'

'Congratulations, Heather,' beamed Sandy.

'Please, don't say that yet! God willing, God willing! But I want you to know something. Whether the child is a boy or a girl, we're going to call it Sandy!'

'Enough, enough!' said Sandy smiling, 'You'll start me off too!'

A police Inspector, DI Ibrahim Moss, arrived to talk to Sandy. He was clearly uneasy about the potential conflict between the Metropolitan Police and the Green Militia. Sandy tried to reassure him. 'Everything that's happened today has been under my authority. And I report directly to Don Mason. As far as I can see, I came across a number of people with a range of injuries, and I had them transferred to hospital. Now it's up to you to investigate the causes of their injuries, and whether any further investigations are necessary. While they are receiving medical attention, they must not be moved, don't you agree? And in my view, they should be treated as witnesses in potential assault cases, and given appropriate protection.'

'I think you can appreciate, Miss Honeyford, that there are certain grey areas here. I mean, about jurisdiction. The Militias have a wide range of powers to investigate and detain. I've been told you brought someone here, Heather Kitson, who was being held for questioning. She has no injuries, is that right? No need for medical attention?'

'Sure—'

'Then you'll have no objection to her being returned once she's seen her husband is OK?'

'Actually, I don't think there is any obligation for her to return, or for you to compel her. She hasn't been officially arrested, nor has she been the subject of any order from any judicial or Revolutionary body. Do you know otherwise?'

'I don't know of any order against her, it's true.'

'And as a matter of fact, as far as I know there's no official authority for detaining Peter Kitson either. Do you know better?'

'I can't say I do,' the Inspector replied. 'But I should advise you, these are not straightforward times. I can do my job as I should do, but I can be overruled in an instant in cases that involve the Militia. What I'm saying is, I can only do so much. I'll do my best, but I can't guarantee that I can protect them. Not good, is it?'

Sandy thanked him for his professionalism. He made it clear he would do his duty, but he wasn't willing to stick his neck out too far. Fair enough, thought Sandy. But she did get him to agree to provide a driver to take them where they needed to go.

She hurried over to Heather.

'We don't have much time!' she said quietly. 'You have to leave now.'

Hurried goodbyes followed. Outside they were ushered into a waiting police car driven by a uniformed officer. A group of waiting Militia officers immediately got into two cars, ready to follow them wherever they were going to go.

'I want you to take us to Green Park tube station,' Sandy told the driver, putting a friendly hand on his shoulder.

'Green Park?' asked Heather. 'I thought we were going to City Airport.'

'I have to do something first,' said Sandy.

They drove out onto the Fulham Road, with the two militia cars making no secret of their pursuit. The two police officers in the front soon made it clear they had no love for the Green Militia.

'I think you've made quite an impression on our Inspector Moss, 'said the driver.

'A good one, I hope,' joked Sandy.

'He said you were "inspirational". His exact words. We're under strict instructions not to let the Militia get their hands on you!'

'That's Mossy though,' said the other. 'There are others only too keen to cooperate with the jumped-up green-jacketed little shits!'

'OK,' said Sandy suddenly. 'Here's what we're going to do—and I need your help. I want you to stop about a hundred yards from Green Park tube station. Can one of you flag down the first Militia car and stall them—any pretext—and we'll dodge down the underground. I'd like the other of you to come with us, to stop anyone from following us. Is that OK? Then wait outside the station for about five minutes.'

The two officers looked at each other. 'Fine,' said one. 'Are you sure you know what you're doing?'

'I don't know what's happening,' pleaded Heather.

'Can you trust me?' asked Sandy.

'God, yes—I trust you like I trust no one else in all this madness!'

'Let's do it.'

As they headed towards Green Park, the officers radioed for back-up, saying they were escorting some witnesses and were being followed by two suspicious cars. Everything was set.

The police car slowed to a stop about a hundred yards before the entrance to the Tube station, and the officer in the passenger seat got out. He walked purposefully back down the road. The first of the Militia vehicles was now two cars behind them. The police officer held up his hand to stop all the traffic. Meanwhile the car with Sandy and Heather inside moved on slowly to the entrance of the station. Two police cars approached from the opposite direction, lights flashing. Another approached from a side road. Now the two Militia cars were surrounded.

Sandy, Heather and Andrea rapidly exited the car and hurried down the stairs, with the other officer hard on their heels. There were no Militia following them, or in the station already.

Sandy said to the officer quickly, 'I want to thank you so much for what you've done today. I can't believe what I've seen today, but I just know that I'm incredibly, incredibly frightened by it. I don't know if I'll see you again, but if I do I'm going to take you and your colleagues out for the biggest meal ever! But there's one thing I'd like you to do. Can you leak out today's story to the press. How Peter Kitson, a former Cabinet Minister, was found beaten up in the basement of GV House, and how a stand-off occurred between the police and Militia? It may not hit the streets here, but I know there's several journalists who slip this kind of thing through to the foreign press and the renegade press on the Internet.'

'I know someone who can do that,' said the officer.

She stood up on tip-toe and gave him a kiss on the cheek. As she did so, she heard his radio. A call was being issued already for the police to assist in the apprehension of two fugitives with a baby, and a description was being given of Heather and Sandy.

'Seems I've gone a little deaf,' said the officer. 'Where are you going to go?'

'Best for you if you don't know!' called Sandy, as she and Heather passed through the barrier.

As they moved out of sight, Sandy explained to Heather what would come next. 'Make your way to Euston. The militia will assume you're on the Jubilee line out to the airport, and that buys us some time. I've got a ticket for you from Euston to Liverpool. There's a train in about forty minutes. You'll meet Joanna there. She'll be waiting for you, in Liverpool. Use this phone, it's not registered to anyone they're likely to be watching. I've given a new one to Joanna too. From Liverpool she'll drive you to Birkenhead, where you can catch the 10 o'clock ferry to Belfast. The Militia don't carry much clout there, though you'll have to dodge the regular police, I expect. Joanna's got some contacts there from her civil rights work, and they'll get you down to the border. Once you're in the Irish Republic, you should make your way to America—anywhere so long as it's a long way away. And take this too.'

Sandy reached inside her jacket and took out the slim tablet computer she had been given inside Green Volunteer House. She tucked it down inside the bag carrying all the baby equipment.

'For God's sake, don't get caught with this. Dump it, drop it in the Irish Sea if necessary, just don't get caught with it. I want Joanna to take it, and do whatever's necessary.'

Heather stopped suddenly and grabbed Sandy by the arm. 'There's only one ticket? What about you? You must be in a lot of danger too!'

'I have to go back. If I'm not there, who's going to fight Peter's corner? I've still got a position to fight for in government, and I don't think Don will deliver me up to the Militia—not yet anyway! And it seems we've got some friends in the regular police. I'll do all I can, I promise. And—there's Martin too. I need to square things with him. Quick, go now!'

After embracing both Heather and Andrea, she watched them disappear down the escalator to the Victoria Line. Then pursing her lips in resigned determination, she sighed and made her way to the Jubilee Line. Back to Westminster, and to whatever fate should befall her.

••

It seemed Martin Lang was not surprised at Sandy's story when she called him on her way from Westminster station to Downing Street. She had noticed often how well connected he was to the government grapevines.

'I'm glad you're safe,' he said. 'You've certainly set the cats amongst the pigeons. Do you think they'll take this lying down?'

'What's the word on the streets—and in the corridors of power?'

'Do you want the truth?'

'Always.'

'They say you're finished in politics.'

'Oh.'

'Me too. The end of ambition. At least with the current lot.'

'I don't see why it should…You should disown me, seriously. Maybe I'm bound for the camps. You don't want to have an eco-felon for a partner!'

'Why did you do it? Talk of sticking your head above the parapet!'

'How can you ask that, Martin? If you'd been there, if you'd seen what I saw....Oh, God, honey—there was no option. You believe in the rule of law, don't you? These people in the Militia—the bottom line is they kidnap people and torture them: assault them, beat them, threaten their families. Joanna has been right all along. God, it was so awful!'

'I hear you had them running around in circles. And is it true you hit Carl Fullerton?!' Sandy could feel the amazement and pride in his voice.

'Not hit. I poked him in the chest and gave him a piece of my mind!'

'In front of everyone? He won't like that. I'm worried about you. I don't think you should go back into the lion's den. You should head for the hills, like Heather and Jo. Maybe we both should.'

'Really?'

'I don't think the ride is going to be any easier from now on. Time for a strategic retreat.'

Sandy thought a while. But she remained firm to her purpose. 'I know it's risky, but I need to take this to Don. He may be angry, but I didn't actually do anything illegal. He needs to hear at first hand from someone other than Fullerton and Malcolm Morton about what's going on. Maybe we can root out this corruption in the Militia—they're not all like that, I'm sure. Get things back on track.'

'Sandy, I think that's a forlorn hope. Mason's got more social skills than Morton or Fullerton, but otherwise he's just the same as the rest of them. Our main hope is to survive until the end of this regime. Look around us: everything is falling apart. They can't survive past the next election. What you've done has raised your reputation with everyone—except your current employers! Let's take a holiday. How does Italy sound?'

Italy sounded great. But Martin didn't sound so great to Sandy. He was obviously concerned for her, but where was his concern for Peter, or Heather, or Joanna? He hadn't asked one question about how they were. And he evidently wasn't concerned about all the other Peter Kitsons languishing in the camps and prison cells. Buoyed by her success earlier in the day, Sandy had made her decision. Now was not the time for running. It was time to press any advantages she might have.

••

The tension was palpable as Sandy was let into Number 10 Downing Street, where Mason had asked to meet her. The staff greeted her rather stiffly, and there was no exchange of pleasantries as was usual in the more informal regime of Don Mason.

She did not have to wait long before being ushered into Mason's office. He was reading documents as she entered. He looked up over his reading glasses, like a head teacher whose patience is being sorely pressed. He invited Sandy to take a seat in one of the armchairs. He remained seated at his desk.

'Sandy—'

'Don, do you know what's been going on at GV House? If you'd seen what I saw. My God, it was terrible! Unbelievable!'

Mason sighed, and leaned back in his chair, twirling his glasses by one leg.

'I don't know what to do with you, Sandy, I really don't. Wait, wait a minute, let me speak now. I trusted you to do a job for us, and what do you do? Cause absolute mayhem, and expose us to serious criticism. What were you thinking of? You discovered something wrong, no doubt. But why didn't you come back to me, or Malcolm, so we could take the necessary steps to root it out? Do you think I wouldn't listen?'

'Don, I want to show you this,' said Sandy, standing up. She walked over to him, taking her phone from her handbag. 'Please, look at these photos. I took them of Peter and the other prisoners. Can you see the punishment he's been taking? Look at this video, as he turns his head. Now listen to the doctor at the hospital detailing Peter's injuries.'

Mason listened to the recording, grimacing slightly as the list of injuries built up.

'Don, this wasn't a one-off aberration. His broken jaw and eye-socket had been festering for months. He was beaten on an almost daily basis. This was systematic. No one has had access to him—not his wife, not a lawyer, no friend or anyone to take his part. So should I have left him there and run to you for help? Maybe. But I thought he could die in that time, or be spirited away by whoever is doing this. Then they could just say I was hysterical, exaggerating.'

'Where are they now, Sandy? His wife and sister?'

'I don't know exactly. Somewhere safe, I hope.'

'Don't you understand, you've sabotaged a criminal investigation! You don't seem to understand the seriousness of what you've done. And don't try to pretend to me this was done on an impulse, after you saw Peter Kitson in a bad way. This was premeditated, in collaboration with one of the government's chief opponents, Joanna Kitson. Do you deny that?'

'That's an oversimplification. I didn't know quite what to expect, and I made plans for several different outcomes.'

'And you claimed to be acting with my authority!'

'Not exactly, Don. I said I reported to you. But I'll grant I used my position to exercise some authority there.'

'And you don't think I'm embarrassed by that?'

'Don! With great respect, your embarrassment hardly seems to be the point!' cried Sandy passionately. 'An agency of this government is illegally detaining people, and beating them to within an inch of their lives! We should be severely embarrassed about *that*! We've got to root these people out, without delay, or else the government, and the Revolution, will be dragged right through the mud.'

Mason sighed deeply. 'Sandy, you have to be aware of the great things we're trying to achieve. The changes we're making have involved ripping up the rule book to some extent. You know that the Second Revolution requires tough measures. We've made no secret of that, have we?'

'Oh please, Don, spare me lectures about how you can't make omelettes without breaking eggs! How on earth does secretly brutalising Peter Kitson and those other poor sods in the basement push forward the cause of the Revolution?'

'You're so exasperating at times, Sandy! And blinded by your old loyalties to the Kitson family and the Liberals! OK, let's be positive now. We're going to clear up this mess. I'm authorising an inquiry into this affair—the brutalising and everything, and as you say we'll root out the individuals who are doing this. I've already asked Malcolm to take the first steps.'

'One thing, Don, you should be aware of. Carl Fullerton was fully aware of Peter's condition. I was briefly shown the interrogation records. Carl interviewed him, and Peter was beaten in front of him. If Carl's involved in running the inquiry, it can only be a sham. He's the one you need to focus on. Seriously. And I think he's far too close to Malcolm now. Mud sticks. Just … get rid of him.'

'I heard you took on Carl today. Not a good person to make your enemy, Sandy.'

'Well, what can I say? His kind thrive on the absence of legal restraint. We need to—*you* need to restore the rule of law before it's too late. And…did you know about Terry Cairns? I heard today.'

'Yes, I heard. It's very sad news.'

'More than sad. He died in unusual circumstances, in one of our camps. Is this normal? I think we need a complete inquiry into how the camps are run. They're out of control.'

Mason exhaled loudly. 'You're on a mission today, aren't you, Sandy? Let me think about this.'

'I know you feel disappointed with me, like you said. But I'm deeply disappointed too. I'd heard rumours, of course. But what I saw was worse than anything I'd heard, anything I could have imagined. And something else disappoints me. You and Malcolm knew that Terry Cairns was one of my oldest friends. Maybe you think he's one of the greatest criminals on earth. But no one saw fit to tell me, and no one has commiserated with me. Perhaps you think I wanted to disown him, or would be embarrassed by him. It doesn't work like that. Some things run at a deeper human level, and if we don't recognise that, we're sunk.'

Mason was nodding slowly as he listened to this lecture and sensed the emotion behind it.

'Point taken, Sandy. I've had enough for now. You've given me quite a lot to think about. I suggest you go home now. I'll call you in the morning to let you know how we move forward. I understand your motives more, but I think it's going to be hard for you to work with us in the same way now. It's a question of trust, don't you think?'

Now Sandy sighed. 'As you say.'

It was inconclusive, but she felt relief that the dramas of the day were at an end, and that she was free to go home. Her next stop, though, would be the hospital.

••

As Sandy left the building, Malcolm Morton, Sarah Turner and Carl Fullerton filed into Don Mason's office.

'What do you think?' Mason asked.

'I think you were very gentle with her,' said Morton.

'Perhaps,' said Mason. 'But you can see why I like her?'

'It's certainly been an extraordinary *tour de force* she's turned in today,' suggested Sarah Turner.

'Yes, indeed,' agreed Morton. 'We could do with more people like her in the party and the Militia. That kind of energy, initiative and authority. Good leadership ability in a crisis.'

'But one fatal flaw: too much human-love and not enough Planet-love,' pronounced Fullerton. 'She could never be a true Green.'

'Huh!' exclaimed Sarah Turner. 'Since when does being a "true Green" involve beating the shit out of detainees, Carl?'

'Yes, quite,' agreed Mason. 'And not just any detainee, but one who happens to be one of the world's most recognisable politicians! Danny's team have sent me a briefing. This story is hitting the world's press already, complete with before and after pictures.'

'Police photos, not Sandy's. It seems the Met is a little leaky today,' said Morton.

'And a little uncooperative. Some issues to resolve there,' added Fullerton.

'It seems there are some key issues to resolve closer to home, Carl,' said Mason angrily. 'Now I knew that Kitson would be on the receiving end of some tough love in the holding camp. But I never expected this degree of brutality. *You* knew, though, Carl, didn't you? You too, Malcolm! What on earth were you doing allowing her to see him like that? It would have been simple to put her off. I asked your advice, for God's sake!'

'And what were you doing allowing him to be in that state in the first place, Carl? These medieval measures have no place in our Revolution!' Sarah Turner interjected.

'Like Don said,' Morton began to explain, 'we know there's to be some tough measures in the Second Revolution. The eleventh hour is no time to be squeamish. We've said before, anyone who can't deal with it, they know where the door is. But I agree this situation is not ideal. We failed to anticipate the extent of Sandy's reaction, and its effectiveness. However, I was using a tactic we've been using with Militia in the camps. By confronting them with something shocking, we get them to show their true colours. Sandy has shown hers, and it's clear she has no place at the same table as us.'

'Is everyone agreed? From now on we do without her? OK,' said Mason, acknowledging the nods of assent.

'The way I look at it,' said Morton, 'is that Don's protégé, Sandy Honeyford, was the final person in the Kitson Circle to try and hijack the Revolution and steer it onto a light green, a Liberal-Green course. We mustn't acquiesce. Don, haven't you always said that every problem is an opportunity to find new solutions, new ways to achieve what we want? We have a choice. Either we squirm in our seats and get all defensive about this: launch public inquiries, and hope we can wipe enough egg off our faces to survive. Or we can take responsibility for what has happened, and use it to our advantage. I mean, while we can't justify what's happened, it will serve as a good example to anyone who wants to sabotage the Revolution. It will be a deterrent to opposition, and an incentive to comply.'

Mason nodded thoughtfully. 'Point taken. We need to face this boldly. I think we're going to face a lot of pressure, all the same. So I think we need to make some moves that seem like we're meeting criticism half-way. Carl, I want you out of London for a while. There's plenty to do in the provinces. In the camps, in improving the quality of the Militia around the country, and in our special projects. You know me, I like good order and attention to detail. I like to set the agenda, not react to it. So I'm personally giving you the responsibility for making sure this never, ever, happens again.'

Fullerton nodded, accepting the implied rebuke and relieved to have the chance to reinforce his authority.

'What about Martin Lang?' asked Sarah Turner. 'He's the last of the Kitson Circle hovering close to the centre of power.'

Mason looked to Morton for an assessment.

'His position is a strange one,' said Morton. 'He's been travelling solo, on his own trajectory, without being in any party or part of any clearly defined group. He's on good terms with people of all persuasions and none. He's also well networked with a wide range of officials, and seems generally respected. Lang keeps his ear close to the ground. To be fair to him, he's done a pretty good job driving forward our reforms at ESCOLAW. But he's a long way from being one of us. I think he's deliberately keeping in the good books of anyone he thinks might replace us after the next election. We've no reason to think he gave Sandy any help or encouragement for her stunts today. But I can't guess how he'll react once he knows all about it.'

'So he stays for the time being?' asked Sarah Turner.

'Probably time to make a clean sweep,' said Mason. 'Let's get someone primed to succeed him in the driving seat, and then side-line him with a special project. That will give him a choice to make—we'll see if he'll stay with us when he sees his ambition being derailed.'

••

Peter Kitson was just being returned from the operating theatre as Sandy arrived in his hospital ward. Asleep, he looked peaceful, but much the worse for wear. She sat on the chair next to his bed. Tenderly she stroked his hair, returning some order to his appearance, trying to make his familiar face return. She carefully avoided the dressings, and gently removed matted blood from the ends of his hair.

She sat back in the chair, thoughts cramming into her head. As she sat there for more than an hour, she noticed that the police were nowhere to be seen. The ward was being lightly guarded by Green Militia, and she had seen more milling around the hospital entrance. It seemed a Green 'normality' was reasserting itself, as Fullerton had predicted.

Wearily Sandy stood up. She leaned over and kissed Peter on the forehead. He stirred a little. She squeezed his hand. Then she slowly began to make her way home.

An hour away from Liverpool Lime Street station, Heather and Andrea had enjoyed an uneventful journey. Heather had spoken to Joanna using the phones Sandy had given them. Joanna would be waiting for her just outside the station. All was apparently going to plan. But she couldn't help worrying about Peter. And Sandy too. Feelings of guilt crowded in. Joanna had said there was no good choice here, only the least bad.

A text came in, from a number she did not know. 'Boy's OK now. Sleeping peacefully. I'm off home. You girls take care. xx.' It had to be from Sandy. Heather smiled. Her worst fears were calmed, but anxiety remained. What now for Peter?

As luck would have it, on the journey she sat opposite a woman travelling with her two young children. They were aged around seven and nine, and helped to keep Andrea amused. Their mother was a very mumsy kind of woman, who talked incessantly about husband, home and children. Despite her fears, Heather revelled in the unrelenting normality of it all.

Back in London, Sandy's ruse of buying flights for them from City Airport had at first completely fooled the Militia authorities who wanted to get her back. Fullerton had charged Laura Colson with seeing that Heather Kitson was safely brought back in, and she was determined to succeed and restore her reputation as a safe pair of hands in the Militia. By 7.30, though, she was becoming alarmed that there was no sign of either Heather or Joanna Kitson at the airport. She reported her fears back to Carl Fullerton.

He debated for a moment the idea of just letting them go. But apart from wanting to continue the investigation that had been interrupted, he was aware that both of these women could seriously embarrass the government from overseas. More than anything, however, Carl Fullerton did not like anyone to put one over on him. He issued a general alert to the Militia to watch out for them at all airports and seaports, and set up a team to track where they could have gone.

Thirty years of ever more powerful surveillance technology coupled with the fear of crime and terrorism had given London the most routinely filmed population in Europe, possibly in the world, and intelligence analysts who were second to none. Within an hour, Fullerton had received a report. Heather was on her way to Liverpool. Joanna had left her office at 4 p.m., had evaded her followers in the Underground and had not been seen since. She had not returned home. So a reception committee would be prepared for Heather Kitson at Liverpool Station, and no doubt her sister-in-law would be found nearby too.

Twenty minutes away from Liverpool, Joanna called Heather, warning her that the place was crawling with Militia, uniformed police and people milling in groups who she guessed were plain clothes police officers.

'What can I do? How can I get through?' whispered Heather as she stood up, moving away to speak more privately.

'I don't know, I don't know.' Joanna sounded desperate. 'I really can't get near the station. I'm in a café just round the corner. Maybe you can try to change your appearance a bit … or can you hide on the train and head back out again?'

All the time thinking, *I'm no good at this!* Yet it was so crucial. Joanna had always feared what the system could do, and fought against it. Now she was encountering just what the system actually does do—to her own family. She felt totally unequal to the situation she found herself in at this time.

The train pulled into the station. Passengers began to get ready to leave. Heather tried hard not to look agitated. The woman opposite was getting her children organised to leave, telling her daughter to zip up her little pink rucksack before putting it on, and telling her to check for toys under the seat. Then she turned to Heather and said softly, 'You're in some kind of trouble, aren't you?'

Heather looked at her, and tried to pretend a relaxed smile—but failed miserably.

'I know who you are. I've known since you got on the train. I've often seen your picture in the paper, and on the news. Well, I used to. What's the problem? And more to the point, can I help in any way?'

Heather knew that time was short. A plan improvised itself in her mind.

'Maybe,' she said slowly. 'Actually, I'm in a bit of a fix. I'm expecting to be arrested—if that's the right word—by Green Militia the moment I get off the train. I kind of escaped, or walked out of, detention in London. My husband's being held. Well, in fact he's in hospital and I know they're coming after me again, and my sister-in-law…. Really, you shouldn't have anything to do with me.'

'Tell me what I can do, and I'll decide if it's too risky,' the woman said briskly, all the time nonchalantly arranging her children and their outdoor clothing.

'OK, I have half an idea. It seems the main reason they want to hold on to me is to have some leverage over Peter. And it's not just me, it's Andrea too. If they get me, I don't want them to get hold of Andrea as well. I wonder... would you be able to take Andrea for me? I mean, just down the platform, maybe out of the station. I'm pretty sure they'll be looking for a woman with a young child. With any luck, you'll be able to hand her back to me outside the station. And if not...if you see me being arrested....could you take her to my sister-in-law, she's—'

'Joanna, is it? I know her, I mean I know what she looks like—from the newspapers. Just tell me where to find her.'

'Actually, she's in a café just round the corner from the station. I don't know Liverpool, but she said to go out the Lime Street entrance and to the right, there's a café called Annie's—'

'I know it. I'll find her, if I have to. But, you'll be fine,' she said, putting a reassuring hand on Heather's arm. 'Give me the bag of Andrea's bits and pieces, you don't want to be carrying that, now.'

A young woman, a student at the University, who was standing close by, ready to get off, suddenly whispered to her. 'I'm sorry, I heard what you were saying.'

Heather looked alarmed.

'Don't worry. But just think: if they've seen you on CCTV, they'll know what you're wearing. I'm about your size—why don't you swap coats with me? And hat and scarf too.'

'No, no,' said her friend standing behind her. 'You shouldn't wear her whole outfit. They'll suspect you of something if they stop you. Here, have my scarf to go with her coat, I'll go without. And when we go out, Janet can go separately, while you and I walk along talking all the time like we're old friends. They won't be looking for someone in company like this. You can wear my glasses too, only don't let me bump into anything!'

Heather found herself agreeing quickly as the train came to a halt. She left the train and began to walk arm-in-arm with a complete stranger, talking animatedly about trivia and trying not to look at the Militia who were patrolling the platform. She watched the woman and her children walk a little way ahead, the woman's daughter carrying Andrea like a dutiful big sister. Behind her, the student wearing Heather's coat got off the train, and casually began to walk after them. Heather noticed a couple of Militia nearby suddenly make a move, as if they had noticed someone.

'Don't look back,' said the student walking with her. 'Did you take everything out the pockets that might identify it as yours?'

Heather nodded. 'Yes. God, I hope she's OK. I should never have dragged you into this! I'm so sorry!'

'You didn't. We forced ourselves into your life. We saw the news about your husband this afternoon before we left, on a foreign news website. I was so angry! I used to believe in Don Mason. Not any more! Oh, change the subject, there seems to be some kind of checkpoint here. Checking tickets, and checking faces too, by the look of it. Just be cool!'

Cool! thought Heather. She'd rarely felt less cool. But she felt a great sense of relief as the woman and her family went through with no fuss. Then as she approached the checkpoint, she heard a commotion behind her. The Militia had stopped the student wearing her coat. The student reacted with dramatic anger, creating a diversion so that her friend and Heather could get further away. Distracted, the Militia officers at the checkpoint waved Heather and the girl through.

Heather felt the relief rising in her. Still she kept her eye on Andrea and the woman's family moving out towards Lime Street. Suddenly she heard shouts and footsteps running behind her.

'That's them!' shouted someone, a man's voice. 'I saw them changing coats on the train!'

'Shit!' said the student with Heather.

'Go!' hissed Heather. 'You're not with me!'

Heather looked behind, and could see three or four Militia officers closing in on her, while others rushed forward from the entrance. She darted to her right, away from her companion, away from Andrea, aiming to lead the Militia as far away as possible. The station was quite crowded, and she had to dodge round people, startling some of them into the path of her pursuers.

She couldn't get far. Militia and police came from all corners, or so it seemed to her. When she realised there was no chance of escape, instinctively she ran towards a uniformed police officer, and threw herself in his arms and his mercy.

'Don't let them take me! Don't let them take me,' she gasped. Then as the Militia closed in and demanded her to be handed over, this refrain turned into a scream. 'Don't let them take me! Please, take me into police custody! You don't know what they'll do! Have you seen what they've done to my husband! Check the foreign news! Oh please, protect me! *Please!*'

A large crowd was gathering round now, and Heather's desperate cries echoed up into the roof. The woman with Andrea had stopped, and looked towards the commotion, as did most people in the station.

'Oh Jesus,' she muttered under her breath. 'What to do, what to do?'

'What's mummy doing?' asked Andrea, with an impish smile.

'She's just talking to those men, sweetie. She'll be with us before you know it. Let's go and find your Auntie Joanna, shall we?'

56: Tactical retreat

They were still there, waiting by the car outside. Martin let the curtain fall back into place, and returned to packing the suitcase. Why wasn't Sandy answering her phone? He wanted to alert her to the welcoming committee outside, but she was not answering. Must be using the Underground, he reasoned.

Time for that holiday, he had decided. A tactical retreat to Italy. A time to consider the options. His mind was racing. Over the previous months Martin had been aware of a shifting of the sands. The GEM had tightened their control on the reins of government. But at the same time, a covert opposition had developed within the ranks of government service. And their main tactics were the time-honoured ones of delay and obstruction. Elections were just over the horizon, and everyone expected that the Green Earth government would not get a second term. Martin knew that Don Mason was preparing another purge of dissidents and obstructive neutrals. But Martin had himself been cultivating those he thought would be most influential in the expected post-Green era after the election.

Sandy's escapades today had thrown his careful approach into confusion. He would now inevitably feel the force of any reaction against her in the leadership. It might not be an instant fall from grace, but he could hardly expect things to run smoothly.

He also knew that this sudden holiday would play badly with the GEM leadership, and he would almost certainly be replaced as President of ESCO-LAW. But falling out with the regime would play well with the reversionary interest, who saw him as a professional and restraining hand calming the radicals.

Now he had faced another, more mundane challenge. As he began to open wardrobes and drawers full of Sandy's clothes, he realised that he'd never packed a suitcase for anyone else before in his life! His parents, his previous partners, Sandy—it was always they who had packed for him. This was a challenge. He took a broad interest in what Sandy wore, for sure. It was another matter, though, to choose her wardrobe for a holiday, and to pack the necessary female items—clothes that go with each other, underwear, make-up, perfumes, lotions and creams. A world of mystery. One that he'd always accepted as being another realm, and had rarely enquired within. In the end he decided it didn't matter. They were wealthy enough to buy whatever was necessary, and Sandy always enjoyed shopping.

He packed a smallish suitcase for two people, and if observed it would indicate a short trip. As he left their apartment he heard the lift coming up, and heavy footsteps running in the stair well. He quickly went through the fire doors to the stairs, and ran up half a flight. He saw Green Militia with police in riot gear burst through the doors onto his floor, then hammer on his apartment door.

'Sandy Honeyford? Martin Lang? This is the police. Open the door now!'

There was silence. Slowly he descended the stairs, softly breaking into a run as he passed his own floor. He heard a loud crack and the splintering of wood as the police broke down his door. Clearly they meant business.

One floor down, Martin ran along the corridor and knocked on the door of some neighbours he knew by sight.

'Mind if I use your fire escape?' he said, trying to sound nonchalant.

Martin went down as quietly as he could. With an ease that surprised him, he scaled the shoulder-high wall at the back of the courtyard, into the alleyway behind. Now he could circle round to the Tube station. With any luck he could head Sandy off before she arrived home. He took out his phone to try calling her again.

At the end of the alleyway, he looked furtively round the corner down toward the main road. He could see two police vans. And Sandy arriving home, walking from the direction of the Tube station. Rapidly she was enveloped in a circle of police and Militia, and hustled into the Militia car. It drove away at speed.

'Shit! Shit!' said Martin softly to himself. 'What do I do now?'

Martin could hear voices as he pressed himself back against the wall, breathing heavily.

'Do we wait for Lang?'

'No point. He's done a runner, for sure.'

'Chickenshit closet Grey, or what? Leaving his woman to take the heat.'

'Don't bother. It's her they wanted. He's nobody—he can wait.'

His ears burning, Martin turned up his collar and briskly crossed the road into the next street. Flight or fight, he wondered. Maybe from his exalted position he could try to pull something to get Sandy released. But that was too long a shot. This action came from the top, from Morton if not Mason.

Bluffing them twice in one day? There was no chance. Best to try to pull any levers amongst his contacts from a safe distance.

He flagged down a taxi, and started on the road to exile.

••

Andrea was asleep, oblivious to everything that had been happening. The responsibility now weighed heavily on Joanna Kitson's shoulders. The woman who had brought Andrea to Joanna had been distraught, and Joanna had calmed and comforted her. Now she herself felt a surge of uncontrollable emotion welling up within her. She hoped that Heather would be fine, and of course Peter too. And Sandy too, who had surprised her so much over the past thirty-six hours. Thirty-six hours when Joanna had barely slept, and that too was now taking its toll. She hoped no harm would come to them, that the publicity this incident was generating would be their protection. All the same, she had been fighting for the rights of detainees for too long to be sure of this.

Now she was sure that she too was being pursued by the Green authorities. It made a big difference. It gave her no platform to campaign from. And she had Andrea's welfare to think of. She found that fear, even panic, gave lucidity to her actions. Knowing that Heather had been arrested, she realised the authorities would soon be able to track her through the phones Sandy had given them. So she had thrown her phone into the back of a street sweeper's truck, and had smiled briefly at the thought of the Militia earnestly tracking the truck around the streets of Liverpool.

As originally planned, she had at first headed for Birkenhead and the ferry to Northern Ireland. But there were too many Militia in the area, and panicking a little she had turned away and retreated across the river. Then she had headed for the Lake District.

Joanna was driving Rachel Dean's car. Her thoughts turned to Heather's old friend. How times had changed for Rachel. Her husband, Mark, had taken his own life following months of intensifying depression. His company had finally gone under as he had feared. Hard on the heels of this, Rachel had been hauled before the Green Student Council at her university. Edicts had been promulgated demanding that all teaching should include a much stronger awareness of environmental factors and issues. Rachel's own specialism, History, was very much in the firing line of this campaign.

The Scrutiny Commission for Higher Education, ESCOHED, had issued 'Guidelines for the Transformation of History in Universities'. They argued that History had once focused on political history: 'heroes and great men'. That had been corrected with the development of studies in social history, economic history, women's history, black history. The histories of ordinary people and the oppressed. Now it was time to add environmental history to the mix. No history could be complete without an assessment of the 'Earth impacts of events and historical processes'. The 'landscape history' of old was not enough. What was the impact of the French, or the American, or the Russian Revolution on the environment? The impacts of the World Wars on the natural environment were as profound as their impacts on society, it was argued. Likewise trends such as urbanisation should be studied as much for their ecological impacts as for their social and economic impacts.

All this was fine, up to a point, Rachel had agreed. But in the wake of Mark's suicide and the depth of his bitterness towards the regime, Rachel had used a lecture to deliver a diatribe against political interference in teaching, and attempts by 'undergraduates who had never read a whole book cover-to-cover' to dictate to professional historians how they should teach. She likened the whole process to 'the Cultural Revolution, and the stifling of free thought and independent learning for the glorification of a semi-literate and politically insecure leadership'.

She was roundly denounced as 'elitist' and 'Greyist'. A poster campaign around the University soon led to her suspension, and in due course to re-education.

So Rachel had given her car keys to Heather before boarding the bus for an eco-camp. Joanna felt a sense of responsibility about this too. She wanted to use Rachel's car in an act of defiance that she hoped would somehow make a difference. In any case, she was sure Rachel would approve of its use to try to protect Heather and Andrea. Now she had to get to safety.

Joanna thought at first maybe she could pay a fisherman from one of the Lancashire or Cumbria fishing villages to take her to Ireland. But this was risky. The GEM enjoyed a high level of support in fishing communities since repudiating all EU fishing treaties and banning all foreign ships from British waters, now redefined as extending up to two hundred miles from shore. Instead she decided on an old friend who had 'downshifted' to live a simple though quite well-heeled life in the western Lake District, complete with his own boat.

A few days later she and Andrea were in Ireland, and the following week in America, where Zara Alderney took them under her copious wing.

She said she was honouring a promise to Peter, whom she described as 'the sweetest man with the cutest accent she had ever met'. An emotional but hard-headed and forceful woman, she had identified strongly with Peter's devotion to his family. Unlike Peter, she also understood power completely, and had been anxious from the start about the vulnerability of Peter's position alongside the likes of Mason and Morton. Horrified at Joanna's tale, with typical hyperbole she promised that the full power and resources of the mightiest nation on earth would be used to free Peter and Heather, and to punish their persecutors.

At the same time, Zara withheld from Joanna the more disturbing news that intelligence reports were bringing in about radical measures being developed by extreme elements in the Green Militia.

V

57: The army stirs

King Henry greatly enjoyed the reputation he had acquired as the 'Green King'. He took a strong personal interest in initiatives both on the royal estates and those funded by the government. He enjoyed his meetings with Don Mason, and Mason always made sure he arrived at the Palace armed with briefings on new projects. Mason wasn't just humouring the King. He found him to have a good knowledge of environmental issues, and often his comments provided useful insights especially in the field of organic farming and sustainable communities.

The King was in the West Country, surveying one of his latest projects, a completely energy self-sufficient farm. It was something he had been researching and consulting on for nearly two decades, and was delighted now to put it into action. This was what some people had called the 'Dream Farm'— one that produced zero emissions, produced all its own energy, and recycled all its water and waste, as well as being an efficient and productive farm. He didn't like the term 'Dream Farm'. It smacked of wishful thinking, and too many people during his life had underestimated him, branding him as a dreamer and ignoring his many practical achievements.

'The "Total Farm", then. What do you think of it, General?' he asked as they walked through the site. It was nearly complete, just a few outbuildings still under construction. The King pointed out with warranted pride the biogas digester and renewable energy generators that supplied all the energy needs of the farm, the rainwater and greywater recycling facilities, the habitat enrichment for the farm animals, the use of only local and recycled materials for construction, and a dozen other attributes that made the farm state-of-the-art in terms of green innovation.

'Very impressive, Sir, very impressive indeed.'

General Matthews knew the King quite well. He was from a military family, and his father had served overseas with the King during his military service in the 1970s. Their two families had often spent time together. He knew the King to be a man who was very independent in his thinking, had strong opinions, but was always open to advice and new perspectives. He was also open to hearing criticism, providing it was phrased in the right way, and it did not come from hostile sources.

Matthews was genuinely impressed. The whole farm had been constructed with a great attention to detail and emphasis on engineering and architectural quality, as was to be expected from his father's old friend. The farm buildings were constructed of local materials, and looked positively idyllic, inspired by English traditional rural architecture, yet incorporating the latest innovations in energy efficiency. He was also struck by the enthusiasm of the people working on the project, from the managers through to the engineers, animal technicians, carpenters, labourers and caterers.

They went into the surprisingly high-tech farm office, kicking off their muddy boots at the door, and settling down on the two sofas in the meeting area. All the furniture too was high quality, commissioned from local craftsmen. They were brought tea, with a formality like a scene from the palace. Staff fluttered past seeing to every need, as they first discussed aspects of the project, and then caught up on family news.

'Now, Mark. You didn't only want to see me about my little agricultural hobbies. I think you have something else on your mind?'

General Matthews nodded. The King exchanged glances with his chief attendant, and in an instant they were alone in the room.

'Well, Mark, feel free to get whatever it is off your chest!'

He had been given a difficult brief. He was not the highest ranking general in the army, but he was highly regarded, and most importantly he had a long family friendship with the Royal Family. His fellow officers expected him to be able to explore delicate issues in a less formal way with the monarch.

'To put it bluntly, Sir, there is a certain amount of disquiet in the service, or rather services, at the moment. About certain...trends.'

'Go on.'

'In a nutshell, it's about the politicisation of the army, and the militarization of the Green Volunteers–the so-called "Green Militia".'

'The Green Militia? Isn't "Militia" a metaphor here, like the Salvation Army? Like, "Onward Christian Soldiers" and all that? Or the Boy Scouts?' The King was speaking with his tongue firmly in his cheek. It was his habit to challenge and tease.

Matthews smiled. 'If only they were, Sir, I'm sure we'd all be a lot happier. No, of course I recognise that from the outset they had a role in enforcing the decrees of the Earth Councils, driving forward the Green Revolution, and all that. So far, so good. But we're concerned that things are going too far.

Now of course, the Army plays no role in politics, nor should it. But when politics comes to us, or when a paramilitary body like the Militia starts to assume a leading role in the realm of security, and carries out that role without proper controls…what are we to do?'

'Hmm. What do you mean, "When politics comes to us"? You don't like the attentions of ESCOMIL?'

'ESCOMIL? As originally set up, not a problem, Sir. The environmental performance of the MoD was a bit of a shocker, all in all. At home and in the field, there was a lot we could improve on. And we have done. ESCOMIL did sterling work. The new emphasis on rapid reaction for humanitarian and environmental purposes—we love it! Much preferable to some of the things we've had to do in recent years.'

'Quite. So everything's fine with ESCOMIL?'

'It would have been. But we think it has gone way beyond its brief. It's one thing having "Scrutineers" amongst us, auditing our environmental practices and giving good advice. It's quite another having them—and ever more and more of them—installed amongst us as kind of political commissars. It seems everything we do is under scrutiny, and gets reported back to the centre. Officers at every level get called to account for their actions. Now these Scrutineers want to have a role in promotion boards, getting the GEM faithful into higher positions. And this is happening in all the services, so I'm told. There's a real issue about Military Intelligence too. They've been fighting a rearguard action about what they see as interference and infiltration. MI5 and MI6 I hear are encouraging them to stand firm—they think they've allowed Malcolm Morton's boys too much leeway. It seems a lot of the pressure is over sharing intelligence with our allies…I'm sure you know what I mean.'

'Broadly, yes. More tea?' The King started to pour the tea. As he did so, a maid appeared as if from nowhere to complete the task. 'Thank you. Now please, we need some privacy—complete privacy if you please!'

'Is it safe to talk without being overheard?' asked Matthews, looking a little disconcerted.

'You know, Mark, my entire life I've asked myself the same question. I think I've found a way to deal with it. It doesn't matter whether one is being listened to so much as to who is doing the listening. I'm pretty sure if it's anyone here, it will only be my people. That is, people who, in their own way, look out for me.'

Matthews did not look entirely convinced. Still, he'd set the ball rolling, and the King seemed confident enough to let him continue. 'The intelligence sharing is two-way, of course. It seems Morton's people are worried about what we in the military are hearing from the Americans, too.'

'And what are you hearing from them?'

'Quite enough to give us cause for concern. Details of systematic abuse in the eco-camps. That the population in the camps is around eight times the official number. That elements of the Militia are being trained up and equipped as combat units. That the government is planning to pull us out of NATO. That another purge is being prepared of senior armed forces personnel.'

'I see.'

'And that there are more extreme elements within the Green Earth government and Militia who plan to take things much further. Deindustrialisation. Population control. Measures that will require some degree of coercion, I'm sure. Is that what the Militia is being prepared for? Or do they expect the army to play a role? If so, I'm sure it would be an unwilling role….'

'All this comes from the Americans? Do they have real evidence for any of this? I mean, they have been known to over-egg things a bit when they want their way, haven't they?'

'If they're half right, then we have problems, I think,' Matthews replied. 'And we've also heard rumours that Mason is going to cancel the elections.'

'Yes, my spies have told me that too.'

'Elections we would expect them to lose…'

'But Mark, if Parliament passes an Act to extend their term of office, what is to be done? They are quite within their rights to do it, even if it's not exactly in the spirit of the constitution.'

'And you would give the Royal Assent to such an Act, even if you suspected it was purely in the interests of one party, and not in the national interest?'

'What are you asking me to do, General? Throw them out of office? Sounds like we're talking about some kind of coup—and you want me to be the centre of it?'

General Matthews looked down for a moment, before looking up boldly and continuing: 'I think the key question, Sir, is about upholding the Constitution. I remember you saying that it's the role of the monarchy in our democracy to preserve the constitution, defend the rule of law and keep everything in balance.'

'Quite so.'

'But what happens if a democratically elected government abuses the powers at its disposal to flout the law, create its own private armed force outside the army and police, sets up its own system of punishment and control to bypass the legal and penal systems, and then misuses its privileges to put itself permanently in power?'

'Put like that, General, it sounds quite alarming. But it also sounds to me as if the army itself is getting quite political these days.'

'Not political, I wouldn't say that. But we have an acute awareness of our role in protecting the nation, and maintaining its stability. And of our loyalty to you as our Commander-in-Chief, and to Parliament.'

'We've known each other a long time, Mark. Let's have some straight talking, shall we. It seems you're saying either: 1) I have to intervene to end this government, or 2) the armed forces will stage a coup to remove them from power. Is that right?'

'Not exactly, Sir. I think it's more: 3) both the King and the army must be prepared to do what is necessary, if or when it becomes necessary. We both have roles as guarantors of the Constitution. We cannot stand by and see democracy being whittled away, and then find it's too late to recover it. Nor can we stand by while one party creates a state within a state.'

'I see. And what if the American intelligence you have received is, shall we say, flawed?'

'Hopefully everything I've told you is wrong: the camps will let everyone out, the Militia will spend their days planting vegetables for the nation, and the elections will run their normal course. But do you think that likely, Sir?'

'I–I have my concerns. But what you are talking about seems a little–a little unprecedented.'

'True. But many other things happening at the moment are unprecedented. If things do turn out for the worse, as many people feel they will, then we need to be prepared. Need to plan for every eventuality, however much unthinkable. In normal circumstances, of course, it wouldn't be necessary. But these are not normal circumstances.'

General Matthews paused, but the King did not reply.

'Perhaps there is something that can be done, rather than waiting to see if the worst comes to the worst,' continued Matthews.

'Go on.'

'Something could be done to regularise the situation. In particular, the situation in the camps. The Mason government could be invited to hand over security at the camps to the army. They can still run the re-education aspects, such as they are. But we, and the Military Police in particular, can make sure that the security is run professionally, and that interrogations don't go the Kitson way.'

'Yes, that was appalling, wasn't it? Mason assures me that they're getting that sorted out. There'll be no repetition of that. The mavericks involved are being brought to book.'

'But are they, Sir? Where is Peter Kitson now? Where is his wife? Where is Sandy Honeyford who blew the lid on the whole thing? We understand that Zara Alderney has taken a very personal interest in their situation, and has asked us to use our best efforts to find where they are and to ensure their safety. It seems their daughter is staying at her house...'

'Along with the formidable Joanna, I understand. And I'm sure Mason will say the Americans are over-reliant on Ms Kitson's information...'

'One thing you could do, Sir, is test the waters. Put what I've suggested to Mason. See how he reacts. And why not simply ask him about the rumours of a ten-year term?'

The King nodded slowly.

'And though I am loathe to say this, Sir, I feel I must. You have identified yourself quite closely with the Mason regime. It would be most unfortunate if you were taken to be complicit with any anti-democratic measures they might take...'

'If they do...'

'I think there's enough evidence of a general slide towards what we fear. One can't leave it too late to do the right thing. Your Total Farm is a sign that you can be a flag-bearer for what is good in the Green Revolution, while they can shoulder the responsibility for what has gone off track. As long as the world has enough time to see that you are not one of them.'

'Quite. How's General Montague's wife, by the way? Is she recovering well?'

The serious discussion was over, leaving the King with plenty to think about.

●●

At their weekly PM's briefing at Buckingham Palace, Mason naturally refused to accept the principle that the army could run the camps.

'It misses the point completely!' he argued. 'I think the camps have largely served their purpose, and soon we'll be moving on to a new phase. Yes, there are too many people in them, and we'll be sending them home soon. The Earth Councils and the Tribunals can play a role in re-educating people within the community, rather than sending everyone away. The truth is, we've been somewhat overwhelmed. But the inmates have taken part in some truly amazing projects, and go back to their communities with new skills and values. When you're next up in Scotland, or over at Sandringham, you should take the opportunity to visit one of our new Eco-communities.'

As for extending their period in office and militarising the Militia, Mason denied them completely. 'Idle rumour,' he assured.

58: In the West Highland eco-camp

'You know, it ain't so bad 'ere. See, I've even lost some weight–the missus will be well pleased! And the work's not so bad. I've always worked outdoors. Bloody freezin', but this tree-plantin', ditch-diggin', navvie-work really, it's fine by me. I'm a good boy! I work 'ard–model prisoner, that's me!'

Sam Sharma was showing Heather Kitson the ropes in the West Highland Eco-Camp. Sam's endless rabbiting was a breath of fresh air after the seemingly endless interrogations and indoctrination sessions. The whole experience had been so terrifying, so surreal.

'Yep, model prisoner I've been. It ain't enough for 'em, though, is it? They don't just wanna change what I do, they wanna change who I am, the bastards. Oh, pardon me, ladies present!'

Heather smiled at Sam's old-fashioned apology for his language.

'Worse than any street-bully I ever met, an' I can tell you, I've met a few of 'em in my time. Y'know, when I was a nipper, my big gob was always gettin' me in trouble. I dunno why, I couldn't resist it! I always 'ad to take the piss outta the bigger kids, especially the ones who thought they was 'ard. Teachers too, and the cops. And the big kids would always thump me! Whack, like that! But in those days, when they thumped you, that was it. Soon I'd be their cheeky little pet, kinda court jester-like. I could say whatever I bloody wanted, and they'd all laugh.

'Not this crew, though. Never laugh–humourless bunch of pricks. Oh, pardon me! Too bloody serious by 'arf. What do they call my problem? "Attitude crime". Not thinkin' right. How am I goin' to deal with that? If they act like stuck-up twerps, how can I think differently about them?

'I thought I was in here 'cos of the bleedin' bins. I could put that right. I want to put that right, and go 'ome to Kelly and the kids. I'll sort out me recyclin' real good and proper, sir. Yes sir, no sir, three bloody bin bags full, sir. "Just do what they bloody want," Kelly says. Not that easy, is it? I can change what I do. I just can't change the way I bloody think about it. I just think they're a load of bloody wankers. Oh, pardon my French, ma'am, gone an' done it again, eh? This lot, they couldn't run my market stall, and they want to run the bleedin' country!'

As Sam was about to apologise for his language again, Heather put her hand on his arm to stop him. 'I've heard far worse. You don't need to mind your Ps and Qs with me,' she said.

'You're very understanding, Miss. But I was brought up not to swear in front of ladies, and I can tell you're a real lady! You know, one thing that gets my goat? All my working life I've been paying more and more for less and less. I mean, to the government and the Council. Take the bins. When I was a lad, some big burley geezer with a big cheery grin would come down our alley into the back yard, hoik a big metal dustbin on 'is shoulder, take it out to the van, empty it, then bring it to the back of the 'ouse again. Ask 'im to take a bit extra, no problem.

'Then they started all this bin-bag malarkey. You have to put the bags out yourself. And they wouldn't take no extra. Saves the bin men coming into each 'ouse. More efficient, they said. Poncey gits. For them it's more efficient 'cos they got every bleedin' 'ouseholder doin' 'alf the work! Then some wanker in Watford strains his back liftin' a black bag. Should learn to lift proper, dozy git! So all the Councils in the country go lary about 'ealth and safety, and the next thing we've all got these wheelie bins to trundle out once a week. Can't leave nuffink by the side, nuffink poking out the top. If the lid's half an inch open, they'll take the top bag out the bin, and leave it on the pavement. They can lift a black bag then, when it comes to not delivering a service, can't they? What a shower!

'Then all this recyclin' malarkey starts. Now we don't just take the rubbish out for them, we have to bleedin' sort it for 'em as well. Council Tax goes up too, to pay for more inspectors to check we're doing it right! That's even before these Green Earth twots come along. Now we 'ave six bins in the back yard! Three big wheelie bins, and three big plastic boxes. No room for no bloody flowers no more! Then they fine you if you mix your plastics with your bottles or some such bollocks.

'Then in the market, more of the same, only with a bunch of wallies snooping around and 'assling you all the time. The more you pay in service charge, for the market stall, I mean, the more you 'ave to do the bloody job that they used to do for 'alf the cost. I wouldn't mind doin' a bit of recycling, but why should I pay through the nose then do it all myself? Don't make no sense. But shhh, Sam, you ain't thinkin' right again!'

Heather smiled. 'Sometimes you just have to toe the line a bit. It's the only way to get through.'

'Sure, you're right. But as I see it, life shouldn't be so complicated. Think about it! Grow something, make something, sell something. That's all there is to it! People been doin' it since we came down from the trees. It's as old as the human race. But now we've always got some plonker with a college degree and a poker up 'is arse tellin' us: "You've got to do it this way, you can't do it that way…!" It does me 'ead in, it does! Then they slap a whole load of taxes on you so they can pay wankers like this to 'assle the 'ell out of you for not doing it the way they want this week!

'Y'know, there's always been people who know how to live your life better than you do. When I was a young man, all these young twerps from the area buggered off to Pakistan or Afghanistan or some-other-bloody-stan, then come back all radical, with straggly beards and dressed like my grandpa. Hundreds of 'em went. Lot of people hushed that up now, 'cos lots of the stupid pillocks never came back, got shot to bits fighting for stuff they didn't know anything about. In Iraq, or Russia, or Kashmiristan or somewhere. One of me mates, Ali, went and 'e comes back an' complained to me, "They kept calling us Arabs, Sam. 'Go home, ya bloody Arabs, we don't want you here!' they'd say". And he kept saying, "I'm not a bloody Arab, I'm English. I'm your Muslim brother!" And they'd chase him off with a pitchfork or a broom— sometimes with guns too.

'That's what comes of mindin' other people's business. Anyway, these earnest young goats all come back to London tellin' us, "live like this, wear this, you can't do that, you can't wear that…" They don't even know I'm not a bloody Muslim, it's just that lots of my friends are! My mum was a Muslim, mind, but my dad was Hindu. You know, they fell in love in India, but everyone gave them 'assle 'cos they're from two different religions. So they run away and come to England. They come to England in the 1960s to escape from bleedin' prejudice and busybodies, can you believe it?

'All they wanted to do was mix in with everyone else, none of this religion stuff. I mean, Dad had the gods up in the house, little statues like, and got me mum to dust them every day, but that was about it. I was the runt of the litter, me, and they decided they want to give me an English name to fit in better. So they called me Samuel. Bloody Jewish name, can you believe it? I loved my dad to bits, but he could never do anything right! Didn't know anything else except his own opinion, but he stuck by it, and he never did no one no harm. Maybe that's what I'm like too, what do you think? I'd like to be, at any rate.

'Well, I married a lovely English lady, my Kelly, and we have a lovely pick-and-mix assortment of kids, and life is good. Then this lot come along, the Green Volunteers, I mean. Just like the goat-boys, only no beards. Someone else to tell us what to do. In my book, people should just *mind their own business*. When people spend too much time minding other people's business, that's when the world goes to pot.'

For Heather, Sam's little speech was both entertaining and disturbing. After all, Peter was a politician, one of the constant busybodies who disrupted people's lives, always wanting to change things in accordance with their view of the common good.

'But Sam,' she said. 'Don't you think there are some people who really want to help people and improve the lives people have?'

'Sure, and I know who you're thinkin' of. Strikes me he was one of the good guys, and there ain't many of 'em. But with all due respect, my love, he may 'ave 'ad the best of motives, but didn't he support those Earth Councils and all that busybody stuff? And his party never did a lot for our area when they was in charge. No, the thing is, nice people can't be good politicians. The mean guys will always stuff 'em. But I don't mean to... Anyway, I heard he had a bad time. How is he?'

'I don't know, Sam. I saw him in hospital, and he wasn't in a good way then. They won't tell me anything. Is there any way of finding out? You seem to know how to handle yourself here...'

'I know me way around the system, that's true. I can sometimes get some news. I can get messages out, but that's easier than getting news you can rely on. This place is like anywhere. People need things, or think they do. And that's all you need for a market, and every market needs a Sam Sharma.'

'I've got nothing to trade with, though...'

'Don't worry about that. In a place like this, everyone becomes resourceful. And I like you, you're a real lady. So I'll see if I can find some news of hubby, out of goodwill. Or on account, perhaps!'

'And Andrea, you know, my little one—did she and Joanna really get away? Do be careful, though. Don't let people think you're part of the so-called "Kitson Circle"–that's not good for your health.'

'Look, you're paying me back already,' said Sam, looking down to the ground.

'What do you mean?'

'I've been in camps for more than two years. I've been questioned and 'arassed by the boys and girls in green, and given jobs to do and had thanks from my fellow "criminals". But you're the first person in all this time who's ever shown any concern for me actual 'ealth and well-being. Like I said, you're a real lady!'

Sam escorted Heather around the camp, or rather to all the areas they were allowed to go. She remembered the camp she had visited in Wales, and this was similar. The inmates, all dressed in orange—it makes them easier to spot if they go walkabout, Sam had said—did not generally look ill-used or malnourished. But not many people smiled. She exchanged glances of recognition with a couple of people, journalists she had come across somewhere with Peter. She was not anxious to renew the acquaintance.

Suddenly Sam took her by the arm and gently turned her round, leading her back in the opposite direction. 'Buses,' he said. 'When the buses come in, make yourself scarce, OK?'

'Why?' asked Heather, puzzled.

'Just take my word for it, life here is better than life anywhere those buses will take you. Let me tell you something, a word of advice on how to survive in life. Me, I learned nuffink at school. I learned to read at home, learned me maths on the market. I learned nuffink, except how not to get picked. Never volunteer. Always do what *you* want, not what others want you to do. Especially if they want you to do it for free. Y'know I spent twelve years of PE lessons going to the back of the queue. Know what I mean? They make you line up to use each bit of gym kit. But the smart ones like me, and the chubby ones too for that matter, spend all their time going to the back of the line. Every now and then a PE teacher says, "Have you gone over the vault, Sam?" "Yes, sir," I says. He doesn't believe it, but all the other kids back me up.

'Same thing here. Always sidle yourself to the back of the line if you want to survive. Some people never learn, though. One girl, Stella, lovely lady really, put herself forward to go to North Camp. When I first come here, I was sent out to help build the cabins there. Very tough work. But I was back here before they started shipping people out there. After that, loads of trucks went past here every day heading for North Camp. I told her not to go, but she wouldn't listen! Said she had to find out what was going on there. "Call it professional curiosity," she said. I called it bloody stupid, but she just laughed. Came back two days ago, thin as a rake and covered in bruises, hasn't said a word to anyone.

'Not only her. Some of the Militia twats as well, they jump on the buses and an' all but some of 'em soon wish they'd decided different-like. The ones who want to prove themselves. Ambitious ones, think they're special, or chosen or something. One girl, unfriendly, serious sort, spouting all the usual bullshit, only really meaning it. She come back looking like she'd seen a ghost. I saw her in the medical centre. No bruises, or anything like that. Just kind of like she was hypnotised. One day, she took herself up to that watchtower over there, and jumped off.'

'Oh my God!'

'Didn't die though. Broke her back and dozens of other bones, so they told me. And she screamed. Hadn't said a word for a week, then after she jumped she screamed through three days and three nights. Then a chopper come and takes her away, still screaming and wailing. Don't ask me what's that all about. Except, don't get on a bus to North Camp.'

'My God, that's so awful, Sam,' exclaimed Heather. 'But tell me about this Stella. I might know her. Is it Stella Walton?'

'Oh, I dunno. Never knew her surname. Nice girl, thirtyish, very lively before she went away. Some kind of journalist, like half the other wasters here. Very nosey. Always wanting me to smuggle messages back and forth. I did it a couple of times, but felt it was kind of dangerous to be around her. I said to her, food and clothing only. Nothing dodgy or political. See, she's a busybody on the other side. Steer clear of the lot of them, I say.'

The hairs had stood up on the back of Heather's neck when she heard the name Stella. And by the description, this had to be her. Sam advised Heather to steer clear, even if she was a long lost twin. But seeing that Heather would not take no for an answer, he pointed out the cabin where she was staying.

Inside the gloomy hut, Stella Walton was resting on a lower bunk in the corner of the room. The bunk above her and the ones next to her were stripped bare, and evidently unoccupied.

'Stella Walton?' Heather asked tentatively.

'Don't come near me!' Stella said urgently, and hoarsely. Then a note of recognition. 'Heather Kitson? Oh, I hope not....' she groaned.

'Yes, it's me, Heather Kitson.'

Heather had been building up stores of anger and resentment against Stella ever since Peter's arrest. Why had Stella dragged them into all this? In truth, these feelings had ebbed and flowed, as she knew Stella was not the whole cause of their problems. They had made decisions too. And the way things were turning out, she knew that Peter's involvement with the Mason government would have been likely to end badly one way or another. Now, seeing Stella again, she felt a confused mix of emotions, but mostly compassion seeing the condition she was in.

Despite Stella's warning, Heather advanced into the room, where she could see Stella better. As her eyes became accustomed to the gloom, she could see someone that she would never have recognised as Stella Walton. Her hair had thinned and was lank and untidy. Her face was emaciated, almost skull-like, her cheekbones very prominent. She coughed intermittently, and seemed to be in pain when she did so. Large brown and purplish bruises like stains on her skin stretched up from under her collar to her jaw.

'What happened to you?' gasped Heather. 'Did they beat you too?'

'No,' said Stella. 'I wish they had. I've been so sick. I thought I was dying. It was so awful. Terrifying too.'

'What was it?'

'They said it was an outbreak of a new strain of flu at the camp. What I had wasn't flu. I heard them talking. It was plague.'

'Plague?' gasped Heather. 'Bubonic plague? Are you serious?'

'The Black Death. I can't describe the pain I was in. Heather, they want to kill us all! That's what this is all about. They want to reduce the population, and this is how they're going to do it!'

For a moment Heather was too stunned to speak. 'It doesn't make any sense! Why would they let you go if they want to kill everybody?'

'Have they let me go? I hadn't noticed!' Stella said bitterly. 'People are dying up there at North Camp, while doctors and Militia in white coats watch it all and record it. Believe me! I was put in a large room with sick people in it. Then I became sick, they watched me for a while, then treated me. As I was recovering, they exposed me to something else—quite blatant. I was in this kind of glass cubicle in their labs, and they pumped something into the air, just like that, and they watched it all. After that I got sick again, really, really, horrifyingly sick. Lumps were springing up all over my body, and I could barely breath. I was sure I was going to die. Then they treated me again, and after a while shipped me back here. They were injecting people with stuff too and ... I saw people die, in agony, while they watched and made notes. They've used me as some kind of guinea pig, to test different diseases on me. I'm sure of it. I don't know if I'm contagious any more, but I warn people to keep their distance all the same.'

'But why bring you back here?' asked Heather, barely able to believe anything she heard.

'Why bring you here at this time, too?' asked Stella. 'They want to see what we know.'

And Heather thought, *she's telling me too much again.*

'As for me,' Stella continued, 'I'm done for. There's no way I'll live through this. Even if they decide to let me go, I must have had so much damage done to my organs, they could pack up at any time. And quite honestly, I don't want to live any more. Except for one thing. To expose what these bastards are up to. Oh, oh, how's your husband?'

'I don't know. In a pretty bad way when I last saw him, nearly a month ago.'

'I'm sorry. They took him, did they? Maybe it's my fault'

No '*maybe*', thought Heather, but she could not bring herself to say it.

'Did he pass on the research?'

'We didn't have a chance, really. Just as we were getting to grips with it, the world caved in. They beat him very badly, you know, Stella.'

Stella sighed a deep sigh, which ended in a spasm of coughing. 'I'm genuinely sorry. Sorry for him, and sorry for anything I've brought on you. But this business is bigger than all of us. We suffer now. But if they're not stopped, how many others will suffer? Doing nothing, or looking the other way, minding our own business—these aren't options. How can we—'

'Oh Stella, don't try and drag me into anything else! I'm the wrong kind of person for all this. I have a two-year-old daughter—and I don't know where she is! I gave her to a complete stranger to take her to safety. Would I have done this if I didn't already know it was really bad? I hope to God she's safe, with my sister-in-law. And I have another child on the way,' Heather said, patting her stomach. 'My first duty is to survive for my children my family. Nothing else! That's all I live for.'

'I won't argue with that,' said Stella after a moment. 'I wish you all the luck in the world. But if somehow you get out before they unleash whatever they're planning...be sure and tell someone, OK?'

'Sure,' said Heather softly, her head bowed.

The following day Heather brought a bowl of soup out to Stella's hut. But Stella was nowhere to be found.

59: The Counter-Revolution takes shape

The Olsen residence in Stockholm was now a hive of activity—counter-revolutionary activity. Patrick Baxter, the former Prime Minister, was a frequent visitor there. He felt more than ever vindicated in his earlier hard-nosed approach to the GEM. If only people had listened!

American envoys came, liaised and moved on. High level discussions were carried on by videoconference with President Wilding and leading members of his administration. A daily stream of EU officials passed through the hall. Britain's membership of the European Union had been suspended, citing the withholding of payments to EU funds and the violating of several treaties and agreements. As Britain's diplomatic isolation increased, so the Olsen house was seen as the seat of the next UK government. The presence of military personnel—British, American and European—added to the sense of purpose and importance.

Colonel Demont Ashton had been appointed by the American State Department to liaise with the government-in-waiting. He was said to be close to Zara Alderney—more than professionally close. His authority and influence were well-respected. Now he, too, was a regular visitor at the Olsen residence.

Sir James Olsen was holding forth about the character of the regime they sought to replace. 'It's not only to do with their politics. This is what happens when people who are naturally subversive get hold of the machinery of government. They are addicted to skulduggery and cloak-and-daggerism. The leopard can't change its spots!'

'James, remember this is our daughter you're talking about!' said his wife, Lady Frances, as she served tea.

'Yes, and she always was subversive. Even her marriage was a subversive act!'

Ashton gave an embarrassed laugh. 'But, all the same, I understand you have a special request.'

'Yes, we have,' said Lady Frances. 'We know she's, as it were, "one of them". Lately, though, it seems she's been out of the picture, politically. We understand that she's not entirely enamoured of all the things that have been going on since those wretched Animalists joined the circus.'

'The long and short of it,' said Sir James, 'is that if the worst comes to the worst, your troops are going to be funnelling in through the East Anglian air bases—those that are left.'

'That's the plan,' Ashton confirmed.

'We'd like you to spare some manpower, if possible, to see that Jessica and our grandchildren are protected. From any backlash, that is. No doubt you'll want to make a bee line for their place anyway—could well be a lot of evidence that needs to be seized.'

'All seems reasonable to me,' said Ashton. 'And no need to be shy about asking personal favours. I'm carrying a long list of personal priorities for Secretary Alderney, though I've a feeling Joanna Kitson is the author of many of them.'

'Ah yes, what a story,' said Lady Frances. 'So many people have their own personal tragedies tied up in these events. Though I hope of course, this tragedy has a happy ending, and the Kitson family can be reunited and live the rest of their lives in peace.'

'Amen to that,' said Ashton. 'I'd like you to tell me more about the family. I've met Joanna, who I think is absolutely extraordinary, and heard a lot about her brother and sister-in-law. It seems they are very close. Zara is very fond of them'

'Well, I didn't know Kitson very well personally,' said Sir James. 'But I heard a fair deal about him from colleagues who worked closely with him. Quite highly regarded. Honest sort of fellow, bags of integrity. But the word is despite spending a lifetime in politics, he never really understood power. Thought it was all about Parliament and majorities. Lot more to it than that.'

'Actually, thinking about the Kitsons, there's a connection with our Martin, isn't there? Martin Lang, that is,' said Lady Frances.

'I've heard of him,' said Ashton.

'Well, he's working closely with Baxter and the Co-ordination Committee now,' said Sir James. 'I always used to think of him as a bit of an unprincipled chancer when I first got to know of him. No fixed principles, always networking to find the best route to the top of the tree, you know the sort.'

'Sounds like the perfect Whitehall bureaucrat,' teased Lady Frances. 'Actually, he's completely devastated by what happened to his girlfriend, Sandy Honeyford. You know, the one who—'

'Yes, I know of her,' said Ashton. 'Joanna never stops singing her prais-es. Joanna has also been in touch with Martin a lot recently. Seems there was an old friendship which cooled while he was close to the Masonites.'

'I'm sure they have a common interest in finding Sandy alive and well,' observed Lady Frances. 'Poor Martin is so downcast. I was trying to give him a little comfort, and you know what he said? He said, "I don't deserve any kindness. I don't even deserve to be thought of as a human being after what I've done, or rather what I've not done". I don't know what he did or didn't do that's so bad, but he didn't at all seem the heartless amoral opportunist of popular rumour. I was worried he's going through some kind of breakdown.'

'Yes, Baxter and I were worried too for a while,' added Sir James. 'But it seems he's channelling all his angst into working to end the regime and to finding his beloved. He seems possessed of a demonic energy. Never sleeps, they say.'

'Well, I'm going to leave you gentlemen here to talk about things I probably shouldn't be hearing. Nice to see you again, Colonel Ashton,' said Lady Frances, taking her leave.

'What's the latest news from Washington then, Colonel?' asked Sir James.

'You know, whenever you ask me that, I always suspect you know more than I do!' laughed Ashton.

'I keep my ear to the ground, it's true,' said Sir James, 'but what I hear is a mixture of fact and rumour. I like to have everything confirmed, not leave anything to chance. I don't want to risk acting on false information or desper-ate optimism.'

'OK, here's what's cooking. President Wilding is determined to act, and is sure he can take Congress with him, on humanitarian grounds. But if the circumstances demand, we act first, get permission afterwards.'

'Yes, we always say it's easier to get forgiveness than permission.'

'Sure. Our satellites and AWACS and, er, the other stuff we don't talk about, they're picking up a lot of noise that's not too good. The militarization of the Green SS is speeding up, for sure. Orders for military equipment from UK suppliers that were originally commissioned by the Saudis and Indone-sians—APCs and other light armour, automatic weapons, helicopters—these are being commandeered and diverted to the Militia. Seems a base in Essex is the main destination. Training seems to be a key issue, and they're drafting in ideologically approved regulars to do the business.

'There's also one helluva lot of activity at the camps in Scotland and Wales. New inmates arriving, shifting them to and from satellite camps. And a lot of Militia movements to and from all the camps as well. Some people there for just a day or two. Something's going down, for sure.

'And the most disturbing thing—a lot of talk of bodies. Deaths. Burials. All very hush hush. People talk and don't talk at the same time. Are you guys hearing this too?'

'A little, but not much,' replied Sir James. 'The thing is, our spooks were caught with their trousers down when the GEM came in. They've been well and truly purged. It seems Mason, or Morton at any rate, had moles coming up through the ranks well before they came to power. We thought we were infiltrating them, but they outsmarted our boys for sure. Still, all is not lost. We've still got some reliable sources inside, and we've been able to build up new resources—mixture of old hands, freelancers and some of our foreign specialists. We've had some news of deaths too. At first we put it down to bad conditions, but it seems there are big differences between the camps. And it's always worse in these satellite camps for some reason. They could be special punishment camps, what do you think?'

'We think it's more than that. These top security satellite camps are the focus for so much Militia activity, we think it must be more. They're building up to something really big. And quite frankly, we don't like it at all.'

'What is your analysis of this "something really big"? ' asked Sir James.

'OK, we think the zealots have taken control of the Militia. Like the lunatics have taken over the asylum. How much the likes of Mason and Turner know about it, we're not sure. But we're sure Morton is in the thick of it. Pearson too. And it's about going beyond the so-called "Second Revolution". These guys want something apocalyptic. A new heaven and a new earth. They want to transform society, and whatever they're going to do, it's really going to hurt. The President thinks it's to do with de-urbanisation. Like Cambodia maybe. Moving a whole lot of people into model communities. They've been building these with forced labour in the camps. Now they want to coerce people into them. Hence the extra armour for the Militia. The other strand we've come across in the chatter is population control. Maybe compulsory sterilisation, Indian style.'

'Too many "maybes" in all this, don't you think? We need more facts. How imminent is all this? And how soon could the combined forces go in?'

'On the first one, we just don't know. There's still a lot of movement to the camps, which means they're still in the preparation phase. As for our combined forces, we reckon about ten or eleven weeks.'

'Ten or eleven weeks? That takes us into May,' said Sir James. 'What if we need a more rapid response? Can we prepare a contingency for that?'

'We may have to, indeed. But we're talking about dealing a decisive blow to end the regime. We don't want to risk half measures that allow the Green Militia to start some kind of guerrilla war. We also need to be sure about the de-greening process and rebuilding a stable government. We've had a few too many regime-change fuck-ups in recent years: we want to get this right first time.'

'Absolutely. We're pretty much prepared for a transitional regime now, restoring the old systems and jettisoning the Green institutions and personnel, and anyone too compromised by them. Lang's been doing astonishing work through his contacts in preparing who should do what, where and when. We have to exercise a seamless transition, with everything working as it should do straight away. Baxter's worried about his legitimacy as caretaker PM, and wants elections within three months for government and local councils too. Says it's essential for stability and a return to the British way of life. I'm inclined to agree.'

'Tall order. Depends on a lot of things. One problem, though,' said Ashton. 'Your Green King. He's a bit tainted, but you Brits are rather attached to your Royals, aren't you? Are you ready to ditch him, or is he essential to stability?'

Sir James looked thoughtful, wondering how much to tell the Americans, especially about his personal reservations. 'We think the monarchy is absolutely essential in the regime change process. They have a theoretical constitutional role, but most of all it's the historic and emotional connection with the people that's important. If he's onside, it'll be much easier for people to accept the legitimacy of what we are doing. A conflict with him would be very damaging. An abdication could be damaging too. Some of our people have sounded him out. Seems he's not irreversibly conjoined with Mason. But he's very emotionally attached to Greenery. He may be a very reluctant passenger on the ride to restoration.'

'Well, our view is that if we want continuity, we need to do a Hirohito on him. Adapt him to the revised order of things. Otherwise, your Royals may find themselves going the way of the Italian and Greek royals. The best thing would be if he could actively support us. Any chance?'

'Not likely at the moment. We've taken some soundings, but he kind of stonewalled the approach. But we've sown some seeds, and we can work on it.'

'How about the humanitarian effort? I hear the food shortages are biting very deep,' asked Ashton.

'In some places, they are. This localised production campaign has been an unmitigated disaster since the subsidies ran out. People depend almost totally on the black market now. But it seems our capacity to produce food remains good, in principle. Another year and it could be a different story. The EU agencies are standing by with food aid. We think the big three supermarkets can restock in a few weeks, but the risk is of being overwhelmed by demand. This is going to have to be well-managed. But we Brits are generally an orderly lot. We'll rise to the occasion, and queue politely.'

So the discussion ranged across the issues, confirming details and highlighting areas where more action was needed. Then they came to the question of prosecutions. Baxter's view was that any prosecutions should be carried out on the basis of British law prior to the Green Revolution. The Americans thought it might be necessary to have a special international tribunal to deal with the whole question of a government committing and encouraging illegal actions.

'The danger is,' said Ashton, 'that there'll be plenty of evidence to catch the small fry, but there'll be room for "reasonable doubt" when it comes to nailing the guys at the top.'

'Martin Lang's been working on that too,' said Sir James. 'He's been detailing all the possible sources of evidence, and is working out an action plan to have them seized before anyone gets a chance to destroy them. We need to have this as a major priority, and the troops on the front line need to know that it is top priority. Actually, Lang has some of his most trusted sources gathering evidence already. He's leaving no stone unturned in his search for Sandy Honeyford, and finding a lot of useful sources in the process. He says we need a Special Commission of Investigation with the power to call in anyone and gather all evidence prior to prosecution. I'm happy with that, and it will give the whole process a clear focus.'

Demont Ashton now prepared to ask the question that had gone begging at the start of their conversation. 'You said, Sir James, that you want us to protect your daughter Jessica when the day comes. How about Dave

Barrington? Are you happy to throw him to the wolves—or at least to Lang's Commission?'

Sir James' face clenched into a long-suffering grimace. 'I don't think there's any option. He's one of the GEM leadership. And he's been in charge of all these Climate Change Projects, running construction sites with forced labour. We know people have been abused in his work camps, and now we hear they're dying from exhaustion and malnutrition. There's no option. He has to face the music.'

60: MacLean back in the fray

It was a grim and cold Trevor MacLean who made the journey east towards Balmoral. He had proposed a Highlands-focused story on the launch of the new model farm on the royal estates there, a Total Farm on the lines of the much celebrated one on the King's estates in the South-West of England. His producer, always under pressure for more genuinely green stories, had given the idea his blessing, despite the admonitions from on high to keep a close eye on MacLean.

In the Inverness BBC centre it had been noted that Trevor MacLean was no longer so annoyingly effervescent and full of himself. Now he could even be described as subdued, and was rarely in the office, preferring to work from home. Life was less risky for his colleagues when he lay low, so these absences were welcomed whenever there was pressure from the Green authorities. The writ of ESCOMEDIA, however, was relatively weak up in Inverness, and though one had to be careful, journalists there did not encounter the same kind of pressures as their colleagues in London, Manchester or Edinburgh. Locally, MacLean's intermittent trips to Edinburgh were seen as a sign that at last he was learning his lesson and was aiming to ingratiate himself with the new powers in the BBC.

In fact, MacLean spent most of his time in Edinburgh closeted with Donny Patterson, building as clear a picture as possible of GEM secret agendas—who was doing what, and when and how population reduction plans would be put into effect. If what they were uncovering were true—always this big 'if' hovering in the background. The concept was so outrageous, they needed to be more sure. But every new bit of information they uncovered, every 'secure' online conversation they tapped into, added to the likelihood.

Donny also became aware of the authorities closing in on their activities. Finally, he had decided it was time to make tracks. He left a message on one of his 'ultra-secure' message boards, telling Trevor that the game was up, and to go with what they had. Donny had also 'rigged' the message board so that after detecting Trevor's last entry and log-out it would delete itself. As Trevor read the message and logged out, an alert announced in red letters,

'This message board will self-destruct in five seconds', in true Mission Impossible style. Geek humour. But all trace of this location had indeed evaporated.

It brought a tired and anxious smile to Trevor's face. It was decision time. Now it was time to do something with all this research. Both he and Donny knew inside themselves that every time they decided they needed more hard evidence, it was also a convenient excuse for delaying the need for action. But neither of them were really the action-hero type.

'A man of action must be a man of limited vision, and a man of vision is usually a man of limited action,' Trevor had said, loosely quoting Dostoevsky.

'Aye, it's great comfort for souls like ourselves who canna do anything in the real world that we're hot on the vision stuff,' Donny had joked.

For people working in the media, there was an obvious course open to them. They knew how to get the news out. They discussed this often. How best to avoid Morton's bloodhounds and get the news out to the foreign press, allowing it to filter back into England. But they recognised a number of problems with this option. It was not so easy to get information to the foreign press—though Donny no doubt had the skills to do this while minimising the risk of detection. Another problem was that it was all deniable. While they had built a detailed dossier, the material was so outrageous that the natural instinct would be not to believe it. Denials by the GEM government would have a high level of credibility.

And that raised the most serious of the problems. From the chatter they intercepted, it seemed as though it would be at least another month before the Green zealots would be ready to put 'Operation Cyrus', as it was being called, into action. Cyrus, the Persian ruler mentioned in the Old Testament who is the Anointed, the Messiah, the Chosen One, who rights a great historic wrong and restores all things. In the files Stella had sent, it was not clear who 'Cyrus' was to be identified with amongst the GEM leadership. Trevor and Donny were now sure that where Cyrus referred to a person, it was Malcolm Morton. He was coordinating the great project of restoration, rebalancing nature, restoring Creation to its rightful order. And his code-name had also become the code for the project itself.

Operation Cyrus was nearly ready, but not quite. The greatest danger was that if they went public with the information they had, Morton and his followers might be panicked into bringing the plan forward, before anyone could stop them. Trevor and Donny felt a great responsibility. On the one hand, they could be the people to put a stop to the madness. On the other hand, they might recklessly trigger the whole thing off.

One thing their investigations had also done was unearth signs of increasing opposition to the Mason regime within the machinery of government. And Donny had intercepted a security briefing intended for Morton's eyes only, detailing surveillance on suspected opposition in the armed forces, and how attempts had been made by the dissidents to win over various parts of the establishment, including the King.

Trevor decided that the best course of action was to attempt a three-pronged attack. He would personally take the information he had to the King, using the launch of the Scottish Total Farm as a pretext to make contact. Donny would wait on the results of that, and from afar would forward the evidence to key 'obstructionist' figures in the civil service and to General Matthews if the attempt to involve the King were to fail. These people were sure to be under close surveillance, so that carried a heightened risk of exposure. Finally, getting the evidence out to the wider media world would be the last option, to follow after several days if both the first two options failed.

So now it was decision time for Trevor. Go or no go.

'You don't have a choice,' said Carrie, putting a comforting hand on his shoulder.

'There's always a choice,' Trevor sighed.

'Not this time,' said Carrie emphatically. 'Not if we want a future for our children, and our children's children. And everybody else's children. And do you know what?'

Trevor looked round at her and smiled. 'No, I don't know what. It's all so crazy, I don't think I know anything about anything anymore.'

'Well, I know something. And I know you. And I know you'll do it. And I know you'll succeed.'

As he rode on the ecobus from Inverness, he did not feel at all certain of success. His heart was full of affection for his wife, but he was sure that Carrie knew him well enough not to believe what she was saying. He remembered the old line that 'behind every successful man there is a very surprised woman.' He'd like to see the look on her face if he got through all this, with mission accomplished. Now that was worth living for.

He went on from Ballater, where the bus stopped, to Balmoral by electric taxi. There were journalists there from the national and international press, and of course most of them had turned up without transport for the last few miles to the farm. It was fun for Trevor to see them compete for the few taxis that were available, and accosting the locals, offering them large amounts of money to drive them there. Several went by tractor, others by bicycle. Trevor had booked his taxi in advance, and being almost local the driver was keen to look after him, despite the incentives he was being offered to ditch his booking.

'You can come back for him of course,' a French journalist was arguing as Trevor arrived.

'That's very considerate of you,' Trevor exclaimed loudly behind him

'Ah, only one of you! Then maybe we can share your taxi!' said the journalist.

'Er, no—I'll take them,' said Trevor, pointing to an attractive all-female media team. 'Can you fit them all in, cabbie? I don't mind if it's a tight squeeze. Be rather pleasant, actually'

The French journalist protested loudly, but with a big smile, as he felt he could identify the masculine reasoning at work here. But Trevor's mind was also working on another level. Arriving to face the inevitable Militia security it would be better to be in the company of other people, especially those who would be seen as no threat, and who might attract more attention than himself.

The women sharing his taxi were Australian, usually based in the Netherlands, and like the other foreign journalists invited over especially for the occasion. And very charming they were too, so Trevor felt. They had lots of questions about what life was like in Scotland, about food shortages and the alleged excesses of the Militia these days. Trevor played these questions with a straight bat. The taxi driver, however, was much more forthcoming. Trevor urged him to silence as they approached a security checkpoint on the edge of the royal estates. Everyone had to show their ID and authorisations to attend this event, which were scanned by the security team. Then they were waived through. So far, no trouble.

It couldn't last, however. Two Militia jeeps came alongside the taxi as it approached the final gate to the new farm. They ordered everyone in the taxi to get out, wanting to see their IDs and authorisation again. Trevor noted the difference in their attitude to the previous security guards. They seemed much tougher and more determined.

'OK—you Aussies are fine, you can go on. But we need Mr MacLean to come with us,' said the officer in command. He manhandled Trevor quite roughly, pulling him by the arm and starting towards one of the jeeps.

'One moment, please,' said Trevor, trying to appear unruffled. 'I fear you've made some kind of mistake—'

'No mistake. Our orders are quite specific.'

'Is there something wrong with my authorisation? Perhaps we can sort this out here...'

The Australian reporters were not willing to stand by and see Trevor be led away unchallenged. One of them began filming the incident, as the reporter, Jeanette, interposed herself between Trevor and the jeep.

'Can you just explain what's happening here?' she asked.

'No, sorry–I don't need to explain my actions here. Now let me pass,' the Militia officer said brusquely.

'Wait, wait, wait,' Jeanette said, still interposing herself between them and the jeep, but smiling all the time. 'Mr MacLean is an accredited BBC reporter, who was on his way to an event organised by the Palace, on Crown lands. Are you taking him away on the orders of the Palace, or is this a Militia action?'

'Can you stop her filming?' the Militia officer barked to his colleagues, who now began to close on the woman with the camera.

Other vehicles with guests and media now began to arrive. Other crews began to film the incident. More Militia arrived.

'Let's get him in the jeep now,' the officer barked to his colleagues. 'We don't want this turning into a bloody circus.'

Two of his colleagues began firmly but quite gently moving Jeanette out of the way, while others helped to hustle Trevor towards the jeep. Trevor decided his best strategy was not to struggle–it wouldn't stop him being put into the jeep, and might detract from the image of his being an innocent victim. Jeanette appeared to acquiesce in her removal, then slipped out of the grasp of her minders, and confronted the Militia office again. But before she could ask any more questions, she was tackled by other Militia and ended up being knocked to the ground.

'Are you getting this? Are you getting this?' she called to her colleagues in true professional fashion.

Trevor was hustled into the jeep, and it began to bump its way up the hill, past the line of vehicles on their way in. Suddenly another car pulled out of the line of vehicles and in front of the jeep. Three large men came out and advanced towards the jeep, waving police ID as they advanced. The senior Militia officer jumped angrily out of the jeep.

'What the hell's going on?' he demanded.

'I have to ask you to remain here a moment. Someone wants to talk to you,' said a police officer.

'Who?' demanded the Militia man angrily.

The police officer did not respond, but just nodded towards the farm. The Militia man turned round, and saw a large Range Rover bouncing towards them from the direction of the farm. 'You should know I have authority to vet all the people coming in here today,' he said sharply.

'Fine. Tell that to the guv'nor, then.'

They waited in silence in the cold wind until the Range Rover arrived. The Militia officer could not see through the tinted windows who was inside. Three men and a woman got out simultaneously. And one of them was the unmistakeable figure of King Henry.

The King shot an angry glance at the Militia officers, then went over to the Australian reporters who had followed the jeep up the hill, filming all the time. He spoke softly to them, putting his hand solicitously on Jeanette's arm and asked if she was alright. Then he turned and stalked up to the Militia officer, who stood mutely waiting for events to unfold, caught between jurisdictions and not knowing what to do.

'Well, sir. I wonder if you'd kindly explain to me what just happened here? Why you're pushing one of my guests onto the ground and hustling another away in a jeep? And I'd rather you didn't try to flannel me—I saw everything from down there with my binoculars. Speak up, man!'

'Erm—I was just explaining to your police...security team...I was just carrying out my job. Our duty is to vet the people coming in here today, check their IDs and authorisation...and I was asked to detain one of the people here to...verify his credentials, and...'

'And where did this order come from, to remove someone from my estates after he'd been cleared to enter?'

'The order came from...above.'

'From above? Did the clouds open and you hear a voice from heaven?' thundered the King. 'You should know that as far as earthly powers go, on this land I am the authority that counts. And you should also learn, young man, how to address your monarch with the proper respect. Have you been taught how to do that?'

The King stared hard at him, like a stern father rebuking a child. The Militia officer didn't reply, but looked down the ground. His republican instincts bristled to respond, but knowing the King's relationship with the GEM leadership felt it would be politic to keep them in check.

At last he responded. 'I'm sorry, Your Majesty, if there's been a mis-understanding. It seems a journalist was assigned to cover this event, even to have a brief interview with you, who is not approved by ESCOMEDIA for this kind of work. He has a track record of trying to misrepresent the Green Revolution, and was assigned to less sensitive tasks. It hasn't worked out like it should, but I was trying to remove him quickly from the scene so that we could review his credentials in a less public environment.'

'Indeed, it would seem it didn't quite work out as intended. We have half the world's media filming it. It seems you've quite upstaged our little celebration of green farming here—and I'm less than pleased by this. Now, who is this villainous character you're trying to abduct from my property? Let him out the car, if you please.'

'Now please, Sir,' said the Militia officer softly. 'We'd be grateful if you'd just let us do our duty with no further embarrassment, then … '

'Then you don't lose face?' suggested the King. 'Now you must understand, I wasn't asking your permission to let him out the car, merely being polite. So let's do the right thing, shall we?'

One of the other Militia guards immediately wilted under the royal stare, and let Trevor MacLean out of the car. Trevor got out of the jeep, and theatrically straightened and brushed down his clothes. He took hold of the hand of the Militia man holding the door open, and shook it in a friendly way, with a gesture of 'I forgive you'. Then he walked towards the King, and bowed his head respectfully.

'Trevor MacLean, Your Majesty,' he said, as he raised his head.

'I know who you are, MacLean. A few degrees either way from here, and you may not have been so lucky, don't you think?'

Trevor smiled graciously at this reference to his controversial programme, and was more than a little pleased that it had had such an eminent audience. 'I am lucky that in this dramatic moment you arrived as a *deus ex machina*—or should I say *rex ex machina*?'

'Very good, MacLean. I think *rex* will suffice.'

Trevor turned to the Militia man, and sensing his great discomfort in this situation decided to add to it. 'You've got no idea what we're talking about, have you?' he said in a stage whisper. 'Never mind. Just smile, you're on worldwide TV.'

And he patted him gently on the cheek. Then he noticed that everyone was looking back down the track to the farm gates, which were now opening to let a silver Rolls Royce come through.

'Ah yes,' said the King. 'I asked my assistant to arrange some suitable transport for you and the young ladies, as compensation for the incivility of your reception.'

A policeman invited the cars waiting to get in to pull over onto the grass to let the Rolls Royce come on the road.

The King was evidently enjoying looking at the mix of reactions on the faces of everyone there. 'How do you like my new toy?' he announced. 'In case you're worried where I'm getting the petrol from, it runs on hydrogen. What do you think of it, Mr MacLean.'

'Very nice, Sir. I thought you might be running it on something more agricultural. I think our Militia friends here have an ample supply of bullshit they seem anxious to share with everyone, isn't that right, Sergeant?' He turned towards the Militia officer as he made this last remark.

'I can see why you're not so popular with the Militia. And why you haven't been on our screens for a while, Mr MacLean. It was a cheap shot,' said the King as they moved away to the car.

'I accept the reproof, sir. I trust you will be more interested in the other things I have to tell you about.'

'Tell me about? It seems I was under the mistaken impression that you were here to interview me, not the other way round.'

Now one of the other Militia officers came over, having received some instructions via his earpiece. 'With respect, your majesty. For your safety, we would like to check over Mr MacLean's clothing and equipment—in the interests of security,' he said.

'Search him? Have you any objection to being searched, MacLean?'

'None at all,' Trevor lied, and held out his arms to be frisked. Then pointing to a female Militia officer, added: 'If it's not a problem, I'd prefer her to do it!'

The King gave him a withering look, while the Militia man proceeded to frisk him.

'And the case. What's in it?'

'Camera. And accessories.'

'We'd like to take these away for examination.'

Trevor grimaced. 'It would be kind of hard for me to do my job without the tools of the trade, don't you think?'

The King looked irritated. 'Are you telling me you think there are weapons, or explosives hidden in here?'

'You can't be too safe, Sir,' said the Militia officer blandly.

'Jackson, are the sniffer dogs out here somewhere?' the King called to one of his security team. 'Never mind, let me.'

With that he opened Trevor MacLean's case and took out the camera and each additional bit of kit in turn, turning them over in his hands, trying various catches and releases. Trevor showed him how they worked, and how pieces detached and reattached.

'Gentlemen, I think we can be assured that this is indeed a camera. Now, if that's all, Mr Jackson here will escort you and your colleagues to the edge of the estate. Good day.'

As they walked to the Rolls Royce, the King looked archly at MacLean.

'Well, this has caught my interest, MacLean. Your being so determined to see me, and their being so determined to stop you. I hope I am not disappointed! Jenkins, wave everybody else through, and make them all welcome. We have Scotland's first Total Farm to show them, and we have to ensure they're more interested in that than in this peculiar little interlude.'

••

Alone with the King and his inevitable attendants, Trevor insisted on doing a short interview first, as planned, to cut in with the footage he would shoot of the farm.

'It's the Scottish angle that's my brief,' explained Trevor, 'so I'd like us to focus on what this means as a prototype for farming across Scotland–and it's wider implications for how we live north of the border.'

The King was happy to talk at length on this, showing a good knowledge of Scottish agriculture and forestry, regional differences and historic factors affecting how land was used. Trevor's dry wit and theatricality made the King relax, and encouraged him to pepper his own observations with witty asides.

Trevor was very pleased with the result, and knew that he could turn this into a first rate piece of television, and one that would on no account offend the Green authorities who would certainly scrutinise it very closely–that is if he were allowed to get so far as being able to put the whole thing together.

'Very well, MacLean. Now tell me what this charade is all about. What is it that's so important that you have to tell me, and they don't want you to tell me?'

'First of all, sir,' explained Trevor, 'what we've just done is construct my alibi. This unique interview is the reason I came, as far as anyone else is concerned. But this is my ulterior motive for being here.' With this he flourished the spare hard drive for his camera.

'This is just what I told the boys up there—additional hard disk space for the camera. But on it I have some very extraordinary material as well. May I show you?'

'Be my guest,' invited the King. 'But please be aware that I have many other guests waiting outside for the grand tour of my biogas engineering techniques and pigsties. Perhaps you can give me the gist in five minutes?'

Trevor looked challenged, but decided he could do this. As a TV professional, he was well used to having to condense earth-shattering news into twenty-second bites. He hooked up the hard-drive to one of the computers in the King's office, and opened the files. He explained 'a colleague's initial work', and how he had built on it. He showed the route through the complex of files, and the 'Executive Summary' he had prepared.

It was all there: the private top level briefings with Morton and others, the budgetary information, the connections with Porton Down, the profiles of the emerging dominant personalities in the government and Green Militia, and the writings that apparently exposed their real agenda. Then evidence of the experimental work at the camps, and the plans for solving the 'humanity question'.

The King looked very solemn and thoughtful. 'It's completely unbelievable. It's so … far-fetched. Of course, I will have to look closer at it. And have to find a way to verify it. I can keep this, er, drive?'

'Of course. But I advise you to keep it to yourself. Or only allow people you trust absolutely to see it, as you decide what action to take. I have to ask you—do any of your staff seem especially close to Mason or Morton, or always seem to want you to take their part?'

'I see. You think my staff has been infiltrated? Hm. You must understand, though, MacLean, that I haven't accepted your point of view yet. And it's not clear to me what I should do even if I accept it is all true.'

'I understand your caution. Seriously, I do. Let me tell you why I have brought it to you. It's the timing. As you can see, there's reason to believe they may take the first steps in the next few weeks. I didn't want to broadcast what I've found out, in case it panicked them into making an early move. What's needed is to pull the rug out from under them in one go, to take away their means of doing anything.'

'And you think I am the person who can do this? You have a much greater belief in my powers than I do!' laughed the King grimly.

'If it's true, then they have to be stopped. As you might imagine, I've thought about this a lot. Actually, I think it's safe to tell you that I have Plans B, C, D and so on up my sleeve. If you don't believe all this, or think it's not your position to do something, then I push it out further, despite the risk of their doing something more quickly. What else can I do? I can't sit by and do nothing, knowing what I know. I don't really know the extent of your powers, Sir—but I believe it must extend to dealing with a government that is acting illegally—or elements of it that are doing so. "May he defend our laws", as it says in the song.'

'Quite.'

'There is something you can do short of changing the government. You can challenge Don Mason on some of it. Not the central issue of population control. But perhaps on the regime in the camps. And on the list of missing detainees. There's some very eminent people on this list—Miles Campbell, for example. Terry Cairns. Peter Kitson. Where are they now? And you could ask to have an independent investigative team flown in to examine the camps—in particular the "North Camp" satellite of the West Highland Eco-camp, now known to the inner circle as New Dawn. It seems that is the centre of their biological experiments. A judicial investigation, or a kind of emergency Royal Commission. And if Mason won't agree with it, then we know that something is up.'

Again the King looked very pensive. 'Mason has assured me that the camps are being wound down, in favour of dealing with people in their communities. He said that by Earth Day, most of the detainees will be returned.'

'By Earth Day? Oh, good Lord! If he's telling the truth, and my information is right, then it's the people who are the delivery system. It means within three weeks they'll be releasing thousands of people from the camps, infected with a deadly disease.'

'I'm sorry, MacLean, I think I've taken in about all I can take at the moment. I've got about two hundred visitors outside waiting to see round my new model farm. You've quite taken the wind out of my sails. And that's a problem, isn't it? I care a great deal about the achievements of the Green Revolution. The way you talk, the Greens are *them*, the bad guys. But I'm one of *them* too, don't you think?'

'It's one reason why I thought to come to you. Someone with integrity on the inside, someone who can combine passion for the environment with concern for humanity. If anyone can influence the course of events, it's you, Sir.'

'I can see through your flattery, MacLean. You're heaping a great deal of responsibility on my shoulders, and trying to sweeten it with fine words.'

'Perhaps I can put it another way,' said MacLean. 'You were born into responsibility. I'm just providing the information you need to exercise it.'

'I'll take your information into account in whatever I do.'

And so it was left for the time being. The King, greatly troubled, proceeded with celebrating the launch of the first Scottish Total Farm. A lifetime of training in masking his feelings, arguably the greatest of British skills, had made him a consummate actor. No one would have guessed the thoughts that were going through his mind. The habits of command were well ingrained in him, albeit in a very limited sphere. However, he realised that his role rarely called for him to exercise actual leadership. Not-exercising-leadership was the cornerstone of constitutional monarchy.

MacLean's had by no means been the only voice calling for him to rein in or depose the Mason government. There had been the informal delegation from the military, and exploratory contacts from Patrick Baxter's 'administration in exile', as well as soundings from several foreign ambassadors and a couple of heads of state, not least President Wilding of the United States.

The number and diversity of the protests and accusations against the government had now convinced him that it needed somehow to be called to account. Most of the complaints had referred to civil liberties, or trade. The foreign press and websites were full of stories of brutality in the camps, and Joanna Kitson had made available transcripts and videos of her brother's brutal interrogations. Now MacLean had brought him face to face with something much worse. It seemed incredible to him, as a natural sympathiser with the Green Revolution. But then a few years ago, the other 'lesser' allegations would have seemed incredible too. Revolutionary excesses had become excusable in the interests of a greater good. But where was revolutionary zeal leading the country now?

As Trevor MacLean joined the farm tour, Jeanette the Australian reporter caught him by the arm.

'Hey, you ungrateful little shit!' she called.

'Whoa, that's a little unfriendly, isn't it?' Trevor protested.

'Since when am I your friend, you pommy bastard? First I rescue you from the Green bully boys. Saved your lousy skin we did. Then you get us slung out while you conduct your exclusive with Henry. Now that's what I call unfriendly!'

'Oh, some private business. But no complaints, please. Thanks to me, you've got some headlining footage of Militia brutality, and a story to tell your grandkids about how you rode in an organic Rolls as a guest of the King of England. Think what I've done for your career and inter-generational status!'

'Well thanks indeed, you smarmy bastard. Now, tell me what you were really up to.'

'That's between my monarch and his loyal subject. I'm sure you know that it's extremely bad form to report a private conversation with the King.'

'Huh!'

'But let me tell you this. There's likely to be some interesting news to report soon. And I'll do everything I can to get you in on it when it happens. I promise. Don't tell anyone I said this, though. Oh, and one more thing. Here's my card, and that's my home number I've put on the back.'

'Crikey, you're a bit forward aren't you?'

'Attracted as I am to you, my lovely, I have another motive. I've got a feeling I may not make it home safely. Oh, His Majesty has promised me some protection, but I feel that protection fades with distance from his august presence. So, if you see me being packed into a Green van, can you call my wife and let her know what's happened? And if later you hear that I have disappeared, you have another story I've given you.'

'What is it with you, Trevor? Why are these Militia guys so worried about you? And why is a busy Head of State happy to spend forty minutes closeted with you? What makes you so bloody special?'

'Ah, Jeanette. I've spent my whole life looking for an answer to that, and I'm afraid I'm no wiser than the rest of the world. But enough about me. Wow, look at that! Isn't that the most amazing pumpy-recycling-thingy you've ever laid eyes on?'

The tour over, The King addressed the assembled guests one final time, pressing on them the merits of this kind of zero-carbon agricultural production. He also announced the setting up of a not-for-profit consultancy to help others in the UK and overseas to go down the same route. PR assistants handed out goodie bags with memorabilia and video files to help the guests remember the day, and to help the media visitors compile reports with the best possible images.

As Trevor was preparing to go, he was approached by one of the King's assistants.

'Mr MacLean, have you enjoyed the day here?'

'Fascinating and delightful, it was,' enthused Trevor.

'I'm glad you think so,' said the official. 'I'm Graham Forsyth, head of the Media Team here. I have a request from His Majesty himself. He'd like you to join us down in London as a special adviser for a few weeks. Would you be able to do that?'

'I would be most happy to oblige,' said Trevor, feeling the immediate relief of not having to run the gauntlet of the Green Militia on the way home.

'His Majesty felt that possibly you'd like to fly down with us tomorrow, in which case we can send a car to collect anything you might need,' said Forsyth.

'You are most kind. I'll call my wife and have her arrange everything.'

'His Majesty asked me to pass on a message. He said that while he values your advice, this guarantees nothing. He said you'd understand.'

'I understand indeed,' Trevor nodded.

The relief Trevor felt rapidly turned to an overwhelming urge to run as far away as possible. From that moment on for the next three weeks, he constantly felt nauseous, butterflies incessantly fluttering in his stomach. It was a feeling like he had experienced in his first days front of camera, only intensified. He tried to tell himself he was an old stager, and this kind of thing shouldn't be happening. But he knew that for all that nervous energy he had invested in his TV career, in the end it that had been only image, career and reputation that were on the line. Now there was so much more at stake.

61: Peter in Utopia

They'd taken Peter Kitson from the hospital two days after his operation, but he did not go back to Green Volunteer House. He was moved from place to place for the next week, never quite knowing what was happening or where he was. He was not assaulted again, and it seemed he had attained a status that left the Militia who guarded him somewhat in awe of him. The GEM leadership had taken a very direct interest in his welfare, and the international media had been full of the ill-treatment he had received. No one, it seemed, wanted to be responsible for any further suffering at this stage.

His new home was in a new eco-settlement in Norfolk, close to the sea. It was a new community built by eco-camp inmates, and inhabited mostly by Green Militia and their families. He was one of a minority of 'revolutionary enemies' assigned to this community. He was not sure of his reason for being there. All the other revolutionary enemies there were fit and able-bodied, and were assigned to a range of physically demanding tasks to help sustain and extend the community.

Different levels of trust were assigned to these offenders. Peter was classed as a 'saboteur'—the worst of the enemies of the revolution. These had to be closely monitored in whatever they did, and attend regular re-education and self-criticism sessions. Lesser offenders, mostly 'Stage Three' inmates from eco-camps, had to learn primarily through the work they did, with weekly self-criticism sessions to correct wrong thinking.

Mason had told the King the truth, up to a point. The eco-camps were to be wound down. Each camp had been involved in the building of new communities designed on 'Green Earth principles'. The communities provided most of their own energy and a large part of their own food. The inhabitants traded with their own local 'currencies'—GETs—Green Earth Tokens representing units of work in their own community. Nothing particularly new in this system, except the extent of it. Money was almost unused within these settlements, though quite a few of the Militia left their homes each day to commute into nearby towns to do 'normal' jobs.

'It's the future,' Jane Johnson told him. 'The way we live will be the way most Britons will live in a few years.'

The Johnsons were Peter Kitson's minders. Three of them in all: husband and wife and the husband's younger brother. No children. In fact, there were no children anywhere in the community. Jane explained that in this transitional stage, the first inhabitants would be those with no dependents. Later, as she began to trust him more, she explained that all those who volunteered for life in these settlements had signed a pledge that they would not have children before the age of thirty-two, and that they accepted the principle that the community would collectively decide on who would have children, according to the need of the community for a 'successor generation'.

Jane was evidently delighted to have been selected for living here. She said there was a list of more than ten thousand people, and she and her husband had been amongst the first hundred to be allocated a home. She clearly revelled in the appreciation of her Green virtue that had led to this selection.

Peter had been living there for one month, and he had found it—tolerable. Extremely tedious compared with his previous life in the free world, but much more pleasant than his experiences of the camps and interrogation. Each night there were communal meals, though people could also cook at home. The communal meals helped to conserve resources, and also contributed to building community spirit—or so it was hoped. Often home-made alcohol flowed, and people became merry or antagonistic. After all, the Greens were just like other people, Peter thought.

The arguments that occasionally broke out were interesting for Peter. Often they were over trivial matters, such as over who was apparently not pulling their weight. But sometimes they were more substantial, and from these Peter could learn something of current events. For example, in one argument it emerged that people in the settlements had much better access to food than those outside. Some idealists thought this unfair, while others argued that it was right and proper to give privileges to people who lived more sustainable lives.

Peter wondered constantly about Heather and Andrea, whether they were safe. Now he worried if they had enough food to eat. He had no idea where they were or what they were doing, and any attempts he made to find out were met with silence or a rebuke.

Rows often flared about vegetarianism and animals. Many of the Militia, including many in the settlements, had been Animalist activists, and were solidly vegetarian. Yet the rules drawn up for settlement living clearly allowed the raising and eating of animals. Jane Johnson was often upset about this. A lifelong vegetarian, she had tried to accommodate herself to this way of things as a compromise on the road to a better future. But the arguments always unsettled her. One time she felt the need to pour out her thoughts to Peter.

'It's clearly against the Declaration of the Rights of Species!' she exclaimed. 'How can we, of all people, live our lives while violating this Declaration?'

'Well, one thing I've learned in the past few years is that it's not what's written that's important, it's what's done,' replied Peter. 'In this brave new world, if you want to change something, just seize the day and do it. There's nothing to be gained by protesting that others aren't abiding by the rules.'

In the past few days there'd been some heated debates, if not exactly arguments. Peter learned that the government had decided that all detainees in the eco-settlements were to be returned to the camps in two weeks' time, and after that were to be returned to their home communities in what was being termed the 'Earth Day Amnesty'. This raised Peter's hopes considerably, but some of the community leaders wanted to resist this edict, arguing that it could leave them critically short of labour while the settlements were still in their infancy. Peter also learned that the leaders at the Climate Change Project work camps were already protesting about a lack of available labour. The eco-camps had almost stopped providing workers to the projects, and rumour had it that they were falling seriously behind schedule. All this encouraged Peter. That the projects were in trouble was now good news, and might be a prelude to either a change of direction or a change of regime.

Over the next few days it became clear that the government would not shift in its order that all detainees should be returned from the settlements to the eco-camps prior to being sent home. However, the local leaders were mollified a little with the news that new settlers from the ranks of the Militia would be coming to replace the detainees, and that they would be allowed to select the incomers, making sure they had the skills to suit the local situation.

So it was that Peter Kitson boarded a bus and headed ten miles inland to the nearest eco-camp, his heart full of hope that his nightmare would soon be coming to an end.

62: Where drama meets history

Trevor MacLean found his new assignment pleasingly non-specific in the first few days. And it was good to be back in London. At first he was worried about the attentions of the Militia, but it was clear the word had been put out that he enjoyed the protection of the Palace. He was being put up at one of the best hotels in Buckingham Gate, and was savouring the creature comforts that came with it. Even in these austere times, class made a difference.

He was, however, concerned at the lack of any clear direction from the King. He had been called upon just the once since his arrival to explain some things in Stella's files. So it seemed that the information he had provided was being looked at, but apart from that he felt he was being kept at arm's length.

Trevor felt that time was growing short, and that it was necessary to put the second stage into action. He was in irregular and cautious contact with Donny Patterson, who had hidden himself away in the far north of Scotland, and at last he felt he had to trigger the next phase—passing on what they knew to the overseas opposition. In a coded conversation apparently only about the weather and fishing, he and Donny agreed to give the King just twenty-four hours more, or take the matter out of his hands.

Breakfasting in cafés was a treat Trevor would normally enjoy, even with a limited menu such as he found now. But his thoughts were burdened with the responsibilities and risks of what he was doing. And he was aware of being constantly under surveillance. He was becoming suspicious of everyone who sat down near him, or who walked in the same direction as him for too long in the streets. He felt the adrenalin begin to flow every time he passed a group of Green Militia on the streets, and anxious every time he heard a police siren.

He noticed something about the Green Militia too in London. They seemed to have become more militarized even during the few days he had been back. They patrolled in army vehicles, and many of them carried some kind of weapon: truncheons, tasers and even guns. This morning, a brisk April morning two weeks before Earth Day, there seemed to be more police and Militia in evidence than ever. And they seemed agitated, alert as if they were expecting something to happen. And then it did.

At first he could hear distant noises, some shouting, chanting, thumping of drums. Other breakfasters in the café began to look up, then exchanged puzzled or anxious glances as the sounds became louder. Through the large glass window Trevor could see Militia and police running, pointing, moving into position, then shouting and taking up different positions. Two armoured cars drew up just outside the restaurant, and riot police in full gear rapidly jumped out and took up position.

'Any idea what this is all about?' asked Trevor, turning to the other customers in the café. They all shook their heads or muttered their ignorance.

'Seems some kind of protest,' offered one of the waiters.

Clearly it was. Suddenly there was a crescendo of noise as demonstrators entered the street. All the streets leading down to Trafalgar Square were now full of people shouting and protesting.

'Food riots!' exclaimed Trevor, now able to pick out some of the slogans they were shouting. He wondered how so many people could have been mobilised like this in the current climate.

Now a tide of protesters was surging towards the police and Militia outside the restaurant. Trevor's instincts as a journalist were now overcome by his preference for self-preservation. The café had an upstairs section which was closed at this time of the day.

'I think it might be safer if we went upstairs, don't you think?' he asked the waiter who was busy locking the door. The waiter nodded, and the customers grabbed their belongings and moved upstairs. An elderly couple called over a waitress and calmly asked her to carry their food and drink upstairs for them. Trevor smiled as he noted their British 'keep calm and carry on' mentality.

From upstairs he had a great vantage point. Opening the tall windows, he crowded onto the narrow balcony with some of the other customers. He could see hundreds of demonstrators in a stand-off with the authorities outside the café. And at the end of the street, in the Strand, he could see hundreds more making their way towards Trafalgar Square. It seemed the ones outside the café wanted to join with the main group and head into the Square too. Some wanted to confront the authorities, others were urging them to go back the way they came and take a different way through. The police and Militia, Trevor guessed, had been stationed there in readiness for the protesters coming down The Strand. Now it seemed they were potentially trapped between two groups of demonstrators.

Someone put their hand on Trevor's arm.

'I wouldn't do that,' a cautious voice said to him. Trevor had started to video the demonstration, using the small digital videocam he habitually carried with him. A personal rather than professional piece of kit, the quality was still just about good enough to use in news reports if required.

Trevor acknowledged this advice from a fellow customer, but chose to ignore it. He was anxious to film any trouble if it developed. A small skirmish did develop between the protesters and the Militia, and one protester was hauled through behind the police ranks, handcuffed and bundled into one of the cars.

Most of the protesters were now trying to retreat, pulling their more confrontational colleagues away. Then Trevor saw a news crew on the corner, behind the demonstrators. He could not make out what network they were with. He swung his camera round to film them. And now along the side road came more demonstrators—and these demonstrators included some people in Militia uniform. To his astonishment, Trevor realised it was a counter-demonstration, a large group of people demonstrating in favour of the Revolution, and against 'Saboteurs, Greys and Obstructionists', as one of their banners proclaimed.

Now the two groups were facing each other, just a few yards apart. The pro-government demonstrators greatly outnumbered the anti-government demonstrators who were outside the café. Then some more police and Militia appeared to force their way in from another side-street and placed themselves between the two groups. The noise from both sides grew very loud, with constant chanting and name-calling.

Now Militia agents and policemen were also filming the anti-government demonstrators, trying to get a visual record of everyone there. As one of them swung his camera upwards towards the balcony, Trevor stepped back to hide his face from them. When he nervously put his head forward again to look down into the street, the Militia had moved aside, and were now letting the demonstrators through to join their fellow protesters on their way to Trafalgar Square.

'Very strange, this,' said the man who had warned Trevor against filming.

'Hm,' nodded Trevor vaguely. He knew what was going on, recognising news management when he saw it, and rehearsing in his mind the stories that would be manufactured that evening by the purged news media.

As the players from each side ebbed away in several directions, Trevor stepped back inside the room, putting his camera in his coat pocket. Immediately he became alarmed. Three large men were now in the upstairs room with him, people he had not seen in the café before. One of them nodded to the others, and before he had a chance to evade them, they had grabbed him and were hustling him towards a door leading back to the customer toilets. A fourth man was there, opening a fire escape, and suddenly Trevor was being half pushed, half carried down the metal stairs to a courtyard at the back of the restaurant, then in through a back door into another building. One of his assailants was holding a scarf tightly over his mouth in case he cried out, but Trevor was too breathless and surprised.

He heard kitchen noises as he was bundled into a dark corridor, then he was pushed into a service lift, where the men relaxed their grip on him a little.

'Not a word, there's a good boy,' one of them counselled, holding his finger in front of his lips.

'Wouldn't dream of it,' Trevor whispered, trying to regain his composure.

'Enough,' said the man, holding his finger up again, only this time more threateningly.

The lift stopped at the fifth floor, and Trevor was bundled out. Now it seemed, the men were trying to act less aggressively, though the threat was still there as they moved along a hotel corridor. Trevor wasn't sure which hotel he was in, but felt sure he was in a good one. He hoped this was a good sign.

They stopped by a door, and one of the men knocked. Immediately they were let inside by another very large man. The room was bright, and Trevor could see two figures sitting by the window, silhouetted by the morning light. Though the windows were closed, the sounds of the demonstration still filtered into the room. One of the figures immediately stood up, and walked towards Trevor with his hand extended towards him.

'Mr MacLean, I'm very pleased to meet you at last,' he said.

Trevor looked him up and down, to try to understand who he might be. He assumed at first Militia, or at least some government agency. He was a tall man, but not as burley as the people who had abducted him. He was smartly dressed in an expensive suit. The cut was traditional, rather than fashionable. A middle-aged man, he stood very straight and correct. The smile seemed forced, more polite than sincere. Must be army or police, Trevor now thought.

'My apologies for bringing you here like this. My name is Mark Matthews, General Mark Matthews—we haven't met, but maybe you've seen my face before in the news, much as I try to keep out of it! Over here I have...a friend. I can't tell you his name, but for the purpose of this meeting you can call him "Paul",' said the man as Trevor cautiously shook the hand held out to him.

'Please take a seat. I think we may have a lot to discuss. Tea?' said General Matthews.

Trevor did recognise the face now, as someone whose picture in the past had cropped up on the celebrity pages in the newspapers. Now apart from seeming older, he seemed quite an imposing figure, exuding a calm authority and great self-confidence. But Trevor remained cautious. All he knew of Matthews was what little he and Donny had found. Could all this be a set-up by the government or the Militia?

'I'm pleased to meet you, I'm sure,' Trevor said as he sat down. 'But I'm a friendly kind of fellow. If you wanted to talk to me, why not just knock on my door? Or give me a call?'

'If only life were so straightforward!' laughed Matthews. 'I'm sure you know why. Talking to you in most circumstances becomes a somewhat, shall we say, public undertaking. I wanted our discussions to be a little more exclusive. I know that within these four walls, this whole suite actually, whatever is said will be quite private. My friend's friends have the technology to make sure nothing is overheard.'

'A good place to bring the girlfriend, then,' said Trevor. 'Or the boyfriend,' he added, nodding towards 'Paul'.

'I'm sure you're right. Now, if you don't mind, I'll get to the point. We know that you have some information that is of great interest to us. And we'd like you to share it with us. Don't ask us how we know, just accept that we do. How you came by it, we don't care. We don't actually know if it has any value, if it tells us anything that we don't already know. We do know that you've passed it on to the King—at considerable risk to yourself.'

'We also know that you've caused quite a stir amongst the government security forces. What happened up at Balmoral hasn't gone down too well. Morton and his people are just waiting for the right moment to get hold of you. But you probably know that already,' added Paul.

There was something about his manner that Trevor didn't like. He was sure he was a spook. And spooks at the moment were in theory under Malcolm Morton's control. There seemed also to be a veiled threat in what Paul had said, a warning to tell them what they needed or else the Militia will get you. Trevor felt intimidated, but decided it would be best to appear that he wasn't.

'It's the problem of always being popular,' he said. 'Sometimes you get to be popular with the wrong people.'

'I understand that—' said Matthews.

'No, I'll tell you what you must understand,' interrupted Trevor. 'I don't know who you two are—except that you're army and you're probably MI5. So I have absolutely no reason to trust anything you say, especially after the way you brought me here. I have no idea what information you're talking about. As a journalist I have a lot of information coming at me all the time. Though it's possible that if I knew who you were, I might understand what it is you're looking for, and might be able to help. So, before I put any trust in you, you must put some trust in me. Tell me what this is all about. Really all about.'

Matthews and Paul looked at each other. It was Paul who spoke first.

'Believe me, Mr MacLean: if we wanted to make you tell us, we could do that. Here and now. Suck you dry and leave the cleaners to take away the shell. But we don't want to do that.'

'Because we think you're on our side,' added Matthews, casting a stern sideways glance at his colleague.

'OK, so you play good cop to Paul's bad cop,' said Trevor. 'Still, you're not hitting me yet, or injecting me with something dreadful, and I'm grateful for that. The point is, what is your side? Tell me, and I'll tell you if I'm on it or not. Then you can get the needles ready if you need to. Are they sterilised? I'd hate to share a needle with the wrong kind ...'

'OK. I'll tell you,' said Matthews. 'But after I tell you, you're committed. As simple as that. You cease to be a free agent, until this thing is over. Do you understand?'

'Go on.'

So General Matthews told Trevor the nature of the opposition to the regime, and the plans being developed for 'regime change'. He told him about Patrick Baxter as the figurehead for an interim government, of Sir James Olsen's extensive network within government, and of the support of foreign governments. He talked of particular concerns the armed forces had about the eco-camps and the militarisation of the Militia, the turning of a free media into a propaganda machine, and how the country might descend into chaos with an economic collapse by the autumn if no steps were taken to reverse the headlong slide.

Trevor was impressed. The way Matthews spoke seemed too genuine, too heartfelt, to be some kind of Militia ruse to get information from him.

'It's worse than you think,' Trevor said. 'Much worse.'

Trevor then told them what he knew of the activities in the camps, the plans for population control, and his worries over what the King had told him about an amnesty for detainees on Earth Day, just two weeks away. Matthews and Paul exchanged anxious glances as he told them about this.

'You have evidence about all this? Can we see it?'

'I have evidence. I gave it to our gracious King. Who, as far as I can see, is sitting on it. Mulling it over. I've been trying to get another audience with him, to persuade him of the urgency. Maybe you can do something to prompt him.'

'You gave the evidence away to someone who sympathises with the regime?' asked Paul.

'I gave it to someone close to the inside. Someone who has influence and who could make a difference. And who I'm sure wouldn't be in cahoots with the likes of Fullerton and Pearson.'

'You gave the evidence away?' repeated Paul, sounding both incredulous and anxious.

'Yes. But don't worry. There are copies. Many copies. In fact I have one here.'

Trevor pulled his camera from his coat pocket.

'It's on the memory card of this camera. In fact, on the memory card or hard drive of several cameras. I poked it right up the nose of several Militia zombies in Scotland. Quite fun, really. One thing: I do want the video I shot today from this drive. I think you'll see it's quite important when you see the news later. Do you have a computer here? Of course you have.'

As Trevor began to transfer his files to General Matthew's tablet computer, Matthews began to talk in more detail about the plans for regime change. If what Trevor said were true, their plans needed to be brought forward. The problem was, they were not ready yet.

Before they could discuss anything more, the noise from outside suddenly seemed to increase. Matthews went to the window and opened it. Chanting had given way to more chaotic sounds, wild shouting and screaming, and the sounds of many people running. Truncheons beating on riot shields, heavy boots running in step, and other footsteps running at speed in different directions.

'They're breaking it up,' said Matthews.

'I need to film this,' said Trevor as he completed the transfer and reclaimed the hard drive for the camera.

'Not a good idea,' said Matthews.

'Not at all,' added Paul emphatically.

'That sounds like gunshots!' exclaimed Trevor.

'Rubber bullets, I should think', said Matthews, remembering the sound from his service in Basra.

'Well, should be safer for me then?' suggested Trevor.

'I expect it's not only the bullets you need to watch out for,' suggested Matthews.

Trevor knew this was right. It would be good to get some film of this, but he did not need to put himself in danger.

'You have other fish to fry, Mr MacLean,' said Paul. 'I can assure you there will be pictures of this. CCTV, security services video. You wouldn't believe how much of it there is for incidents like this in London. Even satellite images. If what you've told us helps to bring down Mason, I can see you get enough of it to fill any number of documentaries. Now, though, I think we need to get you back to your café as safely as possible.'

'What happens now?' asked Trevor.

'Now? It looks like we have to be ready to move before the 22nd, and you should prepare yourself to record history in the making! In the meantime, anything you can do to win the King over to our side would be very helpful,' said Matthews. 'And of course, you haven't met us. When we need to talk to you again, we'll find you.'

••

More police and Militia streamed towards the area around Trafalgar Square; on foot, on motorbikes, in buses and armoured vehicles. Ignoring the advice of Matthews and Paul, Trevor MacLean decided to go for a stroll. After all, he thought, the most direct route to his hotel was across Trafalgar Square. And he was confident that as long as he was circumspect, his Palace press accreditation and BBC pass would be enough to demonstrate that as a journalist he was approved by the Green authorities. All the same, there was always the risk he might bump into the wrong person.

The wind was bitingly sharp as he left the café to head towards the Square. Briefly challenged by the police in the street outside, he headed away from The Strand to find another way in to where all the action was happening. But solid ranks of police and Militia blocked all access to the Square.

The closest he could get was by the church of St Martin's-in-the-Field. From there he could see the National Gallery, with hundreds of Militia gathered just outside.

A police officer spotted him and called to him. 'What do you want here, sir? Are you sightseer or a protester?' There was an edge to his sarcasm, the cultivated sneer as he said 'sir'.

'Just passing through, actually, Officer,' Trevor replied, then he moved forward. Several of the police turned to him.

'No way through here, sir,' said one of the police, 'go in there and the only way out is in a wagon. Doesn't look as if an eco-camp would be your cup of tea.'

'Absolutely,' agreed Trevor. 'Actually, I've got an appointment with the curator of the National Gallery at 10 o'clock. Wasn't expecting this—were you? Could you tell me if I can get in there off the Charing Cross Road, in through the back entrance?'

'Maybe. You'll have to loop round the back way, and see if you can persuade the officers there to let you through. Say, don't I recognise you? On the box—though I haven't seen you on there for a while, have I?'

'No, that's right. I moved into more of a production role—'

'MacLeod, isn't it? No, MacLean?'

'Yes, Trevor MacLean. I'm still with the BBC, but now I'm working with the Palace Press Corps—hence all this arty business.'

'Yeah, yeah, I remember now. I remember you with Mason on the box a few times. You work with him too?'

'Not so much lately, though I'm working on a programme connected to him now. Well, I'd better head on round the back. Many thanks for all your help!'

Suddenly there was a surge in the crowd on the other side of the police ranks, as some protesters were driven that way by a Militia snatch squad. More shots were fired—rubber bullets again, Trevor sincerely hoped.

The Charing Cross Road was lined with armoured vans ready to take away the protesters. Bored drivers and police in riot gear waited their turn to take part in the excitement. Trevor confidently walked between the vans, and into the alley behind the gallery. The service gate was open, and he walked boldly into the delivery area. No one challenged him as he made his way in, till he was about to go up the stairs to the upper galleries.

'You're with the BBC, are you? They're out front, on the steps. Best view from there. Right to-do this, isn't it?' said an attendant.

So, Trevor realised, he was not going to be the only person using this vantage point to film the events in the Square. He thought it would be wise to avoid the official BBC team, if he could, as his presence there was unauthorised. He followed the attendant's direction through the espresso bar towards the main entrance. Outside, at the top of the steps, a BBC team occupied the spaces between the central columns. Trevor darted quickly to the right, concealing himself as best he could on the other side of the end column.

'Our very own Tiananmen,' he whispered to himself. Except, he soon saw, it wasn't. There was indeed real blood down there on the pavement, and he could see people being chased and beaten. It was chilling enough. But there were no tanks, no live ammunition, no army—not the real army at any rate. More on a par with actions in the miners' strike or the poll tax riots. Only somehow more orchestrated. All round the Square, Trevor could see police and Militia hemming the protesters in, not letting them escape, while special squads went in to arrest and cart away protesters.

Some protesters, it seemed, were being almost deliberately driven towards the ranks of riot police, as if to bring them into conflict. Some other protesters, mainly women, had sat down on the floor, and were throwing their arms up and weeping. Militia surrounded them to prevent them from moving, then began to remove them one by one. The Militia in riot gear on the steps began to beat their shields rhythmically, creating an air of calculated intimidation.

After ten minutes, Trevor felt he had filmed enough. He had noticed some of the staff who were going in and out of the gallery entrance looking at him oddly as he stood filming with his tiny videocam. As he started to leave, he couldn't resist taking a look to see who was running the BBC news team, to see if he could recognise any of his former colleagues. And he did. Much to his surprise he saw Danny Malik, now the Minister for Culture, conducting the operations in person. To be caught sneaking away would certainly lead to trouble. And besides, he felt it would be fascinating to get an insight into what exactly was happening here. So Trevor walked as calmly as he could over to Malik and stood beside him surveying the scene.

'Quite a spectacle, eh, Danny?'

Danny Malik looked taken aback for a moment, then a smile gradually crossed his face.

'Trevor! My word, you are full of surprises!'

'In our business, it doesn't do to be too predictable, eh? Take yourself: you certainly exceeded expectations. D-G, perhaps, we might have predicted, but Minister of Culture? We're blinded by your eminence!'

They both stood looking out across the square for a few moments.

'How about you, Trevor? I hear you're very well connected these days too.'

'Yes, it seems His Majesty was bowled over by a piece I did for Scottish TV on his Total Farm. Wants me to help in his campaigns down here too. And you know me, can never resist hobnobbing with royalty! Did you see my piece down on the farm?'

'Surprisingly enough, I did. And equally surprising, it was very good. Have you changed, Trevor? I mean, since your earlier run-ins with ESCOMEDIA?'

'I'm a reformed man, Danny,' Trevor said, putting on his best air of penitence. 'Had a good chance to reflect and mend my ways. You know, we're even living a true Green lifestyle, growing our own vegetables, harvesting our own rainwater—do you want some by the way? It never stops raining where we are. No, now I can see that a lot of what I did before, I did for the sheer hell of causing mischief. I'm one of the good guys now, a lot more serious, would you believe? And as you can see from my film on the farm, I can produce propaganda as good as anyone else in the Corporation these days, don't you think?'

'Propaganda?' said Malik. 'A much maligned concept. Everything we do, everything we report, has to be done from one vantage point or another, don't you think? After all, what is propaganda but the truth as you see it?'

Trevor nodded. 'Absolutely. I used to make programmes trying to balance two points of view, regardless of their validity. I've learned my lesson, and I'll never make a balanced programme again. Artificially balanced that is, as explained in the ESCOMEDIA news guidelines.'

Danny Malik looked closely at Trevor, then sighed and smiled at the same time. 'Have you really changed, Trevor? What did you do to annoy everyone at Balmoral so much?'

'Me annoy them? I think it was more the other way round, Danny. I was poised for my scoop, then suddenly the local yokels go into a panic in case I'm not kosher! My track record since my faux pas down here is completely without blemish. Sometimes those boys can get carried away with themselves, don't you think?'

Trevor knew he could rely on metropolitan disdain for the competence of anyone outside of London. He now turned his attention to the scenes outside. 'Who are all these people anyway? This has taken me quite by surprise, and I don't really know what they're up in arms about.'

'Seems there's a mix of grievances and agendas here, Trevor. Organised by Conspicuous Consumptionists, I'm sure. Has their fingerprints all over it, getting swarms of people to gather suddenly like this. Counter-revolutionaries and saboteurs, and stirring up discontent about shortages and so on. Maybe other agendas too. Look there, being held by those Militia—know who that is? Justin Talbot-Smith, son of a famous father. And, we're sure, the main ringleader of the Conspicuous Consumptionists. There's political agendas in there too, for sure. People who want to embarrass us and bring us down, bring an end to the Second Revolution.'

'But you were ready for them?'

'Sure. We knew about it two weeks ago.'

'And decided to make an example of them?'

Danny smiled enigmatically, then turned again to look out towards the masses in Trafalgar Square. Green Militia were advancing down the steps leading down to the fountains to cut off one group of demonstrators. Truncheons and tasers were being used quite liberally, followed closely by roving camera crews. Danny looked across at the director of the location crew. He was straining to hear something in his earpiece.

'OK, can you run that one again only this time in the south-west corner? The light's better there, out of the shadows … huh? OK, better get some others across there to throw themselves at the shields. I want someone really vicious-looking going for the Militia. Use one of the undercover guys if you have to. The Militia boys should be defensive only, got that? Yeh, call me when you're ready to run,' he said into his mic.

'This has always been my forte, Danny, where news meets drama, with a cast of thousands—what could top it?' said Trevor.

'Yes, history in the making,' added Danny Malik. 'This really could be your field, you know. Stick around, drop the tail-tweaking and the ironic tone, and before long you could be chronicling the most momentous changes ever to take place in this country—or anywhere in the world. We've got plenty of committed reporters, but frankly most of the new crop are too earnest and arse-licking by far. Lack creativity and imagination. The kind of qualities you could provide, as long as you reined in your … maverick tendencies.'

'Are you offering me a job?' exclaimed Trevor incredulously.

'Not a job, not yet. But an opportunity. An historic opportunity—if you can ever tear yourself away from the Palace.'

'I'm most flattered. We could talk more about this, don't you think? But your mentioning the Palace reminds me. I've got a meeting there with the Press Team at 11.30, and I need to go by the hotel to pick up what I need,' said Trevor.

'Sure, sure. Don't let me delay you. Glad to have the chance to meet with you again. One thing—why are you here with us today, Trevor?'

'Ah, Danny, you know me. I can't resist getting a good view of what's going on, from a safe vantage point. So I just talked my way in, and here I am.'

Danny reached out to shake hands. 'I hope you have as much success talking your way out.' He smiled broadly.

As Trevor left, Malik reached for his phone and called to report his surprise visitor. After a short delay he was messaged a report on Trevor MacLean's security status. *Suspect attitudes; suspected association with reversionary interests; current motivations unclear; media work beyond reproach since transfer to Scotland; no evidence of any actual counter-revolutionary activity.*

It was enough to ensure that Trevor was able to get safely back to his hotel.

63: Royal demands

It was the day after the riots. Don Mason was having one of his twice-weekly meetings with the King, and it was not going so well.

Mason was well aware that the King was increasingly the focus of reversionary and counter-revolutionary interests. He had tried to enthuse the King with more details of the plans for eco-settlements, but the King had an agenda of his own for the meeting, focusing on continued stories of ill-treatment and malnutrition at the eco-camps and work camps. And he was plainly getting information from his own sources.

'Now Mason, you say the camps are to be wound down and the inmates released to serve out their time in the community,' said the King. 'But I'm concerned about the conditions in the camps now. I'm still hearing reports of ill-treatment, and it seems as if the regime in the camps is as chaotic as ever—'

'Well, Sir, I'm sure if there are specific allegations, Malcolm will see that they are followed up—'

'Through Carl Fullerton?' said the King, exasperated. 'Can't you see that most of the incidents reported find their way back to his door? No, no, no. What's needed is an independent investigation to establish exactly what the conditions are like, and how people are being treated. When they were first set-up, some degree of irregularity might be expected. But after three and a half years, man, we should be having some stability! And without some degree of regularisation, I have no confidence that the release of detainees will go smoothly.'

'With respect, I really think that all we would do is close the stable door after the horse has bolted. What we need to do now is focus on how to integrate released detainees into the community—'

'I think you're not listening to me, Prime Minister. We have to put an end to this shambles once and for all. Now, I have a list of some seven hundred and thirty people, including some fairly eminent figures such as Miles Campbell, Peter Kitson, Heather Kitson, Terry Cairns and Louise Adams, two national newspaper editors, two chief executives of hospital trusts, several captains of industry, plus no end of ordinary citizens who seem to have disappeared without trace. I can see that the amnesty has every possibility of going wrong if these missing people do not turn up, as I suspect will happen.

'So, there are two things I want you to do. First, take this list and come back to me with chapter and verse on where they are and where they've been. Twenty-four hours should be enough if, as you say, things are not so bad. Secondly, I want your agreement to having a Royal Commission to investigate conditions in the camps. Clearly you'll want to discuss it with your colleagues, but I think the situation is so urgent now, especially with all these people arrested just yesterday in Trafalgar Square. I've drafted some terms of reference, and I'll have an investigative team under Lord Hulton ready to move within thirty-six hours. What do you think?'

'What do I think?' asked Mason, clearly taken aback. 'I think...I think that's not how we normally do things with any kind of Commission, especially Royal ones, if you don't mind me saying so.'

'Well, there are many things we do now that are not the way we used to do them. No, I have reliable information of serious irregularities and suffering, and we have to act fast to put things right. You should agree to this, even if only out of a sense of self-preservation. Once people start coming out, the writs will be flying left, right and centre. And if it seems you and your colleagues failed to take the opportunity to set things right, then it could be you standing in the dock taking it on the chin from the human rights lawyers. This is not something I wish to see happen to one of my governments, and one with which I have identified closely.'

Mason sighed thoughtfully.

'I'll consult with my colleagues on your requests, Sir. However, I do feel your sources must have exaggerated the conditions, and I suspect that they are partisan. It would help us if you could say where your information came from, and we can start to assess its reliability.'

'My sources are various, Prime Minister, and I'm confident of their reliability. I think it would be most appropriate if their reliability were tested through the investigations of the Commission, rather than pass them on to be prejudged by people who might turn out to be the focus of the investigation. And I have a suggestion. A strong suggestion.'

Mason raised his eyebrows in anticipation, but was unprepared for what followed.

'During the investigation process, I'd like the Militia to hand over the running of the all the camps to the army. I've already identified the units most able to take over, and established that they could move in within twenty-four hours.'

Don Mason was lost for words. This was clearly unacceptable, and more than that, was a strong challenge to his authority and the validity of the Green Revolution. He stood up, and gathered his papers together, scooping up the large plans he had spread out for the new sustainable settlements.

'It seems I have many things to get on with, Your Majesty,' he said.

'Indeed,' replied the King. 'I won't detain you any longer in that case.'

••

'I'll see MacLean now.'

The King was pacing up and down the room in deep thought when Trevor MacLean was shown in. Trevor was at once struck by the restrained sumptuousness of the room. An environment in which the King was completely at home, yet one that contrasted sharply with the austere functionality of his 'Total Farm' where Trevor had met him previously.

'Ah, MacLean, do come in. Sit down, sit down.'

Trevor sat down in one of the gilded eighteenth century chairs that generations of monarchs had used for meetings like this. He almost purred with pleasure as he felt the gilt work and upholstery of the chair, and looked across the room at the portraits in gilded frames.

The King did not sit down straight away, but continued his pacing. 'I'm sorry not to have called on you earlier, but I trust you've been able to occupy yourself in the capital?'

'I have indeed, Your Majesty, and most interesting it has been. Just yesterday I was able to film the most stage-managed riot in British history, and interview the Minister of Culture, who admitted it was pretty much all propaganda.'

'Really? Most incautious of him, was it not?'

'I suspect he didn't realise I had my little videocam activated in my coat pocket. You can't see much except copious amounts of pocket fluff, but it picked up the sound remarkably well. Wonderful thing, technology. I can add this to your dossier, though I think it has a different level of urgency. Mind you, the suppression of a free press is quite a significant issue, isn't it?'

'Yes, I fear it is,' said the King. 'Though I have to admit, I was also enjoying a more responsible press. A more restrained press has given my family a little more personal freedom. But, the reason I wanted to see you is that you'll be pleased to know I've been reading and digesting your dossier. And verifying some things, where I can. I'm ready to take things to the next level. But I want to be clear in my mind about certain aspects.'

For the next three hours the King remained closeted with Trevor, asking detailed questions about the people, policies and projects in the dossier, and telling Trevor about the activities now being coordinated through General Matthews. He also briefed Trevor on his meeting with Don Mason.

'It was a test of Mason, in a way. I didn't reveal our hand, but I wanted to test his attitude to letting his camps and the Militia come under scrutiny. He didn't rule it out, but he certainly didn't leap at the idea. He's got until tomorrow to come up with a response.'

'And if he says "no"?' asked Trevor.

'I doubt if he will refuse outright. What would you do in his shoes? Play for time, I imagine.'

'I can't imagine being in that position for one moment—playing for time in order to unleash a biological weapon.'

'The amnesty is planned for Earth Day. People will be released on the Wednesday, to be back home in time for the remainder of Earth Week. Apparently there's to be a media release about it this weekend. That gives ten days to pre-empt it. I'm sorry I didn't believe it all first time round—we've lost some time, haven't we?'

'So, Your Majesty. What are we looking at happening tomorrow? Will you take control?'

'I'm afraid it's the only option now. Mason will be dismissed, and I'll declare a State of National Emergency. Mason is due here at three in the afternoon, and I'll be taking control whether he agrees to my requests or not. MacLean, I want what we do to be done in full view. So I'm asking you to head up the process of liberating the media. Everything that happens, I want on film. Do you have your camera with you?'

'Yes—it's just outside.'

'Then you can start with these.'

The King went to a table and brought over two large envelopes, and emptied from them an array of surveillance devices that had been found in the Palace.

'General Matthews brought in some independent security this morning, and this is what they found when they swept. Though I daresay some of it predates Morton.'

'Phew! You were well and truly under their watchful eye!'

'Tell me, MacLean, do you think they've been playing me all along?'

Trevor thought hard before answering.

'I want a candid answer, not one to flatter me or spare my feelings, if you please,' added the King.

'To some extent, Sir, I think they played all of us—all of us who want a better and greener world. They capitalised on our genuine enthusiasm, and took us to a place where to refuse any apparently Green measure became an impossibility. And you, Sir—they exploited your reputation and held you up as a model, while all the time pursuing a more radical agenda. And maybe they capitalised on your isolation. They were able to support your quest for a Green nirvana and at the same time isolate you from the way the rest of us have experienced this revolution.'

'I see. Then it's time for me to emerge from this world of illusion I've locked myself in, wouldn't you say?'

64: Amnesty

'We cannot agree with this,' declared Malcolm Morton firmly.

After his meeting with the King, Don Mason had called his senior Ministers and advisers to him. They had to decide what to do with the King's demands—or 'requests' as he had put it.

Morton was very disturbed by the new direction being taken by the King. He was aware of an apparently growing number of contacts that the King had with counter-revolutionary elements. And he was also now beginning to absorb the possible significance of the curious meeting that Danny Malik had reported with Trevor MacLean.

'This sudden reappearance of MacLean in the entourage of the King just at the time when he seems to undergo a change of heart can't be just coincidence. MacLean will have to be brought in for questioning'. He looked across at Danny Malik.

'MacLean has been monitored closely for any signs of contact with Stella Walton and the Kitson Circle,' said Malik. 'And we know that the only recorded contact was a telephone conversation in which MacLean very firmly rejected the chance to be involved in anything subversive. All the same, there are questions to ask.'

Sarah Turner, as a die-hard republican, thought Mason had been too indulgent in his dealings with royalty. 'Just say "No". Call his bluff! Then we'll see how far his power extends in reality.'

Doug Cunningham agreed. 'He has status for sure, but he has no right to insist on these matters. I know you have a soft spot for him and his mid-green enthusiasm, Don, but his support is not essential for us. We can move on without him, and if we must, then so be it.'

'The way I think of it,' said Morton, 'is that we haven't got where we are by being defensive. He's making demands of us. So we turn the tables on him. Challenge him on his contacts with counter-revolutionary elements—especially General Matthews. I'll get a list drawn up of his advisers and hangers-on, and we can challenge him on their connections and attitudes.'

Don Mason looked pensive. He knew a crisis point had been reached. As he was about to speak, one of Morton's advisers from the Ministry of Defence entered the room and spoke quietly too him. All eyes turned towards Morton, who now looked very grave.

'You have some news, Malcolm?' asked Mason.

Morton nodded slowly. 'Yes. It's about unauthorised troop movements. We have reports of regiments based in Europe and the Middle East on the move, apparently making their way back to Britain. And joint American and European military exercises departing from their expected plans, with forces concentrating in the Low Countries.'

'Shit,' said Cunningham. There was a stunned silence for a few moments.

'We need a new plan, I think,' said Mason.

Malcolm Morton was disappointed but not entirely surprised by the news. He had been fearing a strong reaction from the forces of counter-revolution.

Gabriella was typically forthright. 'You have to play for time, Don. And the rest of us have to move fast. We bring the Amnesty forward. There's no other option. When do you think they want to strike? And can we hold them back when they do?'

'We need to know if it's practical to bring the Amnesty forward,' said Mason. 'And if we can bring it forward, we need to see how much this will compromise the objectives.'

'What other options are there, Don?' demanded Pearson.

'Get the stuff out of New Dawn, and cover our tracks,' said Don. 'Then we return to subversive mode. We live to fight another day.'

'We need to ask Annie about this,' suggested Sarah Turner. 'Can we get her on screen?'

Within a few moments Annie Lee, wearing her white lab coat, appeared on the large screen at the end of the room. Malcolm Morton briefed her on the expected crisis.

'When you say bring it forward, when exactly are you thinking of?' asked Lee.

'Tomorrow morning,' said Mason.

'Wow. Really?' asked Annie, now looking distinctly troubled.

'Or the other option is to scuttle the ship, and take away everything of value for a future date. Then cover all the traces as far as possible.'

'Bringing everything forward is more practical,' said Annie without hesitation. 'We've already started shipping supplies out to most of the camps. Recalling it and hiding it away is not possible. The best way to reduce stocks is to use it! If you can get all the planned vectors in from outside and anyone needing immunity by tomorrow morning, then that part of it will be OK. Compromised, but doable. The main headache is with the overseas missions. They need more lead time, and I can't see them going to plan.'

'Malcolm, if the Counter-Revolutionaries move in overnight, how long can our forces resist them?' asked Mason.

'As far as we can see the situation, they are not in a position to make a move tonight. But they may be by morning. What we don't know yet is how loyal the armed forces are here. We'll try to get a better picture in the next few hours.'

'Well, we have work to do,' said Mason. 'We must do the best we can. Though we fear the worst, I need to prepare to deal with the King. If he is pivotal to these events, perhaps I can sow enough doubts in his mind to buy some time. But I'm not hopeful.

'Listen now. We always thought our time in government could end abruptly, one way or another. And it looks like it probably will, in the next forty-eight hours or so. Whatever happens, this is only one stage on the journey. So you need to prepare your exit plans, to get away to where you can take it on to the next level. So let's get to it, and do the best we can in the time left.'

As he threw himself into action, Malcolm Morton felt the adrenalin flowing, feeling a mixture of thrill and desperation as he chased up intelligence reports and issued orders to his people in the MoD and the Green Militia. All this time he worked closely with Gabriella Pearson. They rushed forward the plans for the 'amnesty' of eco-camp detainees. The Green Militia worked through the night to get personnel, buses, and biological agents into position, ready to unleash Operation Cyrus on the nation in the morning.

Meanwhile armed detachments of Green Militia were ordered to move into London to take control of strategic locations. The stage was set for a contest that Morton knew he could not win by conventional means.

As the picture became clearer, Morton admitted to Gabriella Pearson that he was a little dismayed at the lack of loyalty in the armed forces. The disloyalty was not universal, but it seemed the strength of traditional attachments outweighed loyalty to the elected government or to the people that he had put in post.

In this sense everything was happening too soon, before the 'greening' or 'harmonising' of the armed forces was complete. As Gabriella reminded him, the basis of Operation Cyrus was surprise. Somehow they had lost the element of surprise, and now the only thing to do was to snatch it back.

While her colleagues launched themselves into action, Sarah Turner returned to her desk and found herself incapable of action. Shortly she went back to Mason's office. 'I need a word, Don. Alone.'

Mason nodded to his staff who immediately left the room.

'Don, we don't have to do this. It's not too late to turn back.'

Mason sighed quietly. 'You're right, Sarah, we don't. But you of all people should know. We've run through all scenarios. We've had every resource at our disposal to probe the alternatives. And in two generations, every scenario leads to disaster. Every year we delay, the Planet dies a little bit more. And the prospects for humanity don't improve either. I wish it were otherwise, I truly do. But we know more now than when we came into office. We know what they were hiding from us. A world of fifteen billion people living at today's level of prosperity—we all know it can't happen. Even half that number doesn't work. The cost of compromise is too high. The only question is the rate at which we destroy the Earth.'

'I'm not sure I can bear this, that's the problem, Don,' said Sarah, tears beginning to roll down her cheeks. 'Does it have to be us?'

Don stood up, and came over to Sarah to hug her. Then he gripped her arms gently. 'Be strong. Be wise. Go to a safe place. The Movement needs you to be strong, for whatever comes next.'

After a few moments, Sarah wiped her eyes, and took a deep breath. Then, nodding her head several times and biting her lip, she left the room.

65: Bullets and vaccines

The citizens of London awoke on that crisp April morning to the sound of armed trucks rolling through their streets; barricades, road blocks and checkpoints being set up and an announcement through all the media of the imminent release of all the eco-camp detainees.

Five hundred miles north, the release of the inmates was announced at the West Highland Eco-camp. This worried Sam Sharma intensely.

'This ain't right,' Sam said, the one sour note amidst all the euphoria. When news of the General Amnesty was announced, the detainees were elated, though taken by surprise despite the odd rumour that had been circulating. Their Militia guards were tired and tetchy, having worked through the night to deal with the practicalities of the Amnesty coming more than a week earlier than expected.

Stocks of plague labelled as 'vaccine' had arrived on the buses that had brought in more than a hundred detainees who had been held at North Camp, or New Dawn as they now preferred to call it. These detainees sat wearily on buses just outside the camp gates, while inmates of the West Highland Eco-Camp stood in line for their injections before being sent on their journey home. Sam Sharma had promptly disappeared, urging Heather Kitson to do likewise. But seven months pregnant, Heather was now quite large, and feeling larger than she looked. And she felt almost constantly nauseous, unlike in her previous pregnancy during which no one could see her without coming out with some cliché about 'blooming'.

There was no bloom in this pregnancy. And no chance of her following Sam into his hiding place, a narrow gap in the roof space of one of the huts. Whatever she did, she would have to take her chances at ground level. Stella Walton's story had alarmed her from the moment these new vaccinations were first mentioned. And even if the vaccinations were genuine, in her condition it was clearly something better to avoid.

She pleaded with the Militia guards who found her, as they forced her along, one holding each arm and leading her into the clinic. She reasoned, argued, begged, struggled and screamed, warning of the potential damage to her baby.

'You won't have to worry about that,' said the most senior Militia officer, Perry Jones, newly arrived from New Dawn that morning. A nurse Heather had not seen before administered the injection as the Militia guards held Heather down in a chair.

Sobbing, Heather was escorted out of the clinic, while other freshly injected inmates boarded buses with cheery smiles, relieved to be on their way home. So it was that on a bright but cold spring morning on the west coast of Scotland, Heather Kitson was 'vaccinated' with a genetically modified version of bubonic plague.

••

Mason was escorted to the Palace by a large bodyguard of armed Militia. He had called the Palace, unilaterally bringing the planned meeting forward to first thing in the morning. While he entered the Palace, more Green Militia moved into position in Westminster and around the Palace.

The King was immensely irritated by Mason bringing the meeting forward in this way, without consulting him or his staff. It was not how Prime Ministers behaved towards their monarch, but he understood the meaning. This was about power, and Mason was asserting his supremacy. The King sighed, but all the same he looked forward to the meeting now that he had made his decision.

Mason was looking out of the window across to Hyde Park, where Green Militia units were establishing themselves, when the King entered the room.

'Prime Minister, you are somewhat ahead of schedule, it seems,' said the King.

'Yes, my apologies for that. But it seems there is a lot of pressing business today,' Mason replied as he took a seat on the small sofa that the King was gesturing to. The King took his seat opposite.

Mason got straight down to business. 'I have the list of detainees you gave me, with details of their whereabouts. But of course it's largely academic, as we've brought forward the Amnesty. No doubt you've heard on the news. And that clears up the other issues, like the camps being taken over by the army.'

'Hmm,' said the King, glancing quickly down the list of names. 'Largely academic? And maybe to a certain extent fictitious? I see here that Terry Cairns is alive and living in North Wales. Yet we've known for some time that the unfortunate fellow died in one of the camps. Did you know that, Prime Minister?'

He tossed the list contemptuously down onto the coffee table. 'I'll have my people check it through for other anomalies. Now, before we get onto other matters, I have to tell you that I won't be granting the Royal Assent to your bill to extend the Parliament to ten years. It's not warranted by the current circumstances, and if you want to take your policies further you will need to get the approval of the electorate. Besides, you have in principle nearly a year and a half before an election has to be called.'

'The Bill has been approved by both Houses of Parliament and by the Green Convention, so we would expect your Assent as a matter of course,' protested Mason. 'Still, Your Majesty, I think that today that is hardly the point. We're dealing in shorter time periods than eighteen months or ten years, aren't we? I mean the unauthorised movements of the armed forces both here and overseas. Do you know anything about these? And if so, could you explain the reasons for them? And can you assure me that you are not involved in any illegal measures to put pressure on—or, God forbid, overthrow the elected government?'

The King looked at him sharply. 'I am Commander-in-Chief of the armed forces in this country, and they are responsible to me. You wish it to be a purely honorary position. To a large extent this is so. But the levers of power in this country are subtle, and contain checks and balances to preserve us from tyranny, whether the will to tyranny comes from the monarch or from, shall we say, other directions. The system is out of balance, and all kinds of wrongdoing and injustices are slipping into the life of the nation.'

He paused as if bracing himself for a confrontation. He knew now was the time to act decisively against Mason. 'Now. Tell me about Operation Cyrus.'

Mason looked startled. 'Operation Cyrus? I have no idea what you are talking about!'

'Come now, man, don't treat me like an idiot!' snapped the King angrily, getting to his feet and starting to pace the room. 'Population rebalancing. The Noah Principle. The shipments between Porton Down and New Dawn! Don't tell me you know nothing about these? Are you not responsible for the actions of your colleagues Morton, Pearson, Fullerton, Collingworth?'

Mason let out a theatrical guffaw. 'The Noah Principle! That old rubbish! Who has been feeding you this nonsense?'

'The amnesty must be halted. We have stopped one of the buses from the North Norfolk camp. It seems everyone on board is seriously sick.'

'We? Who is "we"?' demanded Mason, also standing up. 'So you are involved in a conspiracy?'

The King stopped by the window, and looked out at the Militia assembled at the gates. He turned and nodded to his assistant, who went to the door of the room.

'I see you've arrived mob-handed today. I assume your Militia friends aren't here for a picnic in the park?'

The King walked calmly but assertively towards Mason. 'Let me tell you a little story. Once, as I was greeting people on a state occasion outside the gates, a small boy asked me if those soldiers in the red uniforms and furry hats are real. Let me tell you what I told him. "Yes, they are real. Armed and ready in case of emergencies". You should understand that, Mason, before sending out your toy soldiers on the street.'

'I think it's clear now where we stand,' said Mason sharply, preparing to leave.

'Perhaps not clear enough. You're dismissed, and I'll be appointing a new Prime Minister within the day.'

With that, he nodded to the security guards who had been let into the room.

'These gentlemen will keep you company here until matters become a little clearer. This could take some time. Perhaps you would care for some tea, now?'

Mason sat down, momentary anger giving way to a wry smile on his face. He knew protests would be useless and demeaning.

'Your phone please, and any other communication devices you may have on your person,' said one of the security officers.

'Maybe I should just inform my colleagues and my staff about this… change of circumstances, don't you think?' said Mason.

'I'm sure word will get to them soon enough,' said the King. Then he turned and left the room.

66: Birth-pangs

By ten o'clock in the morning the final buses had left the West Highland Eco-camp. Sam Sharma was not on any of them. Nor was Heather Kitson. Hysterically Heather had fought and screamed, refusing to be taken on the bus. She was sure she had been infected with something, and feared she would die on the bus, or worse still pass it on to people she loved. Finally she began to vomit uncontrollably—from hysteria, as it was too soon for the disease to be having that effect.

'She can stay and fend for herself. A poisoned chalice for the counter-revolutionary forces when they arrive,' said Perry Jones, the officer in charge of this operation. Freshly arrived from New Dawn, he now exuded a calm and steely authority. He felt as if he was Chosen, entrusted with one of the most—no, *absolutely* the most—important task in human history. And he was determined to take it through to its conclusion, repaying the faith that Carl Fullerton had put in him.

Jones noticed the difference in himself now. Previously people would respect him for his ability, but not take him entirely seriously as a leader. Now he could feel the fear and respect his very presence commanded.

It had not been easy. He had seen things at New Dawn that no one would want to see. He himself didn't want to see it—but he took it all in, made himself as hard as steel. He authorised further tests, watched the effects, and supervised the burials. He stood by an open grave as the corpses of the human 'lab rats' (as the Militia called them) were thrown in by other doomed inmates. He had stood there and pronounced 'Mother Earth takes her revenge!'

He had seen the hatred on the eyes of the inmates at New Dawn, and grown strong in their hatred. Their enmity and opposition strengthened his resolve. Now he had demonstrated his abilities of command in the execution of this critical phase of Operation Cyrus. He had heard that the North Norfolk Eco-camp had despatched some carriers earlier, but theirs was a smaller camp, and their evacuation was not yet complete. And they had been given extra resources to move fast to get their selected 'missionaries' to the airports and the centres where the biological agents were to be released. But his, Perry Jones', operation had proved to be the most swift and complete overall, and this was bound to come to the attention of Carl Fullerton and Malcolm Morton.

And he rejoiced too, that the date for his own death was now set: in ten years' time on April 13th, on what would be the tenth anniversary of this great day. As a signatory of the Voluntary Holocaust, he had foresworn having children and had dedicated himself to the salvation of the Earth. And he had taken the genuine vaccines morally secure in the knowledge that his sacrifice of others was bound up in his sacrifice of himself.

Now he looked at Heather Kitson as she sobbed on the ground by his feet. Pity was now an emotion he recognised early, and he had trained himself to expunge all symptoms of it through clear thought and action. This was the remedy prescribed by Malcolm Morton in his *Guidelines for Green Activists Entrusted with Special Missions*.

His clear-thinking led him to meditate on the multiple ironies of his situation. It was his unsuccessful interrogation of Peter Kitson that had led to his being sent away to New Dawn. He had at first considered it as a reprimand, but now he understood that it was to test his abilities and his resolve. And it was he who had first ordered the detention of Heather Kitson, in order to put pressure on her husband. It had seemed so important at the time. But now any information they had withheld was irrelevant. Peter Kitson had revealed little more, and Stella Walton now lay in an unmarked grave in the newly planted woods behind this eco-camp. It had all seemed so important, but now all trace of them would fade forever into the lost world of human history.

Here was Heather Kitson, seven months pregnant. The inevitable death of her unborn child seemed to encapsulate the death of human arrogance, the death of human selfishness on this planet. This is what Operation Cyrus was all about: the birth-pangs of a new rebalanced world through the death-pangs of the human species' boundless egoism.

He could hasten things, and put her out of her suffering, which would come on in a few hours. 'No, let nature take its course,' he thought, and walked away. Any sign of pity at this stage could weaken him for what lay ahead.

After half an hour, Jones and most of the camp personnel had left in their Militia vehicles. Only a handful of staff remained, plus two or three inmates in the clinic—plus Heather Kitson and Sam Sharma. Heather felt the hand on her shoulder.

'Heather, get inside! You'll freeze!' said Sam.

'Sam! Oh, Sam, keep away from me, don't touch me! They've given me something, like poor Stella!' cried Heather.

Sam backed off a little, partly for fear of upsetting her further, and partly out of self-preservation. 'Still, you can't stay outside. Get inside this cabin, and I can make a fire to keep you warm. You've gotta think of the—'

Sam stopped himself abruptly. Heather was thinking of the baby, of course, and could think of almost nothing else.

As Sam led the way inside, Heather asked him, 'How can they do this to us? How can they do this to my child? What kind of people are they?'

'Maybe it's OK,' said Sam, trying to be reassuring. 'We don't know what they put in you. Could be a vaccine, like they say. Could be it won't do either of you no 'arm.'

'Oh Sam, what am I going to do?'

'Well, I'll tell you what I'm going to do, I'm going to get you a doctor. Must be a phone here that works. You just hold on, and keep yourself together, alright?'

As Sam left, Heather called, 'Be careful! They haven't all gone yet!'

'Don't worry,' called Sam. 'I'm a survivor!'

He left the cabin, but came straight back, poking his head round the door.

'And so are you, and the little'un! Alright?' he called.

The camp, normally so full of bustle seemed deserted now. Sam ran as fast as he could to the clinic. Two inmates evidently too sick to move, were lying on beds. One of them looked little more than a skeleton. A third patient with a broken leg, arm and neck-brace was painfully moving himself about the clinic, looking for medicines for himself and the other patients.

'Bloody 'ell,' said Sam when he saw this scene. 'You guys don't look too clever. Hey, is that you, George?'

He recognised the inmate with the neck brace as someone who had worked with him on tree-planting detail, and had tried to run away. Sam thought he was a bit of a boaster—said he used to be in Special Branch. But it was very sad to see him in this way.

'They caught you, then?'

'I gave them a good run, though,' said George softly. 'Took me into North Camp, then back here.' Speaking was clearly difficult for him.

'I don't suppose there's a doctor around, is there?' asked Sam.

'They've all gone, and left us to it. Gave us some more injections, then went their merry way.'

'Oh. That's not good. I think we need to get a doctor or two here pronto. There's a sick woman, very pregnant, in one of them cabins. Heather, you know 'er of course. Do the phones work?'

'Not here, we've tried. Mostly they used the computers for making calls, and they've all gone. Kind of weird. Look in there, in the office. Cleared everything out. And look out the back. Those guys over there—they're burning things. Something's going down, and I think it's all over. But I don't get this bussing everyone out, doesn't make any sense. Maybe—maybe help is on the way. Why else would they be leaving so suddenly?'

'Maybe. But I don't wanna wait on a maybe. I'll skadoodle up to the office, and see if I can phone out from there.'

Sam ran across the site to the camp office. It was empty. Strangely so. All computers were gone, but screens had been left. Filing cabinets were open, with some drawers emptied but others still half full. He lifted a phone. It worked.

'Doctor, doctor ... how do I find a bleedin' doctor?' he mumbled to himself. He was trying to remember where exactly in the UK he was. In his wheeling and dealing he had heard the names of a number of towns and villages, but had no clear idea of how close or far they were. He could dial 999, but that might involve the police and he had no trust in them.

It struck him as strange that here he was in a government punishment camp dialling Directory Enquiries, asking for a doctor to come to somewhere in the middle of nowhere to deal with cases of possible plague. And would they take him seriously enough to send a doctor out to an eco-camp?

Inverness! That was the biggest place he'd seen on his journey as he got closer to the camp, but that still had been a long journey away. And he seemed to remember that was in the east of Scotland, while this was the West Highland camp. But he could call the hospital there, there was bound to be one. They could organise sending the nearest doctor, or something. With some difficulty, Sam was able to persuade them to send help—all he could get them to agree to was to find the person who could get there quickest while they sent an ambulance out from Inverness.

Heather was pacing frantically around the cabin when he returned. 'So stupid! I should have got on the bus! I'd be somewhere where they could help the baby! I could do something!'

Sam tried to calm her, and told her that help was coming from Inverness. She could go to the clinic, where she could be more comfortable. But when he told her of the other patients there, how they had also received injections, at first she refused to go. Maybe they all had the same thing and would die anyway, but there was too great a risk of catching or spreading something.

After a few minutes going over the possibilities, they both went across to the office. The doctors had asked Sam to stay near the phone he had called from. The sun was shining strongly now, welcome after seemingly months of snow and rain. It was still cold, but the sunshine helped to instil in Sam a sense of optimism.

'Let's get you inside,' he said. 'It's quite warm in here. Much better insulated than them cabins. All creature comforts, all mod cons, you see.'

'I don't mind the cold,' Heather said. 'I'm feeling quite warm, a bit feverish actually.'

'You've gone an' caught yourself a chill,' said Sam. 'How long were you sitting out there in the cold? Must have been nearly a couple of hours. That's 'ow long I was up in the roof. Couldn't come down 'cos of all them geezers pulling stuff around and burning it right by the cabin.'

'I hope it's only a chill,' said Heather faintly.

''Ere, look what I've found. Cupboard full of tasers. Fancy going off without all these. Used to be right fond of zapping us with them, bunch of shits. Can't have charged these off their solar power. Take a whole summer of sunshine up 'ere to charge up just one of these, we used to joke. Even them Militia guys used to joke about it, saying like "How'dya like six months of Scottish sunshine?" before letting rip with it. Sadistic bastards, the lot of 'em!'

'We've got to stop the buses!' Heather said suddenly. She slapped herself on the forehead. 'Christ, what was I thinking of? Sam, call them again, whoever you called, and tell them what's happening!'

'Well, I did kind of mention it, but didn't say, like, you gotta stop 'em.'

Heather was soon on the phone to the Infectious Diseases Unit at Inverness Hospital. Doctor John Geddie was not entirely encouraging.

'We're not a large hospital; we're just not geared up to deal with an emergency like you're talking about. We used to have emergency exercises for biological terrorism a few years back, but since the terrorism ended it's been more back to normal as far as treatment is concerned.'

'But you must have some procedures for containment in place. These buses need to be stopped, and everyone on them must be isolated!' Heather pleaded.

'Well, even if you're right, and I've no confirmation of that, then it's the local council that has to deal with that,' said the doctor.

'And they're being run by the people who are doing this! Listen, I'm telling you, this is not a hoax, and I'm not crazy. You recognise me? You can see who I am, Heather Kitson. You know who I am, and you know who my husband is—'

'Mrs Kitson, I am taking you seriously, please believe me. I tried to get the nearest local GP down from Ullapool to get treatment started, but he's about an hour away by car, and he says he's up to his ears with his regular patients at the moment. We've sent up a helicopter with a medical team on board, and as long as it's safe to land they'll be with you and the other sick people in less than an hour. So I take you seriously, but we haven't got the resources or the power to deal with things on a grand scale.'

'OK, the police. There'll be people in the police who can help, or there must be a way of escalating this through the NHS so people are prepared across the whole country. If they are doing this here, they must be doing the same kind of thing from other eco-camps too. Don't you see?'

'Mrs Kitson, you know that bubonic plague is not normally transmitted from one person to another...?'

'I didn't know that. Is that good news for my baby? But you sounded like you were going to say "unless..." '

'The "unless" is: unless it has been genetically modified. I have heard talk about when it comes to bioterrorism. Sorry—can you hear me, it's very noisy here!'

Heather could barely hear for the noise at the other end of the line. Gradually it faded. Now the doctor was talking animatedly with his colleagues. Heather could barely contain her anxiety and impatience.

'Hold on, Heather, please. This is ... we don't know what's going on!'

There was a pause of several minutes. They could hear the doctor talking to colleagues, get up, move away, then return.

'Those were American planes going over. On their way to Lossiemouth, I think. Big transport planes, and dozens of them. And we've just heard that there are tanks on the streets of London, and some fighting too, but no one knows what it's all about. And apparently we've got the army—the British Army—moving into Inverness too. What's that?'

There was another pause of a few minutes while the doctor talked animatedly with others in the background.

'They're saying that the local council has been taken over by a provisional military authority, and the Earth Councillors are being arrested—well those they can track down. Bloody hell, we can start to run a proper hospital again!'

'John, listen to me!' Heather yelled at the phone several times, until the doctor returned to his seat, his face very animated.

'Listen, John. Now you can do it. Stop those buses. Get them stopped now!'

Suddenly the doctor looked serious.

'I'll do it. But Heather, move your face closer to the camera, will you? Turn to the right a little. Is your nose bleeding?'

Now the doctor advised Heather and Sam about how to make Heather comfortable until the medical team arrived. The disease was evidently progressing very fast, with symptoms developing in a few hours that could normally take up to six days. Sam was advised to wear a face mask at all times.

Sam ran to the clinic again to get the items suggested by the doctor. The main thing, the doctor said, was to keep the fever down, make her drink a lot of fluids, and try to keep her calm. For possibly the first time in his life, Sam found himself doing exactly what he was told with a willing heart.

'I'm OK. Now, Sam, phone your wife,' Heather told him on his return. While he was gone, she had tried phoning everyone she could think of. She couldn't get through to her parents—network always busy, or so the recorded message said. And when she called Joanna and Rachel Dean, there was only voicemail.

After tending to Heather, Sam phoned his wife. It took several attempts, but eventually he got through.

'Sam!!' his wife screamed when she heard him say, 'How are you, darlin'?'

Heather smiled as she could hear excited screaming at the other end. Some of his kids ran to the phone and were crowding in front of the camera, waving and shouting ecstatically. He was weeping for sure, but kept his back to Heather to preserve his dignity. Heather leaned back on the couch, enjoying her first encounter with happiness for many weeks.

She remembered how Sam several weeks ago had offered her some other vaccine, and his explanation of why he was putting his faith in it.

'If the greenfly are takin' it, it's kosher. If the rest of us are getting' it, it ain't. Simple as that!'

She had refused his caring offer, for fear of harming the baby. He had taken her under his wing and looked after her. There was no profit in that, but it seemed he had done it without hesitation. Seeing him talk with his family, she understood more about the man, and the pieces seemed to fall into place somehow.

Maybe, she thought, scenes like this are being played out throughout the length and breadth of the land. Then she recalled that many of the lost returning home to loving embraces were probably ticking biological bombs, and her mood of reverie and happiness was replaced by pain and anguish.

'Sam,' she called softly, tentative about breaking into his reunion.

'Yes? Oh, darlin', I'm here wiv a very famous lady, and possibly a rather sick lady too. In the family way too. I'm lookin' after her until the medics arrive. Do you recognise her?'

He turned the phone towards Heather, who sat forward on the sofa. She could see a tearful Kelly Sharma and two of the Sharma children.

'Hello,' said Heather softly, trying to ignore the pain from the cramps that were starting to grip her insides. 'I'm Heather. You know my sister-in-law Joanna, I believe, she took on Sam's case in the early days. Your husband has been very kind to me, you know.'

'Hi, Heather. I'm Kelly. How is he really? He'd never tell me if something was up!'

'Really, he's fine. Fit and healthy despite everything. A very resourceful man, your Sam. And when he's not regaling me with his philosophy of life, all he talks about is you and his family. You know that?'

Kelly laughed through her tears as she listened to Heather's words.

'I'm sorry to interrupt your reunion,' continued Heather. 'But I desperately need some news. What's happening in London? And have you heard anything about my husband, Peter? And my daughter—of course you won't know, but I need to get some news! Can you help me find something out?'

Kelly knew nothing about what had happened to Heather's family, but told her all she knew about what was happening in London. The day had started with an announcement of the amnesty, then suddenly there were Militia everywhere, and soon after that reports of army units moving into the streets of London. About 10.30, they had heard the first shots, and there had been sporadic shooting and a few explosions throughout the rest of the day so far. There was a news blackout, it seemed, with all the channels showing reruns of soaps and game shows. Then a call for calm on all channels, saying rogue army elements were attempting to seize control of the country: people should stay indoors and keep calm. Access to the Internet was being blocked. With no news to go on, everyone was calling each other and rumours were rife. The two older Sharma boys had joined with friends to go and 'take over' the local

Earth Council and Town Hall. Sam protested about their safety, and that they should stay out of politics.

'They're doing it for you, Sam. They want to end this madness and get you back home! They're young men and they can't stand by and do nothing!' said Kelly.

That was all she knew. So Sam and Heather passed to her the news that the military were taking over in Scotland, and the Americans were on their way too. People should keep calm, Sam advised: the cavalry was coming.

67: A very public coup

For Trevor MacLean, the arrest of Don Mason under his nose was the scoop to end all scoops. After some indecision and several telephone discussions with their collaborators outside, the Palace allowed Trevor to interview Don Mason, the recently deposed Prime Minister of the United Kingdom, with the sound of sporadic gunfire providing a dramatic backdrop.

As Trevor took his seat opposite him, Mason was busy eyeing up the sherry and brandy decanters on a cabinet behind Trevor.

'Mind if I have a drink?' asked Mason in a weary voice.

'Not at all,' replied Trevor. 'Be my guest. Or rather, His Majesty's guest.'

'Or the tax-payer's guest,' suggested Mason with a sardonic shrug as he got up to pour himself a large Scotch.

Mason seemed calm, resigned, even relieved as he poured himself a large brandy.

'What's your poison?' he asked Trevor.

'Would be a Scotch,' said Trevor, 'but not when I'm working.'

'Ah, there's the difference. I'm not working any more, am I?' said Mason with a wry smile.

'If I may say so, Mr Mason, you're taking everything very calmly under the circumstances?' said Trevor. 'Considering there seems to be a civil war starting outside...'

Mason smiled enigmatically. 'What do you expect me to do, rant and rave?'

'If you could manage that at least once for the cameras, we'll pay double,' suggested Trevor.

'You're a strange man, MacLean. At the outset, you seemed a good friend to the movement. Then you ruffle some feathers with your incorrigibly flippant and challenging style, and disappear to the back of beyond for a couple of years. Suddenly you're back, right in the centre of things, seemingly a central figure in the counter-revolution. I'd like to know more about what you've been up to all this time.'

'I'm flattered by your interest, of course. But in this kind of situation, I think it's more newsworthy to know what you've been up to this past few years.'

'Maybe. But to me the word "interview" implies a two-way flow of information, don't you think? Indulge me a little.'

'Well, you're interested now, perhaps. But I don't suppose you gave a moment's thought over the past two and a half years as to where I was. For all you knew, I was in one of your camps, being re-educated. Or maybe learning how to die. Actually, I was being a good Green boy, growing my own vegetables and keeping the faith. I did a lot of recycling too. Mainly old news, as new news was a touch too dangerous.'

'What brought you back?'

'I ask myself that. Maybe hunger for a real scoop. But I think most of all, respect for someone else's courage. One of the victims of your revolution. Do you remember Stella Walton?'

'I know the name. Never met her though. I'm told she was one of the Kitson Circle.'

'Actually, Don, you did meet her. At least three times. In the early days. She was always kind to you. But maybe she was beneath your gaze while you had higher things to consider.'

Mason was silent for a moment. Then the penny dropped.

'Your colleague at those first interviews. The researcher. How is she?'

Trevor was feeling quite emotional, and turned away for a moment to collect himself. Mason looked down at his brandy glass, then finished the contents. Trevor knew he had to regain his balance, be more professional to make the most of this occasion, to get Mason talking openly. At last he turned back to face Mason.

'I don't know, Don. It seems she spent a lot of time in the Scottish Eco-Camps. I've been trying to get news. I think she's on your list, but I'm not sure the information on there is correct.'

'The list is pretty worthless, Trevor,' admitted Mason candidly. 'Even more so this morning. If she was in a camp, she'll be on her way home by now.'

Trevor bit back the accusing and flippant comments that sprung into his mind.

'Don, I want to ask you: why do you think you've been ousted from power today?'

'A good question, and a big question,' Mason replied. 'There are two sides to it, I guess. On one side, it's fair to say we lost the impetus, the momentum behind the Revolution after about eighteen months. To be frank, our popular support lasted longer than we expected. There are tougher measures that are necessary to move the Revolution forward, and people are not psychologically ready for it yet. Sometimes we thought we should go slower, but I don't think it would have made us much more popular. We would just have achieved less while allowing opposition to grow.'

Trevor motioned Mason to continue. Mason stood up to refill his glass, pouring a Scotch for Trevor and putting it in front of him. There was an increase in the sound of shooting outside.

'On the other side, it's clear the forces of reaction have been gathering for some time. What's happening today wasn't prepared overnight.'

'And what exactly is happening?'

'Well, stuck here I'm not quite in the best position to know. But from what I knew before I came here, it seems like treacherous elements in the armed forces and the establishment have combined with President Wilding and others abroad who don't like what we're doing, and they're trying to topple a democratically elected government. We had intelligence of the conspiracy forming, and tried to take counter-measures. But the odds seem stacked in their favour, wouldn't you say?'

'You seem philosophical, rather than indignant?'

'I am indignant, but I am not in a position to change things at the moment. You must know that I have always been a man of practical action. Our vision is worthless unless we have the means to realise it. We need power to change things. Power comes in many forms. Running a government is only one of them.

'In the days of struggle, I always used to say that the British establishment is too entrenched to be overthrown. So we had to get inside it, to work with it. Our opportunity would come in one of the periodic crises when the establishment loses confidence in itself and its tacit mission. That happened. But it seems we haven't been able to purge and remould the establishment quickly enough. It has regrouped, and it is coming back at us with a vengeance. In the past, the British establishment has always exercised tolerance towards dissent, but crushes any attempt at subversion with overwhelming force. Once it is secure, it will safely adopt some of the revolutionary ideas as its own. So, assuming they win, I expect some light green measures as a sop to bring about national unity. But it won't be enough.'

'Enough?'

'The central issues will still remain, and become more acute with every year that passes. The struggle is not over. The issues will have to be faced, whether we want to or not. And the worldwide Green Movement will have to find other means to get results if the political process is off limits to us'

'What are the issues we have to face?'

Mason let forth a mild guffaw.

'Come on, now, Trevor? Where have you been for the past four years? Do you want me to revisit all the things we've said in this time? Everyone by now must know what the issues are, even if they don't agree with what how we want to deal with them!'

'Yes and no. It's the so-called "Second Revolution" issues I would like to hear about. Reversing economic growth and reducing population. How crucial to the future of the planet are these?'

Mason hesitated for around a minute before answering, clearly weighing up what he should say. He knew that this was possibly the last time he would be able to put forward his views to the public.

'They are critical,' he said at last.

'Putting the economy into reverse, and reducing the population are critical?'

'Not "putting it into reverse", as you say. But we should not all kneel before the god of endless growth. We can, and shall, have a fully functional economy that does not depend on that. At the moment, our economy is built on consuming too much, and producing boundless waste. Our methods were starting to hurt, sure, but we have been moving in the right direction. More localised, small-scale production and distribution, with the full environmental costs factored in; growing our own food, making our own clothes—in effect for many people taking these activities into the non-money economy...'

'And to achieve this it's necessary to end capitalism?'

'End or transform—I wouldn't want to be hung up on words. For me capitalism is neither bad nor good. It reflects one aspect of human nature: to produce, to trade, to accumulate, to lay something in for the future. But the system we've ended up with cannot last. Whether we win or lose, it cannot last. Today's capitalism is helping to destroy the planet, through reckless consumption in the pursuit of personal gain. It needs to be scaled right back to a truly human scale, to a natural level. I know the process may be painful, and that it will inspire vigorous and selfish resistance.'

'I'd like to be clearer about what you mean by "a truly human scale",' asked Trevor. 'Because the economy we have supports a vast social infrastructure including schools, hospitals, transport systems, social services, police and prisons, and so on and so on. All this becomes if not impossible, then much harder to support if the economy ceases to run at current levels. Unless...'

'Unless?' echoed Mason.

'Unless the population is reduced.'

Mason nodded thoughtfully, but said nothing. Trevor signalled to the cameraman to zoom in for a close-up shot of Mason's face as he restated the question.

'Don, do you think there are too many people on the planet?'

'For sure.'

'And there are too many people in this country?'

'I think most people would agree that there are.'

'And your government wanted to reduce the population? I mean, you were actively looking at ways to reduce the population?'

'It's true that various options were discussed, though no plans were brought forward.'

'And you think you had a mandate for this?'

'Not specifically. But I think we had a general mandate to consider all measures necessary to carry forward the Green Revolution.'

'I see,' said Trevor, as someone came into the room and whispered something to him.

Mason said he didn't mind at all breaking for a moment, and Trevor left the room.

Trevor was ushered into another room, where he was re-introduced to General Matthews and several of his officers. He was then introduced on-screen to Sir James Olsen and Colonel Demont Ashton, who both congratulated him on the work he had done, telling him how his intelligence had been crucial to bringing forward the plans for the invasion.

'We want to show you this,' said Sir James, and the screen switched to a feed from a videophone in Scotland, channelled through the military networks.

'This was filmed a few minutes ago, and we'll go to live pictures in a moment.'

It was film taken by an American soldier of buses being stopped about thirty miles south of Inverness by American soldiers and medics in white contamination suits. People were being helped from the buses, some apparently very sick, others seeming quite healthy. A couple of bodies were also being removed, while the sick and walking were ushered into hurriedly set-up field hospital tents. Trevor watched in stunned and saddened silence.

'I'm afraid there's more like this coming in from around the country,' said Ashton.

'The thing is,' said General Matthews, 'we need these pictures going out there. Live. And the media control system is still clamped down pretty tight. No problem getting it out to the foreign press from the areas where we're in control. But we need people in this country to see what's happening, to help break resistance and show these villains up for what they are. And we want your help and advice. I'm sure we can take control of all the BBC buildings in the city within a couple of hours, but they're quite well defended. A couple of hours is too long, and we want to avoid unnecessary bloodshed.

'MacLean, we know they've been using BBC technical centres to control all the domestic broadcasting. Again, it would take us a while to take control and liberate output. But if we can get the people running the BBC to realise the game is up for Mason, then maybe they'll cooperate. Things can move much faster then. Do you think you can help? Who's left there you could persuade?'

Trevor thought for a while. He realised he now knew almost no one of any influence. In fact, most of those he used to know in the higher echelons never liked or trusted him very much anyway. Still, there was Craig Delaney, although there was no love lost between them. Perhaps it was the best shot.

'I know Craig Delaney. We used to be kind of sparring partners...'

Delaney had enjoyed a successful spell as President of ESCOMEDIA, and had moved back to the BBC as Director-General and was considered a safe pair of hands from the Mason government's point of view.

'We know he's in there. We've tried to contact him, but some minion keeps brushing us off,' said Sir James. 'So you know him personally?'

'Sure,' said Trevor. 'Kind of love-hate relationship. I loved winding him up. He just hated me.'

'Not so good, then.'

'I think it's worth a shot,' said Trevor. 'He's a spineless little shit, and if he's in there he'll be crapping himself, not knowing which way to turn. I think he's playable.'

'Playable!' repeated Ashton.

'I want to set something up first, but it will only take a few minutes.'

Less than five minutes later, Craig Delaney at Broadcasting House had agreed to take a call from his old adversary Trevor MacLean. In part it was curiosity at Trevor's recent re-emergence, and in part his own desperation, trapped in his offices and not knowing which way to turn. In truth, while he was fearful of his position vis-à-vis the government, he was also uncomfortable playing a role that was too propagandistic for his comfort.

'Trevor MacLean, as I live and breathe,' said Delaney, trying to sound nonchalant.

'One and the same, in glorious living Technicolor,' Trevor replied jovially. 'Reporting from the Palace, as it happens. There's some pretty decisive news breaking out here, you know.'

'I heard you're moving in exalted circles now, Trevor.'

'You too, Craig. Except the exalted company you've been keeping is busy biting the dust right now. But you know what? If I turn on the TV now, what do I get? A rerun of *Eastenders*. I think there are more important things happening in the country right now. And you should be showing it.'

'We've moved on since your day, Trevor. Our broadcasting has to be responsible.'

'When was I ever anything else, Craig? But really, have you seen what's going on? Here, take a look out of the window at the Palace here.'

He held up his tablet computer and swung it around the room, so its camera could pick up all the details. Then he moved towards the window. The Palace security men urged him to be cautious, in case of stray bullets. Trevor panned the camera around the grounds of the Palace and across the street, beyond the gates and into the park. Now Delaney could clearly see Palace guards exchanging fire with units of the Green Militia.

'It looks a bit like a pantomime, Craig, with the ceremonial costumes and all, but those are real guns and explosives, and these people are really shooting at each other. And none of this is reaching the good people of Britain. When this is over, they'll wonder what they're paying their licence fee for. What about our mission to inform, educate and...whatever the other thing is!''

'Entertain,' added Delaney needlessly.

'There's a bit of that too, I guess, in a grim kind of way. But that's not all. When I swung the camera round, did you see who I'm interviewing in the room here?'

'No. Tell me.'

'Former Prime Minister Don Mason,' said Trevor, swinging the camera back towards Mason. Mason lifted his refilled brandy glass and smiled sardonically to the camera.

'Good God!' exclaimed Delaney.

'Don't do anything he asks, Craig,' Mason called out grimly.

'This is your big chance, Craig,' urged Trevor, turning the camera back towards himself. 'What's going down here is unbelievably big. And all being filmed live. It will be the largest ever audience for an event like this. And it'll be *you* that makes it possible. Take a look at this, too.'

Trevor signalled to a technician, and now images from around the country were routed through Trevor's tablet to Delaney. He saw the footage from the buses in Scotland, from a Welsh eco-camp being entered by Irish troops, and in Norfolk live film of soldiers in contamination suits examining a pit of bodies at a former work camp. Trevor was shocked too at seeing this—it was more than he had expected.

'This is happening right here in this country, right now, and where are we? We have a duty, a responsibility, Craig, to put these pictures in the public arena.'

'I—I don't know, Trevor. I mean, with all due respect, I know where your sympathies lie, and I need to think carefully about the source of this news. And … I need to discuss it with Juliet—'

'Discuss it with Juliet? Can't you see how she's screwed you over from the first day you met her? Her days are numbered, count on it. For Christ's sake, Craig, make the right decision for once in your life! This is *big*. The Greens are out. The other guys are in. There are troops from all over the world invading this country for the first time since 1688! Are you going to make this happen, or have our news teams got to climb over a pile of bodies to bring the news late to the nation?'

Delaney pondered for a few moments.

'OK. You're on. You're hired! Tell me what we need to do!' he sighed, exhaling long and hard.

'Thank you, thank you, Craig!' exclaimed Trevor. 'It's a brave decision for you, seeing the situation you're in. OK. First we need to set up a live feed to the Palace here. We'll continue the interview with Mason, and everyone can see the reality of the situation. Then later when things are under control, we'll have a broadcast on all channels, I hope, from the King and General Matthews about the interim government arrangements. And you need to get the regional network going. These images from my tablet are important, but the picture quality is pretty crap, don't you think? We need the regional teams out liaising with the liberation forces at the camps.'

'Trevor. Tell me about those bodies I saw…what's been going on?' said Delaney, visibly shaken.

'You'll see. You must have heard rumours about the camps. It's worse than you heard, Craig. Unbelievably worse. All will become clear in the next few hours—with your help. Oh, and one thing. If Juliet Coe is there, and any others of the Green Machine, get security to detain them at once. Take away their phones. But let them watch on TV, by all means. See how they react when confronted with the fruits of their action.'

As the call ended, and Trevor turned away, Mason gave him a light round of applause. 'You're good, Trevor MacLean. Danny said you are. Such a shame you backed the wrong team. You could have done so much for us.'

'Who knows, maybe if you hadn't hounded me into exile and abducted several of my friends and colleagues into your camps I could have done a good job for you. But I don't think so. My fault was in having a mind of my own, and wanting freedom of expression.'

'It's in what you want to express that the problem lies, perhaps,' said Mason, with a shrug.

'In the end, it is only the truth,' said Trevor. 'I have to go for a while now, but I hope we can continue our discussion in a little while. I'm afraid this break will be a long five minutes, but I'm anxious we should resume.'

'Probably more so than I am. I've become just a story to you, Trevor, just an ingredient for resuming your career. I can't promise to say anything more to you.'

'As you wish. But I can assure you, for the last year my life has been so bound up in yours that you are certainly more than just a story.'

After all his research following up Stella's files, Trevor was itching to question Mason further to fill in the gaps and to find out the answer to the big question: how much was Mason at the centre of all this, or had maverick elements gone way beyond what he envisaged?

That would have to wait. There were urgent things to be done. In a makeshift studio across the corridor Trevor was soon anchoring a news bulletin being broadcast to the nation. Footage of the counter-revolution in action was soon broadcast to the nation. Footage of Mason minutes after his dismissal was broadcast, and clips of Trevor's first foray at an interview.

The King made a brief broadcast, announcing the end of the Mason government and the Declaration of a State of Emergency, handing over to General Matthews who elaborated on the details. The police and army were to cease all cooperation with the Green Militia and Green institutions, all of which were declared suspended. All Militia were to return to their bases and await instructions for their decommissioning. Few of the Militia in fact complied with this, most preferring to go home while some attempted to continue resistance. All inmates released from camps who had made it home were instructed to call an emergency medical number at once, as was anyone who had come into contact with released detainees. Everyone was urged to stay where they were until further notice.

Then Trevor outlined the reasons for the overthrow of the government, bringing in comment from Patrick Baxter, political and health analysts, and a statement from President Wilding. The biological attacks initiated by 'rogue elements' in the Militia were analysed in detail, and film of the liberation of the camps was released. From foreign sources, film of the landing of foreign troops and their collaboration with British forces was shown to the nation and to the world.

'The nightmare is almost over,' said Patrick Baxter. 'Never in all the annals of British history have we seen dark days like these, with a government unleashing such terror on its own people. There is work to be done to repair the damage done by the extremists, and we can all pull together to do this. Those responsible will be brought to justice and punished. But our most important task is to restore the British way of life. The illegal Green institutions are now abolished. We must learn from the lessons, and restore our traditional forms of government as speedily as possible, at all levels, purged of the people who have subverted them. Our aim is to have elections within three months, and a return to our cherished democracy. Until then I will head a Provisional Government of National Unity. I undertake to stand down from this position as soon as a new government is appointed after the elections. The freedom of the Press is restored with immediate effect. Media reporting of these momentous events and of the restoration process will be free and unhindered—but journalists are strongly advised to be very careful of their own safety. The Provisional Government suspends all the environmental laws passed since the GEM and their partners came to power. The new elected government will in due course decide which ones they will retain and which ones they will repeal...'

With the force of the media behind it, Trevor felt the counter-revolution had an unstoppable momentum. Privately General Matthews and his staff spoke of their concern about rounding up the willing and unwilling carriers of the plague. The battle was not over yet.

When Trevor MacLean returned to the room where Mason was detained, Mason was on his fifth or sixth brandy, and had evidently been watching the news reports. He looked solemn and troubled, but still had generally an air of calm.

'So, everything is up? Or is it all propaganda from the Grey side?'

'You knew about this, didn't you, Don Mason?' Trevor asked directly.

'All this?' asked Mason, slurring his speech very slightly.

'All this! The genetically modified plague, the process of unleashing biological terror. The experiments in the camps. The malnutrition and the suffering. But maybe you don't like to see the details on-screen in front of you.'

Mason was silent.

'You asked me what I was doing while I was away. Much against my naturally shallow instincts, I did some thorough research. It was Stella who started it off. They've just told me she died in the West Highland eco-camp.'

'I'm sorry.'

'"I'm sorry" be damned!' shouted Trevor. 'You sanctioned all this, right down to bringing forward the amnesty, sending home all these poor people infected with ghastly diseases. Have you any idea of the suffering involved?'

'I have nothing to say at this point—I am still trying to take in what I have just seen, and what's happened today. Do you think I can be held responsible for this? It only hastens our future.'

Mason's voice sounded tired, and a little strangled, as if it was struggling to make itself heard. 'Trevor, I think I could do with another brandy. Last request from a condemned man … '

Mason was struggling at his collar, though it was already undone.

'I'm feeling a little hot, it seems…' he said, and slid slowly to the floor clutching feebly at his collar. Immediately security officials rushed towards him. They could see his collapse was genuine and not feigned. Within twenty minutes he was being whisked to hospital. Leaving Trevor without the answers he was looking for, and feeling emotionally confused. He felt a natural sympathy for a sick man in distress, and wished him to recover. At the same time images of the crimes he appeared to be responsible for were played in a loop as backdrop to the breaking news.

As he had lain struggling for breath, Mason had motioned Trevor to come closer. He was trying to say something, which Trevor caught on the third or fourth attempt. 'Magna est veritas!' Mason had said. Then he closed his eyes, satisfied that Trevor had heard these words.

'What did he say?' asked one of the security guards trying to administer first aid. 'Magnus who?'

Trevor smiled grimly. 'I heard it, but I don't understand it yet. "*Magna est veritas.*" It's Latin. It means: "The truth is great". Well, of course. And so what?'

68: Invisible legions

In his Whitehall offices a short way across the capital, Dave Barrington was watching the news unfold, transfixed by the images on the screens around him.

Malcolm Morton had been rushing around the offices and corridors barking orders to everyone, but it was clear to him that the game was up. He broadcast a final message to the Militia, using an open channel they could all pick up on their headsets. 'Our enemies are getting closer,' he said, 'closer and closer. They don't just want to defeat us, they want to annihilate our worldview. They want to replace the Truth with their lies. We are in the final moments—but only of the first stage. This is the time to be strong, time to keep the faith. And to be ready for what is to come—it's far from over! You will see! Hold fast to the truth, and don't believe their lies!'

As he spoke Morton too saw the images on the screens, watching impassively. Then he spoke briefly with Dave Barrington.

'The game's up, Dave,' he confided. 'We have to leave. We've held them up as long as we can, but these are overwhelming odds. Some of the guys will get through, but this time round there won't be the impact we hoped for. But it's only the first round, Dave.'

He put a hand on Barrington's arm and stared reassuringly and confidentially into Barrington's eyes. Barrington was lost for words.

'Remember what Don used to say? All direct action has to be educational, to take forward the Idea. Population reduction is now truly on the world's agenda—we have taken the first step. Of course people will judge us harshly now. But the world will know that there really is no truly Green path that doesn't include this. We're pioneers, and heroes. Our names will be remembered for all time. We had the strength of will to take the action necessary, however painful. But the job is done for now, and it's time to go back underground.'

Barrington seemed to be in a state of shock. 'Fight or flight' was the way Morton seemed to see it. But as Barrington saw it, fighting was hopeless and fleeing pretty hopeless too. 'I'll stay a while, Malcolm,' he said, quietly.

'Hold the fort a little longer, and see what we can do to protect our people from reprisals.'

Morton sensed both Barrington's despair and a note of reproach, as if Morton was deserting his command and those he was responsible for.

'You must understand, Dave,' he said, 'that I *need* to be elsewhere, to take things forward on the next step of the journey. Our invisible legions are on the march, and I have to support them and reinforce them from elsewhere. You do what you think best. No one else is left, so you take charge. Stand everyone down in a few hours—just try to give me some space to make my exit. OK?'

They looked at each other for a while.

'You know they'll try to hang you for this?' said Morton quietly. 'There's not a lot to implicate you, but if we're gone they'll pin everything on whoever they can. It's your choice. I've always trusted and respected your judgement.' Then he slipped a packet into his hand.

'Vaccines,' said Morton. 'And some capsules. Take one of those if it's the best way out. It will be quick, and you won't suffer much.' Then he left.

Barrington remained somewhat dazed for five minutes, though it seemed longer to him. Then he slipped into organising mode, and began the process of standing down the Militia and the remaining loyal army units. He encountered only token protests. Training-field battles are no real preparation for the reality of armed conflict, and most of the Militia were relieved to hear the order to surrender. Most were also aware that the regular troops they had confronted had been very restrained in combat, and the results could have been much worse for them. Then Barrington signalled to the enemy that the Mason government would offer no more resistance. He sat down at a desk, alone, and waited for the enemy to arrive. He tried to call Jessica, but was unable to get hold of her.

Now he saw on a news flash the body of Peter Kitson being recovered from a bus in Norfolk, barely five miles from the Barrington homestead. He took a deep breath and rested his elbow on the armrest of the chair, his hand supporting his chin.

So much water under the bridge. Now there were American and Dutch troops all over the work camps in Norfolk. No doubt they had called at his home too. He thought about the search that must be going on at his home right now. Big army boots clomping over the wooden floors. The intelligence and forensic experts loading his computers and documents into big plastic bags, labelling them, and putting them into trucks. Maybe they would be tramping all over Jessica's little market garden, digging it over, looking for—whatever they looked for. He was sure they would find nothing of great interest.

He tried to recall the information that would be held on the information systems at the coastal defence projects, and in the work camps. He could not think of anything in particular that could cause him trouble, be used against him. Except maybe the communication records. Maybe the teams there had been busy deleting what they could. He knew where the dangers to him lay: in communications with the eco-camp network, and with people like Carl Fullerton, Gabriella Pearson, and Malcolm Morton. Not to mention with Don Mason himself. Records of communication would certainly exist in more than one place: on telecommunication servers, on computers, phones and other devices.

He knew he would not be the number one target, but he could easily be incriminated by association. Not only by association with the big fish: anything found against his underlings might also point a finger of guilt at him. Even were he to appear purer than pure, people could always point a finger of blame at him and say, 'This happened on your watch. You are responsible.' It was inevitable. He would mount a strong defence. Actions speak louder than words, he felt, and not running away was the first step in demonstrating his lack of guilt. Complete cooperation was the second step.

And Barrington realised he was also motivated by a sense of pride in his achievements. He wanted to act to protect what he had achieved. The coastal defence works, the renewable energy mega-projects, the reforestation and habitat creation—all were tainted by the 'slave labour' used to enable them. But they were viable projects, and he wanted to hand them over to people who would continue the good work—minus the forced labour, of course. The danger was that the new regime would throw the baby out with the bath water. If he could project himself more as the disinterested technocrat, the chances for the continuation of his work would be that much higher.

He was saddened to see clips of Don Mason sipping his brandy, under arrest and apparently indifferent to the fate of millions threatened by or dying from the biological terror. It must be very selective editing, he thought. It also confirmed what he had felt for a while—that Don was losing his touch. He had made too many mistakes, trusted too many of the wrong people. Barrington was one of those who felt that the 'Second Revolution' was too rushed. Power had not been consolidated properly, and they had rushed their undefeated opponents into precipitate action.

He remembered something Mason had once said, adapting Clausewitz's famous statement on war: 'War is the continuation of policy by other means'. Mason had added: 'Subversion is the continuation of policy when war is not possible or desirable'. He had said that more than once in the time of struggle. Now Morton had alluded to it before his disappearance. Once they had used political subversion to undermine the establishment. Now they had gained the means to subvert the human race through biological means. That was, no doubt, why Don Mason had appeared so calm, and Morton so optimistic of successfully continuing the struggle. Only time will tell, he thought. Now Barrington's mood was overwhelmingly fatalistic about the future of the country, and of the planet. But for the time being, he had to attend to his own prospects.

He noticed all the shooting outside had stopped. Maybe it had been silent for a few minutes now. A rather dishevelled civil servant put her head timidly round the door, and announced that General Matthews and a small retinue had arrived. Barrington gestured for them to be shown in.

As formal handovers of power go, it was quite civil and gentlemanly. Matthews informed Barrington casually of his loss of liberty, and asked for his full cooperation. Barrington assured him that this would be forthcoming. He had already assembled a team of senior civil servants to effect transitional arrangements, and these would be ready to meet the leaders of the new regime in Downing Street as soon as they were needed. This show of cooperation seemed to impress General Matthews.

'I assume my father-in-law will be back shortly to take up the reins?' said Barrington, with a forced smile. To Matthews it seemed more like a grimace.

'He landed about half an hour ago, and is already on his way here.'

'Please send him my best regards, and to Lady Frances. Please tell them, for what it's worth, I trust them to look after the best interests of Jessica and the children. If I'm to be the price for their liberty, so be it.'

'Very noble, I'm sure,' said General Matthews icily. 'But I'll pass on your compliments to them.'

69: Liberation

Liberation forces had not yet arrived at the West Highland Eco-Camp when the helicopter with medical help arrived to help Heather Kitson and the other inmates. By this time Heather had become very sick. Sam Sharma had abandoned all caution about contagion, and was cradling her in his arms, holding a cold compress to her brow and periodically wiping away the blood that flowed from her nose and the fluids she coughed up from time to time. Sam rested her back gently on the sofa as he heard the sound of the helicopters.

'They're here, sweetie. Lie back now...I told you they'd come. You're gonna be fine. Both of you are gonna be fine.'

Heather didn't believe him, but smiled as broadly as she could to acknowledge his kindness. Sam ran out of the door to meet the arriving medics. Heather felt feverish, and pain in places where she'd never felt pain before. She was sure she was dying. And she knew what she was going to ask.

Four medics burst through the door with Sam panting behind them, shouting needlessly 'There she is! There, Heather—they've come to save ya, and the little'un!'

A voice called to Sam from outside: 'Quick, Sam, take us to the others.'

Heather heard the sound of several sets of footsteps running away across the gravel towards the clinic.

The medics in the office quickly snapped into action, examining Heather and setting up a couple of drips. They were wearing face masks and disposable gloves, but nothing else to protect them.

'Keep out of the way when I cough, won't you?' said Heather, admiring their bravery and determination.

'If it's plague you've got, in principle it's very curable,' said the tall medic leaning over her, listening to her lungs through his stethoscope. 'But I see it's progressed very fast.'

'Did you bring the incubator for the baby?' asked Heather.

The medic looked up at her. 'Yes, we did. But it doesn't seem as though you are about to go into labour.'

'I know. But—I'm sure I'm dying. I want you to induce labour, or do a Caesarean. If my child has a chance...'

'Let's not rush into that, Mrs Kitson. I want to complete my examination, and start treatment for the both of you. Your child will have a better chance fighting this with the help of your body, than being born two months premature and fighting for life in an incubator. And as for you—childbirth is not what I'd recommend for you at this stage.'

After a few minutes Sam came hurriedly back into the room. 'They're working on George and the other guy now—how's Heather doing, doc?' He could see that Heather looked calmer, even restful.

'The drugs are kicking in. I think she's stabilising.'

'I'd kiss you if I didn't risk passing some lurgy onto you,' said Sam to the doctor.

'How's your hearing, Sam?' asked one of the medics.

'Fine, I think,' said Sam.

The medic cupped his hand to his ear. Sam could now hear more helicopters arriving, and rushed out the door. In a few minutes he was back with a small group of American soldiers, all wearing biological warfare kit.

'Colonel Palmer, US Marines,' announced the senior officer by way of introduction. 'Is this Heather Kitson?'

Sam and the medics chorused that it was.

'Corporal, get Colonel Ashton on the line—he wanted to know as soon as we found her or her husband. Doc—fill me in on the situation here.'

Colonel Palmer had arrived with a small platoon as an advanced guard at the Eco-Camp. He'd been told that the camp had been abandoned, and to secure it for the investigators to move in. He'd also been advised to expect to find some stragglers, and possibly some light resistance. Soon his soldiers had found the two Militia men who had been left behind to destroy documents, hiding in one of the outbuildings. Then they set about securing the perimeter to make a quarantine area.

Heather started to become more animated, but could speak only with some difficulty. 'Colonel, thank God you've come. This is only the tip of the iceberg—the really serious stuff all took place at North Camp.'

'I know, ma'am. New Dawn, they call it. We've got teams on the way there now. Oh. It looks like we've got someone to talk to you. Corporal, pass your phone to Mrs Kitson.'

Heather took the phone. She briefly saw the face of a soldier in uniform, then suddenly Joanna Kitson's face was in front of her as the call was transferred.

'Oh my God, Joanna. I can't believe it.'

'Your sister-in-law's in the States now,' said Palmer.

Tears were streaming down Heather's face now as she heard Joanna ask how she was and telling her that Andrea was safe with her in America. 'I am so happy to see you, you can't believe how happy. Yes, I'm OK. Well maybe not so OK, but I'm in capable hands now. Any news of Peter?'

'No news so far,' Joanna lied through her tears. 'As you see, I've got good connections, and everywhere they go they've been looking for you, and Peter. And Sandy. But there are thousands, Heather. Thousands and thousands. It's unbelievable.'

Suddenly Heather turned to Colonel Palmer. 'Have they stopped the buses?' she asked anxiously.

'We stopped almost all of them now, but there's a lot of people still to round up. We're containing the situation.'

'Heather, you must rest,' said Joanna. 'The Mason government has gone, and the good guys are in charge. You can focus on your recovery, and we'll leave everything else to our friends in uniform. By the way, I've got someone outside to see you, if you're ready to see her...'

'Andrea?'

'Are you up to it?'

'Give me a minute,' said Heather. 'Sam, can you bring me my bag—over there on the desk.'

Obediently Sam fetched her small bag from the desk. Heather got out a small mirror and a hairbrush, and began to tidy up her appearance. Fighting back more tears, she realised this might be the last time Andrea saw her mother. She wanted to look at her best. Then she thought Andrea would probably be too young to remember, but all the same ...

As she brushed her hair and wiped away the signs of tears, Heather talked to Joanna about her 'guardian angel', and turned her phone towards Sam Sharma. Joanna recognised Sam immediately, and was relieved to see that he was alive and well.

'He's a survivor. Or so he keeps telling me,' said Heather, smiling. 'Now bring on my little girl'.

Heather could not restrain herself from weeping as she saw her daughter after so many months. But as she wept she smiled continuously, laughing frequently. Andrea looked older—less like a baby and more like a little girl. Her hair was longer, and tied up in ribbons. Other hands were caring for her, Heather could see. Yes, they were other hands, for sure, but the important thing was that they were caring for her.

538

Andrea twisted round and looked up, presumably at Joanna. 'Is that Mummy?' she asked. It was a short conversation, Andrea shy but obviously quite satisfied that she had a mother and that she was OK.

Suddenly Heather felt more pain rising above the impact of the drugs. She began to feel hot and faint. The medics closed in, and Palmer ended the call to Joanna Kitson. Feeling herself fading into unconsciousness, Heather cried to the doctors that it was time. They had to save the baby.

'Do it, do it!' she yelled.

A female medic was listening for a heartbeat from the baby, while another was manoeuvring an ultrasound scanner back into position. She shook her head. There was no heartbeat to be found. The doctor had been sure from his first examination that the baby could not be saved. By the time they arrived, its lungs had probably already been damaged beyond repair. Even a healthy premature infant could have had problems breathing at thirty-two weeks. When they had first heard the baby's heartbeat it had seemed too weak for it to survive the trauma of birth. So they had decided to focus on saving the mother, hoping that restoring her to health could improve any chances the baby had to survive. Now it was clear the mother was dying too. Normal treatment wasn't working. This disease was designed to resist the usual kinds of treatment.

Sam could see that all was not well.

'C'mon, Doc. There must be something more you can do?'

The doctor shook his head in despair.

'The best we can do here is to make her comfortable. We could try to get her back to hospital, but I don't think she'll survive for another hour to get there. The disease is progressing so fast now.'

The medics with the Marines were now examining Heather too, and advising as best they could. Finally they decided to move her to the camp clinic where they had set up treatment for the other two inmates, though now only one of them remained.

As they carried Heather over to the clinic, Sam Sharma talked all the way, trying to find ways they could save her. 'Look at me. Why ain't I got it? Has to be the vaccine I took.'

'It's too late for a vaccine, Sam—'

'Maybe you can use my blood. Transfusion of something...'

'It doesn't work like that, Sam. If we could do it, we would.'

'Can you make something from my blood, antidote or something?'

'In theory, yes, Sam. But it would take days, if not weeks. And we don't have that long.'

'For Christ's sake, boys, stop telling me what you can't do, and start telling me what you can do!!'

The female medic put a comforting hand on Sam's arm in the sympathetic silence.

'Listen, this is for real,' said Sam. 'Stella told us when she was at North camp they took 'er to the edge of death, then injected 'er with somefing, and she recovered. Wasn't 'ealthy when we saw 'er, mind, but she was still livin'. Maybe they've got some of that stuff here, or at North Camp....'

The medics looked at each other. After Sam explained who Stella was, they agreed it was a possibility—if only they knew where to look. The problem was, as far as they knew North Camp had been abandoned, and probably all the equipment they had used would have been removed or destroyed.

'There was that guy here this morning,' exclaimed Sam excitedly. 'The guy in charge. Don't know his name, but Heather said she'd met him before.'

'Perry Jones,' Heather mumbled through her rising delirium. 'Perry Jones. That's who it was. He's responsible for this....all this...'

Palmer acted quickly, putting out a call to all units to see if they'd apprehended a Militia commander called Perry Jones. At first there was no news. Then after twenty minutes there came the news that Jones had been arrested at Edinburgh airport, where he'd released a canister of bacteria into the airport ventilation system. He'd flown down from Inverness that morning, and was booked on a flight out to Copenhagen. He seemed to be immunised against the disease, and was also carrying some vials of a substance in his luggage that appeared to be a serum to counteract the disease. Now Edinburgh airport was sealed off. No one was to enter or leave, and the planes that had set off since Jones released the toxin were being recalled to Edinburgh or to military airbases.

Sam returned to comfort Heather, who now seemed to be fading fast. He gripped her hand tightly, urging her to keep fighting. Outside the clinic, Colonels Palmer and Ashton were talking quickly by phone, analysing all the options. Saving Heather and Peter Kitson had been an express priority of Zara Alderney, the Secretary of State. But the officers in charge at Edinburgh were reluctant to consider releasing any of the serum until it had been analysed. And if it was the antidote they believed it to be, then it made more sense to them to use it first for the victims in Edinburgh.

'In any case, how long have we got to get some to Mrs Kitson?' Ashton asked Palmer.

Colonel Palmer went back inside to check with the medics how much time they had. And he could see at once the answer. The doctors had all gone quiet. They had stopped attending to Heather, and were moving like sleep-walkers tidying equipment away. Sam Sharma was bent over Heather Kitson, holding her in his arms, and silently sobbing. It was over, and there was no longer a decision to make.

Colonel Palmer sighed deeply, and leaned back against the wall, a sense of despair rising inside him. He'd seen death before, civilian deaths too. But the calculated wickedness of this act struck at him as if he'd been kicked in the pit of his stomach.

He felt nothing could be worse than this. Then he was ordered to move on to join the forward team that had landed at North Camp.

70: Endgame

Most of the buses that had left the camps had been stopped before they reached their final destination. But many of them had already let passengers off to join families ecstatic at their release. Across the country, former detainees from eco-camps, work camps and the new eco-settlements that were closer to major towns were at loose amongst the population, making their way home using the public transport networks well before the Mason government was overthrown and the King had declared a state of emergency.

Confusion, panic and then anger began to sweep across the nation as people heard the news. At first there was widespread disbelief. Many no longer liked the Mason government, but what was happening was beyond the bounds of belief.

Trevor MacLean was handed a cup of coffee and a phone as he came off air.

'You'll want to take this,' said his assistant.

'Trevor—Miles here. Miles Campbell. I'm pleased to see you're in one piece. I don't know how you did it, but I've got a feeling we owe you a lot.'

'Bloody hell, Miles! Let me see you! Where are you? How are you?'

'Oh, I've lost a bit of weight. Otherwise, not bad considering where I've been for the past couple of years. I'm in Shrewsbury—that's where they dropped me off to catch a train.'

'And you're OK? Sorry to be blunt, but have you seen the news? I think you need medical attention right now!'

'Actually, Trevor, I'm as sick as a pig right now. I was doing the stiff-upper-lip bit before. But I'm in a kind of field hospital now, they've set it up outside the main hospital here, to isolate all of us plague victims. God, that sounds odd! They say I'm responding to treatment. But not everyone is. The doctors seem puzzled by that. Seems there's more than one strain of the plague at large here.'

'Yes, so we're beginning to hear from around the country.'

'Trevor, I want to apologise for not standing by you way back when. Michaela told me I had to make more of a stand.'

'No hard feelings on that score,' said Trevor, touched that the former D-G had wanted to take the time to make an apology while he was so ill. 'You probably saved my life, shipping me off to the back of beyond. And it gave me the taste for wearing a kilt and growing vegetables. Miles, there was nothing either of us could have done to make a difference back then. Nothing at all.'

'I don't know. I feel I was in a position to do something ... Tell me about Michaela—any news on her?'

Trevor told him she was safe in Italy, and updated him on several other people from the past that he'd heard about. Then Miles asked him about Juliet Coe. 'I'm sure she was the driving force behind the purges at the BBC.'

'And a lot more,' said Trevor.

Miles Campbell's family in London had a similar experience to thousands more families in the UK. The morning news carried news of the amnesty, and their hopes had been raised. Their hopes were tinged by anxiety until they had a call from him, cheerfully saying he was on his way home. Already he had been feeling sick, but had not wanted to alarm them.

Then came the rumours—of troops in the streets of London and other cities, and of clashes with the Militia. Then they heard the sirens—ambulances on the move, police seemingly everywhere. People working for local councils and the medical professions were suddenly called in to work, and were told to prepare for a major civil disaster. Word of this spread very rapidly, but there was no official news.

Those who could access the foreign media soon began to spread the word to their neighbours that American and European troops were landing in large numbers. Soon, in many cities, police cars were driving slowly through the streets, telling people to stay indoors: not to leave home for work or school; if at work to stay there and not to return home. Buses and trains ground to a halt, and airports were closed.

During this time, however, several thousand families also had tearful reunions with family members who had been detained in the camps. But many of these were already sick, and soon their loved ones were becoming ill too.

Finally the news broke. The 'national firewall' restricting the news media was lifted, and a nation sat appalled at what they saw. Or else they were frantic with alarm, having welcomed the plague into their home or travelled somewhere with possible plague victims.

••

Malcolm Morton's invisible legions were on the march, and he and Gabriella Pearson observed the chaos it was causing with professional satisfaction from their safe house.

Pearson's brow began to furrow. 'Is it enough? They seem to be reacting quicker than we thought.'

'It's better than we could have hoped for yesterday. We moved fast too. Carl has a lot to be proud of,' Morton replied.

Gabriella Pearson nodded.

'And this is only the first foray,' Morton added. 'The world thinks it is taking the battle to us. But everything is moving into place now. From today, we are taking the battle to them.'

They were silent and thoughtful for a while.

'You will miss Don,' said Pearson at last.

Morton nodded, pursing his lips. 'It is the way it has to be. He took us to the edge of the Promised Land, and will watch us enter from the mountain top. Will you miss Titus?'

Pearson smiled. 'In a way. We worked a lot together. For over twenty-five years. Inspirational and infuriating at the same time. He loves our planet like no one else I've ever met. Though a lot of the time it seemed he was on a different one altogether! Do you think of him as a loose end?'

'Not really. He knew we were keeping practical things from him, and it seemed he wanted it that way. We've allowed him to absorb a fair amount of misinformation about what was happening and about what comes next. It will keep the Greys off balance for a while. Long enough, anyway.'

She picked up her tea cup and held it forward to make a toast.

'To the Restoration!' she said.

'The Restoration!' echoed Morton, as Trevor MacLean on the TV fronted scenes beamed in from the camps of white-suited troops discovering decomposed bodies in a large pit.

••

The events of the day were fast and furious, but the day seemed never-ending to Trevor MacLean. By the afternoon he was monitoring reports coming in of a series of reprisals against the Militia, and against GEM and Green officials at all levels, from the Earth Councils to the Convention. After some debate and reflection, he agreed with General Mathews to delay reporting these, for fear of encouraging copycat actions across the country.

News was also filtering through of the agents who were en route with the plague to other countries. Most were caught, though some made it through. But Annie Lee had never stepped out of the shadows, and had slipped away.

Patrick Baxter and the interim government were effectively in control of the country by late afternoon. The plot to export the plague around the globe had been exposed, and all planes had been grounded. Some had taken off but been recalled to base.

Now Baxter was in conference on-screen with Zara Alderney and various intelligence chiefs.

'Some must have slipped through the net,' said Zara. 'We have to have all planes grounded that are carrying people who transferred onto them from a British Plane today. It's a simple as that. Can we track who they are?'

'I believe we can,' said Baxter, referring to the intelligence chiefs.

And they could. Ever since 2001 security measures had been tightened more and more, allowing individuals to be tracked much more easily, especially when they travelled. Morton had made extensive use of this ability, and had extended the surveillance techniques to new levels. Now these levers were in the hands of Baxter's government.

By the end of the day the body count was rising well into the thousands, with tens of thousands becoming sick. As the enormity of the last act of the Mason government became known, the reprisals increased across the country. In Southampton leading members of the Green Earth Council were rounded up and given summary justice. In Manchester an armed mob took the members of the Green Earth Council at gunpoint from police custody and executed them outside the Town Hall, then moved on to round up those members of the Green Militia who had not already fled.

It was towns like Glasgow, Manchester and Norwich that suffered first, as they were the first delivery point for many of the former camp inmates who were released. There the Militia volunteers who slipped through the net released the plague in shopping malls and public transport centres, and the plague spread rapidly with the authorities and medical services always several steps behind. It was clear casualties would continue for several weeks before the plague could be contained by mass vaccinations. Some of the fake vaccines that Annie Lee had ordered to be distributed were used before the authorities realised their purpose, and contributed to the chaos, fear and casualties.

At around one o'clock in the morning, Trevor MacLean finally slumped back into a chair in the makeshift studio at the Palace. The team were still at work decommissioning the studio now that the national media networks had been 'liberated', but the atmosphere was one of awed silence. They had covered the events of the day as they unfolded, and now they dreaded what the next few days would bring.

As he sat in silence, one of the Palace staff came to Trevor, asking him if he would come through to have a word with His Majesty. He was led through some corridors to a small book-lined room. He was motioned to sit down. The King sat motionless, looking a little haggard, but still dignified. He said nothing.

'Tough day,' said Trevor. Half a statement, half a question. It sounded inane, but Trevor always preferred embarrassed words to awkward silences.

'Indeed,' said the King, shaking himself from his reverie. 'It's good of you to come to see me, MacLean. One of the lessons I've learned is to trust your judgement. I wish I'd learned this lesson a little earlier. Maybe even a day or two would have made a difference.'

'I don't think the tanks and planes were ready a day or two ago,' Trevor replied. He felt uncomfortable hearing this kind of remorse, and seeing people suffering in this way.

'I'm considering my position,' said the King.

Trevor nodded slowly. 'Is this not a little—precipitate? Maybe things need to settle down a little. Give us all time to reflect. What you did today was important. Just think what would have happened if you hadn't acted.'

'I think if I hadn't acted, you would have all acted without me. All I would have done would have been to delay things a little.'

'With lethal consequences.'

'Some people have congratulated me,' said the King with distaste. 'I feel only disgust for myself, and what I had done—and failed to do. I not only sympathised with these people, I nurtured them! I helped them into power, helped them to understand the levers of power. In recent months I talked almost every day with Mason, shared his enthusiasms. We poured over our green projects together. My Total Farm and their eco-settlements all came from the same drawing board!'

'We were all on board with them, at least for a while,' said Trevor.

'But you got off the bandwagon! Why did you see through them, and why did so many others see through them, but I remained entranced by them until the last moment?' asked the King with passion.

'You give me too much credit. If they hadn't come after my scalp, who knows how I would have reacted? No, it took someone much braver than me to see through them, and set me on a path I didn't want to follow.'

His thoughts gravitated to Stella, and he felt his sorrow welling up inside him.

'You are a kind man, and a brave man, MacLean,' said the King. 'No, don't try to protest. A modest one too.'

Trevor raised an amused eyebrow. 'No one has ever described me as modest before, Sir!'

'Then I'm glad to be the first. The nation owes you a big debt. A very big debt. As for me? My mind is made up. I will abdicate. There is no alternative. Not immediately—it would seem like I am trying to draw attention to myself, and to usurp the national mood. But I must go. I have a duty to preserve the monarchy, which the country needs more than ever to heal the wounds and bring stability. But I am too contaminated by ... all this. I won't wait to be tried in the court of public opinion, or subject myself and my heirs to the vagaries of a referendum. What do you think, MacLean?'

'Well, three things spring to mind, Sir,' said Trevor. 'One: I still think it's precipitate. I hope you reconsider. Two: if you do abdicate, I can stop calling you 'Sir' and you can call me Trevor instead of MacLean. I keep thinking I'm back at school! And three: if you do decide to abdicate, can you say again what you've just said, only this time with the cameras rolling?'

The King gave a smile from the side of his mouth. 'They said you were an impertinent fellow, Trevor!'

VI

71: Life must go on

London seemed strangely normal to Joanna Kitson as she was driven through. The atmosphere in the city struck her as indifferent to the momentous and tragic events that had been ordered from within its boundaries. Life must go on, everyone kept saying. And every time someone said it, the wounds opened afresh. She knew what they meant, though, and tried not to feel hurt or bitter. For the survivors, life must indeed go on. Otherwise, what was the point of what she was doing?

The car drew up outside the offices in Great George Street, just across from the Houses of Parliament. She walked inside, and was escorted up the marble staircase and into a large oak-panelled room where several people were seated at tables laid out in a large square, while others were standing drinking coffee before the meeting began. Nearly all of them were men, she noted.

As she entered, the chatter subsided. The young woman dressed in mourning black commanded instant respect and sympathy wherever she went, both for her constant stand against injustice, and for the loss she had suffered.

Patrick Baxter stepped forward to greet her with generous sympathy. Behind him she could see Lord Justice Hulton, who would head up the Commission of Inquiry, and Gordon Talbot-Smith, the father of an eco-camp survivor, who would represent the transitional government on it. Across the room, sitting alone at the table she caught sight of Martin Lang working away, apparently oblivious to the comings and goings at the front of the room.

Baxter explained he was attending the inaugural meeting to show that it had the highest level of government support. The investigators would be given all the resources they required. What the government wanted was results. And by that he meant the truth, rather than vengeance or scapegoats.

Beyond the table where Martin sat, a mountain of evidence was beginning to form. Paper documents, disks, video files. The legal process seemed to demand physical objects, not yet trusting to have its evidence stored online, though it amounted in the end to the same thing. Somehow the mountain would add weight to the proceedings.

Joanna was introduced to all the members of the investigating commission. Then as soon as it was polite to do so she made her way over to Martin Lang and touched him on the shoulder.

'Hello Martin,' she said softly.

'Joanna, hi,' he said quietly. He stood up, but did not move forward to embrace her. Joanna was taken aback by the unaccustomed note of self-doubt and the lack of confidence in his voice and posture. He kept his eyes downcast.

'It's me, I'm back,' she said, lightly holding him by the shoulders and embracing him. 'We've been through some hard times. But we're here.'

Martin sighed, and brought his head up reluctantly to look her in the eye.

'I've been hearing all about your energy in gathering all the evidence against the Mason regime. Everyone is singing your praises,' said Joanna.

Martin looked pained. 'I wish they wouldn't. It's too little, too late.'

'Let's sit down.'

They sat in silence for a minute or so, collecting their thoughts. It was Martin who broke the silence.

'I am so sorry about Peter and Heather. Words can't express how... If only...'

'Hush,' whispered Joanna, putting her finger to his lips. 'There are things all of us could have done differently. We lived our life according to one set of rules, one we still believe to be right, and they operated by a different set altogether. They acted in a way much more extreme, more barbaric than we could ever have envisaged.'

'They didn't even give her a chance. No messing around with tree planting or anything. Just straight into the labs as a "lab rat". They think she died about twenty days after her arrest. Twenty days she probably spent in pain and agony. And she was so much better than me ... but here I am.'

She would find Martin was always like this now. He rarely mentioned Sandy by name, but it was always her of whom he spoke.

'Enough now. We owe her a lot too, Andrea and me.'

'Jo, you know I ask myself every day, how can I have been so blind? She saw it. Late in the day, perhaps, but it came from the person she was. And I couldn't see it at all, not until it was too late, and they had taken away the only person I ever truly loved. You understood it too. You understood the value of people for themselves. I never understood that. Sandy made a stand, risked everything for others. Just because it was the right thing to do. I could have helped her. She was everything I ever wanted, and I just let her slip through my fingers...'

Joanna put her hand on his shoulder, and gently massaged it.

'I promise you this,' he added, looking directly into Joanna's eyes. She could see his eyes were moist with emotion. 'I will work night and day until we bring to justice those responsible for the murder of Sandy and Peter and Heather. And for the murder of all the other brothers, sisters, mother and lovers. Then I'll retire from public life for as long as it takes to get myself sorted out. But I'll never, ever, return to being the person I used to be. I promise you that.'

Joanna smiled gently. She sensed that though Martin was chastened and wiser, the old energy, ability and ambition still rumbled beneath the humility and his transformed perception of the world. He had a goal, he would go for it, and he would achieve what he wanted. In time he would be back, she was sure, and was comforted by the thought.

The meeting was called to order. After Baxter had made his welcoming speech and left the room, the Prosecuting Commission began its work. They had a huge amount of work to do, but it was imperative to bring the defendants to trial as swiftly as possible. They considered their options.

Mason had poisoned himself when he saw that his regime was at an end, and was now unfortunately beyond prosecution. Sarah Turner was in custody, but had so far refused to talk to anyone, even her appointed lawyer. She seemed to be going through some kind of breakdown, spending much of her days staring straight ahead, as if in a trance. Morton and Pearson had escaped, and the world was looking for them—so far without success.

That left Titus Whitaker, Dave Barrington, Douglas Cunningham, Carl Fullerton and Juliet Coe as the star defendants, plus many front-line functionaries such as Perry Jones who had carried out the crimes against humanity. Thousands of the Green Militia were now detained in the eco-camps, under the supervision of the army. It would take months to interrogate them all and establish who was responsible for what.

For Joanna, it was enough. She would have liked Mason and Morton to be in the dock, to be brought to book. In time justice would catch up with Morton, no doubt, and Pearson too. But for now it was enough to have meaningful work to do, and to raise Andrea on behalf of Peter and Heather.

The first challenge of her work was to coordinate the evidence-gathering from the eco-camps. The next day she would be flying to the West Highland eco-camp, where a handful of survivors of the experimentation at New Dawn were in intensive medical care. From there she would see the camp where Heather had died, and in due course Peter's final home in the Norfolk 'model community'.

••

As Joanna arrived at the gates of the West Highland eco-camp, a tall American officer stepped forward to greet her. She took his outstretched hand.

'I'm Colonel Palmer, US Marines. I'm honoured to meet you—I just wish it could have been in different circumstances. I have a tent set up here for your team to work from. We can't tell if it's safe enough yet to work in all areas of the camp. But you'll be able to interview the survivors once you're suited up. I'm afraid though that two or three may not last out the day....'

Joanna Kitson took a deep breath, and replied, 'Well, we'd better get started as soon as we can. I want to get every last bit of evidence I can find...'

The camp looked very similar in design to the one she had visited in Snowdonia. Several of the cabins nearer the gate were now being used to house lower-level members of the Militia and Scottish Earth Councils. They had not been assigned work to do, and spent their days sitting and standing around, like regular prisoners. Joanna imagined they had all, or most of them, been inoculated against the varieties of plague. What were they thinking now? she wondered. Were they contrite? Were they planning their defence? Did they profess not to know, or really did not know? These were questions she would need to get to the bottom of, how deep the knowledge of the plans reached down in to the green institutions.

But that was for later. Now Colonel Palmer was taking her into a cordoned off area of the camp where she would find the medical centre, the cabin where Heather had lived her last days, and the central office where she had lived her last moments. She felt curiously numb, unable to take in the connection between the mundane places she saw, and the enormity of what had been done to her sister-in-law. She took a deep breath.

'I should speak to the survivors first,' said Joanna.

'There are only a few. Only one has survived who was left here at the main eco-camp. Your Sam Sharma was instrumental in that. The medicine that was sent over from Edinburgh when we caught Perry Jones, it was used to treat George. But he is incredibly weak, and we're not sure he will survive. There are five others who were abandoned at New Dawn, which is just a mile north of here. We're keeping them all together here. It looks a bit makeshift, but we have the very top people from America working here and at New Dawn, so we'll learn just how to fight this thing. Come on in.'

The medical centre was now completely isolated. A network of white plastic tunnels connected it to a network of tents where scientists and military personnel in protective clothing were working diligently. Joanna passed though these and was led into the cabin that was the medical centre. The half dozen patients were each isolated in their own clear plastic chamber, surrounded by an array of medical and electronic equipment and connected to various tubes.

'This is George,' said Colonel Palmer.

George Cavendish was an almost skeletal figure, a man in his mid-fifties who now looked well over seventy. His yellowish skin was covered in large purple and black bruises. He looked very sick indeed. He was propped up to an almost sitting position, and when Joanna sat down on the chair close to his bed, their heads were almost at the same level, separated by the clear plastic sheeting.

'Hello, George. I'm Joanna Kitson.'

George nodded slowly. 'How are you, Joanna? I am so sorry for your loss.'

His voice was firm and steady, but it seemed to Joanna as if he was speaking from within a cavern, as if his voice was somehow emanating from the back of his skull.

'I've told Palmer and his team most of what there is to tell, but since he said you were coming up here I've been looking forward very much to meeting you. I'm not sure if I am speaking out of turn in your time of sorrow, so forgive me if I say anything inappropriate. But as you can see I am a sick man, and it's possible I don't have a lot of time left. And before I say anything else by way of a formal statement, I want to tell you some things about Heather, at least in so far as I knew her.'

'Oh, please do,' said Joanna, who was eager to hear any scraps of detail about the last days of her family.

'I can't describe the effect that Heather had on us up here in those last months. It's true that she often felt sick, and struggled with her condition, but she brought sunshine into our lives. Our lives were hard, as you can imagine. Long days of hard labour for most of us, then interminable hours of indoctrination and self-criticism. She was assigned to work in the kitchens and serve in the refectory, and that could be hard work. But it seems that everyone there grew very protective of her. And as she grew larger and larger, they looked after her and tried to help her out as much as she would let them. I think with everyone so far from home, the prospect of her having a baby brought some sense of hope, something good to look forward to when everything else was so bleak. And probably something approaching normality, even a sense of family. That was something we all missed dreadfully.

'And the thing is, however rough she felt, and however much she was anxious about her husband, and her daughter, and you—she always asked about others. She would always listen, and ask after us, remember what we had last been moaning on about, and remember what we liked to eat and prepare treats for us. It seems she found some purpose in looking after other people, or maybe that was just her nature. Even the Militia guards and the trustees, who were mostly a callous bunch, warmed to her and sought out her company. And that makes it all the more mystifying to me why they did what they did at the end. It is incomprehensible to me. I'm sorry, I'm upsetting you.'

Tears were streaming down Joanna's face by now, complex emotions pulling her in several directions at once. She wanted to reach out and touch George's hand, but could only put her gloved hand up against the plastic screen.

'This was in the days before I was sent to North Camp. I tried to escape, you know. Got quite far, actually. I'm not as young as I used to be, but I survived quite well up here. Had several extra layers when I came, but they soon slipped away up here! But I used to be a fit man in my army days, and know how to survive in harsh conditions. So I got quite far, down to Fort William, in fact. Stole some clothes and some money and maybe if it had been the tourist season rather than mid-winter I might have been less noticeable and slipped away. But they got me, and then shipped me straight up to North Camp.'

'I've seen your recorded testimony to Colonel Palmer. You don't need to go over that again if it's too painful. I can't imagine what you went through. This is all part of the evidence now. My job though is not only to gather the experiences of everyone who went through this, but to find out as much as possible about the people who did this. Who did what, who was in charge, what did they say, what they might have let slip about where their order came from.'

'I understand. You know I was a policeman. In Special Branch, and anti-terrorism. You know there was only a couple of us assigned to the green underground and the animal rights lot back then. The others, my colleagues, all used to pull our legs about this, about chasing tree-huggers while they tracked down the jihadists. Funny how it turned out. Anyway, I knew some of these people from of old, though I'd never have imagined it could come to this. You know I even met Don Mason once? He bought me a drink! Seemed very affable. It's nearly four years ago now, but I can remember he asked me if I'd enforce laws against eco-criminals in a Green Earth government. Can you believe that? But once they were in power they purged the service. They brought in their own people, a completely different kettle of fish to our previous bosses. You know when the Green Earth government came to power, we were asked by our superiors to step up surveillance on the GEM and their fellow travellers. They even expanded our team. But that didn't last long. They took out the top level, then worked their way down, and that's how I ended up here.'

He paused to take a sip of water.

'One good thing though. I saw it coming. So I made sure I copied everything I had and smuggled it away. I've told Palmer where to find it. It should be good background and help you to join the dots.'

'That's good,' said Joanna. 'And did you come across any of these people up here, especially if they were involved at North Camp?'

George nodded. 'Carl Fullerton. He was here several times, striding about, motivating the Militia. They seemed to treat him as some kind of god, hanging on his every word, rushing to fetch him things.'

'Did he see Heather here?' Joanna remembered their meeting with him at the Snowdonia Eco-camp, and knew that Heather would recognise him.

'He must have done, in the refectory. But I don't know if they talked.'

'And he was at North Camp?'

'I saw him there.'

'He was there in person, and saw people subjected to these experiments?'

'Yes. He was there, and when he came in it was clear who was in charge. He asked about the details, about progress. I remember him putting his arm around the woman who was normally in charge, Dr Clare they called her, and talking to her very earnestly. And I remember him coming over to us. We were isolated, behind glass. All of us sick, some of us dying. And he looked right at me, tipped his head to one side as if somehow sizing me up. Not a scrap of compassion on his face. And then he walked along and stopped opposite this woman called Stella, or "Number 89", as they called her. He turned away to talk to someone, then this other person came over to the glass, and the two of them pointed to her and talked about something. I never felt so powerless, so much at the mercy of another person. Or of other people. It was beyond terrifying. But then, you feel so sick that you just want to die, want it all to end.'

'George, a few people have named this Doctor Clare. And that she is oriental-looking. Was she actually the one in charge? And did you recognise her from any time before? It may not even be her real name. But she seems like a ghost—we know nothing about her or where she came from and have no idea where she is.'

George thought for a few moments. 'I could probably sketch her from memory. I did think she reminded me of someone from the early days, maybe ten years ago, but somehow it doesn't add up. There was a quiet Chinese girl, British Chinese, who used to hang around with Sarah Turner at some of their actions. A student, I think. There were a lot of them who came and went. She was around for maybe a couple of years? I'm not sure. Very quiet, very studious ... I'm struggling for a name, though it should be in my files. I'm trying to recall Sarah Turner talking to her, if she used a name.'

He thought for a few moments. 'It's Annie. Annie Lee. There is a file on her. But she dropped out of the picture years ago. It could fit, if she was one of their infiltrators.'

Joanna looked up at Colonel Palmer, who called over one of his team. They left the room quickly.

'I couldn't swear to it,' said George. 'But it's a lead. And I can definitely identify Gabriella Pearson, Tara Collingworth and Malcolm Morton as visitors to North Camp. I saw them in a meeting room just across from where I was, talking with this Dr Clare and a few of the others.'

Joanna spoke with George for a full two hours. She was worried about tiring him, but he felt energised by having the chance to get everything off his chest, and to feel that he was playing a part in bringing the culprits to justice. Then Joanna went on to talk to the other three survivors, the last of the people from North Camp. They told Joanna of the last dreadful days at the camp, when dozens of new 'lab rats' were brought in, and a new Militia officer called Perry Jones who introduced a tougher regime for those not currently being experimented on, and who coordinated the rushed preparations for the Amnesty.

From Scotland Joanna flew down in a military plane to Norfolk. She visited the North Norfolk Eco-camp, and from there went to the location where her brother's body was taken out of the bus that had been stopped by invading troops. The bus was still there, its doors open, and the area cordoned off as a crime scene. Tents had been set up nearby to house the forensic teams and their equipment. She could imagine the scene: how Peter would have been elated at what he would believe to be his imminent release, and the end of his nightmare. He had been amongst the first to die, so was probably amongst the first to receive the phoney vaccination. Probably he was feeling sick already when he got on the bus, and by the time the bus was stopped was already beyond saving. What thoughts must have been going on in his mind? Joanna felt almost unable to tear herself away from standing in front of the bus, and was eventually guided away from the scene by a soldier.

At the new model community just outside North Walsham, Joanna saw the home and the communal buildings where Peter spent his last few months. Her military escort explained how the community was set up, and gave an insight into how the army had dealt with the people that were found there. The homes were deserted now, and the government had to decide their future.

As she was standing in the kitchen garden of the home where Peter had lived, a car pulled up. Two soldiers escorted Jane Johnson up towards the house, and one of them introduced her to Joanna, who nodded slowly. The two women stood a few feet apart, but said nothing. Eventually Joanna broke the silence. 'This was your home?'

'Yes.'

'Let's go inside.'

Jane Johnson looked around the house. Everything seemed to be exactly as she had left it. She feared that it would have been damaged or looted, but everything was the same, except that she could see the laptop was no longer where she had left it.

Joanna took out her voice recorder, put it into the best position to capture the conversation, and hit the 'record' button. 'Tell me about your life here. I know it hasn't turned out like you expected, but tell me what you expected would happen, how your life would pan out in your model green community.'

Jane explained the purpose of the community, and the way it worked, much as she had explained it to Peter Kitson several months earlier. These communities were to be the new style of living, and they were in the vanguard of this new way of life. 'We talked about ways to limit the population, but it was all to be voluntary. We never talked once about these kinds of measures. I mean, what actually happened.'

This was something Joanna had heard or read many times already. 'Tell me about the role of prisoners from the eco-camps that were billeted here. Why were they sent here, and what did they do?'

'Well, they were here for two reasons. We were short of labour. And the community was unfinished. We were building it as we went along. Running it, and learning to make a new way of life at the same time. We still had to earn a living while we were learning to be self-sufficient. It wasn't a bed of roses, but we believed in it. And the other thing was, well, education through labour. A much better deal than the eco-camps. So it was—it was intended to be—a next step for those who had ... graduated through the camps.'

'How hard was the life for these people—people like my brother?'

'It was better than the camps. They told us that. And we knew it should be, that was what was intended. It wasn't perfect, but you could have something approaching a normal existence.'

'As far as doing forced labour is ever normal?'

'It was meant to be a kind of rehabilitation. That's how we saw it. Though at first most of us here didn't want to take any prisoners, in case it ...' Jane's sentence petered out.

'In case it tainted the purity of the community?' suggested Joanna.

'There was a lot of competition for places in these communities. For those who were selected, it was such an honour, a privilege to be making this new world. Or what we thought would be a new world. But when the food shortages started, we became a bit of a target. So the fences went up. And then the eco-camp parolees were sent along, and they had to be monitored. They wore electronic tags, you know. They would sound if they went past the perimeter. It wasn't heavily guarded, so we lost quite a few—mostly those we were glad to see the back of.

'Your brother ... Peter was an unusual case. He hadn't been earning his points in the camp, but was a kind of special prisoner. We were entrusted with looking after him, and seeing that he was restored to health. But also to see—that is collectively, we were all to see that he didn't escape. I didn't want this responsibility. But it worked out. I mean us all living together. He wasn't worked too hard.'

She lapsed into silence.

'He was always asking for news—of his family, of you. And about Terry Cairns, and someone called Sandy. We didn't know anything, and were told it was not appropriate to try to find out. Come with me, there's something you might want to see.'

They got up and walked into the central corridor of the house.

'This was Peter's room. It's very Spartan, but after what he went through, I think it felt secure, at least.'

'Did he tell you much about what he went through?'

'He didn't dwell on it, but we had a couple of conversations. And it came out in his self-criticism sessions ….'

'How did that make you feel when he told you what he was subjected to?'

'I thought it was wrong. I was shocked.'

'Really? And it didn't make you doubt the whole direction of the Green Revolution?'

'It led to some big arguments in our community meetings. But basically no. I still thought we were on the right track, but that something had gone wrong, and we could put it right.'

'Do you still think it was on the right track?'

'I can't answer that,' said Jane, looking away. 'There was something I thought might be here. They must have taken it. It was a notebook, for his self-criticism. I thought you might want it.'

Joanna was sure she did want it.

'Tell me, Jane. What happened in the last twenty-four hours. You all went to the Eco-Camp, and they divided you into two lines: one to get the vaccine, and one to get the poison?'

Jane Johnson now looked shaken, when faced with the stark reality of the decisions that were made that night. 'It wasn't quite like that,' she said softly. 'We all went to the North Norfolk Eco-Camp the night before. We were told that the parolees were to be released in an amnesty, and they were being brought to a central point for administrative reasons. To process their release and to make sure it happened in good order. They told us that while we were there, we would meet other Green Volunteers and be able to select the ones who would return with us, replacing the people being released so we would not be left short-handed. And when were there, they told us there was a virulent new strain of bird flu, and we were to be immunised against it. So we were. Then we left later in the evening with a handful of new volunteers to join us. Peter, and all the others like him, were to stay overnight and be released in the morning. And they were to have their injections before they left. That's all we knew. Honestly, that's all we knew.'

Finally, she broke down. 'I am so, so sorry for what happened. Believe me, I had no idea.'

560

Joanna waited a few moments and asked, 'And what would you have done if you had had an idea about it?'

Jane was unable to answer, but only shook her head.

'Who here did have an idea, do you think? Who was most connected with the camps, and the inner workings of the Militia?'

Joanna let her questions sink in for a few moments.

'Jane, I want to ask you something. Look at me. I shouldn't ask this question without you having a lawyer with you. So you don't have to answer. My advice is you shouldn't answer. But I want to ask you anyway. Do you feel any responsibility for my brother's death?'

Jane Johnson sat sobbing, and remained silent. She seemed to be nodding.

'Whatever happens to you in terms of the law, you will always have your own feelings to deal with. So if you have any feelings of responsibility, any remorse at all about what happened not just to Peter but to all the others, then I think you should tell us everything you know. If what you are telling me is true, these people lied to you—just like they lied to the whole country. They used you and trampled on your dreams. You owe them nothing.'

'There's another question I've been asking myself,' said Jane, looking up suddenly. 'What if this Operation Cyrus had succeeded? What would we have done here? What would I have done? We would have become the leaders in building the new world. At first we might have believed it was a natural catastrophe, but it wouldn't have been possible to keep up the lie for long. Would I have gone along with it, covering up the crime for the sake of building a Green Earth future?'

'Would you have?' asked Joanna.

'As the least bad option, I fear I might,' said Jane.

••

Ten exhausting and harrowing days later, Joanna was back in London.

Detective Inspector Ibrahim Moss opened the door to the cell briskly, allowing Joanna Kitson to walk in before him. Hearing how Moss had helped Heather to escape from London, Joanna had asked to meet him. She found him an intelligent and affable man, instantly knowing he was someone she could trust, and asked for him to be seconded to the Investigation.

As Joanna entered the interview room, she felt a chill run through her. Dave Barrington rose to greet her, automatically extending his hand, as if to an old friend. Moss interposed himself between them, taking from Joanna the awkward decision as to whether to accept his handshake or not.

Barrington had changed only a little since she had last met him. He was greying a little at the temples, and his hair had begun to recede slightly. Though his face still seemed quite young and his eyes sharp and alert, there were many more lines on his face, and his skin had become somewhat pale and unhealthy-looking. Probably the stresses of high office, then several weeks of incarceration, rarely seeing the sun.

He did not deserve to see the sun, she felt. Then she shook the thought aside, and rapidly snapped into professional mode. She wanted to interrogate him, but was worried her feelings and prejudices could interfere with her assessment. She did not want any unfairness on her part to jeopardise a successful trial, allowing a clever defence lawyer to get him off the hook by complaining of unfair treatment.

Joanna was aware of the broad lines of Barrington's defence. That he was not part of the inner circle. That he was too absorbed with the valuable climate projects—which he would argue still had great value—and so he had failed to notice another agenda develop within the Green movement. It didn't wash with Joanna. She knew how from the start he was so central to the whole GEM project. But there was little documentary evidence to prove it.

'It's been a long time, Dave,' said Joanna as she sat down opposite.

'Around two years, I think,' said Barrington.

'I noticed the invitations stopped coming. How's Jessica? And the children?'

'They're fine. At least, I'm told they're fine. I hope they are.'

The family. Access to them could be used as leverage. But Joanna had refused to even consider going down that route, and Moss respected her all the more for that.

'I believe they are still in Sweden. But I'll try to see that news gets to you.'

'I appreciate that. Listen, Joanna, I'm so sorry to hear about…about Peter and Heather. I was devastated—'

Joanna held up her hand, motioning him to stop.

Barrington sat back in his chair, opening his arms wide in a resigned shrug.

'I understand. Nevertheless, I have said what I have said, and it is from the heart.'

Joanna felt complicated emotions rising within her. She had not expected it to be so hard to begin the interrogation.

Barrington's lawyer also sat back, twisting her pen between her fingers. She said nothing. The ground rules for the investigation, and for possible trials had been fixed. Barrington had promised full cooperation, unlike some of the other defendants. His lawyer would try to protect him from saying anything self-incriminating.

The interrogation began slowly. The Commission wanted to know every possible detail, starting from the beginning of Barrington's association with Don Mason and the GEM. Over several days Joanna and Ibrahim Moss questioned him about the development of the GEM agenda, their aims when placing 'sleepers' into organisations, and their policy aims when they came to power. They questioned him at great length on his role as Communications Director in the early days and then as supremo for the Climate Change Projects. Every detail was probed and questioned, and cross-checked with evidence from other witnesses and defendants.

'I have been writing something that may help you,' said Barrington one day. 'My Memoirs, so to speak.'

'We know,' said Moss. 'We—or at least I—have looked at early drafts.'

'Of course. You're welcome to. It may be short on some details, but I feel I've got limited time. Have you decided the charges yet, and set a date for trial?'

Barrington's manner had become increasingly confident as time had gone on. The interrogations seemed to provide him with a comfortable routine, and any fears of summary justice—the kind his government might have dispensed—had obviously been allayed.

'Details may be important. There's some that I hope you include. Like how two work camps and an eco-camp can be operating within thirty miles of your home, and supply in all over six thousand workers for your Climate Change projects there, yet you apparently know nothing of how they operate and the conditions there. How my brother could be interned in a work camp for eight months there without your knowledge, spend several months in one of your new-age population-balancing eco-settlements, be exposed to plague and sent home to die and poison other people—all without any knowledge on your part. All of it happening right under your nose!'

Barrington's lawyer leaned forward and gestured Barrington to say nothing. 'My client has asserted that he is not aware of any of these circumstances or events. It is unreasonable to expect him to provide details of events of which he knows nothing!'

'It's OK,' said Barrington. 'You are right, of course. It is in the nature of high office that most of the details are hidden from you. That is why it is so easy to promise one thing, while something else entirely is delivered. But I understand Ms Kitson's scepticism in the circumstances. And I am glad that the gloves are off. It is better we are direct. My *Memoirs* are truthful, and I will answer any question truthfully and with candour.'

'OK,' snapped Joanna, now fired up. 'During your time as a government Minister, did you at any time hold the view that the population of the country should be reduced?'

'Broadly, yes. But I never entertained thoughts about it being by compulsion rather than by voluntary methods. Absolutely, never.'

'Did you hear others talk about more drastic methods of reducing the population?'

'There was always wild talk in the movement, but I never heard anyone who mattered seriously advocating population reduction by extreme methods.'

'Not even Gabriella Pearson or Titus Whitaker?'

Barrington hesitated, then looked thoughtful, as if trying to recall something.

'Titus often spoke of such things. You've read his writings. But he spoke of many options, without coming down on the side of, well, extermination. Not in so many words. And certainly not after becoming part of the government.'

'It surprised you when he and Pearson were taken into the Cabinet?'

'I was flabbergasted. But I trusted Don.'

'Do you think Don Mason collaborated with Morton, Pearson and Whitaker in the design and execution of Operation Cyrus?'

Again Barrington paused. 'I am not certain.'

Joanna looked exasperated. Then Barrington continued:

'Don's habit was to create broad lines and then let others get on with delivering what was wanted. But he had a good mind for detail. He liked to be told what was happening. I think it unlikely that he knew nothing. He believed tough measures were necessary. But he never spoke to me about anything as drastic as what actually happened. It's possible that he was deceived. I mean that he was told one thing, and others took it in directions he had not intended.'

'Let me ask you about the eco-settlements. You helped design these according to principles developed by Titus Whitaker in his book *Future Communities and Rebalanced Populations*. You must have realised that the communities you were building were to serve a much reduced population. Whitaker envisaged a population in this country no greater than that in the sixteenth century. No more than five million people!'

Barrington's lawyer again cautioned him not to reply, but he gestured to her that it was OK.

'If that had been the only thing I did, it would be a clear testament to my complicity. But I talked many times with Don Mason about the eco-settlements. It was indeed meant to be a new design for life, one where people could live much closer to and in harmony with the natural world. But it was not the only story. We also made extensive plans for reshaping cities, developing the new Ecopolis, as we called it, in which *millions* would continue to live at vastly reduced energy and resource cost. Think about it! The renewable energy projects that I worked on—that Peter worked on—were on a huge scale, generating enough power to support a population of many tens of millions. That was the aim. It makes no sense to undertake these massive projects if all the time we were following Titus Whitaker's madcap ideas.'

Joanna now felt she was in danger of starting to believe Barrington's story, and it annoyed her deeply. Everything circumstantially pointed to his knowledge of the tough measures that the Mason government had taken. It seemed inconceivable that someone so senior, someone who drew his labour force from the eco-camps and work camps run by Morton and Fullerton, who sat down and planned the shape of the eco-settlements with Pearson and Whitaker, could be in complete ignorance of the extreme measures that they took.

And yet Barrington had clearly marked out the ground for 'reasonable doubt'. As a lawyer, she knew there could be enough there to get him off the hook with regard to the bioterrorism charges. The only way to get him for these would be if someone else implicated him directly. And so far that wasn't happening.

Ibrahim Moss sensed her frustration as the day ended. After some hesitation he said:

'Do you mind if we take a detour on the way back? There's something I want to show you.'

They drove a short way across the city, past King's Cross, into Islington. The market traders were just packing up, and the sun was now low over the buildings. Joanna looked a little puzzled, but recalled it as Sam Sharma territory.

72: Sam's grief

Shortly after his return from the West Highland Eco-Camp, Sam Sharma appeared to be in depths of depression. After the initial rejoicing at his homecoming, in which he seemed fully to share, his mood became steadily more sombre. He spoke less and less to his family, and barely acknowledged friends and colleagues.

Kelly, his wife, was desperately worried. She urged him to take up the counselling offered by the new government for people released from the camps. He attended a couple of sessions, but came home from them as tight-lipped as before. He slept almost as soon as he came home from work, but at night she would find him sitting in a chair, staring at the wall, sometimes with tears streaming down his face. Kelly had read about 'survivor's guilt', as they called it, but had not anticipated anything like this.

One night when she found him alone, he held her gently by the hand, kissed it and said: 'You heard her. She called me her "guardian angel". Some guardian angel, eh?'

'You only did what you could do, love,' said Kelly. 'It wasn't you who poisoned her.'

'So many of 'em. How could they do that to 'em? To so many of 'em? And right at the end, to poison a mum and her child just like that. I can't understand. I saw his face though, you know, the one what ordered it—and he did it on purpose! He could've let her be, but he had to do it! And y'know? I left her there! I jumped up in that roof and I left her there! Tell me what kind of man does that? "I'm a survivor" I kept saying like a pillock...'

'Enough, enough,' Kelly had said. 'You survived, and we wouldn't have it any other way. You survived for us. You tried to save the poor girl, and you comforted her in her dying moments. You did all you could.'

'Not enough,' said Sam brusquely, with a note of finality. He didn't speak after that for nearly a week, until two days before Ibrahim Moss brought Joanna to Islington.

Sam worked gloomily in the market alongside his sons, who tried constantly to raise his spirits. They noticed how he kept looking towards the large recycling bins in the middle of the market. One afternoon he was looking at them and muttering. His sons and friends tried to distract him, but suddenly he flew into a rage and ran at the bins, starting to kick them, shouting incoherently all the time.

'Fuck ya! Fuck ya! Fuckin' bins! This is where it all started! Fuck the lotta ya!'

Furiously Sam pushed the bins, as if trying to roll them right out of the market. He grabbed a large piece of wood, and then a metal pole and began to beat the bins, denting the sides. One of them, gathering some momentum as it rolled, crashed into one of the stalls, causing it slowly to collapse.

'What the hell are you doing, you bloody idiot?!' the stallholder called, as people tried to calm Sam and pacify the stallholder.

Soon the police arrived, and the street trading officer from the Council. But things had moved on. Sam was now demanding bricks. 'Just get me the bricks. Get me the bricks! Don't stand there like a lemon, son! Where are the bricks?'

'He's lost it,' the other stallholders were saying. But there was a huge amount of sympathy and respect for Sam, and many were trying to work out how to humour him and comply with his strange demands.

Soon bricks were arriving, harvested from a nearby building site. Builders in hard hats at first tried to stop this very public pilfering, then watched as events played themselves out, scratching their heads.

'You'll need some cement,' called one of the builders.

As Sam tried to lay the bricks, it was soon evident that bricklaying was not his forte. Friends and family took over, working to Sam's instructions and advised by the workers from the building site. Looking ever more distressed, Sam scurried from side to side, barking orders or muttering to himself. The Council officer remonstrated with the police, telling them that Sam couldn't do that there. Sam stood up, and looked as if he was going to attack the man. The Council officer stepped back warily.

'Steady on, Sam,' said the policeman. 'He's only doing his job.'

'That's when the trouble starts,' shouted Sam, 'when everyone's only doing their bloody job! Bloody jobsworth! Should sack the fuckin' lot of 'em and start again, that's what I say.'

'OK. If you want to let him do this, I won't interfere,' said the Council officer good-naturedly, and settled in with the crowd to wait for what would happen next.

'Topsoil. I need some topsoil. Where can I find some bloody topsoil, anyone?' Sam ranted.

'You got to line it with something,' called someone.

'Better let the cement dry first!' called someone else.

The topsoil he was calling for didn't take long to arrive. It seemed half the community was now bending itself to fulfil Sam's requests. Sam looked across at the plant stall in the market, then shook his head. 'Wrong stuff. Take me to the garden centre, son,' he said.

After forty minutes or so, the Sharma family returned from the garden centre with compost and a car full of plants. Reversing carefully through the gathered crowds, they arrived next to the impromptu raised flowerbed that Sam had had constructed in the former site of the recycling bins.

Sam carefully planted the large selection of Scottish heathers in the flowerbed, then stood back to look at his work. People told him it was beautiful. Some dissidents muttered 'It ain't practical: we've got to put our bloody rubbish somewhere, yeah?'

'I need a board and some paint,' Sam announced sharply.

After a few minutes, he had both. He propped up the board on the side of the flowerbed, and took a narrow brush in his hand. He stood like that, brush in hand, for several minutes in silence. Then he dropped the brush.

'I don't know what to write,' he said softly, and turned away to go home.

••

Joanna stood in front of the flowerbed, tears flowing down her cheeks, as Ibrahim told her the story, or at least the version he had heard.

'I've never been to his house. Where does he live?' she asked.

They found Sam at home, tended by his family. The day of his flowerbed-building he had come home exhausted, and fell into a kind of nervous collapse. He had barely moved or spoken since. Kelly Sharma took Joanna through to see him where he lay on the sofa.

'You've got a visitor. You'll want to talk to her,' she said.

After a while, they left Joanna alone with him, taking DI Moss into the kitchen to make him some tea. Kelly told Ibrahim what Sam had been through, and Ibrahim was able to let the family know a little more about the enormity of what they had found at the eco-camps. From the living room they could hear the sound of talking, and tears from Joanna. They could hear Sam talking about Heather and the camp, and Joanna talking about the whole Kitson family, and especially about Andrea and her future.

Eventually as the daylight faded, they emerged in the kitchen doorway, Joanna holding Sam tightly by the arm, and putting her head against his shoulder.

'It's going to be OK,' said Sam quietly.

'Life goes on,' said Joanna, 'and we're happy about that. At least, as happy as we can be at the moment. One day at a time is how we'll do it.'

73: Annie Lee's journey east

'Her name is Annie Lee, and she's possibly the most dangerous person on the planet right now,' said General Matthews gravely. 'We've only just been able to put a name to the person behind the development of the new plague. We've been trying to get something out of the people we have in custody, but we're not getting very far. As we speak, we're trying to get Titus Whitaker to provide some kind of leads as to where she might be. In her student days she was close to Sarah Turner for a while, but Turner won't say a word other than that "Annie had her own agenda".'

'Some of the documents MacLean unearthed link her to both Porton Down, our former military science centre, and to North Camp,' added Sir James Olsen. 'Some survivors have identified her as being there, but it seems she disappeared the day before the plague was released.'

General Matthews and Sir James presented the facts before national leaders and security chiefs from around the world, via videoconference.

'Her mother—who as you might imagine is in a complete state of shock—has provided us with the most recent photographs we can find. The most recent is from a few years ago, with her brother. He's almost certainly in the clear, but we're keeping a close eye on him all the same. Here's the picture now … and how she might look if she changed her appearance in various ways,' said General Matthews as the pictures flashed up on the screen.

'We're pretty certain that she's not in the UK, and that she's not alone. Our analysts think that she's on a mission, rather than being on the run—a mission to reduce the world's population. Exporting their warped ideas of restoring the natural balance of the world. And, though it's only speculation, the logic of their ideology would seem to steer her towards the areas of greatest population pressure—in Asia. Her own nationality, and her ability to speak Mandarin might indicate that her intended destination is China. But who knows what else might be planned en route? So this is a problem for us all.'

It was Earth Day, April 22nd. Annie Lee at this time was travelling, under a false name and with her hair dyed red, on a flight from Rome to Chongqing. From a tourist capital where she could blend in with the thousands of oriental visitors, to one of the world's fastest growing industrial cities. She flicked between the in-flight movies without concentrating. Just another Chinese traveller locked into their digital world of entertainment. The thought made her smile. But at the same time she was frustrated.

She had sent members of her small team ahead several days before the amnesty, and sent their supplies by special medical courier to prearranged reception points. But when the amnesty was hurriedly brought forward and the country was invaded by counter-revolutionary forces, it had severely disrupted her plans. Her original plan had been to leave a week before Earth Day, the day originally designated to release the plague in the UK. That would have given the time she needed to get everything in place. Had that been possible, outbreaks of plague in Asia could have been timed to start at the same time as in Britain. It would have greatly increased the chance of success, sowing confusion as to the origin of the epidemic.

Instead, everything had been rushed, and now her mission had to take place with—in all probability—all the world's security and medical agencies on high alert. She had had to lie low in first Geneva, then Rome, until she felt comfortable that her movements had not been tracked. So at first forced to rush forward the preparations for the UK, she was now a week behind her mission to export the plague to the wider world. This amount of improvisation made her anxious.

She went over the plans in her mind. Members of her team would enter China from different directions—by road from Kazakhstan, by rail from Russia, and by air into Beijing, Shanghai and Guangzhou. And some too would be arriving into China by boat. Part of the plan was for her team to infect the crews of ships entering China from South-east Asia. There would need to be successive waves of infection. It was dangerous for her to go to China herself. But she had a small network of activists in China, who had risked everything for this moment. She had to be there to support them, and to ensure they could respond fast to changing circumstances if needed. In part, it was a matter of professional pride.

Five hours into the flight, it was time to freshen up. One of her finest products, she felt, were her scented pathogens, which could be taken on board a plane in a travel atomiser in hand luggage. She went to the back of the plane, and discretely sprayed the atomiser into the air. The HEPA filters in the air-handling system would take out some—perhaps even most—of the bacteria. Some, though, would get through, and the contagion could begin. But she knew well the weakness in any system is usually more in people's behaviour than in technologies. Standing near the back of the cabin, she sprayed some on herself.

'Mmm. Smells nice,' said a stewardess who was preparing drinks. 'I could do with some of that.'

Making it easy. Annie Lee offered her the spray, and the stewardess sprayed herself in a fine mist of one of the slower-acting strains of plague. How many passengers on how many planes would she have contact with over the next few days? How many countries would she visit? This stewardess would become an involuntary heroine of the rebalanced world.

Annie had prepared an order of several thousands of the atomisers, which she would collect when her mini-production facility was assembled. In China, there could be no state-sponsored production facility like the one she had created in Scotland. She would need to take everything she had learned and put it to work in the utmost secrecy. Her years as a GEM sleeper were good preparation for this.

Her team would travel all over China using these atomisers. They would give them away. They would sell them to street traders. They would allow them to be stolen. At the same time, there would be mass infections in key population centres that would attract all the attention of the authorities, both the security and the medical authorities. Meanwhile, the vanity of the population as a whole would be enlisted to spread the virus person-to-person by stealth.

As the plane landed, Annie thought of the outbreaks that should already be underway in Western China and in Beijing, set off by her associates.

The plane was taxiing, but Annie soon realised that it was not heading towards the terminal. Instead it was being directed towards a remote part of the airport. Leaning across her neighbouring passengers, she could see through the window other planes that had been diverted to this area. And soldiers—hundreds of them. Ambulances too.

She had half-expected this. The full-on response is the Chinese way. This she remembered from studying the way the authorities had reacted to the SARS outbreak years before, and how they had dealt with anyone arriving from outside whom they suspected of being a health risk.

The captain made a strongly-worded announcement for plane passengers to remain in their seats. The stewardesses tried to keep people calm and in place, but soon angry arguments were beginning with some of the passengers. These halted abruptly when armed soldiers entered the plane and took up positions in the aisles. An officer barked out orders through the intercom and explained procedures. Everyone leaving the plane would be medically examined for a new and dangerous infection that it was necessary to contain. There would be no exceptions.

Stewardesses began to distribute face masks, which the passengers eagerly put on. Some panicked, shouting that they needed to get outside, into the open air. Why keep everyone inside where the air might be infected? In the end there was a slow but orderly exiting from the aircraft. It was a pattern that was repeated all across the country for international flights. Annie Lee was now extremely anxious. She had no symptoms of the disease, but was no doubt carrying it. And she did not know how sophisticated the detection techniques would be. One thing was certain. If she got through, it would be necessary to lie low for months until the emergency measures were relaxed. Patience and discipline. She was sure she had the character for that.

The passengers filed through a plastic tunnel into a large tent, where doctors and nurses were taking temperatures and swabs, while orderlies wrote down details to connect the tests with passengers and the places they had travelled from. Everyone was given a number, and a plastic identity bracelet that was sealed on their wrist.

Now it became clear that another kind of screening was taking place. Young women in their late twenties and early thirties were being separated from other passengers, and taken through another plastic tunnel that led into an outbuilding. There must have been over a hundred women, all anxious, taken from several different flights. As they entered, each had their photograph taken. After a short period of waiting, they then had to stand in groups of ten while a camera filmed them, slowly moving up and down the line several times.

••

'We've got her!' General Matthews exclaimed as he put his head round the door, interrupting a conversation between Patrick Baxter and Joanna Kitson. 'In China, Chongquing airport.'

'Are you a hundred per cent sure?' asked Baxter.

'Positive ID from a camp survivor, George Cavanagh,' said Matthews excitedly. 'And confirmed by Lee's brother. I don't think there's any mistake!'

Patrick Baxter looked grimly satisfied. He turned to look at Joanna, and saw that her face had turned completely white.

'I'm fine, I'll be fine,' she said.

'Can we get her back?' asked Baxter.

'We're working on that,' said Matthews. 'There have been several plague outbreaks over there, so the Chinese are saying they want to deal with her. I think we can work something out with them. There's a lot we need to ask her about.'

74: Experience

'He's over there,' said the orderly standing by the double doors into the garden, pointing to a figure in a wheelchair halfway down the gardens.

Patrick Baxter descended the stone steps of the nursing home and made his way along the gently winding path by the flowerbeds on this warm September morning.

'It seems you have a visitor,' said the nurse, smiling, and turning the wheelchair.

'Howard, how are you?' asked Patrick Baxter, proffering his gift.

Howard Blackstone shielded his eyes with his hand.

'Patrick! Good God! Do have a seat. Do you like my new office?' Howard gestured towards a garden bench nearby with a smile. Patrick Baxter sat down as Howard was wheeled a little closer.

'You're making a good recovery, then?' Patrick asked.

'It seems so. Quite wondrous what they can do with modern surgery, isn't it? Even in three years, since the first op, things have come on a long way.'

'And the outlook is good?'

'Not bad. They keep me going, at any rate. No doubt if Mason and his lot had had their way, the doctors would have been operating on me with flint axes or something! Or they'd have just let me keel over, to keep the numbers down. But Patrick, you've really stepped back from the fray now?'

'I have indeed, Howard. I said three months, and three months it was. I wanted to see us back on track, and I think we are.'

'The country owes you a great debt,' said Howard.

Both men felt emotional for a moment, looking away around the garden.

'It's very beautiful here, isn't it?' said Howard.

'Actually, Howard, apart from seeing how my old adversary is, my main reason for coming to see you is to ask you to play a part in the memorial service in St Paul's—the Memorial Service for the Fallen. A reading, or a eulogy, as you think fit.'

'You're very kind to ask me. But is it appropriate? After all, for several months I was sitting at the same table as …. as those responsible.'

'For a while you were, it is true. But so was most of the country at the time, so to speak. The views of your party better represented the mood of the nation at that time than the true nature of the GEM. We were all "light green", rather than "dark green", so to speak. And you were close to many of those who fell: Terry Cairns, Peter Kitson, and Heather, of course; Sandy Honeyford, Gill MacDonald... I'm sorry. It must bring back too many painful memories.'

'It's OK. They are never far from my thoughts. And I keep asking my-self, why didn't I see it coming? Evan was against going in with them from the start, though he's the first to say he opposed it for the wrong reasons. But you saw it, didn't you?'

'Not at all, Howard. I was much like you, like everyone else. I took it at face value. Who could have thought they would do what they did? That anyone could do such things? More than two hundred thousand souls here, and the thousands who perished in other countries... They still haven't completely contained it in China.'

'But you opposed them from the outset!'

'I did. But not effectively. One thing I did see, and it's why I did what I've done since our return—restore things as much as possible to how they were. Our way of life, our institutions, the way we run our country: they're far from perfect. But they work. We respect them. We abide by them. We respect the rule of law, and accept its judgements, even when we don't agree.

'Look at us, two old stagers, somewhat the worse for wear. We've dis-agreed with each other and poured insults at each other for more than thirty-five years! But we've always been able to sit down and talk over a drink. And we've never thought of shipping each other off to labour camps, or worse. I'm a Conservative, and I love our Constitution, and our way of life. We change, we make progress—but we need to keep the fabric of our civilisation together, and move forward with the consent of all sections of society.'

'Yes. "Conservatism consists in defending the Liberal achievements of a previous generation", as the great man said,' said Howard with a wry grin.

'Don't start, Howard!' said Patrick, appreciating the normality of the political banter. 'But actually, if it makes you happy, I'll accept that formula. Progressives push, Conservatives resist; but somehow we inch forward in the right way. It needs to be the same for progress in the green direction.

'But you know, Howard, one thing I ask myself every day?' continued Patrick. 'Why did I resign? I wasn't strong enough, that's all. If we'd shown the resolution at that time that we showed when we finally brought it to an end...'

'Hindsight's a wonderful thing, Patrick. No one would have supported that kind of strong action at the beginning. Don't you remember the mood? It was overwhelming, like an unstoppable tide. Do you remember all the people in the streets? Not for days, but for months! You can't take responsibility for not doing more. There was no one to back you up. You went, you regrouped, and, thank God, you came back with the cavalry.'

Patrick Baxter drew little comfort from this. 'It happened on my watch...'

'Our watch,' corrected Howard. 'They deceived us all.'

'But how could this happen amongst us?' asked Patrick, with passion. 'How could so many people buy into all that? How many people joined up to the Militia? Tens of thousands! And there were thousands too who bought into the extreme measures. Look how many are facing trial now. Mason and Morton didn't do this alone! They were just the tip of this toxic iceberg.'

Howard looked thoughtful, and seemed overcome with tiredness. His nurse moved forward to him.

'I'm so sorry,' said Patrick, 'I'm tiring you out. I'll go now.'

'No, not at all. Sit, sit. It's good for me to talk. All these things are playing on my mind all the time,' said Howard, his voice a little weak but animated.

'To me, that's the most important issue. The Commission of Inquiry will establish individual guilt, but we need to address the deeper causes,' continued Howard. 'I think it's like this. Have you noticed the age of the people involved? Apart from Mason and Whitaker, almost everyone was under forty.'

'Yes, that's true,' said Patrick, nodding thoughtfully.

'It was primarily a "young" movement. Most of the Militia were in their twenties,' observed Howard. 'You know, this kind of radicalism often takes root when a beleaguered older generation doesn't practice what it preaches. I mean, since the 1980s if not longer we've force-fed the upcoming generations with environmental messages, till we had this overwhelming political correctness where any greenish pronouncement was seen as undeniable. The messages may have been largely right–but we also made them pretty much beyond rational investigation. Then we did nothing! All talk, and bugger all action! The next generation was champing at the bit to do something!

'It's like the young Muslim radicals who brought terror to our streets before–and to countries all over the world. Their parents, and their leaders, would get up every morning and say "Death to America!"–then go to work, do the shopping, go the mosque, and carry on as normal. A generation grew up believing what their fathers and their religious leaders said but never acted on! So they went out, signed up, and really did try to bring death to America and to the rest of us.

'The Nazis were a young movement too. A generation brought up in the First World War, swallowing all the propaganda about Germany's greatness and the evil of the Allies. Then they saw their parents making a peace they didn't understand and trying to live a normal life, as if nothing had happened. It was shameful in their eyes. So the young flocked to Hitler and the people who, as they saw it, upheld the true values they were brought up in. And they wanted to do something about it. You should ignore me, Patrick—I'm rambling, probably the drugs I'm on!'

'Not at all, not at all. So what should be done? Get more balance into our environmental education, more debate and so on?'

'I don't know if I have the answers. The green messages came at us from every side: school books, government campaigns, the media, campaigning organisations. Our own party programme, for God's sake! It was a mood we all bought in to. Much of it had value—it just left us off balance, and unable to resist those with a darker agenda and a will to extreme action. I guess what we have to do in future is talk and campaign less, and do more of the fewer things we talk about.'

75: Magna est veritas

The work of the investigative commission was moving forward. It was now acquiring a professional and bureaucratic solidity that added weight and stability to the process. Every day the risk of its being a kangaroo court diminished, and legally weighty cases were being constructed against the key defendants. The feeling was that justice would be done, and would be seen to be done.

There were loose ends that all concerned were keen to tie up, and significant gaps in knowledge that they were anxious to fill. There was a great of deal of evidence about how the camps had been run, how people had been mistreated, how they had been experimented on, and how Operation Cyrus had developed and been put into effect.

But for Martin Lang, Joanna Kitson and the rest of the team of investigators there were not enough answers to the 'why?' questions.

Carl Fullerton was talking openly, even boastfully, about his role in events. But he studiously avoided implicating Don Mason or any of the other leading figures. His evidence and that from the Militia records were quite damaging to the defence of Dave Barrington and Sarah Turner, providing details of contacts and joint activities between their departments from the inception of the camps right through to their emptying. All the same, he would not point the finger directly at them or say 'we were all in this together'.

It became more important to understand the role of Don Mason. Yet Mason was gone, leaving the part he played enigmatic and open to every possible interpretation. It was Mason who planned the process of taking power, who drove the revolution forward, and who always seemed to keep the closest eye on what his government did. He helped to plan the eco-camps, the climate change projects and the new model eco-settlements. It was he who brought the Animalists into power and instigated the 'Second Revolution'.

Throughout his career, he spoke of the need to take tough measures, of the need not to shirk hard decisions, not to be seduced or weakened by 'Greyist morality'. But at the end of the regime, there was little in the way of hard evidence to confirm that he personally authorised any of the brutality and state terrorism that took place. In fact there was growing evidence that the

GEM itself had been infiltrated from the outset by the Animalists, and that key figures like Malcolm Morton and Juliet Coe straddled the two movements and had developed their own creative synthesis.

There was another key figure too who was not talking, despite the confidence of Gabriella Pearson that he would. Titus Whitaker had lapsed into silence when faced with any direct questioning. He was reported to be affable and communicative, in that he would talk about anything except what had happened while he was in government. There were concerns about his mental stability, as he was prone to ramble, and lose track of where he was, and to whom he was talking. But people who had known him before said that was normal for him. Joanna Kitson felt sure that if he could be encouraged to open up, he could provide key insights into the relationships at the top level of government, and the motivations of all concerned.

Now the Americans and the British intelligence advisers were offering to try out 'more persuasive techniques' on Whitaker and the other defendants who would not speak. To Joanna's dismay, Zara Alderney tried to persuade her it was time for a more robust approach. She wondered how Zara, who had only shown kindness and humanity in her dealings with the Kitson family, could operate such different private and professional standards. It remained important for Joanna to stay true to her principles; but she justified it pragmatically, saying the defence lawyers would have an easy task rebutting confessions gathered through forceful methods.

During the weeks following the end of the Mason government, Joanna met Trevor MacLean on several occasions. He found her charming and attentive; she found him amusing and entertaining. Underneath his flippant and iconoclastic façade, however, she recognised a man with deep knowledge of the events that had taken place, and a soul much moved by what had happened. He had a mission, it seemed, to bring everything out into the open, to leave nothing lurking in dark corners, as he put it.

'I hear you've been offered some pretty high ranking jobs in the media,' Joanna said when they met one day in the café where she had met Sandy Honeyford some months before. 'And refused them all, I also hear.'

'I see it is impossible to keep things from you,' said Trevor, smiling. 'I'm still the same greedy bastard, holding out for more money and complete editorial independence.'

'I don't believe a word of it,' said Joanna firmly. 'You need a break from this, don't you? I certainly do.'

'It's not so much a break, Joanna. I'm actually pining for the hills, and my life up there. How long did I live in London? Longer than I care to remember. Don't get me wrong, I still love the buzz here, the metropolitan air, the chance to get under the skin of self-important people and annoy the hell out of them. But—after I've finished this work, pulling together all I can about the GEM, the Animalists and all their hangers-on, I'm sure I can't go back to the media world I lived in before. Not just like that. It would be too empty. Too vacuous. Although actually, the vacuous is my true milieu. But I've got in too deep this time: I should be skittering over the top like my usual butterfly self. Now I need a chance to ... restore some balance, to borrow a phrase.'

Joanna didn't buy his self-deprecatory assessment. She realised though, that it was his way of dealing with the things that he had witnessed.

'Trevor, I want your help,' she said suddenly and confidentially. 'With Titus Whitaker.'

'Whitaker?'

'Yes. You know he's not really opening up.'

'You think I can help you to get him to talk?'

'You've told me about your research into him. You've read most of his writings, and through Stella Walton's files you also know how others reacted to him—I mean people who bought into what he believed—and how they interacted with each other. I think you may be able to get him to talk: that's one of the things you're good at anyway, getting people to talk. He probably won't answer questions directly, but if you can talk about the wider issues of his philosophy, establish some kind of rapport with him... It doesn't have to be a friendly rapport: it can be adversarial. But if you can establish some common language, get on his wavelength...'

'On the same wavelength as the mass-murdering guru of la-la land? I may never recover.'

'You'll do it then? You can film the interview—they're all recorded anyway, though hardly up to your standards. And once the trials are out of the way, anything we have can be used openly.'

'I know, I know. Actually, I'd like to talk to him. And to all of the others, too. As long as I can use disposable gloves if I have to shake hands with any of them.'

••

Titus Whitaker had been warned that he was having a special visitor. He showed a mixture of surprise and pleasure when Trevor MacLean came into the room. Trevor's was a face he saw almost every day on TV. He confessed to watching a lot of TV during his enforced leisure.

'Maybe you could write a book,' said Trevor. 'David Barrington is.'

Whitaker seemed to scowl slightly when Trevor mentioned this, but made no comment. Trevor looked closely at Whitaker, thinking 'the camera's going to love you'. Whitaker looked like the archetypal ivory tower academic—or at least the public perception of one. He still had quite a good head of hair, though he was over sixty, but it was somewhat on the wild side. He habitually swept it back from his temples with his hands. His eyebrows were wild and untrimmed. He wore a light, slightly worn jacket with ill-matching and equally worn trousers. He fitted the mould of TV 'boffins' too, to some extent, with exaggerated gestures and facial expressions. When he thought hard about something, his face creased into a thousand folds, as if every ounce of energy was being squeezed into the thinking. When he laughed, it was an open and generous laugh. When he wanted to make a point, he looked over his glasses directly into the eyes of the person he was talking to.

'If you're not writing a new book, maybe we can discuss some of your older works,' said Trevor.

'You've dipped your toes into them for your journalistic research, I expect,' said Whitaker with a dismissive tone.

'More like full immersion baptism, I'd say,' said Trevor. 'I've chosen them as my *Mastermind* special subject, as it happens.'

Whitaker smiled. 'Do carry on, and I'll see how well you've learned.'

They started with Whitaker's most famous and influential work, *The Equality of Species*. Trevor probed and teased him about the definitions he used, and alleged inconsistencies. After a cagey start, Whitaker began to rise excitedly to the challenge.

He argued strongly against the dominant theories of human rights, as being arbitrary and self-contradictory. After demolishing human rights theory, and the impossibility of basing moral equality on any notion of 'factual equality', he outlined his basis for the equality of all species.

It seemed as if he was beginning to frame a new book in his mind. At times he addressed Trevor directly, at times the camera, and at other times no one in particular as he became more animated. Quoting Jeremy Bentham, he then said: ' "*The question has to be not can they vote, or can they reason, or can they talk—but can they suffer?"* In different ways all organisms, all life-forms can suffer. Not in the same sensory and emotional way we humans can experience it, but in the experience of loss. Loss of capacity, loss of movement, loss of habitat, loss of opportunity to do what it is their nature to do—and ultimately loss of existence: at both the individual and collective level.'

By this stage Trevor's head was swimming as he struggled to reconcile this abstract approach to suffering with the reality of the hundreds of thousands of people who had lost their lives, many of them in extreme agony.

'Titus, Titus,' he said, holding his forehead with one hand. 'Let's just stop and think a little of how this plays out at ground level. I had coffee with Joanna Kitson the other day—'

'Ah yes, the formidable Ms Kitson,' smiled Whitaker.

'You recall what happened to her sister-in-law?'

'Oh,' said Whitaker, looking down. 'I see where you're going...'

'Do you? Do you *really*? I hope you can explain, because I don't understand. Heather Kitson, seven months pregnant, was injected with a highly virulent disease that killed her and her unborn baby. Was that not suffering? And that suffering was inflicted by one of your disciples, Militia Commander Perry Jones. Was that right? Was that morally right?'

Whitaker now looked very anguished, and lost in deep thought for a moment.

'It...should not have happened. Not like that...'

'Is their suffering not different to the suffering of an ant trodden underfoot, or a tree cut down in a forest?'

'Factually, the suffering is different. But morally...'

'Morally, they are equivalent?'

Whitaker now looked very pained. 'The deaths and suffering that have occurred, have occurred in a context ... where the human species has inflicted massive and unnatural suffering on the whole of the natural realm. We ... we had to take steps that were not to our liking, but were necessary. Necessary to restore order and balance into the natural world. What we did was not right, when seen at the individual level. But at the collective level ... Overall, it was not wrong if it achieved what it is intended to achieve.'

'Everything can be justified if we look away from the direct effects, and gaze at some distant horizon, don't you think?'

'No. But in some cases you *have* to look at the bigger picture. All governments do this. They will bomb a city, knowing there will be "collateral damage"; send in drones to assassinate an enemy, and wipe out his family at the same time; or storm a building where hostages are being held, knowing that innocents will probably die. They do it because there is a bigger picture. Look at President Wilding and his predecessors: they've strafed and bombed Middle Eastern and Asian villages. They've kidnapped suspects around the world and tortured them, to save their precious democracy from its enemies. It's just a question of knowing the scale of the bigger picture. Ours covers the whole of the natural world.'

Trevor was trying to keep his distress in check. The important thing was that Whitaker was talking. 'Why you, Titus? Why did you get involved? I mean, you had a respected if controversial academic career as a moral philosopher, then this! It is documented that you were part of the Loch Lomond meetings when the plague solution was carried forward, and the Ultimate Cull planned in detail. We know Morton's key role in it all. We've even got the speech he made when he told Militia leaders this would be "an unwritten chapter in history"—we've got that because some half-witted prick in the Militia wrote it down! But what I don't understand is how a man like you, with your sensitivities and intellect, could get his hands dirty in this way, working with people like Morton and Fullerton and Perry Jones.'

Whitaker was nodding as he listened to the question. 'Conviction. It's about conviction. If I was right in theory, then I should have the courage to see my ideas through, whatever the cost to my "sensitivities", as you put it. I had the vision, but I also had the responsibility to put it into action. You only have to see me to know I'm not the most practical of people—certainly no man of action. But the work needed to be done. And I found the people to do it with. Had I the power to carry it through all on my own, I hope the process could have been—cleaner. But the world is as it is. What kind of moral hypocrite would I have been if I had had the vision, then stepped back while others carried it out, just so I could sit smugly in the purity of my vision? I was in amongst them. And my hands are dirty. Like a gardener's hands are dirty, but only to restore the beauty of the garden.'

Trevor could not speak for a moment, taking in the force of Whitaker's oblique confession.

'So: Operation Cyrus,' said Trevor softly. 'Cyrus. Samson. Whose idea was all this Biblical imagery?'

'I don't know, actually. It emerged. From separate strands originally, then the concept merged into one as ideas turned into action.'

'Who is Cyrus? Are you Cyrus? Was it Mason?'

'Cyrus? He's the Persian king in Biblical times who restored all the displaced people to their homelands. The liberator, the restorer, the anointed one, the original *Messiah*. Brought the Jews home from exile in Babylon. It's certainly not me! Why do you think it is one person? It's a principle, a concept. A representative figure.'

'Maybe a grimly ironic one too, when you think of people being injected with a deadly disease, then released from captivity and returned to their homes?' suggested Trevor.

'I hadn't thought of that,' said Whitaker, seemingly appreciative of the insight.

'And Mason?'

'Don Mason? He is not Cyrus. Maybe he is Moses. Led us to the Promised Land, but was unable to enter it. He looks down from the mountain top as the new nation enters.'

'You're toying with me now,' said Trevor.

'And don't forget,' said Whitaker, as if lighting up at a sudden inspiration. 'Cyrus was the king who restores all things. An anointed king. Maybe the "king" aspect might give you a clue...'

'You don't mean—now you are playing games!'

Whitaker threw his head back in laughter. Trevor was intrigued by his character, and repelled at the same time. He hadn't expected a man with a sense of humour. But it was truly repellent how quickly he diverted his mind from the deaths he had caused.

'Why is it *our* responsibility to rebalance nature?' asked Trevor. 'I mean, we're just one kind of organism sharing this planet. Why this inconsistency in your views? All species eat, reproduce, attack and devour other species. Nature red in tooth and claw, and all that. Why is it *our* responsibility to do something about it? Giraffes and goats, elephants and locusts can devastate an environment. But in your view it is only humans who have a duty to make good the devastation? Why should we not be as careless of the environment as every other species?'

Whitaker looked surprised. 'Everything has its place, and acts according to its nature. The moral faculty in humans is part of our nature, and we must act accordingly. It is underdeveloped for sure. We mostly use it to be "moral" in relation to our own interests.'

'But how can you know that rebalancing nature is the right thing to do? It is one of many possible choices.'

'You are asking me about the legitimacy of my moral viewpoint. It is rational, rational from beginning to end, with no compromises on the basis of sentiment or self-interest.'

'Is that enough? Aren't there other bases for being moral? Like protecting and defending one's own? Or love? Don't these matter?'

'They matter. There are different circles of morality. But the larger circles have to take precedence over the smaller ones. It is not an easy choice. We have all made sacrifices. All of our followers have sacrificed the chance of personal fulfilment, of a personal future through their own children. Malcolm, Gabriella, Juliet, Carl and thousands of others, have all vowed to be childless. Hundreds have voluntarily given their lives to help reduce the plague of humanity on the face of the earth. People like me and ....and others.... who already had families have renounced them, and any favouritism towards them. The hard choices are also hard choices about ourselves. Those of us who took the vaccine also set a date for our own deaths, dedicating our time until then to serving the cause of rebalancing the planet. Like Don Mason's heroic death. He chose not to stay beyond his fall from power. This is a truly noble and heroic calling.'

Whitaker was gazing out through the window into the far distance.

'You don't understand how our people can have made the hard choices that they did,' he continued. 'It's no problem doing what is required if you have no conscience. But to overcome your conscience to do what is right—that is living to a higher morality. This is the struggle we face. And you cannot underestimate the heroism of those who have committed themselves to this course in spite of their instinctive—and selfish—moral sense.'

'Let me ask you again: how did you know that population reduction is the right thing to do? It might be possible to justify, but how did you *know* it is right? Know it in a way that demands such a sacrifice from you?'

Whitaker turned towards Trevor and looked him steadily in the eye. 'Don't you see? Nature seeks its own balance. One species or another can distort the balance, but only for a while. Nature asserts itself, in whatever way it can, to restore the balance. You still don't see?'

Trevor was shaking his head.

'Why has there been the growth in Green consciousness? Why have so many people joined with us to undertake this great work? *Nature is working through us, working through me.* I am doing this because I have to do this. My role, as Gabriella often said, is to be the piper who leads us to reason. We may be frustrated now, because the selfish forces at work in one species is still at work, impelling it to expand at the expense of others. But the collective force of nature at work in me and those thousands of others will only get more insistent. It will prevail.'

' "For want of me the world's course will not fail:
When all its work is done, the lie shall rot;
The truth is great, and shall prevail," ' quoted Trevor.

' "When none care whether it prevail or not",' interrupted Whitaker excitedly as he completed the quote. 'Exactly. "Magna Est Veritas". Let me tell you the fundamental mistake the Light Greens make—I mean the Kitson Greens and their ilk. Even many of the Deeper Greens, the Jessica Barringtons of this world. They think it's all about saving the planet for their children. As if the continuation of our own selfish species was the necessary condition for taking environmental action!'

'But if we're not saving it for our children, who are we saving it for?'

'Does there need to be a "who"?' asked Whitaker.

There was a pause as Trevor digested the implications of this.

'Titus, when did you and Don Mason agree the population reduction programme?' asked Trevor.

Whitaker went silent for a few moments, shifting his position in his seat a few times before continuing. 'This may surprise you. Don was not committed to this course for some time. He wanted to keep his options open. Hmm. And it was Cairns who in the end convinced him there was no other way.'

'Terry Cairns?' Trevor gasped.

'You think it's ridiculous. But it's how it happened. I found Don's delaying tactics frustrating, and Gabriella found it frustrating beyond belief. But for Don, Terry Cairns was his last hope. That's what I believe, his last hope. Faced with the enormity of what we had to do, and his responsibility for it as the Leader of the Revolution, Don was struggling with his conscience. His Earth-Conscience, I mean. His Earth-Conscience was on one shoulder reminding him of the suffering of the planet, and his human-conscience on his other shoulder, urging him to take the easier path of selfish humanity. His weakness was the weakness of us all, and he so much wanted to give into it. It's one reason for his drinking! He knew the choices he faced. To him Terry Cairns was someone who might actually make a middle path work, a softer green option. A future in pastel shades. Yes, yes. A more gradualist path. And I think Cairns felt Don's desperate need to find another way, and he tried hard. But the numbers did not add up. They never could, could they? And when he finally told Don and Sarah that it really, really couldn't work, Don was crestfallen.'

'So Cairns could only foresee economic collapse,' said Trevor, 'and all that would entail. For him that meant turning back, didn't it? But for Mason, it meant the descent into hell was the only way. Yes?'

'I wouldn't put it that way,' growled Whitaker. 'But a difficult and testing journey can be hi-jacked by good intentions. It nearly was. Even after Cairns fell, Don was still looking for another way. Even as the Ultimate Cull was being planned, he met almost daily with Dave Barrington to enthuse over those far-fetched plans for a techno-Green Utopia.'

'I thought Barrington was one of you?'

'Hmm,' said Whitaker, noncommittally. 'For Don there was always more than one way. He knew his goals. But he wanted to take the world with him too. He was even prepared to work with the likes of Wilding. "Patience. Patience and discipline," he would say. But there wasn't going to be time for that.'

'Especially when he found the Americans were not to be trusted?'

Whitaker nodded thoughtfully.

'What happened there? What is the truth about Louise Adams and this story about spying? Was it real, or paranoia?' asked Trevor.

'We Animalists were not in government then, so many things happened that we only heard about second hand. Malcolm Morton told it to us like this, after his ... thorough investigations. Louise Adams, ah, such a charming young woman, quite brilliant really! Such a shame. Very close to Sarah Turner, but not admitted to the inner circles. Not completely. We never knew it, but she had been assigned by American intelligence many years before, in a more or less casual way, to keep an eye on us deep green and animal rights activists. Back then it wasn't high on their security agenda, not at all. But they obviously thought we might be worth watching, and maybe it was something for a trainee spy to cut her teeth on. One can only guess about that really. But it seems she did in time come to see the Truth, at least up to a point. Without knowing she was doing it, Sarah had converted her to be really one of us! And Louise had the kind of economic brilliance that we lacked in the Movement. Sarah relied on her more and more. And then of course she came to know

Terry Cairns. In some ways, Cairns and Adams were an odd couple: different parties, big age difference. But they shared a similar outlook. They wanted to make the new world work using the tools of old world economics.'

'What happened?'

'It was inevitable, inevitable. They couldn't come up with a workable policy like this—how could they? You simply can't support a population of sixty-five million at the same time as massively scaling down economic activity. Cairns was right all along, though I think he genuinely tried to believe he could make it work. I said Don was crestfallen at Cairns' failure. But he wasn't the only one. Louise Adams saw it too. But she saw what Cairns did not. She understood that there was no question of Don turning back. And she knew more about the deeper Green alternatives. What's more, she saw Malcolm's and Don's closeness to us, and other so-called "extreme" views. So at some point, not long before her fall, I think, she got back in contact with her American handlers and began to feed them insights into our possible plans. It was a massive breach of trust, massive. The Cabinet was shell-shocked for a while after they found out, completely shell-shocked. And after that, there was only really one way. Our enemies had revealed their hand. At the same time, we were becoming sure it would be hard to win a second election. More than hard—probably impossible. It was act now, or ... probably never.'

'And—did you have any part in what happened to Terry Cairns and Louise Adams?' asked Trevor.

Whitaker shook his head. 'None at all. Though now I've heard the reports ... of what happened.'

'Let's talk numbers, Titus,' said Trevor. 'What was your target population? Four or five million, as you mention several times in your writing?'

'I think one can dwell too much on numbers. You need to understand where we, as a species, have taken the unsustainable path. And how it has unbalanced life on Earth. It's in our constant quest for security and safety. Have you read my essay, *The Place of People on a Predatory Planet?* It's all in there. All other life on Earth plays its part in consuming, and being consumed. But our sheer dominance of the Planet has step by step reduced our exposure to the predators which, in the state of nature, would keep our numbers in check. We want only to consume, and yet be free from all danger of being consumed ourselves. It is an illusion, for we all must die in the end. But our quest in the meantime for self-preservation and perpetuation of the species does untold damage to the balance of life on Earth. This is why we need to *restore humanity to vulnerability.*

'Let me tell you what I mean when I say I am proud to say I am an Animalist. It is not, or not only, about rights for animals. It is about restoring humanity's own true nature as an animal species, rather than being the destructive and self-indulgent demi-gods we have made of ourselves. So—to answer your question! We need to bring the numbers down, down to a point where a *natural* balance can be maintained.'

'So reducing the UK population is only the start. You needed to bring down population across the whole world,' said Trevor, more as a statement than a question.

'How could it work otherwise?' asked Whitaker.

'And so—someone you do know about: Annie Lee,' said Trevor. 'You know she's been caught? In China. Tell me all you know about her.'

Whitaker smiled. 'I'm tired now. I've enjoyed talking to you. And I think I've given you enough to be going on with.'

After this there was no more Titus Whitaker would say.

••

As Trevor left the room he met Joanna Kitson. She had been watching the interview on a screen. Inside, she was smouldering at Whitaker's avoidance of the human issues, and the way he referred to 'the Kitson Greens and their ilk'.

'I feel like I've just been taking some strange hallucinogenic drug,' said Trevor, blinking a little theatrically, as if emerging into daylight.

'You got him to talk more than he has done before. So thank you, Trevor,' said Joanna.

'You know what I want?' said Trevor. Joanna shook her head.

'I hear they've found some more pits at New Dawn. I want Whitaker to get his "gardening hands" really dirty. I want him—and those who signed up to his insanity—to wade in there and exhume the bodies. I want them to identify their victims, and compile lists of all their relatives, all the people who suffer their loss. Then we can see if he feels the garden is more beautiful at the end of the day from his dirty work! And we can see if remorse is anywhere on his moral compass.'

'You're not the first to say that. It may happen. But I'm against it.'

'Why?' exclaimed Trevor, wide-eyed.

'Because we have to be better than they are. No work camps. No humiliations. No degradation. No re-education. It's a slippery slope, and I don't want to get on it.'

76: Barrington's defence

Joanna Kitson switched off her reader, and put it on the arm of her chair. Dave Barrington's memoirs. The inside story. Self-justifying, but not without insight. The last chapter played on her mind. Barrington had written:

Now that several months have passed since the end of Don Mason's government, the first truly Green government in history, how can I sum up what happened in those years? How can we weigh up its achievements and failings?

The world has already passed judgement. We lost control of extreme elements in the Movement, and that resulted in actions of unparalleled wickedness. All of us at a high level share some collective guilt for this. Most of all I am guilty of blindness to what was taking root amongst us. Malcolm Morton's complicity in the moves to forcibly reduce the population is something I still find hard to believe. He was with us from the beginning, and I can say I never heard him say anything to make us think he supported such drastic, murderous measures: not until the last day, in fact.

Now the evidence has been compiled, and his leading role is completely clear, from the moment he recruited the Animalist guerrilla Carl Fullerton to head up the Green Militia. It is also clear now, that just as we had 'sleepers' at work in government and industry, we were not the only group to do this. Animalist cells did likewise, and it seemed they were also embedded amongst us from the beginning. To understand what happened is not to excuse it. It is unforgivable, and I have deep regret where my role in pushing through the Climate Change projects overlapped with other projects of a more sinister nature.

Now we move towards the trials of those deemed to be responsible. Don Mason, of course, is no longer with us. Malcolm Morton and Gabriella Pearson, the two prime movers in all this, have evaded capture. Daily there are rumours as to where they might be, but it seems the authorities looking for them are nowhere nearer to finding them. Annie Lee—of whom I'd never heard until after the fall of our government—is on trial in China, and when found guilty faces immediate execution.

So that leaves me as one of the top leaders left to face prosecution. I have been charged with 'crimes against humanity' and corporate manslaughter, but the case against me, it seems, will focus on the poor conditions in the work camps and suffering amongst the detainees used to move forward the projects I controlled. I am told there is no case being made against me in relation to population reduction measures. In any case, I face a long period behind bars. Even were angels to testify in my defence, it would be politically impossible to let someone of my status in the Green Earth Movement escape without punishment. What will be, will be.

What concerns me more is that we did make real achievements—and these are being trampled underfoot. The Consumptionists dance in the streets, like Cavaliers let loose after years of Puritanism. All the environmental laws and regulations we introduced are suspended, and most will not see the light of day again. Our renewable energy programme is also suspended, while they review all the options, including even nuclear power. How unthinkable that would have been four years ago at the time of the nuclear catastrophe!

When all is said and done, when we have been tried and convicted, what can we say? We tried to make a difference: to green our future and to save the Planet. We failed. Our failure, however, does not mean the problems have gone away. As our achievements are undone one by one, it means the problems are in fact becoming more acute with each day that passes.

Though the methods of Morton and his followers were wrong in the extreme, we still need to ask ourselves the hard questions: How much longer can the world go on increasing production, consuming resources, polluting the air, the land and the sea, wiping out one species after another, and robbing our children of their future? My accusers have one philosophy—'eat, drink and be merry: for tomorrow we die'. Till then we are free to suck our Planet dry. So I stand here accused, and have to answer for my actions. But one thing is certain. The time will come when my accusers will have to answer for the consequences of their actions.

Then our children and grandchildren will point their fingers and ask our generation, 'What did you do to save the Earth?'

77: Another truth

Joanna Kitson felt she was in danger of succumbing to the same nervous exhaustion as Sam Sharma. After visiting the camps, seeing her brother and sister-in-law finally buried, throwing herself into her work and seeing the mountainous evidence of horror upon horror growing before her eyes, she felt it was time to do as everyone was urging her: to take compassionate leave.

Two things, two missions in life, kept her going. Her commitment to justice propelled her, just as it had always done. The Commission of Inquiry took up much of her time. Most of her old human rights cases were now closed. Her clients were either released, or they were no more. Now she found she had relatives of former Green Militia coming to her, to see if she would help them get their loved ones released from detention that seemed to have no end in sight. She weighed the arguments, but invariably she refused. Someone else can fight for their rights, she felt.

The other mission in life was Andrea. Joanna had never asked to be a mother—or an aunt for that matter. These things just happened in life, it seemed. As far as she could recall, she had never been in love, not really head-over-heels in love. So far there had never been a man she wanted to marry, let alone raise a family with. Colonel Ashton was caring, gallant, attractive and, in the most sensitive way, pressing his attentions on her. But in this time of grief and activity, there was no time for romance. And she feared lest her grief lead her into unwise decisions.

The unconditional love of a child, though, was irresistible and had to be returned. And in her devotion to the child, Joanna expressed her devotion to Peter and Heather too. Joanna had always felt herself to be unsentimental. Logical, reasonable, even powerful, was how she had always liked to see herself.

Now, as she dressed Andrea or listened to her chatter, she felt she understood much more. At times she reflected on what she now knew, and which the likes of Malcolm Morton and Gabriella Pearson with their ideology and their poisons could never understand. She understood the future of the planet not as something abstract to be balanced and managed, but as a small and vulnerable person you hold in your arms, and sing to sleep each night.

10845426R00331

Printed in Great Britain
by Amazon.co.uk, Ltd.,
Marston Gate.